Jesse 'n Will
and
The Gaslight Knights

J.L. Fredrick

To John —
Enjoy!

J Fredrick
"Jord"
2-22-19

Lovstad Publishing
www.Lovstadpublishing.com

JESSE 'N WILL
AND
THE GASLIGHT KNIGHTS

First Edition

ISBN: 1542894689
ISBN-13: 978-1542894685

Printed in the United States of America

Cover design by Lovstad Publishing
Cover photos by Joel Lovstad

For my big brother, Ralph
Feb 4, 1943—Nov 14, 2002

Novels by J.L. Fredrick

Another Shade of Gray
The Gaslight Knights
Across the Dead Line
Across the Second Dead Line
The Private Journal of Clancy Crane
Unfinished Business
Piano Man
Dance With a Tornado & Other Short Stories
Thunder in the Night
The Great Train Robbery of Monroe County
Mad City Bust
September Ten
Aftermath
Cursed by the Wind
The Other End of the Tunnel

Non-Fiction

Rivers, Roads, and Rails
Ghostville
Etc., Etc., Etc.

Jesse 'n Will
and
The Gaslight Knights

PART 1

JESSE

1

Lizzy and Emma Hawthorne stepped off the train. They had just returned from one of their frequent visits to Milwaukee, and as usual, Jesse wheeled the luggage cart onto the platform where they stood waiting. Usually, they took their brown leather satchels, and without even a word of thanks, strolled off in the direction of their huge old mansion on South Main Street. But this time it was different. This time there was a large trunk in addition to the usual luggage -- much too large and much too heavy for them to carry. That trunk was about to change Jesse's life.

Disliked by almost everyone in town, these two old spinsters had lived in that huge old mansion on South Main Street since before there *was* a South Main Street, and they had the best racket in town, as Jesse would soon discover. Identical twins, they were often mistaken for each other, and even at the ripe old age of eighty, they displayed the vitality of people half their age. Little was known about them by anyone, and few cared to know anything. Emma and Lizzy weren't too popular in social circles -- their self-centered personalities left something to be desired, and their house was becoming an eyesore. What had once been a regal estate was slowly transforming into a hideous, weed-infested half acre of ugliness no one wanted to go near, and quite often the property was fuel for rumor.

When Jesse arrived at the house that evening with the trunk, a cordial invitation brought him inside to elegance he would have not expected.

1

From the fabulous oriental rugs to the intricate crystal chandelier, the front parlor was a showplace of fine craftsmanship. It was obvious that the Hawthornes were anything but poor.

Emma and Lizzy took a liking to Jesse, and as he sipped the tea Emma insisted he stay for, she dug to the bottom of a battered old purse, and then handed him a silver dollar. Somehow, he knew this was the beginning of a profitable relationship. A whole new era was developing -- an era of new influences, opportunities, and experiences that would change Jesse's life forever.

Within a short time Jesse was visiting the Hawthornes' house frequently, and this marked him as a less than desirable person to many townspeople. He hadn't really changed, but for some reason there were those who shunned anyone associated with the Hawthornes. But Jesse wasn't about to let those attitudes interfere with his new-found source of income. He had established some goals. Next spring he would complete his education, and that would allow him to pursue meeting those goals. Certainly he could endure the next few months, even though he felt somewhat abandoned -- even by his friends at school.

His association with Mr. Kelly, though, never altered. Julian Kelly didn't seem disturbed at all over the Hawthorne affiliation. In fact, he encouraged Jesse to ignore the adversities and to keep focused on his goals. Julian's son, Donald, was still his best friend, and he, too, encouraged Jesse to seek his fortune. At least the Kellys recognized Jesse for who he really was, and they weren't influenced by rumors started by people who didn't know him the way they did.

Jesse had lived in the Kelly household since he was ten years old, and now he was considered part of the family. His mother had died when he was only three; he could barely remember her. Mr. Kelly wasted no time in beginning to provide for Jesse's welfare on that chilly November day in 1920 that stood out most clearly in Jesse's childhood memories – the day he became an orphan. His father had been a sawyer for Kelly Logging and Lumber since he was a teen, but on that day he miscalculated. Unable to escape on a slippery, frozen hillside, David Madison lost his life to the unmerciful force of falling timber. He left behind his only son, Jesse.

Before nightfall that day, Jesse had a new home, a new family, and future he had not even considered until then.

And now, seven years later, Julian Kelly still looked out for Jesse's welfare, and it was he who signed Jesse's school report card, and it was he who was teaching Jesse to drive his Model A Ford pickup truck.

Jesse grew up quickly and his perception developed to a keen edge. He didn't dispute the word of the man who had taken him in, readily accepting him as one of the family, but he knew the real truth behind Mr. Kelly's reluctance to hire him at the mill: there was too much risk of Jesse's reflections on the tragic accident that had taken his father's life interfering with his safety, as well the safety of other crew members.

Instead, Julian used his influence to place Jesse in a less hazardous work environment. A few days after his fifteenth birthday, Darwin Anderson, the general manager of the railroad depot, visited Jesse. It was quite evident that Mr. Kelly had arranged the meeting, and equally evident that his influence had landed Jesse in the position of potential employment. There was an opening for a freight and baggage handler at the depot, and the job was Jesse's if he wanted it. Elated, Jesse contemplated the offer for at least three seconds and accepted. Two hours after school, Saturdays, and maybe full-time during the summer -- that was the deal -- and because Mr. Kelly was in the shadows of the negotiations, that deal was as good as gold.

At first, Darwin Anderson wasn't the most pleasant man to work for, but Jesse recognized the challenge of pleasing a man few could ever please, and from that he soon learned the value of solid work ethics. Show up on time, do the job to the best of your ability, don't complain about anything, and stay until the job is finished. Those simple philosophies -- if practiced regularly -- earned high marks in Anderson's grade book, and Jesse made certain he remained on the honor roll. His diligence proved exemplary; his dedication, superb; his attitude was like none Anderson had ever observed. He could count on Jesse to complete any task put before him, and within a few weeks, he required little if any supervision.

Never before had the Westby Depot seen a baggage smasher quite like Jesse. The regular commuters grew to expect his smiling, cheerful greeting on the platform, and he was always ready to assist them with their suitcases and trunks. There were those who were aware of his star-crossed childhood, and perhaps out of pity, but mostly due to their gratitude, slipped Jesse a little loose change. On a good day the tips far exceeded the modest wage he earned.

Every night, Jesse stood on the corner of Main and State Streets, watching the cars chug past and imagining himself in the driver's seat of each one. And now that there was a motorcar dealership just down the street with a brand new Model A sedan displayed in the front window, he could spend hours gazing at the shiny machine and dreaming of the day when one just like it would be his.

One night, as he stood there on an almost deserted street, staring through the showroom glass, the rumble of a car engine broke his concentration. The car stopped next to the sidewalk just behind him. The mirrored reflection in the huge window was that of the biggest, classiest car -- the likes of which Jesse had never seen in real life. The Packard's gleaming chrome grille and headlight pods sparkled under the gas street lamps. The hood seemed a block long, flanked by a spare tire nestled behind each front fender. It was very black, and its presence was almost intimidating. Jesse was in awe, scrutinizing every square inch of the long sedan. He couldn't believe this car was actually there in front of him.

The rear passenger door window slowly rolled down, revealing a smartly dressed man -- black suit, white shirt, and black necktie.

"Hey. Kid. Can you tell us where Lizzy Hawthorne's house is?"

It would have been simple to tell the man to just turn around and backtrack three blocks, but Jesse was so taken by the beautiful car that his instructions seemed a bit complicated.

"Why don't you just jump into the front seat with Karl and show him the way?"

Jesse didn't think twice about the offer to get a ride in that car, and in the wag of a lamb's tail he was sitting next to the driver on the plush, gray mohair seat.

"Turn left at the next corner."

When they pulled into the driveway, the man in the back seat leaned forward and put a hand on Jesse's right shoulder.

"You're all right, kid... my name's Al. We'll be here all day tomorrow conducting some business with Lizzy, and if you'd like to make some pocket money, I'll pay you five dollars to come back tomorrow and wash my car. Think you can do that?"

"Sure... I'd love to wash this car!"

And with that, Al stuffed a dollar bill into Jesse's shirt pocket as gratitude for his help, and sent him on his way.

Jesse didn't know who Al was, but five dollars was a lot of money -- it didn't matter who he was. He could wash the car in the morning and still get to the depot in time for the noon train.

As promised, a five-dollar bill was waiting for Jesse when the job was completed, and a formal introduction was made while tea was served in the Hawthornes' front parlor. Jesse had read in the newspapers about Al "Scarface" Capone, but he never dreamed he would come face to face with such a noted celebrity -- especially this one. Capone had become one of the most powerful men of the age -- the Chicago Mafia boss. Challenged by many, he was defeated by none, and those who stood in his way were quietly -- and sometimes not so quietly -- rewarded with sudden elimination. His bold reputation was well-known throughout the land; people's respect for him was surpassed only by their trepidation.

It must have been Jesse's calm attitude that captured Capone's interest in him. There seemed to be an immediate trust between them -- Al sensed that the association did not threaten his security in this town, and Jesse knew his discretion regarding his acquaintance with such a powerful figure would certainly ensure friendship.

In the months to follow, Capone made regular visits to Westby -- the Hawthorne house was a safe overnight stop between Chicago and Couderay, where the construction of a fortress hideaway on a four-hundred-acre tract was under way. Couderay was Capone's choice for the safe-haven retreat, some four hundred miles to the north, as the crow flies, from the infernal gangland battlegrounds of Chicago.

The Hawthorne mansion played into the scheme of things in another capacity, too. For a couple of years, Emma and Lizzy had made it available as an outpost for Capone's growing business -- bootleg liquor and prostitution -- in exchange for a handsome share of the profits. No one seemed to know how the association between Capone and the Hawthornes originated, and Jesse never asked. But he suspected the frequent rail trips Lizzy and Emma made to Milwaukee must have had something to do with it.

After a few months, Jesse was a trusted confidant of the Capone entourage during their stays in Westby. He saw a different side of Al, a man so many feared and loathed. To him, Al Capone was a generous, caring man. Al Capone was a friend. Al treated him like a little brother, and almost always avoided exposing Jesse to acts of human violence. The relationship grew stronger with every visit.

The business alliance between Capone and the Hawthornes strengthened, too. At first, small amounts of liquor began arriving on furniture delivery trucks. Because the Hawthornes weren't the most beloved people in the city and everyone knew they had boarders coming and going most of the time, few paid any attention at all to the trucks. Although Jesse knew what was going on, he made no one aware of the knowledge, or of his association with Al Capone. It would remain the best-kept secret in town.

In time, the traffic to and from the Hawthorne house increased. Out-of-towners, mostly, and eventually a number of locals, were making late-night visits to the house, and because of the prohibition laws, those patronizing it didn't want to lose this convenient supply line. The secrecy of the illicit operation remained intact. And when the public finally learned who the kingpin really was, Jesse began to realize the magnitude of Capone's influence. Even though this underground business was becoming more known, no one in the quiet community of Westby was eager to invite the violence plaguing Chicago and other big cities into their own back yards. No one in this town was eager to wake up in the middle of the night to the sound of machine-gun fire. No one was eager to see their town destroyed by bombs and fires that would surely result should they openly oppose the quiet invasion that so far wasn't really hurting anyone.

Opposition did come, but not in the form of an attempt to block Capone's operation. Instead it came as competition, and Jesse's impression of Capone's power was reinforced.

The Lynch brothers, Henry, Tom, and Wendell, were rednecks who farmed a rugged territory northwest of town. They were the lords of some three hundred acres -- ninety percent of which was steep hills, rocky bluffs, and timber. It wasn't unusual to hear tales of someone being shot at upon unknowingly wandering onto their land while squirrel or rabbit hunting. That turf was theirs, and so was the wild game thriving on it. For years, that area was renowned as the "Lynch Law Land," and to avoid the possibility of coming home with buttocks full of buckshot, or worse yet, not coming home at all, everyone avoided the Lynch property. That made for the perfect location of a corn whiskey still, and the Lynch brothers recognized a lucrative supplement to their income from a ragtag farming venture.

But the Lynches' reputation didn't stop -- or even slow down -- Capone's reaction when the competition started cutting into his profits. One night, a larger-than-usual entourage accompanied Al when he arrived at the Hawthorne house. Seven men -- instead of the usual three -- followed Capone in from the two cars parked in the back yard, out of sight from Main Street. Capone took Jesse aside. There was an element of danger involved in the mission he described, but Jesse was the only one he could count on as a guide to escort his men to the Lynch distillery, located in the hills, and every precaution would be taken to ensure Jesse's safety. Capone's men were highly skilled in covert operations like this one, and all Jesse had to do was lead them to their destination. *They* would do the rest.

Jesse wasn't absolutely sure what *the rest* was to involve, but he was certain this wouldn't be a social visit, much less a business call. But it sounded like an adventure Jesse couldn't pass up. His loyalty to his friend was surpassed only by his enthusiasm. He knew those hills and valleys as well as anyone, and he was quite sure he knew just where the still would be located – in an obscure ravine deep within the perimeter of the forbidden territory, accessible only on foot through a heavily wooded area at least a mile from the nearest road.

The explosion heard on that clear, placid night rattled windows and sent every dog for miles around into a howling frenzy. Heads popped out of doorways, searching the clear night sky for an unexpected thunderstorm. Jesse was the only person in all of Westby who knew the true origin of the mysterious rumble, but he said nothing. The Lynch brothers got the message quite clearly, though. They never attempted to rebuild their still.

2

To anyone else, the chain of events that occurred during the next few months would have been nothing out of the ordinary. Jesse saw it a little differently, but he had no reason to discuss his observations with even his closest friends. His association with Capone had gone unnoticed, and he wanted to keep it that way.

Two very attractive young women arrived with Mr. Capone one night. As Jesse unloaded the truck that followed Al's car into the Hawthornes' back yard, he thought he was merely moving more boarders into the upstairs bedrooms. But most of the crates and boxes were more bootleg liquor. Only a few actually contained the new residents' belongings.

Secretive conversations were regularly being conducted between the Hawthorne sisters and Capone now, and Emma and Lizzy were making more frequent trips to Milwaukee. They weren't saying much about these trips as they always had in the past. And each time they returned, their baggage included a trunk that Jesse knew wasn't among their departing luggage. It seemed quite unlikely they would be purchasing clothes or souvenirs in such quantities. Jesse was always instructed to deliver the trunks to the cellar through the outside entrance at the rear of the house, and when he did, the previous two or three trunks would be lined up along the wall -- open and empty.

The two women who had moved into the house were becoming rather popular among the single male population, entertaining different boyfriends nearly every night. Then, just before Al was to return after serving a ten-month jail sentence out East for carrying a concealed weapon, the women simply vanished. No one saw them leave town, and they were never seen again. Al was quite upset with their disappearance, and that's when his association with Emma and Lizzy Hawthorne began to deteriorate. Just as he had witnessed the rise of the quietly booming business, Jesse was now watching it crumble, piece by piece. Although his alliance with Al remained intact and strong, he sensed there was something amiss. An apparent dispute over money loomed within the Hawthorne house with Al's every visit. But Jesse knew it was not a matter for him to become inquisitive about, and Al wasn't volunteering any explanation.

On a hot, muggy July late afternoon, the strangest of all events occurred. The Hawthornes had been away on one of their Milwaukee excursions for more than a week. The house was empty -- or so Jesse thought. Capone

7

arrived earlier than usual, and it was only because there was no scheduled train that day that Jesse happened to be walking through the park and noticed Al's car parked in the driveway.

The previous November's stock market collapse had brought the public to its knees. The onset of the Depression had taken its toll on the small midwestern community of Westby in epic proportions. The few businesses that were still surviving were operating on a shoestring, and the population was steadily shrinking because there were few jobs to keep families fed. The once-thriving railroad, which had maintained a daily schedule of freight and passenger trains through Westby since the town was established, was now on the verge of extinction, and Westby was not much more than a whistle stop most of the time. The weak economy was affecting people in every walk of life, and Jesse was no exception. With the greatly diminished rail schedule, he now had a lot of extra time on his hands, so the sight of Capone's big, black sedan gave his spirit a boost. He sprinted across the nearly deserted road to greet his friends, whom he spotted around the corner at the rear of the house.

Jesse greeted Al with a cordial handshake. "Good to see you, Al. Did you have a nice trip?"

"Hello, Jesse. I wired Lizzy last week... told her I'd be here today to collect. Needed to get away from Chicago for a few days anyway."

Jesse tried to offer an explanation for the Hawthornes' absence. "Emma and Liz aren't here... They--"

Before Jesse could finish, Capone interrupted. "Oh, they're here, all right... but they're laid out on the sitting room floor, dead as a pair of mackerels, and the inside of the house stinks worse than a morgue without ice. Looks like we ain't gonna collect today, and we won't be doing business here any more."

"But Boss... what about that last trunk that isn't here yet?" one of his assistants asked in a whisper.

"Forget it." Al replied quietly and calmly.

Jesse knew exactly what those words meant: Al wasn't coming back here. Ever.

"Does that mean I won't be seeing you any more?"

"Not unless you come with us right now to Couderay, and work for me there. This wasn't a very profitable operation, anyway."

Even though he was devastated by the thought of ending this relationship, Jesse wasn't ready to leave Westby just yet. "No. Thanks for the offer, but I have to stay here. As soon as I save up enough money to buy my Model A, I'll come visit you."

Capone put his hand on Jesse's shoulder. "I know you've been saving a long time for that car. How much are you short?"

8

Jesse didn't have to think about the answer -- he knew the figure exactly. "Three hundred and fifty dollars."

Al dug into his pocket, produced an impressive bankroll, and began counting out bills. "Here. Take this. It's enough to get you that Model A... and maybe a little left over."

"But Al. I can't--"

"Take it. It's yours. Just remember -- you didn't see me here today. Now, I hafta get outa here. Give my regards at the funeral."

Capone and his boys were in the black car and speeding away before Jesse could make another attempt to inform them that the Hawthornes would be returning on the next train. This had all happened much too quickly for Jesse to fully digest it, but two things were certain -- Al Capone was gone, and there were two dead bodies lying on the parlor floor. Jesse didn't understand how the Hawthornes could have returned without his knowing, but now it seemed they had -- and they were dead.

For more than an hour he sat on the park bench across the street while the local constable and the undertaker removed the corpses from the house. It wasn't until after the crowd of curious onlookers dispersed that Constable Wade Sheppard spotted Jesse, strolled across the street, and informed him that the two bodies weren't the Hawthornes. He had found no identification, so he didn't know who they were. But Lizzy and Emma could probably supply that information when they returned.

In just a few short hours, Jesse's life had made another abrupt turnaround. Truly strange circumstances surrounded him now. These changes didn't trouble Jesse, nor did they comfort him. They were just peculiar. He had an unbelievable amount of cash in his pocket but a somewhat abandoned feeling in his heart; an extraordinary sense of freedom, yet a sense of being imprisoned by responsibility.

The Hawthorne twins did arrive the next day on the train, as Jesse expected they would. He had been commissioned by Constable Sheppard to inform them of the unfortunate circumstances and to direct them to the constable's downtown office upon their arrival. Their behavior seemed a little odd to Jesse as they waited for him to retrieve their baggage, and when he told them of the incident, he suspected right away that their reaction of surprise was somewhat artificial, but he played along with it, giving them no reason to believe he knew there was something fishy about the situation.

After Sheppard had interviewed Emma and Lizzy, they asked Jesse to deliver their luggage -- all but one trunk -- to the Hotel, where they would stay while the house aired out. It was then that Jesse realized they had much more with them on this trip than usual -- as if they knew in advance they would not be returning to their own home right away. There was definitely foul play in the air, and whatever had happened, Emma and Lizzy Hawthorne had hidden it well. Constable Sheppard was showing no interest in detaining them for any wrongdoing, and Jesse wasn't about to utter a word of his suspicions to anyone.

As usual, the trunk was to be delivered to the cellar. Lizzy assured her sister it would be safe there for the time being. There was little chance that anyone would enter the house -- by now the whole population of Westby was aware of the incident. Everyone would steer clear of the mansion, and that would ensure the trunk's security.

But Emma and Lizzy didn't count on Jesse's curiosity. A couple of days passed, and he couldn't stop thinking what might be in that trunk. It was apparent to him that its contents must belong to Al Capone as he recalled the comment about "the last trunk" one of Capone's men had made. And now the Hawthornes were confident that Al would not return to claim it, and they were concerned about its safety. Certainly it must contain something of value to warrant their concern.

A week had gone by when the Hawthornes appeared at the railroad depot at mid-morning on the day the Milwaukee-bound train was scheduled to stop in Westby at noon. There was no cargo to ready for loading, so Jesse was keeping himself busy with a broom until passengers started showing up.

"The house is still quite unpleasant, so we're going to Milwaukee to stay with our friends there for a couple more weeks," Lizzy told Jesse. "Would you haul that trunk -- the last one you took to the house -- back here and get it in the baggage car with the rest of our things?"

"I sure will... isn't much else to do here today, so I'll have plenty of time."

Jesse knew what they were up to -- they were taking the trunk back to Milwaukee to ensure that its delivery to its rightful owner would never take place. Once it was on the train, Jesse would never see it again.

At high noon, the twins watched as Jesse loaded all their belongings into the baggage car, including the mysterious trunk. As he slid the heavy door shut and closed the latch, they were satisfied that their precious cargo was safe, and they boarded the Pullman to settle in for the long journey ahead. Jesse stood on the platform, just inches from the cars as they slowly rumbled along the steel tracks destined for the big city. He was experiencing disbelief about what he had just done. But somehow, he knew in his heart it would all turn out for the best.

Timing spells success or failure when attempting to make a plan come together. Jesse had pulled the pin on a grenade that would surely blow up in his face if he couldn't make everything fall into line. He was committed, now, to carry out a scheme, the details of which he had not spent a great deal of time considering. He had often dreamed of the day he would leave Westby and be freed from his restricted life. But suddenly he found himself at the doorway to the world, and knew he wasn't completely prepared to go charging through it. He also knew that if he didn't seize this opportunity, the door might never open up for him again, and he could be trapped here for the rest of his life, never knowing what might have been awaiting him.

Now it was a matter of putting the rest of his plan into action. Jesse's biggest dream would soon become reality; the very next day he would own a Model A Ford, a monumental event in his life.

Darwin Anderson was not pleased to hear Jesse's resignation, but all his efforts to convince Jesse to change his mind were in vain. The chips were on the table; Jesse was leaving town, and there was no chance of stopping him.

Julian Kelly, though, was as proud as a new father when he saw Jesse step out of the new Model A pickup parked in front of the lumber yard. He had watched Jesse grow up, helped him through a traumatic childhood, filled the void of absent family, and just seeing the fine young man Jesse had become was all the reward he needed. Now he was being honored as the first to admire Jesse's new truck, and he spoke only words of encouragement when he learned of Jesse's intentions to seek a better life.

Within a couple more days, the preparations were nearly all made. Everything Jesse owned was barely more than most people packed for a week's vacation. He had never been one to accumulate possessions, and now as he was preparing to journey into the unknown; his burden was light and his cares were few. For the last five years, he had saved nearly all the money he earned at the depot and from the Hawthornes, and the money Julian Kelly gave him was still unspent, too, and it was all safely hidden away in a cigar box at the bottom of a foot locker now resting in the bed of the truck. He would never tell anyone the truck was bought with Al Capone's final gift. And no one would know he still had $423 tucked away in that box. In terms of a 1930 economy, Jesse was moderately wealthy, but that was to remain his secret, even to Julian Kelly.

Jesse's last day in Westby – Sunday – was spent with the Kellys. It was as if Thanksgiving had arrived early. Mrs. Kelly prepared a feast second to none, complete with roast chicken, dressing, sweet potatoes, and corn. Jesse couldn't have hoped for a better send-off. The Kellys were special people in his life, and now they were proving that fact more than ever before. The message they were sending was: "Jesse... if things don't work out for you, you always have a home to come back to." Although he had deep feelings for the Kelly family, he was quite certain he would not return to Westby for a long time.

His excuse for leaving that night instead of waiting until morning was that he had never seen the city lights of LaCrosse at night from Grand Dad's Bluff, and this may be his last chance to do that. But his true motive for making the departure that night was something he could tell no one. It had to remain his secret. He couldn't be anywhere near Westby the next day when the train arrived from Milwaukee, and he could accomplish the final step of his plan under the veil of darkness. He had one more stop to make before he left town for the last time. There was something he had to get from the Hawthorne cellar.

3

Jesse Madison didn't leave much behind as he drove away from Westby that balmy August night in 1930. The engine purred; the new truck rumbled along the country road toward the bluffs overlooking the Mississippi River. Images of the past raced through his mind. Vivid recollections mapped out the course of his first twenty years; where he had been was no mystery and why he was engaged in this particular trip at this particular time was quite clear. But the future seemed nothing more than a blur of uncertainty. Somewhere in northern Wisconsin he hoped to reunite with an old friend and perhaps discover the beginning of a bright new future.

Like a snowball rolling down a hillside gathering mass, a force had grown inside him, pushing him to this edge, until he made a decision that went against everything he had ever learned about honesty and respect; a decision that would put his honor at risk, and his safety in jeopardy. But he believed it was a risk worth taking, and now he only had a few hours to distance himself from Westby without leaving a trail that anyone could follow.

He navigated through the dark, moonless night to the out-of-the-way spot he knew high atop the bluff above La Crosse. That's where he would stop for the night and sleep in the bed of the truck under the stars. Reality was setting in. He began to feel the magnitude of his freedom as the wind blew through the open window and the sweet pine forest aroma filled the cab. Jesse was living his dreams. No longer did he have to stand on a street corner in Westby and imagine himself behind the wheel of passing cars. No longer did he have to imagine what the rest of the world was like, just by looking at pictures in books because now he was behind a steering wheel, and that steering wheel was guiding him to real places.

The early morning sun trickled through a canopy of lofty hickory and oak trees rustled by a brisk breeze. Jesse sat up, squinting into nature's living room. He had slept like a rock, and now he wondered if this was just another dream. But when his bare feet touched the ground, and the long, soft grass tickled his toes he knew this was not a fantasy. It was all very real, and it was the most magnificent feeling he had ever experienced. Now he recognized how sheltered his life had been, dwelling in the confines of Westby. He had only been away for one night and already he felt like a new person, restricted only by his own inhibitions, and at this moment he was more positive of his destiny than ever before.

His attention focused on the cargo in the truck bed and he recalled the mission demanding his immediate action. It was the very reason he couldn't leave a trail, and why he had left town without telling anyone of his destination. He carefully untied the rope securing the blanket draped over the trunk -- Al Capone's trunk -- the trunk the Hawthorne sisters thought they were transporting back to Milwaukee. By now, they surely would have discovered the stack of old newspapers he placed in another identical trunk to simulate the weight of this one, and likely as not, they would be on the morning train arriving from Milwaukee. *And they would be looking for him.* Jesse chuckled out loud at the thought of his successful deception. He might not be standing here laughing had they investigated the trunk's contents before boarding the train. But they didn't, and now he was in possession of the property the Hawthornes attempted to steal from Al Capone. His mission was to deliver it to the rightful owner -- a good deed that would repay Al for his generosity, and was certain to re-establish a lost association that held a promise of employment.

But if the Hawthornes were back in Westby, he was still too near, and there was too much at stake to linger here very long.

The trunk was securely locked, and although Jesse's curiosity was staggering, he knew it had to stay locked until it reached its destination. That would ensure Capone's trust, and greatly improve their alliance.

He covered the trunk with the blanket, tied the rope around the bottom, and prepared to continue the long journey. According to the map, Couderay was due north, and because he had never traveled much, his concept of distance, at best, was less than average.

La Crosse was a busy place. There was far more activity on the streets here than Jesse was accustomed to in the small, rural community where he had lived all his life. He had visited the city several times, but never alone, and now as he neared the heart of the largest commercial hub in this part of the state, he began to view it differently. The multi-story buildings seemed to generate an intimidating energy. All around, people bustled about in their daily routines, and because there was little chance he would see even one familiar face among them, Jesse realized that he was really *alone*. But he was determined to face the world, even if he had to do it alone, and he would learn to ignore the loneliness.

State Street led right to the Mississippi and ended in Levee Park on the banks of the main channel where the riverboats docked, and Front Street began its southward course past a half dozen warehouses, several grain elevators, and the coal yards. For the first time, after numerous visits here, Jesse noticed how the beauty of the park with its many majestic oaks and maples and meticulously kept flower gardens seemed to collide with the less attractive sector of the city.

Despite the profound contrast, the park was a perfect spot to spend a few minutes studying the map. This would be his first venture beyond this point to the north. His instincts told him to chart a path along the river that was now casting a strange magnetism. His sudden attraction to the river puzzled him; the river had always been there, but never before had it drawn his attention quite like this.

Not far out of the city, the highway reunited with the riverbank. The loneliness that was once hanging over him like a light fog seemed to evaporate, and was quickly replaced with passion and intrigue. Before him, in its radiant splendor laid the great unknown. Glistening sunlight danced on the water, and in the distance farther upstream, majestic bluffs towered beside the river like custodial sentries; it was a magnificent sight.

Mile after mile, Jesse soaked in the grandeur of the Mississippi River Valley and the different culture that it cradled. Little settlements he passed through seemed to be huddled around piers jutting out from the shoreline, and boats appeared to be more important than cars to the people living there. Life was geared to the river, and the highway was just a convenience for people like Jesse to discover the magical charm.

He rounded a curve just south of Fountain City; a clear view of the river opened up. Another sight bolstered Jesse's enchantment: out in the main channel the regal beauty of the grandest river steamer he had ever seen glided effortlessly downstream. It was a floating fortress of elegance. Long and sleek, the gleaming white vessel was vividly garnished with gold scrolls and stripes, and high above the third deck, gray smoke curled from the crown-like tips of the shiny black twin smoke stacks, lingered for a while, and then was whisked away by the breeze. A giant American flag waved lazily from a mast at the stern, and beside it, an equally large banner boasted the ship's coat of arms.

Jesse steered his truck to the roadside and stopped. A huge boulder just beyond the wooden guardrail served as a better vantage point. It was a picture so magnificent, he had to embrace it for as long as it would last, until the boat was completely out of sight. Even then, it was difficult to take his eyes off the mighty waterway, and return to his designated course.

The little town of Alma snuggled into the hillside, shadowed by six-hundred-feet high sheer rock cliffs overlooking the Mississippi. A stretch of the highway formed its Main Street and several narrow alleyways, terraced into the hillside, serpentined with the steep contour. Stairways, some made of stone and some constructed with wood, sharply ascended the hill, connecting Main Street to the other roads. Peeking above the treetops and dotting the slope were scores of house roofs, and a church steeple proclaimed its watchful vigil over the hamlet. Most of the business places huddled along the main road, many of them with the river splashing at the foot of their stonewall backsides. Near the center of the market strip, a large, grassy levee graced the river's edge, and from it a massive boat dock protruded out over the water, with fishing boats and pleasure craft moored to its upstream side.

Nearly as busy and crowded as the streets of La Crosse, this little river village had everything -- a butcher shop and fish market, a dry goods store and a green grocer, a gas station and a pharmacy, a post office, a hardware store, and a small lumber yard. Toward the north end of Main Street, stood the majestic Alma Hotel. But there was one big difference -- the atmosphere here was warm and affectionate. Jesse strolled the sidewalks; everyone he met cordially greeted him as if he were a next-door neighbor. It was almost like being back home with the beauty of the river just outside the front door. In this picturesque setting, Jesse discovered the essence of a lifestyle he could learn to love, and until now he didn't know it existed.

Several hours had passed when he noticed the sun, sinking lower in the west. Although he wanted to remain there forever, he knew he was committed to a mission that commanded his departure. He had to pick up the supplies he needed and press onward. But he would never forget Alma.

4

Jesse had developed a fascination with the river and now it was almost like saying good-bye to an old friend as he turned the steering wheel, pointing the Model A up the hill into the forest-covered slopes. The road snaked along a ravine flanked by tall peaks that seemed to touch the sky. Driving deeper and deeper into this wilderness, civilization along the riverbanks quickly disappeared behind him. Perhaps someday he could return to enjoy more of the place he had learned to love within just a few hours.

The fiery red western heavens caught Jesse's eyes in the rear view mirror as he crested the long, winding grade. He pulled to the side of the road, stopped, and stepped out of the truck. He was at the top of the world again, looking out over the breath-taking view of the horizon on the other side of the river. It would be dark soon, so finding a place to stop for the night was in order. Traveling through this beauty during darkness would be a waste, and he didn't want to miss a single inch of it.

Up ahead, Jesse saw a dirt road meandering across the ridge to the east - - a likely route to an obscure overnight hideaway. The land on this plateau was nearly void of trees, but a field of waist-high corn was evidence that a civilization did exist there. There was no sign of human habitation nearby, and Jesse liked the quiet solitude he had found. This was quite clearly a trail less traveled; it didn't seem likely anyone would bother him way out there.

About a mile off the highway, the dirt road appeared to end at the edge of woods. Obviously it was taking him no farther, as if it were dictating his choice of campsites. Just before the dead end Jesse saw something lying in the middle of the roadway; in the shadows of dusk it looked like a body. He stopped the truck and cautiously got out to investigate. A sigh of relief exited his tightened chest when he saw the body was that of a large dog. It appeared to be badly hurt and panting short, shallow breaths, apparently exhausted by the pain of injury, and unable move.

"Aw... ya poor mongrel. What happened to you?"

Jesse gave no thought to the danger element; he knelt down beside the critter and gently stroked the fur on its neck and shoulder. He saw there was a nasty gash just below the dog's left ear and another on its hind leg.

"I'll bet you got hit by a car out on the highway, and ya' just couldn't make it any farther than right here."

A meek whimper turned into a growl; Jesse quickly pulled his hand back and leaned away from the animal.

"Hey! Take it easy, boy. I'm just tryin' to help ya."

Too weak to carry out any further attack, the gray dog just laid there, panting, staring into Jesse's eyes.

"Well, I can't just leave ya here like this, but I don't know what to do to help ya, either. Are ya thirsty? Ya want some water?"

The injured dog tilted its head at the sound of Jesse's voice. Its eyes were permanently fixed on Jesse's every move. A water jug and iron fry pan was within easy reach in the truck bed.

Another growl warned Jesse not to get too close, but Jesse knew if he let his fear show he would have conceded to defeat, and this beast clearly was in no condition to mount a threatening attack. He set the pan of water on the ground and pushed it within the dog's reach with his foot. The mongrel sniffed at the pan and just continued to stare at Jesse.

"Okay... you can have a drink whenever you get ready. Now I'm gonna find some firewood."

All the while Jesse constructed a teepee arrangement of sticks he had gathered for the campfire, he kept talking to the dog. Even though he knew he wasn't being understood, somehow that strange creature filled a void in the loneliness of the night, and it was strangely comforting to have someone -- or something -- to talk to. He rambled on and on about his days at the railroad depot and about the night he led Capone's boys out into the Lynch property to blow up the moonshine still, and how he was on his way to find Capone again, to deliver the trunk to him.

Jesse expected the dog to eventually regain his strength and simply run off into the night. But instead, the dog just lay in the same spot, periodically lapping at the water and eventually rested his chin on his outstretched front paws, seemingly contented, and not fearful of Jesse's presence, as long as Jesse kept his distance.

The can of pork and beans Jesse set on a rock next to the fire didn't seem to arouse the dog at all, but the pound of wieners he unwrapped from the butcher paper sent out a signal.

"Oh. I s'pose you're hungry too. I guess I can share my dinner with you."

Jesse tossed one of the wieners on the ground at the dog's front paws. It vanished in one gulp, as did the second one, and the third.

When the fire had died down to a heap of embers, Jesse announced, as if talking to a roommate, that he was going to bed. As he settled into the truck bed and gazed up at the stars, he wondered if his guest would still be there in the morning.

One lonely, fluffy white cloud drifted silently by as Jesse opened his eyes to the gloriously blue sky. He stayed perfectly still, watching the cloud transform into dozens of different shapes until it disappeared from sight. When he finally began to stir, a movement near his feet drew his attention; on the open tailgate of the truck laid last night's dinner guest. Jesse's stirring had aroused the dog too, as his head lifted and his watchful eyes trained on Jesse.

"Well... good morning, boy. I didn't expect to see you still here." Jesse tried not to make any sudden movements and slowly sat up. The dog did the same. Jesse cautiously extended his hand toward the beast, but the friendly gesture was not graciously accepted, and in a split second the dog was back on the ground twenty feet from the back of the truck where he casually sat on his haunches and just stared at Jesse.

The silvery-gray fur glistened in the morning sun, and except for the bloodstains on his hindquarter and the side of his face, he was beautiful and sleek. But there was something peculiar about him. Jesse realized that he had been trying to befriend a very non-domestic creature of the wild.

"You're not just a dog... are you? You're a wolf."

The animal's head cocked to the left and then to the right as Jesse spoke. "Well... I'm glad to see you're feelin' better. How 'bout another cold wiener for breakfast?"

The rustling of the butcher paper was now a familiar sound, and the smell of the wieners drew his keen nostrils into the air, sniffing at the aroma.

"But ya gotta come over here and get it." Jesse knew he could use the food as a means to gain the wolf's trust. He laid the wiener on the tailgate, sat back against the truck cab, and began munching on his cold breakfast.

Within a couple of minutes, the tempting meat scent overpowered resistance and the muscular gray mass of fur leaped up onto the tailgate. His dining etiquette lacked, but then what could be expected of a wild animal? Jesse held up another wiener -- the last one. Progress was under way and this was perhaps his only chance to lure the wolf closer.

Trepidation was gone from both man and beast; Jesse boldly held out the tempting fare, and the wolf stepped cautiously nearer. The tasty wiener distracted the wolf long enough for Jesse to pet the silky fur on the back of his neck.

The food was soon history and so was the petting. The wild creature still wasn't convinced that this kind of contact was safe, quickly backed away, and once again jumped to the ground. Because the wolf had passed on many opportunities to rip him apart, Jesse was certain this otherwise feared, savage renegade didn't pose any threat to him, although now that the wieners were gone, that concept was subject to change.

It hardly seemed likely -- or even possible -- that the rules of nature could allow such a mingling of man and wild beast to occur. Apparently, the rules had been altered on this hilltop. Jesse had plucked the thorn from a lion's paw, and now the lion was showing his gratitude with friendship.

The butcher shop in Alma was just a few miles back down the hill and down river. Going back there wouldn't be so bad; it would give Jesse another opportunity to be next to the river again, and he did need more food. But would the wolf still be here when he returned? Probably not.

"I know you don't understand a single word I'm sayin' to ya, but here's my plan. I'm gonna leave some of my stuff here while I go get some more food. Maybe you'll know I'm comin' back again. Of course I'll understand if you decide to take off while I'm gone."

The wolf seemed to have a certain degree of attraction to Jesse. Limping, it paced back and forth, keeping a close watch on Jesse's every move, but from a safe distance.

For a reason Jesse couldn't quite comprehend, he felt a strange sort of covenant with the animal, and he hoped the animal sensed that same bond.

Jesse's fascination with the Mississippi River had not diminished. A block from the butcher shop, the irresistible sights and sounds lured him to the water's edge. Tied to the dock was a stern-wheel steamer, the Russell Walker. He had seen the majestic, two-hundred-foot-long craft, or one like it, cruising down the river just north of La Crosse the day before, and there it was, bigger than life within touching distance.

His comprehension of the river had not yet reached a level of high expertise by any means, and his knowledge of the large vessels sailing upon it was even less, but there was little doubt in Jesse's mind that operating a boat like this one carried a colossal measure of prestige. Everyone involved with keeping it afloat took a great deal of pride in its dazzling appearance. Even though they were not in their homeport, and there didn't seem to be any passengers coming or going, the crewmen busied themselves with a spit and polish routine as if they intended their boat to be the most attractive one on the Mississippi. They were scrubbing the outside walls with long-handled brushes and polishing the windows to a squeaky-clean luster. One young fellow was repainting the brilliant gold spindles of the upper deck railing with the passion of a world-class artist. Whatever their task, it was clearly a labor of love. This gallant vessel was their life.

Jesse could only imagine the extraordinary sense of satisfaction one would feel being a member of that elite fraternity. Deep down inside, he wished he were among them.

High above the work detail, the riverboat pilot stood near the ship's wheel in the pilothouse, busily jotting entries in the log. His silvery beard and the crisp black jacket adorned with gold buttons rendered the distinction of command. He noticed Jesse's admiration of the fine craft, and when their eyes met he raised his hand with a respectful wave, acknowledging Jesse's interest. Jesse returned the gesture. Shaking the President's hand couldn't have been more gratifying.

Time had a way of slipping by that day too, as he wandered about the village, frequently taking advantage of the shade under storefront awnings. He watched the coal trains from the north rumble by, and the fishermen returning to the docks with their day's catch. The flow of area farmers coming and going constantly changed the expression of Main Street. If it hadn't been for the predetermined destination and his loyalty to a friend, Jesse might have aborted any further travel, or at least postponed it for a while. This place felt good.

Dark, threatening clouds were tumbling over the horizon in the west. An occasional rumble of distant thunder signaled the approach of a storm; the hot, still, sticky air was beginning to cool; a ghostly breeze sporadically whistled through the treetops. It didn't appear likely that the Walker would be casting off on its return to the homeport of Winona until the storm had passed. Deckhands were preparing the vessel for rough weather, lashing additional mooring ropes to the mammoth posts supporting the boardwalk pier, and closing the shutters over all the windows. Jesse entertained the thought of holding up in the town too; the hotel might be a better place to wait out the elemental harshness that was slowly closing in, but then he remembered he had left some of his belongings up on the hilltop. He'd have to go back for them.

He was about to bypass the butcher shop and just hurry back to his campsite, but then he thought of his original intention to return to town.

"I'd like some bones," Jesse told the butcher. "You'd never believe what happened up on the hill."

"Got some soup bones," the butcher said.

"That'll be just fine. There was this wild wolf, and..."

Jesse recited his experience to the butcher while the bones were carefully wrapped in paper.

"Oh, that must be Lobo," the butcher replied. "Ol' Man Weaver's critter."

"He's somebody's pet?"

"Yeah, Weaver raised him from a pup. Kinda funny, though... nobody but Weaver can even get close to him."

"Guess he was hurt too bad to get away from me."

"I'll tell Weaver that you found him... he's been kinda worried 'bout that mutt. Hasn't seen him in a while."

Jesse took the package of bones and hurried off to his truck.

It wasn't surprising that the wolf was nowhere in sight when he arrived at the campsite. But at least now he understood the nature of the beast – if it really was Lobo that had been his overnight guest.

The wind was considerably stronger up on the ridge, and the view of the thunderheads, still miles beyond the river, rendered the obvious explanation for battening the hatches on the Russell Walker. Lightning bolts pierced the intimidating, charcoal sky, some of them making contact with the rugged Minnesota terrain beyond the bluffs across the wide river; the hazy, gray columns of a torrential rain seemed a logical reason to head back to the protection of the hotel. But the brunt of the fury was clearly taking a course toward the north; it appeared as though the hilltop would not be in its path. Jesse gathered up his things and stowed them in the pickup box, and then just sat there on the open tailgate, intrigued with the cinema playing on the grandest theater screen known to man. The earlier feeling of need for seeking refuge seemed unimportant now. The worst of the storm was going to miss him.

"Whatya got in the truck?"

The gravelly voice coming from behind him sent a chill down Jesse's spine. He jumped to his feet and spun around, only to see the large caliber rifle barrel pointing right at him; at the other end was a bristly, black beard and a pair of beady eyes staring at him from under the brim of a tattered black hat. This was not a social visit.

Jesse raised his hands out of instinct. "Who are you? If this is your land, I'm sorry I came on it... and I'll leave right away."

"Shut up! This ain't my land, and I couldn't care less that you're here... now... whatya got in the back of the truck?"

"N-nothing. Just my clothes and stuff."

"Well, I don't believe you... you got any money?"

"No sir." Jesse's eyes shifted to the footlocker in the truck bed, and then back to the grizzly character. He knew instantly he had made a mistake by looking at the cargo.

The stranger's stare briefly trained on the two chests in the truck box and then fixed on Jesse again.

"Open up that big one. Let's see if there's anything in there I might want."

"I can't. It's locked and I don't have a key. It's not even mine. I'm just delivering it to a friend... and I don't even know what's in it."

"Then toss it down here on the ground," the stranger demanded. "We're just gonna have to bust it open. A locked trunk must have something in it worth locking up."

Jesse wasn't about to argue with a gun barrel at point-blank range. He climbed into the bed, hoisted Capone's trunk over the side and dropped it to the ground in front of the stranger.

The thunder's volume increased, and Jesse thought he heard another familiar sound that blended with it, but the stranger was oblivious to the growl erupting from the front of the truck. His intentions were clear in his mind: if the trunk contained anything of value, he wouldn't think twice about killing his victim and making off with the spoils. He had done it before. There were no witnesses. And this was a pretty easy target.

Jesse sensed what was about to happen. He was going to die at the hands of this ruthless rogue. He had no means of defense.

The growl was more distinct this time and was accompanied by a blood-curdling snarl. Even the stranger noticed it that time; he turned to see where it had come from, but it was too late for a bullet to ward off the jaws full of razor-sharp fangs. Jesse heard the growling and snarling and the terrified screams from the stranger; he saw a gray blur as the wolf set his teeth into the forearm holding the rifle, and despite the man's efforts to get free, his strength was no match for the ferocious beast. The gun dropped to the ground, butt-first, jarring it hard enough to cause its discharge with a deafening blast. Jesse heard the bullet zing by as it sliced through the air just inches from his right ear. He fell to his knees.

The blast startled the wolf too. He released his deadly grip long enough for the man to scramble back to his feet and escape in a dead run, his arm and hand painted bright red by blood gushing from the torn flesh. The wolf ran after him and caught him almost instantly, snarling and biting at the man's legs. Jesse just watched in awe, thinking the man was sure to meet his fate before this was over. But then, as if the wolf were satisfied that the stranger was no longer a threat, he ceased the chase and just watched the stranger running away until he was out of sight.

Paralyzed with fear, Jesse stood beside the truck holding his breath as the wolf trotted toward him. Was he going to be the wolf's next victim?

The terror quickly dissipated; the wolf's eyes no longer beamed the glare of a bloodthirsty animal and his movements were not those of attack. He sat on his haunches at Jesse's feet, leaned against Jesse's leg and looked up into Jesse's eyes as if he were seeking approval of a good deed.

Jesse kneeled down slowly and cautiously began stroking the fur on the animal's neck. Miraculously, the wolf allowed the petting to continue, and he was even showing signs of enjoying the contact. He was finally accepting Jesse's friendship.

"Lobo," Jesse said, recalling the butcher's story.

The wolf perked his ears, responding to his name.

"I don't know where you came from, but I'm sure glad you showed up in the nick of time."

Man and beast had come to terms by virtue of the bizarre situation. Combined efforts had allowed them both to survive potential disaster. There would be a tomorrow.

5

Sleeping across the seat of a 1930 Model A pickup truck wasn't the most comfortable accommodation, but it was the only option to stay dry. The overnight tempest that still lingered with snarling thunder and rain driven by a biting wind created less-than-desirable camping conditions. Jesse had already proved to himself that he was a survivor, not to be defeated by a little adverse weather. The storm was sure to pass. The sun would shine again, and everything would be just fine. But for right now, snuggled in a dry blanket, even these cramped quarters were somewhat comforting. Even Lobo seemed quite content curled up in a furry ball on the floorboards. Although he had been sleeping for several hours, the rain falling on the rooftop cast a hypnotic spell on Jesse. There just didn't seem to be a good reason to move, and the dismal day offered little invitation.

It was mid-morning when the rain stopped and the sun began peeking out between the clouds now and then. Jesse sat up behind the steering wheel.

"Well, Lobo... looks like the storm is over. I'll bet you're ready to get out and stretch your legs."

Lobo jumped up into the seat beside Jesse and sniffed at the fresh, rain-cleansed gentle breeze through the open window. Jesse didn't have to be reminded that they both had been confined in the truck cab for several hours. They both needed to find a tree.

Once Mother Nature's call had been answered, Jesse knew he was alone again. Lobo would not return from the forest where he disappeared. He was a wild creature, meant to run free through the hills. Jesse had perhaps helped Lobo survive, and Lobo, without a doubt, had saved Jesse. Their meeting was by chance and the companionship brief. But now the score was even, and each had their own and very different calling. Jesse was saddened by the thought of Lobo's permanent absence, but then he realized how privileged he must be to have experienced such a rare acquaintance with nature. It was something he would not soon forget.

"Good-bye Lobo..." Jesse said softly. "...And don't get hit by any more cars out on the highway. Maybe we'll meet again, someday."

The mile of dirt road back to the highway was nothing but mud. The Model A struggled along and Jesse gave a sigh of relief when he finally made the turn onto the highway. On the paved road was where he would stay from here on, at least until the ground dried up a little. His mission had already been delayed by a couple of days and there would be no point in losing any more time by getting stuck in a mud hole.

The road twisted and turned among the corn and grain fields that were nearly washed away in some places. The severity of the storm was more evident as the miles went by. Huge oak trees lay uprooted and roof tin from nearby barns littered the countryside. Up ahead, the mangled windmill wreckage was toppled onto the remains of what had once been a small shed. As Jesse surveyed the wrath and destruction left in the wake of an apparently furious gale, he felt quite lucky that he had not been in the path of this monster.

Gradually, the roadway began its decent down heavily wooded slopes into a broad valley. The low land was the catch basin for the deluge, and this otherwise peaceful-looking dale, was the pathway of a raging brown flood. Dodging rockslides and tree branches strewn about by the cyclone, Jesse paralleled the rushing, overflowing creek, exercising caution in not getting too close to the edge where the muddy water was within just a foot or two from spilling onto the road. Just ahead, the highway made a swooping curve where a bridge spanned the swollen stream. One glance at the bridge stopped Jesse dead in his tracks. Water sloshed up onto the deck and the far end of the bridge was completely submerged. The road headed for higher ground on the opposite side of the creek, but getting there appeared quite impossible. Turning around and backtracking to the Mississippi River seemed like the most logical thing to do. There was bound to be an alternate route farther north.

As Jesse maneuvered the Model A back and forth, the weight of the truck was more than the rain-softened earth beside the road would hold. The bank caved in, taking with it the rear wheels of his truck. In a heart-stopping moment Jesse felt the sudden downward lunge, and in that same moment he pictured him and his truck plunging into the floodwater. Although the Model A stopped short of the water's edge, the cargo in the truck bed did not. Jesse's footlocker and Capone's trunk went sliding out the back, tumbling down the embankment, and into the water. As he peered out the rear window, Jesse watched his entire collection of worldly possessions, including all his money, bobbing like a toy boat in a puddle. If he got to it quickly enough, he'd be able to retrieve his footlocker, but Capone's trunk was floating away. He knew he had to try to recover it; when the footlocker was on solid ground he took off running along the creek bank with hopes the trunk would float close enough to grab it out of the water. Less than a half-mile downstream, the road curved away from the creek and back up the hillside. Beyond that, trees and brush prevented any rapid negotiation along the creek bank. Luck had to be with him or surely the trunk would be lost.

Jesse stood at the curve in the road and watched the trunk as the current carried it farther away. He wondered if it really was worth chasing. He still had no idea what was in the trunk, but his loyalty to Al compelled him to keep trying until there was no apparent hope of its recovery.

He started fighting his way through the weeds and brush, trying desperately to keep the trunk within his view. Downstream a ways, a high knoll shadowed with trees jutted out from the far bank where the creek curved around it. Jesse saw a young boy sitting on a log. The boy appeared to be watching all the flood trash floating by, and the trunk seemed to catch his attention. With a sudden jerk, the boy sprang to his feet and started running toward the next bend where the current shot the trunk close to that bank. Just as it came near him, the boy grabbed for it. His feet spit out from under him, then a splash, and the boy vanished into the muddy, swirling water.

The recovery of the trunk had abruptly transformed into a treacherous rescue mission. Saving that boy from being swept away by the current was far more important than retrieving a trunk, no matter what was in it. Jesse started crashing through the weeds even faster, hoping to see the boy come back to the surface, but all he saw was the trunk floating farther out of reach.

He had almost given up when he spotted what appeared to be a logjam. Perhaps the trunk got caught there, and with a little luck, the boy too.

Jesse neared the trapped debris; the domed top of the trunk was barely visible among a snarled mess of tree branches, weeds, and all sorts of miscellaneous flood trash. But there was no sign of the boy. The rushing current had carried him away and there was nothing more Jesse could do to save him.

With a heavy heart, he decided to retrieve the trunk and try to forget about the tragedy he had just witnessed. Getting to it without falling into the water might be a trick, but at least the trunk wasn't lost.

He cautiously stepped onto a log that seemed lodged tightly enough to support his weight. It wiggled a little but didn't come loose or sink any deeper into the water. The other end of the log was hung up on a large rock, and from there he might be able to reach the trunk handle. What he would do with it once he got it up out of the water, he didn't know, but he would worry about that later.

Just as he reached with his fingertips barely touching the trunk's leather handle, another hand grasped at the top and a dark-haired, freckle-faced head popped up from behind it. Startled, Jesse jumped back nearly losing his balance. He wasn't expecting to ever see the boy again.

"Where did you come from?' Jesse yelled over the roar of the gushing flood.

"What difference does it make?" the boy answered. "I caught your trunk... now are ya gonna help me get outa here or what?"

With a daring leap Jesse jumped to another rock without concern of its steadfast mooring. He was on the other side of the trunk where he could see the boy had all he could do to keep from getting swallowed by the undercurrent as he desperately clung to a tree limb. Jesse steadied himself with a tight grip on another branch and reached toward the boy with his free hand.

"Grab my hand... I'll try to pull you up." Jesse yelled. His adrenaline was pumping and his heart was pounding. He couldn't let this poor guy drown. And with all his strength, he grasped the boy's forearm and gave a mighty tug. The assistance allowed the boy to get a better grip on the limb and he pulled himself partway out of the water. Another tug from Jesse and the boy was up on the rock, his feet still dangling in the muddy, brown water.

"Are you okay?" Jesse asked.

"I think you pulled my arm out of joint... but other than that... I guess I'm okay. I just need to catch my breath."

Jesse had cheated the angry waters from claiming a life, and this deliverance bestowed on him the highest sense of gratification he had ever known. Tragedy was no stranger to him; the deaths of his mother and father were still clearly engraved in his memory, even though it was a long time ago. But this time, he had the power to control a tragic fate. For that he was grateful.

The drenched boy sitting on the rock at Jesse's feet was thankful, too, that Jesse had not given up the search for the lost trunk. He knew he might not have survived had Jesse not arrived when he did.

"Guess I ain't never been that close to diein' and I can't remember ever bein' quite so scared," the boy panted. "Thanks for pulling me out... now we'd better get your trunk out of the water too."

With the boy's help, hauling the trunk up onto solid ground was an easier task than Jesse had originally anticipated. They sat on the creek bank with the trunk at their feet.

"Sure am glad you came along when you did. What's in the trunk, anyway?"

Jesse stared at the trunk for a few seconds and then turned to the boy. "Don't know. It's locked. It belongs to a friend of mine. I'm going to deliver it to him. He's got a place up in Couderay."

"Never heard of it. Where's it at?"

Jesse shrugged his shoulders. "It's up north from here. Don't know how far -- maybe a hundred miles. But now my truck is stuck in a ditch up the road. That's how the trunk fell into the creek. I was trying to turn around 'cause the flood was up over the bridge and the side of the road caved in."

Bewildered and discouraged, Jesse thought about his truck and the predicament he was in, now that his pride and joy lay helpless in that ditch. The ecstasy of liberation suddenly evaporated and a feeling of doom crept into his already dampened spirit.

"If I help you get your truck out of the ditch, can I go with you to... to..."

"Couderay... I'm going to Couderay."

"Yeah... Couderay. Can I go with you to Couderay?"

"Well... what about your folks? You can't just run off like that. Where's your home?"

"Oh, I'm not from around here. My step-dad lives in Milwaukee... and I don't know where my mom is. She left over a year ago. I hopped on a freight train last month. Couldn't stay with that bastard stepfather any more. He beat the crap outa me every chance he got... for no reason. I just couldn't take it any more, so I ran away."

The boy's voice quivered, and tears trailed down his dirty face. In his mind, Jesse questioned the validity of the boy's story at first, but then he realized the boy's sincerity; honesty certainly wasn't an issue to doubt. Although it had been many years, Jesse was all too familiar with loss of family. He had been fortunate to be blessed with a guardian like Julian Kelly, but it seemed this lad was not so lucky.

"What's your name?" Jesse asked.

"Will... Will Montgomery." The boy wiped the tears from his cheek with the back of his hand. "I'm fourteen, and I can take care of myself. So if you don't want me to go with you... I... I can get along just fine."

He was holding back the tears, but the quiver was still in his spoken words. He was trying his best to display his toughness, but uncertainty and a degree of fear was penetrating through the curtain of courage.

Jesse accepted the situation at face value. Sitting there beside him was a scared young boy who had nothing but the ragged, dirty, wet clothes he was wearing, a darkened past and a hazy future, if he had any future at all. Jesse couldn't refuse to help a soul so desperately in need of a friend, and it might not be so bad to have a traveling companion for a while.

"So... where have you been stayin' all this time?"

"Most of the time I sneak into farmers' haylofts at night, and there's always cans full of fresh milk in the milk house and usually a garden that's good for a handful of carrots or somethin.' And now and again, there was a farmer's wife that would prob'ly wonder how that loaf of bread she left on the back porch to cool just disappeared without a trace. But last night... the barn I was sleeping in ... the roof got blowed off in the storm. I thought I was gonna get killed!"

"Well..." Jesse pondered for the right reply. "If you help me carry this trunk back up to the road to my truck, we'll find you some dry clothes. Mine probably won't fit you very good, but at least they'll be clean and dry. And you won't have to raid any more gardens and milk houses or sleep in any more barns, and the next town we come to, we'll stop and buy you some clothes that fit... that is... if we ever get my truck out of the ditch."

"You mean... I can come with you?"

"Yeah... you can come with me."

Will's frown surrendered to a beam of sunshine. Never before had he been offered such kindness and generosity. Growing up in the shadows of a big city atmosphere, and under the iron fist of a barbarous, unscrupulous, abusive stepfather, he had learned the characteristics of that life style, and until today he believed the entire world consisted of nothing more. Scrawny, undernourished, and dirty, he was a little rough around the edges in outward appearance, but his senses were keen, and deep down inside there was an industrious, ambitious giant eager to flourish. Will knew the difference between right and wrong, but lately his will to survive had led him into a fiendish way of life. He was now quite proficient at popping the lids off milk cans in the middle of the night without making a sound and snatching apples from a produce market when the storekeeper wasn't looking, and he had developed a certain degree of accuracy in judging the size of blue jeans and shirts hanging on a back yard clothes line. But now he felt lost in a cruel world, and Will was ready to accept the security of companionship.

By the time they had lugged the trunk nearly a mile back through the thicket shrouding the creek and another half mile up the road to the marooned truck, Jesse had revealed nearly his entire life history by virtue of a thousand questions spewing out, one after another, in the typical fashion of a fourteen-year-old who had been deprived of conversation for over a month. But when Capone's trunk hit the ground beside Jesse's footlocker, Will's enthusiasm melted away. Even to a fourteen-year-old, it appeared quite unlikely that freeing the truck from the mudslide would be an easy task.

Jesse surveyed the predicament. The truck sat at a forty-five degree angle with the headlights pointed toward the treetops. The front tires were still on the solid road surface but the rear wheels were buried in mud up to the axle. They were going to need help, and plenty of it.

"First..." Jesse said, directing his attention to Will, "...let's get you cleaned up and into some dry clothes." He opened his footlocker and pulled out a bar of soap and a towel. "There must be some cleaner water around here somewhere... over there... on the other side of the road."

A small pool of clear rainwater had collected in a sandy pocket at the foot of the road bank. There was no shyness as Will stripped off his dirty, wet shirt and jeans and began scrubbing away the layers of filth from his five-foot-four scrawny body. Jesse couldn't help but notice the many scars vividly revealing evidence of Will's brutal past; he understood why Will had run away from home.

Jesse's jeans were at least six inches too long and four sizes too big around the waist. Two of Will's size could have fit into the shirt. With the pant cuffs rolled up and a piece of twine for a belt cinching up the waist band like a potato sack, Will looked more like a scarecrow -- but a clean scarecrow.

Jesse had given in to compassion, reluctantly accepting a temporary responsibility to help Will survive until a more permanent home could be found for him. But as the days would pass, survival would become a team effort and as if their brotherhood was meant to be, the bond between them would grow.

The flood was receding quite rapidly. The far end of the bridge that earlier had been completely under water, was graced with only a generous layer of mud, and the roar of rushing water no longer echoed through the valley. Birds sang and squirrels chattered under a cloudless sky. It was difficult to imagine the nasty conditions that had prevailed the night before as the afternoon hours painted a portrait of natural beauty.

The most beautiful sight and sound to Jesse was that of the heavy-duty dump truck rumbling down the hill. A road maintenance crew was there to check the condition of the bridge, knowing the flood could have possibly caused some damage. The big truck and a twenty-foot log chain snatched the Model A up out of the sinkhole with little effort.

With warnings of more hazardous road conditions farther up the highway, the truck driver convinced Jesse that his best option was to return to the River Road, as it might be at least a couple of days until this route was safely passable.

It seemed like a good time to check into the Alma Hotel.

6

Jesse wasn't exactly a stranger to the streets of the busy little river town. He had been there several times during the past few days. And the town wasn't so big; it would have been difficult to get lost. Will had been there too. Fortunately, he was no longer wearing the clothes he had swiped from a laundry line at the edge of town, and he hoped the grocer wouldn't recognize his sparkling, clean face and neatly combed hair.

Hancock's Dry Goods Store was their first stop. Eager to make a sale, a tall, slender, bald-headed clerk with a yellow tape measure dangling from his shoulders met them at the door.

"My little brother needs some new clothes. He lost all his in the flood last night. Do you think you have some jeans and shirts in his size?"

The merchant eyed Will with his many years of experience in the clothing business and confidently replied, "I'm sure we can find something to fit... right this way."

Will beamed with excitement as the man led him down the isles of garment racks filled with new apparel. This was the first time since his mother left that he was going to have new clothes from a store. Or, maybe it was Jesse's unofficial adoption that brought out the ear-to-ear grin. A few hours ago he was a lost, lonely, homeless kid with nothing but uncertainty to call his own, and now, a feeling of security suddenly surrounded him -- he had a big brother.

"Pick out two shirts, two pairs of jeans..." Jesse stared down at Will's bare feet. "...And some socks and a pair of shoes too."

Jesse assured Will and the store clerk that he would be back to pay the bill, but while the new wardrobe was being fitted he would be just down the block securing a room at the hotel.

As he strolled down the sidewalk toward the hotel, he realized an element of responsibility had once again crept into his life. Responsibility wasn't anything new to him, but this time it didn't feel like an obligation. Will was capable of taking care of himself -- he didn't need a babysitter -- just a little guidance. In Will's case, experience had been a poor teacher.

Jesse was so involved with the analytical approach to accepting the responsibility of Will's care that he didn't notice he was being watched from across the street. He wasn't aware of the deep-seeded revenge and the hateful greed that, by chance, had found him here. He wasn't thinking of danger, nor did he have a reason to suspect that his safety was in jeopardy by delaying the journey to Couderay another day or two. Ignorant of the danger, Jesse was flirting with another calamity.

"That will be two dollars a night... in advance."

Jesse laid four dollars on the counter and signed his name in the register.

"You'll be in room number three at the top of the stairs. There's a toilet just down the hall." With an artificial smile, the desk clerk handed Jesse a key. "You might have to jiggle the lock a little... that one sticks sometimes."

Will stood just inside the door of the clothing store eagerly waiting to show off the new attire. The stiff, new blue jeans, crispy red and blue plaid shirt and shiny black shoes complimented the proud smile on his face.

"Wow! Look at you. You look like a real person again," Jesse said jokingly. Seeing the joy in Will's eyes made him feel good. He knew that he had done the right thing. "How much do I owe you?" Jesse asked the merchant.

"Twelve dollars," the clerk replied, "and I've got the other pants, shirt and socks... and yours that he borrowed right here. He was pointing to a bundle sitting on the counter wrapped in brown paper tied with string. Jesse pulled the cash from his pocket, counted out the twelve dollars and handed it to the clerk.

"Thank you... and come back again."

Will picked up the bundle; they headed out the door.

"Boy, Jesse... you must be rich!" Will was quite impressed with the roll of money Jesse had pulled out of his pocket.

"I've been saving for a long time." That was a matter Jesse didn't want to discuss out in the open and quickly changed the subject. "Tomorrow we'll get you a suitcase to put your stuff in. But right now, let's get something to eat. The food smells real good at the hotel. Are you hungry?"

That was like asking if the Pope was Catholic. Will hadn't eaten a sit-down meal for a long time, and although he wasn't very big, his starved appetite was more closely matched to that of a lumberjack. Not a single breadcrumb remained on the plate when he was finished.

The truck was parked just outside the dining room window where Jesse had it within plain view. He had not been too concerned about it, but suddenly a troubled expression erupted like a volcano.

"What's wrong, Jesse?" Will asked. He peered out the window at the truck and the bearded man standing next to it scrutinizing the contents in the bed. His right arm was wrapped with a bloodstained white bandage.

Jesse recognized the man who barely escaped with his life from the hilltop where Lobo had nearly ripped him to shreds and had almost made a meal of him. The scoundrel obviously recognized Jesse's Model A and the trunks in the back. He had no way of knowing that Jesse had removed the cash from the footlocker after almost losing it twice. But persistence prevailed. Jesse thought maybe the man was attempting to recover the rifle, which was still buried in the mud on the hilltop. Whatever his motive, Jesse knew precautions were necessary.

Other hotel patrons exiting the front door had scared off the villain by the time Jesse and Will cautiously peeked around the corner at the top of the entrance stoop. He was nowhere in sight, but Jesse sensed an eerie presence of the man who had unsuccessfully tried once before to rob, and perhaps kill.

"C'mon Will. Help me carry the trunks up to our room. We can't leave 'em out here."

Their second story window provided a view of Main Street, and beyond, to the Mississippi River vista. Reflections of the setting sun danced on the gentle waves; gulls and swallows skimmed just inches above the surface in a feeding frenzy.

Feeling a little more secure in the safety of a locked hotel room, Jesse sighed in relief and flopped onto the big bed. Will didn't feel the anxiety or the threat, but he was confused about Jesse's concern. Curiosity produced questions, and then Jesse saw the need to explain the situation, which he had avoided before. He told Will about the origin of the mysterious trunk and how he had deceived the Hawthornes to gain its possession, and of his association with Al Capone and why he was so desperately trying to return the trunk to him. He told the story of his experience with the wolf, and the bandit, who was lurking in the alleys somewhere outside the hotel.

Like a child hearing a bedtime story, Will listened intently with wide eyes and dropped jaw. Little had he realized until then that he was becoming a part of this incredible drama.

Now that Jesse had told his whole story, he thought he should know something more about the kid that he'd taken under his wing. "So how did it come about that you ran away from home?" he asked Will, and for the next hour he listened to Will's account of his last month as a nomad:

"My Mom left me with Harley a year ago. He's my step-dad. Ain't no wonder why she left him; he ain't nothin' but a drunken bum. Got fired from six jobs in eight months. I hardly ever saw him sober. We didn't have much food 'cuz whenever he did have some money he'd manage to find a jug o' hooch, even with the pro'bition. Harley got awful mean when he was on a drunk. That's how I got all these scars – well, most of 'em. The neighborhood kick ball games got mighty rough too. But Harley give me most of 'em. Once, he pitched me right out through a window. Lucky for me we was on the ground floor at the time.

"And then I started hearin' some folks saying how something bad happened to the stock market in New York City and everybody started gettin' real worried. I didn't understand what was goin' on, but I do know a lot of people lost their jobs and all their money and some folks even lost their homes. There were people lined up on the streets looking for food and work. It got real crazy.

"Didn't really change things for Harley though 'cuz he didn't work much anyhow. He just kept gettin' ornerier all the time and rantin' 'bout the gov'ment and takin' out his anger on me.

"Then one day I just couldn't stand it any more. I stuffed some of my raggedy clothes into a pillowcase and headed for the railroad yard. I'd heard some of the old hobos talkin' down there 'bout all the places they'd been ridin' the rails, and I'd hardly never been outside the city so it sounded pretty exciting. And a hobo's life seemed pretty easy – they didn't have to work; they didn't have to go to school; they didn't have to answer to nobody. They didn't seem to have nothin', but hobos always seemed happy to 'low the rich folk mind the world's affairs.

"I saw this one tramp watchin' me. Guess I must've looked a little lost and he motioned me to come over to his fire where he was sittin' and cookin' somethin' that sorta smelled like coffee in a banged up tin pot. Said his name was Johnny. "He was about the only friendly one around that day. I guess everybody was kinda riled up, just like Harley, 'bout losin' jobs and money, and maybe that's why they were hobos. Most of 'em were all eyein' trains comin' and goin,' sizin' up boxcars for their next ride.

"Johnny told me he'd been a hobo nigh on fifteen years. I 'spect that's why he wasn't angry and mean – he'd been out there since long before all the trouble with the stock market started.

"Then he give me some advice; said he could tell I was new at this hobo stuff 'cuz of my shiny white pillowcase. "It'll never last. Gotta get you a canvas bag, or a carpetbag – one that'll take some tossin' around," he told me.

"He pointed out the trains that was fixin' to pull out soon and what direction they was headed. I figured west was where I wanted to go. East was where New York and all that stock market trouble was – didn't want no part of that. South went to Chicago – just another big city, prob'ly no better than Milwaukee. And north – I'd been to Sheboygan once and that didn't seem too exciting. I remembered reading 'bout Montana in school, and I knew it was west, and that's where I decided to go.

"I wandered on down amongst some older boys that said they was goin' to Nebraska to work on a cattle ranch. They were all concerned about me gettin' hurt 'cuz I was so small. They thought I might fall and get run over and cut in half by the wheels. I certainly didn't want that, and they all agreed they'd help me get on, when the train started moving.

"And so they did. Ol' Johnny was absolutely right 'bout my pillowcase – it didn't last a hundred feet of the trip. 'Course, that could've been 'cuz I didn't have much travelin' experience and I dropped it just as one of the big boys boosted me up into a boxcar. I nearly cried when that happened, but I couldn't let the other boys see me cry. I pretended like it weren't no big deal. After all, the only stuff in that bag was a shirt missin' most of the buttons, socks with holes in 'em, and a pair of raggedy old blue jeans. I didn't need 'em anyhow.

"The train rattled and shook and rumbled along through the city, and in an hour or so we were passin' by farms with cows and cornfields. Then the train slowed down some when we passed through small towns, but it didn't ever stop.

"Before long the dark seemed to swallow everything up. The other older boys that had been talkin' and carryin' on all the while were quiet then, and the rumble of the train wheels made me drowsy too. But I felt pretty confident. I had took that first step – the hardest step, I thought – and tomorrow would be a new day and I would be away from Harley for good. I didn't even know for sure where that train ride was taking me, but I had all night to think about what I'd do the next day – or whenever that train came to a stop. I had eighty-five cents in my pocket and I thought breakfast would be a good idea.

"As hard as I tried, I couldn't stay awake. Starin' out through the black night seein' nothin' but shadows of trees now and then put me to sleep. I'd wake up once in a while, but when I realized it was still the middle of the night I'd drift off again.

"It was the brakes squealing that woke me. The train was barely moving; it was just startin' to get daylight, and I could hear a lot of yelling and cursing goin' on. Then one of the older boys came over to me and said, "Get ready to jump! The bulls are coming!"

"Well, now I had heard all about the railroad bulls. They're like detectives that roust out anybody tryin' to hook a free ride, and sometimes they could get real mean. I could see we were amongst big hills and right beside a big river. I didn't know where we were, but I didn't care. I just didn't want to get caught up by the bulls. When my feet hit the ballast rock I was down, spread-eagle in a heartbeat. My knees and elbows stung from grinding 'em into the gravel, and I figured I'd added a few more scars to my collection. I could hear the older boys scramblin' away and it sounded like someone was chasin' them. The bulls didn't see me, so I got up and tried to run, but my legs hurt so bad, all I could do was limp along. Now I understood what Johnny meant when he told me this was a dangerous business if you didn't know what you was doin.'

"I managed to get into a clump of trees and out of sight. Daylight wasn't quite in full bloom yet; it was dark and creepy there in the trees, but I decided to just stay there until my knees stopped hurting so much. I sat down next to a huge tree, leaned against the trunk and I think I must've dozed off for a spell.

"The rumbling train wheels woke me sudden. Well, now there weren't any chances of jumpin' on that train even if the bulls were gone, and I wasn't sure if I wanted to jump onto any train just yet. I was more interested in feedin' my grumblin' belly, and there was bound to be more trains.

"The caboose clickety-clacked down the tracks and I didn't see anything of the older boys that had helped me. I began to realize I was alone. That scared the dickens outa me at first, but when I thought about it, I had been on my own for quite some time. The only difference now being that I didn't have Harley addin' to my scar collection.

"I wondered about Harley and how he was getting along, now that I was gone, not that I cared, mind you. I wondered if he had even noticed yet that I was missing, not that *he'd* care. All in all, I 'spect the parting was the best way for both of us."

"So how did you end up way out here?" Jesse asked, impressed with the saga so far.

"Well, the days went by; one week sorta melted into the next. I spent so much time wanderin' around the countryside I guess I lost track of the days. My eighty-five cents was gone, but I always managed to scavenge something to eat.

"Haylofts made a good bed at night, and whenever I needed a clean shirt, I'd hunt for a clothesline somewhere with laundry hangin' out to dry.

"Then, last night when the sun went down I could see the sky boilin' up a witch's brew of a storm. I headed for the nearest barn I could find 'cuz I knew if I didn't I'd be gettin' soaked mighty soon.

"The wind howled and rain poured down; the thunder sounded like dynamite blasts right outside the barn. After just a little while, the wind roared even louder and stronger and the whole barn shook. Then with one loud crash the roof peeled away from the walls. Thought sure I was gonna get killed. Next thing I knew I was drenched 'cuz there was no roof left at all. I dug into a hole in the hay and just stayed there until it got quiet again.

"It was still dark, but I could hear voices, and then there were lantern lights scurryin' all around the wreck. I waited for a bit, and then I snuck away into the darkness before somebody was bound to catch me.

"I stumbled around in the dark for a while until I happened onto a rocky overhang on the side of a bluff that gave me a little protection from the rain. I was wet and miserable, but by that time I was pretty tired, and even on a bed of hard rock I fell asleep.

"When I woke up the rain had stopped. It was daylight, but there weren't any blue sky. I sat there thinking about the night before, and how this rock den would be much safer than any barn, and that I might just stay right there until the bad weather passed.

"I heard a faint roaring sound that kept getting louder. I thought about the roar I had heard just before the roof parted company with the barn, but this roar wasn't anything like the wind. It sounded more like a waterfall, and it's a darn good thing I decided to find out where it came from.

"Just past the trees I found a creek; the muddy brown water was racin' along and almost comin' over the banks. I looked back toward the rock den and realized that my little hideaway would be filled with floodwater in no time. I sure couldn't stay there.

"That's when I went up on that little hill and saw your trunk come floatin' down."

"Quite a story, Will," Jesse said.

"Whatya s'pose is in there?" Will asked. He kneeled down in front of Capone's trunk and laid one hand on the lid.

"All I know," Jesse replied, "...is that the Hawthornes knew and they sure were eager to take it back to Milwaukee. Must be something valuable."

Just across the hall, another hotel guest quietly entered his room.

7

Will was still sound asleep. He didn't move a muscle when Jesse carefully slipped out of the bed, pulled on his jeans and quietly slid the chair in front of the window. Jesse gazed out across the still river as the soft morning light gently caressed the waking day. Pillows of pure white fog hung motionless over the water, as if suspended in time. The serenity was like a magnet to Jesse's eyes; he imagined himself on the deck of a magnificent riverboat gliding along the glassy surface, and he could almost feel the gentle breeze on his face and hear the crisp, cheerful banjo serenade.

On the street below, only a big yellow tomcat strolled casually down the sidewalk. The whole town was still asleep.

Rays of golden sunlight began cutting through the trees high atop the bluff behind the hotel, burning away the patchy fog. That must have been the wake-up call. Gradually, the traffic flow increased and within a short time the little town was alive with activity. There seemed to be a moderately steady stream of people entering and leaving the hotel front door just below Jesse's window. The aroma of fried bacon and eggs filtered in. Obviously, breakfast was being served in the dining room downstairs, and apparently, this was a popular early morning stop for many people.

Jesse patted Will's shoulder. "Wake up sleepy head. It's time for breakfast."

Jesse scanned the crowded, chattering hotel dining room in hopes of finding an empty table. There were none.

An arm rose above the crowd motioning them to come to a table. Jesse made eye contact with the man seated alone at a table large enough to accommodate four. The gentleman nodded and motioned again; the invitation was clearly intended for him and Will.

"Y'all are entirely welcome to sit here... that is if you're wanting to have some breakfast." He didn't smile, but he didn't frown either, as he removed his white hat from the table and placed it on the vacant chair beside him.

Jesse had the distinguished-looking, red-haired man pegged as someone of importance. "Thank you, sir. This is mighty kind of you. My name is Jesse, and this is Will. We're just passin' through... had to stay here 'cause the road is washed out by the flood."

"Guess that's why I do all my traveling by riverboat. Don't have much need to get too far from the river."

His hand went up again, this time signaling a waitress. "Get these boys plenty of bacon and eggs. They look mighty hungry. And put it on my bill."

"Thank you, sir." Jesse was rather astonished that this stranger was offering to pay for their meal.

"No need to call me Sir. The name is Eddy Morgan... but everybody calls me "Spades.""

Will's usual curiosity sprang into action. "Why do they call you "Spades?""

"I've been riding the river nearly all my life, and poker is how I make my living. Spades seem to be my lucky suit... never lost a hand with just a pair of aces as long as one of 'em was a spade."

Spades Morgan was from Missouri and the picture of a typical riverboat gambler. The chocolate brown three-piece suit with a gold watch chain dangling from the vest pocket, crocodile skin boots, and the off-white ten-gallon hat proclaimed his rank among the high rollers. His precisely groomed, waxed handlebar mustache and ruddy, expressionless face punctuated the statement. He was a professional whose reputation was known, respected and often feared from New Orleans to St. Paul. Only the shrewdest poker players -- or unsuspecting fools -- would sit across the table from Morgan. He'd toy with the fools simply for a means of entertainment until a keener opponent came along to challenge his skill, and rarely did he walk away from the table with less than when he started.

Morgan knew more about the pair of youngsters than they were aware; he had just arrived at the hotel the previous day as Jesse and Will toted the trunks through the front entrance. Overhearing their conversation that night gave him enough information to formulate a fairly accurate draft of their situation.

Jesse and Will began devouring the platefuls of scrambled eggs and bacon; Morgan leaned toward them and spoke in a near whisper as to not be heard by anyone else but them. "The scoundrel who tried to rob y'all is Pete LeFever. I saw him sneakin' 'round town yesterday. He's not someone y'all want to mess with... probably the worst critter I ever came across. Pete's wanted in every state south of the Mason-Dixon. That's probably why he's way up here in the north where nobody knows him."

When Morgan started his words of warning, Jesse didn't give much thought to his knowledge of what had happened regarding the crook up on the hill, but as Morgan went on to mention "Capone's trunk," Jesse stopped chewing and looked across the table at Morgan with a puzzled, surprised stare.

"How do you know about Al's trunk?"

Spades saw the concern in Jesse's eyes. Just as he had trained himself to never display emotion -- whether he was at the poker table or not -- he had also acquired the ability to read the expressions of others; he knew Jesse hadn't filled his inside straight. There was no reason to let the tension mount. Jesse was calling Spades' bluff, and it was time to lay the cards on the table.

"I heard y'all talking in your room last night. My room is right across the hall. Don't worry... I'm not going to steal your trunk. But you'd better be careful as long as LeFever is in town."

That explained how Morgan knew of his mission, but Jesse couldn't help but wonder who else had heard them talking. He was beginning to realize that the trunk was creating more trouble than he had counted on. Now it seemed even more urgent to get it to its destination.

Spades Morgan would be boarding the Lake City Queen, a gallant side-wheeler due to dock at this port at four o'clock and depart at five. A planned rendezvous with a high stakes game was on his agenda. Will and Jesse would be there too, to bid him a farewell.

As promised, Will got his suitcase, and by mid-afternoon he and Jesse had explored nearly every square foot of the town. Jesse had plenty of time to think about Morgan's advice, making him more aware of the possible danger. Pete LeFever could still be somewhere near, although he hadn't let himself be seen. With a reputation like his, if Morgan's identification was correct, it was understandable that LeFever would stay out of sight.

A few people started to gather around the boat dock anticipating the arrival of the Lake City Queen. It might have just been an ordinary, everyday occurrence to most of them, but to Jesse this was an event. Not only was he there to say good-bye to Spades Morgan; he wanted to feast his eyes on yet another grand river vessel.

A seven-piece band assembled on the upper deck filled the air with joyful Dixieland jazz; passengers lined the railings of the majestic white and gold floating hotel. They seemed so happy -- waving, laughing, and swaying in rhythm with the lively music.

With the precision of a watchmaker, the well-seasoned, steady hands of the pilot guided the huge craft within inches of the pier and a half dozen crewmen leaped to the dock with choreographed accuracy, tethering the boat to a gentle stop. A fifteen-foot-long gangplank was lowered to the levy from the bow, and a sharply dressed steward greeted the boarding and departing passengers.

It was almost five o'clock when Will spotted Morgan walking down the gradual incline from Main Street and sprinted off to meet him half way. Jesse couldn't hear their conversation, but it appeared as though Spades had taken a liking to Will. He actually smiled as they talked, strolling toward the dock.

There was no time for lengthy farewells. "Good-bye, Jesse. Good-bye, Will. If you ever get to St. Louis, look me up. I have a state room on the Silverado."

"Good-bye, Mr. Morgan... and good luck in the game tonight."

The big boat shuddered as the steam engines propelled the giant side paddle wheels, churning the water into frothy whirlpools alongside the hull. The Queen gracefully backed away from the dock, turned, and slowly started upstream toward Lake Pepin. Jesse and Will leaned on the dock rail and watched silently until she was out of sight around the bend.

In just hours, Jesse and Will would resume their journey, too, but for the moment, Jesse was content to dawdle along the rocky river bank, enjoying every remaining minute before he had to leave the river valley. Will had wandered off on his own and that afforded Jesse some time to contemplate the options dangling before him on threads of enticement -- options he had not even considered until that day -- options he never knew existed until fate delivered him to that river town. He saw a different kind of sunset there, and he was touching a different kind of lifestyle. His ears were attuned to the different melodies that place was singing, and all his senses were synchronizing with this new world.

Ever since the day Capone offered him employment, Jesse's thoughts had been focused in that direction, but gradually he was realizing there was so much more to explore -- so many discoveries to be made and so many dreams to be followed. Now that he had found one new interest -- the river -- he wondered what other discoveries would unfold in his path, and how could he possibly commit his dedication to Capone and a concept, about which he knew so little? For as long as the relationship with Capone had lasted, it had always been a good one. Al had always been an admirable friend, but Jesse also knew there was another side to Capone – a side that he had not yet seen.

Good, bad, or indifferent, Al's trunk still had to be delivered. Perhaps a different light would be shed on Jesse's uncertainties when he reached Couderay. Maybe a career did await him there. Or maybe not. At any rate, Jesse wasn't making any premature decisions.

His awareness of reality, at that very moment, had slipped away. Jesse stood at the edge of the water on a flat slab of sandstone, relaxed, silent and still, gazing across the river and trying to imagine what might lie in the far away hazy hills on the other side.

A voice interrupted the serenity with an icy chill. It was a voice Jesse recognized, and one he had no desire to ever hear again. Hoping the voice was only his imagination he turned around to look. Not more than six feet away he could feel the heat of revenge burning in the eyes staring at him. Once again, he was on a defenseless collision course with doom.

"Guess you ain't so tough... now that you ain't got that flea bag mutt to protect you."

Pete LeFever held his bandaged right arm out for Jesse to get a good look at the bloody, painful wound. He had been stalking Jesse for the past hour waiting for the right opportunity. There, isolated from the rest of the world, he would even the score, and this time he was quite certain that his unfair advantage could not be challenged.

The concealed steel-gray Colt revolver tucked into Pete's belt became clearly noticeable as he parted the front of his jacket. Jesse wanted to run, but there was nowhere to make an effective escape; sudden fear had his feet glued to the rock where he stood, face-to-face with obsessive malevolence. A fatal threat was breathing down his neck. Jesse wasn't sure what LeFever's intentions were, but he was almost certain it wasn't to invite him to tea.

"Your dog nearly ripped my arm off... and now you're gonna pay!" Pete used his left hand to remove the pistol from his belt, cocked the hammer, and leveled the barrel toward Jesse.

"Now, give me the key to your hotel room... I believe there's a trunk in there that I want."

It was hard to understand why this man was so obsessed with gaining possession of a wooden box of which he didn't know the contents, but if the trunk was all he wanted, Jesse was ready to give it up. He felt his whole body trembling as he slowly slid his fingers into his pocket to retrieve the key.

As he extended his shaky hand offering the key, Jesse saw a rock the size of a grapefruit hurtling through the air, and had Pete not leaned forward to accept the key, the projectile might not have found its mark. It slammed against LeFever's right temple with the driving force of a wrecking ball, and the side of his face was instantly streaming with blood. He dropped to his knees and collapsed into an unconscious heap on the rocky river bank.

"Jesse! Are you okay?" Will's frantic voice startled Jesse almost as much as the flying rock had. He came crashing through the weeds and stood at Jesse's side. They both stared at the limp body lying at their feet.

"D'ya s'pose he's dead?"

"I... I don't know. But I don't think we're gonna hang around to find out. C'mon, Will... we're getting out of this town right now!"

Only minutes had passed when they climbed the stairs to the second floor of the hotel. Jesse nervously jiggled the key in the lock and swung the door open. He took one last look out the window at the fiery red horizon beyond the river, but there wasn't time to linger. Vacating the area before

LeFever regained consciousness and hunted them down -- if he was still alive -- seemed to be the logical priority. The fact that they might have done society a favor by decommissioning a most-wanted outlaw didn't enter Jesse's thoughts. He just wanted to get away as quickly as possible.

With a white-knuckled grip on the steering wheel, Jesse aimed the Model A out of town and northward up the river highway. Images of the close encounter with tragedy settled in. He was beginning to realize what a dangerous place this world really was.

Sitting silently in the seat beside Jesse, Will just stared out into the twilight. Mixed emotions swirled in his head: he was eager to seek new adventure; he was glad they were not going to be confronted by Pete LeFever again; he was thankful he had met Jesse; he was disappointed that he wouldn't be sleeping in that big, soft, comfortable bed again that night.

8

They traveled through the darkness over countless hills and passed through at least four small towns where there was little sign of life. Over two hours earlier they had crossed the bridge that indirectly brought the two of them together, and now in this unfamiliar territory all Jesse could do was follow the road. But one thing was certain: they were far enough away from Pete LeFever. It wasn't likely that he could be a threat to them any more.

An abandoned logging trail that hadn't seen use in years offered a welcoming invitation; Jesse turned the truck off the highway just far enough to be under the cover of the fragrant pines. His eyes were burning from staring into the unknown beyond the reach of the headlights. It seemed like a good time and place to rest for the night.

"Where are we? Are we lost?" Will asked as they spread a blanket on the ground over a thick, soft layer of pine needles.

With little concern for the possibility of being off course, Jesse replied calmly. "Nope. The highway will take us to another town... sooner or later."

The balmy night air was refreshing, and the bed of pine needles was almost as soothing as the bed in the hotel had been. For the first time in several hours, Jesse's tension eased; he stretched out and gazed up through the pine boughs at the stars. It was so peaceful and quiet, and it required little effort to get comfortable in that tranquil sanctuary. The only sound he heard was Will's snoring.

Not far from where they had been camped, the road came to a clearing where it intersected with another road, and at the crossing stood a welcomed sight. A sign on the roof of a modest, white building said "Sheldon's Gas & Grocery." The roof extended to form a canopy over a single gas pump; a faded red sign on the sidewall of the structure encouraged passers-by to *"Drink Coca-Cola."* Another sign at the side of the road named the place "Cougar Crossing" – it was like an oasis in the desert. Jesse suspected the truck was nearly out of gas, and he and Will were hungry and thirsty.

Jesse rolled the Model A to a stop beside the gas pump; a squeaky screen door swung open and a hardy "Good mornin'" echoed under the canopy. Sheldon always had a cheerful greeting for any customer – even strangers.

Jesse instructed Will to go inside: "Pick out some groceries while I gas up the truck and make a few maintenance checks... and don't steal anything. I've got enough money to pay for everything we need." Jesse wasn't absolutely certain that Will had completely shed all of his old bad habits.

"Fill 'er up right to the top," Jesse said. Sheldon prepared to pump the gasoline. All the while Jesse inspected the oil and water levels and Sheldon continued the fueling process, they exchanged conversation about the weather, the Model A, and where Jesse had been and where he was going. Lately, Sheldon hadn't seen too many people other than the local farmers and the truck drivers delivering goods to the store. Times were rough and business was slow; he and his wife, Rachel, were just getting by.

Sheldon washed the windshield and Jesse was looking over all the tires when another car chugged to a stop in front of the country store. It seemed a little odd to Jesse that the man and woman exiting the Chevrolet coupe wore long coats in such warm weather. They quickly entered the store where Will was patiently waiting at the counter with a log of smoked sausage, a box of crackers, four apples and two bottles of orange soda. He was carrying on a pleasant conversation with Rachel, who in a few short minutes had developed a fondness for the freckle-faced boy.

Will paid little attention to the strangers coming in the front door. Rachel was accustomed to seeing less-than-desirables wandering in from time to time, but for some reason she felt uneasy with this peculiar pair. They seemed a bit nervous as they immediately went to an obscure corner of the store behind a gondola; Rachel could see only their shoulders and the back of their heads, and their occasional glances toward the counter. Her uneasiness subsided when Sheldon and Jesse entered, and Sheldon was by her side behind the counter.

Before the storekeepers had finished tallying the cost of the groceries and gasoline, the cloaked strangers produced an element of surprise that was merely a by-product of their poor planning. From under the long overcoats they wielded sawed-off, double-barreled shotguns. Quite clearly, they had no intentions of making a purchase. Rachel suddenly realized the origin of her ill feelings when she had first seen them enter; her worst fear during all the years of running a country store in such a remote location was becoming reality.

"Don't nobody move. Just stay put, 'n nobody'll get hurt!" the gun-toting woman yelled in a commanding voice.

While the other man held the storekeepers, Jesse and Will at bay with the intimidating firearm and a dagger-sharp sneer, the woman stuffed a cloth flour sack with goods from the store shelves. When the bag was full she returned to the counter.

"Now... give me all the money from the cash register... and don't do nothin' stupid."

Rachel pulled back the handle on the side of the register, her hands shaking from fright. The drawer popped open with a ding that echoed through the deathly quiet room. Thirty-two dollars in small bills represented a whole week of receipts, and to Rachel, handing it over to these crooks was like handing her soul to the devil.

Sheldon noticed that the sight of the cash had momentarily distracted the man's attention. Trying not to be obvious, he slowly moved his right hand nearer to where a Winchester rifle lay hidden under the counter. The man's attention was suddenly restored as he noticed Sheldon's foolish attempt to produce a weapon. With a quick jerk, the shotgun was trained on Sheldon.

With the bagful of booty slung over one shoulder, the woman was at the front door encouraging her partner to follow. Her plan was to disappear quickly, as they usually did after such raids, always keeping one step ahead of the law. But her partner recognized a possible threat; Sheldon's ability to reach for a weapon still remained. He knew the need to better his odds against retaliation. He grabbed Will, locked his arm around Will's neck, and shielded himself with the body of a defenseless child, and then stepped backward to the door. Will struggled, but his size and strength presented little challenge.

Jesse anticipated Will's release outside, but by the time he and Sheldon reached the door, Will had already been stuffed into the Chevrolet, and it sped away.

Sheldon aimed his rifle at the speeding coupe.

Jesse grabbed the gun barrel and pulled it down. "Don't shoot! Will is in that car!"

In the confusion of the moment, Jesse knew there wasn't time to discuss a plan; he also knew that he was more capable of making chase. His compassion for the aging storekeepers turned to angry fear; Rachel and

Sheldon were spared from immediate danger, but Will was not. Jesse had to take control of the situation and quickly convinced Sheldon to give him the rifle and more ammunition.

"Call for help," Jesse commanded. "I'll try to follow them."

Jesse coaxed the Model A to its top speed along the dirt and shale road. He feared the crooks had made good their escape, but after several miles he noticed dust in the air, and at the crest of a hill up ahead he saw a concentrated dust cloud, and the car creating it. As long as he could keep the dust cloud in sight, and if he didn't get too close, allowing them to discover they were being followed, he wouldn't jeopardize Will's safety.

Mile after mile, the road dust was getting heavier and almost like driving through fog. Jesse knew he was closing in. Suddenly the air was clear. Obviously the car had turned off the road. Jesse stopped and peered out the rear window of the truck cab. When his own dust settled, he saw another trail cut through the trees. That had to be where the other car had disappeared.

The trail was no more than a sandy dirt path through the timber; Jesse spotted fresh tire tracks on the bare dirt. He was confident that he was still on the bandits' heels.

The trail took him deep into the forest. After inching his way and carefully scrutinizing the woods in all directions for signs of the car, he saw a clearing up ahead, and what appeared to be a house. Jesse stopped and stared for a few minutes, trying to detect any movement. There seemed to be none.

He thought it would be best to get his truck out of sight, and cautiously guided it between the trees off the trail. He would investigate the house by getting closer on foot, and the rifle would not leave his hands.

It was a ramshackle of a place, obviously abandoned long ago. Nearly all the windows were broken; weeds flourished all around the weather-beaten, old hovel, and a small woodshed and outhouse, nearly rotted away, stood next to a large pond. The brown Chevrolet coupe was parked beside the shack. Jesse had found the secret hideaway; surely Will was being held captive inside. The challenge of rescuing him without bloodshed was frightening, but Jesse had a rifle and plenty of ammo, and although he had never been much in favor of violence, he was ready to do whatever was necessary to get Will out.

Jesse didn't really know what to do. An hour or two passed and he hadn't come up with any ideas. All he could do, for the time being, was to stay hidden in the bushes at the edge of the clearing with a watchful eye on the house. There hadn't detected any activity, and he was too far away to hear any voices. He desperately wanted to get next to the house so he could peek in a window, but in broad daylight that would be too risky. He thought about returning to the country store to recruit some help, but if the crooks left while he was gone he might not ever find Will again. Although the chance of Will's presence in the house was good, there was no way of being absolutely certain, and until he knew for sure, Jesse would stay right there.

By mid-afternoon Jesse's hunger was becoming unbearable. There was no food in the truck; he and Will had left Alma in haste, unable to acquire supplies as planned. The unscheduled interruption that morning at the country store had definitely curtailed any dining arrangements. Just behind the house, across the clearing, Jesse was sure he saw what looked to be blackberry bushes, and they appeared to be heavily laden with berries. Birds were frequenting the bushes and seemed to be dining quite well on the succulent fruit. Jesse made his way through the brush around the perimeter of the clearing and indeed, he found lunch. The blackberries were ripe, plump and juicy. He had eaten several handfuls of berries when he heard the squeaking door hinges at the rear of the house. He ducked further back into the brush and weeds to avoid the risk of being seen. His hunger had proven to be a stroke of luck; he was in position to see some activity.

He expected to see one of the crooks, but instead he saw Will emerge from the darkened doorway. Will stepped over to the edge of the open porch and began to urinate. His hands were tied together, creating some difficulty. Behind him, in the doorway, a shadowed figure watched to make certain the lad did not try to run off. Now Jesse knew Will was in the house, but he still had no rescue plan. He contemplated an element of surprise, but busting into the house with the rifle ready to fire, if need be, seemed too hazardous, uncertain of what he would find inside. And way out there in the middle of nowhere, the possibility of help arriving anytime soon was quite slim. No one else knew where the chase had led, and it was hard telling if anyone was even looking.

"What would Capone and his men do in a situation like this?" Jesse thought. He recalled the night he led them to the Lynch still, enabling them to perform their dirty work in the cover of darkness. That seemed to be a good idea in this situation, too. But this wasn't an unguarded whiskey still - - Will's preservation was at stake.

Perhaps it was a good thing that Jesse couldn't hear the conversation inside the house. He may have panicked upon hearing some of the options being considered regarding Will's disposal. Or, he may have had second thoughts of lingering there in the woods after dark with talk of the high population of hungry timber wolves in that area. Most of the chatter was intended to scare Will, and it was definitely working. The couple wasn't considering the boy's adoption, either. Will had served the purpose of their safe exit from the store that morning; now they were faced with the burden of getting rid of him. Shadows grew and dusk settled in; Jesse's frustration grew as well. He felt helpless and weak. He knew nothing about the desperadoes, other than that they had robbed the country store, and they hadn't done that very well. They weren't professionals, but nevertheless, they had Will.

Complete darkness would soon be to Jesse's advantage, allowing him to maneuver closer to the house. It was like waiting for an overdue train; Jesse had done that many times, and he had learned the art of patience.

He considered a few options: what if he disabled their car? Maybe flatten all the tires? Or, maybe if there was some way to lure them out of the house through the front door, he could sneak in the back, free Will and sneak out again into the woods. But what kind of disturbance would draw them both out, leaving Will unguarded long enough for him to get inside, undetected? Noise was apt to cause them to barricade themselves even tighter; they were hidden away in a place far off the beaten track, and even with a temporary sense of security, they would probably still have their ears tuned to approaching intruders. Noise wasn't the answer.

The sky was getting darker; a lamp had been lit inside the shack. It didn't appear as though the occupants were making any plans to leave anytime soon. In the dim light, Jesse saw the man sitting in a chair with his feet propped up on another chair; he appeared quite relaxed. The woman was seated at the table with her eyes buried in the pages of a book, and Will was in a chair on the opposite side of the table with his hands tied behind the backrest. Jesse focused on the flame in the lamp. That was it. He knew how he would lure the scoundrels out of the house.

Jesse figured their transportation was their most valuable asset. Their car was the one thing they would try to protect and save should it be threatened, especially way out there, miles from civilization. As Jesse stared at the lamp flame, he envisioned a fire blazing around the car, and the two hoodlums frantically trying to extinguish it. That would give him the opportunity he needed to rescue Will. As a bonus, the fire would render the car useless; Jesse and Will could escape, free from the risk of pursuit. The plan could work, but Jesse would have to prepare carefully; he'd have to be ready to act quickly and effectively at precisely the right moment.

Cautiously, Jesse made his stealth surveillance of the house, the car, and the surroundings; he visualized every necessary move. There was plenty of dry grass, weeds, and other forest debris to pile around the car, providing adequate fuel for the fire. He picked out a spot where he would make his retreat once the blaze was started -- a spot where he could see into the windows and where he had a clear view of the car. He rehearsed in his head, over and over, each and every move. Success depended on well-thought-out strategy, and its flawless execution.

Everything Jesse needed was in his truck. He twisted off the gas tank cap on the cowl of the Model A. From his footlocker he pulled a flannel shirt and began feeding it into the open gas filler until only the cuff of one sleeve was left to hold onto. He reeled the gasoline-saturated garment back out of the tank and replaced the cap. His pants pockets were bulging with ammunition, matches, and his jack knife. He was ready to do battle.

Just as before, the thieves were paying little attention to the outdoor sounds of the crickets, owls, or the distant baying wolves. Will's head bobbed as if he were falling asleep. There would be no better time to start the show.

Crouching beside the Chevrolet coupe, Jesse cautiously turned the door handle, praying the hinges wouldn't squeak. With the door partly open he squeezed the gasoline from the shirt onto the seat upholstery, allowing some to trickle onto the running board. He placed the shirt on the ground just below the open door and heaped the dry grass, twigs, and leaves over it. The strike of a singe match was all that remained.

By the time Jesse had circled the rear of the house and taken up his predetermined position, the flames were just beginning to consume the front seat of the car. No one inside the house had noticed the trouble developing outside; Will looked as though he were sound asleep. But his head jerked back and his eyes widened when the woman gave out a shrill scream. The man jumped to his feet and bounded toward the front door yelling at the top of his lungs. "GET ANOTHER BUCKET!" In seconds, the woman was out the door too, with what looked like a large kettle. Jesse hadn't counted on there being water vessels within easy reach. The pond was about fifty feet away and they were on their second trip when Jesse reached the back door. But by then, the car was engulfed in flames. Jesse knew it would keep them busy for a while.

Will hadn't developed any fondness for his captors but he wasn't too fond of being left alone tied to a chair inside a burning building either. All he could see were the flames, and from where he sat, he thought the front porch was on fire. He struggled to get himself free, but with no success.

"Will... are you okay?" Jesse had his jack knife ready to cut Will's hands free.

"Jesse! How did you find me?" Will was quite astonished with Jesse's arrival.

"Shhhhhh. I've been here all day. I followed you here," he explained quietly while he sawed through the rope around Will's wrists and ankles. "When you get out the back door, run as fast as you can into the woods out back. My truck is just down the road a ways. C'mon... follow me."

When Jesse stood up after cutting Will's ankles free, he spotted another bonus -- the stolen money was sitting on the table. He grabbed the stack of bills and stuffed them into his pocket.

With lightning bolt speed they darted out the back door and into the woods. Jesse stopped to make sure Will was still right behind him. He saw the glow from the blaze, and the black smoke billowing up into the still, moonlit sky. He could hear water splashing onto the burning car, but he was confident that it couldn't be saved.

Jesse wasn't concerned whether or not the sound of his motor was heard as he backed the Model A out of the trees and raced down the dirt road. They would be miles away before the crooks discovered that Will was missing, and without a car they weren't much of a threat.

The only place Jesse knew to go was the country store at Cougar Crossing. It would be many hours till daylight and the store was the one place he and Will could seek safety for the night.

The place was dark. The sign in the front window said "CLOSED." Jesse stopped the motor. "We'll just wait right here 'til morning," he said. But Will never heard a word. He was already asleep, safe and secure with Big Brother.

A sharp wrap on the window glass woke Jesse. He opened his eyes to bright morning sunshine.

"Are you boys all right?" The man standing at Jesse's window was the County Sheriff. "Sheldon called me early this morning and said you were here. We didn't 'spect to ever see you again. Come on inside... Rachel's got a fresh pot o' coffee brewing, 'n I'd bet you could stand some breakfast."

Sheldon and Rachel were delighted to know the boys were safe, and they -- as well as the Sheriff -- were astounded as Jesse retrieved the money -- all thirty-two dollars -- from his pocket and laid it on the counter. Sheldon was pleased that his rifle was being returned.

The Sheriff already knew with whom he was dealing -- Sheldon had given him a description of the robbers. "Shotgun Shirley" and "Slug" McNally were a couple of nomad bandits who had drifted into the north woods from the Kansas plains, and they had been terrorizing the whole northern half of Wisconsin for three months, holding up stores like this one, managing to always stay one step ahead of the law, disappearing after every strike. Because of their gypsy-like nature, they were unknown, except by the many rural small business operators falling victim to their pillaging, one-time visits.

Between gulps of the ham sandwiches Rachel made for them, Jesse and Will described in detail their entire ordeal, including directions to the hideout, deep in the woods. The Sheriff's eyes lit up, thinking he might be the one to finally capture those outlaws, ending their reign of terror. Apprehending the McNallys would certainly renew his dignity as a Sheriff and restore the confidence of the citizens he served. He needed to round up a few deputies and pay a surprise visit to the abandoned shack that they had never thought to search out before.

By nine o'clock, a platoon of heavily armed men gathered outside the store. They arrived by the truckloads and some came on horseback. All were eager to begin the hunt, and they were determined to bring back the trophy.

But all they found was the charred remains of the Chevrolet coupe and an empty shack. Once again, "Shotgun Shirley" and "Slug" had slipped away without a trace.

The excitement was over. As quickly as they had assembled, the throng of overalled temporary deputies dispersed. The search had been abandoned. There were just too many square miles of dense forest, and without a single clue to indicate the direction the bandits were headed; it seemed useless to send thirty men tramping out into the wilderness after them.

Jesse and Will spent most of the afternoon keeping Sheldon and Rachel company. The word had spread throughout the countryside of the storekeepers' misfortune, and although no one knew they had recovered the stolen money, patrons from miles around stopped in that day to buy something, whether they needed it or not. It was their neighborly way of helping to ease the pain of devastation. But even with the frequency of customers coming and going, Sheldon and Rachel seemed quite grateful for Jesse and Will to linger. They owed a debt of gratitude to the two courageous youngsters who saved their day, and who had nearly enabled the capture of the wanted criminals.

9

No one in the little town of Couderay was particularly helpful when it came to locating Capone's place. It was as if he didn't exist. But Jesse knew he was in the right town. Capone had talked about Couderay too many times for him to be mistaken about the name, and Al had even pointed it out on the map once.

Unlike Alma, Couderay seemed to lack the complaisance of the river valley culture. In comparison, the atmosphere in Couderay was abrasively harsh. Jesse was just a little disappointed. What he didn't realize was the trusted pact Al shared with the people. Just as Jesse's trust and confidential alliance in Westby had kept Capone's presence there at a very low key, Al had the same relationship with almost everyone in Couderay, too. He brought prosperity to the remote village and its residents in grand proportions. The construction of his fabulous mansion, capable of providing his protection from any adversary, created good-paying jobs for the Indian Nation populous, and the entire area felt the positive effects from the imported wealth, as the money cascaded into local businesses, creating even more employment opportunities for everyone. Recognizing the source and understanding the premise, Couderay denizens were less receptive to other outsiders, and although they wouldn't admit to personal relationships with Capone, he had many friends there. His generosity had earned respect -- and protection. And because Jesse and Will were outsiders, their reception was less than Jesse had anticipated.

There had to be a way to find Capone's place. The trek had been long and challenging, plagued by thieves, storms, floods, and more thieves; Jesse had resolved to right the Hawthornes' plunder, and to reunite with a friend. He had been through too much to give up. Perplexed, he perched on the running board of his truck, and with despair written on his face, he leaned against the door. He tried to recall anything Al might have said to indicate where his search should begin.

A droning buzz kept getting louder. The sibilant sound was not totally unfamiliar to Jesse, but not common either. After a few seconds of studying the noise, he identified it. He looked up, scanning the cloudless sky for its origin. What seemed to be little more than treetop level, the silver and blue twin-engine plane, with its belly shaped like the hull of a boat, swooped by. As quickly as it had appeared, it was gone.

The sight and sound of the plane jarred Jesse's recollection. Al had once mentioned that the shipments of liquor to Couderay were flown in by landing the amphibious plane on the lake adjacent to the house.

A young man about Jesse's age leaned against the storefront wall, sipping from a soda bottle. Jesse noticed he had been there for a while and he certainly didn't appear hostile. In fact, he looked downright friendly, and if anyone would render any assistance at all, it might be him to do it.

"Which way do I go to get to the lake?" Jesse asked, mimicking the boy's relaxed lean against the wall. Perhaps an inquiry regarding the lake, rather than Capone, would produce a favorable result.

The boy looked around to make sure no one else was hearing his cooperation. "There's just one road leading north out of town. The lake is about six miles. You lookin' for Mr. Capone?"

His knowledge of the quest took Jesse by surprise. "Well, sort of... but how'd you know that?"

"Heard you asking some other people, but you're wastin' your time. You ain't gonna get in there. That place is guarded day 'n night. No stranger has ever gotten even close." He discretely pointed to the intersection down the street.

Jesse acknowledged the direction. "But I'm a friend of Al's. I'll get in."

Engaging in an argument with someone who didn't understand his relationship with Al was the last thing Jesse wanted right then, and this contact seemed to be the friendliest one in town; there wasn't much point in tarnishing a new friendship with conflict right from the start.
"I'm Jesse Madison, and that's Will. Guess I don't have to tell you we're new in town."

"Luke Jackson." He smiled and accepted Jesse's handshake.

Luke was the oldest son of a potato farmer. His mother's dressmaking talents helped support the family and although they were not wealthy people, they always seemed to have everything they needed to sustain a modest lifestyle.

Now that the spring planting and mid-summer cultivation had produced twenty acres of an anticipated bumper crop of spuds, there were some leisure hours between the daily chores to enjoy summertime pleasures before the fall harvest began.

Jesse felt the warm and genuine welcome from Luke -- an enthusiasm not encountered with anyone else he had approached so far. He had struck harmonious chords with at least one friend there.
Luke didn't give the impression that he ever made any personal contact with Capone, but then neither did anyone else. Perhaps he was just conforming to a community standard.

The last six miles of the journey seemed to take forever. Jesse was anxious to see Al again, and the fabulous house he spoke of often. He would soon be sitting in the lap of luxury contemplating the future, and he knew he was within spitting distance of making a decision. He would either accept the terms as they were presented, or he would walk away. There would be no compromising. There would be no middle ground.

A large, impressive wrought iron gate blocked the entrance. There was no sign of a mansion, but Jesse was certain this had to be the place. Nowhere on this route had he seen such a distinctive signature to indicate a style, the likes of Al Capone, and the two sentinels tending the post confirmed his conclusion. They were typically dressed like all the other Capone associates Jesse had encountered on previous occasions in Westby -- the dark suits and white shirts were almost a trademark and the Thompson machine guns they toted left little doubt. These guys weren't hunting rabbits.

Will slid down in the seat as the pair of Tommy Guns faced off with the

Model A headlights. The gate guards had not been alerted of any welcomed visitors arriving that day, nor were they expecting any deliveries from town. Their standing orders were quite clear: no one was to pass through the gate, uninvited, without the proper credentials. Period. The truck and its occupants were unfamiliar to them, and this was as near to Mr. Capone's fortress as any stranger would get. And by the stern expressions the gunmen displayed, there was no question that they intended to fulfill their assigned duties.

"I thought you said these people were your friends!" Will whispered hysterically.

Jesse realized he was arriving unannounced and the two guards didn't recognize him. How could they? They had never seen him before. He reluctantly tipped his head out the side window to speak.

"I'm Jesse Madison from Westby. I'm here to see Al, and I have a trunk to deliver to him."

The two men staged a brief conference and concluded they had never heard the name mentioned by Mr. Capone. This scenario was quite simple and their sarcastic response required little thought. "I'm sorry, but your name doesn't seem to be on the guest list. Turn your truck around and get out of here... right now!"

"But I'm a friend of Al's. He told me I could come to work for him. Just ask him."

"Sure he did. Mr. Capone ain't here... now turn around and get lost."

Jesse couldn't believe he had come this far, risked his life -- and Will's -- attempting to perform a good deed, and he wouldn't be afforded the satisfaction of showing his gratitude with the recovered trunk.

"Would you at least see that Al gets his trunk back?"

Jesse's persistence was now on the verge of annoyance to the gatekeepers. Apparently, they were familiar with the Trojan Horse story, suspecting the trunk may very well be some sort of booby trap sent by rivals. Capone did have his share of enemies too, and they knew it. They would have no part of accepting the unknown parcel.

One of the men came closer to Jesse's open window to make certain the intruders clearly heard, and understood, his emphatic instructions. "I'm tellin' you for the last time. Point this truck down the road and don't ever come back here again."

Jesse had seen more than his share of gun barrels aimed in his direction lately. This situation was getting a little too tense, and it was quite clear that he wouldn't gain entry to Capone's domain. The reception was very convincing, and it definitely seemed in his best interest to just comply with the command and drive away; there was no point in pressing his luck any further.

Jesse had reached a decision. He knew now that a career in Capone's world was not for him. The rejection at the gate didn't envelope him in disappointment, entirely. But this decision also left him in a state of confusion as well. Pursuing Al's offer was a thought of the past; Jesse's desire to travel to Cicero no longer existed either. There he was, in a small town in Northern Wisconsin that seemed to offer little satisfaction for his interests. He had already gotten a taste of being an outsider there. The cold shoulder treatment from most of the people was evidence enough to indicate an unpleasant future in Couderay.

Jesse couldn't return to Westby. The Hawthorne sisters had certainly discovered the trunk switch, and he feared facing the consequences that might await him there, not to mention the destruction his pride would suffer by returning, admitting his failure of finding something better than Westby.

But there did exist a positive outlook. Now that he had been exposed to the world beyond the confines of his hometown, he had discovered the enchantment of the Mississippi River and the enticing lifestyles of the people living along its banks. Surely there existed other horizons with equal or superior amenities, and Jesse was inclined to seek them out.

And what about the trunk? Now that its delivery was refused, did it mean that it and its contents rightfully belonged to him? It certainly didn't belong back in the Hawthornes' possession, and after all the trouble it had caused and the effort to preserve its safety getting it this far, no one justifiably deserved it more than Jesse -- that is, if it did indeed contain something of value.

And what about Will? He was just a kid, and he needed and deserved a home and a family to care for him -- something Jesse couldn't provide long term. They had been through a lot in the past few days and there was no one Jesse felt closer to than Will, but Jesse was uncertain of his own clouded future.

After an "I told you so," Luke made it quite clear to Jesse and Will why the people of Couderay had not been so receptive to their request for help in locating Capone. It all made sense to Jesse. He knew Al Capone and he understood the power that Al commanded. It was fitting that the citizens of Couderay would want to protect the source of their newfound prosperity.

"I can't help you get into Mr. Capone's place, but I can take you to another place where nobody'll bother us." Luke seemed eager to get out of town too; he was beginning to feel the sharp stares from people passing by and he wasn't ready to sever the new friendship.

Luke was speaking of the long-abandoned Northfield farm, several miles out in the country. It was a place where he went occasionally when he wanted to be alone. Living in a household with two brothers and four sisters -- all younger than him -- getting away for a little solitude, sometimes became an urgent requisite for maintaining his sanity. The Northfield farm wasn't too far from his home, and it offered a peaceful privacy intruded upon by no one else.

As they all climbed out of Jesse's truck and found a shady spot under a crab apple tree in what once was the front lawn of the old, but remarkably well-preserved brick two-story house, Luke told the legend connected to the abandoned dwelling and its long-gone occupants, and why the farm had remained empty and unused for so many years.

"Nel and Isaac Northfield once lived here. They homesteaded the land and over the years became quite successful. They replaced the original tiny log cabin with this house."

Luke directed his listeners' attention to the other buildings on the property. "They built that big barn and the chicken coop and the other sheds with the timber they cut from right here to clear the land for crops. They had cows, chickens, geese and sheep. Sold the milk, eggs, and wool to the rest of the settlers who were mostly lumberjacks then, and the general store in town and nearby lumber camps.

"Isaac worked himself to death, and after he died, Nel refused to leave the farm, even though she could no longer manage the hard work. She sold all the livestock... all except a dozen white geese.

"Every day she would coax the gaggle of geese down to the river where they would swim and forage for food. One by one, the geese began to disappear. Nel claimed it was snapping turtles in the river that were killing the geese. By the time all the geese were gone, Nel's mind was all but gone too. And even though she had no geese, she still went through the motions of flocking the non-existent birds to the river, calling to them by name when she thought they were swimming too far from the bank.

"Then one day Nel disappeared too. Some people speculated wolves killed her. Some thought she might have fallen victim to hostile Indians from Canada. No one knew for sure... her body was never found.

"But several months after she disappeared, a neighbor stopped by one day to check on the place only to find Nel and twelve white geese in the front yard. Astonished with her presence, he approached her to welcome her home, thinking she had just ventured off somewhere to get some more geese. As if ignoring her visitor, she -- and the geese -- vanished into the house -- without opening the door!

"When the neighbor told his story to the townsfolk, naturally no one believed him, convinced that he had become just as loony as Nel had been. So on several occasions, others went to the farm and soon returned to town, white as tablecloth linens, all telling the same story of seeing the old woman and the flock of geese... but none of them ever spoke with her, as she would vanish when they came near.

"In no time, the place was deemed "haunted" and no one ever since has gone near it."

Will huddled close to Jesse as the story progressed. Jesse though, seemed intrigued. Luke noticed that Will appeared a little uneasy with the tale, especially as they were sitting under the apple tree in the very spot where the ghost of Nel Northfield had been sighted.

"Don't worry Will. I've been here a hundred times and I've never seen Nel, or the geese. But I don't tell anyone that. As long as everyone thinks this place is still haunted, they'll stay away... and I like to come here to be alone."

"Have you ever gone inside the house or the barn?" Jesse asked curiously.

Luke didn't want to admit to any degree of fear, but his hesitant response indicated that he believed in the possibility of a ghoulish presence within the structures.

"N-no... and I'm not going to."

Jesse was uncertain how much of the legend he actually believed. It was clearly a saga that had been passed on from older generations. Luke told it with absolute sincerity, and he definitely had no intentions of entering any buildings on the property.

"I'm sure you can stay here as long as you want," Luke explained. "No one ever comes back here. You can't see the place from the road. Nobody will ever know you're here."

Jesse peered down the long driveway that was mostly shaded by gleaming white birch and silvery-leaved poplars. Luke was right. It would be impossible to view this place from the road. And if the farm still maintained the ghostly reputation Luke characterized, keeping the local people at a distance, it positively would yield all the privacy anyone would ever need.

"There's a spring over there by the creek. That's where I build a fire and sleep when I camp overnight. And there's plenty of firewood all around."

Luke was returned to his chores awaiting him at home, and after a quick trip to a grocery market in town, Jesse and Will found themselves back at the Northfield farm. The sun was settling behind the treetops, but there was still plenty of daylight left -- enough to gather a substantial heap of firewood and prepare the site for a campfire dinner and a good night's rest.

Will was a little nervous about spending the night there. Luke's ghost story was fresh in his mind and he couldn't help glancing toward the house now and then, expecting to see Nel Northfield and her geese.

"You don't really believe that tale, do you?" Jesse still wasn't sure, himself, if he believed it or not, but to help Will feel more comfortable, he had to be as convincing as possible. His attempt must have been effective. Will soon found relief from his fear. If staying here was okay with Jesse, then it was okay with him, too.

It wasn't long until Will's courage allowed him to leave Jesse's shadow. His free spirit once again came out of hiding and led him on an exploration along the riverbank. Daylight was fading rapidly and fireflies dotted the still evening air with thousands of tiny flashing beacons. It was hard to imagine how anyone could associate this serene haven with any kind of violence or unpleasantness -- it seemed like such a waste.

At last, Jesse seized the opportunity to sit back, relax, and contemplate. So far hardly anything had happened quite the way he had anticipated. A trip that should have only taken a day -- two at the most -- had transformed into nearly two weeks of chaos. Perhaps his present situation would have turned out differently had he not taken the time, that very first day, to satisfy his intrigue with the Mississippi River. Only his choice to loiter there initiated the string of further delays. Had he pressed onward to his destination instead, he wouldn't have been caught by the storm. But on the other hand, he wouldn't have found Will or met Spades Morgan. He wouldn't have seen the riverboats up close, or encountered the phenomenal experience with Lobo. Of course, he would not have been nearly killed -- twice -- by Pete LeFever nor would Will have been kidnapped by Shotgun Shirley and Slug. But he wouldn't have had the opportunity to heroically recover the stolen money for Sheldon and Rachel either, and that good deed in itself seemed to tip the scales in the right direction.

Fate played a big role in the recent chain of events that directed Jesse to this very moment in time and to this very spot in the universe. But more significantly, it afforded him exposure to reality and a reason to seek unexplored options. He had nearly made a tragic mistake. Had fate not steered him differently, he might be a member of Capone's army, and he was thoroughly convinced that he had no desire to be connected to that society with any degree of commitment.

As Jesse stared into the flames of the fire, trying to sort out the maze of scrambled impressions, Will found it difficult to penetrate the barrier that seemed to surround Jesse. Will's mind was clear, and his body refreshed after a swim in the creek. He set aside all the trials of the past few days, and his adolescent, fourteen-year-old spirit wasn't pondering the future, either. Reality to him, at that moment, was the fire's radiant warmth on his bare skin, the star-speckled, black, night sky, and the sound of frogs chirping their nightly ritual songs in four-part harmony. Nothing else seemed to matter, to Will.

Two days passed; apparently, Luke's evaluation of the present-day Northfield homestead was accurate. Not a single person – or ghost – had invaded their paradise. The privacy allowed Jesse and Will to grow closer, becoming more like brothers with each passing hour. Will was beginning to idolize his new protector -- he would do anything to please Jesse. No one had ever treated him as an equal before; no one had ever taught him the values he was absorbing from Jesse. Influenced by a rowdy neighborhood gang, life in the big city had made Will unruly and coarse, but now he was learning dignity and self-esteem, and how to be a respectable human being. He wanted to be just like Jesse.

The noon sun was hot and there wasn't a cloud in the sky; it seemed like a good time to cool off with a dip in the creek, and while they were at it, all their clothes needed washing too.

They stood waist-deep in the cool water, scrubbing their jeans with a bar of hand soap; Will saw the opportunity to raise a question that had been on his mind all day. "Do you s'pose... I mean... would it be okay with you... if... ah... if I changed my name... to Madison?"

The query caught Jesse off guard. "Well, I don't know if you can just do that. And why? Aren't you proud of the name Montgomery?"

Will replied without hesitation. "What's there to be proud of? Daniel Montgomery left me and my Mom when I was five years old... and then my Mom left me alone with that drunken bum, Harley. See all these scars? Harley put 'em there. Why should I be proud of the name Montgomery?"

Jesse was rather impressed with the logic emitting from the youngster, whether it was right or wrong. Will had not altered his explanation of the prolific scars, and now, his choice of a name change was nothing short of flattering. Feelings of guilt bolted through Jesse. He had planned to talk with Will about finding a family he could live with, but now that seemed like a heartless response in return for Will's adoration and affection. Maybe he could continue the boy's care for a while longer. Abandoning him now would only create emotional pain -- for both of them.

"I guess... if that's what you really want to do, it's okay with me," Jesse replied.

Will's toothy grin and freckles beamed with delight. "Okay. It's official. From now on my name is William Thomas Madison." He threw his arms around Jesse's torso with a joyous hug. "Thank you Big Brother Jesse... thank you."

Will's self-coronation ceremony continued; he splashed his way out of the water and tossed the pair of jeans he was laundering aside. Standing tall and proud on the bank he raised his arms, triumphantly proclaiming for the whole world to hear, "MY NAME IS WILLIAM MADISON."

10

Whippoorwill whistles echoed through the hazy pre-dawn tranquility, accompanied by the babbling murmur of the river current rippling along the shoreline rocks. Jesse sat up and breathed in the crisp freshness of the new day. Will was soundly asleep and last night's campfire was no more than a heap of gray ashes. There was just enough light to reveal mere silhouettes of the forsaken brick house and the towering barn. For the first time, seeing those forms in this light, Jesse could feel the spooky ambiance, but he quickly convinced himself it was just his own imagination creating the eerie impression.

During the past couple of days of exile from the rest of the world, Jesse came to realize that his life had once again been altered. Now there was Will -- a *brother*, to whom he had given a new lease on life, and as he sat silently, gazing at the boy's peaceful slumber, Jesse discovered his true feelings and the fondness for Will that he had developed, even though at first he might have considered Will somewhat of a burden. But now, that had all changed.

Jesse's thoughts began to focus on the subject that had taken him so far from home. Al's trunk now belonged to him. He had acted honorably all this time, protecting it, and respectfully observing Al's privacy by keeping it locked and the contents undisturbed. But now the circumstances warranted a look inside. He could think of no legitimate reason for it to remain a mystery any longer. It was finally time to unveil the encrypted secret.

The relentless hand of time had deposited a generous layer of rust on the iron hook holding the barn door securely closed. It was vividly apparent that no one had opened that door in decades, and although he knew his intrusion was insignificant, a bit of guilt followed Jesse through the doorway. But once inside he would certainly find something he could use to pry open the trunk lock. Darkness concealed most of the barn's interior except for the faint illumination near the open doorway and several windows. Finding anything in there was not going to be easy. As he cautiously stepped farther inside he could sense the vast, hollow emptiness within. It was like stepping into the pages of forgotten history that was remembered only as the remnants of a ghostly legend.

In the corner to the left of the doorway, Jesse could make out the vague shapes of familiar objects -- an overturned wheelbarrow, an anvil, and a wooden bench. Above the bench, an array of tools hung neatly on the wall.

"This must've been Isaac Northfield's workshop," Jesse thought as he inched his way closer for a better look. Among the various hammers, axes, and saws, was just what he needed -- a crude-looking crowbar. There was no need to continue the search any further. He plucked the bar from its peg and turned back toward the exit just as the squeaky door that he had left open slammed shut and repeatedly bounced against the sill, sending crackling echoes through the cavernous building. Jesse felt the hair on the back of his neck stand up; the tingling sensation paralyzed his ability to move, or to even breathe. Was Isaac Northfield's ghost about to punish him for stealing his crowbar? Jesse stood silently staring into the darkness, expecting havoc to erupt. But he only heard the howling wind outside and a sudden clap of thunder. Relieved that he had been spared from doom, Jesse scurried out the door, realizing that once again his imagination had taken the upper hand. Dawn was ushering in a thunderstorm, and as quickly as it seemed to be approaching, the best thing to do was to awaken Will, gather their belongings and seek shelter -- in the barn.

Still a little groggy, Will obeyed Jesse's instructions; he rolled up the blankets and slung them over his bare shoulders. Jesse scooped up all the dry clothes they had washed, and with wind-driven raindrops stinging his face, he briskly headed for the barn. Will was right on his heels. They were well inside before Will's sleepiness wore off and the reality of being inside the barn finally hit him. "I-is i-it s-safe to be in h-here?"

"Of course it's safe," Jesse said. "It's better than being out there in the rain."

"B-but what about the g-ghosts?" Even after three days and nights without incident, Will still remembered clearly the Northfield lore, and nothing had yet convinced him to disbelieve it.

"If there were still any ghosts here I think we would've seen 'em by now." Jesse had a knack for easing Will's uncertainty about almost anything. So if Jesse said it was okay, then it must be okay.

The barn did little more than reduce the storm's intensity. Missing shingles and broken wallboards permitted the vicious weather to penetrate. But through the center of the barn, directly below the roof peak was a loft, under which seemed to be dry and better protected from the invading elements. The blankets and clothes were draped over the side of a manger, and Jesse was content to sit there calmly. Will though, was as restless as a long-tailed cat in a room full of rocking chairs, listening to the creaks and moans and groans the old structure produced as the wind and rain pounded against its exterior. His imagination was dredging up voices, footsteps, and honking geese, and he was sure he saw a whole parade of creatures lurking in the shadows.

The thunder crackled and rumbled long after the rain stopped.

Rainwater was still dribbling from the leaky roof as streaks of bright yellow sunshine began peaking through the larger openings like dozens of tiny spotlights. Will could plainly see they were alone, but he was still ready to get out of there. As he bounded toward the doorway, he heard the squeaky board that immediately snapped under his weight, sending his left foot plunging through the floor. All his weight was supported on the next board under his right knee, and that board broke as quickly as the first. As if a monster had swallowed him, Will disappeared. Jesse's hasty reaction, in an attempt to come to Will's aid, found him crashing through the rotted wood floor, too. The five-foot drop was hardly enough to cause any serious injury, but the fall was quite startling. After a few seconds the shock wore off, and they realized they were merely a few feet beneath the floor in a shallow pit. The large hole they had created overhead let in enough light to expose the mortared rock floor and walls surrounding the small room. Jesse couldn't help but laugh, although Will wasn't so quick to recognize the humor in falling through a floor. It only renewed his uncertainty about being in *that* barn.

"Why is there a cellar under the barn?" Will's question did raise a point; its placement did seem a little odd. But then Jesse recalled something he had read in a book long ago, and he explained his speculation as if he were an authority on historical facts.

"The pioneers always had places like this to hide in case of renegade Indians attacks. There were probably plenty of them around when the Northfields built this place."

Will looked around as he contemplated Jesse's theory that seemed logically satisfying to his curiosity. Propped against one wall he saw a ladder, and just above it appeared to be a trap door in the ceiling -- definitely a better exit route than the one by which they had entered.

The unlatched barn door had been swung open by the wind. Beyond the building's shadow, rain droplets clinging to the tall grass and weeds glistened in the brilliant blaze of sunshine. Will was almost to the doorway when he stopped abruptly. He held his breath. He couldn't believe what he saw on the front porch of the brick house. Will and Jesse were no longer the only intruders there -- they had company.

The storm's roaring rage had masked the arrival of the dark green sedan parked beside the house, and the two people standing on the porch definitely weren't ghosts. Will recognized them all too well. He backed away from the door and turned to Jesse who was just emerging from the tiny cellar.

"It's them! They're here!" Will whispered in frightened excitement.

"Who? Who's out there?" Jesse's first thoughts were that Will's imagination was working overtime, and that he thought he had seen the

Northfield spirits. "Are you seeing ghosts again?"

"No! It's those two crooks who robbed the store! They're up by the house. I saw 'em plain as day. I know it's them."

In near disbelief, Jesse crouched beneath a window and peeked over the sill through the dirty, cracked glass. There was no one on the porch, but the door was open, and he knew that car had not been there before.

"Will, you weren't seeing things this time. Are you sure it was Shirley and Slug? They didn't see you did they?"

"I'm positive it's them, and I don't think they saw me."

The McNallys had escaped the arm of the law that was not long enough to stop them a few days ago, and early that morning after trekking miles on foot, they found another country general store near Spooner that became their ninth target this month. Not only did they get away with a gunnysack full of groceries and the money from the cash drawer, but this time they made off with the owner's car, too. And as fate would have it, they just happened to find their way to this abandoned farm at the end of a dead end road. Jesse's truck was behind a clump of brush near the river, out of view from the house, so Slug and Shirley were totally unaware of anyone else being there. The condition of the premises indicated a long absence of habitation, and a good bet that this was a safe hideout.

"What are we gonna do now?" Will whispered. He trembled with the thought of the menacing danger those two sinister characters posed. "D'ya think they're lookin' for us?"

"No. I think they were just lookin' for another place to hide... and it's just a coincidence they showed up here."

"How are we gonna get outa here? That's the only road out. They'll kill us if they see us here... you set their car on fire and they had to buy another one."

Jesse snickered. "They didn't buy that car. They prob'ly stole it."

They sat there watching the house for a half hour and saw nothing. Jesse was hoped that Nell Northfield's ghost would appear and scare off the bandits hunkered down in the house. But he was quite certain that wouldn't happen. The next best option was to sneak out the back of the barn and hike to Luke's place. It was just a little more than a mile, and Luke would know how to reach the Sheriff.

"What were you boys doin' at the Northfield place?" This Sheriff wasn't as friendly as the last one they encountered a few days before. It had taken him an hour to arrive at the Jackson farm, and his attitude was that of a gorilla being disturbed during naptime.

"We were just camping down by the river and we ducked into the barn to get out of the storm this morning, and when we came out they were there... in the house."

"Who was there?" Sheriff Dodson was a bit confused. The message he had received apparently didn't include any details.

Jesse realized that he had some explaining to do. "A few days ago we were at Sheldon's Gas Station, over at Cougar Crossing when they got held up by Shotgun Shirley and Slug McNally. They took my little brother hostage. I followed them in my truck to a cabin out in the woods. I set their car on fire that night to distract them so I could rescue Will, but they got away before the Sheriff got there the next day. Now they're in the house at the Northfield farm. They've got a dark green Ford sedan now. And my truck is by the river out past the barn. We didn't dare drive by the house... that's why we walked over here."

Now all the facts were falling into place. Sheriff Dodson had heard the account of the Cougar Crossing hold up, and just that morning, the Sheriff of Washburn County alerted Dodson of an incident there. "Must be the same banditos who robbed the Spooner General Store this morning and stole Charlie's car -- he has a green Ford sedan."

Dodson's attitude changed. He didn't seem too concerned about the trespassing issue any more -- if there even *was* an issue. Now it was his turn to have a go at capturing these wanted criminals. "You boys stay right here. Don't go back out to the Northfield place until I tell you its okay. Understood?"

"Yessir... we understand."

The Sheriff turned to Luke's father. "Tom, make sure these boys stay put. I wouldn't want 'em gettin' hurt out there."

Mr. Jackson acknowledged Dodson's mandate; he walked the Sheriff back to his car.

"Oh, by the way..." Dodson turned around to direct one last question to Jesse. "...How long did you say you've been camping out there?"

"About three days." Jesse responded.

Dodson rubbed his chin and stared at the ground. "You didn't by any chance happen to see a little old lady and some white geese, did you?"

Jesse chuckled. "No sir, didn't see anything like that." Only Luke and Will understood why Jesse found a bit of humor in the Sheriff's query.

After Dodson drove away, Luke, Will, and Jesse settled down at a picnic table with a pitcher of cold lemonade in the shade of two towering white pines. Luke wanted to hear every detail of the story, all the way back to the hold up at Sheldon's. He had delivered sacks of potatoes there several times in the past, so he knew Sheldon and Rachel fairly well.

It didn't take long for Jesse to understand why Luke treasured the opportunity to get away and to be alone once in a while. Six overly-energetic, screaming youngsters insisted on playing their game of tag, with the picnic table as the center of their universe that only extended ten feet in any direction. The two oldest girls -- Laura and Jean -- seemed to be competing for Will's attention, neither of which was attaining much success. Will was a little flattered, but not very interested. Finally, Luke had enough of the irritation and shooed the siblings off to another part of the yard.

Jesse was becoming a pretty good storyteller, and with a little help from Will now and then, one episode spawned another -- and another -- and another. The chronicles went on for hours; Jesse was beginning to realize that his life wasn't so dull after all.

Luke was captivated, exhibiting no signs of losing interest. His intrigue manifested with eagerness to hear more. The only stories he usually heard were the Paul Bunyan yarns told by old lumberjacks of the area, and he was certain most of them were nothing more than exaggerated fairy tales. But Jesse's stories were real and believable.

And then it started. The ear-stinging distant volley of gunfire echoing across the rolling hills interrupted Jesse's recital. The three boys could only speculate on what was happening at the Northfield place. They sat and listened while the combined forces of Sheriffs and Deputies from four counties unleashed their revenge with a hailstorm of lead.

It was a battle between the law and the lawless, and the latter was pitifully outnumbered. There was no escaping this time.

By nightfall the shooting stopped. It was hard to say if the confrontation was over, or if darkness simply put it on hold. The eerie stillness through the night only added to Jesse's anxiety. His brand new truck and everything he owned was out there in that war zone, and nothing short of a miracle could insure its safety. He was unable to fall asleep, dreading what he might find when he was allowed to return to the campsite. Luke sat beside him at the open bedroom window overlooking the hills and the forest and the darkness that hid the Northfield farm from their view.

"When this is all over, where will you go?" Luke tried to ease the tension with a little conversation.

Jesse had been giving that subject some thought over the past few days; his response came swiftly and easily. "Maybe Missouri, maybe Texas, maybe even Florida... someplace where it's warm all winter. I don't like winter."

"Whatya gonna do when you get there?"

"Guess I'll have to find work of some sort. I've got a little money saved up. Me 'n Will can get by for a while 'till I find a job."

"Sure wish I was goin' to Florida... don't think I want to raise taters all my life." Envy of Jesse's adventurous lifestyle oozed from Luke's words.

"So... why don't you come with us?" Jesse didn't give much thought to the possibility that Luke would take the offer seriously, but he recognized Luke as a compatible friend, and there was no harm in extending the invitation.

The wheels were turning inside Luke's head; Jesse realized his proposal was receiving some serious consideration.

"Ya know, my Pa 'n me have been talking about this all summer," Luke said. "He thinks I should get out on my own now that I'm grown up... 'n maybe he's right."

It wasn't hard to tell that Luke's mind was no longer trained on the unfolding drama at the Northfield farm. Instead, his imagination was traveling cross-country to places he only knew as pictures in books and dreams in his heart. But he questioned his own courage to leave the only home he had ever known, and the security it offered.

Sunrise caught Jesse and Luke finally napping after a long, sleepless night. Whether it was the sounds of the resuming firefight that awakened them, or maybe the magnificent aroma of the fresh coffee and pancakes from the kitchen downstairs, they were wide-awake and ready to meet the challenges of the new day. After breakfast, Luke and his Dad would start preparing for the potato harvest, and Jesse and Will would tag along, just for something to pass the time.

By late morning the storage shed was clean and ready for the new crop. Tom Jackson took pride in his work; everything had to be just right. In two weeks he would be hiring the crew and the harvest would begin.

Jesse kept an ear to the air, monitoring the gunshots that were much less frequent than they had been earlier; it had been quite a while since he had heard any shots. Staying out of harm's way, as they were ordered, kept everyone at the Jacksons' from knowing the current developments occurring just a mile away. But the news had traveled quickly to other places. Newspaper reporters from cities as far away as Minneapolis, Duluth, and Rhinelander were already swarming like vultures, hovering over a carcass in the desert. The numerous country store heists had scarcely been noteworthy, but now the two-day standoff and capture of the McNallys was about to become a monumental event of the region.

Shadowed by three reporters, Sheriff Dodson showed up about four o'clock that afternoon with the news everyone was awaiting. He had not slept since the previous morning, and his exhausted, drained expression was proof of that. But his stamina prevailed as he made the proclamation.

"The McNallys have been taken into custody. Norman -- that's Slug's real name -- has a couple of bullet holes in him, and that's prob'ly why Shirley gave up and surrendered. They're both behind bars in the County Jail."

Dodson took off his hat and wiped the sweat from his forehead with his shirtsleeve. Everyone suspected there must be more to the story, and by the extreme sorrow that came over the Sheriff at that moment, they knew tragedy must have struck. He went on to explain that one of his deputies was mortally wounded during the gun battle. Jimmy Kendall was Dodson's best friend and his best deputy. And now he faced the dreaded obligation to inform the family that Jimmy wouldn't be coming home.

"These newspaper reporters are gonna want to ask you a few questions. They already know you boys are the ones who led us to the McNallys. When you're done with them, I guess it will be okay for you to go get your truck." Dodson leaned toward Jesse and spoke softly. "And if I were you, I wouldn't stick around out there too long. There will be more reporters, and they'll hound you to death."

"Okay," Jesse said quietly. "Thanks for the tip... and I'm really sorry about your deputy."

The Sheriff tipped his hat in a gentlemanly fashion, got back in his car and drove away as the news men launched a barrage of questions aimed at Jesse and Will. "Why were you at the farm?" "When did you first spot the McNallys?" "How did you know it was them?"

The questions spewed out fast and furious; the reporters frantically jotted notes as Jesse and Will told the saga of their experiences with Shirley and Slug. Those three journalists knew they had struck pay dirt by lingering a while longer than the others, who were already enroute to their home offices with the hottest story of the day, and wanting to be among the first to tell the world of the gallant capture, and the tragedy that went along with it. But only those three would share the exclusive account of the hold-up at Cougar Crossing, Will's abduction, and Jesse's heroic, single-handed rescue. Jesse and Will were nobodies, but with the next morning's edition of at least three big city newspapers, their drama would be thrust into the limelight, and thousands of readers would accredit them with delivering the loathsome felons to justice.

Jesse and Will gave little credence to their act of crime fighting. They were glad the thieves were taken out of circulation, and they were pleased that they had done their part to help accomplish that. But they wanted to get on with their lives. Returning to the Northfield farm and reclaiming their campsite by the river, despite the Sheriff's advice, was their top priority. They probably wouldn't stay there much longer, but it did serve as their home base at the present.

Jesse thanked the Jacksons for the warm welcome and the accommodations he and Will had enjoyed, and appreciated. "It's time for us to be movin' on, but if we ever get back this way again we'll be sure to look you up."

Mr. Jackson offered a cordial handshake. "You come back anytime. Our door is always open... and good luck."

Luke decided that saying good-bye at that moment wasn't among his greatest desires. "I'll walk part way back to the river with you." And with that, he, Jesse and Will struck out across the meadow.

"When do you think you'll be leaving?" Luke asked.

"Tomorrow sometime, I figure." Jesse wasn't about to make any commitments on a schedule.

"Okay. I'll see you again tomorrow before you go. I'll meet you down at the river. Don't leave until I get there."

The enchantment of the place seemed to be gone as they approached the deserted farm buildings. Not a single windowpane in the entire house remained unbroken -- the ones that were left were marred with bullet holes, and the whole house was riddled with the permanent reminder that a gun battle had taken place there. The green Ford sedan was equally perforated; its windows were shattered as well. Glass shards and bits of brick littered the ground all around the house. Its charm of undisturbed antiquity was stripped and gone forever.

The barn, however, showed little evidence of the skirmish; it appeared to have escaped the brutal shower of lead. Only a few stray bullets had left their splintering endorsements on the walls, but they were hardly noticeable.

Jesse picked up the crowbar that he had dropped there the previous morning as they passed by the barn door.

"What's that for?" Will asked.

"I found this in the barn yesterday morning before the storm hit. I'm gonna use it to pry open Al's... *my*... trunk."

Not one bullet had found its mark on Jesse's truck, nor did anything else within their campsite appear to be disturbed. It was all just the way they had left it the previous morning, as if nothing more than a rainstorm had interrupted their day.

Jesse perched on the log next to the fire pit and gazed into the woods across the river, trying to block out thoughts of the event that had occurred only hours earlier, just a couple hundred feet away. He had more important things to consider. His uncertain future was in the balance, and he wondered where his fate would take him next. The world was obviously full of surprises and adventure -- Jesse knew he had only scratched the surface.

11

"**W**here are we going tomorrow? I heard you tell Luke last night we're going to Texas. Are we going to Texas?" Will's curiosity was mounting. Jesse hadn't spoken of any future plans, and Will was anxious to relocate. Being in such close proximity to the Northfield homestead looming in the backdrop still raised goose bumps every time he glanced in that direction.

Jesse fidgeted with the crowbar. "We'll keep going 'till we find a place we want to call home. Don't know where that is 'till we get there."

He stared at the trunk in the bed of the Model A. A sense of guilt was still simmering a reluctance to break it open. But there was no one else around to witness the act, and after all, he *did* declare its ownership. It was his to do with as he saw fit.

The chisel point of the pry bar made fairly easy work of removing the lock. A couple of sharp jabs and a little prying, and, at last, the mystery contained in the box that Jesse had been safeguarding all this time finally was unveiled. He carefully opened the lid. Suits. Black, pinstriped, silk-lined, men's three-piece suits -- a bit rumpled and damp, but they were new and very high quality garments, but hardly worth protecting from life-threatening consequences. Jesse didn't know whether to laugh or cry as he pulled the suits, one by one from the trunk, tossing them in a heap on the ground. His mind's eye flashed visions of Will nearly drowning trying to retrieve the trunk being swept away by the flood, and the deadly intentions glaring from Pete LeFever's eyes. Then he envisioned Al Capone and his men as Jesse had always seen them -- dressed in apparel just like this.

Will looked on with impulsive curiosity, but his enthusiasm diminished to disappointment with each garment added to the pile. He wasn't anticipating anything in particular, but there was nothing too sensational about a bunch of clothes.

As Jesse plucked the last jacket from the container, his idea of fueling that night's campfire with the useless garb -- and the trunk -- seemed to be a fitting disposal, and an end to the curse its possession had bestowed. He would be rid of it once and for all.

"What's that?" Will asked, when he noticed something else that had been hidden under the clothes at the bottom.

Four gray lumpy canvass bags, tied shut with leather lanyards lined the bottom of the trunk. They each pulled one of the bags out, untied the cords and carefully dumped the contents on the ground. Will's eyes enlarged to the size of small pumpkins and Jesse's lower jaw dropped nearly to his knees. Stunned by the sight, they silently stared at the bundles of money -- more money than either of them had ever seen before.

"W-O-O-O-O-O-W!" Will exclaimed with quiet excitement as he fondled a pack of ten-dollar bills. "Where did all this money come from?"

Jesse lifted the other two bags from what he now considered a treasure chest. They, too, held similar amounts of cash. "Prob'ly from a lot of people in Milwaukee who bought bootleg moonshine from Capone."

All the pieces of the puzzle fell into place, and the chain of events back in Westby made more sense to Jesse. Liz and Emma Hawthorne were acting as couriers between Al and his associates in Milwaukee, transporting the large sums of money back to Westby for Al to pick up there. No one would ever suspect two little old ladies on a train to be affiliated with the Chicago gangster, or that their baggage disguised all that loot. He understood why the Hawthorne twins had staged their deaths, knowing precisely when Al would arrive at their house, and that he would be the one to find the two dead bodies they planted there, appearing to be Emma and Lizzy, which would put an end to their business relationship with Al, and provide their opportunity to abscond with a small fortune that could never be traced. Their clever scheme of deception to rid themselves of Capone's control was almost perfect -- except they underestimated Jesse's perception and ingenuity.

The Hawthornes might have been successful too, had Jesse not been so clever. They had always entrusted him to handle their luggage to and from the railroad depot, and there was no exception to the rule for their final step to pilfer the trunk intended for delivery to Capone. They knew the contents, and if they could secretly transport it back to Milwaukee, the riches would be theirs. But they didn't account for Jesse's loyalty to his friend. They would have been wiser to cut Jesse in, but greed commanded their poor judgment.

And so it went unnoticed that Jesse pulled off an equally shrewd scam by switching trunks -- a shell game that the Hawthornes didn't know they'd lost for several days, when it was too late for a rematch.

With the stroke of a crowbar, Jesse had become instantly wealthy beyond all imagination. Maybe just pocket change to Capone, but to Jesse it was a fortune.

"What are we gonna do with all this money?" Will asked.

Jesse thought a moment, considering the options he could bring to mind at that instant. "Nothing. We'll stash it under the seat of my truck, and we won't tell *anyone* about it. I'll think of something later."

The smashed trunk and fine suits made for quite a bonfire later that evening; in a short time, it was all reduced to ashes -- even the tin hinges and latches melted into indistinguishable clumps. Jesse felt nothing but relief as he watched the sparks from the fire fluttering into the air, knowing the trunk would never again attract a thief's attention, nor ever again fall into a raging flood. The curse was gone forever.

Satisfied that not a trace of it remained, Jesse settled back on his blanket. The reality of sudden wealth slowly began making its impact. Nothing seemed unfeasible now. Knowing there must be several thousand dollars in those bags, he knew he had more money than he had ever dreamed possible; the future didn't look quite so discouraging after all. But what would he do with that much money? Economic instability made banks a bad risk; leaving it hidden under the seat of his truck for the time being was, perhaps, the best solution. There would be plenty of time to think about it later. He drifted into a deep sleep.

"Jesse! Jesse! Wake up!"

Jesse opened his eyes only to see and feel Will frantically shaking him. He squinted in the bright morning light, still incoherent from the abrupt awakening.

"Someone's here! Up by the house!"

Screams and moans of mental anguish were sounding from that direction. Jesse quickly sat up and slipped on his shoes. His senses were beginning to align with reality and he recognized the fact that they had visitors. The voices he heard were distressed, but he couldn't quite understand what they were saying. He'd have to get closer to determine what was going on.

One man was standing at the rear of the Ford sedan, and another was walking around it, emitting the pitiful cries upon surveying the ravaged automobile. "Just look at my new car! It's ruined! My new car is ruined!"

Obviously, this man was the owner of the sedan, and the last victim of the incarcerated crooks. Jesse cautiously approached him. "Is there anything I can do to help?"

Charlie was a little startled by Jesse, but his expression of surprise immediately returned to that of devastated depression. "I'm glad they caught those bastards, but look at what they did to my car. Sheriff Dodson told me there was some damage, but he didn't say it was totally destroyed. I just got this new car two weeks ago... and look at it now."

Jesse eyed the broken windows, the hundreds of bullet holes and the three flat tires. He could feel the sorrow that Charlie must have felt as he climbed back into his friend's car and rode away.

"Who was that?" Will quizzed as Jesse sauntered back toward their camp.

"Charlie. That's his car, and he runs the store that the McNallys robbed.

Guess he figured his car wasn't worth taking home."

Another voice called out. "Jesse! Will!" The voice was familiar. Luke came crashing through the weeds past the barn with a bedroll slung over his left shoulder and a brown leather satchel in his right hand.

"I talked it over with Pa last night. He thinks it's mighty kind of you to let me travel with you."

Jesse and Will displayed a look of surprise with Luke's announcement.

"Is it still okay with you?" Luke sensed he might be intruding where he wasn't welcome.

Jesse looked Will in the eye. "I guess I did sorta invite him to go with us. How 'bout it little brother? Is it okay with you?"

Will shrugged his shoulders. "Sure... why not?" He was ready to agree to anything if it meant leaving the Northfield place.

Jesse gave it some thought. Luke had developed the courage to explore the unknown adventures awaiting him beyond the boundaries he knew, and he was anxiously waiting for Jesse's approval. There was no reason to deny Luke's eagerness to discover the world, just as Jesse was doing, and there might be better safety in numbers.

"Okay," Jesse said. "We'd better load up and get started. Luke... do you know the best way to get back to the Mississippi River? We'll follow the river south."

Ecstatic with the acceptance, Luke responded. "Just south of Rice Lake there's a highway west to the St. Croix River. There's another road that follows the St. Croix down to the Mississippi."

And then they were three. Within minutes the Northfield farm was only a memory as the crusaders started their journey in search of tomorrow. Each new horizon held the promise of adventure, and together they would chase the sunsets and pursue their dreams.

Cruising down Main Street in Rice Lake, Jesse spotted a glass-fronted building with a bright blue oval-shaped Ford sign painted on the wall. He turned the truck toward the side of the street and stopped. A dark blue Model A sedan sat just inside the huge showroom window.

He handed Will a couple of folded bills from his shirt pocket. "You and Luke go get us some food and cold drinks. I have some business to take care of. Be back here in an hour."

An hour later, Will and Luke returned to the truck with a bag of groceries, just in time to see Jesse shaking hands with a well-dressed man inside the window.

But Jesse didn't tell either of his traveling buddies of the business he conducted while they were gone. They would reach the Mississippi, and beyond, before the new Model A sedan was delivered to Charlie at the Spooner General Store, paid for in full with part of the windfall, and a note on the front seat that simply said: "Good luck, Charlie. I hope you like your new car. Your friends, Jesse and Will."

They were only a few miles from the St. Croix River that afternoon when lightning bolts began to dance beneath a boiling canopy of dark, ominous thunderheads in the sky to the west. The threatening weather seemed to be closing in; Luke started feeling a bit uneasy. "Looks like a bad storm rolling in. Maybe we should stop somewhere."

Jesse peered up at the black clouds through the windshield, reminiscing his recent experiences with the darker side of life. "We will, but don't worry. Storms fade away."

12

The cool autumn wind whistling in from across the Minnesota prairies, and the green of the forest giving way to the brilliant ambers, oranges, and reds – prominent signals that winter was waiting in the wings -- were reasons enough for the trio to seek refuge in a more temperate environment. Their sights were set on reaching Missouri, where they would escape the northern winter's brutal, icy bitterness.

By far, Luke had endured the most severe winters during his lifetime in northern Wisconsin. But even with his hardy adaptation to winter weather, his tolerance level was wearing thin.

Jesse just plain hated winter. He'd *always* hated winter. He thought back of all those bone-chilling days spent on the railroad depot platform, with the frigid wind piercing into his very soul, numbing his senses and transforming his spirit into a solid chunk of frozen dismay. Even though, only a few steps away, the huge potbelly stove stood at the center of the depot's main hall, radiating tropical warmth, where he could revive his chilled body, it could do nothing to change the season outside. Jesse just plain hated winter.

Will didn't voice any opposition to a warmer climate. When he ran away from Milwaukee he had never given much thought to pending difficulties such as keeping warm. Jesse's plans seemed quite different from what Will expected his destiny to produce, but he had learned to trust Jesse, and if Jesse believed Missouri should be their destination, then Missouri sounded good to him, too.

Distance meant very little to any of them. None were seasoned travelers, although Jesse and Will were starting to get the hang of it. They knew Missouri must be a long ways, but it was just barely into September.

They still had a month, or so, until the really cold weather would set in. Because none of them had any steadfast plans in mind, there didn't seem to be any really good reason to be in any great hurry.

Jesse still entertained a craving for the big river vessels. There was some magical magnetism that lured his interest and continued to weave hazy visions of the future in his mind. He could never lock in on a clear picture, but a voice inside his head kept encouraging him to seek out the answers to his curious affinity. It was as if someone was calling his name, but he could never quite identify the face.

Will was beginning to feel a mysterious attraction to a world with which he was unfamiliar. He knew of the ships that navigated the Great Lakes. Many times he had wandered to the waterfront at Milwaukee's east side and watched as the mammoth freighters maneuvered in and out of the harbor. But this was different. His interest was more than likely spawned by Jesse's influence, but a certain charm of the river's pageantry did create an appealing atmosphere.

Of the three, Luke was the only one who had ever actually been on board one of the big boats. He had once helped his father transfer a truckload of potatoes from their fields to the deck of a cargo riverboat on the St. Croix. He wasn't sure if it was the immense size of the craft, or the hard work involved, that was more memorable. But now that Jesse was dramatizing a marked interest in the world afloat, Luke realized that this was indeed a fascinating concept.

It would be a couple of days and a couple of campfires later when they arrived in LaCrosse. The journey's progress was slow, as every time they spotted one of the mighty steamers churning its way among the islands and sandbars, they would stop to watch until it was out of sight, and only its smoky signature lingered in the air above the water. No matter how many times Jesse saw them, each one was as intriguing as the first. Nothing had ever captured his interest with such intensity since the day he had his first ride in a motorcar -- the day Julian Kelly took him for a drive to the sawmill -- the day his passion for the automobile was born. He knew without a doubt that the river was about to open a new avenue into the future, and yet another chapter of fascinating discovery.

Luke, in all his nineteen years had never set foot in a big city. Although LaCrosse was small compared to Chicago or Milwaukee, to him it was big, and like a kid on his first trip to the circus, his eyes widened more and more as they approached the center of town. The concourse of tall buildings; the red brick-paved streets; the traffic; the throngs of people. On nearly every street corner a young boy stood with a canvas bag draped over his shoulder and waving a folded newspaper, chanting an enthusiastic plea to the passing public to part with a dime for the morning daily news.

This was the height of the harvest season. Rows of vendors offered everything from freshly picked apples to zucchini, and in the crispness of the morning, scores of basket-toting shoppers were milling about, seeking the firmest head of cabbage, the sweetest apples and the plumpest pumpkins.

Block after block, they passed by storefront after storefront. Luke was in awe. He had entered a spectacular new world.

All this was old hat to Jesse -- he had been here many times. Will had spent his whole life, until about three months ago, roaming the streets of Milwaukee. Until he jumped that westbound freight train, he could only imagine that rural America existed at all. But he learned quickly how to survive outside the city, and likewise, Luke would learn the ways of the street.

Jesse's attention naturally gravitated toward Levee Park. But this time it wasn't the park's pleasantness that lured him there. This time, the park was his portal to tomorrow. It was from there that he could stroll along the docks, fill his lungs with the river air, and feel the magical power that was beginning to control his every thought. There, he could satisfy a hunger he didn't fully understand, yet he desperately wanted to pursue.

When they first saw the River Serpent, there was nothing too impressive about her. Weather-beaten, drab, and scarred with age, the Serpent had been the typical steamboat white once, but now a mixture of soot and dust was sun-baked onto every surface, and the remaining grayed paint was wearing thin. Nothing like the gallant vessels Jesse had admired during his last encounters with the river, there was little one could call prestigious about the Serpent. Less massive than many, the Serpent was clearly a working vessel, unlike the glittery showboats that primarily transported passengers and provided them with Broadway style entertainment, elegant dining, gala events, and gambling during their voyages up and down Mid-America's inland waterways. She was nothing more than a hundred and twenty feet of floating loneliness.

The entire main deck was intended for cargo, the forward third of which was open to the elements. Although the upper decks housed passenger accommodations, the space seemed limited and appeared to lack any elegance at all. Cosmetically, the Serpent was an unattractive old scow, but even though the luster of distinction seemed absent, she was surrounded by a certain radiance of dignity.

It might have been that there were no other big boats docked there that day -- only smaller fishing and pleasure craft -- making the choice of closer inspection quite simple. Whatever the reason, Jesse was drawn to the Serpent like a monkey to a stack of bananas.

The main deck was empty. Not a sign of creature or man stirring anywhere. The loneliness rendered a rather eerie setting compared to the beehives of activity they had witnessed on other vessels. It seemed odd that such a fair day was going to waste on idle time.

"Aye, Mates!" The strong greeting sliced through the gentle breeze and aroused a half dozen squawking gulls perched on the end of the pier.

The boys tipped their heads back to focus on the open pilothouse window above the upper deck where a gray haired man wearing a faded blue shirt and a black seamen's cap leaned out with his hands planted firmly on the sill. A hardy grin lit up his gray bearded face. He seemed glad to have visitors.

Jesse started to explain their presence as if they had been caught with their hands in a cookie jar. "We were just looking at your boat... we--"

"Well, then. Permission to come aboard granted! I'll let you get a closer look."

They hadn't expected this kind of welcome from a total stranger, but they weren't going to pass up an opportunity like that.

He met them mid ship on the main deck, and spoke with a Scandinavian inflection and rhythm that was common in this part of the country. "Captain August Bjornson, but you can call me 'Augie.' And you are...?"

Augie offered his hand to each of his guests as they announced their names.

"Jesse Madison."

"William Madison."

"Luke Jackson... pleased to meet you, sir."

Augie Bjornson, now in his mid-sixties was an ex-Merchant Marine. He had served aboard ocean-going vessels until shortly after the close of the Great War, but he never got the deep waters out of his veins. Augie had sailed around the Horn more times than most people go to the grocery store in a year -- sailing was second nature.

When he returned to the Midwest after a long career on the high seas, he realized how much he missed that life, so he gathered up his sea legs, spent his entire life savings for the down-payment on the River Serpent, and took to the river, "tramping" as it was called -- steaming from town to town with no set schedule -- transporting cargo and passengers up and down the Missouri, Ohio, and Mississippi.

Now, age was creeping in on the Serpent, and on Augie as well. Together they had logged more river miles than he cared to remember; his sea legs were getting shaky. A lean year had weighed heavily on his enthusiasm, especially now when he was finding it more difficult to keep a reliable crew, and the old ship just didn't have the pizzazz necessary to keep up with the changing times.

Augie loved the river, and he loved a good poker game, too. He had learned the art of gambling on the high seas as a young sailor, and there had been times in recent years that his luck and a deck of cards would yield a handsome supplement, but lately he didn't seem to do much better than just break even.

A lengthy tour of the River Serpent revealed the lack of attention -- cosmetic features, mostly. Nothing a good coat of paint wouldn't cure. She was solid and sound and quite worthy of the river. Only the fading of time suppressed the gracefulness that had so carefully been pieced together by skillful hands.

Just ahead of the huge stern paddlewheel were two powerful steam engines and boilers, silent, and ready to thrust their brute strength into propulsion. All that was missing was an engineer and a fireman.

When the tour reached the upper deck where the passenger cabins were, Augie couldn't resist telling the boys of the Serpent's claim to fame. "Charles Lindbergh rode on this boat once, 'course that was before he got to be famous."

It needed a little cleaning and maybe the floor could have used a fresh layer of varnish, but the passenger quarters were nicely appointed -- honey-colored oak woodwork accented the pale blue walls that surrounded a huge living room area containing tables and chairs and sofas, commonly referred to as the "main saloon" on river boats. A long, narrow corridor led from the back of the room to the rear of the boat that was lined with twenty oaken doors opening into small but adequate cabins, each large enough to accommodate two people. A window let light into each one.

To the front, overlooking the bow, an open-air deck lined with benches provided fair weather lounging and observation. The magnificent, panoramic scenery, bountiful in the river valley, could not be viewed from a more advantageous spot.

Augie ushered the boys along the "Texas Deck" above the passenger deck, where the crew's quarters and the galley sprawled over half the vessel's length, and crowning the superstructure, the glass-walled pilothouse offered a view in every direction. Nestled among an array of levers and switches and gauges, the stalwart cherry wood steering wheel, polished to a mirror finish boldly proclaimed that this was the point of command.

Just below the pilothouse were the dedicated Captain's quarters. It served as his office, his dining room, his own private pub and his bedroom. Hot in the summer and cold in the winter, that was where Augie Bjornson called home.

Over the years, the Serpent's cargo bay had been host to every imaginable kind of freight -- cotton bales to horses; household furniture to gunpowder; farm machinery to printing presses. Even a few barrels of moonshine whiskey occasionally found their way from Kentucky to Minnesota aboard the Serpent, hidden away among the amassed freight, and conveniently lost from the ship's manifest papers. Augie spoke of his accomplishments proudly. His ship had served him well. But now the decks were bare and the crew's quarters were vacant, and he feared his glory days were nearing an end.

A few encouraging sparks of optimism still flickered in Augie's heart. Now that three eager, energetic, strong young men were showing such enthusiastic interest in the Serpent, perhaps he had the makings of a new crew, inexperienced as they were. At least two of them were big and strong, and Will -- he was no Charles Atlas, but he had spirit, and he would make a fine cabin boy. Augie was a shrewd, but honest businessman; he recognized the opportunity to revive the momentum of his life-long profession, if only long enough to return the Serpent to his Missouri homeland where he could retire among his friends.

To avoid the threat of pandemonium, by hastily suggesting any premature plans, Augie made an offer to the boys they couldn't refuse. "If you need a place to sleep for a night or two, you're welcome to stay here on the River Serpent. As you can see, there's plenty of room. You can use a couple of the cabins on the passenger deck."

Will recalled that August day in 1927 -- three years earlier -- when he shinnied up a lamppost along Wisconsin Avenue in Milwaukee, because he was too little to see the parade from within the crowd. He wanted to catch a glimpse of "Lucky Lindy." The debonair young pilot had made aviation history; Charles Lindbergh was an American Hero, and he was Will's hero too. Will saw Charles Lindbergh that day, and because he was clutching onto that lamppost, ten feet above the crowd, Will was sure he had made direct eye contact with Lindy. That was the closest he had ever been to a celebrity; the moment would live in his memory forever.

"Can I have the cabin that Lindbergh slept in?" Will was as excited as a kitten in a shoelace factory; he had the good fortune to sleep in the same bed where Charles Lindbergh once slept.

"Sure, you can." Augie replied with a big grin. "That would be the Tennessee Stateroom."

Augie didn't really remember which cabin Lindbergh had used, but he saw the wonderful excitement in Will's eyes; he didn't want to spoil the youngster's thrill by admitting uncertainty.

"Wow! This is great! Thanks, Augie!" Will's enthusiasm carried him in a dead run to Jesse's truck. He gathered up his suitcase and headed straight for the famed cabin.

"Augie?" Jesse's curiosity peaked. "Why do all the cabins on the passenger deck have state names instead of numbers... like hotel rooms?"

"That's always been a tradition," the Captain responded, "...that the passenger cabins on a riverboat bear State names instead of numbers. That's why they're called "Staterooms.""

The next couple of days, life was grand. Two blocks from the pier, downtown La Crosse offered just about anything Jesse, Luke, and Will could possibly want, and to them it was almost like strolling through a carnival, complete with hot dogs, taffy apples, popcorn, and a moving picture theater.

But the glitter of the city was secondary, as quite often, they would find themselves huddled around Augie Bjornson aboard the River Serpent, intently listening, while he spun tales of the river, the cities and villages nestled along its banks, and the grand boats. He was a great storyteller; the strong Norwegian accent seemed to add a unique flavoring. Every time another boat, large or small, would tie up at the dock, it would remind Augie of another story. The boys never tired of the old sailor's yarns, and little by little, they learned the riverboat jargon.

Luke and Jesse knew they should be making their way south; the cold weather wasn't going to hold off forever. But the wheels had started turning in Jesse's head. All the while they had been in La Crosse, an unequalled friendship was generating with the riverboat captain, and the sensation of a purpose for that kept looming in Jesse's subconscious. Finally it surfaced like a whale coming up for air. Augie had been hinting at getting a crew together, and maybe that was the answer to their search for a better tomorrow.

It was late afternoon. The *Capitol* was docked about fifty yards downstream, and Augie had combed his hair, splashed on some of his best toilet water and meandered toward her, anticipating a reunion with a fraternity of river men, and perhaps, a poker game. He knew he would find both on the *Capitol.*

Alone on the Serpent's upper deck, Jesse, Luke, and Will conducted their own fraternity meeting.

Jesse evaluated the situation. "Augie's been havin' some bad luck, lately. I kinda feel bad for him. He doesn't have a crew, and I think he wants to keep sailing. We're looking for jobs... maybe we can talk him into hiring us. Whatya say we help Augie get this boat back on the river where it belongs?"

Will thought it was a fantastic idea. He couldn't think of a single thing stopping them.

Luke had some concerns, though. "But we don't know anything about sailing."

"You didn't know how to drive a truck either, until your dad taught you how. We can learn. Augie's probably a good teacher."

"How much d'ya suppose the job pays?"

"Who cares? Anything is better than what we have now."

"What about your truck, Jesse?"

"Maybe I can talk Augie into letting me put it on the boat. There's plenty of room on the cargo deck. When we get down south, we'll find a place to live, and we'll unload it there."

Luke had heard so many colorful stories and legends from Augie that he was almost convinced; steamboating on the Mississippi could be an incredible adventure, and there certainly was no better way to experience all the exciting grandeur the Captain had described in his stories.

"Okay... let's do it. Let's learn how to be river tramps."

13

The cool September night air had little effect on Jesse as he lay on the Tennessee Room bunk, unable to sleep with the excitement of new adventure dancing in his head. Will seemed to be peacefully settled in his "Lucky Lindy" bed, but Jesse could hear Luke's restless stirring in the Ohio Room across the hall. Faint but jubilant, spirited dance music coming from the *Capitol's* Main Saloon had stopped. In the eerie stillness, Jesse listened for Augie's footsteps on the stairway to the Texas Deck. He was sure that Augie would be delighted to hear the trio's decision to seek a riverboating career aboard the River Serpent.

How could anything have turned out more perfectly at a time when the future held so much uncertainty? Jesse wasn't so concerned about financial security -- he had a plentiful supply of money -- but he still yearned a meaningful existence. So far, his entire life had been a roller coaster ride; for the first time he could recall, he was beginning to see some direction. The path leading to an ultimate destiny was gradually defining itself from the foggy depths of unpredictable vagueness. He wasn't staring into a well of indecision any more. And now the only remaining element needed to open the door to the future was gaining Augie's approval and acceptance.

The long, reverberating baritone wail of a steam whistle heralded the approach of a barge towboat out in the main channel to the coal yard downstream. Squawking gulls sounded close enough to be perched on the bedpost. Jesse opened his eyes. It was morning, and he realized he had fallen asleep without hearing the Captain's return. The hour had finally arrived to announce the good news. His feet hit the floor with a thud; he shook Will's shoulder.

"Wake up, Willy. It's time to get up."

Luke was already up, dressed, and returning from the privy when Jesse headed down the hallway with that same destination in mind.

A benchmark day was ahead of them. This was the day they hoped to become real rivermen. Jesse had been pondering this day for a month; Luke and Will were just as exalted with the endeavor.

They found Augie sitting in the Main Saloon with a pot of coffee on the table. His face wore a blank stare. An air of exhaustion clung to him like moss on a tree branch. Obviously, he had not slept all night.

"G'mornin' Captain!" Jesse nearly exploded with cheery enthusiasm.

A solemn "Mornin'" was the only reply.

Jesse suspected that it was not the best time to discuss business, but his proposal couldn't wait. The boys pulled chairs up to the table, like they had done so many times before, to hear Augie's great river stories. But this time, it was their turn to do the talking.

"We know you're wanting to get the Serpent back on the river, and we talked it over last night. We want to be part of your crew. We'll help you get the boat ready. How about it, Captain? Will you hire us on your crew?"

Augie stared across the room. He tried to smile but it required more effort than he could collect. Something was terribly wrong. The boys had never seen Augie in such a state of depression. Not quite certain if it was just fatigue settling in, or if it was because of a few too many "toasts" to the fraternity the night before, they eagerly awaited Augie's answer as he took another sip from his coffee mug.

"Yesterday," he began with a sorrowful tone, "...I would've jumped at your offer. In fact, I was scheming to make a similar proposal. I could tell you fellows took a liking to this old boat, but I'm afraid I have some bad news."

Augie took another sip of coffee.

"Last night I got into a poker game over on the Capitol. The stakes got a little too high, and I got a little too bold, and now the River Serpent belongs to Blackjack McDermott."

"Who's he?"

"A gambler... from New Orleans."

A bolt of lightning striking the center of the table couldn't have produced a more shocking blow. Jesse wanted to make sure he understood what Augie had just said.

"You lost your boat in a poker game?"

Augie looked down at the table, nodding his head in shameful disgust.

He hated to admit that he was no longer Captain of the ship.

"McDermott will be here this afternoon to look her over. He said we could stay for a couple more days until we made other arrangements."

The stark reality began its cruel impact on the boys. They had suddenly been robbed of their ambitions. Their spirits melted like a scoop of ice cream on a hot sidewalk.

"So what are you gonna do now?" Luke asked the Captain.

"Oh... haven't thought much about it yet, but I'll prob'ly catch another southbound tramp back to St. Louis, or maybe there's a boat out there in need of a pilot."

A more important question for the boys to answer now was "what were *they* going to do?" There certainly wouldn't be another opportunity like the one that just slipped away. As much as they disliked the idea, the next best option was to pack up their belongings and continue their southward ply, as originally planned. Saying good-bye to Augie would be difficult, but at least they had experienced the privilege to enjoy his unforgettable friendship.

The rest of the morning, and into the afternoon hours, they sat in the Saloon, listening to the thumps, as Augie rummaged through his quarters, packing his memories into boxes. There was little to say. It seemed as though Augie had given in to defeat.

At 2:00 o'clock, sharp a bit of a disturbance broke the stillness aboard the Serpent. The boys detected voices coming from the lower deck, and between the snippets of undistinguishable speech, noises like the heavy end of a billiard cue slamming against an oil drum echoed across the empty cargo bay. Jesse and Luke ran out of the Saloon and perched halfway down the staircase, overlooking the main deck. Augie had heard the ruckus too, and he followed, but he went to the bottom of the stairs, leaned against the railing and folded his arms across his chest. Will stood beside him mimicking the stance.

Blackjack McDermott and his valet had begun their inspection. As they ambled from engine room toward the stairs, they mumbled something about the boilers, but Jesse couldn't make out the exact words. All he could think about was how much McDermott reminded him of an overweight bulldog waddling along, and how his assistant's voice sounded like poorly tuned strings on a bass fiddle.

Dressed in a light gray suit and derby hat, McDermott was short and nearly as wide as he was tall. An equally stubby, fat cigar protruded from the corner of his mouth, and his chubby, ringed fingers clutched a brass-handled walking stick, obviously the instrument responsible for the boiler banging.

Otis, his assistant, appeared quite the opposite. Nearly six feet tall and skinny, his darker colored suit hung on him like a limp dishrag on a nail, pants legs four inches too short. On his head of black, greasy hair, sat a derby as well, but at least two sizes too small.

What a pair. Luke thought they kind of looked like an exclamation mark and a period searching for the end of a sentence.

"Good afternoon, Augie." McDermott's scratchy voice penetrated the air with a distinct tone of arrogance. "Came to take a look at my boat."

Augie gave a single nod, but he didn't speak. There was no need to be pleasant, and a guided tour was out of the question. The Serpent belonged to McDermott. He could discover its details as he wished, and without Augie's help.

Luke and Jesse graciously slid over to one side, making plenty of room on the steps for Otis and McDermott to pass. Without the slightest acknowledgment of the boys' presence, they made their ascent to the Saloon deck. Jesse had already concluded his evaluation as to the character of the new owner. It was less than admirable. McDermott was rude and arrogant, and he obviously had no feelings of remorse. He had crushed Augie's livelihood, and he probably accomplished it by cheating.

The inspection didn't take long. It was hard to tell if McDermott's grunts and snorts coming from the upper decks were sounds of approval, but Jesse and Luke, still sitting on the staircase, concurred that it really didn't matter. They were more concerned about Augie, and the devastation he must have been feeling. It seemed bad enough that he had lost his boat, but losing it to this man -- of all people -- Blackjack McDermott -- made it seem even worse.

Will rejoined Jesse and Luke on the stairs as McDermott and Otis lured Augie to an obscure spot where their conversation would not be heard.

"Isn't there something we can do?" Will asked Jesse.

Jesse had already been contemplating some devious plans, but they involved criminal acts, and his better judgment quickly dictated their dismissal.

"I don't think so, Willy. It would take nothing short of a miracle to get the Serpent out of McDermott's hands now. Best thing we can do now is stay out of the way and let Augie handle it the way he wants to."

By 4:00 o'clock the steamer *St. Paul* had docked beside the Serpent, and a gradually increasing number of passengers began filing down the loading ramp. Some were headed for the busy downtown La Crosse streets, and many were transferring their suitcases to the *Capitol*. Roustabouts scurried back and forth between the two big steamers with wheeled carts loaded with crates and trunks.

Jesse, Will, and Luke had domineered a wooden bench at the edge of the park, near the sidewalk leading to downtown. It offered a clear view of the activity on the docks. They sat watching and discussing how great it might have been to become a part of riverboat life. But for some reason they could not explain, the glamour of those big, elegant riverboats didn't seem to have the magnetism any more -- not since the Serpent's quaintness had settled into their souls. They felt just as cheated as Augie.

Suddenly, Will perked up. He stood. His eyes were fixed on the ramp at the bow of the *St. Paul*. Jesse hadn't seen that much joy on Will's face since the day at the Northfield place when he officially changed his name. It wasn't clear to Jesse what had excited Will, and by then Will was already dodging pedestrians making his way toward the St. Paul at a Kentucky Derby pace. When Will stopped running and took up a stride with a gentleman walking toward the park, Jesse felt a smile warming his own face, and he, too, trotted off to meet them, leaving Luke sitting alone and confused.

"Hello... Jesse, isn't it? Sure didn't expect to see y'all here," the man said.

"Yessir... and Hello to you too, Mr. Morgan. It's good to see you again."

Spades Morgan, all that time, had been hopping from one tramp boat to another, all the way to St. Paul, Minnesota and back, doing what he knew best -- gambling. Now it was time for an overnight stay at a La Crosse hotel before boarding the *Capitol* for passage back to St. Louis.

"I see you're still haunting the river docks. I thought y'all were going up north somewhere to work. You had a trunk to deliver. Did you get it there?"

"Yessir, but things didn't work out so good, and that trunk? Well, it wound up firewood, and that's why we're back here."

Jesse wanted to avoid any more discussion regarding the trunk or anything related to it. He had managed to keep the money a secret to everyone, other than Will, and he wasn't ready to change that scenario just yet.

"Mr. Morgan, I'd like you to meet Luke Jackson. He's travelin' with us now, too. Luke, this is Spades Morgan. Me 'n Will met him in Alma on our way up to Couderay."

Luke was taken by Morgan's stone faced expression. He was a little uncertain of the degree of friendliness behind a face that didn't smile, but a cordial handshake convinced him that Morgan's personality didn't necessarily match the blank, statue-like outward appearance.

"Pleased to meet you, Mr. Morgan, sir."

Just then a sparkle in Morgan's eye suggested something had triggering a recollection. He turned to Jesse and Will. "Say, didn't I read something in the newspaper the other day about you boys... something about catching a pair of bank robbers?"

Jesse's face flushed. He stared down at the ground and his foot pawed at some pebbles in the dirt where the grass was worn away in front of the park bench.

"Well... yeah. You prob'ly did. But they weren't exactly bank robbers, and we didn't exactly catch 'em. We just stumbled onto 'em and told the Sheriff where to find 'em. The lawmen did the rest."

Nonetheless, Spades Morgan was impressed with the courageous performance, and even more impressed with Jesse's humble reluctance to accept the credit that the news media had given him and Will.

"So... what brings you famous bandit hunters to La Crosse? More bank robbers?"

Jesse giggled. "No. We were on our way to Missouri. Stopped off here for a while and we got hooked up with Captain Augie Bjornson."

Spades glanced back toward the dock. "That's his boat... the River Serpent. Good man, that Augie is. And I'll bet y'all are gonna be rousters on his boat."

It didn't surprise Jesse that Morgan knew Augie Bjornson. There seemed to be an honorable camaraderie among the rivermen -- at least among the good ones. And it also seemed favorable to Jesse, at that point, that Morgan had already spoken auspiciously about Augie. That would certainly make it easier for Morgan to understand his feelings of distress.

"Well, Mr. Morgan... you're partly right." Jesse paused, and his expression turned solemn. "Augie *is* a good man. We've become good friends, and yes, we *were* going to be on his crew, but..." He hesitated again.

"But what?" Morgan was too well trained in the art of reading faces; he detected Jesse's anguish, and he didn't have to hear the words Jesse spoke to anticipate a bit of adversity entangled in the reply.

Jesse felt compelled to finish his statement, but he struggled with mixed emotions about interfering with Augie's business. He didn't know if this was the suitable time to announce, to anyone, something that Augie would prefer to be kept quiet. But Spades was a friend, and as long as he had voiced a high opinion of Augie Bjornson, he must know Augie well, and he would certainly treat the information with discretion, preserving the dignity Augie deserved.

Jesse's voice quivered. "Well, as of this morning, the Serpent doesn't belong to Augie any more."

"What? Augie sold his boat?"

"Not exactly."

"What, then?"

"He lost it in a poker game last night."

"He what?"

"Augie lost the Serpent in a poker game, over on the Capitol last night, to a gambler from New Orleans... Blackjack McDermott."

Morgan rarely displayed emotion. It was his nature. But at that moment, he twinged with disgust. The name 'Blackjack McDermott' would never have appeared on Morgan's list of friends. They were rivals, and rather than being subjected to McDermott's repulsive morals, Morgan avoided his presence altogether. It had been that way for a long time.

"McDermott," Morgan blurted. Even speaking his name made him sick. "McDermott. That good-for-nothing, slough scum weasel. Is he here now? I thought I smelled something peculiar when I got off the boat."

Morgan peered at the *Capitol* for a few seconds. Then he gazed up into the sky at the wispy gray clouds, and then at the darker clouds banked on the horizon.

"If that bag o' slurry is on the *Capitol*, then I guess I'll just have to wait for another south-bound. I'd sooner stay here all winter than to be on the same steamer all the way back to St. Louie with... him."

Morgan had made his point. He detested McDermott. Jesse, Luke, and Will didn't have a clue why Morgan harbored such a strong attitude toward the man who probably hoodwinked Augie, but now they were satisfied that their first impressions of McDermott that afternoon were right on the mark.

"How could Augie have let that happen?" Morgan's question didn't seem to be directed to anyone in particular, but more of an out-loud thought.

"Don't know," Jesse replied.

Luke joined the conversation, now that he was convinced Morgan was on their side. "He's taking it pretty hard. He hasn't said much of anything all day since he told us the bad news this morning."

"Can't say as I blame him." Morgan said. "Augie's been up 'n down the Mississippi at the wheel o' the Serpent for as long as I can remember. Can't imagine what it'll be like... Augie not bein' in that pilothouse, I mean." Morgan's eyes drifted back to where the River Serpent lay tied to the dock. It looked so forlorn, like an abandoned, ragged teddy bear left behind on a trash heap. In the late afternoon long shadows, only one lamp giving off a pale, ethereal glow through the Captain's quarter's windows revealed the only sign of life aboard the Serpent. "I wonder what that swamp skunk intends to do with her."

Jesse wasn't too fond of entertaining that thought. Instead, his curiosity regarding Morgan's plans seemed more interesting. "If you're not takin' the Capitol back to St. Louis, what're you gonna do?"

Morgan looked back up to the sky that was darkening by the minute with low, slow-moving, heavy billows of gray. "Looks like more rain comin'. Won't be any boats goin' any direction for a while, I 'spect. With all the rain up north lately the river's plenty high. There'll be more boats, so I guess I'll just stay at the hotel in town for a few days. Say... would you boys care to join me for supper tonight? The hotel serves a roast beef fit for a king. It'll be my treat."

Luke's mouth started to water. They hadn't exactly suffered from the lack of nourishment recently, as Jesse was suspiciously and miraculously producing the means for a bellyful of food every day. But just the thought of a steaming hot slab of juicy roast beef -- the kind Luke's Mom prepared nearly every Sunday -- almost brought tears to his eyes. He desperately hoped that Jesse wouldn't decline the offer.

"Can Augie come too?" Will had already finalized his acceptance to the invitation.

Morgan pondered Will's request for a moment. "Will... I wouldn't mind a bit, but we best leave Augie alone to deal with his affairs."

It was up to Jesse to give his stamp of approval. Will and Luke looked as though they were ready to commit a lynching at the nearest tree if he showed the slightest sign of reluctance.

"What time should we be there?" That seemed like an appropriate way to say yes.

Morgan pulled a gold watch from his vest pocket, snapped open the face cover and made a brief study of the time. He needed enough time for a hot bath, a shave, and maybe a brandy and a cool glass of wine at the speakeasy just down the street from the hotel, where he was well known and welcomed any time.

"Eight o'clock. Meet me in the hotel lobby at eight o'clock."

Morgan turned to commence his hike toward the long-awaited bath. Jesse suddenly remembered that La Crosse wasn't a one-hotel-town like Westby. "Which hotel?" he called out to Morgan.

Morgan stopped, turned, and replied matter-of-factly. "Why, The Stoddard, of course." He resumed his stroll toward downtown.

The boys returned to the Serpent's Saloon deck where their clean clothes and other belongings were still safely stashed in the staterooms. They stepped lightly, knowing the boat would be forbidden territory within a matter of a day or two, or perhaps, hours. The pungent aroma of some unidentifiable cuisine filled the air; they heard a kettle rattling across the top of the cook stove in the galley. Augie wasn't renowned as a fine chef, but over the years he had learned to make do, in the absence of a cook, from time to time.

Jesse felt the need to play the role of Big Brother as they approached the cabins. "Now Will, get ready for supper. I'm going to tell Augie we'll be out for a while, and see if there's anything he needs help with." He looked at Luke, assuming Luke would also take the hint to spruce up a bit, without any prodding.

Will mumbled a protest. "What's to get ready? I'm hungry... isn't that ready enough?"

"Go wash your face and comb your hair... and put on a clean shirt. We're going to a nice restaurant, not a hot dog stand. Morgan was nice enough to invite us to supper and the least we can do is show up looking like gentlemen... not a bunch of hooligans."

Will was reminded of the dignity and self-esteem -- the values that he had been learning from Jesse ever since their first day together. Obedience to his Big Brother had never been a problem before, and it certainly wasn't a problem now either. He instantly retrieved a bar of soap and a towel and headed off to the washroom.

Before Jesse turned to seek out Augie, he smiled at Luke. "Make sure he washes the back of his neck and behind his ears too... sometimes he forgets those spots."

Luke grinned and nodded. "I assure you your little brother will be squeaky clean by the time you get back."

Jesse knocked on the open galley door. He knew it probably wasn't necessary, but as far as he was concerned, Augie was still the Master of his domain, and just barging in without announcing himself first would show little respect.

"Come on in, Lad. You don't have to knock."

"Are you okay, Augie? I mean, is there anything I can do for you?"

"I'm just fine, Lad. A little tired and a little hungry maybe, but I'm doin' just fine."

Augie seemed to be in better spirits -- better, at least, than he had been that morning. Maybe it was just a charade, but if it was, he could win Actor of the Year, hands down.

"Me 'n Luke 'n Will are going uptown for a bite to eat. Thought I'd see if we could bring you back something. But I see you're... cooking."

"Just boilin' up this catfish I caught today. That's all I need. Thanks for askin' anyway."

"That's funny... I didn't see you fishing today."

"'Course you didn't. Don't have the patience to sit with a fishing pole in hand, but I always have a line dangling over the side of the boat. If something's on the other end when I haul it in at night, then that's my supper. And tonight a big ol' channel cat found his way right into my cooking pot. Now you and the others just go on into town and have a good time. I'll be just fine."

"Okay. We'll see you in the morning."

Augie didn't say another word. He just waved his big spoon in the air and went back to stirring the fish soup.

A light rain began to fall as the boys hurried around the corner at Main and Third. They had passed by the graceful, brass trimmed glass doors leading into the Stoddard Hotel lobby several times before, but they had never ventured inside.

Culture shock set in. Luke's mouth dropped open; he stood paralyzed by the sight, gaping at the twenty-feet-high ceiling and the crystal chandelier, valiantly suspended aloft by a golden chain. White and gray marble pillars shone like mirrors. Polished mahogany lined the walls, and Victorian sofas and chairs, upholstered in regal red velvet, were strategically positioned around the giant room. Signed, glossy eight-by-ten photographs of people they didn't recognize hung in gilded frames on every wall. Exquisitely dressed people strolled about, some of them briefly pausing to gaze at the pictures. But Spades Morgan was nowhere in sight.

Will didn't seem nearly as awed by the extraordinary surroundings. This was nothing new to him. He had darted in and out of many exclusive establishments like that in Milwaukee, just to be an irritating aggravation to the "rich snobs" inside. The only difference at the Stoddard was that he didn't have to sneak by a doorman, and one of the "rich snobs" at the Stoddard would be buying him a roast beef supper.

Questions were welling up inside Luke's head. He was beginning to notice oddities surrounding his new friends; peculiar suspicions loomed. Jesse had never mentioned anything about living in Milwaukee, yet his little brother spoke of his experiences there. Jesse seemed to have a lot of money, and he had talked about his friendship with Al Capone. And something strange did happen back in Couderay, but Jesse probably wasn't telling the whole story. And how did Will get all those abusive scars? Certainly not from Jesse; the two shared a better relationship than that. They were standing in a fancy hotel lobby, waiting for a rendezvous with a man who just stepped of a riverboat from St. Paul, dressed in a three-piece suit and a gold watch. Just who were these guys?

Jesse nervously looked at his watch. It was five minutes past eight. He hadn't really noticed how out of place he and his companions appeared. His only thoughts were about Spades Morgan and the plan Augie had triggered.

"He's not going to show up," Luke whispered. "Why don't we just get a hot dog somewhere and go back to the boat?"

"He'll be here. He's just waiting for the rain to let up... and besides, I have to talk to him... tonight."

"Just who is Morgan? Or should I say... *what* is Morgan?" Luke couldn't hold back his curiosity.

Jesse eyed Luke as if something peculiar was taking him over the edge. "Morgan is a professional gambler... I thought you knew."

Luke's eyes opened wide. "Oh, great! Milwaukee! Capone! Money!

Mysterious scars! And now you're getting us mixed up with professional gamblers! This is just great! What's next? We gonna kidnap the Pope?"

His sudden hysteria was drawing some attention. A distinguished-looking gentleman in a black tuxedo approached the boys. The calm refinement was overwhelming. "Unless you gents have some official business here -- which I dreadfully doubt that you do -- I'm afraid you'll have to take your quarrel outside immediately. You are disturbing the other guests."

Jesse was grateful that this stranger had intervened, but he was also quite embarrassed. "Yes, we do have business here... we're meeting someone for supper."

"Yes, I'm sure you are. Now, please leave."

"But we really are meeting someone," Jesse protested. "We're waiting for--"

"Is there a problem here, Malcolm?" The strong but quiet voice came from behind Luke and Jesse as a hand fell on each of their shoulders. They had their backs to the entrance and hadn't noticed Morgan coming in.

The tuxedoed desk clerk made eye contact with Morgan and abruptly transformed his stern grimace to an artificial smile. "Ahhhh, good evening Mr. Morgan, sir. I don't believe your dinner guests have arrived yet, but I'll-"

Jesse interrupted the formal fakery. "We were waiting for Mr. Morgan."

Morgan leveled a poker-face stare into Malcolm's eyes that seemed to drill right through his brain. "These three fine young gentlemen are my dinner guests."

Will took his best shot too, as an official member of the insult firing squad. "Yeah, Malcolm... ya big turd."

Spades ruffled Will's hair. "You tell 'em, kid." Then he turned to Malcolm again. "Is our table ready?"

Malcolm's face had taken on a brilliant shade, nearly as red as the sofa behind him. "Your table for four is waiting," he said meekly. "Right this way."

Will sat next to Morgan. That was a given. Jesse took the seat directly across from Will, leaving Luke face-to-face with their generous host. Luke had calmed down considerably, but Jesse could sense he was still a little uneasy. He didn't know what had lit Luke's fuse in the lobby earlier, and he hoped the conversation here wouldn't get him going again. Jesse had a plan, and he wanted Luke to understand he was acting in the best interest of everyone present -- including Luke.

It was Jesse's only chance to seek Morgan's help. The bad weather was playing right into his scheme, keeping any of the boats from leaving that port for a while

Will wasn't aware of Jesse's attempt to recruit Morgan for the purpose of getting Augie's boat away from McDermott. He and Morgan had hit it off so well, back in Alma, and their meeting at the Stoddard was turning out to be a repeat performance. Jesse didn't have the heart to push Will out of his spotlight, and Morgan seemed to be enjoying Will's trivial questions about gambling, life on the riverboats, and if he had ever gotten into any gunfights with other gamblers. Eventually, Will asked a question that Jesse wished he wouldn't have. "Did you ever see any more of Pete LeFever?"

"No, I didn't," Morgan replied. "But you know? I heard some folks from Alma talkin' the other day. They said they saw ol' Pete come stumblin' up to Main Street from the riverbank, delirious. Had a bloody knot on his head the size of a Joo-ly sweet potato. Didn't know where he was or how he got there. They figured he must've taken a pretty nasty spill on the rocks down by the river. The Sheriff knew who he was though, from his picture on a Wanted Poster in the Rogue's Gallery. They put him in irons 'n shipped him back to Louisiana on the next train."

"But he didn't fall. I beaned him with a rock. He had a gun pointed at Jesse and I let fly with the biggest rock I could throw, 'n--"

Jesse kicked Will's shin to shut him up, and then he looked around the room to see if anyone else was paying attention. It didn't seem they were.

Morgan leaned over and quietly spoke some good advice in Will's ear. "If I were you, I'd keep that story to myself." He winked at Will.

Jesse was relieved to know that his Little Brother had not killed the man, and no one was the wiser about what had really happened that afternoon in Alma.

Luke had definitely enjoyed the succulent roast beef, but he was twitching and squirming, and Jesse noticed a slight tremble now and then. It was puzzling. Luke had heard Jesse's stories about Capone, and about their wild adventures with Shotgun Shirley and Slug, and he had even heard the one about the bandit on the hilltop -- Pete LeFever -- but he had never reacted this way before.

Jesse gently patted Luke's knee; it seemed to give a calming effect. Later, he would try to get to the heart of Luke's turmoil, and perhaps cure the ailment, if that was possible. But at that moment, saving Augie's boat was the urgent business at hand, and that might take some fancy footwork.

"So... Mr. Morgan..." Jesse saw his chance to gain Morgan's attention.

Morgan leaned over the table toward Jesse. "I wish you'd stop calling me "Mr." Just call me Spades. Everyone else does."

"So... Spades... how did it come about that you hate McDermott so much?"

"That swamp slime. Well, I guess y'all deserve an explanation... now that

I've been ranting on about it. You see it goes back a few years."

Will and Jesse leaned forward with their elbows and forearms firmly on the table, and even Luke decided he should listen, too, and he leaned forward, to hear every word.

"I never did like McDermott much, from the first time we ever met. He was always one of the crooked ones, and then one time, I figured out how to beat him at his own game -- his marked deck and all."

"How'd you do it?" Will broke in.

"Secret, son, secret. Can't be divulging my trade secrets." Morgan continued with the story. "We were under a full head of steam late one night along the Louisiana bayou up from Baton Rouge, heading for Natchez. Full moon overhead, and hot, God it was hot. We'd been at the table for about an hour, 'n I had taken him for a few hundred bucks by then, when this young newlywed Cajun farm boy -- Jacques Dupree -- asked if he could get into the game. I tried to chase him away, but McDermott saw an easy target and encouraged the poor sucker to stay. I couldn't bear to take the young man's money, so I got up 'n walked away."

"So, what happened then?" Will asked.

"McDermott let Dupree win a few hands. The Cajun took the bait and McDermott reeled him in. The antes kept getting higher, and the bets kept getting bolder, and after about two hours, McDermott cleaned him out of every penny the sucker had."

"But isn't that what gambling is all about? Hookin' a sucker and reeling him in?" Jesse asked.

"Ahhhh... but there's more to the story. It didn't end there, and this is the part that bred my utter hatred for McDermott. Dupree left the table penniless and destroyed. He'd lost his life savings, and I guess he couldn't bear to face his new bride, so he walked up onto the Texas deck, pulled a revolver from his belt, put it to his head and pulled the trigger.

"A half hour later, McDermott had the nerve to go to Dupree's widow -- Jenny, was her name -- and he demanded that she give him Dupree's gold watch he saw her take from the corpse, as Dupree had been a little short on the last hand. They say she threw the watch at McDermott, then threw herself off the upper deck into the black, swirling eddies below and drown.

"To this day, when the moon is just right, you can still see the ghost of Jenny Dupree walking the banks of the Mississippi up from Baton Rouge, calling for the soul of her dead husband, and she's even been seen on some of the riverboats all along the Mississippi."

"Woooow!" Will exclaimed. "Did all that really happen?"

"Every bit of it. And that's why I hate that greedy, heartless, cheatin' bastard."

After hearing the story, Jesse knew just how to convince Morgan to help get the Serpent away from McDermott. He smelled the scent of revenge, still lingering over the table long after Morgan's voice had gone silent, and it would be the perfect ploy.

"Think you can still beat him?" Jesse asked.

"McDermott? Hmf. I could beat that slop bucket with one eye closed and my mouth stuffed with cotton. He's a lousy poker player. The only reason he keeps winning is because he knows how to cheat... and I know all his tricks."

"How would you like to get some revenge... for Jenny Dupree... and win the Serpent back for Augie?"

Still not realizing Jesse's plot, Will jumped in with his own idea. "Why don't we just sneak the Serpent out of the harbor in the middle of the night and hide it somewhere?"

Morgan chuckled at Will's suggestion. "Son, it's pretty difficult to sneak a steamship... even in darkness. Too much noise, and hiding a boat that size would be like hiding a zebra in a petunia patch. No, I like Jesse's idea better."

Luke was intrigued by the conversation flying across the table, but he didn't care to offer anything to it. Unsure of what the results might bring, he still felt apprehensive, and maybe just a little frightened. He could picture all of them, and the Serpent, victims of sabotage -- the retaliation of an angry, destroyed gambler who he already knew to be less than honorable. The image he saw had grim possibilities, and he really didn't favor that picture.

"How long do you think it will take?" Jesse asked Morgan.

"I'll have that bottom feeder in a game in less time than it takes a snag to sink a steamboat." Morgan jerked his watch from its pocket. "I figure we'll be at the table by midnight. 'Course, I'll have to play him all night... wear him down, you know... to make it look good."

Jesse thought that this was a pretty monumental favor to ask of Morgan, without offering him some compensation for his efforts. The only thing Morgan stood to gain was the satisfaction of beating McDermott at a game that he was already confident he could win. But there was always the remote possibility of failure, too.

"How much money do you want for starting the game? Will a thousand dollars do? I can give you a thousand bucks right now."

Luke's eyes got just about as big as the dinner plates on the table.

Will's head jerked back and forth from Jesse to Morgan, as if he were watching a ping-pong volley.

Morgan was taken by surprise, although he didn't show it. He didn't expect such a proposal, and he had already intended to soldier the game on his own -- as a favor to his friends. "Keep your money, Jesse. You may need it. The pleasure is all mine."

Will nearly ruptured with excitement. "Can we come and watch? Huh? Can we?"

"No." Morgan's answer was quite final. "Can't take any chances with even the slightest distraction. McDermott, the sewer rat that he is, well... I just don't want you there. Don't want nobody there. This is going to be between me and him."

Disappointed but still enthusiastic, Will was persistent. "Will you come over to the Serpent 'n let us know as soon as it's over? That's where we sleep, you know. I've got the bed where Lucky Lindy slept."

"You can count on it, Will. I'll be there." Morgan looked at his watch again. "Now y'all get on to bed. It's nearly ten o'clock, and I'll see y'all in the morning."

Jesse stood up; Luke and Will followed his lead. He offered his hand across the table to Morgan. "Thank you, Spades, for everything. The roast beef was delicious. The best I ever ate. And we appreciate what you're doing for us tonight. You're a good man and a good friend... we're lucky to have met you."

Morgan graciously accepted Jesse's handshake and his praise. "Thank you, Jesse, for such kind words, but it is I who is so fortunate to have met such good friends. I won't let you down, I promise. And I rather enjoyed your company tonight. We'll do it again sometime."

The rain was still coming down just hard enough to keep the puddles in the streets rippling and replenished. The air felt remarkably warm for that time of year, and it smelled fresh and clean, although an occasional whiff of coal smoke drifted by. The rain was refreshing to Jesse -- it was his assurance that neither the *Capitol* nor the *St. Paul* would be leaving any time soon. It was his assurance that there would be a poker game that night. It was his assurance of hope for Augie.

"Funny," he thought, as he and Luke walked side-by-side, and watched Will running into the darkness toward the river. "Funny how so many good things come with the rain."

14

The party lights were burning brightly aboard the *Capitol* and the *St. Paul*. The rain had bullied the remaining passengers and staff off the open decks and into the Saloons of both vessels, and there seemed to be a rivalry going on between the resident jazz bands of each boat --

each number getting louder and faster. Occasionally, the music would be nearly drowned with the sound of the boilers steaming off as they fed pressure to the engines running the electricity generators. As if isolated from the rest of the universe by a sea of darkness, the *Capitol* and *St. Paul* existed as independent entities, alive with gaiety, their occupants temporarily ignoring the looming shadows cast by a failing economy.

But next to the *St. Paul*, the Serpent lay still and dark. Even the lamp in Augie's quarters had been extinguished just before Luke and Jesse reached the gangplank. They paused there a few moments, taking in the spirited interludes between the tunes. Jesse was about to suggest the investigation of at least one of the soirees, but then he realized that Luke probably wanted to talk, and in the quieter atmosphere of the Serpent's empty Saloon would be more suitable. He was curious, too, to discover the origin of Luke's sudden unusual behavior at the hotel. Speaking hardly at all since the temperamental outburst, Luke definitely had troubling thoughts, and he probably needed to get them off his chest.

As they climbed the stairs to the upper deck, Jesse could only speculate the possible logic for Luke's abrupt change in character. Maybe the vastness of the world beyond the surroundings to which he was familiar was just too overwhelming. Maybe he was afraid of uncertainty. Maybe he didn't possess the emotional stamina to endure adventure. Maybe he didn't feel the same sense of freedom and independence that Jesse had experienced. *Maybe he was homesick.*

The Saloon was lit only by the glow from the *St. Paul's* lights splashing through the windows. Augie had obviously turned in, as there was not the slightest sound of stirring in his quarters. Will was perched at the window in the Tennessee Room with his nose pressed to the glass, his eyes fixed on the neighboring boat, hoping to catch a glimpse of Morgan through the St. Paul's windows.

"D'ya think he'll win?" Will asked, not breaking his stare as Jesse entered the room.

Jesse wanted to sound positive. "Of course he'll win. He always wins. Now get out of those wet clothes and go to bed. Starin' out that window ain't gonna help Morgan one bit. We'll know first thing in the morning."

"But I'm scared, Jesse."

"Scared? Scared of what?"

"I'm scared that McDermott will do something bad to Morgan like he did to that guy... Duper... a long time ago."

"Dupree. His name was Dupree, and nothing like that is going to happen to Morgan. Morgan's too clever to let McDermott get the best of him. Now go to bed. Everything's gonna be just fine... you'll see."

Will got undressed and climbed into the Lucky Lindy bed, pulling the covers up to his chin. At that moment, more than ever, Jesse recognized the importance of his Big Brother role in Will's life, and he thought of the words Morgan had spoken: "...It is I who is so fortunate to have met such good friends."

"Thank you, Jesse." It was as if Will were reading Jesse's mind. Jesse knew precisely what Will meant -- no other words were necessary. He gave a twist to the knob on the oil lamp, and then from out of the darkness he heard Will's meek but deliberate voice again. "I love you, Jesse."

Jesse paused in the doorway; the words penetrated deeply into his soul. Jesse couldn't recall those words ever spoken to him before. He didn't have to evaluate their sincerity. He knew they were.

"I love you too, Will," Jesse whispered. "Good night."

Had his attention not been drawn to yet another emotional crisis, Jesse might have sat down and bawled, but instead, he savored the good feeling as he headed into the Saloon where he knew Luke would be waiting. Now that Will was at peace, he needed to do the same for Luke -- or at least try. "Boy," he thought, "...this big brother stuff is demanding. But I don't mind. I don't mind at all."

Luke sat on a sofa in the dim light; elbows on knees, chin in hands, he stared at the floor. He had taken off his rain-dampened shirt, and his tanned skin, still moist from the rain, glistened in the rays of light from the *St. Paul.* Jesse's shirt was quite damp and uncomfortable as well. Removing it didn't seem like such a bad idea, so he did, draping it over the back of a near-by chair. He sat down next to Luke. Several minutes of silence passed. Jesse sensed that Luke was waiting for him to cast out the first line.

"Good thing it started raining... so the boats didn't leave, huh?"

Luke just kept staring at the floor. That wasn't the topic he had hoped for. "Yeah, I guess."

Jesse held is watch up in the light from the window. "Well it won't be long now 'till Spades and the sewer rat start their game."

"Yup... suppose so." Still not the subject matter Luke wanted to hear.

Small talk wasn't working. Jesse thought he'd better get right to the point. He laid his hand flat on Luke's back. "C'mon Luke. What's wrong?" he asked.

Luke gave a brief glance in Jesse's direction. "Nothing."

Jesse didn't expect that answer. It clearly was going to require a little more coaxing. "There must be something wrong. You've been acting kind of funny all night. C'mon... you can tell me. Will's prob'ly asleep by now, and there ain't nobody else 'round... you can tell me."

Luke leaned back, pinning Jesse's hand between him and the sofa. "Ain't nothin' wrong. It's just that nothin' seems right."

That didn't make much sense to Jesse, but it was a start. "I'm sure everything is gonna turn out okay, if it's savin' the Serpent that's worryin' you."

"It's not that. I'm not worried about how things will turn out. It's about what's already happened."

"What do you mean?" Jesse wasn't sure where the conversation was going, but it probably had something to do with Luke's tantrum in the hotel lobby, when he babbled on about Milwaukee, Capone, money, and whatever else he had thrown in about gamblers, and something about kidnapping the Pope. Jesse wasn't sure how *that* fit in.

"I don't know, Jesse. I'm just real confused right now."

Jesse thought *frustrated* was more the case. "Confused about what?"

Luke looked Jesse in the eye. "About... about... you... mostly... I guess."

"Me? What's so confusing about me?"

Luke thought a moment, searching for a good place to start. "I guess I don't know you as well as I thought I did... and maybe it was a mistake for me to come with you."

The pieces of this puzzle were starting to fall into place. Jesse suddenly realized there were many secrets that he had kept from Luke. He had been playing Simon Sez without a full explanation of the rules. And maybe it was time to clear the air. But there was one question he needed answered first.

"Luke... are you homesick?"

"Gosh sakes, no!"

"Then why was it a mistake to come with me 'n Will? And why am I such a mystery to you?" Jesse had a pretty good idea what the response would be, but it would be better to let Luke take the lead. There was no need yet to volunteer answers that had no questions.

"Well, I'm just a poor farm boy, 'n when we first met I thought you 'n me had a lot in common..." He hesitated. It was like walking barefoot through a rattlesnake pit -- he wanted to get to the other side, but he didn't want to suffer snakebite in the process. "...Now I don't know if I have the right to pry into your personal life," he said, as if he had changed his mind about saying any more at all.

"Luke..." Jesse put a gentle but firm grip on Luke's forearm, and his face took on the most sincere expression known to mankind. "...You are my best friend, next to Will, and you can ask me anything you want. I promise I'll give you honest answers. I swear on my mother's grave that I've never lied to you yet. Maybe I haven't told you everything, but I haven't lied. Ask me anything you want -- personal or otherwise. I don't have anything to hide from you any more."

Luke's tension eased. He had failed to see the genuine person in Jesse before then, but there were still doubts lurking about. "What got me thinking about all this was Will, this afternoon. When we were getting ready to go to supper, I saw him with his shirt off and all the scars... like he'd been beat. 'N look at you. Not a mark on you. I know you have the same last name, and you call each other brother, but you've never mentioned once about living in Milwaukee, and Will talks about it every once in a while. I don't get it. Are you really brothers?"

It was bound to surface sooner or later, but it was nothing Jesse was ashamed of, and in fact, as of a half hour ago, his fondness of Will had flourished into brotherly love. He was proud to call Will his Little Brother.

"Blood brothers... no. Will ran away from his stepfather in Milwaukee a couple of months ago. Jumped a freight train that would take him anywhere away from there. And me? I grew up in Westby 'bout thirty miles from here. Orphaned as an only child when I was ten. I pulled Will out of a flood after he fell in tryin' to save my trunk that was floatin' away. Would've drowned too, if I hadn't got to him. He needed some love and understanding, and I gave him that. Bought him some clothes, fed him, took care of him. And he's taken care of me too... saved my life once, in fact."

"When he clobbered that guy in Alma with the rock?"

"Yup. I would have been a goner if Will hadn't snuck up on him with that rock. Ol' Pete LeFever was about to fill me full o' lead. Wanted that trunk awful bad."

"But you 'n Will have the same last name. Is that just a coincidence?"

"No. Will's last name is, or was, Montgomery. By the time we got to Couderay, we'd been through a lot, savin' each other's hide. Well, you know all about the crooks at Cougar Crossing and the Northfield place. One day while we were campin' out at the Northfield farm, he asked me if I'd mind if he changed his name to Madison, 'n he started calling me his Big Brother. Guess I kinda liked it myself. By that time, I was gettin' pretty fond of him. The brother stuff... well, it stuck. Guess now I'd do just about anything to protect him from harm. And I guess that makes us... brothers."

"Jesse?" Will's voice startled Jesse and Luke. They hadn't noticed Will come into the room; they had their backs toward the State Rooms. Dressed in only his under shorts, Will plopped down on the sofa beside Jesse.

"What are you doin' up?" Jesse asked, a little embarrassed, and wondering how much Will had heard. "I thought you were asleep."

"Couldn't go to sleep. Heard you talkin' out here." Will huddled up close to Jesse and rested his head on Jesse's shoulder. "You left out one thing."

"And what would that be?" Jesse knew that Will had probably heard the entire conversation so far.

"I wasn't the first one to call us brothers. When you took me into that store to buy me clothes, you told the store clerk I was your little brother."

Jesse thought about it for a moment. "Yeah, I guess you're right." He turned to Luke. "It was much easier to say that then. Didn't want anyone to think I'd kidnapped the little rascal, or that he was really a runaway. Couldn't stand the thought of him gettin' shipped back to a home where he got beaten all the time." He turned back to Will. "Why don't you go back to bed? Luke 'n me have a lot of talkin' to do yet."

Will looked up at Jesse with pleading, puppy dog eyes. "Please let me stay out here with you. I'll be quiet as a mouse. I promise. Please let me stay."

Jesse couldn't possibly say no to that. He turned to Luke again. "It's okay. Anything you say to me, you can say in front of my Little Brother."

Luke winked and nodded his approval. At first he had been disappointed with Will's arrival, but Will's presence seemed like an asset to keeping the facts straight.

"Did you really know Al Capone? Or were you just making that up?"

"Yes. I really know Al Capone. We were good friends for a long time. He used to come to Westby quite often. He had a business arrangement with a couple of old ladies there. I did odd jobs for them now and then, and that's how I got to know him. Then when they tried to steal that trunk from him, I switched it with another one, and that's when I took off for Couderay -- with the trunk -- to return it to him. He'd offered me a job, but when I got there... well, he wasn't, and the guards at the gate didn't know me."

"And where does Spades Morgan fit in? How did you get tangled up with a professional gambler?"

"Oh, I wouldn't call it gettin' tangled up. Me 'n Will met him in Alma. He was in the hotel room just across the hall. Took a likin' to us, I guess. Bought us breakfast one morning. Warned us about LeFever... guess we didn't listen good enough. We said good-bye when he boarded another riverboat, and we never saw him again 'till today."

"About that trunk. I know you didn't deliver it to Capone's place. It was still in your truck when you came back to town. What happened to it?"

"Burned it. The night before you showed up at our camp we'd already busted it open."

Will perked his head up, glaring at Jesse. He wanted to remind Jesse of the oath they had made, not to tell *anyone* about the money, but he had promised to be quiet in exchange for a berth on the couch and Jesse's shoulder as a pillow.

"It's okay Will. Luke needs to know about this too."

Will accepted that; Jesse knew best. He curled his legs up on the remainder of the sofa and repositioned his head on Jesse's chest. Barely able to keep his eyes open, he was asleep within minutes. He didn't have to hear any more. Will already knew the rest of the story.

"So... what was in the trunk?" Luke resumed the questions.

"Suits. A dozen or so. Black suits," Jesse continued.

"That's all? Just a bunch o' suits?"

"And money. About ten thousand dollars, I guess."

Luke's eyes widened and his jaw dropped. "Te—te—ten th-thousand bucks? Wow. That explains it."

"Explains what?"

"That you could offer Morgan so much money at suppertime... to get him into the poker game."

"I probably would've given him more, if he would've asked."

"Aren't you afraid Capone will come lookin' for his money?"

"Naw. He doesn't even know I have it. The old ladies in Westby are the only ones who know that, and I *know* they won't come looking, and I won't go back there any time soon, either."

"You mean to tell me that you're totin' around ten thousand bucks that you stole from Mr. Capone, 'n you're not just a little nervous 'bout that?"

"Nope. Didn't really steal it. I tried to return it, but the guards wouldn't take it, so I guess that makes it mine. God knows I damned near got shot 'cause of that trunk. And Will almost drown tryin' to save it. I wouldn't say that I stole it."

"But... ten thousand bucks!"

"Well... not that much any more. I bought that new car."

"What new car?"

"In Rice Lake. I bought a new car for the storekeeper, that got his all shot to hell in the gunfight at the Northfield place. Remember? When we stopped and I sent you and Will to get us some food? Wasn't gonna tell anyone I did that."

"Jesse Madison? You are one amazing character. You took in Will. You catch crooks. You buy a car for a total stranger, and now you're willing to risk all that money to help Augie save his boat. Jesse Madison? You are just amazing."

It was good that the light was dim; Luke couldn't see Jesse blushing. To avoid any more of the embarrassing praise, Jesse thought he'd better change the subject. He was curious about Luke's degree of honesty as well.

"Luke... tell me one thing. Did you really get your father's blessing when you left home? Or did you just run away without tellin' the folks you were leaving?"

Now it was Luke's turn to get caught in something just a little short of the whole truth. He thought of just sticking to his original story, but after listening to Jesse's soul baring, he couldn't lie. All of Jesse's cards were face up on the table, and although there wouldn't be a winner or a loser, it didn't seem to matter that Luke didn't have an ace in the hole.

"Oh... they knew I was gonna take off. Ma cried, 'n my brothers 'n sisters begged me not to go, 'n Pa? Well... I didn't exactly get his blessing. He thinks I should be satisfied growin' taters the rest of my life, just like him."

"But you told me that he'd been encouraging you to get out on your own."

"I just said that 'cause I thought if you knew the truth, you wouldn't want me to come with you."

"And that's the real reason you thought it was a mistake to leave home, right?"

"No! No, I really did want to leave."

"Luke, will you do me a favor?"

"What?"

"Write them a letter. Let them know you're okay."

Will started to snore.

15

M organ snapped open his pocket watch. It was five minutes to six. Likely as not, the boys would still be asleep, and there wasn't much point in waking them at this early hour. It had been a long, grueling night; Morgan was tired. He wanted, more than anything else, to return to his hotel room and feel the soothing comfort of a soft pillow on the back of his neck. But he had promised the boys he would pay them a visit that morning and deliver the results of the game with McDermott -- whatever the outcome.

It was barely daylight. The dawn was already revealing signs of another dreary day ahead -- one of those days when everything the morning touched took on shades of white and gray, like an unfinished painting. The air wasn't cold, but it wasn't warm either. The heavier overnight rains had stopped, and only an occasional sprinkle was felt, as if the clouds were trying to shake loose the last few droplets left in them. Not the most pleasant conditions for a walk, but walk he would, until a more reasonable time to knock on a Stateroom door.

The blocks passed by under Morgan's feet and his eyes gazed amid the gloom; the sound of McDermott's raspy voice haunted him and the words it was speaking sent an icy chill from the base of his scull all the way down to his tailbone. "What's the matter, Spades? Lost your Midas touch over the years?" the voice kept saying, again and again.

Morgan despised that man. The past six hours had reminded him of that; he clearly remembered why he had avoided McDermott all those years. Time had nearly allowed him to wash from his memory that horrible night just north of Baton Rouge, and the sound of one single gunshot piercing through the darkness, the blood-curdling screams of panic-stricken passengers, and the sight of beautiful, young Jenny Dupree, still wearing her long, white wedding dress, disappearing silently beneath the black waters.

Morgan thought that McDermott might have changed with the passing of a decade, and that he might have absorbed some human values. But he had not. And his voice kept echoing in Morgan's head: "What's the matter, Spades... What's the matter, Spades... What's the matter, Sp..."

Morgan snapped open the gold watch again. 6:25. He had been walking for a half hour. If he turned around right then, he would reach the docks just before seven, and that seemed to be a reasonable time to arrive at the Serpent.

All the while he walked back to the docks, he couldn't stop thinking about that vile creature, and worst of all, when the *Capitol* departed for St. Louis later that day, McDermott would be aboard, but Spades Morgan would not.

Morgan stood on the gangplank, one step away from the main deck; he paused and looked at his watch one more time. Two minutes to seven. "Perfect," he thought. But everything wasn't perfect. He dreaded setting foot on that vessel. It held a haunting, uneasy feeling. But he had a mission to complete.

"What's the matter, Spades? What's the matter, Spades? What's the..."

"For Chrissake. It's only a boat," he thought. He stepped onto the deck and walked toward the stairway.

The staircase was just as he remembered it; the hardwood steps were a little more worn, and the entire craft seemed to have lost the sparkling charm it once had, but otherwise, it hadn't changed much.

Augie's cheerful greeting met Morgan at the top of the stairs. "Spades Morgan! Haven't seen you in a while."

"Good morning, Augie. How've y'all been?"

"Gettin' ready to retire, as a matter o' fact."

"Good for you Augie." Morgan patted Augie's shoulder. "But we'd miss y'all out on the river."

"Well... all good things have to end sometime, and I reckon this is my time." Augie's smile melted away. "If you're lookin' for passage back to St. Louie, ya better catch the *Capitol*. I'm sure the Serpent ain't gonna get up a head o' steam for quite a while."

"I see..." Morgan wanted to avoid a discussion of Augie's recent loss, and he was quite certain that that was where the conversation would lead. "Actually, I'm here to see Will and Jesse Madison. They told me last night that they had a Stateroom on the Serpent. Are they here now?"

"How in blazes d'ya know Jesse 'n Will?"

"It's a long story, Augie. I'll tell it another time, okay? Right now I gotta talk to the boys for a minute, and then get back to the hotel for some sleep. Up all night, y' know."

Augie chuckled. "Rough game last night?"

"Yup, but another time, Augie... another time."

Augie pointed to the Saloon. "You'll find 'em in there. I think they're still sleepin'. Gotta go downtown for a while. See ya later, Spades." Augie trotted down the stairs.

Morgan stood in front of the Saloon door.

"What's the matter, Spades? What's the matter, Spades? What's the matt..."

Morgan swung the saloon door open. "It's just a boat," he thought. He stepped inside.

If he had possessed a camera at that moment, the picture it would have captured would be priceless. He quietly walked across the room to a chair near the sofa where Luke and Jesse sat sprawled out, sleeping. Jesse's left arm was wrapped around Will, curled up with his head resting on Jesse's lap; a flannel shirt substituting for a blanket covered most of him. He was clutching Big Brother's arm like a small child would hold his favorite teddy bear. It was a portrait of peace and youthful innocence -- a picture Morgan would always carry in his memory.

Spades thought about his lovely wife, who had departed this earth long ago, and about his son, who was just about Will's age; Morgan hadn't seen his son in several years. He thought about the choices he had made as a younger man, wondering what his life would be, had he not chosen the river as his companion. Fate had delivered him to this moment, and it was one moment that he wished could last forever.

Morgan disliked the thought of disturbing this scene of tranquility, and briefly entertained the idea of returning at a later time. "No," he thought. "I made a promise."

Morgan pulled back a wooden chair; it made a scraping sound on the floor. The noise woke Jesse. His eyes opened slowly. He didn't notice Morgan right away. He blinked a few times, adjusting to the morning light. Freshly-brewed coffee aroma drifted into his nostrils; he squinted toward the coffee pot and three sparkling, porcelain cups that Augie had left, like Santa Claus leaving gifts to be discovered on Christmas morning. Reminiscence of his talk with Luke slowly came into focus, and his last recollection of the night before was that of him covering Will with his shirt. They had fallen asleep in the wee hours, after revealing the secrets that they had kept from each other.

Jesse's eyes fell on Morgan. "Mr. Morgan!" he whispered in quiet surprise.

"Good morning Jesse," Morgan replied with his usual stone-faced lack of a smile.

Jesse gentle jabbed Luke in the ribs, and rubbed Will's chest. "Wake up! Wake up! Spades is here."

Luke abruptly came to, and he was quickly alert. "Oh... good morning Mr. Morgan."

Reviving Will was a slower process. He squirmed a little, moaned, and gripped Jesse's arm tighter.

Jesse shook Will again, a bit more aggressively. "Wake up, Will. Spades is here," he said again, trying to coax Will out of his slumber. Will rubbed his sleepy eyes with his fingertips; laboriously, he sat up. His dimpled cheeks drew out a joyous grin as he jumped up to greet Morgan. But then he suddenly realized he was nearly naked -- except for his under shorts. That had always been okay in front of Jesse -- but Morgan? Morgan wasn't exactly a stranger, but he certainly wasn't family, either.

Jesse saw Will's self-consciousness, and wrapped the big, flannel shirt around him again. It fit Will like a kimono, but it was the perfect solution to the red-faced predicament.

Luke rose to his feet. "Excuse me, but I have to use the privy." He felt a little awkward, too; no one, other than his family, and maybe Jesse a time or two, had ever seen him without a shirt, although his muscular, farm-grown physique left little room for shame. He grabbed his shirt and headed off down the hall.

Will quickly dismissed his embarrassment. He stretched and yawned, and dove into a one-sided conversation with Morgan. "G' mornin' Spades. Boy! You look pretty tired. Didn't you get any sleep last night? Would you like some coffee? Augie left us some coffee. He makes real good coffee!" He bounded to the table, poured a cup of the brew, and with both hands carefully delivered it to his guest.

"Thank you, Will." Morgan took a sip.

Jesse and Will had become accustomed to Morgan's expressionless manner. They grasped its origin and could rationalize its importance, considering the profession, but in most cases it left them at odds with trying to identify his mood at any given time. They usually had to rely on his spoken words. He was quite good at disguising an ace in the hole, or a deuce, if the situation called for it.

Jesse, though, could sense a certain anxiety, and he began to fear the worst.

Almost afraid to ask, Jesse couldn't hold back another second. "So, how did the game go? You *did* have the game with McDermott, didn't you?"

Morgan nodded, obviously too exhausted to speak any more than was absolutely necessary.

"W-well?" Jesse was prepared for the news he didn't really want to hear. He had made an effort to help a friend, and if the results were less than favorable, life would still go on. He looked at Will and saw shards of disappointment forming. Will would be the one to suffer most, and right then Jesse wished that he had never attempted such an immeasurable task.

Morgan reached into the breast pocket inside his jacket and pulled out a folded piece of paper. "Here, Will. Give this to your brother." He held the paper out within easy reach.

Will walked the four short steps and handed the paper to Jesse. Knowing not what to expect, Jesse's hands trembled. He unfolded the paper holding it at arm's length with one hand, and hugging Will with the other. Will put an arm across Jesse's shoulders, ready to comfort his Big Brother, in the face of bad news. He had noticed Jesse's emotional alarm.

Jesse stared at the paper. He read the handwritten words, then looked up at Morgan with disbelief. The document didn't make sense to him at first; he read it again.

At La Crosse, Wisconsin, USA
On September 10, 1930

I, J.D. McDermott of New Orleans, Louisiana, USA, do hereby relinquish all legal rights of ownership of the steamship "River Serpent" to one Jesse Madison.
Sealed by my hand this day --- J.D. McDermott
Witnessed --- Edward Morgan

"What y'all are reading is for real, Jesse. That piece of paper is as legal as a Courthouse Judge." And Morgan was as serious as an Old Maid in a bingo parlor.

"But... but... this can't be." Jesse was still in disbelief.

"Sure it can." Morgan said.

Will was coming apart at the seams with curiosity. "What does it say? What does the paper say?"

Jesse couldn't speak. He handed the paper to Will.
Will read until he got to the word *relinquish*. He didn't know the word's meaning, nor could he pronounce it.

"It says, Will," Morgan announced, "that your brother, Jesse Madison, is now the owner of this boat."

Jesse finally caught his breath. "But Spades. How can this be? You must've won the game with McDermott. Doesn't that make the Serpent yours?"

"Jesse... what would I want with a riverboat? 'Specially this one.

Besides... if the boat is given back to Augie, it should be yours to give. It was your idea in the first place."

"But it was you who took the risk. The Serpent should be yours."

"I won enough money off McDermott to make it plenty worth my while. I don't want the damn boat. That paper says it's yours... and that's that."

Jesse was having a hard time accepting the concept. It was more of a shock than if Morgan had not been successful.

"Tell us 'bout the game! Tell us how you beat that ol' swamp scum!" Will still hadn't gotten past the word *relinquish,* but it didn't matter. He wanted to hear the details.

"Another time, Will. I'm pretty tired and I need some sleep... back at the hotel. I'll tell you another time." Morgan started to leave, but half way across the room he stopped. "Oh. Will. I almost forgot." He was digging into another pocket. "I won this off the ol' swamp scum, too. Thought y'all would like to have it for a souvenir." He held out his hand and dropped a gold pocket watch into Will's outstretched, cupped hands.

"Gee, thanks, Spades! But are you sure you want me to have this?"
"Of course, I'm sure. I don't want it. Already got one."

By the time Luke came back from the privy, Morgan was gone. He seemed more relaxed.

Will fondled his new watch. It wasn't exactly new -- a bit scratched and a little dull from wear in spots, it appeared quite old. But that didn't matter to Will. It was a present from Spades Morgan, and that made it worth cherishing.

"So... was Morgan successful? Did he beat McDermott out of the Serpent?" Luke asked. Apparently he hadn't heard any of the proceedings in the saloon.

Jesse handed Luke the paper. "Here... see for yourself." He wasn't keeping any more secrets from Luke.

Luke reacted much the same way Jesse had at first. "Wow! Is this real?"

"Morgan said that paper is as legal as a... as a..."

"As a Courtroom Judge!" Will chimed in. "And look at the gold watch he gave me. He won this off ol' Swamp Scum too." Will had officially nicknamed McDermott. Of all the pseudonyms Morgan had used, he liked that one best.

"Does this mean me 'n Will gotta call you *Captain Jesse* from now on?" Luke was joking, of course, but Will didn't think it sounded half bad.

"Of course not," Jesse said sternly. "I'm not keeping the Serpent. I'm givin' her back to Augie."

16

What could possibly be more rewarding? What could be more gratifying? Giving the Serpent back to Augie rated somewhere between returning the thirty-two dollars to Sheldon and Rachel, and pulling a drowning boy from a raging flood.

Jesse had envisioned a more ceremonious event, but he couldn't hold out through the rigors of pomp and circumstance. When Augie finally returned to his cabin, about noon, Jesse, Will and Luke marched to his door; their faces beamed with pride. Jesse handed the paper to Augie. "With a little help from a friend, we've gotten the Serpent back," he blurted, "...and we're officially turning her over to you, Captain."

Augie studied the paper with intense concentration. It hardly seemed possible that the boys would be exercising some cruel prank. He didn't know how they had accomplished such a feat, nor was he sure he wanted to know. He peered at the signatures on the paper. He knew Morgan's word to be as sound as a gold brick. He and Morgan had been friends for many years, and not once had Morgan ever done anything to make him doubt that.

Augie stood in silence, trying to think of the right words to say; the boys waited eagerly for his response. They knew he must be overwhelmed, and they could understand the delay.

"I don't want the Serpent back." Augie offered the paper to Jesse again.

"What? What do you mean?"

"I've had plenty of time to think about it the past couple of days. I've made a good living on this boat, and she don't owe me a thing. I've decided to retire, and I don't want her back."

Augie was serious. He didn't want to own that boat.

"But Augie! We saw how sad you were when you told us you had lost her, and we thought nothing would make you happier than to get her back."

"Oh, I'm happy that you got her back, all right. And I appreciate your efforts. I really do."

"But Augie, what are we gonna do now?"

"Well, by the looks of that paper, Jesse, you own the Serpent now. I'd suggest that you hire a crew, book some passengers, and take her down the river. That's what you wanted to do in the first place, wasn't it?"

"But we don't know anything about running a riverboat. All we ever wanted was to be on your crew."

"You'll learn -- just like I did. Now if you don't mind, I have to take some of my things over to a boarding house in town."

He turned his back on the boys, picked up a tattered old suitcase and a small box and headed for the stairway. Jesse, Luke and Will followed closely behind him like honeybees competing for the same flower.

"But Augie! You can't just leave like this. This boat is your life. You love this boat."

Augie continued his descent on the stairway to the main deck. "Not any more. She's not mine to love. She's yours now."

Jesse stood at the bottom of the staircase as he watched Augie near the gangplank. He had one last chance to convince Augie to stay.

"Okay!" He raised his voice to make sure Augie heard. "I'm commissioning you to be the Captain of my boat."

Augie stopped in his tracks. He turned to face Jesse and just stared for a few seconds. "Are you offerin' me a job, Lad?"

"Yes. I'm offering you the job of Captain on my boat."

"Can you afford to pay me what I'm worth?"

Without hesitation, Jesse replied. "Yes. I'll pay you well. And we'll be your cubs."

Augie stared down at his feet a long moment, and then looked back to Jesse. "I'll think about it. I'll let you know." He turned and walked away.

Jesse felt like he was just waking up from a bad dream. Nothing seemed quite real. The *Capitol* and the *St. Paul* were gone, and the few people who had been lingering after the departures were no longer there, either. The docks were deserted, except for five men loading crates from the pier onto trucks. It was all so quiet, compared to just a few hours before.

"D'ya think he'll come back?" Will wasn't as aware of the consequences as Jesse and Luke were.

"I don't know," Jesse said after a brief pause. "But I think we'd better hope 'n pray that he does."

Reality finally began to sink in; once again, Jesse was in possession of property -- someone else's property, he thought -- that he would just as soon return to the rightful owner. But just like Capone's trunk, the Serpent wasn't being disposed of so easily. A trunk was one thing. He could load that in his pick-up truck and haul it away. But a riverboat presented a bit more of a challenge; he didn't know quite where to start in devising a solution.

By five o'clock, Luke was addressing Jesse as "Captain Jesse," and there wasn't any point in objecting to the title. Jesse was the Captain, whether he liked it, or not.

Augie's voice cut through the stillness. "I won't be your Captain, but I'll be your pilot, 'n I'll teach you all that I can in one trip, down to Cairo and back to St. Louie. Then you're on your own."

Jesse breathed a sigh of relief knowing that Augie had returned.

"But I want five hundred dollars a month. I'm a Master Pilot, y' know. I figure it'll take 'bout that long to make the trip. Think ya can afford to pay me that much?"

Jesse would have been willing to pay three times that amount, just to have Augie's expertise on board. He was so overwhelmed with the acceptance, he just nodded and offered his hand to seal the agreement.

It was just like old times -- sitting around a table in the saloon, listening to Augie tell stories. But now it was different -- the boys were students, and they had a lot of learning to do. They listened to every word.

"We'll have to hire a crew. I just saw Charlie Benson in town a while ago. He was my best engineer. Said he'll come back, and he knows a couple of good firemen to stoke the fireboxes. And a cook... we'll need a good cook. I'll talk to Henry tomorrow, and Mildred -- the waitress at the hotel -- she'll pack her bags in a heartbeat. She'll be the chambermaid. With all the banks closin' up, shouldn't be a problem finding a clerk."

"What about me? What's my job gonna be, Augie?" Will asked with exploding enthusiasm.

"Well..." Augie scratched his bearded chin. "Jesse is the Captain, and it's his call. But if I were him..." he winked at Jesse and continued. "...If I were him, I'd give you the most important job of all."

"What's that?" Will was ecstatic.

"Will, you've got just what it takes to be the best cabin boy on the river. You'll make sure the passengers are taken care of properly, 'n you can assist the clerk when he needs help... a very important job."

Jesse didn't want Luke to feel left out. "How 'bout Luke... what will he do?"

"Luke should be your First Mate. He'll oversee all the deckhands and rousters. Both you and Luke will be my pilot cubs. Both o' you gotta learn how to take this ol' tub up 'n down the river."

The conversation went on into the night. Jesse, Luke and Will absorbed every ounce of riverboat protocol that Augie had to offer. Just as Jesse had predicted, the old Captain was a good teacher, and in just a few short hours, he was confident of their abilities. Everything was going to turn out great.

Although Jesse was only an infant to this grand, new world, he knew the time had come for him to start taking command. People who knew the business -- people he could rely on for advice and expertise -- would soon surround him. But he also held the purse strings, and there was no better time to make sure everyone remembered that one important fact. "As the new Captain of the Serpent, I think we should adjourn." He looked at his watch. "It's late, and we all have to get an early start tomorrow. Tomorrow we're gonna start givin' the Serpent a fresh coat o' white paint. Luke... you'll be in charge of seeing that gets done. And Will... you'll be in charge of cleaning the staterooms and gettin' 'em ready for our passengers. Augie... after I get the paint from town, and hire some hands to help with the painting, you and I will go find our crew. And I'm sure there's a lot more details we gotta work out."

Luke stood at attention and gave a respectful salute in recognition of the new commander's orders. "Aye, Captain."

Will duplicated Luke's action, and they headed for the staterooms to turn in for the night.

Augie was impressed with Jesse's ability to take charge. There was no doubt in his mind that Jesse Madison was destined for success. The next day would mark the beginning of a new era for the Serpent, and Augie was glad he had decided to remain a part of it.

Jesse turned out the light as he climbed into bed. Will's concerned voice probed the darkness. "Jesse? Now that you're the Captain, you'll still be my Big Brother, won't you?"

"Of course I will. You'll always be my Little Brother. You can count on it. Now go to sleep."

Jesse closed his eyes. The previous night he had gone to sleep as "Big Brother Jesse." That night, he was going to sleep as "Big Brother *Captain* Jesse."

17

Within five hours the next morning, Jesse had secured the employment of six more young men to help with the painting project, and purchased what appeared to be every bucket of white paint that existed in the entire city. By mid-afternoon, the Serpent looked like a giant, spotted gray and white jigsaw puzzle, as each painter worked vigorously on his assigned section. Luke seemed to have the work detail well in hand. Mildred, whom Augie had already sent down to help Will with the cleaning, had five of the passenger cabins looking fit-for-royalty.

By late afternoon, Jesse and Augie had acquired an engineer, Charlie, and the two firemen, John and Cyrus. Charlie was quite familiar with the Serpent; he and his firemen were in the engine and boiler rooms, assessing the condition of the machinery and preparing for some much-needed maintenance that would begin the next day. Lester Collins, the newly appointed clerk, gazed into the tiny office just outside the saloon at the top of the stairs. It was considerably less spacious than the office he had occupied at the failing bank, but times were hard, and he needed a job, and he finally agreed that the accommodations would do.

Mildred had prepared a mouth-watering boiled ham and potatoes by sundown. The painters, engineer, firemen and the clerk had all gone home for the evening. Will, Luke, Augie and Jesse clustered at a table in the saloon, sharing the fine supper and traded progress reports on the Serpent's face-lift.

Luke was pleased to announce that five of the six painters had agreed to stay on as roustabouts and deck hands. He didn't know how many were required, but if more were necessary, those five had friends who were seeking work too.

Will reported that he and Mildred had half the staterooms ready, and when all of them were done, the Saloon and galley were next on the list.

Augie assured that Charlie would have the engines and boilers tuned and running like a Swiss watch within a few days.

Jesse was quite delighted with the enthusiastic performance of his crew. So far, everything about this new venture was running smoothly and taking shape far beyond his expectations. "I appreciate the hard work you all are doing. There's a lot more to be done, but I promise that you all will be rewarded for this someday."

Those words could have gone unspoken, for Will and Luke had long since grown to trust Jesse's good judgment; they had freely committed themselves to his able leadership. Augie had grown to admire him, too. Jesse was an ambitious young man with the makings of a fine riverboat Captain.

Mildred cleared away the dishes from the table; Will twirled his gold watch on its chain. He was thinking about Morgan and wondering if he would ever see him again.

Augie stared at the annoying antics. "Where did y' get the gold watch, Will?"

"From Morgan. He won it in a poker game. He gave it to me... said he didn't need another one."

Jesse glared at Will, hoping he wouldn't say anything more about the poker game that won the River Serpent from McDermott's greedy hands. He wanted to keep that information confidential.

Will caught a glimpse of Big Brother's dirty look; he took the hint. "The only thing I don't like about it..." Will paused, popped open the watch lid, and held it so Augie could get a better look. "...It has McDermott's initials inside the cover. See? J. D." He had associated the engraved letters with McDermott's signature on the paper assigning the Serpent's ownership to Jesse.

Augie turned the timepiece, inspecting every detail, and then held it so the light clearly reflected the inscription. He studied the watch some more, snapped the lid shut and laid it on the table in front of Will. Augie's face turned pale, and sadness stole the sparkle from his eyes.

"Those aren't McDermott's initials," Augie said quietly.

"Then whose initials are they?" Will was puzzled.

"Kind of a coincidence, I guess. That's probably why McDermott wanted it, and why he carried it around for ten years."

Will was persistent. "If J. D. isn't McDermott, then who is it?"

Augie stared at the watch; he hesitated. His voice trailed off as he spoke the name, "Jacques Dupree."

Too many other events, happening so quickly, had caused Jesse to nearly forget Morgan's tale about Jacques Dupree; hearing Augie's brief comments restored his recollection.

"You know about Jacques Dupree?" Jesse asked, a little astonished.

The room became deathly quiet, and all eyes focused on Augie. Even Mildred stopped cleaning.

"Everybody on the river from here to New Orleans knows about Jacques Dupree," Augie said. "Sounds as if you know the name too. Spades must've told you, I reckon."

"Yeah, he did tell us." Jesse sensed there was more to the story than he, Will, and Luke had been told.

"I'm surprised Morgan didn't tell you 'bout the watch."

"What about it? What about the watch?" Will asked.

"That's the watch McDermott took from Dupree's bride just before she jumped in the river 'n drowned."

"Well... he did tell us about a watch, but he didn't tell us it was this one." Jesse was curious how Augie was able to identify this particular watch.

Mildred went on about her dishwashing chores. Augie's eyes drifted around the room; he was searching for a way to change the topic. Jesse wanted to move on, too; he saw the emotional pain that Augie dredged from his memories. But Will wasn't quite finished yet.

"Morgan never told us. Augie, what was the name of the boat that it happened on?"

Augie looked at Will for a moment, then at Jesse, and then stared off across the room at nothing in particular. "The River Serpent. It happened right here on the River Serpent... ten years ago this last July."

There was no better way for Augie to disconnect from the conversation than to excuse himself and announce his departure. "Thank you Mildred, for that wonderful supper. It's getting late. I think I'll go back to my room now. I'll see all of you in the morning."

Mildred was just finishing the cleaning chores. She wrapped a shawl around her shoulders. "I'll walk with you into town. It's right on my way." Arm-in-arm, she and Augie disappeared into the night.

The boys were shocked by the information; they sat in silence for a few minutes after Augie and Mildred had left.

"Well that might explain it," Jesse said.

"Explain what?" Luke asked.

"Why Augie has had a tough time of it the last few years, even though he doesn't want to admit it. This boat has a bad reputation. He said it himself. Everyone on the river knows about Dupree, and they know he died on the Serpent. People can be superstitious about that sort of thing."

"But there isn't much we can do to change that now," Luke said. "That all happened ten years ago."

"We can't change what happened ten years ago, but we *can* change what happens from now on. Luke... tomorrow I want you to paint over the name. Cover it up so good that it will never be seen again."

"What then?" Luke asked curiously.

"Then... we'll change the name. I'll go into town tomorrow and hire a sign painter. There's bound to be one of them in a city this size."

"Change the name to what? What are we gonna call her?"

"Anybody got any suggestions?"

Will was quick with a response. "Why don't we call it The Madison? I see a lot o' boats on the river named after the owner. You're the owner... so you can call it The Madison."

Jesse thought about that for a minute. He looked across the table to Luke; a request for approval was in his eyes.

"It's okay with me, Captain. She's *your* boat."

18

I t was a day or two after the sign painter had finished his work before Augie became accustomed to the fact that the River Serpent *wasn't* the River Serpent any more, although he was quite impressed with the improvements. The gleaming new white coat glistened in the sunlight, and the brilliant sapphire blue that trimmed the deck railings and some of the window frames rendered an appearance of distinction that had been absent for so many years; he knew now that his old boat had fallen into good hands. Clearly, the new owner's pride was second-to-none. Jesse seemed to have natural instincts propelling him, and he always seemed to ask the right questions. His experience at the railroad depot proved to be an asset, and the years of close proximity with Julian Kelly had rubbed some good business sense onto his character.

Augie wasn't the only one to take notice. The boat that many people had once ignored was attracting the curious attention of nearly everyone passing by, and no one recognized her as the Serpent. She was beautifully sleek and gently touched by graceful elegance. No longer could any man look upon this boat with scorn. The Madison, in her infancy, was receiving the admiration she justly deserved, and it wouldn't be long until she took to the water, finding her place among the river royalty.

As the hours ticked by, it became more evident that the Madison Packet Company was off to a good start. Thanks to Augie and his connections, the cargo bay was filling to capacity. Jesse's Model A was hardly visible as the rousters stacked crate after crate around it. By the time Emil Johnson showed up with fifty barrels of river clamshells, destined for the button factory at Lansing, Iowa, there was barely enough room to accommodate his cargo. He had always been Augie's regular customer -- a hog farmer from along the banks at Betsy's Slough, near Fountain City. He harvested the clams from the river, fed the meat to his hogs, and sold the shells to the button factories farther down the Mississippi.

Dozens of would-be passengers had seen the handbills around town, announcing the departure of the Madison for destinations south, all the way to St. Louis, and had reserved their first class berths. There seemed to be little reluctance to travel on the steamship that had once held a gruesome image in the public eye. Augie was impressed, and he realized even more that Jesse had made a smart move by changing the name and the appearance.

In the late afternoon hours of the day before the scheduled departure, Jesse stood on the dock beside the sternwheeler; he gazed across the river, hoping the weather forecasts for fair skies would prevail. His ship was ready: coal bins full, food pantry well-stocked, fresh water barrels filled, maintenance complete, a full crew complement, cargo bay loaded to capacity, and the staterooms were filling quickly. The time was near. There was no turning back, and the last thing he wanted was for Mother Nature to cast an ugly shadow on his long-awaited dream.

A pleasant but business-like woman's voice broke into his daze. "Excuse me. I saw the poster in town stating that this steamship is offering first class passage to St. Louis. Where might I find the Captain?"

Jesse was somewhat stunned by the appearance of the quite attractive, thirtyish woman in a long, dark blue silky dress; the tails of a black shawl draped over her shoulders and fluttered in the breeze. Her auburn hair was pulled back into a knot; her smile nearly paralyzed Jesse. She stood beside an enormous trunk mounted on wheels, and several smaller suitcases were piled on top of it.

He cleared his throat. "Captain Jesse Madison... at your service, Ma'am."

"Yes, of course," the woman replied. "Where can I find this Captain Jesse Madison?"

"*I'm* Jesse Madison."

"You? But... you're so... *young!*" Her big brown eyes scanned every inch of Jesse's six-foot-tall frame and finally came to rest on his smiling, dimpled, blushed cheeks. Obviously, she was expecting someone more like Augie, but it didn't seem like the time or place to disagree about how old a riverboat Captain should be.

"I've just arrived by train from New York," she explained. "And I am seeking passage by riverboat to St. Louis. When will we arrive there?"

Jesse was confronted with a question to which there was no accurate answer. "This is a tramp boat, Ma'am. We'll be stopping in at least two dozen towns along the way. Maybe two weeks. If you're in a hurry, Ma'am, maybe you should--"

"Perfect," she interrupted, before Jesse could suggest the faster railroad. "I'm a photographer and a painter. I'm opening a gallery in St. Louis and I want to make a lot of pictures of the river scenery. I hear it's beautiful this time of year."

"Yes, Ma'am... it is."

"Two weeks and five hundred miles on the river. That's just perfect." She was thrilled with the opportunities awaiting her. "By the way... my name is Sadie Perkins." She offered her hand to the handsome young Captain.

"Pleased to meet you, Ma'am."

"I'll want the largest stateroom you have available. And I'll need your permission to set up my camera anywhere on the boat to get some good photographs during the trip. Will that be all right?"

"All the staterooms are the same size, but I'm sure we can take one of the beds out to give you more space. And I don't think it'll be a problem for you to set up your camera anywhere you like." Jesse motioned to Luke, looking on from the gangplank. "I'll have my First Mate get a deck hand to carry your luggage up for you, and at the top of the stairs, Mr. Collins will arrange for your accommodations. If there's anything else I can do for you, just let me know."

"Oh, Captain... you are a dear. You're a dream-come-true." Sadie couldn't resist giving Jesse's cheek a lustful little kiss.

Jesse awoke at six a.m. This was the day he had been anticipating. All the hard work that went into preparing for this very morning was about to pay off. In three hours, the steam whistle atop the Madison's pilothouse would sound. The mooring ropes would be reeled in and the huge paddlewheel would begin turning. His spirit was charged with excitement as he scurried along the Texas deck, knocking on each crewmember's door to make sure everyone was awake, alert, and ready to gather in the crews' dining room for breakfast. This would be the last time, perhaps, until they reached St. Louis that they would all eat a meal together, and it was the first time Jesse would see his entire crew together in one place. He had his inaugural speech all planned and memorized, and as soon as Augie arrived, he would take a stand at the head of the table and make his official oration.

Charlie, John and Cyrus were already in the engine room getting ready to stoke the boiler fireboxes; they were making the last-minute inspection of the machinery. Henry and his assistant had been in the galley since five o'clock, preparing for the breakfast meeting. Mildred had arrived just minutes before, ready to help serve the hungry crew their bon voyage breakfast. She made it quite clear to everyone that this was the last time she would wait on them -- from there on, they were on their own, as her duties were on the deck below, satisfying the needs of the *paying* passengers.

"Willy... go down below to the engine room 'n fetch the engineer and his men. Get them up here for breakfast." Jesse was as nervous as a long-tailed cat in a room full of rocking chairs. Even though he had been the *Captain* for some time, he was just starting to feel the impact of being an authority figure, and the responsibility that went along with it. This very moment, to him was like the President-Elect stepping into the White House for the first time. The command of the boat and its twenty-one-member crew was in his hands. Augie had coached him well and had prepped him for this moment, but he still couldn't help feeling a little jittery.

Two men strolled down the sidewalk toward the pier in the pale first light of morning. Augie's freshly pressed black trousers and gold-buttoned jacket were as crisp as the morning air. A turtleneck sweater peeked over the collar of his jacket, nearly a perfect color match to his neatly trimmed gray beard. He walked proudly -- a man who respected the river, and the river respected him. He knew he was about to take off his Captain's coat for the last time and drape it over the shoulders of his successor. But it didn't cause him sorrow. Augie had faith in the young new Captain, Jesse Madison.

Walking beside Augie, Lester Collins was all business. He had handled the finances of several riverboat companies at the bank where he worked; the job was nothing new to him. His sharp mind and a steady hand could handle any accounting problem put before him; he was a wizard with numbers and business. Jesse Madison's purse strings were in good hands.

"Mr. Collins," Augie said, "...we're lucky to have acquired your services.

Jesse is young and he doesn't have much experience when it comes to riverboats, but I intend to teach him all that he needs to know. I trust that you will serve him honestly, as you have done for me in the past." Augie's voice clearly indicated that Mr. Collins would be seeking another job if he tried to pull any shenanigans.

"Yessir, Captain. You can count on me. I will do my best."

"Good. And don't call me *Captain* any more. I'm just a pilot now. You'd better get used to calling Jesse your Captain from now on."

As they topped the stairs to the Texas deck, they found Jesse pacing in front of the dining room door. When he saw them, a bit of relief fell upon him; he grinned.

"G'mornin' Augie... Mr. Collins."

"Good morning Captain," they replied.

"I've been waiting for you. The whole crew is in there eating breakfast, and I think I'm ready to talk to them as their Captain... just like you told me. C'mon in and have some breakfast. You too, Mr. Collins."

Augie blocked Jesse's approach to the door. "Before we go in there, Jesse, I have something for you." He removed his jacket and held it open for Jesse to slip his hands into the sleeves. "This is yours now... you're the Captain."

"But Augie. I can't take your coat."

"Of course you can. It's my gift to you. It's practically new, and I want you to have it. You're the Captain, and you need to look like one. Wear it proudly, Captain Jesse Madison."

Jesse slipped into the jacket. It fit his broad shoulders quite well, although the rest of it was a bit large.

"There..." Augie said with a wide smile, "...now you look the part of a riverboat Captain. Now, go in there to address your crew."

All heads turned to the door as Captain Jesse walked in. There wasn't room for everyone at the table. Jesse tapped Will and Luke on their shoulders and motioned for them to make room for Augie and Mr. Collins. They had finished eating anyway, and quickly relinquished their seats.

Jesse stood before his crew. All eyes were on him, eagerly awaiting his message.

"As the Captain of the Steamship Madison, I want to welcome all of you aboard as my crew, and I want to thank you for your efforts in making this day a success. At nine o'clock, we will be steaming out of La Crosse. That's less than three hours away. We have a full cargo bay and a long passenger list. I expect everyone in this room to treat our passengers with respect, and to handle the cargo with care. I expect everyone to give an honest day's work for an honest day's wage.

"Now, you all know my First Mate, Luke Jackson, and my brother, Will.

They deserve my special thanks right now. Without their help, we wouldn't be here. And many of you know Augie Bjornson. He's the best riverboat pilot on the Mississippi. We can all be thankful that Augie will be in the pilothouse.

"Our passengers will start arriving soon and you all know what your jobs are. We have a busy day ahead, and if you encounter any problems, my door is always open. Luke and I will be spending a good share of our time in the pilothouse with Augie... that's where you can find us. Now let's get ready to steam to St. Louis."

Augie had been looking around the room at many faces he knew, but there were many unfamiliar faces, too -- some who may not know steamboat protocol. He rose to his feet and beckoned the crew's attention. Almost everyone still recognized Augie as an authority figure, and the erupting chatter abruptly ceased the moment he began speaking.

"I was the Captain of this vessel for twelve years, and I must say, Captain Jesse has assembled a fine-lookin' crew. I have just one thing to say to you all now: *he is the Captain of this boat*, and you will give him that respect. The first person I see showing any disrespect to the Captain, I will personally throw him overboard whether he knows how to swim or not. Now... get to work ... all of you."

The younger members accepted those words as Gospel; they scrambled for the door to take up their assigned duties. The older, more experienced ones, though, knew Augie, and they had heard similar speeches in the past. They understood exactly what he meant: Augie would never *really* throw anyone overboard, although, in some cases, over the years, it might have been the better alternative.

As the crew filed out onto the decks, Jesse put a firm grip on Will's shoulder. Will was dressed in a new, spiffy white shirt and a black bow tie that Mildred had taught him how to knot. His hair was combed and his remarkably clean face wore a smile from ear to ear.

"You're lookin' pretty sharp today, Little Brother. How are ya doin'?"

"This is great, Jesse... I mean *Captain* Jesse. I can't wait to get started." Will was just as excited about this day as Jesse was.

"Well, we'll be under way soon enough. In the meantime, you have an important job to do. Help Mr. Collins and Mildred get all the passengers settled in. Show them to their rooms 'n help them with their luggage... okay?"

Will nodded and grinned. "Aye, Captain." He went bounding down the stairs to Mr. Collins' office.

There was one person Jesse had hoped to see before the Madison steamed away from La Crosse. Spades Morgan hadn't made his presence visible for many days, and Jesse thought he would have certainly said good-bye before departing on another boat. Jesse felt indebted to Morgan, and it would have been grand to extend the much-deserved gratitude to him. But as he started his rounds, he remembered that Morgan's home was in St. Louis, and he could find Morgan there.

Everything seemed to be running smoothly by 7:30. A slow but steady flow of passengers boarded; the rousters delivered luggage to the Saloon deck. Charlie and his firemen had the boilers building a head of steam, and the smaller engine that ran the electric generator chugged life into all the lights throughout the boat. Will and Mildred scurried about like cocker spaniels in a fireplug factory, assisting passengers in finding comfort. The entire boat was a whirlwind of activity.

Jesse couldn't help but thinking about the first time he had laid eyes on the vessel. How empty and desolate, lonely and forgotten it seemed then. The contrast he was viewing made him feel good – modestly, he gave himself credit for reviving her back to life.

He stood on the main deck at the head of the gangplank, greeting the passengers as they came aboard. Some of them he recognized from the day before, when they made their early reservations. And of course, lovely Sadie Perkins came prancing up the walkway with a parasol propped on her shoulder. She was dressed more casually, but still, quite a striking woman.

"Oh, Captain... it's so nice to see you again." Her flirtatious style seemed a bit bold to Jesse, but he didn't mind at all -- having a pretty lady, the likes of Sadie Perkins, on board all the way to St. Louis might make the trip more enjoyable.

"Good morning, Miss Perkins. I believe Mildred has your stateroom ready for you. My Bittle Lother -- my Lither Brottle – ah -- my... *Little... Brother... Will...* can show you to your room. I hope you find it to your liking."

"Your little brother? You have your little brother with you on this boat?"

"Yes ma'am. He's the Cabin Boy. I'm sure you will find him quite charming."

"Yes... well if he's half as handsome as you, Captain, I'm sure I will." She strolled off toward the stairway.

It was against Jesse's better judgment to be flirting with one of the passengers this early in his new career. There seemed to be a struggle commencing between his good common sense and a love bug that had crept under his shirt collar. "I can't let this interfere," he thought, "I have too much to learn and do."

Just then another man and yet another beautiful, young girl -- younger and prettier than Sadie -- approached him on the deck. They were each carrying a suitcase. The man appeared to be an average, middle-aged typical American seeking no more than the joys of riverboat travel. The fringes across the breast of his brown leather jacket swayed with his walk.

The man stuck his right hand out toward Jesse. He seemed a bit nervous. "I'm Tobias Aldrich, and this is my daughter, Jennifer." She batted her eyelashes and bobbed a little bow.

Jesse returned the handshake. "Captain Jesse Madison."

"We're wantin' to go to St. Louis. I saw a sign that said this boat's goin' to St. Louis. You got any rooms left?"

"We had some this morning, but you'd better check with the clerk at the top of the stairs."

"Thank you. Come along Jennifer. Let's see if there are any rooms."

Jennifer couldn't take her eyes off Jesse. Even half way up the stairs she was still staring back at him. She *was* rather pretty -- long blonde hair and dazzling blue eyes -- about seventeen or eighteen, Jesse thought. Her father seemed nice enough, too, but there was something peculiar about his nervousness that Jesse couldn't quite put a finger on.

It was 8:30 -- a half-hour until departure time. So far, there had been no problems, other than Mrs. Johnson's luggage getting delivered to Sam Gustov's room, and vise versa. The bags were almost identical, and it was an honest mistake on Will's part.

Luke and Jesse had made their final rounds and were in the pilothouse, receiving a few last-minute procedure lessons from Augie before leaving the dock. They hadn't been there long when Jesse noticed a sharply dressed man in a white ten-gallon hat, toting a suitcase, walking toward the pier. The hat brim covered the man's face, but it looked like someone familiar.

"Excuse me Augie, there's a passenger I must greet. I'll be right back."

Spades Morgan had reached the top of the stairs and was standing at Mr. Collins' office when Jesse spotted him. "Spades!" Jesse said with delight. "It's really good to see you. I was hoping we would see you again before we left. Are you joining us for the trip?"

Morgan's usual poker face hadn't changed. "Yes Jesse, I am. I hope there's a stateroom available."

"There are two left," Mr. Collins said.

"Good. I'll take one... all the way to St. Louie." Morgan reached in his pocket for a wallet. "She's a good-lookin' boat, Jesse. I've been watchin' her take shape. Kinda curious 'bout the name though."

Jesse didn't want to talk about the acquisition where others would hear. "She's mine now, but we'll talk about that later, okay?" He put his hand on Morgan's fingers to prevent them from retrieving the money from his wallet. "Put your money away, Mr. Morgan... this trip's on me."

"Well, thank you Jesse, but that isn't necessary."

"But I think it is." Jesse waived to Will. "Will... come and show Mr. Morgan to a vacant stateroom."

Elated with the sight of Morgan, Will came running, picked up the suitcase and led Morgan to none other than the Tennessee stateroom.

Mr. Collins thought he should question Jesse's action. "Captain... Sir... you can't be giving free rides to your friends. It's not good business."

"Never mind that, Lester. If it weren't for Mr. Morgan, you wouldn't have this job. None of us would be here. I'll explain later."

Three short blasts from the steam whistle was Augie's signal to the Engineer and Firemen -- fifteen minutes to departure. Jesse ran up the stairs to rejoin his fellow officers.

From the pilothouse, they could see everything going on down on the dock and the bow. One by one, the mooring ropes were unwound from the dock posts and hauled onto the main deck. The deckhands hoisted the gangplank up from the dock. The Madison was free of all bonds to the shore. Black smoke billowed from the tall chimneys. An arm-waving crowd had gathered along the pier to see their families and friends off, and to witness the beginning of the Madison's maiden voyage. Jesse's heart was racing. This was the most exciting moment of his life.

"Now, watch, listen, and learn." Augie's foot stepped down on the whistle pedal. A thick, white stream hissed from the three brightly polished brass cylinders atop the pilothouse, gradually swelling into a splendid triad of sound, proclaiming the departure of the steamship Madison.

At the stern, the mighty paddlewheel began to rotate, slowly at first, then picked up speed, churning up the Mississippi water, tossing and whirling thousands of tiny, glittering droplets into the air.

Jesse and Luke could feel the tingling vibration through the soles of their shoes as they watched the dock and the row of warehouses retreating away, but the sensation of movement was nearly non-existent; it was as if the rest of the world was moving and they were standing still.

Augie steered the boat backwards at an angle up river, and when she was far enough out into the channel, the current caught the bow and gently swung her around, pointing her straight down the middle of the river. Augie stepped on the pedal again, giving the signal to the Engineer to set the paddlewheel into forward motion. The paddles slowed and stopped momentarily, and then began churning again, pushing with the current down river.

The Madison was under way to St. Louis.

19

No one aboard the Madison noticed the two brown-suited, shifty-eyed men among the crowd on the dock as the big boat drifted out into the main channel. To the travelers, they were just two more faces in the throng of well-wishers. But they had come there for a purpose, and had arrived just minutes too late to end a pursuit that they desperately wanted to close.

Hired by another man in Sheboygan, the two had tracked their suspect across the state, always one step behind him, and always missing their chance of capture. They knew he was aboard the Madison -- they caught a glimpse of him on the deck as the boat backed away from the dock.

"Where is that boat destined?" one of the men asked another spectator.

"St. Louis, Missouri," was the reply. "I think the first stop is in Lansing."

Lansing was on the opposite side of the Mississippi. But there was an afternoon train leaving Brownsville scheduled to arrive in Lansing by early evening. They would be on that train, and they would catch up with the Madison there. Finally, they knew where the chase would end.

Augie stood with steady hands on the wheel and eagle eyes fixed on the river ahead. A helmsman of supreme coolness, judgment and skill, he possessed an intuitive sense of the water and an uncanny feel for the vessel beneath his feet. He embodied a medley of quiet courage, poise, and endurance that had earned him admiration and praise among his peers.

Flanking this man of unmatched river wisdom, Luke and Jesse knew if they absorbed all they could from him, their success was within easy grasp. They carefully listened to his calm but firm lessons on how to *read* the river, detecting the deepest channel by the color of the water, the patterns of the swirls and the height of the waves. They observed and listened as Augie pointed the craft, gracefully careening around wing dams and sand bars, like a ballet dancer performing in slow motion amid a silvery, glittering stage.

Occasionally, the sound of a bell would drift through the open pilothouse windows. Many residents living along the river banks had bells on their yards facing the channel, and sounding their bell as the riverboats passed was their way of saying, "welcome." People on the river loved the big boats.

Augie would answer the greetings with a couple of short toots from the steam whistle; it always yielded hearty waves of friendly acknowledgment from the onlookers. On a hillside near Genoa, the entire student body of a tiny country school amassed in the front yard, joyously waving their greetings to the Madison; the pretty, young teacher stood on the front steps, her hands on her hips, patiently waiting for the boat to pass out of sight, so class could resume. The people on the river -- even the youngsters -- adored the big boats.

Lansing was not much farther. High water and swift currents allowed the Madison to make exceptionally good time that day. So good, in fact, that Sadie Perkins was feeling a bit frustrated. The high rocky bluffs that caught the afternoon sunlight, and the colorful autumn-hued forests, passed by too quickly. She poked her head through the open pilothouse door.

"Oh, Captain..." she sang with a flirting tone, "...would it be possible to slow down a bit? I'm missing so many wonderful pictures."

Jesse quickly recognized an opportunity to show Augie that he had been paying attention to the lessons. "I don't think so, Miss Perkins. We have to maintain a speed faster than the current... otherwise the boat is too hard to steer."

Augie thought that was an excellent reply.

Sadie began studying the view from behind the pilot that encompassed the river vista through the front windows. Her artistic eye saw a magnificent shot, and she suddenly forgot about her previous request. "Oh, Captain... this would make such a wonderful picture... you and the pilot standing at the wheel, and the view of the river in the background through those windows." She studied the setting some more. "Could I set up my camera right here and take that picture?"

"You'll have to do it quickly," Jesse replied, after getting a nod of approval from Augie. "We'll be arriving at Lansing soon."

While Sadie gathered her equipment on the deck below, Augie offered some instructions. "Luke, it's time you made your rounds. Make sure the deck hands are ready to tie up, and the rousters should be ready to start unloading the barrels of shells, and find out if there are any passengers gettin' off at Lansing. Mr. Collins should be able to tell you that. You might have to locate their baggage."

"Yessir." Without hesitation, Luke sprang into action. When he was completely out of earshot, Augie leaned toward Jesse. "Treat him well, Captain. Luke will make a good pilot. I think he has what it takes."

"How d'ya know that so soon?"

"Oh... I just know. I've taught many cubs... and I just know -- Luke will be a good pilot."

Sadie reappeared at the door with her tripod-mounted camera. "Okay, Captain... now if you could turn this way just a little." Not only did she want the dramatic setting captured on a negative, she was using this as an excuse to capture the handsome young Captain, as well.

Luke alerted his crew of the nearing port. The planned schedule included only as much time docked at Lansing to allow off-loading the button factory's freight. There would still be enough daylight to reach the overnight stop at Prairie du Chien. Only three deck passengers were to disembark at Lansing, and there was little chance that anyone would board there; anticipated confusion wasn't an issue. Luke decided he would locate the departing luggage.

The three suitcases weren't difficult to find -- they were practically right in front of all the rest, displaying tags that clearly said "Lansing" in bold, black letters. As he double-checked the names, just to be sure, a movement in the far cargo bay corner, near Jesse's truck, caught his eye. He had accounted for all his crewmembers, and it didn't seem likely that any passengers would be -- *or should be* -- mulling around the cargo. He thought he had better investigate. Climbing over several large crates, he found a narrow pathway that led to Jesse's Model A. Luke knew there was no other easy route away from that corner -- he had supervised the freight loading. If there were someone in the corner, it would be impossible to escape without being seen.

A dark-haired boy sat huddled on the floor behind the truck. His clothes were tattered and dirty, and he looked quite bedraggled. Clutching a ragged blanket, rolled up in a wad, he shook with fear.

"Who are you?" Luke asked.

"R-Reggie Pierce," a meek voice muttered. He dropped his face into his hands and began to sob. He knew the consequences; he had been caught once before. He would be humiliated in front of crew and passengers, and then he would be put off the boat in a strange place, with nothing more than his pitiful life and a ragged, dirty blanket, only to be scorned by yet another city full of uncaring strangers. And if he was lucky, he might find a garbage can in a back alley containing a few scraps of discarded food. If only he had not awoken when he did and began to stir, he would not have been caught, and perhaps he could have saved himself from the pending humiliation. He could have snuck off the boat in the cover of darkness at the next stop, and could have chosen his own destiny, but instead, he had no choice but to meet his dreaded fate.

"What are you doing here?" Luke asked. He could tell Reggie was terrified, and he tried to be as gentle as possible.

Reggie sensed a touch of compassion in Luke's voice -- perhaps an explanation, of sorts, might deliver him from the precarious situation. But it was difficult to get the words out between the sobs. "I... I... I'm trying ... to get to... St. Louis... my... uncle lives there... I think... but... I have no money...

to get there."

Luke understood that Reggie was a stow-away. Nothing could have been clearer. But Luke viewed the incident in an entirely different sense, and started putting together all the facts that seemed obvious. Reggie -- if that was really his name -- was truly a lost soul, apparently without a family anywhere nearby. He spoke with an accent -- British, Luke thought, but definitely not native Wisconsin. And a boy who appeared to be about sixteen wouldn't be crying like that if he hadn't fallen into some extremely unfortunate circumstances. And he certainly wouldn't be hiding in the cargo bay of a riverboat, with nothing more than a blanket to his name, if he had adequate means of support. Not unless he was, perhaps, evading some sort of predator.

Luke kneeled down in front of Reggie, placed his hand on the sobbing boy's shoulder and spoke softly. "When was the last time you had something to eat?"

"Yesterday... I found some bread in a trash can behind a bakery in that last city."

A long, steady whistle blast, signaling the Madison's approach to Lansing, slashed through the chugging noise of the nearby engines. Luke knew he must immediately return to the pilothouse. "My name is Luke. Stay right here, out of sight. I'll bring you some food as soon as we leave this port. We won't be here very long... okay?"

Reggie was shocked that he wouldn't be marched off the boat, or tossed onto a muddy riverbank in strange surroundings, and he was thankful that such a caring individual had discovered him. He wiped away the tears from his cheek with a corner of the blanket. "Thank you, Luke. You are very kind."

Luke started back to the pilothouse with urgent haste. He knew he couldn't disclose the cargo bay discovery to anyone. Even if Jesse understood, Augie would surely disapprove, and it could only mean disaster for the poor boy. He had a plan in mind, but some more careful thought was necessary first. There would be time for that during the layover at Prairie du Chien.

A large island lay between the main channel and the Lansing docks. Augie stayed on course with the channel, explaining that it was necessary to always approach the docking point from down stream. Maneuverability was best against the current, and that was why he was passing around the island instead of heading straight for the pier.

"Now watch, listen, and learn," Augie said. "Luke... you're gonna to take her in at Prairie, so pay close attention here."

The Madison's bow gently nudged the sandy riverbank; deck hands lowered the gangplank to a boardwalk, ten or fifteen feet away. The huge paddlewheel continued to slowly rotate, keeping the boat hugged tightly to the shore, as more deck hands reeled out a massive rope from each side and wrapped the ends around mammoth posts to contain any further movement. The distinct whistle had attracted a small group of onlookers at the foot the town's Main Street, dead-ending at the river's edge. But Luke and Jesse weren't paying much attention to them. They had been concentrating on Augie's skillful maneuvering of the big boat with such finesse, and his deliberate communications with the engineer. He made it look so easy.

"Oh, Captain..." Sadie Perkins' voice, pleasant as it was, buzzed in Augie's ears like a pesky mosquito. "How long will we be docked here? Do I have enough time to walk into town? I'd love to take a picture of that church steeple."

"We'll only be here an hour," Jesse responded immediately. "There's only a few hours of daylight left, and we hafta make Prairie du Chien before dark. You have one hour."

Again, Augie was impressed with Jesse's assertive answer. There was no doubt in his mind that Jesse was learning the art of command very quickly.

Luke hurried down to the main deck with three objectives: The departing passengers needed their luggage; the rousters needed prodding to get the freight unloaded; he had to be sure that the unregistered guest in the cargo bay was not discovered.

Ambition was at its peak; the roustabouts carted the open-topped barrels onto the dock where they were inspected and counted by the button factory receiving clerk. Luke handed over the last of the three suitcases; he scanned the dark corner where he had last seen the stow-away, and he saw nothing but crates, bags, and the roof of Jesse's truck. Apparently, Reggie Pierce was heeding his instructions, and he was staying out of sight.

Henry had prepared a tray of ham and roast beef sandwiches, as a late afternoon lunch for the crew. Jesse and Augie were eating at the table in the crew lounge when Luke entered. Luke knew he had enough time to return to the cargo bay to deliver the promised fare to Reggie, but he would have to make an excuse for eating on the run. "I have to check some stuff on the freight deck. I saw a crate that might've tipped over. I'll eat my sandwich on the way." He poured a large mug of lemonade, wrapped a sandwich in a napkin and started for the door.

"D'ya want me to come with you?" Jesse asked.

"No! I can handle it. You stay here and enjoy your lunch, Captain. I can handle it just fine."

Jesse didn't question the gesture of commitment and responsibility. He trusted Luke's judgment and competence.

By then, the barrels were nearly unloaded, and the rousters and deck hands were filing up to the lounge for their lunch. When the last one bounded up the stairs, Luke sought the dark corner. Reggie's eyes lit up as he unfolded the napkin. To him, a simple roast beef sandwich was like a Thanksgiving feast -- it was the best food he had eaten in days.

"Now I hafta get back up to the pilothouse. We'll be getting under way soon. Stay outa sight, and tonight, after dark, I'll come back with some more food. We'll have time to talk then. I think I know how to get you outa this mess you're in. Okay?"

Reggie just nodded. His mouth was too busy chomping the sandwich to speak.

A shrill, high-pitched whistle echoed across the river valley. Jesse recognized the sound from his past. It wasn't a steamboat whistle; it was a train. He peered back toward the port of Lansing that was three hundred yards behind the boat. A locomotive towing six Pullman cars, a baggage car and a caboose was just coming to a stop near the dock where the Madison had just left, minutes before. "I hope there's no one getting off that train who wanted to get on this boat," Jesse said with concern.

"Too late now," Augie replied. "If there is, they'll catch up to us in Prairie. They've got all night." Showing little concern for the bad timing, Augie persuaded Luke to take the helm. There was nothing but open water and a wide channel ahead. This was a good time for the cub to start getting a feel for the craft, when there was little danger of putting safety in jeopardy.

There *was* someone getting off the train, desperately wanting to board the Madison. The two men who had helplessly watched their prey escape that morning at La Crosse, stood on the Lansing pier, and once more stared out across the vast waterway as the blue-trimmed white ship steamed away.

"Where will that boat stop next?" one of the men asked the workers loading the shells onto a truck. One of the workers looked down river to the Madison that appeared no bigger than a dime on the southern river horizon. "Prairie du Chien... she'll be tied up there for the night, I reckon."

Only the roof peaks reflected the copper tones of the last rays of sunlight. The Madison glided past the Prairie du Chien waterfront, lined with brick and tin-walled warehouses. Its destination was a strip of shoreline just to the south, where the water was too shallow for the bigger barges, but deep enough for the flat bottomed boats like the Madison.

Passenger ferryboats coming in from points along the Wisconsin River tied up there, and it was close to a coal supply.

With Augie close at his side, Luke duplicated the maneuvers he had watched his mentor perform so effortlessly at Lansing. Here, there was less current near the shore, and a wide berth granted Luke a comfort zone for his first attempt at making contact with the levee. When the bow was pressed against the beach and the loading ramp began to lower, Luke took in a deep breath and exhaled with a sigh of noble contentment. He felt like a prince, proud, and pleased with his performance.

Augie was pleased too, although it was he who had sent all the signals to the engineer. "You brought her in like a real pilot. Well done. Now go tend to your other duties while I put today's entries in the log."

Jesse understood why Augie had spoken so confidently about Luke's abilities as a pilot. He wasn't jealous of Luke's achievement. Instead, he was quite relieved to know that a promising new pilot, being taught by the best, stood in the Madison's ranks, and somehow, that idea lessened his worries of failure.

Mr. Collins had requested a meeting with Jesse, so they could discuss the current financial status -- operational expenses, income revenues, and a lot of other topics with fancy titles that Jesse was certain he wouldn't understand. He had entrusted Lester Collins to handle all the legal mumbo-jumbo from the very start, and there was no reason to change any of that. But as the owner and Captain, Jesse felt obligated to hear the accountant's reports, and it seemed like a good time.

Lester wasn't in his office; Jesse decided to peruse the saloon and meet some of the passengers who would be getting ready to sample Henry's evening cuisine. He hadn't seen or talked with Will since that morning, either, and he was curious to see how Little Brother was fairing among all those strangers.

Beautiful, teen-aged Jennifer Aldrich met him at the doorway. She batted her thick eyelashes and flashed a timid little grin. "Hello, Captain," she said in a shy, seductive schoolgirl tone. "I was hoping I would get a chance to talk to you again."

"Hello, Miss Aldrich. Are you enjoying your trip so far?"

"Oh, yes! I just love your beautiful boat... and the scenery along the river is so... so... romantic. Don't you think so?"

"Ah... sure... I guess it is."

"Father is in the stateroom taking a nap, and I was wondering if you'd like to go for a walk along the riverbank with me."

Jesse scanned the room. He spotted Will pouring coffee at a table, surrounded by several dainty, elderly women.

"Maybe later, Miss Aldrich. Right now I have to talk to my Little Brother, and then I have to meet with the clerk. Maybe after supper."

"Well... all right, then. After supper. Don't forget." Jennifer was pouring more charm than Will was pouring coffee. She batted her eyes some more, and walked away.

Jesse strolled to the table where Will administered a generous helping of charm, as well as coffee. "Hello, ladies. I'm Captain Jesse Madison. Is everything to your liking? Is my Little Brother taking good care of you?"

Mrs. Johnson gave a surprised look. "So you're Captain Madison? And Will is your brother? I can certainly see that handsome runs in the family. Will is such a little doll. I think I'd like to take him home with me."

Will's face reddened with embarrassment.

Jesse grinned. "I'm sorry, but I don't think I can let you have him," he said.

"Well... okay," Mrs. Johnson came back. "But if you ever change your mind, you let me know." She pinched Will's cheek; he turned a brighter shade of red.

A couple of tables over, Spades Morgan sat with his eyes buried in a book. He was alone, and ignoring the surroundings.

"Hi, Spades. Are you having a pleasant trip?"

Morgan looked up from the book to see Jesse and Will sitting at the table. "Well, hello Jesse. Will has been pampering me all day... guess I've never been treated this well on any riverboat before. You boys are doin' a fine job."

"Spades told me all about the game with Swamp Scum!" Will announced to Jesse.

"Not so anybody else heard, I hope," Jesse replied.

"Don't worry, Jesse," Morgan said. "That conversation was in my stateroom behind closed doors. Nobody else heard... that's our secret."

"Good," Jesse replied. "I kinda want to keep that just between us. Now if you'll excuse me, I hafta find my clerk. He wants to go over a few things. If there's anything at all that you need, Morgan, be sure to let us know... anything at all." Jesse went off to find Mr. Collins.

He hadn't quite reached the doorway when Sadie Perkins' sweet voice called to him.

"Oh, Captain..." Sadie arose from a chair and stepped between Jesse and the door. "I just wanted to let you know that I have had a wonderful day aboard your boat, and, oh yes... you were absolutely right. Your little brother is perfectly charming. Will is such a little dear." Her smile weakened Jesse's knees.

"I'm glad you're enjoying the voyage, Miss Perkins."

"Oh, heavens, yes I am... and it looks like such a lovely evening for a stroll through the town. Would you care to join me? I would be most delighted."

"Sure... I think I would like that, too. But first I must meet with my clerk. We'll have supper, and then go for that walk."

There didn't seem to be any need for concern of Will's ability to cope with strangers. Quite obviously, he had won the hearts of everyone on board. Knowing Will like Jesse did, it wasn't difficult to understand why.

And what about his own heart? Sadie Perkins was hopelessly carrying it away. But just a walk around town couldn't hurt -- just one, innocent, little walk.

The chill October night settled in. Massive oceans of clouds swept across the black sky; only an occasional star twinkled through the haze just briefly, before it was snuffed out by another wave of the gray surf. Most of the crew had ventured into the city to seek various forms of entertainment, as had many of the remaining passengers, who would be continuing on to destinations farther down the river. But some stayed on board to make their own entertainment. It was discovered that one of the voyagers was an accomplished banjo player, and another, picked out melodies on a guitar; their music had everyone singing and dancing, and forgetting that the journey had been temporarily halted until the next morning.

Luke wasn't among them. He and Reggie Pierce had snuck off the boat and found a cluster of huge rocks along the riverbank where they could talk privately.

"Where are you from?" Luke asked.

"England... Liverpool, England."

"How did you get here?"

"A steamer...'cross the Atlantic, and then by train, mostly, the rest of the way."

"And why are you here?"

The answer to that question wasn't a simple one. Reggie had been expecting the need to explain the reason, and he had thought about it all afternoon. The truth would be his best alternative in return for Luke's kindness; somehow, he sensed that Luke would understand. "My father sent me away to a private school three years ago. I think he was just trying to get me out from under foot... he never did like me much. But last spring, near the end of my third year there, I was expelled, and I just couldn't face my family again. I would've been the disgrace of the entire borough. My father had sent me money for my summer vacation in Switzerland. But I bought a ticket for a steamer to America, instead."

"Why didn't you just go to Switzerland?"

"My father could've found me there. I figured he would never find me in America."

"Why were you expelled from the school?"

Reggie's expression turned solemn. He knew he would be confronted with that question, too, but he was still confident that Luke would understand the truth. "I was training for the Rugby team... Rugby is kind of like your football here in America. I wasn't very good at all. There was another boy, Stephen Hobbs, a Prefect, two years older than I, and one of the best players. He was helping me train, and we became good friends... very good friends." Reggie looked into Luke's eyes, trying to detect a reaction, only to see intense interest. "One Saturday afternoon after practice, Stephen and I snuck off to our secret hiding place like we often did... the luggage loft above the garage where Mr. Metcalfe, the Head Master, kept his motor car. We'd been up there quite a while, and we were so involved with what we were doing that we didn't hear Mr. Metcalfe coming up the stairs... and we got caught."

Luke displayed a puzzled frown. "What d'ya mean... got caught?"

"I was afraid you wouldn't understand." Reggie paused, fearful of continuing. "We... we had our clothes off, Luke. We had our bloody clothes off."

Astonished, Luke said nothing.

"They called me his bum-boy... and maybe I was, but they didn't understand. Our friendship was something special. We were there because we both wanted to be there." Reggie began to sob. He feared he had just destroyed the only alliance he had known since he arrived in this strange, vast land.

"So then you were both expelled... you and Stephen." Luke's words flowed out with a tone of sympathy.

"I was," Reggie said, as he wiped away his tears. "Stephen was a Prefect. A senior in high standing, and he was about to graduate. Mr. Metcalfe knew there was a lot of that sort of thing going on. It was bound to, in a school like that. But Stephen was always one of his favorites. He didn't want to ruin Stephen's future, so he kept it all quiet and let Stephen graduate."

Reggie covered his face with his hands. "I suppose you hate me now, don't you?" His voice was quiet and muffled, but it suggested an air of relief; he had vented the anxiety.

"No, I don't hate you." Luke put his arm around Reggie's athletic shoulders, offering some comfort. "I understand. It's all right. I really understand."

Luke and Reggie sat in silence for a few minutes, just staring across the dark river. Off in the distance, near the Madison, Luke could just barely identify the silhouettes of two people walking away from the boat, and he desperately hoped they wouldn't come his way. He listened to the voices; one was quite familiar – Jesse; the other was a woman's voice. They sounded happy, enjoying each other's company. As they strolled toward the streets of town, Luke heard them talking about photographs and scenery; he thought the woman had to be that women photographer, Sadie Perkins.

When the couple had disappeared into the depths of the city, Luke remembered why he originally started the conversation with Reggie. "If you still want to get to St. Louis to see your Uncle -- "

"I don't have an Uncle in St. Louis," Reggie interrupted. "I just said that. It was the only thing I could think of at the time."

Luke was reminded of a similar statement he had made to Jesse that night in the saloon after supper with Morgan. "Then why do you want to go to St. Louis?"

"I've been trying to find employment, but there are no jobs anywhere I've been so far. I haven't any money left, and I lost all my clothes. All I have is this blanket. I heard that I might find work in St. Louis."

"What happened to your clothes?"

"I was sleeping in a railroad freight car coming across Ohio. When I woke up, everything was gone. Someone must've stolen everything, except my blanket. I was using it for a pillow."

"Well, I have some extra clothes... nothing fancy, but they'll do. And if you're interested, I'll talk to the Captain. Jesse's my best friend. That was him walking with the lady. I'll tell him I hired you as a deckhand. Then, when we get to St. Louis, you'll at least have some money."

"But where will I stay? In the cargo deck where I was today?"

"Nonsense. You'll stay with me. I'm the First Mate, and I have my own room up on the Texas deck." Luke gazed up into the sky. "Looks like it might come a shower, and it's kinda chilly out here. C'mon, let's go up to my quarters and find you some clean clothes."

Overwhelmed by Luke's sincerity and warm touch, Reggie knew why he had felt confident about his messiah's acceptance.

20

A knock came at the door of the second floor room in a hotel in the middle of town.

"Yeah... what d'ya want?" the grouchy voice answered from inside.

"There's a steamship docked at the waterfront, bound for St. Louis, Sir," the bellboy informed the occupant. He was earning a handsome tip in exchange for keeping an eye on the river, and for relaying the information.

"What time is it?"

"It's seven o'clock in the morning, Sir."

"What boat is it?"

"Sir?"

"The boat... what's the name of the damn boat?"

"The Madison, Sir."

"Never heard of it. Is it a nice boat? Don't want to ride no cattle ferry."

"Yes Sir... it's a very nice boat, Sir. Would you like me to find out if they have a stateroom available, Sir?"

"Yes! Of course! And find out what time it leaves ...the sooner the better. And be quick about it."

"Yes Sir. I'll be right back, Sir."

Jesse heard the muffled voices through the wall. He rubbed his eyes and glanced over to lovely Sadie, lying in the bed next to him. The affair was not a dream.

"For Chissake! Seven o'clock." He had thought that he would awake much earlier, and that he would be back on the boat before anyone realized he wasn't in his quarters.

"I am the Captain," he thought. He hastily slipped on his clothes. "And it's no one's business to know where I've been all night."

Sadie began to stir.

"I'm going back to the boat," he said softly. "You can take your time... we don't leave for another two hours." He leaned over the edge of the bed, giving Sadie a tender little kiss. "I'll see you later."

Day two of the journey was about to begin. Nothing seemed out of the ordinary, although Jesse didn't have too much to compare. Just one day, and he thought that had gone quite smoothly, thanks to Augie.

Jesse trotted up the stairway to the Texas deck, pausing only long enough at his quarters to slip into his Captain's jacket, and to make sure Will was awake.

Will stood in front of a mirror, attempting to make his bow tie more presentable. He peered at Jesse's reflection in the mirror and talked to it instead of turning around. "Where were you all night?"

"I stayed at a hotel in town." Jesse didn't want to reveal any more information than he had to, and tried to change the subject. "Are you ready for another day on the river?"

"Sure. But why didn't you sleep here last night? I was worried about you."

"Well you don't have to worry any more, Little Brother... everything is just fine."

That didn't really answer Will's question, but he was relieved to know Jesse was safe. "I saw you walking into town last night with that lady photographer."

Jesse stopped abruptly at the door. The thought occurred to him that Will might be a bit more perceptive than he was giving him credit for, and Jesse certainly didn't want rumors to start. "You just keep that to yourself, Little Brother... okay?" He drilled a stare of expectant obedience into Will's smirk, that he could only see in the mirror.

Will just nodded. He was still having trouble with the bow tie.

Jesse bounced into the pilothouse where he knew he would find Augie. "Good mornin' Augie." His cheeks were a little red with embarrassment, expecting that Augie might know about his walk with Sadie, too. "Everything under control?" Jesse asked, trying to avoid conversation of his private encounter.

"G'mornin' Captain. The coal bins are full, and we'll be ready to get under way by nine sharp."

"Think the weather will hold? Looks kinda dreary."

Augie glanced at the barometer and tapped on the glass. "Don't think it'll rain any more. I'm more worried about fog when we get a little farther south."

"I see we lost quite a few passengers... think it'll fill up again?"

"Made this stop a hundred times over the years," Augie said. "Always a good stop for takin' on more passengers. But you better look into the problem brewin' on the main deck. Seems to be a trouble maker on board... a crewman."

Jesse began to feel tension building in his gut. The smoothness had gained some ripples, and maybe he hadn't been paying enough attention. "What's the problem?"

"Don't know for sure, but I heard some arguing among the deckhands this morning when I went down to check with Charlie. I think you ought to look into it before we get under way."

Just then, Luke appeared, ready to begin the day's cub lessons. "Good morning Jesse... Augie."

"Good morning Luke," Jesse returned. "Do you know anything about the trouble with the crew? Augie says there's a troublemaker. Know who it is?"

"Well, I do know there's one hand that doesn't get along too well with the rest of them -- Hollingsworth. But I thought Stieger was gonna straighten him out."

"C'mon Luke. We're goin' down there right now to take care of this before it gets out of hand. We don't need any troublemakers... right?"

The unity of the crew had begun to jell remarkably, considering the short period of time they had been working together. Hollingsworth was the exception.

One of the more experienced deck hands, Deke Stieger, was certainly making Luke's position a little less demanding. He was a big, muscular fellow whom the other crewmen had learned to respect, right from the start. Deke knew the ropes -- he had even worked for Augie on this boat at one time. His grizzly, intimidating appearance was a valuable asset when it came to keeping the other hands in line.

Mike Hollingsworth was lazy, and he chose not to heed Deke's warnings; one confrontation after another was rapidly escalating the dispute. Deke's patience was wearing thin. It was only a matter of time until unwritten justice would send Hollingsworth over the side, and as his going-away present, he might take with him two blackened eyes and a broken nose.

Luke and Jesse lit on the cargo deck about the time justice was being administered. They heard Deke's dominant voice, and he wasn't reciting the Morning Prayer. Several other crewmen circled around Deke, who had Hollingsworth pinned to a wall with one hand, and was delivering intermittent, attention-getters with the other.

"You don't curse at me and get away with it, you lazy little twit," Deke said in a powerful tone, and then landed a closed fist solidly onto Hollingsworth's cheekbone. That one drew blood. Quite clearly, Mike Hollingsworth was no longer capable of any form of defense, much less, mounting the slightest bit of retaliation.

"That's enough, Mr. Stieger!" Jesse yelled. He and Luke held Deke's arms to prevent a beating from becoming a murder.

Hollingsworth collapsed to his knees, doubled over with his arms folded across his stomach, moaning in pain and humiliation.

Jesse and Luke dragged Deke away from his victim. Deke struggled at first, but then he realized he was resisting the top ranking officers, and he quickly succumbed to their wishes.

Jesse instructed another rouster to escort Hollingsworth to his quarters. "And all the rest of you, get back to work! The show's over." He glared at Stieger, and then at Luke. "Does somebody want to tell me what's going on? And why wasn't I informed about this problem before now?"

"We thought we could handle it without bothering you, Captain," Luke said. He realized that he had made a mistake.

"Luke... this is not how we will handle these matters on this boat. And Mr. Stieger? I value your know-how. You're doing a bang-up job. But you can't be kickin' the crap outa any crewmember. If you have any more problems like this, you come see me about it before you decide to kill off the crew. Got it?"

"Yessir."

"Good. Now I've been told that Hollingsworth has not been getting along with the rest of the crew -- I'll deal with that right now." He turned to his

First Mate. "Luke, make sure everything else is goin' the way it should. We get under way in an hour. I'll see you in the pilothouse later."

Blonde-haired, eyelash-batting Jennifer Aldrich cornered Jesse on his way to Hollingsworth's cabin. "Hi, Captain Madison. I looked for you last night. Did you forget about our walk?"

"N-no. I didn't forget, but something came up. And I really don't have time to talk right now, either."

Purely disappointed, Jennifer wouldn't give up her chances of gaining the Captain's attention. "Well, then, maybe later? When you're not so busy?"

"Sure... we'll talk later, after we get back on the river and I'm not so busy. I promise."

Jesse knocked on Mike Hollingsworth's cabin door. The day was off to a bad start, and he dreaded the discussion he was forced to conduct.

Mike sat on his bunk; a far-away look was in his eyes. He dabbed the bloody cheek wound with a handkerchief.

"Are you okay? You're lucky you didn't get killed down there."

Mike remained silent, reluctant to make eye contact with Jesse. Apparently, he wasn't too eager to contribute his view of the situation.

Jesse got right to the point. "I've heard some complaints about you, Mike. My First Mate tells me that you aren't getting along with the rest of the crew very well, and obviously, from what I saw down on the cargo deck, Stieger doesn't exactly consider you his best friend."

"Yeah... so what are ya gonna do about it?"

Jesse didn't know Hollingsworth very well, but he understood the problem: Mike possessed a hostile attitude, and the beating hadn't humbled him. "The way I see it, Mike, you have two choices. First... you can dump your bad attitude into the river, start doing your share of the work that you're getting paid to do, and try to get along with everybody else."

"And what's my second choice?"

"I don't think I should have to explain that one," Jesse said firmly.

Mike knew that his future on the Madison looked quite dim. Rather than facing Stieger again, he chose the easier solution. He packed up his personal gear and stormed off the boat. Jesse didn't see any point in trying to salvage the relationship; it would only result in more problems later. None of the other rousters made any attempt to convince Hollingsworth to stay, either. They were all glad to see him leave.

Luke was just closing his cabin door when Jesse came through the breezeway.

"We just lost a rouster," Jesse said. "Hollingsworth quit. Packed up his things and walked off." Jesse sounded a little concerned. "Think we can get along with one less on the crew? There really isn't time, right now, to find someone. We'll be under way in a half hour."

This wasn't the best news for Luke; the crew was already short-handed. But it did simplify the justification for another issue. Luke wanted to tell the Captain about Reggie, but it involved answering too many questions that Luke would rather avoid. "I guess we'll have to. Maybe at the next stop I can scout around for someone to take his place."

"Yes," Jesse nodded. "That sounds like a good plan."

"I'll talk to Stieger right now... let him know what's goin' on." Then as an afterthought, Luke added, "By the way. I saw you walking into town last night with the lady photographer, and I noticed you didn't come back 'til early this morning."

Jesse didn't see any humor in Luke's taunting remark. "That's none of your concern. Just keep it to yourself, Luke."

Jesse ascended the stairs to the pilothouse. In comparison, this day was developing into a disaster.

As Jesse approached the pilothouse door, he saw Augie and Spades Morgan with their backs to him; they were talking, unaware of his presence.

"Never thought I'd see you on this boat again," Augie said. "Not after what happened down at Baton Rouge."

"That was a long time ago, Augie. Times have changed. This boat has changed. But now that you brought it up, there's something I've been meaning to tell you about that for a long time."

Jesse ducked around the corner to conceal his eavesdropping.

"I saw more of what really happened that night than I have ever told -- to anyone," Morgan continued quietly. "When I came up to the Texas deck that night, I intended to talk to Dupree... to try to help him if I could. That's when I heard the gunshot, and by the time I got to him, McDermott was hovering over his body."

"You mean McDermott was already there?" Augie said. "He told me he ran up the stairs *after* he heard the shot."

"That's what he told you, but that's not the way it was. Looked to me like he was planting the gun in Dupree's hand."

"What? You think McDermott was the one who pulled the trigger?"

"Can't say for sure, Augie. But I do know that McDermott had been eyeing Dupree's gold watch during the poker game, and I know Dupree was light on the last hand."

"So why, for heaven's sake, didn't you say anything about it back then?"

"Didn't want to get involved... had enough problems of my own then."

"Did McDermott know you were there?"

"Sure he did. That's the only reason he didn't get the watch off Dupree's body right then. He knew he'd been caught. When he saw me standing there, he started babbling about how the boy had just pulled out the pistol and blew his own brains out. By that time, there were other people around, too, and then you showed up. Remember?"

"Too well, Spades. I remember all too well." Augie stared into the morning haze.

It seemed to Jesse that the conversation had ended. It was a good time to make an entrance. "Well, good morning Spades."

"Morning, Jesse. I was just having a little chat with your pilot about old times. Hope you don't mind."

"Not at all. Stay as long as you like."

"Actually..." Morgan looked at his watch. "...I think I'll go to my stateroom and nap for a while. I woke up much too early this morning."

Augie glanced at the clock. It was fifteen minutes to nine. He sounded three short blasts with the whistle. "Where's Luke? He should be here now."

The Madison had crossed the Mississippi, stopped briefly at McGregor, and it was, again, riding the current of the main channel. The early morning crisis had passed, although it was not entirely resolved. Jesse sat on the lazy man's bench behind the pilot. Luke had been at the wheel since the gangplank was raised at Prairie du Chien, and Augie continued a steady pace of verbal coaching. "You've got to know every detail of the river... every landmark and every island..."

"But there's too much to remember." Luke said. "How can I possibly remember every detail?"

"You've got to. In time, Luke, you'll get to know every tree and every stump on both shores as well as you know the inside of your own house."

"Why do I need to know all those details?"

"*Because*, Cubby, when you come back up the river, you won't be out in the main channel like you are now, going downstream. You'll be hugging the shoreline where the current isn't so strong. You have to know the shape of the river at every bend, and remember where the wing dams are, and..."

It all seemed overwhelming to Luke, but Augie's confidence in the young cub's ability was reassuring. Luke was beginning to feel the reactions of the boat with his every command of the rudder, as if it were a part of him, and his sense of recognizing what the water's surface told him, like words on the page of a book; he knew the rest would become second nature, too. He started scrutinizing the landmarks and burning them into his memory. His only desire was to become a pilot with the skill equal to that of his teacher.

Will appeared, and sat down beside Jesse. He seemed a bit nervous as he whispered, "You'll never guess who got the last stateroom."

"Who?" Jesse asked.

"Swamp Scum McDermott."

"I thought that voice at the hotel this morning sounded familiar. But why is he on this boat? I thought he went back to St. Louis on the Capitol."

"He did... but he got off the Capitol at Prairie du Chien and got involved in a big poker game at the hotel. He's been stuck there all this time."

"Does he know what boat he's on?"

"He didn't at first. But by the time he figured it out, we were already under way."

"So... how far is he going?"

"Looks like we're stuck with him all the way to St. Louis."

"Does Morgan know?"

"I don't think so. Morgan's still in his stateroom. He told me he was going to sleep a while."

Another crisis was brewing; Morgan and McDermott, together on the same boat, and especially this boat, posed a potentially dangerous combination. Perhaps, nothing short of posting a guard at the two stateroom doors would prevent a distasteful occurrence. "But this isn't a prison ship," Jesse thought, "and we can't spare the deck hands for that kind of duty. We'll just have to make sure the situation doesn't get out of control."

The next landing at Cassville was several hours ahead. Jesse announced to the pilot and his cub that he would be tending to other matters; he excused himself from the pilothouse.

As Jesse passed by the clerk's office, Mr. Collins hailed his attention. "Just thought you might want to know, Captain," Lester said discretely. "There are two men on board... identified themselves as Pinkertons... said they were looking for someone who they thought was on this boat."

"Who are they looking for?"

"They wouldn't say. Just said that they had been tracking someone clear across the state, and now that person was on this boat. They paid for passage all the way to St. Louis and told me not to alert anyone of their identity."

"You've met everyone on this boat, Mr. Collins. Who do you think it might be? A passenger? Someone on the crew?"

"I don't have the foggiest idea."

"Where are these men now?"

"The last I saw of them, they were sitting at a table in the corner of the Saloon. They're wearing brown suits, and their names are..." Lester looked at the passenger register. "... Simms and Pulaski."

"Okay. Thank you for that information, Mr. Collins." Jesse wandered into the saloon.

Inclement weather had kept almost everyone from enjoying the scenery from the outer decks. Sadie Perkins, though, was braving the cool, damp air, with her camera pointed toward the dense, gray, riverbank forests, anticipating a picturesque moment. That afforded Jesse the opportunity to seek a promised conversation with Jennifer Aldrich. She was sitting alone and she appeared quite bored.

"Hello, Miss Aldrich. Mind if I join you?"

"Please, do." Jennifer's spirit perked up the instant Jesse spoke. He had triggered a teen-aged crush the very first time their eyes met; Jennifer was obsessed with becoming the center of Jesse's interest.

"I don't have anyone to talk to," she said, as Jesse sat down beside her. "And Father stays in the stateroom most of the time. He hasn't been well lately."

Jesse knew it wasn't any of his business, but he couldn't help but express just a little sympathy. "Oh. I'm sorry to hear that. Is there anything I can do to help?"

"Oh, no. It's better if he's just left alone. He needs his rest."

"Well, then. We'll let him get all the rest he wants." Jesse's eyes scanned the saloon as he spoke; he was more interested in spotting Simms and Pulaski, and trying to determine whom they might be hunting, rather than hearing about some illness.

Jesse's eyes found the Pinkertons, but they weren't watching anyone in particular. The two men were trying to be inconspicuous, and to everyone else in the room, their shrewd presence went unnoticed.

Jennifer, desperately trying to win Jesse's attention, saw that he was preoccupied. "My father and I are going to St. Louis. But I guess you already know that. We're taking a family heirloom to someone who is willing to pay a lot of money for it."

Jesse acknowledged Jennifer with a nod, but his thoughts were still focused on the Pinkertons' mystery.

Jennifer continued babbling, but in a whisper. "Father found a large diamond on the farm when he was a little boy. It was probably brought there by the glacier, thousands of years ago... at least, that's what we've heard."

Jesse's attention was slowly starting to catch up with Jennifer's saga as she rambled on.

"But the times have been so hard and he has been so ill."

"So why hasn't he seen a doctor if he's so sick?"

"He says he can't afford a doctor. That's why we're taking the diamond to St. Louis. Father said we will be quite wealthy when we get there."

It was plain to Jesse that the young girl was merely trying to impress him, or she was seeking sympathy. A few people around the room were taking notice of her flirting antics; Jesse felt uncomfortable with the relationship that, perhaps, should have been avoided. He needed to escape.

"Yes, well it has been nice chatting with you, Miss Aldrich, but I really must go now. Perhaps we can talk another time."

"Yes, I really do hope so." Jennifer batted her eyelashes.

Jesse walked away; he could almost feel Simms' icy glare. Who were these guys after? he thought. The boat was full of candidates -- it could be anyone. Jesse even gave consideration to himself. After all -- he had made off with Capone's cash. Could Capone have sent these men to find him and the money? There wasn't any reason for Luke to be wanted – wasn't he just an innocent farm boy? But Will. Will was a runaway; his stepfather could be attempting to locate and drag him back to Milwaukee. And what about the rest of the crew? Other than Augie, they were total strangers until a few days before the Madison set sail. Of all the passengers, Jesse knew only one before the voyage began -- Spades Morgan, but Morgan had been scarce for a week, or so. Who knew what mischievous endeavors he could have found? And then there was Blackjack McDermott. If no one was after *him*, there probably should be.

A whole boatload of candidates, indeed. The more Jesse thought about it, the higher he placed himself on the list. Ten thousand dollars, in cold, hard cash, certainly warranted a manhunt. The guards at the gate in Couderay could have informed Al about Jesse's visit, *and* the trunk he tried to deliver. Was this to be the end? Jesse's head was swimming in a pool of frightening visions. He knew Al could be a ruthless man, and dispatching a couple of his men, posing as Pinkerton Detectives, wasn't beyond him. Worst of all, Luke and Will's safety was in jeopardy, as well.

Jesse stood at the railing on the Texas deck, staring down into the waves radiating from the hull.

"Oh, Captain!" Sadie's voice was like a life raft floating toward Jesse. Her words were no longer those of a whining, demanding passenger; Sadie was an intimate friend. "Is something bothering you? You look troubled," she said with a comforting tone.

Sadie was the last person he wanted to make aware of the situation. His feelings for her were much more than just friendly; alarming her with the sudden development of anxiety could be detrimental to their relationship. "No, I just have a lot of things on my mind right now."

"Well, I hear there's a nice hotel in Dubuque -- the *Julien Inn*. We *are* stopping at Dubuque overnight, aren't we?"

"Yes."

"We could slip away again tonight. It would give you a chance to relax."

Jesse thought about the comments his comrades had made that

morning. "I don't know, Sadie."

"Are you afraid of falling in love, Jesse?"

Jesse wasn't expecting such a right-to-the-point, shocking response, and he couldn't remember if that word had slipped into the previous night's passion. "No... well... maybe... just a little."

"So am I, Jesse. But I think it's too late. I'm afraid that I am very much in love with you. No one has ever made me feel the way you do." Sadie's eyes sparkled with sincerity.

Never before had Jesse ever experienced the tingling sensation that he felt at that moment, either, but he liked it. He wanted to express his mutual feelings, but he feared that his words would come out sounding stupid. "Okay. I'll meet you at the *Julien Inn* later tonight, after I'm sure everything is in control here."

"All right then. I'll wait for you there."

They embraced, and for a few brief moments, the chilly dampness transformed into tropical warmth.

Morgan emerged from his stateroom. Many miles of riverbank had passed by while he napped, but he had traveled the Mississippi so many times, over the years, that a few glances at the surroundings quickly oriented him to location; the Madison was nearing the Cassville Levee.

That stop didn't hold much interest for Morgan. If it had been an overnighter, the *Denniston Hotel* would yield a good poker game, but this late in the season, the risk of no other southbound boat was too great. It wasn't worth giving up his stateroom on the Madison. He even dismissed the idea of taking a short walk along the levee.

He looked around the saloon, as several passengers appeared to be gathering their belongings in anticipation of their journey's end; that meant a comfortable chair might soon become available. That's when Morgan saw the one man whom he detested more than any other on the face of the earth -- J. D. "Blackjack" McDermott. Their eyes met. Each was equally astonished with the other's presence, and neither man was about to offer a greeting -- friendly or otherwise.

Will saw Morgan and immediately came running. "Hi, Spades. Did you have a good nap?"

"Yes I did. But what's Swamp Scum McDermott doing here?"

"He boarded at Prairie du Chien this morning, just after you went to your room. I was going to tell you, but I didn't want to disturb your nap."

"But what's he doing on this boat?"

"Guess he got stranded. The Capitol left without him. He was all wrapped up in a poker game at the hotel."

"Hmf. Serves him right. And now, I suppose he's going all the way to St.

Louis."

"Yeah. Guess so."

"Well, I think I'll go for that walk when we land at Cassville after all."

Luke learned a new docking technique at the Cassville Levee -- maneuvering the boat parallel to the bank -- and although he didn't get it precisely right on the first try, Augie assured him that he would have another shot at it, in Ice Harbor at Dubuque.

Cassville was to be just another brief stop of only an hour. A few pieces of cargo would be unloaded and a handful of passengers were terminating there. The weather conditions hadn't changed much from the gloom that had been with the Madison all day, and none of the remaining voyagers were in the mood for a short walk. Not even Sadie Perkins had a desire to venture off in search of a picture.

Augie kept a close eye on the low clouds that were beginning to smother the hilltops. "Make sure this stop is a short one," he told the Captain. "We can still make Dubuque before the fog sets in. Fog can be deadly to a riverboat... so hurry things along."

Jesse caught up with Luke in the crew lounge. Luke was heaping a plate with enough food for two. When he saw that Jesse was taking notice of a glutton's portion, he knew he had to make an excuse. "I'm really hungry... haven't eaten much all day. And I think I'd like to go to my quarters to have my lunch." Luke had kept Reggie a secret so far, and if it could remain that way for just a little longer, he could introduce the newcomer at Dubuque, as someone he had found there, and no one would have to know that Reggie had been a stow-away.

"Okay, Luke," Jesse agreed. "But before you go, there's something I want to talk to you about. It'll only take a minute."

"Sure, Captain. What's on your mind?" Luke set the plate back on the table.

Jesse glanced toward the door to make certain no one else was about to enter. "Luke? Is there any reason that I don't know about... anything you haven't told me... any reason at all, that someone might be following you?"

"Why? What do you mean?"

"Well, there's a couple of guys on board, Pinkerton Detectives. Mr. Collins told me they are looking for somebody on this boat, but they wouldn't say who."

"And what makes you think they'd be after me?"

"I don't. I just thought--"

"Well, you thought wrong. They wouldn't have any reason to be looking for me."

"Okay. That's all I wanted to know." Jesse turned for the door.

"They could be after you. You're the one who stole all that money from

Mr. Capone. Did you think of that?"

"I didn't *steal* that money. And yes, that thought did cross my mind."

"So what are you going to do?" Luke's frown indicated concern.

"I don't know... guess I'll just have to explain what happened and hope they'll understand." Jesse looked at his watch. "Now go eat your lunch. We have to get back on the river.   Augie thinks we can beat the fog to Dubuque... and don't say a word about the Pinkertons to anyone."

Jesse swiftly descended the stairs and joined Mr. Collins, who was on his way ashore to collect a freight bill.

"Have you heard anything more about the detectives?"

"Not a word," Lester said.

Luke cautiously opened the door to his quarters.   Jesse's news had stirred his curiosity about Reggie.

"I brought you some food." He sat on the bed beside his guest.

"Thank you, Luke. Did you talk to the Captain?"

"Well, yes I did... but not about you.   Can't do that until we get to Dubuque."

"When will that be?" Reggie asked eagerly.

"Tonight. I'll talk to him tonight."

"Then... does that mean I won't have to hide any more?"

"I hope so, Reggie." Luke allowed a bit of concern into his voice.

"There's something wrong, isn't there?   Something went wrong." Reggie's smile suddenly vanished, as if he knew that he was about to hear bad news.

"No, Reggie... nothing is wrong. But I do have a question for you, and you have to tell me the truth, okay?"

"Okay."

"Is there any reason the law might be chasing you? I mean... have you done anything illegal?"

"Like what?"

"Well, you didn't steal something or kill somebody, did you?"

"No, Luke. I'm not a thief... or a murderer."

"How about your father? Could he be trying to track you down?"

"My father couldn't possibly be trying to find me here. He's probably searching for me by now, but he thinks I'm in Switzerland. Why are you asking me all these questions?"

"Oh, I just thought I should ask you all this before I have a talk with the Captain. You do understand, don't you?"

"Yes, I think. But you *are* going to get this job for me, aren't you? So I can stay here with you?"

"Sure, Reggie. I'll get you the job. But you have to stay out of sight until

142

tonight. You can't let anybody see you."

"Okay... I can do that. How long will it be?"

"We'll be in Dubuque in just a few more hours, and right now I have to get back to the pilothouse."

The gangplank lowered and the deck hands secured the Madison to the pier at Dubuque; Luke sighed a breath of relief. His docking procedure had improved.

The engines were stopped. Little whiffs of black smoke drifted from the stacks and mingled with the heavy, moist air. The Madison had won the race with the fog, but only by minutes.

Luke gazed down at the dock. Dozens of people had been watching as the Madison pulled into the harbor, and he couldn't help thinking that he had performed quite a show for them.

"You've done a good job today Luke," Augie said with pride. "You'll make a darn good pilot... I've never seen a cub handle a boat that well after just two days."

Augie turned to Jesse. "And you're making a fine Captain, too, Jesse. I've heard nothing but admirable remarks from everyone on board about your diplomacy." Augie looked at his watch. "Now, as all pilots do, I'm going into town. I'll see you in the morning."

Luke and Jesse wallowed in the compliments a while as they remained in the pilothouse, watching the scurry on the dock below. Augie gave a little wave as he strolled away with Spades Morgan and Lester Collins at his side. Not far behind them, McDermott waddled up the sidewalk.

Several youngsters had assembled on the pier, feeding on the wonderment. One of them made eye contact with Jesse, grinned and waved. Jesse thought back to the day when he stood on the levee at Alma, admiring, and dreaming, and waving. Now it was he who was enthroned in the grandest spot on earth, returning greetings to the dreamers.

Luke and Jesse felt like kings at that moment, realizing their greatest accomplishment. The whole world seemed to be at their fingertips. Anything seemed possible.

On Will's way to his cabin, Will saw that Jesse and Luke were still in the pilothouse. He climbed the stairs, flung open the door and plopped onto the bench. It had been a busy day for Will, keeping the travelers pacified during the bad weather. "Hey, Little Brother. I'm glad you're here," Jesse said. "I have something important to say to you and Luke."

Luke leaned back and sprawled his arms across the big steering wheel.

"I've been thinking," Jesse continued. "Now that we've made it this far without sinking or running aground, it looks like this is going to turn out pretty darn good. And it wouldn't be that way if it wasn't for you two."

Luke smiled appreciatively. Will blushed.

"I told you before that you would be rewarded for your efforts, and I intend to keep my word. I want to make you both my partners, as owners of the Steamship Madison."

"Are you serious?" Luke couldn't think of anything else to say.

"Of course I'm serious. I want you to be my partners."

"But why?" Will asked.

"So if something happens to me, you'll still have the boat."

Will chuckled. "But nothing is going to happen to you."

Jesse hoped Will was right, but he was secretly worried about the detectives, and he would have made a bet that Luke was aware of his fear, too. But under no circumstances was he going to mention any of that to Will. Jesse knew how Will had reacted to things that scared him, and Jesse had enough issues to deal with.

"So how about it? I'll have Mr. Collins draw up the papers to make it official."

Luke and Will exchanged surprised stares. First, Will gave a jerky little nod. Then Luke. They all joined their hands together in one big massive handshake. It was unofficially official -- they were partners.

Nine o'clock once again gathered the less-adventurous passengers in the saloon, singing and dancing as the banjo and guitar players led them into another joyous night of entertainment.

Jesse thought it was a good time to quietly disappear to his rendezvous with Sadie. Luke had left an hour ago, apparently in search of a replacement for Hollingsworth, and Will seemed quite tired after a hard day. He was probably asleep.

Simms and Pulaski remained seated at the corner table, and Jesse certainly didn't want to draw their attention. He had noticed them peering toward him on several occasions, but they would quickly turn away when he returned a glance. Puzzling. What were they waiting for?

As Jesse walked toward the *Julien Inn* at Second and Main, he had the strange sense that he was being followed. He could hear the clicking footsteps on the sidewalk behind him, and he could feel his heart pounding. He quickened his pace. When he reached the front door of the hotel, he looked back. Simms -- or Pulaski, he wasn't sure which -- was not far behind.

Sadie was waiting in the lobby. She didn't have to speak. Her eyes said it all, and a loving kiss confirmed it. They hurried off to her room on the second floor.

Sadie had never looked more beautiful. Her warm touch, the subtle fragrance of her perfume, her silky hair, her soft, delicate skin, had never been more soothing. She was a Goddess -- the only woman Jesse had ever loved.

Noticing Jesse's tension as she gently massaged his neck and shoulders, Sadie knew something was interfering with his ability to relax, and if the night were to be one of ecstasy, she would have to bring him out of his tense mood.

"Why are you so tense tonight? Is there something wrong?" she whispered close to his ear.

"It's been a very trying day, Sadie." Still reluctant to say too much, Jesse turned toward her, took her hands in his, and gazed deeply into her eyes. He wanted to forget about the fight on the cargo deck that morning. He wanted to forget about the conversation he had overheard between Augie and Morgan. He wanted to forget about the man who had followed him to the hotel. He wanted to ignore his anticipation of a knock on the door at any moment. But those visions kept tumbling around in his head, and if anyone deserved an explanation, it was Sadie.

"I think someone followed me here."

"Well, that doesn't sound so terrible. A lot of people would come here at this time of night."

"But this was someone from the boat... one of the Pinkerton Detectives. They told my clerk they were looking for someone, but they wouldn't say who."

Sadie was a little puzzled. "What detectives? And why would they be following you?"

An hour went by as Jesse explained his involvement with Capone, and about the trunk. He felt safe telling Sadie the whole truth, and somehow it seemed necessary.

"...And that's why I think they might be after me."

"But don't you think they would've at least talked to you by now?"

"That's what's so puzzling. I don't know what they're waiting for."

"Maybe they're not after you at all. Maybe there's someone else they're chasing."

Someone else. Yes. The Pinkertons had to be after someone else. And the man who followed him from the boat was just coming to the hotel for a room. That was the most appeasing thought Jesse had entertained all day. Sadie had put his anxiety to rest, at least for the night.

21

Morning broke with the rumble of thunder and the wind whistling through the cracks in the windowsill. Jesse pushed back the curtain. It did not look like a good day for river travel. The meanest-looking black and purple sky was threatening a delay.

Still remembering the Pinkerton following him to the hotel the night before, Jesse looked over his shoulder now and then, as he walked back to the harbor. No one was pursuing him. Perhaps Sadie was right. Maybe the detectives weren't after Jesse Madison.

Jesse saw that Augie was already in the pilothouse, and other than a few rousters moving about on the main deck, there wasn't much activity. A strong west wind dispersed the smoke from the cook-stove chimney. Henry was preparing breakfast, and breakfast was a welcomed thought.

Luke and Reggie sat at the table in the crew lounge, eating scrambled eggs and bacon. Jesse put in his order for the same and sat down with them.

"Captain," Luke said. "I'd like you to meet our newest member of the crew. This is Reggie Pierce."

"Glad to meet you, Reggie Pierce." Jesse responded, and shook Reggie's hand. "Have you worked on a riverboat before?"

"No sir. But I'm willing to learn. Luke has taught me a lot already."

Reggie's British accent caught Jesse by surprise, but he seemed energetic and eager, and certainly able-bodied. Luke appeared quite enthusiastic; there wasn't any reason to doubt the First Mate's judgment.

"Okay, Reggie. Welcome aboard. The pay is thirty-five dollars a month and all your meals... and what ever you do, don't get on Mr. Stieger's bad side."

Henry brought in Jesse's plate.

"Now if you'll excuse me," Jesse said, "I think I'll eat my breakfast in my quarters."

Will was at the mirror again, having another difficult episode with the bow tie. He said nothing, and he appeared quite depressed.

"Hi, Will," Jesse said. He sat down to eat.

Will offered no response.

Attempting to get a reaction of some sort, Jesse joked, "Are you having trouble with that tie again? Maybe you should just throw it away."

Will spun around, dropping his clenched fists to his sides. "Are you going to spend every night at a hotel with Sadie?" His tone was half disappointment and half anger.

Jesse felt the broadside hit. "Why do you say that?"

"I got pretty lonely here all by myself."

"Will, I'm sorry. Last night you looked so tired. I thought you went to bed."

"I did... but only because I was so lonely. Everybody left and there wasn't anybody to talk to."

"What about Luke? Why didn't you go talk to Luke?"

"He was busy with that new guy, Reggie."

Another storm was brewing, but this one wasn't in the sky. Jesse sensed the bitterness: Sadie had stolen Will's Big Brother. Will had grown accustomed to the attention Jesse always gave him, and some degree of neglect had sewn a seed of conflict between Will and Sadie -- the two most important people in Jesse's life. He knew he had to make the storm fade away.

"Tell you what," Jesse said. "Where ever we are tonight, we'll go to a nice restaurant for supper. Just you and me."

Will's eyes lit up. He was thrilled that Jesse was making such a generous offer, but he didn't want to be selfish. He knew Jesse's feelings for Sadie were strong; Will thought she was okay, too, as long as she shared Jesse. He was willing to compromise. "That would be great. But I really wouldn't mind if Sadie came along too."

"Okay. It's a date. You and me and Sadie... supper tonight."

Expressionless, Augie sat in the pilothouse, gazing out beyond the harbor. The wind had picked up and the river boiled with waves.

"How long do you think it will last?" Jesse asked.

"Hard to say. All we can do for now is just wait it out."

Torrents of rain hit the window glass like a bludgeon; the boat rocked as gusts of wind pressed against its side. Jesse strolled through the saloon, greeting the few early risers who were enjoying the hot breakfast that Mildred and Will were catering. Detective Simms was just being joined by his partner at the corner table, and at the far end of the room, J. D. McDermott grumbled to Mildred about the eggs being cold and the bacon too well done.

"Captain, I want to register a complaint." Jesse didn't know the soft-spoken passenger. He assumed the complaint couldn't be regarding the eggs and bacon. The man hadn't been served his breakfast yet. Jesse sat down to listen.

"This morning when I woke up, a blonde-haired girl in a white dress was standing just inside my doorway. Put quite a scare into me."

"What was she doing there?" Jesse asked.

"Well, I asked her that very question. She said her name was Jenny, and that she was looking for her husband."

"Didn't you see her come in?"

"No! She was just... there."

Jennifer Aldrich was the only person on the passenger list who answered that description. Jesse had thought all along that there was something strange about her, and now he knew why. The only reason she would be entering another passenger's room, was if she planned to steal something. She certainly wasn't searching for a lost mate.

"Is anything missing from your room?"

"No. Not that I could tell. But Captain? There's something else quite peculiar about the incident."

"Oh? What's that?"

"Well, I looked away for just a couple of seconds, and when I looked, she was gone."

"I'll look into this right away. Don't worry. This won't happen again."

"Thank you Captain. I hope we don't have a thief on board."

Jesse knocked on the Aldrich stateroom door. There was no answer. He knocked again, but still no answer.

Jesse had not seen Mr. Aldrich since the day when he and Jennifer boarded at La Crosse. That, alone, seemed odd. After hearing the passenger's complaint, Jesse understood Jennifer's peculiar behavior, but before the situation got any worse, he had to find her right away. He scanned the saloon, thinking he might have overlooked her earlier, but she, or her father were nowhere in sight. Simms and Pulaski seemed to be watching Jesse once again, as if they had some particular interest in his activity. Temptation to finally confront them nagged at his conscience, but finding Jennifer was more important.

Jennifer was leaning on the observation deck railing, gazing at the storm clouds. Jesse leaned against the railing beside her. She seemed delighted that he was there.

"Hi, Jesse. Do you mind if I call you Jesse?"

"No, I don't mind."

Jennifer batted her eyelashes. "Stormy weather can be so romantic. Don't you think so?"

Jesse wanted to avoid that conversation. "Miss Aldrich, I'll get right to the point. Another passenger said he saw you in his stateroom this morning. He thought maybe you had some intension of stealing something. Is that true?"

"Why, that's ridiculous! I haven't been in anybody's room... except mine."

"But he described you. You're the only blonde-haired girl on this boat."

"Well, whoever he saw, it wasn't me. I can assure you of that."

Jesse noticed her yellow dress. The complainant had said that she wore a white dress that morning, but that didn't prove a thing; she could have changed. Obviously, she was lying, but without any solid proof, there was no point in making any further accusations. He started to walk away, but then he remembered another curious notion. "By the way, I haven't seen your father since La Crosse, and he didn't answer the door when I knocked. Is he okay?"

"Oh... ah... yes. He's a very sound sleeper."

Jesse knew that Jennifer was hiding *something.*

22

Several days passed; the Madison had made more than a dozen short hops between small towns. The air was warmer. The river was deeper and wider. The trees along the banks were greener.

Not a single day had gone by without a passenger complaining or commenting about the young, blonde-haired girl invading someone's privacy, or in some way, presenting herself as a pest. All the claims were much the same: if the girl spoke at all, she said that she was looking for her husband, and then she always disappeared. But Jennifer still emphatically insisted that she was not the culprit.

Jesse was right at the threshold of sleep when a knock on his cabin door startled him into abrupt consciousness.

"Sadie. What are you doing here? It's past midnight."

"I'm sorry if I woke you, but you must come to my stateroom right away. There's something you have to see."

"Couldn't it wait until morning?"

"I don't think so. You should see this right now."

Reluctantly, he agreed. "Okay. Give me a minute to get dressed."

Sadie's stateroom looked more like a laboratory than a bedroom; Jesse understood why she traveled with such a large trunk. It contained all her film developing equipment, and that night she had processed a number of the photographs that she had taken during the trip. Tacked to the wall were twenty-three pictures of the river and its beautiful surroundings, selected moments in time captured in pictorial stillness.

"Here," Sadie said. "This is the one I wanted you to see."

Sadie had not only recorded scenery and river towns, but also, the people and activity on the boat as well. The picture she handed Jesse was a long shot of the Texas deck; the Madison's wake trailed in the background, and Will was leaning on the railing with his back to the camera. Next to him, stood a girl in a white dress.

"This is a very nice picture," Jesse said.

"But there's something rather strange about it," Sadie added.

Jesse took another look, but he couldn't see anything peculiar. "What's so strange?"

"When I took that picture, the girl was not standing there."

"What do you mean? Of course she was there. She looks like Jennifer Aldrich, one of our passengers. She had to be there. She's in the picture."

"Well, she's in the photograph, all right. But I'm telling you... she was not there when I tripped the shutter. Will was standing there alone."

"You must be mistaken, Sadie." Jesse studied the picture; it certainly was Will, and the girl did resemble Jennifer Aldrich. "If she wasn't there, then how do you explain the image in the photograph?"

"I don't know, Jesse. I just don't know."

"Can I take this with me? I want to show it to Will in the morning."

"Sure. Maybe he'll confirm that I've lost my mind."

When Jesse awoke, Will was already struggling with his bow tie in front of the mirror, and now that Jesse was sleeping in their quarters again, Will was in much better spirits.

"Will? Do you remember the day when Sadie took your picture on the Texas deck?"

"Yeah. She snuck up behind me. I didn't know she was there. Why?"

"Well, do you remember if Jennifer Aldrich was anywhere near when Sadie snapped the picture?"

"Jennifer Aldrich? Hell no. She was the reason I came up there. I had to get away from her."

"Why?"

"Because she kept pestering me all day with silly questions about you, Jesse."

"About me!" Actually, that didn't surprise Jesse too much; Jennifer had been flirting with him the whole time. He handed the photograph to Will. "Look at this... it's the picture that Sadie took that day."

Will stared at it with a puzzled frown.

"Who is the girl in the picture?" Jesse asked.

"I don't know. That *is* me, and that does look like Jennifer Aldrich, but she wasn't there. No one else was there."

"Are you absolutely sure?"

"Positive."

Will and Sadie couldn't both be wrong. But there *was* another person in the picture. If it wasn't Jennifer Aldrich, then maybe Jesse had been wrongly accusing her of the pesky mischief. Maybe there was another girl on board who he had not noticed. Not likely, but possible.

It was time to confront the Detectives. If they really were who they claimed to be, Simms and Pulaski would possess the skills to eke out a solution, and the problem could be squelched. Jesse still felt a certain amount of uneasiness about who they were after, and the possibility of it being Jesse still haunted him. But this mysterious marauder aboard his boat was creating too much disturbance among the other passengers. He had worked too hard to suppress an old reputation of the vessel and to regain its appeal to the traveling public, to have it washed away by sixteen-year-old Jennifer Aldrich, or whoever was responsible for the strange occurrences. He had to face his fears, and arrange a private meeting with Simms and Pulaski.

"Mr. Collins?" Jesse stepped into the clerk's office and closed the door.

"What can I do for you, Captain?"

"Do you know any more about who the Detectives are looking for?"

"No. Haven't heard a word. They're keeping tight-lipped about it."

"And do you have any clue about who is breaking into the passengers' rooms?"

"Nothing for you there either, Captain."

"Well I think it's about time I had a little talk with the Detectives. Will you arrange a private meeting with them in my quarters."

"Certainly. When?"

"As soon as possible. I'll be there waiting."

"I'll tell them right away, Captain."

Jesse sat in his room staring at the safe where all his money, along with the revenues earned by the boat was locked away. He thought about the grim possibility that it could all be lost with the gamble he was about to take. But it had to be done. The security of the Madison's passengers was more important than his own selfish interests. If Simms and Pulaski were there to retrieve Capone's money, so be it; if they weren't, even better. Jesse would do anything in his power to defend Will or Luke, should they be the prey. Anyone else was on his own.

A chill went down Jesse's spine as a knock on the door announced a visitor. Jesse quickly made himself look busy shuffling some papers on his desk. "Come in. The door's open."

The door swung open revealing only one man, Pulaski or Simms; Jesse wasn't sure which.

"Captain Madison?" the man asked.

"Yes. I'm Captain Jesse Madison."

"Your clerk said you wanted to see me about something. I'm Detective

Walter Simms." He extended his hand with the introduction and made the impression he didn't have a clue why he had been requested to meet with the Captain.

"Please... sit down." Jesse nodded to an empty chair. "My clerk tells me that you and your partner are looking for someone." Jesse kept his eyes focused on the papers as he spoke.

Simms reacted with surprise. "Well, yes... we are. But no one was to know about it."

Jesse looked up at Simms. "Mr. Collins has orders to inform me about everything that happens on this boat," he said with authority.

"Well, if you must know--"

"Yes. I must know."

"It seems that you have a jewel thief aboard your boat."

It was Jesse's turn to act surprised. He was relieved, too; the word "jewel" inserted into Simms' statement clarified that Jesse Madison wasn't the suspect that the detectives were trying to apprehend.

"Jewel thief? I guess that explains why nothing has turned up missing. No one on board has any jewels for her to steal."

Simms appeared a bit puzzled. "What do you mean by that?"

"Several passengers have been complaining to me and to Mr. Collins that a blonde girl has been entering their staterooms uninvited."

"Oh?" Simms perked up.

"I've talked to Jennifer Aldrich about it, but she denies doing such a thing."

"*Jennifer* Aldrich?" Simms acted as though all this was news to him.

"Yeah. Jennifer Aldrich. She fits the description everyone gives. But she always manages to disappear before they can call for help."

"But Captain--" Simms tried to interrupt but Jesse continued.

"Or it could be *this* girl." Jesse slid the photograph across the desk and pointed. "Sadie Perkins took this picture a few days ago, but no one knows who the girl is, and I haven't seen her, either."

Simms studied the photo a few seconds, seemingly uninterested. "But Captain, it's not Jennifer Aldrich we want."

"Then who are you looking for?"

Simms lowered his voice to nearly a whisper. "Her father... Toby Aldrich. He stole the only remaining "Wisconsin Diamond" from the man who found it, some forty years ago. We've been tracking him for over a month."

"So, what about Jennifer? What are we going to do about her?" Jesse was convinced that she was the girl everyone had seen.

"We'll have a talk with her, and then seeing as how the jig will be up, we'll arrest her father and get them both off your boat at the next stop."

"Why didn't you arrest him right away?"

"We wanted to follow him to St. Louis. We found out that he planned to sell the diamond there. We wanted to catch him red-handed."

"Should I get Jennifer in here now? We'll be landing at Hannibal in a couple of hours."

Simms thought a few seconds. "Yes, I suppose that would be the best thing to do. But wait until I talk to my partner first."

23

Nearly everyone on board had either been exposed to the mysterious passenger that no one could positively identify, or, at least, had heard accounts of her intrusions.

Spades Morgan and J. D. McDermott were still at odds, avoiding contact with each another.

And nearly everyone had grown to detest McDermott's pompous and overbearing attitude toward this crew, and every other crew of every other riverboat, who he openly regarded as a trying lot of simpletons and dolts. Augie spent most of his time relaxing on the lazy man's bench in the pilothouse, while Luke handled the navigation, reading the river charts and the river like he had done it all his life. Luke never seemed to tire of his newfound love for the river and the feel of the boat under his feet.

Reggie was learning the value of staying on Stieger's good side, even though he didn't like Stieger much, and he looked forward to every night when he could spend time with his new best friend, Luke.

And Will still struggled with the bow tie every morning, but refused to give up until it was just right.

Jesse was feeling pressure. He had weathered many storms, but this one seemed to be everlasting. There was less time to spend with Sadie, and it was only a matter of days that they would have to say good-bye. Their lives would have to take different paths, once they arrived in St. Louis. It was painful to think that he may never see Sadie again.

But the security issue had reached a point that demanded Jesse's full attention. Some of the passengers were almost to the panic stage, and the Madison risked a bad image, again. Just hours before, Jesse had considered Simms and Pulaski a menace, but now, they seemed to be the Madison's only salvation.

Jesse stood at the doorway just inside the saloon. Pulaski sat at the usual corner table alone; he gave Jesse an inconspicuous nod. Jesse knew that Simms must be ready and waiting for Jennifer's arrival in the Captain's quarters.

"Hello, Miss Aldrich." Jesse tried not to make his approach sound like another attack on her integrity. "There's quite a romantic view from the upper deck. Would you like to go up there with me?"

Jennifer batted her eyelashes. At last, the handsome young Captain had given in, and now *he* was suggesting a romantic interlude.

"Of course. I'd love to."

Jesse realized that strolling from the saloon with Jennifer could be a detrimental image, but he could appease his actions later, when the other passengers knew Jennifer was no longer on the boat.

Jesse and Jennifer stood at the railing on the Texas deck, gazing off into the lush forest caressing the riverbanks; a dozen gulls hovered close by, escorting the Madison on its journey downriver. Jesse had that far-away look in his eyes as Jennifer bid for his attention.

"This is such a beautiful place. I'd love to live here someday... right on the banks of the river."

"Yeah, me too." Jesse harbored not the slightest bit of affection for Jennifer, but he had to put on a good act to lure her into his quarters; she couldn't be given a reason to suspect a trace of deception. "Let's go to my room," he said in a lustful tone, quite certain she wouldn't refuse.

Jesse closed the door; Jennifer's expression turned to anguish when she spotted Simms. She knew at that moment that she had been tricked; she fired a hateful glare into Jesse's eyes. Jennifer had seen Simms every day in the saloon, but she had no idea that he was there to apprehend her father.

"Jennifer?" Jesse began. "This is Walter Simms with the Pinkerton Detective Agency."

Jennifer thought that she was, once again, being accused of the intrusions. She started to cry. "It's not me who has been breaking into the staterooms," she said, tears rolling down her cheeks.

Jesse crossed the room, sat on his bunk, as to get out of the way. Simms could handle it from there.

Simms disregarded the emotional display. "That's not the real reason you're here."

"Then what do you want from me?"

"I and my partner, Mr. Pulaski, were hired to find your father, and to recover the diamond."

Jennifer looked at Simms, then turned her eyes down to the floor. She said nothing.

"We know he's on this boat, and I'm sorry to have to tell you this, but we must arrest him and take him back to Sheboygan. That will happen when we land at Hannibal in about an hour."

Jennifer spoke meekly. "But he's not on this boat."

"What? We saw him on this boat as it was leaving La Crosse."

"He got off that night in Prairie du Chien... said he'd meet me again in St. Louis when I got there."

Simms' face paled. If Jennifer was telling the truth, Tobias Aldrich was already in St. Louis, and that meant the diamond was long gone.

Jesse offered his observation. "That explains why there was never an answer when I knocked on their stateroom door."

Simms knew that Aldrich was a sly character, and Toby might do anything to keep a step ahead of pursuit, but he wasn't ready to accept the story. "Well, Miss Aldrich is going to take me to her stateroom right now. We'll see if Toby is there or not."

"But he's *not* there. He's not on this boat."

Simms stood. "Come on, Jennifer. Let's go have a look... right now."

Jennifer unlocked the stateroom door and swung it open; Simms and Pulaski poised themselves to apprehend the man who had eluded them so many times. The room was empty, except for Jennifer's clothes hanging about. Only one bed had been slept in, and there was no sign that any man had ever been there.

The hunt was not over. Toby Aldrich was still at large. Again, he had cleverly slipped away.

Augie watched a nearly full moon peek over the southeastern horizon in a clear dusk sky. The Madison steamed nearer to the lights of Hannibal.

"From here to St. Louis we can easily navigate through the night. With a full moon and the search lights it will be no problem."

"But aren't you tired? You and Luke have been in the pilothouse all day."

"Captain, its your call. But Luke and I can take the wheel in two-hour shifts. And I want to give Luke some night experience anyway."

Jesse looked at Luke. "Is that okay with you?"

"Sure." Luke replied. "I'll let the crew know, so they can divide up into shifts, too."

"Better put someone at the gangplank to tell any passengers who get off the boat," Augie suggested. "Wouldn't want anyone to get left behind."

"What about stops?" Jesse asked.

"Ain't nothing much between here and Clarksville. We'll be there by morning. Then we're only a day or so from St. Louis."

It was decided. The Madison would coal up at Hannibal and steam on through the night, making up the day lost during the storm at Dubuque. Luke set off to inform the deck hands; Augie made the masterful approach to Hannibal.

There was one passenger Jesse wanted to inform, in person, of the schedule change.

"Hi Sadie. There's been a change in--"

"Don't "Hi Sadie," me! You two-timer!" she snapped.

"Sadie. What's wrong?"

"I saw you prancing off with that little blonde hussy to your quarters this afternoon."

"But Sadie! You don't understand. I was just—"

"Oh! I understand, all right. I thought we had something special, but I guess you're sharing it with every single woman on the boat."

"No, Sadie! You don't understand. Jennifer is—"

"I don't want to talk about it. Just go away!" Sadie slammed her stateroom door in Jesse's face.

"Thank you, Captain. If you hadn't come to us today, we'd still be sitting there watching an empty stateroom," Detective Simms told Jesse, and then he and Pulaski escorted Jennifer Aldrich away. Their plans were to catch a train to St. Louis, and to use Jennifer as the bait to finally catch up with her father. The diamond was probably gone forever, but at least, they could bring its thief to justice.

Sadie hadn't come out of her stateroom. Now that Jennifer was off the boat, Jesse thought that maybe he'd have a better chance to convince Sadie of the misunderstanding. Perhaps the next morning would be a wiser choice, though, when she had calmed down a bit.

An hour out of Hannibal, a ruffled banner of black smoke trailing behind the Madison hung over the water in the moonlit, still night. Half the crewmembers were in their quarters, as was Luke. Augie had volunteered to take the first watch until midnight.

Most of the passengers were relieved to hear the news about Jennifer Aldrich. With Jennifer gone, they all felt more at ease, as the musicians gathered in the saloon for another night of song and dance. But one by one, the passengers began to tire, going off to their staterooms, until only a handful remained.

"Shouldn't a young fella like you be in bed by now?" Morgan said; he sat down beside Will.

"Naw... I'm really not tired. And besides, someone has to keep an eye on things."

Will had been keeping an eye on the obnoxious, fat gambler, sitting alone at a corner table, shuffling a deck of cards and trying to entice an unsuspecting sucker into a late-night game, but there were no takers. McDermott had disappeared, and Will had not seen him leave, but he didn't care, either.

"Well, if it's all the same to you, Kid, I think I'll take a walk on the top deck, and then turn in for the night."

"Okay, Spades. See you in the morning. We'll be in St. Louis by tomorrow night, you know."

"Yep. I know. It'll be good to get home again. See y'all in the morning."

It was just after midnight when Will decided he needed some fresh air. The cigar smoke in the saloon was burning his eyes. He climbed the stairway to the Texas deck. As he passed the crew quarters where all the lights were out and everyone was sound asleep, he heard voices coming from the stern. They were familiar voices -- Morgan and McDermott. Will stayed in the shadows, out of sight; he listened and watched.

"J. D., don't lie to me," Will heard Spades say. "I saw you kill Dupree... right there, where you're standing now."

McDermott looked down at the deck beneath his feet, visualizing Jacques Dupree's dead body lying in a pool of blood, just as it had over ten years ago. He could feel the pistol in his right hand, and he could see the gold watch dangling by its chain from the buttonhole on the dead man's vest.

Morgan took one step closer. "You followed Dupree up here." He took another step closer.

McDermott looked up at Morgan. His sneer turned to frightened terror. McDermott stepped back. "No! It was an accident."

Morgan took another step. "You pulled out the gun."

McDermott stepped back. "No! It was his gun!"

Morgan stepped closer. "You pointed the gun at him and demanded that he give you the gold watch."

McDermott matched Morgan's movement with another step backwards. "No! I was just trying to scare him!"

Morgan took another intimidating step. "When he refused to give you the watch that was a wedding gift, you pulled the trigger."

"No! No! It was an accident! I didn't mean to kill him!" McDermott took two steps back.

Morgan stepped closer. "Then you put the gun in his hand... to make it look like he shot himself."

Another step backwards. "But he did! He did shoot himself!"

"No, J. D. *You* shot him. I saw you do it. Stop lying."

McDermott was nearly out of backing space. "But I'm not lying! It was an accident! I swear!"

Morgan took one more step. "You tried to take his watch, but then you saw me."

"No! That's not how it was! I was checking for a heartbeat! I didn't kill--" McDermott ran out of room trying to back away from Morgan, bumped into the railing, lost his balance and went over the side, plunging into the dark water.

No one on the saloon deck heard the splash. They were noisily involved in their own rendition of *If You Knew Suzie Like I Know Suzie.*

Morgan stood silently. Not a muscle moved.

Will ran out of the shadows to Morgan's side. He, too, stood there silently for a few moments, as he and Morgan watched McDermott thrashing in the water, getting farther and farther away.

"Shouldn't we do something to save him?" Will asked calmly.

"Swamp Scum? No, if he survives, and I'm afraid he might, another boat will pick him up. If he doesn't, no great loss."

Another minute of silence went by as McDermott disappeared out of sight in the darkness.

"I saw and heard the whole thing, you know. You never touched him."

Morgan said nothing, but he knew Will would never volunteer the episode to anyone.

"Did you really see him kill that guy?"

"Yup. Just like y'all saw this tonight."

"Are you going to tell anybody about it? I mean, about that night, ten years ago?"

"Nope. And I hope y'all will keep it our secret, too."

"Why don't you want to tell anybody?"

"Because... we're not lucky enough for him to drown. He'll be back. And if I ever see him again, I can always use that murder against him. I'd rather have the pleasure of tormenting him with it, than send him to jail."

"Why?"

"Because Jenny Dupree took care of my son, after my wife died."

Morgan didn't have to say another word. Will understood the connection, and the real reason why Morgan hated J. D. McDermott with such passion.

"Well... good night, Spades. I'll see you in the morning."

Will went to bed, but he couldn't sleep.

24

Will reached for the watch in the pocket of his jeans hanging on the bedpost. He couldn't see the hands on the watch -- it was too dark. But he knew it must be at least three o'clock. It seemed like an hour since he had heard the scrambling of footsteps during the shift change, and he was still wide-awake. He wondered if Morgan was having this difficulty in falling asleep. Probably not.

Will dressed quietly, and carefully closed the door, as not to disturb Jesse. He paced to the stern and back to his cabin door, and back to the stern again. He could hear Luke and Reggie talking and laughing, occasionally. He couldn't imagine why they were awake at this hour. The paddlewheel churning in the water was the only other sound.

He paced back and forth a dozen times or more. Then, about mid-ship, on his way forward, a sweet, feminine voice called Will's name. He stopped and turned. Only the moon cast any light, but he could see her quite clearly -- young and pretty, with golden hair that glistened in the soft light.

"Who are you?" he asked.

"I'm Jenny," the girl said.

Will peered at the girl's long, white dress. "You're the girl in the picture, aren't you?"

"Oh, I don't think so. No one's taken my picture since my wedding." Sadness shrouded her answer.

"But you are! You're the girl in the picture that Sadie took," Will insisted.

The girl didn't seem too interested with her presence in a photograph. "I've been close to you many times, and I can always hear your watch ticking. I can hear it now."

Will wrapped his fingers around the watch in his pocket, but even he couldn't hear it. "You must have mighty good ears to hear that."

"May I see it... please?" she begged.

Will retrieved the watch from his pocket and held it out in front of him. "Sure, but it's awful dark out here."

Her eyes fixed on the watch. "May I hold it?"

"Sure. I guess so."

She caressed the timepiece, as if it were a newborn child. Holding it in the palm of one hand and gently dragging her fingertips across it, and then clutching it tightly, she pressed it to her bosom. "Oh, Jacques. I've found you at last," she said lovingly, almost crying.

"Jacques?" Will was a bit confused.

"Yes. This is my husband's watch. His love is still with it."

"No, that watch was..." Will's eyes widened. He stared at the girl. "Jenny? Jacques? You're...!" He was too astonished to say any more, much less, inform the girl that she had drowned, over ten years ago.

A door opened behind him. "Will? Is that you?"

He turned around to see Luke and Reggie poking their heads out of the doorway. "Who are you talking to?" they asked.

He turned back to the girl. She was gone. He made a scan of the entire deck, but the girl was nowhere in sight.

"N-no one." His voice quivered. "No one... I guess I was just talking to myself. Sorry I woke you."

The Madison had docked at Clarksville before dawn. No one was stirring yet when Jesse awoke, and he was surprised to see Will, still sound asleep. Usually Will was the early riser.

Jesse peered out the window into the hazy morning sunlight. Gulls and swallows skimmed gracefully, just inches above the glassy water. Off in the distance, an eagle appeared from nowhere and snatched his breakfast fish from the surface in one swift, elegant swoop. It reminded Jesse of that morning in Alma, as he sat at the hotel window gazing into a near mirror image of the one before him. That was the day he began to imagine his life floating along the currents of the Mississippi. That was the day he began to really hear the music, and to feel the heartbeat of the river. That was the day he began to realize that his destiny *was* the river. And now it was all so very real. If he died tomorrow, his dreams would have been grandly fulfilled.

"What time is it?" Will sat up, rubbing his eyes.

"A little after seven -- time to get up."

Will dressed, went to the mirror and began his ritual morning struggle with the bow tie.

Clarksville claimed only a few passengers who had boarded at Hannibal the night before, and by the time the fifteen-minutes-to-departure whistle sounded, more people had taken their place, preparing for the long day's journey. A yearly festival had just ended in Clarksville, and now there was an abundance of travelers waiting to return to St. Louis. The saloon was crowded, and it buzzed with conversation and laughter. Even the outer decks offered standing room only.

Mildred handed Will a plate of poached eggs and crispy bacon. "I believe this one's for Mr. Morgan," she said, knowing Will always wanted to wait on Spades.

Will threaded through the crowded room with the plate balanced on the fingertips of one hand, high over his head, and twirling the napkin-wrapped silverware like a baton with the other. He had become quite good at it, and many of the passengers were finding his unique delivery quite entertaining.

He carefully placed the plate on the table in front of Morgan. "Good morning, Spades." He winked.

Morgan returned the wink. Their communication needed no explanation. He and Will shared a secret that would remain just a wink for all of time. Will turned and started to walk away, then stopped abruptly; he remembered the spine-tingling incident at three o'clock that morning.

Morgan was the only person alive who would believe him. He leaned closely toward Morgan and whispered, "I saw her last night."

"Who did you see?" Likewise, Morgan whispered.

"I couldn't sleep, so I took a walk on the Texas deck and she was there. I talked to her, too."

"Who? Who did you talk to?"

"Jenny Dupree."

Morgan raised one eyebrow and continued to butter his toast.

"She asked to see my watch, so I let her hold it."

"And?"

"And then she just vanished!"

Morgan took a bite of the toast, chewed and swallowed. "Better not tell anybody else. I doubt they'd believe you."

"You believe me, don't you?"

"Of course I do. We'll talk about it later. Now go serve your other guests. They look hungry."

Jesse socialized with the passengers a good share of the late afternoon and evening hours. It would be the last chance to enjoy the many friendships formed over the last couple of weeks. But his real motive for staying in the saloon was the hope of seeing Sadie. She hadn't left her stateroom all day. Mildred delivered her meals to her door, and every time Jesse knocked, her only reply was "I don't want to talk right now."

Jesse desperately tried to tell her, through the closed door, how badly he felt over the misunderstanding, and that there was never anything going on between him and Jennifer Aldrich -- that it was just an act, to lure her to the Detectives. But there was never a response from behind the door.

Dusk turned to night; Jesse stood at the railing just outside the pilothouse, staring off into the darkness. He could hear the talented jazz musicians on the Saloon deck; they were returning to St. Louis after the festival, and their buoyant Dixieland melodies captivated the crowd. The atmosphere surrounding the Madison was joyous, and Jesse wanted to be happy. But his heart was broken, and it was only a matter of hours until they arrived at St. Louis; Sadie would be gone forever.

Jesse felt a firm hand fall onto his shoulder. Augie was feeling a bit melancholy, too; he knew his days on the river were nearing and end.

"Beautiful night, isn't it?" Augie said as he leaned against the rail.

"Yeah. Sure is." Jesse's voice crackled.

"Something bothering you, Captain? You seem a little troubled."

Jesse hesitated, then realized he had to seek moral support from someone, and there was probably no better choice than Augie.

"Sadie won't talk to me anymore."

"Oh. So it's the scorn of a woman that has you lower than a swabbie's mop."

"She thinks I'm two-timin' her."

"All because of Jennifer Aldrich, I'd bet."

"Yeah. But she won't listen to an explanation, and now we're almost to St. Louis, and I'm running out of chances."

"It's not a matter of chance, Jesse."

"What do you mean?"

"Well, first of all... do you love her?"

Jesse swallowed the lump in his throat. "Yeah. I guess I do."

"Some good advice for you. You can't be *guessing* at this point. You have to be sure."

Jesse just listened.

"Sadie Perkins is a strong woman," Augie continued. "Takes a lot of courage to do what she's doing."

"Yeah, she's got guts, all right."

"She's using that little ordeal with Jennifer as her own excuse."

"Excuse? Excuse for what?"

"Sadie realizes that the two of you are going to part soon. Her behavior now is her way of easing the blow... so good-bye won't be so painful."

"So... what should I do?"

"Jesse, I'll ask you again. Do you really love her?"

"Yes. I really do love her."

"Then tell her that, like you mean it. Go after her and let her know you're not willing to give up."

"Thanks, Augie. I think I understand now."

From the description Will rendered to Morgan while they sat at a corner table and the music masked their conversation from everyone else, Morgan was strangely convinced that Will had had an encounter with Jenny Dupree. Morgan knew he'd never provided Will with any of her physical qualities, and even the picture taken by Sadie Perkins didn't reveal her face. Yet, without hesitation, Will verbally painted a perfect image of her, right down to her big, dark eyes and the dimple on her chin, her slender figure and flowing golden hair.

Will realized that ghosts weren't so bad after all, and that he really wasn't afraid of them any more. But he was devastated by the loss of the gold watch Morgan had given him.

"Are you sure you didn't just misplace it somewhere?" Morgan quizzed.

"I'm positive. Jenny took it."

"Well, don't worry about it. I know a good watchmaker in St. Louie. We'll get you another one -- with *your* initials on the cover."

Jesse was milling about through the crowd when he overheard Morgan's last words. "Get you another what?" he asked.

"Oh, Will lost his pocket watch. I'm going to get him another one," Morgan replied.

Preoccupied with his search for Sadie, Jesse would have said "Okay. That's nice" to a reply of "The boat's on fire!" He just kept scanning the throng of people, hoping to catch a glimpse of Sadie.

"Have either of you seen Sadie tonight?"

"No," Will said. "I think she's in her stateroom."

Jesse knew another knock on the door would be in vain. It hadn't worked before. He had to be patient for a better opportunity.

They listened to the band play for a while. Jesse realized there was someone else missing. Even in this congestion, J. D. McDermott would be hard to overlook.

"I haven't seen McDermott all day. Have you seen him?" Jesse asked.

"Ahhhh.... no. I haven't." Will winked at Morgan, hiding the gesture from Jesse.

Morgan suggested that J. D. might have gotten off the boat at the last stop, and just like at Prairie du Chien, he had been left behind.

Will shrugged his shoulders. "Or maybe he fell overboard."

"Come on, Will. Get serious." Jesse said. "Look around. Check his stateroom. Make sure he didn't have a heart attack or something."

Will didn't object to the search. He knew he wouldn't find J. D. McDermott anywhere on that boat.

25

The tall buildings of St. Louis came into view. Luke's heart raced a little with his thoughts of his accomplishment, but his hands stayed steady. He had navigated the Madison over half of the five hundred mile trip down the Mississippi. Never in his wildest dreams had he imagined such an undertaking, but he had done it admirably.

"Captain! We're coming up on St. Louis," Luke announced.

Jesse didn't move. He'd fallen asleep on the lazy man's bench about three o'clock in the morning. Several landings to let off passengers, and one stop for coal had caused a later arrival at St. Louis, and he just couldn't stay awake any longer.

Luke gave a long, steady blast on the whistle. It brought Jesse to his feet. The bright daylight was alarming at first, but Jesse's eyes gradually adjusted, and he realized they were just minutes away from landing at the

St. Louis levee.

"We did it, Luke." Jesse stood beside his pilot, peering out over the bow, watching the St. Louis skyline moving toward them. It was as if they were standing still, and the rest of the world was coming to greet them.

Jesse's thoughts suddenly turned to Sadie. Luke and Augie were so busy conversing about the landing procedure that they barely noticed him slip out the door. He had to be on the main deck by the time any passengers disembarked. Sadie was not leaving this boat without hearing his petition. The talk with Augie the previous night had opened his eyes to see clearly that Sadie didn't want to hear any more excuses. She wasn't looking for explanations -- she probably already knew the truth about Jennifer Aldrich. What Sadie wanted was a commitment, and Jesse was prepared to make one.

Many of the passengers who had boarded at Clarksville were gathered on the cargo deck, anticipating to set foot on St. Louis soil as soon as the gangplank hit the levee. Stieger directed the landing crew, and after doing it so many times their performance was precise.

Since Sadie was not among the departing passengers filing down the walkway, Jesse saw an opportunity to compliment Stieger and the rest of the crew.

"Mr. Stieger." Jesse spoke with authority.

"Yes Sir?" Stieger responded.

"Job well done," Jesse said with a smile.

"Thank you, Sir."

"Looks like your crewmen are working very well together, now."

"Yes Sir. They are."

"As soon as all the passengers are off the boat, and the freight is unloaded, tell the men they can take the rest of the day off."

"I'm sure they'll be glad to hear that, Sir."

"Well, they've earned it, I'm sure."

"Yes, they've all worked hard."

"Just make sure they all understand that they're expected back here tomorrow morning. We have a lot of work to do."

"Yes Sir. I'll tell them." Stieger started to walk away, but then he turned back to Jesse.

"Oh, Captain?"

"Yes, Mr. Stieger."

"That new guy -- Pierce." He nodded toward Reggie, who was exerting enthusiastic energy into securing the stern mooring line.

"Is there a problem with Pierce?" Jesse asked.

"No Sir, not at all. It's just that he has mentioned he was only going as far as St. Louie, but I think you should try to keep him on the crew. I like him. He does a good job."

"Okay. I'll talk to him, and I'll mention it to Luke, too."

"Thank you, Captain."

A few of the First Class passengers were beginning to come down the stairway from the Saloon deck. Spades Morgan was among them. If there was any man on the face of the earth whom Jesse felt more indebted to, it was Morgan. Without his help, this grand old boat would be in the hands of J. D. McDermott, Augie would be a defeated old man, and Jesse, Will and Luke would probably be stumbling aimlessly about the countryside, chasing rainbows and sleeping in the bed of a Model A pickup truck. There would never be an ample way to repay Morgan for his kindness, or for the risk he took at the expense of his own pride.

Morgan set his suitcase down and offered his hand to the Captain. "You've done a magnificent job, Jesse."

"Thank you, Mr. Morgan. I hope this isn't our last good-bye... I mean, we *will* see you again, won't we?"

"You can count on it."

"Well there's a stateroom here on the Madison for you anytime you want it -- no charge."

"I'll remember that, Jesse. Y'all take care."

Morgan picked up his suitcase and headed down the gangplank. When he reached the levee he called back to Jesse. "By the way... I think Will was right. I think J. D. *did* fall overboard. But I wouldn't worry about it too much if I were you."

Jesse laughed. "Yeah, right." he said. Morgan's stone-faced expression still kept Jesse wondering if he was just joking.

There still was no sign of Sadie. Jesse had been near the only exit from the instant the gangplank was lowered. It didn't seem likely that he could have missed seeing her.

Will came running. "Jesse! Mr. Collins wants to see you. Right away."

"What does he want? Did he say?"

"Something about a message for you."

Jesse entertained the thought of waiting until he had talked to Sadie, but Lester wouldn't have said "right away" if the message weren't unimportant. The clerk's office was at the top of the stairs, and Jesse knew he could still keep an eye on the only route to the main deck.

"Okay. Tell him I'll be right there."

Jesse's heart was pounding. Missing Sadie on this, his last opportunity to reconcile their relationship would be his worst mistake. He couldn't let her slip by.

Mr. Collins was at his desk in the tiny office, carefully jotting entries in a journal.

"You wanted to see me?" Jesse said, standing in the open doorway.

Lester finished the entry; he wasn't easily interrupted.

"Yes, Captain. I just received this message from the Captain of the Steamer Danbury." He picked up the note, handed to him by a courier, a few minutes earlier.

"What does he want?"

"He saw us come in from the north, and he wants to know if we're continuing on downriver, and asks when?"

"Why does he want to know all that?" As Jesse spoke, he noticed two rousters starting down the stairway, carrying a large trunk. He knew it was Sadie's -- it had wheels under it.

Mr. Collins seemed a little irritated with Jesse's lack of attention and began to speak louder. "Seems they have some cargo, and not enough room. He wants to know if we'll take it."

"Where's it going?" Jesse saw the blue dress whisking past the door.

"To Cairo."

"Where's Cairo?" Jesse inched his way out of the door, where he could see down the stairway.

"At the southern tip of Illinois."

"How much freight is it?" Jesse asked. Sadie was almost to the bottom of the stairs.

"It's fifty cases of--"

"Three days. Tell him we leave in three days, and we'll take his cargo." Jesse was already starting down the steps when he finished speaking.

Mr. Collins sat with a bewildered stare, and mumbled to himself, "...Dynamite. Fifty cases of dynamite."

Jesse reached the head of the gangplank just as Sadie was nearing the far end, pulling the wheeled trunk.

"Sadie! Wait," he called out.

She glanced over her shoulder, but kept walking.

Jesse stopped, took a deep breath, and called out again. "I'm not willing to give up this easily, you know."

Sadie kept moving away.

"I'm sorry that I hurt you," he said in desperation.

Sadie heard Jesse quite clearly, but acted as if trying to ignore his words.

"I love you, Sadie."

Sadie stopped as if she had struck an invisible wall. She turned and stared at Jesse. "Are you saying that you want to start over?"

"No. I don't want to start over. I want us to pick up where we left off two days ago."

A hint of a smile came to Sadie's face. "Come see me next time you're in town, Captain. I'll be moved into my house on Fulton Street by then."

"Okay. But how do I find it?"

"I don't know... remember? I'm new in town, too." Sadie kissed the air, smiled, and turned away, resuming her lonely walk into the city she was about to call her home.

PART 2

Will

A note to the reader:

The Depression years delivered our great country into a state of incomparable distress. It was a time of political and financial unrest; nearly all the nation's money was in the hands of a select, powerful few, while the balance of the population lived in poverty. To many, it meant devastation, and to some the ultimate end.

But to Will Madison, it was the time for a new beginning. It's 1932, two years after the Madison steamed out of La Crosse on its maiden voyage down the Mississippi. Will Madison tells the continuing saga, as only he knows it.

26

I t was an August Saturday afternoon. Mountains of white fluff drifted across the bluest sky I'd ever seen, and if it hadn't been for a west breeze stirring up the air a bit, the heat could've melted the brass bell on the pilothouse. The *Madison* was tied up at St. Charles for a long weekend. Not all of the maintenance chores were done, but 'cuz it was so hot, Jesse had given everyone the afternoon off to do whatever they wanted. Most everybody was tired and not in the mood for anything that involved sweat. A few of the crew had gone for a swim. Some of us sat in the shade on the open part of the cargo deck. Right then it seemed to be the coolest spot on the whole boat. Mildred, the chambermaid, the only woman on our crew, was off shopping somewhere, and I think Henry, our cook, and his assistant was in town picking up supplies and groceries. Lester, the clerk, had been in his office on the saloon deck, shuffling papers and numbers, but Augie and the engineer came by and talked him into goin' with them to find a cold drink at some speakeasy.

I was sittin' on a couple of burlap sacks of grain. With one layin' flat and the other standing upright, they made a darned good place to lean back and relax. I was thinking about how nice it might be to get away for a while — not that I disliked our life on the river; I truly loved it. I couldn't think of any other job I'd ever want, even though I'd never had a job before to compare this one with. After all, I was only sixteen, rather small for my age, and as strongly as I'd deny it, I was somewhat dependent on Jesse and the rest of the guys. Sometimes it was almost embarrassing how they looked after me and protected me if I ever got a little too close to danger, but at the same time, it made me feel real good to know that I was among a great bunch of friends that were willing to do that for me.

I thought about the past two years—since I ran away from home, if where I lived could be considered a home—and all the adventures I had had in a world that was both magnificent and frightening. I didn't miss my life back in Milwaukee at all, or the neighborhood gang—especially Tommy Horton, who picked on me all the time. He was a bully—a big kid, at least a head taller than everyone else—and he *thought* he was better than anyone else just because he was the only one of us who could bat a baseball over the fence. And I certainly didn't miss Harley, my despicable stepfather—I desperately hoped I would never see him again as long as I lived. And surprisingly enough, I didn't miss my mother, who had left me to the wolves when I was thirteen.

Now I had Jesse. He meant more to me than anyone else in the whole world, and I couldn't imagine life without my big brother. In the face of danger, Jesse stood tall and strong, and I stood in his shadow. He always seemed to know what to do when things went wrong, and I knew that I wanted to be just like him. He was the only family I had now, and I knew that whenever things got tough for me, he'd always be there—like the time last winter when I got really sick and couldn't get out of bed for a whole week. Jesse was there by my side, night and day, it seemed, taking care of me and assuring me that I would soon be well again. That's the kind of guy he is—always looking out for the rest of us. It was comforting to think that such a wonderful person had adopted me as his little brother.

Others around me, too, made me feel like I was a part of their family. Augie seemed like a grandfather to me, although I didn't know what a grandfather was *supposed* to be like 'cuz I never had one around when I was growing up. He'd tell me stories about the river and take me for walks along the riverbanks in the little villages we docked at on our trips up and down the Mississippi. I'd pick up bits of worthless junk from the mud, and he'd say, "Better hang on to that—it might come in handy some day." After he'd said that a few times, I built a little wooden box to keep all my treasures in.

Augie kept telling me, "Next month will be my last on the *Madison*," and "It's finally time to retire now that Luke has pretty well mastered handling the pilothouse." But when the first of each month came around, he was still here. I guess he loved the river and being on a riverboat so much he couldn't bear to leave it. The years were creeping up on Augie, though, and every day I noticed he was climbing the steps to the pilothouse slower and slower.

Mildred was a top-notch chambermaid; she'd been with us since the very start, too, and although there were more glamorous jobs available on fancier, bigger riverboats, she chose to stay on with us. "The *Madison*," she'd say, "is my home now," and she'd always fuss over me like a mother hen, making sure I ate proper meals and had clean clothes to wear, and that my bowtie was on straight when I helped her serve dinner to the first-class passengers in the saloon. She always smelled like lilacs, and rarely did I see her without a warm smile—like it was permanently painted on her face.

I never did tell Jesse or anyone else about Luke's and Reggie's big secret; Luke had discovered Reggie Pierce as a stowaway on the cargo deck the day after we steamed out of La Crosse and had kept him hidden until we needed a deckhand and he could hire him on. No harm ever came of this secret, which slipped out one night when Luke, Reggie, and I were alone in their quarters playin' penny-ante poker, but they made me promise not to tell Jesse. I couldn't see any harm in keeping this secret, so I agreed to honor their wishes. But the secret was even bigger than that: everybody on the crew knew what was going on between them, including Jesse and me, so it really wasn't a secret, but it didn't seem to bother anyone that they was sharing quarters and spending most of their off time together behind a locked cabin door.

Reggie was a runaway, too, from Liverpool, England. His speech sounded a little different, and I loved to listen to him talk—and I would've done anything to have muscles like his.

I had just about dozed off sitting there on those grain sacks. Half asleep, I could feel beads of sweat trickling off my forehead and down my cheeks, but I didn't feel like moving even my hand to wipe them away. There weren't any passengers on board, so I was wearing an old brown T-shirt and some blue jeans I had cut off at the knees 'cuz they were a little ragged and covered with white paint blotches. I was so sweaty I probably looked like I'd been swimming. I could hear Reggie and Luke talking near by.

"Hey Willie... wanna walk into town with us and get an ice cream?" Luke asked. He knew how much I favored ice cream.

I opened my eyes, squinting into the bright sunlight. The rest of the crew had disappeared, and I just barely caught a glimpse of Jesse headin' up the stairs to the Saloon deck. Luke and Reggie were leaning on the rail, shoulder to shoulder, with their backs to the river. Neither of them had a shirt on and they were drenched, not from sweat, but 'cuz they had just climbed out of the water after a swim. "Sure," I said. I got to my feet and started walking toward them.

I could see another riverboat much bigger than the *Madison* plowing through the water about thirty yards out, headed for a mooring on the levee. It must have been a diesel engine boat, 'cuz an air horn blasted instead of a steam whistle like ours, and just as the horn sounded, I saw something: in the path of the boat, a man was floating in the water. I couldn't believe he didn't hear the horn and swim out of the way. All I could do was yell, "LOOK OUT!" and point toward him, alerting Luke and Reggie to the disaster I was sure was about to occur.

Reggie spun around to look, and before anyone else had a chance to think about what to do, he mounted the rail and plunged into the river, all in one swift, graceful motion. I could see the boat's pilot spinning the wheel, trying desperately to avoid colliding with the man in the water, but a boat that size doesn't react quickly. Reggie came to the surface between the bow of the boat and the floating man. I could see now that the man was quite young, and I thought he might be dead. As the bow of the boat came closer to the man, Reggie reached him, swung his left arm around his chest, and began paddling frantically with his right arm. But he couldn't move fast enough, and I heard a dull thud as the hull struck his head. He lost his grip on the young man and disappeared under the water. The young man was pushed off to the side, and he bobbed in the waves, but Reggie was nowhere in sight.

"REGGIE!" Luke yelled out, and the next thing I knew, he had dived into the water, too. "REGGIE!" he yelled again and again, searching in all directions and fighting the waves splashing in his face. I kept frantically looking too, but no Reggie.

I grabbed the rail so tightly that my knuckles turned white. I stared down at the surface of the water, and I could see the terror in Luke's face as he thrashed around and kept yelling Reggie's name. By now the other boat sat pressed against the levee, about ten yards downstream, and three or four of her deckhands wrestled with the mooring ropes, tying her up. The young man's body floated toward the shore and was soon close enough to the bank that I thought I could get hold of him and pull him out of the water. I ran to our gangplank and jumped down to the levee, only a few feet from him. I don't know where Jesse came from, but all of a sudden he was there, too, helping me drag the man up onto the stony sand beach next to the bow of the bigger boat. Tall and lanky, the young stranger had no shirt, his skin was a sun-baked golden brown, and his hair was so blonde that it looked almost white against the sand. His head flopped to the side away from me. I now realized that he was just a boy—probably no older than me, and now his life had ended, I thought. As he lay limp on the sand, I noticed the silver rings that he wore on both hands.

"Is he dead?" I asked Jesse quietly.

"No, I don't think so," Jesse said. "I saw his eyes twitching a little."

More strangers, probably from the other boat, started gathering around us, and then I heard Luke call out, "Jesse! Help me get Reggie up!"

It had all happened so quickly, and I was so deeply involved with the boy, that I guess I didn't think to tell Jesse about Reggie's fate. Jesse jumped to his feet, and the whole crowd around us scurried over there, some trying to lend a helping hand and some just gawking. I stayed kneeling by the boy for a few moments, just staring down at him, not knowing what to do.

Soon they had Reggie up on the levee. He was sitting up, but hunched over, coughing and gasping for air with deep, raspy breaths. I left the unconscious young man and went over to them, too. Luke rubbed and patted Reggie's back and shoulders, and it looked like Reggie was going to be okay in spite of the fact he'd just been run over by a riverboat and was a little groggy from a bump on the head.

For several minutes everyone crowded around Reggie, eager for him to stand up and walk on his own. Suddenly it occurred to me that Golden Boy, as I had secretly named the young man, needed attention too. I turned to see how he was doing, but he had disappeared! I went quickly to the spot twenty feet away where he had been just minutes ago, apparently near dead, I thought, but only some wet sand and pebbles showed that he had been there. I peered about at the people in the crowd and scanned up and down the levee; Golden Boy was nowhere. I gazed down into the river water, and at the boat, and across to the opposite shoreline, and then back to the wet spot on the sand. My eyes caught the sparkle of something shiny on a rock, and I knelt down to investigate; it was a silver ring, like one of the rings I had seen on Golden Boy's long, slender fingers. I picked it up and clutched it tightly in the palm of my hand. Golden Boy was gone, but he had left this ring—for me, I was sure; it was his gratitude for saving his life.

"Where is he?" I heard Jesse say. I looked up, somewhat dazed by the visions of recent moments in my head. Reggie and Luke staggered toward the gangplank, Luke's arm around Reggie's waist, steadying him; the rest of the crowd seemed to be dispersing. The excitement was over.

"I don't know where he is," I said to Jesse. "He just vanished." I didn't say anything about the ring; I grasped it tightly in my fist, hiding it from sight.

"Well," Jesse said, looking a bit surprised. "Guess he must've come to and run off."

I looked at my clenched fist and then up at Jesse. The thought of showing him the ring crossed my mind, but for some reason I decided not to.

Jesse put his hand on my shoulder. "He's okay, Will... no need to worry about him now."

It wasn't that I worried over his well-being; I was curious about his identity. I had a strange sort of fascination with this mysterious Golden Boy.

"C'mon," Jesse coaxed me. "Let's go get that ice cream I heard Luke promising you a while ago."

I guess I was still in sort of a trance, thinking about what had happened, and about the mystical connection to the unknown that I held in my hand. Jesse's suggestion of ice cream slowly penetrated the whirlwind of thoughts in my head. "Sure," I said, after his words finally registered. "Ice cream would be good." I slipped the ring into my pants pocket.

But I couldn't stop thinking about Golden Boy. Who was he? Where was he from? Why had he been floating like a dead man in the river? How did he slip away without anyone seeing him? Where did he go? Why did he leave the ring behind, and did he really mean for *me* to find it? I tried to imagine him standing upright, but all I could see was his still body lying in the sand, his wet, golden-brown skin glistening in the sunlight, and his tangled blonde hair pasted to his forehead. I tried to imagine what his real name might be, but all I could think of was *Golden Boy*.

When we had walked nearly halfway to the ice cream parlor, I asked Jesse, "Is Reggie gonna be okay?"

"Sure," he replied. "He took a little bump on the noggin and swallowed a little river water, but he'll be just fine."

"Who d'ya s'pose that boy was?"

"Don't know. Never saw him before."

"Why d'ya s'pose he was floatin' in the river like that?"

"Don't know that, either."

"Think we'll ever see him again?"

Jesse just shrugged his shoulders and shook his head.

27

That night, Jesse secretly arranged for Henry to prepare a special supper to surprise everyone, and we all ate in the main saloon, where usually only the first-class passengers and the captain dined. It was nothing new to me, 'cuz that dining room was where I spent a lot of my time when there were passengers on board, and I usually ate my meals at the captain's table, too, after everybody else had been served and all the dirty dishes were toted back to the kitchen.

Any other time we were in port for a long weekend, Henry got a day or two off and everybody was on their own as far as chow was concerned. This time, though, Jesse invited the entire crew to stick around for Saturday night, but he didn't say why. Now we knew. It was his way of telling the crew, "Thanks for your loyalty." He was always doing nice stuff like that. Sometimes it was a picnic in the city park and sometimes tickets for everyone to see a show at the opera house in town. This was one of those rare times when not a single stateroom was occupied, and we had the whole saloon to ourselves. There wouldn't be any passengers on board till Monday, when the Madison headed down the Mississippi to Cape Girardeau, and then on to Cairo, and then maybe up the Ohio River to Paducah.

The delicious aroma of Henry's famous fried chicken filled the room; the crewmembers and their wives and sweethearts dug into the feast. Henry had even snuck a few bottles of homemade apricot wine in from someplace, but he wouldn't say where. Earlier in the day, Jesse had sent a message over to the *Silverado* inviting Spades Morgan to the dinner party, but word came back that he had left for New Orleans on the *Natchez* a few days earlier.

Reggie received his share of attention that night—it seemed like everyone had to give him a pat on the back for his heroic attempt to save the life of a stranger and for risking his own life to do it. And Luke got plenty of pats, too, for saving Reggie. I guess no one realized that it was me and Jesse who actually pulled the stranger out of the water, but neither of us really cared, and we didn't say anything about it.

When supper was finished, we all sat around the tables sipping the wine, and the room was buzzing with talk and laughter, but I was still thinking about Golden Boy. I reached into my pocket to wrap my fingers around the ring. Jesse noticed my terrified expression as my fingers searched an empty pocket.

"What's wrong, Will?" he asked me quietly.

I couldn't tell him about the ring, much less that I had lost it. "Oh, nothing," I said. I remembered that after we returned from the ice cream parlor, I had changed clothes, and the ring must still be in the pocket of my ragged cut-offs. I waited for an opportunity to sneak up to our quarters on the Texas. Not that I needed the ring for any particular purpose right then, but I knew I'd just feel more at ease with it safely in my pocket. Until I found a better place to keep it, that's where it would stay.

It was dark by then, and I had to light a lamp in our quarters. I was probably the only cabin boy on the entire Mississippi that shared quarters with the captain. Of course, I was probably the only cabin boy whose big brother *was the captain!*

My old jeans weren't where I had left them. I searched everywhere, but they just plain weren't there. Then I remembered—it was Saturday. That was the day Mildred gathered up Jesse's and my dirty laundry for washing. How she found the time to do all the chores she did on that boat was beyond me. What with all the bed sheets, table linens and the cook's aprons, it seemed like she was washing all the time, but as far as clothes were concerned, Jesse and I were the only ones she did them for — everybody else did their own laundry.

I ran to the laundry room, almost at the far aft end of the Texas deck. Mildred would have left our basket in there, and the cut-offs would surely be in the basket. But they weren't. Where else could they be? I panicked, just a little. The thought of losing that ring scared me, although I didn't know why. I hadn't yet examined it closely, and I didn't know if it was valuable. I felt like it was a present to me from Golden Boy, and it didn't matter if it was valuable—I just didn't want to lose it.

By the time I got back down to the saloon, they had shoved the tables out of the way and were playing records on the Victrola, and everybody was dancing. Mildred already had her apron on, and she asked me if I would help her clear away the dirty dishes before somebody knocked a table over and broke 'em all. I wanted to ask her about my old jeans right then, but it was just too noisy. I hadn't seen our crew so happy and having such a good time in quite a spell. I figured it must be the wine.

We loaded the dishes into the dumbwaiter. I knew when we went up to the kitchen to unload them it would be quieter, and I'd have a chance to ask about the jeans then.

"Mildred?" I said while we toted the dishes to the washtub. "Did you by any chance pick up my old jeans for the wash this afternoon?"

"I did," she replied.

"Well... I looked for them in the laundry room, but I couldn't find them."

"No... you probably couldn't."

"Well, then... where are they?"

"Those things were so ragged—not even worth mending —both your cheeks were fixin' to stick out soon. I tossed 'em down the garbage chute."

As soon as the dishes were in the washtub, I darted down the stairs to the cargo deck, where the garbage chute emptied into a big, wheeled bin. On the way past the saloon, I could see that everyone was still having a pretty good time, and it wasn't likely that anyone would see me digging in the garbage.

I lit a lantern and stood beside the bin, which had sides too tall for me to see over. I pulled myself up on the framework until I was teetering on the edge of the bin on my belly. The bin was about half full, and the most recent deposits were the kitchen trash from Henry making supper—potato peelings, meat market wrappers, and the like. I stretched down to paw through the mess, trying to catch a glimpse of my old jeans, and next thing I knew, I lost my balance and went headfirst into the muck. *Wearing* the garbage wasn't exactly my idea of looking through it, 'specially considering I had on my best clothes. Mildred would not be happy with me at all. So while everybody was up in the saloon enjoying the party, there I was, up to my armpits in garbage. But I figured that as long as I was there, I might as well keep looking for my old jeans and the ring in its pocket. Just under the top layer of potato peelings and some soggy cabbage leaves, blotches of white paint told me I'd found my old jeans. But my joy in retrieving them quickly melted away when I fumbled through the pockets and found them empty. It was too dark to search any more. I'd have to come back in the morning to try again.

By then, I felt so bad that I didn't want to go back to the party. I snuck back to our quarters, got out of my smelly clothes, ran down to the laundry room and slipped them into the basket, ran back to my room, climbed into bed, and doused the lantern.

"How could I have made such a mistake?" I thought. "How could I have let this happen?" Then it occurred to me that the ring could have fallen out of the pocket when Mildred picked the jeans up from the floor, and that maybe it rolled into some corner. I jumped out of bed, relit the lamp, and began the search. I examined every square inch of the floor, including the parts under the beds, but no silver ring.

I hardly slept at all that night thinking about the lost ring, and Golden Boy, and the party that I had missed, and I dreaded the idea of digging through the garbage bin in the morning. I don't think I was ever so disgusted with myself as I was that night.

The next morning I woke up bright and early, long before Jesse did. Mildred was already in the kitchen washing last night's dishes. I guess she'd just left 'em there 'cuz she didn't want to miss the party.

"Well, good morning, Will," she said. "Want to have some breakfast with me?" Her warm smile made me feel good.

"Sure," I said. "What should we have? Oatmeal or eggs? I'll help."

"I think I'd like eggs," Mildred replied.

"Me, too." I got the round wire basket of eggs from the icebox and took an iron skillet over to the gas stove.

"And what are your plans for the day, now that you're up so early?" Mildred asked me.

I hadn't planned on telling anyone about the ring or about my scheme of sifting through the trash bin, but perhaps Mildred would feel sorry for me and offer some advice, or maybe she'd even help me. "There was something in the pocket of those old jeans you threw out yesterday, and I really need to find it," I said.

Mildred just stood there, looking at me with pity in her eyes, and wiped her hands on a dishtowel. "Oh, Will," she said. I could detect a certain amount of disgust in her voice, and I knew I was in for one of her lectures. "How many times have I told you to empty your pockets before I pick up the laundry?"

I lowered my head and stared at her shoes. "Quite a few times," I mumbled.

She kept wiping her hands. "And didn't I tell you just last week that I would start keeping any money I find in them?"

"Yes, ma'am."

Mildred tossed the towel aside and put her hand in her apron pocket. "I wasn't going to give this back to you right away, but I don't want you digging in the garbage, either." She held out her open palm, and on it sat the silver ring. "Is *this* what you're looking for?"

My eyes were about to bulge out of my head. I gasped and almost quit breathing, and I could feel my heart thumping in my chest. Time seemed to come to a halt, and I knew my face was turning as red as a ripe tomato. If only I had asked Mildred about it last night, I could have avoided falling into the garbage bin and I could have had a little sleep. But now my secret was out. Mildred knew about the ring.

"Y-yes," I stuttered. "That's it." I reached out and took the shiny ring from Mildred's hand. This was the first time I had seen it clearly, without having to hide it from other people, and it was even more impressive-looking than I had thought. It was a wide, flat band about as big around as a nickel, and there were two squiggly lines all the way around it and four evenly spaced four-pointed stars etched between them. I thought it was the most beautiful ring I'd ever seen.

"That's a pretty ring. Where did you get it?" she asked.

I hadn't thought about explaining how I acquired it, 'cuz I hadn't planned on showing it to anyone—not yet anyway. But Mildred had seen it, and she knew it came from my pants pocket, and I did have to come up with some kind of story. "Oh, I found it on the levee the other day, and I didn't want to ask if anyone lost it, 'cuz then *everyone* would try to claim it."

I wasn't sure if Mildred would buy that story, but it was the best one I could think up on the spur of the moment.

"You know, Will, I think you're absolutely right. You know what they say... finders keepers."

I nodded my head in agreement, relieved that Mildred wouldn't make me try to locate the ring's owner. "D'ya think it's valuable?" I asked.

She peered closely at it. "Looks like maybe it's pure silver... could be worth a lot."

"How much?"

"Fifty dollars... maybe more."

"Wow! D'ya think?"

"Yup. I think you made quite a find there, Will."

"I sure don't want to lose it again. What d'ya think I should do with it?"

"Well the best place to keep a ring from gettin' lost is on your finger."

That made sense. I slipped it onto my finger, but it was like fitting a wagon tire to a soda straw.

Then Mildred had another suggestion. "You could always get a nice chain and hang it around your neck under your shirt. It would be safe there."

That idea sounded excellent. "Where can I get one?" I asked.

Mildred folded her arms. "There's a jewelry store on Main Street, but it's Sunday, and they won't be open today. Tell you what... I think I may have just what you need in my jewelry box. I'll get it out for you later."

"I'll pay you for it... I have some money saved up."

"Oh, no... it'll be my present to you."

"Thank you, Mildred. But can we keep this a secret? Just between us?"

Mildred smiled and frowned at the same time, like she suspected there was more to the story than I was letting on. "Sure. Now, let's have that breakfast," she said.

28

There were fewer steamers on the river now; we had been noticing the sharp decline in the past months. We'd been seeing a decline, too, in the freight, and the passenger rosters weren't nearly so long. Jesse said it was because the railroads were taking over; they were faster and they went to more places where riverboats couldn't. But then I heard the talk in the saloon when the first-classers gathered and gossiped mostly, 'cept what they were talkin' about mostly didn't sound much like gossip.

They talked about politics a lot, and how President Hoover was to blame for the crisis – the "Depression" they called it – the worst the United States had ever faced. They'd talk about how practically every bank in the country was shut down, and about how their neighbors' and relatives' life savings were wiped out by the bank failures. Then the subject would arise of how some people had to cut out eating entirely on some days, and that children were suffering from malnutrition, and then there were the grim stories about some fathers committing suicide because they couldn't find jobs, and they were unable to feed their families.

When I heard all this, I'd think about when I still lived in Milwaukee, and some of my friends at school would tell everybody they were quitin' school so they could go to work, to help put food on the table. Some of the older boys were leaving home – maybe to pick cotton down south or harvest wheat out west – because there were too many mouths to feed at home. But now, listening to the conversations in the saloon, it sounded like the farmers were suffering most of all, and they could barely afford to pay their hands a mere seventy cents a day. I wondered what those boys from my school in Milwaukee were doing.

Then I'd hear some of the men discussing how there were so few young people able to go to college, and even if they were fortunate enough to stay in school 'till graduation, there weren't any jobs for them. There were hundreds and thousands of youngsters, simply wandering about the country, undernourished, begging for food and old clothing.

Hearing that, I thought about Golden Boy, and I wondered if he was one of them, lost and homeless. I'd recall his slender body, like maybe he didn't have enough to eat, and no shirt might mean that he didn't have any clothes. I wished we were back in St. Charles, so I could look for him and rescue him from such a dismal existence, just as Jesse had rescued me.

Early Wednesday morning, we docked at Cape Girardeau, where we would be tied up a good share of the day unloading freight, and reloading supplies to be delivered to a dozen or more plantations between there and Cairo. As usual, at least twenty fellows waited on the levee with their stacks of bundles – most of them were the plantation owners' sons. I knew that because I had seen many of them before on our trips up and down this stretch of the Mississippi, and I had talked to some of them at one time or another. The Madison was one of the few tramp steamers left that would stop right at their plantations along the river, so they usually waited for us to pick them up at Cape Girardeau, where they came to buy their supplies.

By mid-morning, the big machine we had loaded in St. Louis sat on the dock, ready to be hauled to a factory somewhere in Cape Girardeau. It was so bulky that part of the railing on the cargo deck had to be dismantled in order to load it, and now Reggie and a couple of other deckhands were putting the railing back together. I watched them for a while from up on the open-air part of the Saloon deck. Not far from where they were working, I saw a young man up on the levee, eager for his turn to load his stack of packages. He looked familiar, just like Ricky Henderson from my school in Milwaukee. I hadn't seen Ricky in nearly three years. He never looked up so I couldn't get a good look at his face, but I was almost certain it was him. I figured at least one of the boys from my school had found work on a southern plantation, and even though I didn't know him very well, somehow, I felt happy for him.

"Ricky," I yelled down to him; I waved my arm over my head to get his attention. He gazed around, as several others did down there, not as to answer the call, but merely to satisfy his curiosity of who was calling. Then he looked up at me, and I immediately lowered my hand. It wasn't Ricky Henderson. I don't know which was worse: the embarrassment of calling out a name of someone who was nowhere around, or the disappointment that he wasn't. I backed away from the rail just as a strong hand grasped my shoulder. I nearly jumped out of my skin; it took me by such surprise. The touch of that hand, I knew well, and the sound of Jesse's voice seemed like instant relief.

"Will, what's wrong?" Jesse said.

"I-I thought I saw an old friend from Milwaukee down on the levee, but it wasn't... and then you scared me, sneakin' up on me like that."

"Milwaukee?" he said with a puzzled stare. "You gettin' homesick for Milwaukee?"

I shook my head. "No. I don't ever want to go back there again."

"Okay. I promise we won't ever go back to Milwaukee." Then he gave me one of his big brother bear hugs, like he always did when he knew I was upset about something, and that made me feel much better. Then he pushed me away at arm's length. His expression was that of concern.

"We have a bigger problem right now," he said.

"What?" I asked.

"Augie took sick a while ago. Mildred is looking after him in his quarters now, and you need to get back into the saloon to take care of the passengers – you know, coffee and tea – well, you know what to do."

"Is Augie okay? Does he need a doctor?"

"He's just feelin' a little faint and wanted to lie down for a while, and you know Augie. He wouldn't call a doctor if he was dying."

Dieing! Augie was an old man, nearly seventy. I didn't see any humor in Jesse's choice of words. I rather wanted to look in on Augie, but Jesse insisted that I return to the saloon.

"We'll be shovin' off soon... about twenty minutes. Luke's in the pilothouse alone; I'll be up there 'till we get under way. Mildred will be down to help you as soon as Augie is feeling better, okay?"

"I can handle it, Captain," I said, strolled into the saloon, grabbed a coffee pitcher and started making the rounds.

The steam whistle sounded and it didn't seem like twenty minutes had passed, although they probably did; I could see the hills around Cape Girardeau moving slowly away from the saloon windows. I kept watching the door, expecting Mildred's smile, and her lilac perfume following her into the room. The hands on the clock seemed like they had stopped completely.

Conversation among the gentlemen resumed. It hadn't changed much; they were talking about the economy and politicians again. I heard one man say, "The severity of this Depression is undermining the American people's sense of security." I didn't know exactly what he meant; security to me was being on that riverboat with Jesse, and three squares a day.

Then another man said, "I made the mistake of accepting Hoover's reassurances during the '28 campaign that the United States had come nearer to abolishing poverty than had any other nation, but it's clear now... that isn't so."

Yet another man came to Hoover's defense. "I agree with President Hoover. Our prosperity is just around the corner. We shouldn't interfere in any way with the automatic process of natural recovery."

They went on and on, arguing about Hoover's policies, citing numerous occasions when America had fallen into economic slumps, and had always recovered. I think I learned more about American History in that one afternoon, than I had in all my eight years of going to school every day.

The Madison made several landings, mostly on the Missouri side of the river, where the cotton plantations boasted huge white mansions within a quarter-mile from the riverbank, like tiny islands in a sea of cotton fields. Mildred still hadn't returned, and the jabbering in the saloon never stopped.

"This country is ready for a new President," one man said, "And Franklin Roosevelt is just the man we need in the Whitehouse."

"The Governor of New York?" another man added. "Why, he's a cripple. The country's in bad enough shape... we don't need a man crippled by polio in Washington."

"He's got a cocky smile," another of the men said. "I don't trust him."

"It's too bad that Will Rogers declined the nomination. He certainly would've gotten my vote."

"Mine too. The way he talks... well... he doesn't sound like a politician."

"But Roosevelt's got this New Deal."

"New Deal, New Shmeal. All that's just a happy phrase, a gimmick to make people feel better."

"Well, the way times are now, we certainly need something to make us feel better."

I didn't know much about politics, but I did know about Will Rogers. He had starred in a couple of moving picture shows I had seen, and I recalled hearing one of his speeches on the radio last fall when he told the public that we had more money and more corn and wheat than any other country in the world, and yet, our people are starving, and that America would be the first in history to go to the poorhouse in an automobile.

I gathered from listening to all the arguments that the man those gentlemen expected to become the next President of the United States, Franklin D. Roosevelt, his only asset was that he *wasn't* Herbert Hoover. Tired of Social Studies and political debate, I thought some fresh air, out on the open deck, was in order.

The refreshing southern breeze tickled at my face, and the gushing rumble of the paddlewheel boards hitting the water offered a pleasant change from the saloon chatter. Up ahead, the river sparkled almost red from the setting sun. Nighttime would soon gather us up, and we were still a long way from Cairo.

Even in the breeze, I could smell the lilacs. Mildred was near. She leaned against the rail beside me; her face smiled, but I could tell she was troubled.

"How's Augie?" I asked.

Mildred drew a deep breath and let it out. "He's had a rough time of it all afternoon, but he's sleeping now."

"Is he going to be okay?"

"I don't know, Will. I hope we can talk him into seeing a doctor when we get to Cairo."

"Think he'll go?"

"Don't know. You know how Augie is about doctors."

"D'ya think it'd be okay if I looked in on him?"

"Sure. I'll serve the passengers their supper while you sit with him. But don't disturb him... he needs to rest."

Sitting in a room with a sick old man wasn't very high on my list of fun things to do. But this was Augie, a very special person, and being here was better than listening to a bunch of strangers complaining about how bad off the country was. I had plenty of my own problems to worry about. Well, at least two or three: I worried about Augie; he looked so pale and weak. I worried about the boys from my school not having homes or food or clothes, and I didn't even know why I should be concerned about them. I worried about Golden Boy back in St. Charles, and I wondered if I would ever see him again.

I patted my chest with my fingers, hunting for the ring hanging inside my shirt. It wasn't there. I hadn't noticed that the flimsy chain had broken; the ring and the chain were bunched up at my belly.

I knotted the loose chain ends together, but I wasn't sure if it was safe to put around my neck again. What if it broke again, and what if next time I lost it all together?

Augie looked so frail and helpless, but he slept peacefully, and he seemed to be breathing quit normally, for a person sound asleep, I thought. It didn't appear that he would be awake anytime soon, so that I could talk with him. I was bored.

With the chain looped around my pointer finger and my hand in a fist, I twirled the ring around in the air, slowly at first, and then faster and faster. Suddenly, the chain slipped off my finger; it and the ring went sailing like the projectile from a catapult. The cabin door was open to let some cool air in, and to let the ring out, it seemed. I heard it bounce off the wall across the breezeway and hit the floor. I jumped off my chair and made a leap toward the open door, just in time to witness the most devastating sight. The ring slid across the deck, dragging the chain with it, under the rail and over the edge. I ran to the rail, staring down into the black water rushing past the hull, two decks below me, certain that the ring was lost forever, resting somewhere on the muddy bottom of the Mississippi River.

I felt the tears welling up in my eyes. How could I be so stupid? How could I be so careless? How could I ever forgive myself for letting my treasured ring be lost with such a foolish act? My ring was gone, and so was my connection with Golden Boy.

My vision was a little blurry from the tears that I couldn't hold back; I peered down into the dark. I was in total disbelief that I had betrayed a friendship, even before it was made, and I was willing to do anything in exchange for another chance.

It was at that moment that I began to believe in miracles. Maybe there really was a Santa Claus, and maybe there really was an Easter Bunny. There, in the dim light from a lantern on the cargo deck, I saw a sparkle, just on the outer edge of the cargo deck railing. Could it possibly be? I thought. Yes! The ring! *It had to be the ring!*

My eyes were adjusted to the twilight up on the Texas. I squinted in the blinding bright lights as I darted across the Saloon deck to the stairway leading onto the Main deck, hoping that no one would get in my way. At the bottom of the stairs, I jerked around and raced forward, across the bow deck, and then aft to mid-ship, just below the breezeway on the Texas. I held my breath and cautiously leaned out over the edge.

If miracles really do exist, then one occurred that night on the Mississippi, just north of Cairo. Sometimes I wonder if it was the spirit of Golden Boy that reached out at that critical moment, and entangled the chain on the end of the bolt where Reggie repaired the railing.

But for whatever reason, it was returned to me; the ring was in my pocket, and that's where it would stay 'till I could get a new, stronger chain.

Mildred, Jesse and I took turns sitting with Augie all that night, while the Madison was tied up at Cairo. He seemed to be getting along better, but Mildred insisted that someone should stay with him, just in case. When he finally woke up in the morning, both Jesse and I were in his cabin. I hadn't slept much at all, and I don't think Jesse had, either.

Augie woke up kind of slow, and when he finally came around, he didn't know where he was at first. Jesse had to explain, many times, that we were at Cairo, and not Cape Girardeau. I had never seen Augie so out of sorts; I just sat in the corner worrying and feeling kind of useless. I guess I was so tired by then that I couldn't concentrate on what was goin' on around me anymore. Jesse realized that, and he told me to go to bed and get some sleep. So I did.

When I woke up, we were almost to Paducah, fifty miles up the Ohio River from Cairo. I had slept right through all the whistles.

I went to Augie's quarters, carefully pulled the door open, and peeked inside. Augie was asleep, and no one else was in the room. I closed the door, hardly making a sound, and headed up the steps to the pilothouse. Luke stood at the wheel; his eyes intently studied the river ahead.

I had admired Luke, right from the very beginning. He always seemed so calm and levelheaded. Just a farm boy when Jesse and I first met him, Luke had grown spiritually more, I thought, than any of us had. He had taken his cubbing under Augie's skillful talents quite seriously; he had earned his pilot's license a few months back, and now, in the face of adversity he took total command of his post with the nobility of a worthy professional. Although he was just a few years older than me, I looked up to him, not just because he was the second highest-ranking officer on the boat, but more, because I considered him a valued friend, and I knew Jesse thought of him in the same way.

He glanced just briefly in my direction; I took up a position next to him.

"Hi, Will," he said, looking straight ahead.

"Paducah, huh?" I said.

Luke just nodded.

"Where's Jesse?" I asked.

"Probably down below, checking to see how much coal we need."

"Has he said anything about Augie?"

"Not much... just that he was still a little dizzy and weak, and that he'd probably stay in his quarters for a while longer."

"I've been sleepin' all day."

"Yeah, I know," Luke chuckled. "Jesse said you were out like a light."

"I didn't sleep at all last night."

"Up with Augie?"

"Yeah. Did Augie go see a doctor?"

"Nope. He flat refused."

That didn't really surprise me. "Oh. Well, I better go help Mildred in the saloon."

"Okay, but you won't be servin' any suppers. Not many passengers goin' to Paducah today."

"But what about tonight... on the way back?"

"Ain't goin' back tonight. We're layin' over in Paducah."

"How come? We don't ever stay overnight in Paducah."

"'Cuz I'm the only pilot now. I gotta sleep sometime, ya know."

The freight we were supposed to pick up at Paducah, goin' back to St. Charles, had wound up in Cairo by mistake, and we caught up to it there the next day. Only a half dozen first-class passengers, and maybe that many deck passengers, boarded at Paducah, making for a rather unprofitable two days from Cairo and back. I stayed up most of the night again with Augie, 'cuz I'd slept all day; my days and nights were getting all mixed up. But eventually, Augie started getting his strength back and feeling a little better, and after a few days he didn't need anyone to stay with him every night. Jesse, though, wouldn't allow him to take a shift in the pilothouse alone.

Only seven staterooms were occupied on the return trip to St. Louis from Cairo, and we gained only three more first-class fares and a small amount of cargo at Cape Girardeau. I'd never seen the Madison so empty for such a long distance. I guess this thing they called the Depression was mounting into a pretty serious situation.

Even though a whole different troupe of people was on board, I heard much the same conversations in the saloon all the way back to St. Louis, as I had heard going down to Cairo, several days before. They talked about the banks closing, all the poor people without jobs, businessmen teetering on the brink of failure, and schools that were unable to pay the teachers. And they talked about Franklin D. Roosevelt and his "New Deal."

29

Two and a half weeks seemed a long time for the Madison to make the trip we'd just completed. It usually took half that, but with Augie gettin' sick and Luke the only pilot, we couldn't very well keep her goin' night and day. Luke had to sleep sometime.

I was happy to be back at St. Charles. Mildred had promised she would take me to the jewelry store as soon as we arrived, so I could get a new neck chain for my ring. This time it would be a stronger one; I wasn't taking any more chances on losing it again. And this time I would buy it with my own money.

We tied up at our usual spot on the levee, about a hundred yards downstream from the Silverado, and as usual, a half dozen other boats were between us. I wondered if Spades Morgan had returned yet from New Orleans. I hadn't seen him for a long time and I was anxious to show him the ring, and ask him if he possibly knew of Golden Boy. Spades had been around there for years, off and on, and he seemed to know just about everybody; I could trust Morgan to keep my secret.

A few cars and trucks passed along the road next to the levee; some stopped to wait for passengers getting off the boat. From the Hurricane deck, just in front of the pilothouse, I had a good view of everything going on. Reggie and another deckhand were helping a truck driver load some crates from a furniture factory in Cincinnati into a big truck. I knew all about those crates, 'cuz Lester had sent me over to the warehouse in Cairo to fetch the freight bills, and to see to it the crates got delivered safe and sound to the Madison.

When the last crate was loaded, the truck driver scribbled on some papers, handed a copy to Reggie, climbed into the driver's seat, and drove away. Reggie and the other deckhand turned and walked toward the boat, wiping the sweat from their faces.

Then I saw him. The truck had been hiding from my view a small patch of scrubby maples across the road, and now with the truck gone, I could see him standing there at the edge of the grove, his shirtless, golden brown body, his wavy blonde hair, and the silver rings sparkling in the sunlight. He seemed to be looking right at me and grinning, and I thought I saw him wave, although, he might have just been swattin' at some skeeters. For a moment, I couldn't move. I wanted to yell a hello to him, but I didn't want to even wave, for fear of calling attention to his presence. Then he turned and slowly meandered into the shadows.

Reggie, already on his way to Lester's office with the freight bill, hadn't seen Golden Boy – I was sure of that. I spun around to look up at the pilothouse, to see if Luke had noticed. Luke's eyes were buried in the pilot's log, and he was too busy making the daily entries to notice anything.

I ran to the stairs, and I doubt that I even touched a third of the steps on the way down. Reggie said something to me as I flew past Lester's office, but I didn't pause long enough to hear what he said. I was glad to see that all the passengers were gone; I wouldn't get caught up in a mob of people on the stairway to the main deck, trying to make my way to the gangplank at the bow. Running across the levee, my eyes focused on the grove of trees across the road, and I didn't notice the car speeding at me 'till the blare of the horn nearly scared the Bejezus out of me. "Watch where you're going," the driver screamed at me, but by then I was safely out of his way, and I didn't pay much attention to him.

When I reached the edge of the trees, I stopped running. I looked all around, but Golden Boy was nowhere in sight. Once again, he had vanished; disappointment overwhelmed me. I wanted to meet him. I wanted to know his name. I wanted to be his friend.

I looked both ways down the road before I started across, kicking at the gravel with each step. At least I knew the mysterious boy must live somewhere near, and there was a good chance that I would see him again.

"Will? Are you in there?" Mildred's voice sounded simultaneously with a knock on the door. I sat on the edge of my bunk, fondling the ring, slipping it onto my finger and then off again, wishing my finger was big enough to fit it.

I pushed the door open. The smell of lilacs accompanied Mildred's painted-on smile.

"If we hurry, we can still make it to the jewelry store before he closes," Mildred said.

I dug out my pocket watch – the one Spades Morgan bought for me in St.

Louis. It was 4:30.

Jesse had finally convinced Augie, an hour before, to go to the hospital for an examination. The pains in his chest had gotten worse again. Jesse had walked to the gas station in town, where his truck was parked, and drove Augie to the hospital. They wouldn't be back for at least an hour – maybe longer. There was enough time to go to the jewelry store before supper.

"Okay," I agreed. "Let's go."

A spooky stillness hung everywhere on the boat. The end of that trip marked payday; all the crew was probably in town. Only Lester remained in his tiny office, juggling the books, like he always called it; he was getting ready to put the cash box in the safe, up in Jesse's quarters. Everyone else was gone, except for Luke and Reggie – I knew they were in Luke's cabin.

"If the Captain gets back before we do," Mildred explained to Lester, "tell him we'll be back by 5:30."

"Will do, Ma'am," Lester said. He never looked up from his work.

The jewelry store was a tiny little shop on Main Street. Bells jingled as we pushed on the door and went inside. A middle-aged man, nearly bald, and wearing a snow-white silky shirt, sat behind a glass showcase that stretched from wall to wall across the room. On his long, beaked nose sat a pair of strange-looking spectacles, with a black-rimmed little magnifying glass mounted in front of one lens. The glass shelves, inside the case, were lined with all sorts of sparkly gold and silver things: watches, rings, necklaces, earrings, tiepins, cufflinks, bracelets, and even silver spoons, fancy serving trays, sugar bowls and cream pitchers. I was quite in awe, staring at all of the dazzling ornaments.

The jeweler twisted the magnifying glass away from his eye, so it looked more like a miner's lamp in the middle of his forehead. He peered over the top of his spectacles toward me, and forced an artificial smile. "What can I do for you, young man?" he asked.

"I'd like to buy a neck chain," I replied, digging the ring out of my pocket, "to hang this around my neck, so I don't lose it." I held the ring for him to see.

A strange expression came onto his face, sort of surprised, like he recognized the ring. He took the ring, held it delicately between his thumb and forefinger, with his pinky pointing straight up. He studied the ring for a few moments, and handed it back to me. I hoped that if he did recognize it, he wouldn't say anything that Mildred would hear. She was busy eyeing the earrings at the far end of the case. I held my breath.

"I see," he said. "I have some very nice chains right over here." He pointed to the other end of the case. I started breathing again.

"I think this one would be just perfect," he said. He spread one of the chains from the case on a black velvet pad. Each link was twisted into a figure eight, and they shimmered like a string of tiny Christmas lights. It looked just the right length.

"How much is it," I asked.

"That one is only seven dollars."

A lump formed in my throat. "I only have six dollars. Do you have one for *six* dollars?"

"I'm sorry, but that's the lowest priced chain I have."

Mildred had been eavesdropping. She nudged my elbow; in her hand was a shiny silver dollar. "Buy the chain if you really want it," she whispered.

"But Mildred, I—"

"Go ahead. Get the chain."

I could feel my face turning red. But somehow, I knew Mildred wanted me to accept the dollar almost as much as I wanted the chain.

We strung the ring on the chain, Mildred snapped the clasp behind my neck, and I handed the jeweler seven dollars. With the ring secure and hidden under my shirt, Mildred and I smiled as the little bells tinkled when we walked out the door.

Jesse frowned pitifully. He stood in the doorway to the nearly empty saloon; Mildred, Luke, Reggie and me were about to sit down for supper. We'd been waiting for him, but by eight o'clock everyone was too hungry to postpone the meal any longer. Four oil lamps cast a soft orange glow flooding over the white linen tablecloth; we didn't have the generator running. The aroma of ham and fried potatoes hung in the air.

We all looked at Jesse silently, anticipating him to speak. I could tell by his droopy face and the glassy stare, that he certainly didn't have *good* news about Augie.

The four of us shared Jesse's sorrow, as he finally spoke. "Augie's had a heart attack," he said softly. His voice quivered. "And now he has developed pneumonia, too."

We were stunned. Nobody knew what to say. The joy I had been doting over my new chain slithered away.

"But he *will* recover, won't he?" Mildred asked, after a few moments of silence.

Jesse hesitated, staring about the room, avoiding eye contact with anyone. "The doctor wouldn't say too much, only that Augie needed to be in the hospital for a few days where he can get the proper care."

"Can we go see him tomorrow?" I asked.

"No, Will, not for a while," Jesse said. "The doctor said we shouldn't disturb him for a few days, because he needs total rest."

"So, what are we gonna do now?" Luke asked.

Jesse regained his composure and calmly said, "We'll carry on just as we always do. We'll do the regular maintenance and get the boat ready for another trip to Cairo. We can't let this stop us from doing our job."

"Okay," Mildred said. "Let's eat our supper now. No need for the *rest* of us to get sick from malnutrition." She spoke with a tone of encouragement, but I knew she was worried.

No one spoke at all while we tried to eat. The knives and forks clinked on the plates, but the food disappeared rather slowly. Our appetites weren't quite what they'd been.

When we finished, Mildred, Reggie and I cleared the table, while Luke and Jesse talked.

"We'll need another pilot," I heard Luke say.

"Yes, I know," Jesse said. "We can ask around tomorrow, and if we have to, we'll drive down to St. Louis on Friday."

To me, it seemed like Jesse and Luke were taking Augie off the crew roster prematurely. I guess I didn't realize, right then, the serious nature of the situation we faced.

Thursday morning, I was well on my way to gettin' another pair of jeans in the proper condition for cuttin' off at the knees. I was supposed to be paintin' the railings around the Texas, but as usual, nearly as much of the white and blue paint found its way onto my jeans, as onto the railing. But nonetheless, I was quite pleased with the outcome of the railings – *and the jeans.*

Jesse had already driven to the hospital to check on Augie's condition, and on the way back he'd met up with Luke at the Silverado, to inquire about any pilots wanting to hire on with the Madison. Like many of the excursion showboats, the Silverado stayed tied up most of the time, 'cuz people didn't have the money for too much pleasure travel. That left the possibility of an available pilot.

By then, the whole crew knew about Augie. Spirits were low, but everybody seemed aware that the times were gettin' rough, and we all knew we had to work a little harder to keep the Madison attractive and appealing to the folks that did travel.

Jesse made his rounds on the Madison with a big notebook under his arm and a pencil stuck behind his ear, stopping every once in a while to jot down things that needed repair or cleaning or painting, just like he and Augie had done together. This time, though, Luke walked beside him. They inspected the paddlewheel, and they decided that two of the planks should be replaced, 'cuz they had big cracks in 'em. We only had one spare plank; Jesse said he would go to the lumber mill, and on the way he would arrange for a coal barge to bring some coal.

Just then, I heard Lester's voice joining in their conversation. He sounded a little upset over a Special Delivery letter he had picked up at the Post Office that morning; he was reluctant to say much about it where the crew might hear. I leaned over the rail, tryin' to hear 'em better; all I heard was Lester saying, "All three of you should come up to my office so we can talk about it." *Three of you* meant Jesse, Luke and me. Whenever something important needed executive decision, he'd call us together, 'cuz legally, the three of us shared ownership of the Madison, although, I seldom had much to offer in business affairs. If Lester wanted to see all of us, I knew it had to be something big. At first, I feared it might be some bad news about Augie, but Jesse had just been to the hospital, and the hospital was just across town, so that wasn't too likely. I ruled out that it might be something about a new pilot, 'cuz it was too soon for that.

Lester, Luke and Jesse started forward to the stairs; I stepped back from the rail. Imprinted on the front of my T-shirt was a blotchy blue stripe from the wet paint on the rail. It was a dandy stripe. I liked it, although, I thought it might ruffle Mildred's feathers a bit when she saw it.

Scrunched together in the clerk's closet-sized office, Jesse, Luke, and I stared at Lester as he retrieved a paper from his top desk drawer. I had no idea of what to expect.

Lester held the paper out toward Jesse. "They've cancelled our insurance," he said.

Jesse took the paper from him and began reading.

Then Lester added, "We've got 'till midnight next Friday."

"They can't do that," Luke said.

"Well, whether we think they can or can't, *they did*," Lester said.

"But why?"

"According to that letter," Lester explained, "they have determined that this boat is too old; she's outlived her usefulness as a *safe* conveyance of passengers and cargo. They think the Madison is too much of a risk."

"But we just replaced the boilers last winter, and overhauled the engines and the rest of the machinery this spring."

"I know, Luke," Lester said. "But none of that seems to matter to the insurance company. The boat is just too old."

"What should we do?" Jesse asked. "Buy a new boat?"

Lester shook his head. "With the economy the way it is, you'd better hold off on that for now."

"Then, what do you suggest?"

Lester rubbed his chin. I could almost hear the paddlewheel churning in his head. "We should shorten our trip next week. That will give us some time to drive down to St. Louis. We'll talk to them. Maybe they'll negotiate.

If not, we can contact other insurance companies."

"Okay," Jesse said. "We'll only go as far as Cape Girardeau. We could be back by Thursday. Is that enough time?"

Then Luke had a thought. "Have they ever *seen* the Madison?"

"Yeah," I jumped in. Finally I could contribute to one of our business meetings. "We could take the boat down to St. Louis so they could see first-hand she's in tip-top condition."

"Only if it comes to that," Lester said. "Look around. The Madison is old, and quite frankly, I'm surprised they've let us get by *this* long. No. We'll show 'em all the maintenance records and daily logs, and perhaps they'll see she's still performing up to standards, without any major problems."

"Do you think that'll do it?" Jesse asked.

"It's worth a try."

As if we didn't have enough to worry about, right then, with Augie in the hospital, and the bad economy gnawin' away at our very livelihood, some big shot, sittin' in some fancy office in St. Louis, was tryin' to put us out of business. To me, it just didn't seem fair. But Jesse stayed calm. He told me and Luke not to mention any of this to the rest of the crew, and not to worry; everything would be just fine by the end of next week. For the first time since I had known him, Jesse's words didn't ring true to me.

30

The whistle sounded our Monday morning departure signal right on schedule. Only a few first-class passengers came on board, and they were already settled in their staterooms; there wasn't much for me to do in the saloon until we hit St. Louis, where our largest number of traveling clientele always boarded. I stood on the Hurricane deck, 'cuz Luke had told me to stay out of the pilothouse, where I usually rode during the departures from St. Charles. That day, we had a new second pilot; he didn't want anybody else but Luke or Jesse in the pilothouse, and once the Captain delivered the departure commands, Jesse should not be there, either. That was the protocol to which he was accustomed, and Luke thought we should show a bit of courtesy in honoring the new pilot's wishes. After all, it *was* proper riverboat protocol.

I thought about Augie lying in that hospital bed, sick and helpless; I knew he wanted to be here with us, and I wished he were here with us, too.

My eyes caught a movement among the trees across the levee. I studied the shadows, wondering if I had just imagined the motion there, and then out of those shadows he appeared – Golden Boy. The riverbank retreated slowly away. The Madison backed out into the middle of the river to catch the current. I made my way aft and gave a feeble little wave; the St. Charles levee disappeared behind us. Once again, I had missed an opportunity by only minutes. "Good-bye, Golden Boy," I whispered.

At St. Louis, as expected, the Madison took on a fair amount of cargo bound for Cape Girardeau; the staterooms nearly filled. We had been back on the river for over an hour, with Jim, the new pilot, at the wheel. Jesse sat at the Captain's table in the saloon, nursing a cup of coffee; Luke sat beside him.

Unlike our last trip, this group of passengers seemed more reserved – not the boisterous chatter about politics and the bad economy like before. I was glad of that, but a little bored with such a subdued crowd. I sat down beside Jesse, hoping for some conversation. Mildred came over, too, and sat down.

"Is everybody happy and comfortable?" Jesse asked.

"Quite," Mildred replied.

"They sure are quiet today," I added.

Just then I noticed, through the saloon windows, the bow of another boat breaking the waves beside the Madison. It was the Robinson, a bigger and faster side-wheel excursion vessel out of New Orleans. She was overtaking the Madison, as she had done on several occasions. I heard the usual whistle signals between the two boats, and watched the Robinson pull up to where the stern was right even with the window. I knew she'd soon be out of sight, so I paid little attention. But then I noticed we were staying right with her.

Luke first noticed the rumble, and then Jesse noticed the vibrations in the floor. I noticed it too. Murmurs arose from around the room as the passengers took notice. A race was on. Racing was an honored sport among riverboat pilots, especially if they won, but it was dangerous.

I saw the fire in Jesse's eyes. "What the devil is he doing?" he said. Jesse pushed his chair away from the table. "C'mon, Luke." They stormed out the saloon door, heading for the pilothouse. I followed.

"WHAT ARE YOU DOING?" Jesse yelled as he threw open the pilothouse door.

"Just a little race, Captain," Jim said, grinning from ear to ear. "I want to see what she's got."

Jim had signaled to the engineer for more steam – that which was beyond the limits of safety. I could plainly see that Jesse and Luke were producing enough steam from under their collars to power us all the way to Cape Girardeau, without firing another shovel full of coal.

"Luke!" Jesse said, "Go down to the engine room. Tell the engineer to cut her back and vent off the boilers, NOW!"

Luke was gone in an instant.

"Jim, what the hell do you think you're doing?" Jesse said to the new pilot again; Jesse's temper was on the edge.

With arrogance enough to fill a dump truck, as if he thought he could win this battle, and put Jesse out of the pilothouse with his proper protocol, Jim turned toward Jesse. "Ain't no harm in a little race down the river, and *I'm* in command here—"

"Like hell you are!" Jesse's voice blasted; the knuckles on his clenched fists were white. "It's my utmost concern to look out for the safety of this boat, its passengers and crew, not to mention the cargo that we have been entrusted with by the customers that my clerk works very hard to keep!"

Jim's eyes were as big as Half Dollars.

"Furthermore," Jesse went on, his voice still hammering at Jim with anger, "I'm not willing to give you or any other hot-shot pilot the freedom of risking a boiler explosion, just so you can have a little fun racing with another boat!"

I heard the steam venting behind us. The Madison slowed to a normal pace. The Robinson pulled away.

"But Captain, I was only—"

"You were only nothing! We're here to move passengers and freight! Safely! Not to race! Don't *ever* do that again, or I'll put you off at the next sand bar! Do I make myself perfectly clear?"

"But Captain, I—"

"The next sand bar!"

"Yes, sir."

Luke returned, panting and sweating.

"Jim," Jesse barked. "You are relieved from duty for now."

Jim glared at the Captain.

"Luke," Jesse said, a bit calmer. "Take the wheel."

As Jim stepped aside and Luke assumed control, I could see that Luke had already planned to start his shift a little early. I thought the incident was over, but Jesse hadn't finished with Jim.

"Now go to your quarters, and let me know when you've come to your senses, and that you're ready to pilot this boat safely."

Jim strutted out the door and down the steps to the Texas, sneering all the while.

Jesse called out to him. "And just remember – you're on *our* boat now, and you will *never* be in command. Understood?"

Jim didn't look back. He just raised his hand, as to acknowledge Jesse's statement.

Although Jim seemed to be an accomplished pilot, I hadn't liked him much, right from the start. Maybe it was because I resented his being there instead of Augie. He wouldn't talk to anybody but Jesse and Luke, and even then he was quite bigheaded. I guess he was one of those self-important kinds of pilots that thought the world should kiss his feet, and that all living creatures should bow when he passed by. I didn't like him, and now I knew why.

Late that afternoon, I sat at our corner table, next to the dumbwaiter, where Mildred and me usually sat if there was nothing to do for a few minutes. Mildred always had a book or a magazine handy there, although, she rarely spent much time reading them. One elbow on the table, holding my head up with one hand, and rolling the ring between my fingers with the other, I drifted into a daydream sort of daze. Quiet as it was that day, I could hear the paddlewheel planks slapping the water, and the steam generators venting every now and then.

My thoughts took me to far-away places; I envisioned poor Augie in the hospital back in St. Charles, and I tried to picture him like we first met him in La Crosse, always full of spirit and endless stories. I saw myself, a scrawnier kid, climbin' a lamppost in Milwaukee on that day in 1927, so I could get a look at Charles Lindbergh in the parade. I wondered what New Orleans was like, thinking about all the things Spades Morgan had told me about it. I worried about Golden Boy – where he'd find a place to sleep that night, and if he had anything to eat.

"Go out and get some fresh air. You look half asleep," I heard Mildred say.

I sat up quickly. Mildred closed her book and laid it on the table. "We'll be serving the supper in about an hour," she said. "You can take a break 'till then."

It didn't sound like such a bad idea. I hadn't seen the new pilot making any amends to Jesse yet, so I thought Luke would still be in the pilothouse. I hadn't been there the entire trip, so far, except for the few minutes when Jesse laid into Jim for racin' with the Robinson. I decided to go talk with Luke for a while.

I was all the way inside when I realized it was Jim at the wheel. I froze like a stone slab.

"Get out!" Jim snarled when he noticed I was there.

"I thought Luke was at the wheel now," I said.

"Well he ain't. Get out. No cabin boy belongs in the pilothouse."

Apparently, Jim had talked to Jesse, but his arrogance still lingered. His remarks cut me like a saber. I wanted to remind him that I was one of the owners of this boat, and that the Captain was my brother, but I elected to pass on any confrontation, and I'd let Jim learn those particulars on his own.

By suppertime, most of the passengers had regained their ability to talk to one another, and the saloon didn't seem so much like a tomb anymore. Of course, the topics mostly were politics and the economy, and one old lady kept complaining about her rheumatism actin' up, like she was the only person in the whole world that had any problems. But there was a couple of scruffy-lookin' men that didn't talk at all. They'd boarded at St. Louis, and they'd kept to themselves the entire time; I thought they acted kind of peculiar. I didn't think much more about it, 'cuz I'd seen a lot of peculiar people on the boat at one time or another.

Luke and Jesse sat alone at the Captain's table. In passing, I heard them discussing the new pilot's egotism, and his stupidity for trying to outrun one of the fastest excursion boats on the Mississippi. Another time by, I heard Luke questioning Jim's true abilities as a riverboat pilot. And when I brought them their apple pie dessert, Jesse said to Luke, "If we ever catch him pulling a stunt like that again, he's done as a pilot on the Madison."

Luke replied, "I'd just as soon not give him the chance. I think we should make this his last trip."

"He kicked me out of the pilothouse this afternoon," I said.

"He did, did he?" Jesse gave Luke a grimaced look.

"Yeah, I thought Luke would be up there, and I just wanted to talk to Luke for a while."

"Well, don't fret over it, Little Brother," Jesse said to me.

We put in at Cape Girardeau Tuesday afternoon. With fewer stops than normal, the Madison arrived there earlier than the usual schedule, but some of our regulars, the plantation boys, waited on the levee, just the same. They would be disappointed, maybe angry, to find out the Madison wasn't going on to Cairo. I wondered how Jesse would explain it to them, and not lose their loyalty.

After all the first-class passengers had left the Saloon deck, I happened to see Luke heading for the pilothouse, and Jim coming out. Mildred was busy changing bed sheets in the staterooms, and I had finished putting out the clean dining table linens. I wanted to be in the pilothouse, and then was my opportunity.

It felt good to be there again, watching the people below scurryin' about, and I knew Luke welcomed my company, anytime I wanted to visit.

"You got the wheel for the first shift back?" I asked Luke.

"Sure do," Luke said.

"Good." I paused while I watched Reggie cart some boxes to a waiting truck. Luke watched him, too. "I sure don't like that new pilot much," I said.

"I don't either, Will. I just hope he doesn't get us all in trouble before we get back to St. Louis."

"What d'ya mean?"

"I don't know. I just don't trust him."

"I'm glad we're goin' right back from here," I said. "Been worryin' about Augie."

"Me too. Reggie and I have been sayin' a little prayer for him every night... and you should too."

Then, Jesse came in.

"Capt'n," Luke greeted Jesse.

"Luke, we're makin' a change in the schedule."

"How's that?"

"We'll go as far south as the big bend," Jesse said, meaning about twenty miles north of Cairo. "I've been talkin' to the plantation supply runners. I told them we'd go that far, but then we've got to head back north. They agreed to that."

"Won't that put us too far behind schedule?" Luke asked.

"I talked it over with Lester, too. We should be okay."

"You *do* know that the weather report is for heavy fog down there tonight, don't you?"

"There's enough daylight left. We should be able to get down there and back before the fog sets in."

That was Jesse – always lookin' out for someone else. That time it was the plantation boys.

A few of the passengers grumbled a little when they realized we were headed south out of Cape Girardeau. I was glad I had been in the pilothouse, so I could explain the reason for the slight detour. I poured on the charm, like syrup over pancakes, and most of 'em were okay after that.

We dropped off the last of the plantation boys on a sand bar at the big bend; Jim was at the wheel again, and I could just imagine he was in his glory up there in the pilothouse, ordering the engineer to give him full steam against the current.

Despite a cloudy, dreary day, the hot air seemed to stick to my skin. Darkness would come sooner that night because of the clouds, and I hoped it would cool down a bit then.

After the supper was served, the saloon cleared of dirty dishes and the floor swept, my working day ended. I strolled down to the bow, where I found Reggie, just sitting on the deck with his arms wrapped around his knees at his chest. I sat down beside him and stared off into near darkness up ahead. We watched the searchlight beam, cutting bright white streaks through the haze, bouncing from shoreline to shoreline, picking out the white navigation markers. The river was as smooth and glassy as a morning pond. The air was so still that the only sound was the paddlewheel churning the water, more than a hundred feet behind us. Up ahead, the lights of Cape Girardeau on the west bank came into view, but with the tight schedule, we wouldn't be stopping there. Reggie and I were free to sit on the bow and watch it go by.

"Sort of reminds me of nighttime in Liverpool," Reggie said in that Brit accent I loved to hear.

"Oh? Why's that?" I said.

"The haze, and the lights reflectin' on the water... and sometimes it's so bloody foggy you can barely see three meters in front of you."

I didn't know how far was three meters, but it sounded like pretty thick fog. "You homesick for England?" I asked.

"No, not much. I like it here in America."

"Don't ya miss your friends there?"

"A trifle, but I've got better ones here."

The Cape Girardeau lights were getting nearer, but they were also getting dimmer. Within minutes, it seemed, thick fog rolled in from all directions, and we were buried under a heap of white muck. It was like the searchlight was trying to poke its way through a giant bowl of Henry's breakfast oatmeal. The fog had reached its highest stage of perfection.

I expected that the Madison would suddenly slow down, or maybe even stop, but it didn't. I held my breath, remembering that a maniac was in the pilothouse; at a time like that, the pilot must know all the answers, and know them right now, but I feared Jim didn't. I remembered what Luke had said about him getting us all in trouble, and then, to make things worse, I recalled Augie's words: "Fog can be deadly to a riverboat." I had seen plenty of fog before, but nothing like that. Reggie must have been feeling right at home.

I heard heavy footsteps up on the Texas, and voices that sounded like Jesse and Luke. I ran to the stairs and up to the pilothouse as fast as my legs could carry me. I knew Jim was in trouble again, for not slowing down, and I wanted to be there to see the fireworks.

"The levee is still three hundred yards dead ahead," Jim was saying. "I need the speed, or the current will take me off course." Jim's arrogance multiplied with every word he spoke. "Leave this to an expert. I know what I'm doing."

A moment later the searchlight beam revealed the tree line. In the fog, the blackness of the trees looked like the side of a mountain caving in on top of us. Instead of three hundred yards dead ahead, Jim had been *dead wrong* on both counts. Luke violently pushed Jim aside, jerked the telegraph lever to Full Astern, and started turning the wheel. The boat shuddered as the engines stopped, and immediately reversed the paddlewheel. She slowed a bit, but the forward momentum carried her on. The trees and the riverbank kept bearing down on us.

Then there was some crunching and banging noises, and the Madison creaked and moaned as she stopped dead with a sudden jerk, her bow pressed into the mud, just below the surface, and nearly touching the bank.

Luke quickly pushed the telegraph lever to Slow Ahead to help hold the boat in position, leaned out the open front window, and screamed to the deckhands below, "TIE 'ER UP – NOW!"

I could see Reggie leading the mooring ropes onto the bank, and wrapping them around trees. The lines tightened like a guitar string as the current drifted the boat sideways just a little.

Luke set the lever to Stop, gave Jim another brutal push out of the way, grabbed a lantern and said, "I'm going below to check the hull for leaks." He glared at Jim. "And you better hope and pray that we're *not* taking on any water!"

Now it was Jesse's turn to lay into Jim. "Go to your quarters AND STAY THERE! I don't want to see your face again tonight!"

"But don't you want me to help?" Jim said.

"NO! I don't need any more of your kind of help! Now GO!"

Jim left, and then Jesse turned to me. "Check on the passengers. Make sure everyone is okay, and tell them that everything is under control."

Everything *wasn't* under control yet, but the passengers needed to think it was. I went to the saloon, while Jesse walked the bank to determine where we landed in relation to the Cape Girardeau levee. All was quiet again, at least for the time being, and, naturally, some passengers had been startled into muteness, but some were inquisitive.

"No," I explained to them, with more quiet charm. "We didn't hit any sand bar... in this fog it was difficult for the pilot to pick out a good landing spot."

"Where are we?" "Is there any damage?" "How long will we be here?" "Can we go ashore?" The questions fired at me as if I were the target for the main prize at a shootin' gallery.

"Everybody! Things are under control. The Captain is looking for a better place to tie up right now, and we'll probably be here 'till the fog lifts a little. Just stay calm and remain in the saloon or your staterooms for now. The boat may be moving again soon."

That seemed to calm everybody's anxiety for the most part, and I thought I had handled it quite well. I said nothing of the fact that we were right back at Cape Girardeau, where we started from many hours earlier, but it was just as well that I didn't.

When Jesse returned, about a half-hour later, he, Luke and I met in front of Lester's office. Lester was a nervous disaster; he shook so bad that he had to sit down in his desk chair. Luke reported that he had inspected the hull from under the Main deck, bow to stern and there didn't appear to be any damage or leaks, that he could tell, and that all the crew was accounted for, with no injuries. I said all the passengers were okay, but a bit restless. Then the Captain informed us that the crashing and banging we heard, when we ran aground, was the hull of the Madison plowing into several small fishing skiffs tied up at the bank. None of them seemed to be damaged, except for a little one that had been swamped.

"We're only a hundred yards downstream from the levee," Jesse said. "Back 'er outa here, Luke, and we'll tie up next to a couple of other boats there."

The fog was so thick that we could barely see the other two steamers until we were right next to them, but Luke, the master that he had become, put the Madison right along side them, smooth and gentle as a fresh-picked cotton boll. Jesse and I just watched silently at the pilothouse windows, and let Luke do what he knew best.

"We'll recheck everything again in daylight," Jesse told Luke. "But don't put any of this in the log... we can't chance the insurance people seein' it."

"What about Jim?" Luke asked. "What are we gonna do about him?"

"I'll deal with him in the morning. I'm afraid I might kill him if I tried talkin' to him now."

"What if he says something to the insurance people?"

"Don't worry about that. He won't be around to say nothing."

I didn't know exactly what Jesse meant by that, but I hoped his plan didn't involve a secret burial, although, I thought Jim probably deserved it.

Dawn came with the fog still wrapped tightly around us, although, in the daylight, it didn't seem quite as severe as it had the night before. The crew busily checked everything, and Reggie even swam around the boat looking for any damage to the hull.

Tied up next to us, the Santo Domingo, a glamorous casino excursion, out of Natchez, dwarfed the Madison with her two-hundred-foot-long and forty-foot-wide hull, four decks tall. The Madison almost looked like a toy, next to her.

The crew aboard the Santo Domingo seemed to be having their share of problems too, but much different from ours. Policemen swarmed everywhere, even guarding the gangplanks, so no one could get off.

Luke wouldn't think of leaving the port until the fog lifted a little, but one of the police officers boarded the Madison, instructing him not to, anyway. The Police had already searched the Belle Flower, a smaller vessel than the Madison, docked on the opposite side of the big boat, and we would be next.

"What's this all about?" I heard Jesse ask the policeman.

"How many passengers boarded this boat since last night?" the police officer asked.

"None. We came in because of the fog… not to pick up any more passengers. We're almost full."

"Hmmm. You've had *no one* depart or board since you've been here?"

"No sir."

"From what direction did you arrive?"

"South."

"Hmmm. Where are you bound?"

"St. Louis."

"See anything suspicious on your way in?"

Luke joined in. "No sir."

"How many passengers you carrying?"

Jesse turned to Lester, still a bundle of nerves. "Thirty-six first-class," Lester said.

"Hmmm. And none of them from here," the officer said.

"They all boarded here, but yesterday afternoon," Jesse explained. "We dropped off a few plantation supply runners downriver, and then we got caught in the fog on the way back."

"I see. Don't mind if we take a little look around before your departure, do you?"

"Not at all," Jesse said. "What are you looking for?"

"Couple of men. Seems the Domingo got robbed last night by two men that somehow got on board without bein' on the passenger list. Cleaned out one of the ship's safes, and about thirty staterooms rifled… jewelry, money, that sort of thing. You know."

Jesse's eyes widened. "Lester," he said, "go check the safe."

Lester hurried away. I grasped at my chest to feel the ring through my shirt. I knew it was there, but the mention of missing jewelry triggered my instinctive reaction. Then I started thinking about the two peculiar characters that I had seen in our saloon on the trip from St. Louis, but I kept it to myself. We had enough problems without getting any more involved with that one, too. Those men were long since gone, and we'd probably never see 'em again.

Lester returned, and he reported that everything seemed to be in order.

While four police officers searched the Madison and questioned a few of the passengers, Jesse told Luke and me to find Jim. He wanted to see him right away.

We went up to the Texas, thinking we'd find Jim in his quarters, but instead, he stood leaning on the rail overlooking the paddlewheel. I couldn't help but stare at his smug-looking expression as we neared him.

"What are you looking at, you little worm?" Jim sneered when he saw me.

Luke put his hand on my shoulder. "This *little worm* just happens to be the Captain's brother, *and* one of the owners of this boat."

"So what? He's still just a cabin boy."

Jim didn't know when to stop swallowing his own feet.

"The Captain wants to see you in front of the clerk's office... right now," Luke said.

"What about?" Jim asked.

Right then, I knew Jim's paddlewheel wasn't making full revolutions. What *else* could the Captain possibly want with him? It was clear why the Captain of the Silverado had given him up so easily.

"C'mon," Luke said. "Let's go."

Jesse was waiting.

"Mornin' Capt'n," Jim said.

Jesse wasn't in the mood for any pleasantries. "Jim, last night you endangered our crew and passengers, and you damned near wrecked our boat."

"What's this? A court-martial?" Jim said with another sneer.

"Shut up!" Jesse commanded. "I don't like your attitude, and I won't have you jeopardizing our safety any more."

"Sorry... it won't happen again." Jim's face turned solemn.

"I gave you a second chance after that stunt you pulled the very first day, and you're absolutely right... it *won't* happen again. Get your gear together, and get off our boat. Pick up your pay on the way out. The clerk has it ready."

"My gear is already together."

"Then get it, and hit the levee."

We all watched Jim climb the stairs to the crew's quarters on the Texas, looked at each other, but didn't speak a word. A minute later, Jim walked up to Lester's office. Lester handed him an envelope. Jim shoved it in his pocket and headed for the stairs, without even a glance toward us. Jesse and Luke followed him down, escorting him to the gangplank. I saw Jesse talking to the policeman standing there, probably explaining why someone was leaving the boat. A couple of minutes later, the officer nodded; Jim walked down the ramp, and slowly faded into the white fog.

"Visibility is four hundred yards," Luke said. "We can still make St. Louis by midnight Friday if we leave right now."

The police had concluded their inspection and had given us the all clear. Our boilers were hot, the passengers settled in, and the crew was ready. Neither the Santo Domingo nor the Belle Flower, though, looked as if they were preparing to move.

Jesse hesitated, but then he gave the departure command. Our three-toned whistle sounded a long blast, and the paddlewheel began churning up the muddy water; the Madison backed slowly away from the Cape Girardeau levee, turned, and started our journey to St. Louis.

By ten o'clock that morning, we enjoyed a cloudless blue sky and a balmy southern wind pushing at our backside. Everybody, crew and passengers alike, were relieved to know that the pilot that almost left us stranded in Cape Girardeau was probably piloting a park bench, right where he belonged.

Luke put in some long days, sleeping only a few hours each night, and pointing the Madison upstream at the first light of day. Jesse and I took turns in the pilothouse, keeping him company; sometimes he'd let me take the wheel when we were in clear, open water, so he could rest his eyes, but I knew he was sitting back there on the lazy man's bench the whole time, with one watchful eye on the river ahead.

It was 11:30, Friday night, when the Madison nudged the St. Louis levee, and by the time we tied up the emptiest boat we'd ever come home with at St. Charles, the sun poked through some pinkish-gray clouds on the eastern horizon. The trip had been hard on everyone. I was tired; Mildred seemed exhausted, and poor Luke looked like he might sleep for a week.

Henry had breakfast -- soft-boiled eggs, bacon and biscuits -- waiting in the crew lounge. We ate heartily and talked little. No one realized, then, that that was the last breakfast we would eat together for a long time.

31

Unlike most other Saturdays before a Monday departure, the decks of the Madison lay empty and still. Only Henry and his assistant stirred about, carrying on board boxes of kitchen supplies and groceries, as they usually did, preparing for the next trip, and like clockwork, the small harbor tug towed in a coal barge to be tied up alongside. The firemen would be back later in the afternoon to fill our coal bins and to help the engineers with the regular maintenance of the boilers, engines and the rest of the machinery.

Jesse and Lester had packed up all the maintenance records and logbooks right after breakfast, loaded them into Jesse's truck and set out for St. Louis, hopeful of returning by nightfall with the renewed insurance papers in hand. Mildred was sound asleep in her cabin, and I suspected Luke and Reggie were sleeping, too, 'cuz I hadn't heard or seen anything of them since breakfast. After Henry finished his work, he left. I had slept several hours before we arrived at St. Louis, and again until just before we tied up at St. Charles; I didn't feel tired, but I did feel very alone.

I roamed the decks like a lost puppy. I didn't know why I felt so abandoned; Jesse would only be gone for the day, Mildred, Luke and Reggie were near, and I was certain that many of the crew members would be there later on for the usual Saturday get ready routine. But now the boat seemed so lonely and forgotten, like she had been left somewhere on the beach of a deserted island. I sat on the two equally forgotten grain sacks, gazing across the vacant cargo bay floor; the scene reminded me of the first time I set foot on those decks nearly two years ago. I remembered how Jesse had so carefully loaded, on this very deck, his Model A truck, with all that money hidden under the seat, and how he and I had snuck the money bags up to the safe in our quarters late one night, when no one was around. I recalled how that floor was rarely seen since, because it was always covered with freight, sometimes stacked up to the beams under the Saloon deck. But now it was bare again, just like that first time we saw it; Augie's cheery smile and Norse brogue wasn't there to cheer me up. Everywhere I looked, all the surroundings seemed just another shade of gray.

"Would you like to walk with me to the hospital? To check on Augie?" Mildred's voice echoed in the void space. I didn't realize 'till then that it was almost noon. Half the day had slipped away.

Suddenly a strange fear swallowed me. As much as I wanted to see Augie again, I felt afraid of what I might see at the hospital. I gathered my courage.

Reluctantly, I said, "Sure."

Mildred and I walked across town, hardly talking at all. I kept thinking the whole time that I shouldn't have come, dreading the sight awaiting us, and painfully wondering what I would possibly say to Augie, once we arrived. Part of me wanted to turn back, but part of me wanted to let Augie know that I missed him, and that I was eager for him to be back with us on the Madison.

The smell of iodine and rubbing alcohol hung in the air like invisible fog. I could almost taste it. Pale gray walls seemed to close in on us, and everyone spoke softly, their voices like secretive whispers. A deeper depression choked me as we approached a tall desk and the white uniformed nurse standing behind it.

Upon Mildred's request to visit with Augie, the nurse frowned and informed us that Mr. Bjornson had taken a turn for the worse over the past couple of days, and that the doctor didn't want him exposed to any degree of excitement. "But I guess it would be okay if you looked in on him... just for a few minutes," she whispered, as if she were sneaking us around the doctor's orders.

I hardly recognized Augie; his face was pale and withdrawn, his body thin and frail. With a slow, laborious movement, he turned his head toward us; a distant, questioning stare was in his eyes. Mildred leaned down and gently kissed his forehead. "Hello, Augie," she said softly. He didn't speak.

I stepped closer, laying my hand on his. "Hi, Augie," I whispered. His hand felt almost cold; his weak fingers slowly wrapped around mine. Augie looked toward me, and although his lips couldn't form a smile, his eyes did.

A few moments went by. I felt the grip of Augie's fingers lessen, and then he closed his eyes. What little color was left, drained away. He was gone, but I knew he had waited for me before he donned his wings.

Mildred spent most of the afternoon in her quarters; all I could think about was that I wished Jesse were there. The reality, I don't think, had completely set in yet when the crew started arriving. I noticed a few watery eyes among them as the announcement was made to them of Augie's passing, and I didn't see Luke for quite a while. But everyone knew they had a job to do, and they went about their work. They accepted the fact that Augie would never be back; they would never hear his cheerful greetings; they would never again look up at the pilothouse and see his friendly smile beaming down at them.

With Jesse absent, Luke was in command. Once he regained his composure after the initial shock, he stepped in like the professional he was, and I admired him even more for his emotional fortitude. It was his strength and determination that day that kept us all going, even in our deepest sorrow.

Luke made the rounds that day with the big notebook, and I began to realize more, the importance of my role on the Madison, when he asked me to join him. No one grumbled that day about any tasks assigned to their attention. Somber, intense faces tackled every chore, and by the end of the day, under a flag flying at half-mast, the Madison gleamed, fit for royalty.

Mildred made ham sandwiches for Luke, Reggie and me. At nine o'clock when Jesse still hadn't returned, we all sat down in the saloon, where a colorful arrangement of wildflowers Mildred had gathered, and two

205

slender white candles burned brightly, adorning the Captain's table. Conversation was scarce. Luke informed us that the crew was still unaware of the insurance problem, and that we weren't to say anything until Jesse came back; we wondered what was keeping Jesse and Lester so long. But other than that, not much was said.

It was then that I realized that I had not shed a tear all day, and I couldn't help wonder if that was wrong. Augie had passed away. *Augie*. One of my dearest friends, and I had not shed one, single tear. He had died holding my hand, and I had not cried for him.

With a heavy heart, I slowly climbed the stairs to our quarters, closed the door behind me, and leaned against it. I said a little prayer for Augie, and I cried.

Jesse still hadn't returned by Sunday morning. I walked up the levee to the Silverado, where Spades Morgan made his permanent home in one of her staterooms. This wasn't a place for a kid to hang out, but the personnel there had come to know me quite well, 'cuz I frequently visited Morgan whenever I had the chance. I didn't know if Spades had returned yet from New Orleans; I hadn't seen him.

Golden Boy hadn't been around where I could see him lately either; I wondered if, perhaps, because he was probably a homeless nomad, that he might have moved on. I hadn't stopped thinking or worrying about him, but there were just too many other things happening to go out searching for him. Although I thought of asking Morgan about him, the subject never came up.

"Is Spades Morgan back from New Orleans?" I asked one of the custodians.

"Yes, and I seen him just a few minutes ago... I think he's in his stateroom," he told me.

I didn't bother to check the gambling rooms where Morgan often spent his time. I remembered him telling me that he made a point of never gambling on Sunday mornings. I knew just where to find his stateroom, the Carolina.

I knocked on the door. Morgan's poker face greeted me. "Come on in, Will. Good to see you again," he said.

The staterooms on the Silverado were much bigger, and fancier than those on the Madison. Velvet drapes, the color of blueberries, graced the windows; soft, satin-covered chairs with claw foot legs rested on thick Persian wall-to-wall carpet; a gold-framed mirror, and a huge painting of snow-capped mountains and pine trees hung on the walls. In the middle of the room, a single white rosebud in a sparkly clear vase sat on a gray marble-topped table. All that luxury was why Morgan preferred the

Silverado. I couldn't blame him.

"How are things on the Madison?" Morgan asked.

"We've had our share of problems," I said. I paced around the room, not knowing exactly what words to use about Augie. "Had kind of a bad trip last week." I stared for a moment at the few trinkets lined up on the bureau top, and the two small photographs propped up there. I had seen them many times. One was of a beautiful young woman, Morgan's wife, who had died long ago, and the other was of a cute little toddler, their son, clutching a floppy-eared stuffed rabbit.

Morgan sat down in one of the fancy chairs. "Why was it a bad trip?" he asked me.

"The new pilot almost wrecked the boat in the fog down at Cape Girardeau. Jesse fired him."

"New pilot?"

"Yeah."

"Why—"

"Augie got real sick a couple of weeks ago..." A lump the size of a watermelon caught in my throat.

Morgan didn't say anything. He just looked at me with his usual blank stare.

I swallowed hard. "Augie died yesterday."

There was silence for a few seconds, and then I detected sorrow in Morgan's words, "Yes, I know, Will. I heard this morning."

Morgan finally broke another long period of silence. "How are you getting along, Will?"

"I'm doin' okay," was all I could get out. I wanted to tell Morgan how badly I really felt, but I figured he already knew that.

"How's Mildred takin' it?"

"Pretty hard. She cried a lot, but she's doin' better now."

"How about Jesse?"

"Jesse and Lester ain't here. They're in St. Louis on business. He doesn't know yet, and we don't know where to reach him." With that, I felt myself wanting to cry, but I fought it off.

"And Luke?"

"Luke's okay too, I mean, we're all pretty sad, but Luke's been the one keepin' us all from goin' crazy."

"A fine boy, that Luke."

I just nodded, and we sat in silence again for several minutes.

"When's the funeral?" Morgan asked.

"Don't know yet. Mildred is taking care of all that. She knows the preacher at the little church on the edge of town."

After another long pause, I said, "Morgan? We're the only family Augie's got, and… well… will you come to his funeral?"

"Of course I'll be there, sittin' right next to you, Will. I wouldn't miss something that important."

I glanced up at Morgan, and I tried to smile.

"And don't you worry none," Morgan said. "Augie has a lot of friends on the river. Plenty of 'em will be there."

The crew started gathering on the Madison's Saloon deck early Sunday evening. It was almost like one of our parties that Jesse would throw, but there was no music playing on the Victrola. There was no singing and dancing. There was no laughter, and there was no Jesse.

I wasn't quite sure which caused me more pain that night: Augie's death, or Jesse's absence. That was the first time in two years that Jesse had been away for so long; it seemed strange, not to feel the security of Big Brother. Luke and me knew that there was good reason for him to be away, and I suspected, by then, that Reggie knew it too. The timing was just all wrong.

I sat close to a window, where I could watch the road across the levee, hoping that the next lights appearing there would be Jesse's truck. Each time that car lights passed by, without stopping, my spirit sank lower. Someday, I thought, I would have to become accustomed to Jesse's absence; someday our lives would take different paths, to fulfill our individual needs, and to pursue our own dreams. But at that very moment, I wasn't ready for that. I desperately wanted Jesse to be there. I couldn't imagine any other needs or dreams, other than riding up and down the Mississippi River on that boat, just like always, unless, of course, I could learn to be a good pilot, like Luke, and spend my days in the pilothouse, steering the boat, instead of being cooped up in the saloon most of the time, listening to the passengers whining for more coffee and arguing about politics.

I noticed Luke standing on a chair, calling for everybody's attention; when he had it, he stepped down.

"The Madison will not depart tomorrow as usual," he began with a somber expression.

At first, I thought he would reveal our confidential insurance problem, but he didn't.

"As you probably all know by now," he went on, "Augie's funeral will be on Wednesday at one o'clock, in the Good Shepherd Lutheran Church. I'm sure you all want to be there."

Mildred had already told me that; it wasn't news.

"With due respect to Augie," Luke continued, "we will remain in port until next week. Mildred, Will, Reggie and I will be staying here to look after things, so there is no need for any of you to report for duty, unless we call for you. I just need one or two volunteers to stay here on Wednesday, during the funeral."

A couple of the newer deckhands that hadn't gotten to know Augie all that well, yet, raised their hands. Luke nodded. I peered out the window at the passing car lights.

After the grieving crew left, Luke and Reggie headed off to their quarters. I said good night to Mildred, and climbed the stairs to seek the comfort of my bunk. I said another little prayer for Augie. I worried about Jesse. But I didn't cry.

32

I awoke Monday morning only to see Jesse's bunk untouched. He would be back later that day, I assured myself. It seemed logical that he and Lester had not been able to complete the insurance business on Saturday; that was the best explanation I could think of at the time.

I heard some pans rattle, and I poked into the kitchen.

"Good morning, Will," Mildred said. "Ready for some breakfast?" She scooped up a couple of bowls of oatmeal.

Mildred seemed a bit more cheerful now; her painted on smile was only half there, but the lilacs were in full bloom.

"Sure," I said, even though I didn't feel very hungry.

We carried the bowls into the crew's dining room; I sprinkled my oatmeal with brown sugar and cinnamon and began eating.

"D'ya think Jesse will get back today?" I said to Mildred, halfway through my oatmeal.

"I don't know. I sure hope so," she said.

"What d'ya s'pose is taking 'em so long?"

"That insurance stuff, I imagine. They must've run into some difficulties."

"You *know* about the insurance?" I said.

"Jesse explained it to me just before they left."

"Who else knows?"

"Just Lester, Luke, you and me."

It didn't surprise me that Jesse would have told Mildred, but Lester deemed it an issue to remain unknown to the rest of the crew, as it might cause alarm, and maybe panic; we couldn't risk the loss of such good crewmen.

I understood a little about the business end of running the boat, after being on it for two years, and from helping Lester at times. I knew we couldn't operate without insurance, in case something bad happened, and I did know that Lester and Jesse appeared quite concerned about the problem.

Another urgent matter loomed before us – Augie's funeral – a matter that Jesse knew nothing about, yet. I wondered which was more important: the insurance problem or Augie's funeral. But I didn't want to question Mildred about it, now that she seemed a little more at ease.

Then Mildred calmly said, "I have to pick out some nice flowers for Wednesday, and take care of some matters with the funeral director." Her voice began to race a bit. "Then I have to see the Reverend at the church. I'll be gone most of the day... and I made some sandwiches for you and Luke and Reggie. They're in the icebox. And be sure to tell Jesse where I am if he gets back, and—"

"We'll be just fine, Mildred," I interrupted.

Mildred looked at me and smiled. I think she finally realized that she was no longer talking to a little boy.

What would I do to occupy my time, when there was nothing to do? Most all of the chores to ready the boat for the next trip were done; a few windows still needed washing, and I had noticed a couple of spots that could stand some touch-up with a paint brush, but I didn't feel much like working. Luke and Reggie had wandered off to buy new shirts for the funeral; I didn't want to be too far away, in case Jesse came back; going for a walk along the levee or visiting with Morgan was out.

Some cane fishing poles rested on pegs along the walls on the Texas. They didn't belong to anybody in particular – anybody could use them during their off-duty time. I found an empty tin can, dug up a few earthworms, baited a hook and dangled it into the river off the cargo deck.

After about an hour of monotony, I hadn't caught anything. I didn't care. I didn't *want* to catch anything, and if I had, I would've thrown it back. I watched several other riverboats coming and going. I waved to the pilots as they passed by, and I wished that Augie would have gotten well, so that we could be on the river, too, where we belonged.

I kept one eye on the road, expecting to see Jesse's truck come into view. It didn't. Then, I'd glance over to the grove of trees just beyond the road, thinking about Golden Boy; I hadn't seen him in quite some time, and I wondered where he might be. Poor Golden Boy was probably wandering around somewhere, feeling just as lost and lonely as I.

Bored with the fishing and the watching, I jerked the wormless hook out of the water, dumped the rest of the worms overboard, and returned the cane pole to the pegs. I'd never been too keen on fishing, anyhow.

A bucket of water, some rags, and six windows outside the saloon took up a little time; I hoped Luke and Reggie would come back while I was busy cleaning the windows, so they would see that I was doing something constructive, but they didn't. I don't know how I managed it, but in the process of dumping out the dirty water, the bucket somehow overturned in the wrong direction as I hoisted it to the railing top; soaked from bellybutton to shoelaces with the slimy stench, I stood there a few moments, feeling almost as bad as I had the night I fell into the garbage bin. As long as I was already wet, and my clothes were a mess, I thought it was a good time for a bath.

When I climbed out of the tub and dried off, I stood in front of the big mirror in our privy, taking in big gulps of air to puff up my chest, and flexing my biceps, like I had seen Reggie do several times. I looked at myself more closely, exhaled and relaxed my arms. I studied the fellow in the mirror staring back at me. I noticed that I wasn't that scrawny little kid anymore; I was at least a half a head taller than two years ago, I had arm muscles that were actually identifiable, my ribcage didn't stick out, and my shoulders were filled out and broader. Admittedly, I wasn't the muscular mass I saw in Reggie or Luke, nor was I the towering, six-foot column of sturdiness, like Jesse. But I wasn't the puny little twerp that Jesse pulled out of the flood, either.

I just stood there for a couple of minutes staring at the naked body in the mirror. I realized, then, that I had grown up some physically, and that I was more equal to Jesse, Luke and Reggie, something that I had not considered before. And after spending the last two years living among them and working alongside mostly other adults, I had matured spiritually as well, more than if I had stayed in Milwaukee, amidst a band of schoolboy misfits. Of course, I had picked up a few bad habits along the way too: I could smoke a cigarette and drink a mug of home-brewed wine with any of 'em, and my poker playing ability even surprised me, sometimes.

I was pleased with the newly discovered developments I saw in myself. It made me feel good to think that I shouldn't be looked upon as some helpless, little kid, that needed protecting; I was proud of the person I had become.

But then I thought about all those years that I had dreamt of becoming an adult, about ridding myself of all those childhood woes, and about doing the things adults do. Over the past two years, I had schooled myself on being an adult; I had learned the responsibilities of caring for myself. I had Jesse, mostly, to thank for that.

I had also witnessed the dismal complications and painful difficulties that accompany adulthood. What had seemed so temporary, and easily overcome, at first, the condition that they called the Depression, had levied crippling blows to even the most powerful men, reducing some to an identity that resembled something not much more than a dry leaf in a whirlwind.

I had lived the disappointment of rejection, the fear of danger, the terror of disaster, the agony of loss; I had faced it all with courage and the determination to survive. Now that I was within reach of the status I had so long desired, it almost seemed like I had been grasping for something no man would ever want. I wished, for a moment, that it could all go away, and that I could reclaim my youth, and start over. But even I knew that wasn't possible; my life had to continue on, from that very moment in time, and I had to play with the cards that I was dealt.

Abruptly interrupting my thoughts, the door opened with a jerk. Luke and Reggie briefly stopped dead in their tracks, as if they had been startled by an oncoming locomotive. They looked at me, and then casually walked toward the washbasin. In the hastiness of the moment, when I decided to bathe, I had failed to bring dry clothes with me. I froze with embarrassment for my nudity. I thought of running to my quarters as fast as my legs would carry me, but then it occurred to me that I had no reason to be ashamed. I wanted Luke and Reggie to take notices of the real me.

"If you want," Luke said, "I'll go with you tomorrow and show you the store where we got some nice white shirts for Wednesday." He looked at me while he scrubbed his hands. "You could probably use a bigger one that fits a little better."

I glanced, once again, at my image in the mirror. I smiled. It wasn't so much the fact that I probably needed a new shirt, but a *bigger* one. I think Luke noticed.

As promised, Luke escorted me into town to the clothing store on Tuesday morning. Considering the circumstances, even though I had just taken another giant step toward independence, Luke's companionship that day seemed reassuring. Jesse's absence, especially now that Augie was gone, had left me feeling so alone, and even adults, I thought, had the right to feel lonely.

Luke had always been another port in a storm for me, whenever Jesse was beyond reach. Most of the time, though, the pilothouse was the only place we ever met alone, because he usually spent his off-duty time with Reggie. But as we strolled around the town, after buying the new shirts, with no particular destination in mind, and in no hurry to return to the boat, we talked about things that we had never discussed before. We talked about the insurance problem that Jesse and Lester were attending to, and how operations on the Madison would have to change, now that Augie was no longer with us. We talked about the economy and how it had affected our profits; even politics entered in, and I was proud to be able to offer my views on the subject, although, I was just repeating statements that I had heard among the passengers during recent trips. I built the courage to ask Luke about piloting, and if he would teach me as his cub, like

Augie had taught him. He said he would, and that he thought it was a good idea, but that it would be hard to find another cabin boy to fill my shoes. I guessed that he meant he admired my abilities, and that made me feel good.

We stopped at a little café for lunch; we listened intently to the conversations around us, instead of talking; we heard the same old gripes about the bad economy, and how the people hoped a new president would lead the country into better times. We heard them mention Franklin Roosevelt and the "New Deal," but no one seemed to know what the New Deal really meant.

Most of the afternoon, Luke, Reggie and I lounged on the Saloon deck, occasionally playing a few hands of penny ante poker, while Mildred ironed our new shirts. We worried about Jesse's return in time for the funeral, and about how we would tell him the news.

All the talk about Jesse not making it back in time caused a great deal of uneasiness. I knew he'd be back, and I didn't want to hear any more of it; I decided to take a walk over to the Silverado, to visit with Morgan.

He wasn't there. Disappointed and discouraged, I walked the levee, alone, to clear my head of all the turmoil; it didn't seem to work. I climbed the stairs to the pilothouse, stood at the wheel, and imagined myself in total control of the Madison, steaming down to Cairo, reading the eddies and dodging sandbars, sending the commands to the engineer, and sounding the whistle as I made the graceful approach to the docks.

Then, reality settled back in, and I recalled the scratches left on the cargo deck walls, retrieved the paint bucket and a brush from the engineer's tool room, and went directly to work.

A few of the deckhands, their wives, and girlfriends, started to converge on the Madison Wednesday, late morning, dressed in their finest attire, like I had never seen them before. We had all agreed to meet there, and to walk to the church together.

Jesse and Lester still weren't there; I paced nervously around the decks, watching the road for Jesse's truck.

"Couldn't we postpone the funeral 'till tomorrow?" I asked Mildred. "I know Jesse will make it by then."

"We can't keep the Lord waiting," Mildred said.

"But *He* wouldn't mind," I said. "Especially when He *knows* it's Jesse we're waiting for."

"But all the people are here today."

"I'd bet *they* wouldn't mind either," I said.

All the begging and pleading that I could possibly muster wasn't going to change Mildred's way of thinking. I detected a bit of irritation, so I finally gave up. I think she wanted this to be over; Augie's passing had been hard on her, and when he was finally laid to rest, she could feel more at ease.

Just the thought of Jesse not being there devastated me. I could barely begin to imagine the degree of guilt and regret he would to endure; I knew Jesse, all too well.

At 12:30, everyone gathered on the levee at the Madison's bow, and we began our sorrowful walk to the church. I noticed that there were a good many more riverboats tied up there than usual. And still, no sign of Jesse's truck.

I'd never been to a funeral, but I had an idea of what it would be like. I hadn't even been to church much, since my mother left; that was the only real memories that I had of her. I recalled her telling me that "God takes care of fools and babies," and I always figured that I must fit into one of those categories, because He'd certainly done a good job of it so far. After Mom was gone, Harley never went to church. A few times, Jesse and Mildred and I went, if we happened to be tied up at one of the river towns on Sunday morning, and a church was near. Only a time or two had we attended a service at this one, but it had been long ago.

Nearly the whole Madison crew was gathered on the lawn, outside the church, and then I knew why I had seen so many riverboats tied up at the levee that day; Captains and crew members from other boats were there, too, and it was plain to see that Augie was well-known, and had been well-liked by so many people. They were there to pay tribute, and to say their final farewells to a lost friend. I recognized many of the faces from encounters on the river, but I knew very few of their names – at least, I couldn't remember them on that day.

But the most important riverboat Captain, Jesse Madison, was not among us.

Surrounded by the people who were dear to me – Luke, Reggie, Mildred, Henry – all helped to ease the anxiety of what was to come. But another person that I so wanted to be there, wasn't – Spades Morgan. A very special person, Morgan had touched all our lives; if it hadn't been for his help to save Augie's boat, none of us would be together, and Augie's passing would have perhaps gone unknown to any of us.

I thought it seemed strange that Morgan was nowhere in sight when everyone started filing into the church; he said he would be there to sit beside me.

We sat in the pews near the front of the church, and I made sure that there was room for Morgan and Jesse. Somehow, I just knew; *they would be there*. I stared down at the floor by my feet; I was afraid to look toward the front, to Augie's coffin, draped with an American flag and surrounded with flowers of every color. If I looked, I would cry, I thought, so I didn't.

I listened, as the most beautiful, most precisely perfect organ music that I had ever heard, began to play. I remembered hearing church organs before; the novice players sometimes stumbled from key to key, trying desperately to find the right note. But this performance was perfect. I closed my eyes to listen, without visual distraction, to every note and every chord, in their pleasing, comforting exactness.

Then I felt a nudge against my arm. I opened my eyes and looked to my left. There, sat Spades Morgan. His usual stone-faced expression glanced toward me, nodded, and winked. Then Jesse followed, stepped across in front of me, and sat down to my right. He put his arm around me with one of his big brother bear hugs, but that time, it felt a lot different; Jesse's tears dripped on my shoulder. Morgan leaned close to me and whispered, "I went to St. Louis and found him for you."

"How did you ever find him?" I asked.

"I know all the hotels in St. Louis," he said.

Just then the organ stopped playing, and the Minister began the service with an opening prayer. I felt safe and comforted, with Jesse on my right and Morgan on my left.

When the organ started playing again, and the Preacher motioned for the congregation to stand as they sang a hymn, I glanced up at Morgan. He took my hand firmly in his and gave an affectionate squeeze. He stared toward the front of the church, and I thought I saw the sparkle of a tear starting to form in the corner of his eye. His hand squeezed a little tighter. Rarely had I seen Morgan show any degree of emotion, but I was seeing it then, and for good reason, I thought.

While we were standing, I had a better view of the front of the church. Briefly, I looked at the coffin. My eyes drifted toward the organ. I gasped. The nape of my neck tingled, and then my whole body seemed to go numb. For the moment, I forgot about the tear in Morgan's eye. I forgot about why we were there. All the singing voices around me slipped into oblivion, and the whole world seemed to stop – all except the organ music. I questioned what my eyes saw; had I become so wrapped up in the emotion of the day that I was beginning to see things that really weren't there? I must be dreaming this entire event, I thought, but then I felt Morgan's hand squeezing mine. I looked down at his hand; it was real. Everything around me was real. It was no dream.

Again, I focused on the organ and the person responsible for the magnificent sounds it produced. There, before my very eyes, I watched his fingers gliding over the keyboard, caressing each note as it went on its way to join the wonderful multitude of sound that filled the church. There, before my very eyes, playing the most beautiful music I'd ever heard, was Golden Boy; his golden brown arms extended from a silky royal blue robe, his bare feet slowly danced on the foot pedals, and his glistening blonde hair fluttered as he bobbed his head in rhythm with the music.

How could that be? How could a homeless, wandering boy have found his way to that organ bench, and be creating that splendid sound? How could that urchin of the earth appear there, that day, groomed and refined, as if he were the offspring of royalty?

Then it occurred to me that I had been influenced into assuming he was poor, lost and homeless, with no one to protect him. Apparently, I had assumed wrong, and then I felt better, relieved to know that I wouldn't have to worry about his welfare. But, aside from the fact that he no longer needed my help to survive, I still desired his friendship. I had nurtured an unseen bond between us, and he had left, for me, a token of that friendship.

I tried to concentrate on the Preacher's voice, but his words seemed as distant as the moon and the stars. I couldn't stop thinking about the discovery I had just made. Now and then, I would glance over to where Golden Boy sat. Twice, I thought our eyes met, but he turned away quickly.

When I was able to concentrate again on the service, an eloquent eulogy rolled forth, tears flowed, and murmuring sobs seemed to be coming from every direction. I didn't have to look at Jesse to know his muffled weeping was among them.

Another long prayer was read, and then, as we sang the last hymn – the hymn Mildred had chosen, because she knew it was Augie's favorite, *Onward Christian Soldiers* – I took notice of the words. It was then that I began to understand their real meaning. It wasn't the cadence for Augie's march to the great beyond, but instead, it was intended for *our* benefit; it was Augie's final message to us.

The ceremony ended. Six crewmen from the Madison carried the casket down the center isle and out the front door to a waiting hearse. As we all filed out behind it, another familiar hymn drifted through the air. Chills went down my spine as I listened to Golden Boy play *Amazing Grace*. I had never heard it played so superbly.

I could still hear the organ when we began walking the quarter-mile to the cemetery. Mildred, walking arm in arm with Jesse, sniffled and continually wiped her tears away with a white hankie. I had never seen Jesse looking so sad. Morgan kept one hand on my shoulder the whole way. Luke and Reggie walked behind us, so I couldn't see their faces, and I didn't turn around to look.

Assembled around the gravesite, the Minister led us in reciting the Lord's Prayer. It was then that the reality of the day brushed against my soul. We were there saying our final good-bye to our beloved friend.

33

I was beginning to believe that the parade of people coming and going on the Madison would never end that afternoon and evening. I'd never shook so many hands. Captains, their pilots, and nearly all the crew from at least twenty riverboats filed in and out; townspeople and businessmen and their wives dropped by, all expressing their sympathy to all of us on the Madison for our loss. Even some of the fishermen we saw frequently on the river stopped in, and I think there were a few people that came by just to get a free cup of coffee. But Mildred graciously poured a cup for anyone who wanted one, and we all accepted the cards and the handshakes, as we tried to smile with each greeting. I stayed pretty close to Jesse the whole time.

Slivers of guilt poked at me now and then; that day was intended for honoring and remembering Augie, and mourning for his loss. I had done plenty of that; I was, indeed, sad that he would no longer be with us on the Madison; I felt sad that we would never take the walks along the riverbanks, and that I would never again hear his wonderful stories, or see his smile tucked into that gray beard. I was truly heartbroken that he was gone.

But, perhaps, I was also a little too much in a hurry to put it behind and move on. Or maybe it was so many other things racing around in my head that continually distracted me into a state of daydream. I wanted all those people to be gone, so Jesse could make his announcement that the insurance problem was resolved, and that the Madison would resume its regular schedule.

I envisioned myself standing beside Luke in the pilothouse, the spokes of the wheel planted firmly in one hand, and the telegraph lever in the other, my eyes focused on the river ahead, as Luke coached me around islands and sandbars.

Then my thoughts would drift back to the scene at the church – not the people, or the Preacher's sermon, or even the flag-draped casket and flowers – but instead, the barefoot organist. The sight haunted me. Now that I knew he wasn't homeless and hungry, and that I shouldn't worry about his well being, Golden Boy still remained a mystery.

"Turn her into an excursion vessel," I heard one Captain say to Jesse. His words jerked me from my dream state.

"Convert the cargo deck into more staterooms," another Captain said. "The railroad has all but taken over the freight business."

Jesse nodded in agreement with the older, more experienced men. "Yes, we've considered that," he said, but his voice didn't carry much enthusiasm. I think he was just being polite; his thoughts were far from remodeling the Madison, considering the current state of affairs.

It was well past seven o'clock when the last guests left the boat; my arm felt like it had shaken every hand from there to New Orleans. Most of the crew left, too; only Reggie and one other rouster helped Mildred gather the coffee cups left scattered about, while Luke, Jesse, and I stood silently leaning against the cargo deck railing.

"C'mon," Jesse said to Luke and me. "I want to talk to you alone... up in the pilothouse."

It was difficult to distinguish that invisible line between Jesse's agony over Augie's death, and the matters of setting our course back on track. Plainly, the shock of Augie's death, though, overshadowed anything else he might've had on his mind.

"I can't believe Augie's gone," he said. There was a quiver in his voice.

"Guess we're *really* on our own now," Luke said, his voice solemn and shallow.

I just stared down at my shoes. Although I felt badly about Augie and I already missed him deeply, I had been through so many of those conversations that usually resulted in tears, and I hoped that it would pass quickly. But I knew that Jesse hadn't yet been afforded the opportunity to vent his sorrow, the way the rest of us had; I would struggle through the suffering as long as it took – just for Jesse. I think Luke felt the same.

"If it weren't for Augie," Jesse said, "we might not be here... together."

"Yeah," Luke said. "It's kinda hard to believe we've been on this boat for two years."

I decided to be a part of the conversation. "Just think of all the good times we've had."

"And all that we've learned," Luke added.

"And all the good friends we've made," I said.

Luke said, "And I'd bet that Augie would want us to just keep on doing what we've been doing."

Jesse looked at us, tried to smile, and then abruptly turned our discussion in another direction. "I didn't get the insurance," he said, and then deep vertical furrows appeared on his forehead, like a plowed field.

Luke and I exchanged staggered stares, bowled over with the statement we hadn't expected to hear.

"You mean—?" Luke started.

"We don't have insurance," Jesse said again.

"So, what are we gonna do?"

Jesse took a deep breath. "Lester and I talked to at least a dozen or more agencies in St. Louis. All but three turned us down flat."

"And what about the three that didn't?"

"They're taking it into consideration... wouldn't give us a commitment, one way or the other."

"Do you think—?"

"Don't know. I have to go back next week to see them again. We're dead in the water 'till then."

"What will we tell the crew?"

"Nothing... for now," Jesse said.

"But they're expecting to go back to work next week."

"Then keep them busy with maintenance."

"Everything is done. We have to tell them something."

"Well, then, tell them we're waiting for an insurance inspection... you won't be lying to 'em."

"Okay," Luke said. "But I don't think they'll be too happy."

"I've talked this over with Lester. You can also tell them that we'll pay them half their wages for next week," Jesse said.

Luke glanced around the room, as if he were out of comment.

Then I said, "That'll work... I'm sure they won't mind a little paid vacation."

"Right," Jesse agreed.

Luke left the pilothouse quietly, looking distraught with the outcome, but I think he knew that we had no choice in the matter and that it was the best solution for the immediate dilemma.

Jesse and I stood there in silence for a few moments. I could tell that there was something else troubling him, but it might have been leftovers from the previous conversation. He appeared as though he wanted to talk; he'd take a breath to speak, but every time, he'd settle back down, like he had second thoughts of what he was about to say.

Eventually he said, "So, how have you been getting along, Will?"

"Okay," I said. I wanted to avoid speaking of Augie's death. "But I worried about you."

That made Jesse feel good. I could tell by the little curl of a smile that formed on his lips. Then the wrinkles came back to his forehead and concern filled his eyes.

"I --," he hesitated for a moment, "I found Sadie while I was in St. Louis."

"Sadie?" I must have looked puzzled for an instant.

"Yeah, Sadie. You remember her, don't you?"

"Sure, I remember her. But I thought you—?"

"I – I never stopped loving her, Will."

"But it's been so long. What's she doing now?"

"She has her photography studio, but business is kinda slow now."

"Do you still love her?"

"More than ever."

"Does she still love you?"

"She has a little boy now."

"Oh. She got married to someone else."

"No, Will. She's not married."

"Then how--?"

"You remember all those nights on that first trip that Sadie and I went to the hotels?"

"Yeah, I remember."

"Well... little Philip is my son."

I didn't know what to say next. I was flabbergasted. At first I felt a little anger, but I quickly realized being angry at a time like that, wouldn't help either of us. Then a bit of jealousy came over me, but that didn't feel right, either. Apprehension then took its place in the lineup, and I settled on that one.

"Are you going to marry Sadie?" I asked.

"If she'll have me," Jesse said.

"Does that mean you'll live in St. Louis?"

"Probably."

"And I won't see you any more?"

Jesse looked at me as if I had gone daft, put his arm around my shoulders with one of his tender, Big Brother bear hugs and said, "Will, I told you a long time ago that you'll *always* be my little brother, and *nothing* will ever change that."

I pushed him away. A little anger festered inside me again. Even I had figured out that everything doesn't stay the same forever, and Jesse seemed to just be humoring me with idle talk.

"What about the boat?" I said.

"We still have the boat, and just as soon as I can get this insurance mess straightened out, we'll be back on the river again... just like always."

But everything *wouldn't* be just as always – at least, it didn't seem to me. Augie wouldn't be with us, we risked losing some of the crew, and now Big Brother had a family he would run off to, and maybe we wouldn't even port in St. Charles any more, but at St. Louis, instead. I *hated* St. Louis.

I let all the advancements toward adulthood slide right down the garbage chute. I allowed myself to believe all those assumptions, slipping into a rather childish way of thinking – *without* thinking. Out the door I stomped, and headed aft, down the Texas, pouting, and feeling like I had been rejected and already abandoned, when in fact, I knew that was not the case at all.

I heard our door open and close. "Will," I heard Jesse call out to me, but I kept walking. Then I heard a knock on another door; it had to be on

Luke's door, because his was the only other cabin occupied on that end of the boat. That door opened, and closed. I knew that Jesse had gone into Luke's quarters. On tiptoes I made my way to Luke's window, hoping to hear their conversation, but I couldn't make out everything they were saying. I did hear Jesse saying something about leaving again on Saturday, to go back to St. Louis, and Luke's reassurance that everything on the Madison would be fine. I thought I heard Jesse mention my name, but the rest of it was too muffled to understand.

I didn't stick around there long enough for Jesse to catch me eavesdropping. By the time he came out, I was at the railing overlooking the paddlewheel, doing some heavy thinking about the mistakes I had just made.

The night was calm, but with all those horrible thoughts jumbled up in my brain, I wasn't. Confused, jealous and a little angry, with myself mostly, I felt like I had bitten into a sour green apple with no place to spit it out. A tremendous change in my life was about to occur, I thought, that I wasn't prepared for. I feared Jesse was upset with me for pushing him away; I knew that I should go to him, right that very minute, and make amends, but in the end, my foolish pride stood in the way, and I decided to let Jesse come to me, when he was ready.

Jesse hardly spoke to me for the next two days before he left for St. Louis; he and Luke stayed busy, running around town, taking care of business, and apologizing to the regular customers for the Madison's delay in getting back on schedule. If it hadn't been for Reggie and Mildred, I wouldn't have had anyone to talk with.

I sat on the edge of my bunk Saturday morning and watched Jesse pack his clothes for a stay in St. Louis. He said nothing, not even a "good morning." I felt terrible about how I had wrecked our relationship with a few thoughtless words.

"I'm sorry," I said to him.

Jesse stared at me a few moments, like he was waiting for me to continue, and then went back to his packing.

"I'm sorry I said all those things the other night," I said, hoping it would get a conversation started.

Jesse said nothing. He just kept putting clothes in his suitcase, and I thought he was ignoring me.

"I'm sorry I pushed you away and walked out," I tried again.

He closed the suitcase, snapped the latches, and stood there, gazing out the window. Then he stepped close to me, put his arm around my shoulders, like he usually did, and said, "We'll talk about it more when I get back." He looked into my eyes and smiled.

Right then, a warm sensation wrapped me like a blanket; I didn't want him to go away again, but I knew that he had an important mission to accomplish, so we could get the Madison back on the river. I almost asked Jesse to take me with him, but then I remembered how much I disliked the big city, and I didn't want to interfere with another important matter, to which he would certainly be attending – Sadie, and his son.

"But I want to talk about it now," I said.

"Will, I promise we'll talk when I get back. Right now I have to be going... I'm late already."

34

"**Y**ou know that boy that played the organ at Augie's funeral?" I asked Mildred.

She paused in the middle of ironing and folding some laundry, squinted a bit, as if trying to recall, and said, "Yes, I know who you mean."

I knew Mildred wasn't anywhere near the boat that day we pulled Golden Boy out of the river, so she *couldn't* have known it was him; I didn't think Jesse had noticed him at the organ either, and no one else but me and Jesse had really gotten a good look at him that day on the levee. Now that Jesse was long gone to St. Louis, and Luke and Reggie were somewhere in town, Mildred and I were alone. I felt safe in asking.

"Do you know his name?" I said.

Mildred slowed her folding pace as she thought. "No, I can't recall ever hearing his name."

"He sure plays good, don't you think?"

"Now that you mention it, I've heard him play at that church on Sundays before, and yes, he is very good."

Mildred was usually a good source for information, and that time, she had handed me a jackpot. I thought I had asked enough questions for the moment; I didn't want her to get curious about why I was curious, although, I had no logical reason that my curiosity should be kept a secret. I left her with the ironing, strolled up to the pilothouse, sat down on the lazy man's bench, and began scheming. If Mildred had seen him at the church other Sundays, perhaps he would be there that Sunday too, and perhaps that was my best opportunity to finally meet Golden Boy. So far my luck hadn't been too good.

I reeled the chain up out of my shirt and admired the mysterious ring that had never left its place, hanging around my neck. What would I say to

Golden Boy when I did finally meet him? Would I ask questions? Would I simply say, "Hi, my name is Will?" Would I mention the ring? Or would I begin by complimenting him on his wonderful music? I finally decided that situation would handle itself.

I went back to the laundry room.

"Mildred? Are we going to church tomorrow?"

She looked at me with surprise. I guess that wasn't so unusual, as I had never made such an inquiry before.

"Well, no... I'm going to see my sister in Kansas City. My bus leaves at seven o'clock in the morning. But I suppose I *could* take a later one."

Mildred knew that I rarely left the immediate vicinity of the boat alone, except to visit Morgan on the Silverado, now and then. She must've thought I needed an escort.

"Oh. I didn't know you were leaving," I said.

"I told Jesse... thought he would tell you."

"No, he didn't. You're coming back, aren't you?'

"Well of course I'm coming back," she said, as if I had said something to offend her. "I figured this would be a good time. Might be my only chance 'till winter, and I hate traveling in the winter. But I'll take a later bus, if you really want to go to church."

"Oh, no. You don't have to change your plans. I'll go by myself."

"Are you sure?"

"I'll be fine."

By the time I arose on Sunday morning, Mildred was well on her way to Kansas City. She had baked a big pan of biscuits for us before she left. We didn't have the electric generator running, so I hadn't heard Luke's radio playing, but I had heard Luke and Reggie talking and moving about, into the wee hours of the morning. I knew they'd still be asleep 'cuz they were up so late.

I ate a few biscuits with jam, hurried through a quick bath, and put on my best pair of trousers and my new white shirt. I watched the clock like a schoolboy waiting for recess; I didn't want to be late for church.

Walking alone, along the outskirts of town to the church, seemed a bit strange at first. The sense of freedom and independence slowly crept in with every step. I tried to reason why I had been so apprehensive to wander on my own for the past two years. I concluded that I had just been too dependent on Jesse as my security blanket; I had become almost a hermit on the Madison, knowing I was safe there from the harsh, unfair elements of the outside world.

But that day, the environment looked different to me. It felt good to be walking alone. I was older, I thought, and better equipped to handle life's difficulties; I wasn't a scrawny, vulnerable kid who needed constant protection. I had come a long way since my days in Milwaukee. Then, I started thinking about all the grief and suffering that other people endured, and how close that it was striking home, and how I didn't envy Jesse's position as the bellwether of our faltering enterprise. I sincerely hoped that there really was a "New Deal," whatever that meant, coming in with the new President.

I tried to put all that out of my mind. I didn't want to think about trouble.   I was about to embark on a new friendship that I was certain would change my perspective, and break my self-imposed restrictions.

I selected a seat near the front of the church, where I had the organ in plain view. Barefooted Golden Boy, once again, filled the expanse with magnificent sound, as the worshipers ushered in and filled the pews around me.

Then it got quiet and the service began. There were the usual prayers, the reading of the Scriptures, and we sang a hymn or two, and then the Preacher took to the pulpit and began his sermon. His topic, that day, involved children, and how, as they were confirmed and grew older, they seemed to drift away from the church. The words drilled into my ears, and for a moment, I thought he was talking directly to me.

I glanced around the congregation, without turning my head too far; I noticed that he was right – the chapel was filled with adults and their small children, but very few youngsters my age, give or take.

"I was discussing with the church council the other day," the Preacher's sermon went on, "about the problem we have with pigeons nesting in the bell tower. One of the councilmen suggested I should baptize and confirm those pigeons, and we'd probably *never* see them again."

A few muffled chuckles echoed among the usual coughs and baby cries.

With the final hymn sung, the ushers filed everyone out, while Golden Boy played on, performing masterfully. I waited outside on the lawn, watching the people shaking hands and greeting one another, as they ambled off, some to cars parked in the street, many, just continuing their journey on foot to homes somewhere in the town.

The organ had stopped. Almost everybody was gone, and I expected Golden Boy to eventually come out, but only the Preacher appeared at the door. He saw me, smiled, and waved. I waved back, and then he disappeared into the church, closing the door behind him.

How could I have missed Golden Boy? I thought that I had been watching closely, but apparently, not closely enough.

All that week, Luke, Reggie, and I stayed close to the boat, knowing that Jesse wouldn't return until Friday, and that Mildred would be gone that long, too. Luke informed the crew of another week's delay, and most of them seemed satisfied with the paid time off. Lester dropped in, now and then, to shuffle papers and juggle a few numbers, but we didn't talk to him much. Each day, boredom would set in, so we'd hunt up some little chore that needed doing; by Wednesday night, Reggie had put a fresh coat of red paint on the paddlewheel planks, Luke had the pilothouse sparkling like a jewelry shop, and I had washed every window on the Saloon deck, at least three times.

By Thursday afternoon, I was ready to get off that boat for a while. I announced to Luke that I would visit Morgan.

I think that I might have disturbed Spades from a nap, but as always, he graciously invited me into his plush stateroom.

After the usual "Howdy, how are you? I'm okay" routine, and after I had taken my usual lap around the room, examining the trinkets and the pictures of Morgan's wife, and the little boy holding the stuffed rabbit, I sat in a chair next to Morgan.

"What was it like when you were a kid?" I asked him.

"What d'ya mean?" Morgan said.

"Was there all this kinda trouble? I mean with money and politics, like there is now?"

"It was worse."

"How?" I couldn't imagine a time when things could be much worse than what we had right then.

"Money? We didn't have any," Morgan said.

"How did you get along without any money?"

"Barter."

"What's barter?" I asked.

"That's when you trade a half-dozen chickens for a pig."

"Huh?"

"Will, I was born and raised in a much different society than you know here."

"Where was that?"

"Austria... I came to America when I was 15, and I'd lived in an orphanage since I was 7."

"Were you parents dead?"

"No... my mother was declared insane and was sent to an institution; the state took me away, to the orphanage."

"What did your father do?"

"He had a little farm, and he was a carpenter."

"So you lived in the orphanage for eight years?"

"My Aunt Sophia, who already lived in America, fought with the Austrian government all that time to get me out of there, and when she finally succeeded, my mother had been released from the mental institution, hired a lawyer to regain my custody, and we were living in Vienna."

"So, what happened? How did you end up in America?"

"My father had been killed in a train wreck in the mountains. Aunt Sophia knew that my mother was in no condition to care for me, or provide me with a good home. So one day, about two weeks after I got out of the orphanage, she showed up in Vienna, scooped me off the street, and we traveled for days by train into France, where we boarded a steamship and came to America."

"Wooooow. Your Aunt Sophia kidnapped you?"

"I guess you could call it that."

"And your mother never came looking for you?"

"I doubt if she even cared that I was gone."

"So, what did you do when you came here?"

"I worked on my Uncle's cotton plantation in Louisiana, went to school and learned English. After a few years, I got real tired of the farming, got a job on a riverboat, and that's when I met Maria."

"Maria. Was that your wife's name?"

Morgan nodded. "We got married in 1917, and a year later, little Matthew came along."

"That's the little boy holding the rabbit in the picture," I said, glancing toward the photograph.

Morgan nodded again. "When Maria died, he was only two years old, and Jenny Dupree took care of him when I was away on the riverboat. Then, when she drowned, Matthew was adopted by a family in New Orleans."

"And you've never seen him since?"

Morgan gave me one of his stone cold stares. It was always hard to read his emotions by facial expression, 'cuz he rarely changed his expression from the trained poker face he always wore. But I could tell that he was either upset with me for poking into his private business, or that he just didn't want to talk about the subject any more. I understood why.

Morgan taught me a couple of card tricks, and by then, it was time to go back to the Madison for supper.

No one but me knew about Jesse and Sadie getting back together; Lester probably knew, but I guessed that Jesse had sworn him to secrecy, and I certainly wasn't about to say anything. I almost expected Sadie and little Philip to be with Jesse when he returned on Friday morning, so he could proudly introduce to us the newest member of the family. He was alone.

Jesse had little to say before we reached the pilothouse. His face showed concern, but his eyes glowed with optimism as he peered out into the late summer haze. Luke and I sat on the lazy man's bench, eagerly anticipating good news. Jesse leaned against the wheel and folded his arms across his chest.

"The boat has to be in the very best possible condition," Jesse said.

"It *is*," Luke said, as if he thought Jesse hadn't noticed our efforts.

"I'm sure it is, by the looks of things," Jesse said. "But go over her again, with a fine-tooth comb. Make sure everything is absolutely perfect."

"Why? What's going on?" I asked.

Jesse gave a little grin. "The insurance company is sending someone out here to inspect the boat, and I suspect they'll be pretty picky."

"That's great! I'm glad they're at least gonna look," Luke said. "When are they coming?"

"Next Friday."

"That's a whole 'nuther week."

"I know, but that's the soonest they can get here."

"But a whole week?"

"We're at their mercy, Luke. It's not a matter of *our* choice."

"And in the meantime, we're sittin' here, not makin' a dime."

"We'll just have to live with it, for now."

"What about the crew?"

"Get as many of 'em here as you think you need, and check every square inch, and tell the engineers to be mighty particular with all the machinery. We can't take any chances."

"Aren't you gonna be here?"

"I'll be back by Wednesday or Thursday, but now that I have this insurance thing taken care of, I have another matter to handle." Jesse looked at me and winked.

I knew, for sure, that Jesse hadn't told anyone else about Sadie.

At least the crew would receive another half-week's pay for doing very little. We had been so thorough already; chances of finding any major projects were slim. A few of the crew grumbled a bit when they heard the news, and some threatened to quit, but they were abruptly brought to their senses when reminded, by the more willing crewmen, of the lack of available jobs.

Everyone was to report for work Monday morning; Luke didn't want to play favorites, and the more help we had, the sooner we would be ready for the inspection.

Bedraggled and tired from the long bus ride from Kansas City, Mildred returned Saturday afternoon, a short while after Jesse pointed his Model A back to St. Louis. Even the lilacs seemed a bit wilted, and the spring in her step, subdued. She appeared quite relieved, though, to hear the insurance problem was well on its way to resolution; she prodded a little smile, seeing how nice the Madison looked. I explained the task before us, and even though I thought there was little to do, Mildred immediately started verbally listing a number of cleaning chores. But because she was so tired from the trip, she quickly abandoned the thought of mops and cleaning rags; she dedicated the rest of the weekend to repose.

I helped Mildred with her luggage. All the while, the news of Jesse and Sadie burned a hole in my upper lip. I wanted to tell Mildred, but Jesse would probably be upset with me if he found out that I had spilled the beans. I just bit my lip.

"I suppose Jesse is in St. Louis again," Mildred said.

"He left an hour ago," I replied.

"That's good," Mildred said. "He needs to spend some time with Sadie now."

"You *know* about Sadie?"

"Yes... he told me. Said he told you, too, but no one else. We have to keep it hush-hush."

It dawned on me that Mildred was Jesse's confidant, too. The only woman on board, she played the Mother role for all of us, me and Jesse in particular.

"Think they'll get married?" I said.

"I'd say it's almost certain... 'specially when there's a little one now."

I nodded in agreement; Mildred had said enough. I told her to enjoy her day off, and I decided not to bother her about going to church in the morning. I went on my way, feeling good about everything.

35

There I was again, in my new white shirt, standing at the church door, watching families enter, and listening to that magnificent organ music bathe the morning.

All through the service, my thoughts wandered among all my recollections of the mysterious, barefoot organist, and how, before, I had worried about whether he had a place to sleep, or food to eat. I doubt that I heard much of the church service at all; I stood when the congregation stood, and I sat when they sat. I just couldn't stop thinking and wondering why Golden Boy had been so elusive, or how I could have missed seeing him leave the church last Sunday, or to where he disappeared every time that I saw him. Perhaps he didn't *want* my friendship. Perhaps, he lived right there in the church, and that's why I didn't see him come out.

That didn't seem logical. I had walked entirely around the church the day of Augie's funeral; I knew of only one small addition attached to the back, probably the Preacher's office, and no other room for anyone to live. But there was a back door, I remembered, and I hadn't watched it. I *would* watch the back door after the service ended that day.

Poised within its view, I watched as the back door produced several people: some members of the choir that sang that day, and two ushers; their duties were completed.

The organ music trailed off. Nearly everyone had dispersed; I heard the front door close. I waited.

Disheartened, and almost ready to walk away, thinking that I had, once again, been unsuccessful, the back door opened. A woman appeared first; her stunning dark hair contrasted with her powder blue dress. She didn't seem to notice me, as she carefully negotiated her high-heeled shoes down the three steps. Not far behind her, followed my purpose for waiting – Golden Boy, the woman's son, I thought, dressed in a crisp white shirt, creased black trousers – *and shoes.*

"You played very well today, Andrew," the woman said.

"Thank you, Mum," I heard Golden Boy reply.

Just then, a bit astonished, he caught sight of me, as his eyes spanned the twenty feet of lawn between us. Then he gave me a little smile, but said nothing. Matching the woman's stride, he glanced sideways once more toward me, and then the woman looked my way, too. She smiled, turned her head forward again, and they continued walking, side-by-side, across the lawn to the street and disappeared around the corner.

I wanted to follow them, to see where they lived, but my feet seemed anchored in the grass where I stood, and just as well, I thought. They might think I was stalking them, should they notice me.

A ripple of relief passed through me. From out of the deepest, darkest depths of despair, I singled out that vision of Golden Boy's smile, when he had realized that I was there. That alone, seemed to make the day's efforts worthwhile.

Luke carried the big maintenance notebook under his arm, while I followed him around the decks most of the day, Monday. Just as we had suspected, the Madison required very little work, but everybody kept busy somehow; now and then, we'd have to send someone to the hardware store in town for a handful of screws, or a new bolt, needed to replace a rusty one. Never before had there been so much attention paid to such minor details.

After a certain amount of apprehension, cleaning out Augie's cabin proved to be the toughest job we faced, not that it was physically difficult.

Augie had left behind a room that was neat and tidy, and because he never saw the need for unnecessary material things weighting him down, the task demanded little effort, but summoned up emotional mountains in Luke and me. Augie could *never* be replaced, but we knew that his memory would live on; his spirit would continue to walk these decks, maintaining a watchful eye on the Madison, for as long as she existed.

I imagined that cabin to become mine. Nothing had yet been said about hiring another pilot; after our hair-raising experiences with Jim, that would be a touchy subject for a long time. The possibility of Sadie staying on board, sometimes, did exist. Jesse and she would need their privacy, and I would certainly have to move out of the Captain's quarters sometime soon. Although I wanted to suggest that idea to Luke right away, I thought I'd better wait for Big Brother to return.

For some reason, Luke seemed a little edgy the next day. The whole crew was back again, scurrying about the boat like an army of ants, but not much of anything was left to accomplish. The Madison looked like new, inside and out. Even without bright sunshine that day, everything beamed with freshness, like a big smile sitting there in the water, as if she were being launched for the very first time.

Luke sent everyone home after Henry's beef stew lunch. They could do no more.

"She's still an old boat," Luke said to no one in particular.

I gazed around, admiring what I thought to be the best-looking boat on the river. "But she looks great," I said.

"Let's hope the insurance inspectors see it that way," Luke said. "She's *still* an old boat."

I knew at that moment that Luke was trying to hide his feelings, deep inside, where eyes could not penetrate. He worried about the insurance crisis, and although I had become confident that the dilemma would soon be history, Luke's restlessness spilled onto me like water out of a leaky bucket. I looked around some more. As good as she appeared to me, there was no denying – the Madison *was* old.

"I'm going for a walk," I said. It seemed the best way to exit from the sudden tension that I felt.

Luke's brows furrowed; his stare fixed on the grayness of the day. Luke wouldn't look directly at me. He just nodded.

I walked past the tall, sturdy cedars that lined the churchyard; my destination, I thought, was the cemetery where Augie was buried. But halfway there, I realized that the sight of his gravestone, etched with the likeness of the Madison above his name, would only bring more sadness, and I didn't want to be sad that day. Pieces of puzzles floated about; my mind reached for them and tried to sort them. Walking faster, I pointed myself in another direction, heading out into the rolling hills and the forest.

I knew it was only a few hours, but it seemed as though I had been walking for days. A gray, overcast sky kept me from using the sun for any sense of direction; the woods appeared the same, everywhere I looked. It kind of reminded me of when I ran away from home; I had roamed the hills and forests then too, sometimes not knowing where I was, for days. But I wasn't concerned. Even though I'd never ventured too far away from the boat until then, I knew that the river and St. Charles couldn't be very far away, and that I was bound to run across one of them sooner or later.

The peaceful stillness soothed like a warm bath. I had plenty to keep my mind busy, and with no birds singing or squirrels chattering, there was little to distract me from my thoughts.

I wondered what would happen to the Madison if Jesse were not successful in getting the insurance. She was ours, lock, stock and paddlewheel, and at least, we still had a roof over our heads. But that didn't help satisfy my dreams of one day becoming a pilot. I had given that more thought than anything else since Augie died, not that his passing opened up the job. Rather, it was then that I had realized that all things don't stay the same forever; I couldn't stay a cabin boy the rest of my life, but I didn't know any other lifestyle, than the one on the river. I remembered the life I had back in Milwaukee, but I hated the big city, *any* big city. I'd been in St. Louis a few times, and I didn't like it there any better than Milwaukee.

Now that Jesse and Sadie were back together and they had a little boy of their own, I wondered how long it might be 'till they would get married. Maybe Jesse would give up the riverboat, and move to St. Louis. Then I'd never see him. I wanted to think that didn't bother me, and that I was happy he had a family of his own, but deep down inside, I could feel a little bubble of resentment and jealousy, bouncing around like a ping-pong ball. My big brother meant the world to me, and I hated the thought of him not being around.

The sky seemed to be darkening a little. My belly grumbled. I hadn't eaten since noon, and I was getting a bit tired, too. The trees towered above me with their eerie, shadowy faces; their spooky voices seemed to be saying to me, "You shouldn't be here alone." On a tree trunk beside me, I stared at a green-and-orange-colored fungus that I was sure I had seen once before. In a patch of soft, bare dirt I saw a footprint. I set my foot down beside it, and then took it away. The footprints were identical – I had been walking in circles all afternoon. Changing directions so many times, I was confused about which way to go. Misery bored into me. I was tired and hungry, *and I was lost.*

Listening to my stomach growl, I sat down on the log of a fallen tree. Laden with soft, fuzzy moss, it was almost like sitting on a theater seat. I thought I would rest a few minutes and make some logical choice of which way to go before I set out again. With elbows on knees, and my face buried in the palms of my hands, I sat there, disgusted and discouraged.

I heard twigs snapping, like I had heard under my own footsteps. At first, I thought it might be an animal, a deer perhaps, and then I felt the log wiggle. I thought if there were some ferocious beast on that log beside me, I didn't want to look. I didn't want to see its hideous fangs that were about to tear me to shreds and devour me. I held my breath, waiting for the snarl and the gnashing of teeth, and the blow that would kill me dead. I pictured my lifeless body being dragged across the forest floor to some remote cave, where my bones would never be found.

But only a gentle voice said, "Lost?"

I jerked my head up and turned toward the voice. My whole body tingled. I nodded, almost disbelieving my eyes. So taken by the sight of him, my voice wouldn't produce sounds. I reached out to him and touched his golden brown skin, just to make certain that he was not a mirage. He looked down at my hand against his chest, and then into my eyes. Golden Boy's smile came easily, and without pretence.

"C'mon," he said. "Follow me. I'll show you the way back to town."

He jumped to his feet and started out in the direction opposite of the one that I would have chosen. Motioning for me to follow, he said, "C'mon, it's not far."

I forgot about my hunger and exhaustion; I sprang to my feet and followed his lead. He stayed quite a ways ahead of me at a fast pace, now and then, looking back to make sure I was still there. My legs started to ache, trying to keep up; I thought that I would have to stop. But just as he had told me, it wasn't far, maybe a half mile. I figured he would see that I had stopped at the edge of town to rest my tired legs, and that he would wait for me. I looked all around, but he had vanished again, like a fly disappears, once you finally locate the flyswatter.

I felt rather foolish right then, first, for getting lost, and second for not talking to Golden Boy when I had the chance. After all that time that he had been such a mystery to me, and then, when the opportunity to make a new friend sat down beside me, I let him slip away again. Now, he seemed even a bigger mystery.

36

Time seemed to pass rather slowly when it came my turn to stand watch, while Luke and Reggie went into town. Mildred was gone too, so I sat alone in the pilothouse, waiting for Jesse to return.

I imagined myself at the wheel, steaming down the Mississippi to Cairo, and then I flipped through the pages of river charts, picturing in my mind what every bend looked like, navigating around every island and making every crossing. I could feel the whistle pedal under my foot, sounding the triumphant signal of our arrival to every landing along the way. It was a magnificent vision.

I kept flipping the pages, and the charts took me beyond Cairo, farther south to Natchez, Baton Rouge, and New Orleans. Perhaps, if we did convert the Madison to an excursion vessel, those places would soon be ours to see; I craved the taste of new adventure, and I would be right there, in the pilothouse, to savor every moment.

So deeply submerged in my pool of dreams, Jesse's footsteps on the stairs mingled with all the other sounds of my fantasy: the chuffing engines, the churning paddlewheel, the brilliant song of our distinct whistle and the brass bell atop the pilothouse, the joyous clamor of a saloon full of passengers, the deckhands yelling out signals to each other, the hissing boiler vents, the jackstaff flag flapping in the breeze, the cries of gulls circling about, the distant whistle shrieks and drones from other boats, the water slapping against the hull as our bow cut through the gentle waves – all the familiar sounds that had become a natural part of my life.

My mind's eye scanned a mile-wide river, somewhere along the Louisiana bayous, when Jesse's hand came to rest on my shoulder. Like lifting the needle arm from a record on the Victrola, all the sounds in my head stopped, and there I was, in the stillness of a docked craft at the St. Charles levee.

"Are we ready for the inspection tomorrow?" Jesse said.

"As ready as we can be," I said. "C'mon... I'll show you all the stuff we did."

I gave Jesse a tour, pointing out the details as we went along; it was easy to see his pleasure with the results of the efforts everyone on the crew had put forth. His eyes beamed with satisfaction as he marveled at every piece of machinery, polished to perfection, the freshly painted paddlewheel, the decks all scrubbed to a satiny luster, the saloon, radiant with hospitality.

Eventually, we made our way back to the pilothouse. Jesse glowed with a certain radiance, too; I knew that he was pleased with the boat's appearance, but there was obviously something more to it. He paced around, from one side of the pilothouse to the other; watching him almost made me dizzy.

"We cleaned out Augie's cabin," I said.

Jesse kept pacing.

"I was thinking... maybe I could move in there... if it's okay with you."

Jesse just paced.

"Luke and I were talking about me cubbing as a pilot... we need another pilot, you know."

Jesse stopped and stared at me for a moment. "Of course. That's a great idea," he said, but he was so occupied with other thoughts, that I wasn't sure if he really understood what I had said. He went back to pacing.

"But we'll have to find another cabin boy," I said.

Jesse stopped his pacing a couple of feet short from running me over.

"The paddlewheel fell off yesterday," I said.

Jesse looked at me with a strange sort of stare. "What?"

"Not really. I was just checking to see if you were hearing *anything* I said."

"Of course I heard you. Yes, you can move into Augie's old cabin, if you want, and yes, you can cub with Luke, and yes, we'll get another cabin boy."

He *had* been listening. But by the way his face twitched like a bush full of birds, I knew that something else was on his mind.

"Are you worried about the inspection tomorrow?" I asked.

"No, not really."

"Then why are you so nervous? You're making me dizzy with all that pacing."

"Will, I promised you we'd talk about this when I got back from St. Louis."

My fears of Big Brother casting me aside were long gone; we were much too close for that to ever happen, I thought. I wanted to erase the memory of my foolish actions and words that I had said to Jesse the week before. "Let's just forget about all that stupid stuff I told you," I said. "I wasn't thinking straight. You're not still mad about that, are you?"

"Sadie and I got married last Saturday," Jesse said.

I didn't know whether to laugh or to cry; I hadn't expected to hear those words – not just yet, anyway; I wasn't ready for something like that. As strongly as I had resigned myself to accept the inevitable, the news still hit me as a bit of a shock. For the past two weeks, everything had seemed to be moving along about as fast as grass grows, and then, suddenly my world went spinning out of control, leaving me in the dust.

"That's... great," I said. "But why didn't you tell me? I thought we'd all be invited."

"Sadie and I decided we didn't want to make a big fuss about it... you know... because of Philip."

I fought off the feelings of resentment. I couldn't allow that to send me crashing into another one of my temper tantrums, that could foolishly destroy the relationship and security that I had grown to trust. Any kind of negative reaction, at that moment, could have turned Jesse against me again; I certainly didn't want that to happen.

"Does Mildred know?" I asked.

"Not yet... you're the first."

"Are you going to live in St. Louis?"

"For the time being... until I can convince Sadie to move here."

A look of concern must have appeared on my face, although, I tried to hide it.

"Don't worry about that," Jesse said. "There's plenty of room in our house. You can stay there too."

Living in a big city again didn't appeal to me in the least, but I couldn't let Jesse know, right then, that I wanted to decline his invitation. Perfectly content with my own quarters on the Madison, I preferred staying right there, at St. Charles.

"But someone has to stay with the boat... I can do that," I said.

"Suit yourself, but I want you to know that you're welcome to come live with us. It was Sadie's idea."

Still fighting my emotions, I turned for the door. "I'm gonna start moving my stuff," I said. I stopped in the doorway and turned back toward Jesse. "Oh... and... congratulations, Big Brother."

Jesse smiled. "Thanks Will."

The move into my very own private cabin proved to be a joyous event for me; it marked another milestone on my road to independence, even though it was only a few feet down the Texas deck, and right across the breezeway from Luke's door. I was making up my bunk when Reggie came in.

"Want to join us in some poker?" he asked.

I surveyed the room that still required some organizing. "I don't know... I've got a lot of work to do here," I said.

"Aw, c'mon. This'll all still be here later."

"Well – "

"The Captain and Luke and me are gettin' up a game. Come and join us."

With not much daylight left, we decided to light a few lamps in the saloon. We settled in around the Captain's table with a gallon jug of sarsaparilla that Jesse had brought back from St. Louis, and a deck of cards.

It had been a long time since the four of us had gathered like that; the occasion certainly warranted a little celebration.

By then, Jesse had announced his marriage surprise to Luke and Reggie. I felt a little more at ease, and we all enjoyed the thought that the insurance crisis would soon be over.

"And as long as we're celebrating," Jesse said, raising his glass over the table, "here's to our new pilot cub."

Luke and Reggie raised their glasses toward me; I felt like I had just been dubbed into knighthood, and for a few moments, I could hear a choir of a hundred angels singing "Halleluiah." It was official: soon I would be walking among the ranks of the most prestigious men on the river.

"And Reggie," Jesse continued. "You have served the Madison well. Now that Luke is officially the First Pilot, I am promoting *you* to First Mate."

Luke and I joined Jesse in the toast. By the beam of delight I saw on Reggie's face, I was sure that he heard the angels singing, too. Exaggerated dignity overwhelmed us, as we accepted the offerings of congratulations from each other, and then we topped off our private little ceremony by clinking our glasses of sarsaparilla together over the center of the table. It was a grand moment.

With all of the official business out of the way, we could get on with the poker game; I commenced to relieve the other three of their stacks of pennies.

"Will, you've been hangin' around with Spades Morgan too much," Luke said, after I had won four straight pots.

Morgan had taught me some finer points of the game, but luck hung on me, that night, like wet laundry on a clothesline. It seemed that I just couldn't lose.

37

I t was about three o'clock in the morning when all that sarsaparilla I drank woke me with a high degree of urgency. I stumbled around in my dark room to locate the door; still half asleep, my instincts were all that navigated me along the Texas deck to the privy. We always left a lamp lit in there, just for emergencies such as this one.

My senses slowly started to wake up, as I stood there relieving myself; they were telling me that something seemed strangely out of the ordinary. It felt as though the boat was moving, but I knew that couldn't be possible. I figured it had to be my grogginess that was scrambling my head. When I finished, I opened the door and peered out into the night. A few moments went by while I focused my eyes on the shoreline, and a few more moments passed until the sight finally registered. Black silhouettes of trees slid by, and there were no other boats, anywhere; the St. Charles lights were only a faint glow on the dark horizon. I tried to convince myself that it had to be my imagination, or that I was just dreaming, and that, at any second, I would wake up and find myself in the comfort of my bunk. The more I mentally struggled with the bizarre situation, the more it became real; we were no longer tied up at the St. Charles levee. The Madison *was* moving; we were adrift on the current.

"JESSE! LUKE! WAKE UP! JESSE!" I ran to Jesse's cabin and pounded on the door. "JESSE – WAKE UP!" Then I dashed to Luke's cabin door, pounding and yelling his name.

"What's goin' on?" Jesse called out as he threw open his door. All I could see of him was his white nightshirt. Then Luke appeared, dressed only in his underwear.

"We're *loose*, and we're *drifting*," I said.

It took Jesse and Luke a few seconds to realize what was happening. "Oh my God!" Jesse yelled. "Get Charlie! We need to get up steam!"

"But Charlie isn't here… he's at home," Luke said. "We're the only ones on board."

"What are we gonna bloody do?" Reggie said. His voice, like the rest of us, was frantic.

"All right… everybody calm down," Jesse said. "We need an engineer to start the engines. Get some lights on so we can see what we're doing."

"Will," Luke said. "Take a lantern up on the Hurricane deck and watch for boats coming upriver… make sure they see us. Reggie! Go with Jesse to the engine room and help him fire up the boilers. I'm going up to the pilothouse… I'll try to steer her the best I can."

I could see the boat was turned and floating sideways. If another boat, coming up the river, did not see us, the collision would break the Madison in half. But there was no steering it without any power to the paddlewheel. Luke was making an effort, without any results; the Madison drifted, twisting and turning however the current of the Big Muddy dictated.

I paced back and forth across the Hurricane deck, ready to wave the lantern, should any other boats come into sight. Reggie had lit several lanterns; we would be slightly visible, but we still had no control, and without steam, we had no whistle to sound any signals. We were quite helpless.

"Will, can you go down to my cabin? Get me some clothes?" Luke called out to me from the pilothouse door. "You better get some clothes on too… it's cold up here."

It *was* a bit chilly; in all the excitement I hadn't noticed until then. I hurried down to the Texas, slipped into my jeans and a shirt, went to Luke's quarters and grabbed the clothes from the floor by his bunk.

Luke shivered as he dressed. "We better hope we can get up enough steam before we reach the bend at Pelican Island," he said.

I stared into the downriver darkness. "How far is it?" I asked.

"Near as I can tell, about two miles... maybe less."

Dark smoke started pouring from one stack, and a minute later both stacks spewed like volcanoes ready to erupt. Jesse and Reggie had been successful, but it would take some time for the steam to build great enough to power the engines. At the rate we were drifting, Pelican Island was much too near.

"What'll happen if we don't?" I asked Luke.

"The current will crash us into the bank at the bend."

"We'll have enough steam before that, don't you think?"

"I hope so," Luke frowned.

Minutes seemed like hours. Luke and I stood silently waiting and listening for the boiler vents to whistle. All we could do was stare into the black, moonless night; Luke knew that it was useless to try steering any more.

"Luke!" I said, pointing over his shoulder. "Isn't that the tip of Pelican Island?"

The stern of the Madison was aimed downriver. Luke turned quickly to look. Just barely visible, at first, Pelican Island looked like a fiendish monster, rising up out of the river. The bank we would crash into was less than a half-mile ahead. We needed steam – *and soon*.

Like a song from Heaven, the boiler vents let out a hiss. Luke slammed the telegraph lever to Full Ahead. In the eerie stillness, we could hear the first chugs of the engines, and I could see the tension melting away from Luke's face.

"Now all we need is the search light," he said. "Go down and tell them to get the generator fired up."

Just as I darted for the door, a loud crack rang out; the paddlewheel stopped as abruptly as it had started.

"Now what?" I said.

"The drive pin on the pitman arm sheared," Luke yelled, and like a pair of scared rabbits, we both raced down to the Main.

Jesse and Reggie were already feverishly working on the broken machinery by the time we got there.

"Why did the pin shear?" Luke was in near panic.

"Something must be caught in the wheel... nothing seems to be wrong anywhere else," Jesse answered. He sounded a little calmer; he didn't realize how close we were to disaster.

I ran out onto the deck with my lantern, trying to get a look at the paddlewheel. Leaning out over the railing, and holding the lantern up high, I could see the problem: our mooring ropes had entangled around the paddleboards.

"LUKE! I SEE THE—"

Next thing I knew, a sudden jolt tipped me over the rail. I heard the paddlewheel planks cracking, just before I splashed into the water, and when I came back up, the current was swinging the Madison's bow around toward the riverbank.

I wasn't a very good swimmer; it took me a while to reach the bank.

"Will!" I heard Jesse screaming. "Where are you? Are you okay?"

"I'm up here on the bank," I yelled back. It all seemed like the worst nightmare that I had ever experienced; I wasn't sure just how I had gotten to the bank, and the light from Jesse's lantern didn't reach far enough to let him see me.

Then I heard Reggie yelling, "Luke... help me get a line over to the bank. Let's get her tied up!"

I took a couple of deep breaths, and staggered along the rocky bank to where Reggie and Luke fumbled in near darkness, trying to wrap the mooring rope around a small tree. By then, the Madison's stern had swung out away from the bank again; the force against the little tree uprooted it from the soft soil as easily as if it were merely a tuft of grass.

While the bow was still close to the bank, I grabbed for the railing and flung my legs up onto the deck. Reggie and Luke thrashed in the water for a bit, and then made a lunge to grab hold of the gunwale. Jesse reached down to them and pulled them up.

"Of all the bloody luck," Reggie grumbled.

"Well we can't give up yet," Luke said. "Jesse, let's get that pin replaced." Then he turned to Reggie, still sitting on the deck. "Try to figure out how to get those ropes untangled from the paddles."

"What should I do?" I said.

Luke didn't hesitate. "Go up to the pilothouse ...watch for other boats. If you see any coming, you know the whistle signals. And turn on all the lights – the searchlight too. The generator is running now."

Alone in the pilothouse, it occurred to me that that was my first official duty as a cub pilot; I only wished that it were under better circumstances. Nonetheless, I had an important job to perform.

Cutting an icy blue streak through the darkness, I bounced the searchlight beam from shoreline to shoreline; I could see we were in no danger of any oncoming craft. But it seemed we were moving much slower, and the far end of Pelican Island, much nearer. The current had thrust the Madison on a course across the river; we were headed into the shallows along the island. That was a good thing, I thought. With very little momentum there would be no damage to the hull if we nudged a sandbar. I tried turning the wheel, but just as before, there was still no response.

Then I heard a splash that sounded very much like a body hitting the water. I wanted to run aft to see what was happening, but I knew my duty, as a pilot, required me to stay in the pilothouse, no matter what. I couldn't hear any screaming, so I figured everything must be under control.

A few minutes later, Luke entered, offering me an update on the progress. "Reggie is in the water with a hacksaw," he said. "He's gonna get the rope cut away, that's tangled on the wheel."

"Did you get the pin changed?" I asked.

"Yeah."

"Anything else broke?"

"Looks like one plank on the wheel is completely broken, and three others are cracked pretty bad, but I think we can make it back."

"That's good."

"We were lucky... this time." Luke panned the searchlight beam all around to get his bearings. "Maybe you should go down below and help Reggie haul in those moor lines."

I would have rather stayed there in the pilothouse, but I was the cub, and Luke was my master, officially, so I turned for the door.

"And Will?" Luke added. "When you're done down there... better come back up and help me navigate back to St. Charles." His teeth chattered when he spoke, and his whole body vibrated with shivers.

"I'll bring you some dry clothes when I come back," I said.

No other landing at St. Charles could compare to the relief that I felt on that one, even though that one meant a little hard work, helping Reggie with the mooring lines, a task that I usually watched from the Hurricane deck. I doubted that Jesse would ever want to shovel another lump of coal again, and Luke was just plain glad that this ordeal was over.

We all sat at the table in the dining hall.

"How did we get loose?" Jesse asked.

"The lines were cut," Reggie said.

"What?"

"When I tied up just now, I saw the ends of the old lines. They'd been chopped off."

Luke's eyes widened. "Who could've done such a thing? We could've been killed." We'd better go to the police."

"We can't do that," Jesse said.

"Why not?"

"That will mean some bad publicity, and we can't afford any of that now.

The insurance people can't find out that this ever happened."

Jesse looked at his watch, and then he stood up quickly. "The insurance people. They'll be here in three hours for the inspection." He started pacing. "Reggie, get rid of those cut mooring lines. Luke and Will, start removing the broken planks from the wheel. I'll take the truck over to the lumber mill and get some new ones. We can't let them see the damage, and we certainly can't let them see we were the victim of vandals."

Tired as we all were, we went to work. Jesse drove off in his truck. Luke and I found the wrenches, and we began unbolting the planks, and I saw Reggie tossing the short pieces of rope into the river.

Captain Jameson, from the Silverado, out for an early morning stroll along the levee, stopped to satisfy his curiosity. "Didn't I see you boys painting that wheel just last week?"

"Yes sir, I believe you did," Luke said.

"You must enjoy replacing wheel planks," the Captain joked.

"No," Luke replied. "We just now spotted a couple of cracked ones... thought we should replace 'em. Can't be too careful, you know."

"You gettin' back out soon? I've noticed the Madison has been tied up here longer than usual."

"Yeah, since Augie died. But we'll be out again soon."

"Yes, sorry about Captain Bjornson. He was a good man."

"We'll all miss him."

After a short pause, the Captain spoke to me. "Will, I haven't seen you visiting Spades Morgan lately."

"Oh, I've been kinda busy, I guess."

"Yes, well do stop over and see him... he's been asking about you."

"Tell Spades I'll come over later today... if you see him."

"I'll be happy to relay the message. Say! What ever happened to my pilot that hired on the Madison?"

"If you mean Jim," Luke said, "we fired him, down at the Cape."

"Oh dear... why?"

"He was a little too hard on the equipment, and he had a bad attitude."

"That sounds like Jim. Well, enjoy your work, boys. I must be going now."

Captain Jameson walked away. Luke looked at me. I looked at Luke.

"D'ya s'pose it was *Jim* that cut the lines last night?" I said.

Luke squinted in thought. "I didn't think he'd be dumb enough to ever come around here again, but I wouldn't put it past him to get a little revenge."

"Think he'll try again?"

"He might. We'd better post a guard out here all night, from now on."

We had just finished with the paddlewheel when two men, smartly dressed in three-piece business suits, walked up the gangplank. We knew right away who they were, and why they were there.

"Where might we find Captain Madison?" one of them asked.

"I'm Captain Madison," Jesse said.

The two men exchanged glances. "I'm Ogden Thorp, and this is my associate, Gregory Williams. We're here for the insurance inspection."

"Yes, I know. I've been expecting you," Jesse said. He put his hand on my shoulder. "This is my brother and partner, Will Madison." Then he turned toward Luke. "This is my other partner, Luke Jackson, and this is my First Mate, Reggie Pierce."

Thorp and Williams exchanged another glance, and then offered a handshake to each of us.

"You boys are quite... young... to be the owners of a riverboat, aren't you?" Thorp said.

Jesse's face took on a frown, as if offended by Thorp's statement. "We may be young, but we learned from the best, and we've been operating this boat up and down the Mississippi for two years now."

Thorp and Williams looked at each other again; Thorp shrugged his shoulders. "Very well, Captain. Give us a tour, and we'll need to see your pilot's certification, and the daily logs and..."

Jesse and the two men started up the stairs to the Saloon deck. "All the records are in the office," Jesse told them, and then their voices just faded away.

I was so exhausted that I though I might fall asleep, standing. The old grain sacks weren't as inviting as the thought of my bunk, but they'd do. I sat down. Luke and Reggie sat down beside me, and we just stared out over the river.

"How did he do it?" Reggie said.

"Who? What?" I asked.

"Jim. How did he manage to chop through those ropes without anyone hearing or seeing?"

"Everyone else was asleep, just like us," Luke said. "What worries me more is that he might try it again."

"Shhhhhh," I whispered. "Here they come."

We watched Jesse, Thorp, and Williams amble down the steps and then slowly make their way to the engine room. The insurance men peeked inside for a few moments, and then started walking toward the gangplank.

"Very well, Captain. Thank you for your cooperation. We'll let you know later next week."

"Thank you," Jesse said. He offered a handshake. "We'll be waiting to hear from you."

The suited men left.

"That was it?" Luke said. "*That* was the inspection?"

"I think all they came here for was to make sure there really *is* a boat," Jesse said.

"Well great. We go to all the trouble of making everything perfect for them, and they don't even look."

"They noticed," Jesse said. "They commented on the Madison's appearance. Said she looks good."

"Oh. Anyway... I'm going to bed. Think I'll sleep all weekend."

38

The church had become a place of solace for me. Even though my conscious intentions had been somewhat different, I began to realize how comforting that place was. It was a place to where I could carry my burdens and lay them down; all the troubles of the outside world seemed to scurry off into hiding.

Scanning the faces within view didn't produce the woman I had seen exiting the back door with Golden Boy. Certain that she must be there, I studied the heads and shoulders of those to the front of me, until I singled out the powder blue dress and her beautiful dark hair, almost lost among the others around her.

Golden Boy sat at the organ, as usual; his face showed signs of deep concentration, and he seemed absorbed in the music that he played. His fingertips made their precise, effortless movements on the ivory keys; his bare feet did their calculated slow dance on the pedals.

A few times during the sermon, I caught a glimpse of him looking my way. The corners of his mouth curled into a hardly noticeable smile; I knew that our eyes had met. Perhaps he was chuckling inwardly, thinking of the day that he had rescued me from the woods – or – perhaps, this would be the day that he would acknowledge my friendship, and allow our voices to mingle in conversation.

Very much like the previous Sunday, and the Sunday before that, the scene on the sidewalk in front of the church seemed almost routine, the same smiling faces, and the same handshakes, and the paths each family engaged, were quite predictable. And like the final curtain coming down on a stage play, seen many times before, the final measures of the organ music faded into predictable silence, the stout, wooden front door sounded its predictable closing clunk, and I waited.

The dark-haired woman came through the back door, cautiously navigating the three concrete steps. This time she noticed me standing in nearly the same spot as I had been the week before, acknowledged my presence with the same warm smile and said, "Good morning."

I returned the greeting. "Good morning, Ma'am," I said. I raised my hand shoulder-high with a casual wave.

On the lawn, she stopped and turned toward the open door, waiting for her son to join her. I saw him emerging from the shadows inside; his crisp white shirt vividly contrasted with the darkness. He closed the door behind him.

Golden Boy spoke to his mother, but his eyes were on me. "Mum? The Reverend said it would be alright if I came to practice tomorrow afternoon." His words were loud and clear, as if he intended for me to hear them.

"But Andrew. You know I have students coming to the house for lessons. I can't get away tomorrow," his mother protested.

"That's okay. I can come alone." Golden Boy stole another glance toward me as he spoke.

"Well, I suppose that would be okay," his mother said.

They turned and started walking across the churchyard. Without looking back, as if he knew that I'd be watching, Golden Boy secretively extended his arm behind him, with three fingers clearly silhouetted against the back of his white shirt.

I stood there a few moments in awe, wanting to speak, but I couldn't. Once again, I felt hypnotized by the mystery casually walking away.

When they were nearly out of sight, my mind returned to reality. I replayed the scene, once or twice, before the proverbial apple plopped on my head. Golden Boy – Andrew – had staged that clever little performance, as a confidential communication to me: he would be at the church, the next day, without his mother there, and three fingers meant three o'clock. I could only assume his signals were an invitation for me to meet him then. Why our meeting had to be kept such a secret, I didn't understand, but I thought that he must have a good reason. After all, I had kept my awareness of him well guarded, too.

I took my time walked back to the levee, thinking of how I would sneak away the next day at three o'clock. It wouldn't be too difficult – word from the insurance company wasn't expected until later in the week, so the Madison wasn't going anywhere, and there certainly was no maintenance to be done. Jesse would still be in St. Louis; Luke and Reggie would be on the boat to look after things, and they rarely objected if I wanted to go for a walk. No, it wouldn't be difficult at all, I thought.

My eyes fell on something shiny that had been trampled into the sand near the mooring posts where the Madison was tied. I stooped down to pick it up; it was only a gold-colored, metal coat button, but I thought that I would toss it into the box of my worthless, riverbank trinket collection.

The organ's resonance escaped the confines of the vacant church through an open window, in snippets of harmonic melody, repeated time and again, until they were perfect; the finished products finally linked together, to form a complete, flawless refrain, from start to end.

Each time there was a pause at the ending of a song, I reached for the door latch, and then the music started flowing again, and I pulled my hand away, deciding not to interrupt that persistent dedication to practice. But eventually, I thought that I couldn't put the meeting off any longer. I gently pulled the door open, just wide enough to slip through, and cautiously inched my way up the center isle. There, inside, the music swelled to robust enormity, gloriously powerful, yet soothing. The bass tones vibrated in my chest, while the trebles danced a ballet on the back of my neck. It was magnificent.

Golden Boy glanced up from the keyboard; without missing a single note, he kept playing. The last chord echoed a few moments within the vast space. He dropped his hands to the bench.

"I've been waiting for you," he said.

"How did you know I'd be here?"

"I didn't. But I hoped that you understood my signal yesterday."

"I figured it out."

Golden Boy looked at his wrist, as if searching for a watch that wasn't there. "Do you know what time it is?" he asked me.

I pulled out my pocket watch. "Three-thirty," I said.

"Mum has students 'till five. C'mon." Golden Boy motioned for me to follow him out the back door. Once outside, he unbuttoned his white shirt, slipped it off, folded it and tucked it into the corner beside the steps.

"I'm Andrew Lorado." He extended his hand to me.

"I'm Will Madison." The introduction was finally official with a handshake. We started walking into the country.

Andrew stared at me for a moment, as if a little curious. "Madison... that's the name on the boat."

"Yeah, my brother and I own it."

"Wow. You've probably been everywhere."

"Well, we brought her down the Mississippi from Wisconsin, and now we just go from here to Paducah and back, but sometime soon, maybe we'll go to New Orleans."

"We used to live in New Orleans," Andrew said. "But that was a long time ago. Mum got a teaching job here, when I was five years old... been here ever since."

"What does your Mom teach?"

"Music. But now the school can't afford to pay all the teachers, so she gives private piano lessons to kids at our house."

"So that's how you play so good."

Andrew's dark suntan disguised a blush quite well. "I started playing the piano when I was six. Mum made me practice every day. Now she thinks I can be a concert pianist some day... says I'm a natural for it."

"What does your father do?"

"He's a construction engineer for the railroad, so he's not home much."

At least Andrew *had* a father; that's more than I could say, and I really didn't want to get on that subject.

"Thanks for showing me the way back to town the other day," I said.

Andrew chuckled. "I saw you out there, and you looked kind of lost."

"Why didn't you wait for me that day? I really wanted to thank you then."

"I was late getting home. And I didn't talk to you at the church because of Mum."

"Why?"

"She doesn't like me hanging around with other guys... thinks I'll get hurt so I won't be able to play the piano, and I was afraid you might say something about pulling me out of the river. Don't want her to know about that."

The incident at the levee, the first time that I ever saw Andrew, had slipped away from my thoughts during that, our first real conversation. I stole a peek at Andrew's hands, and I saw the faint band of lighter skin around the ring finger of his left hand, where a ring had once been, and on his right, a silver ring, nearly identical to the one dangling on the chain around my neck.

I was certain that Andrew knew that it was me who had pulled him out of the river, but I wondered if he had any suspicion of my possession of his ring. The thought of mentioning it crossed my mind, but I decided to wait for a better time.

"I sneak out once in a while," Andrew continued, "when Mum is busy giving lessons and she won't notice that I'm gone. All my shirts are white, so I take them off, so I won't be spotted so easily."

"What would she do if she knew you were out here now?"

"She'd probably chain me to the piano leg."

We had walked only a short distance in the general direction of where I had been lost a few days earlier; Andrew seemed a bit peculiar to me at first, as he led me along the trail. He knew that terrain as if it were his own back yard; there was little chance of getting lost again. His eyes and ears absorbed every detail of every sight and sound, like the scout of an expedition charting unexplored territory; his senses seemed alive with adventure.

"C'mon," Andrew said to me. "I'll show you a haunted house." He turned off the trail, forging his way through the brush. I didn't want to get lost, so I stayed close behind him, never letting him out of my sight. We trampled through the tall grass across the lowlands along the river, and then into more heavily wooded, rolling hills. When we reached a small clearing, Andrew stopped, keeping well within the shadows.

"There it is," he whispered and pointed. Across the clearing, about a hundred feet away, the shadowy outline of a structure lay tucked in among the trees. Hardly visible, the brown walls blended with the surrounding forest so well that I had to study the shadows to distinguish its single story, lifeless shape. To me, it looked like just an old abandoned dwelling, but Andrew appeared quite intrigued with it.

Not exactly what I had expected from our first encounter as acquainted friends, I peered at the old house, trying to determine what Andrew found so interesting about it. He remained silent, and by his facial expressions, I began to realize that inside him lurked a very complicated character. I thought about what he had told me of himself, so far, and it didn't seem so strange that he hadn't spoken much. Apparently, his life was being restricted from contact with other people, and he probably lacked practice in conversation.

"What's so interesting about this old house?" I asked.

"Shhhhhh," Andrew whispered. "Sometimes I can hear the voices." His eyes stayed focused on the house.

"What voices?" I whispered.

"The ghosts."

Just the way that he said "ghosts" made the hair on my arms bristle; I stared, and I listened, but all I heard was a squawking crow and a distant boat whistle. I still didn't fully understand Andrew's fascination, but the concept began formulating.

"Do you hear them now?" I asked.

Andrew shook his head. "No, and there isn't any smoke coming from the chimney."

"Smoke?" I glanced for a moment at Andrew's intense stare toward the house. He noticed that I appeared puzzled.

"Yeah, sometimes I see smoke coming from the chimney, but there's never a fire in the fireplace."

"Who lives here?" I asked.

"No one."

"If there ain't no fire, then where does the smoke come from?"

"Don't know. I've looked in the windows, and the place is empty, and there's no fire, but smoke comes out the chimney, and I hear voices."

"What do they say?"

"Can't tell. They're too muffled to make out the words." Andrew broke his stare and sat on the ground. I sat beside him.

"I heard about this place a couple of years ago," Andrew went on, "and it took me a while to find it. Everyone else is scared to come out here, so I come here alone. You're not scared, are you?"

"No, not at all. So this is where you always disappear to."

"What do you mean?"

"I've seen you many times, but you always disappear when I try to find you."

Andrew gazed about the treetops, as if he were searching for a reply.

"I thought you were a homeless drifter when I first saw you, and I worried about you."

He stared back toward the house, and then into the trees again.

"I was afraid you didn't have clothes... or food... or a place to sleep."

Andrew looked into my eyes. I could sense his appreciation for my past concern.

"And then I saw you at the church, playing the organ. I knew then that I didn't have to worry about you any more... but I still wanted to be your friend."

Andrew's smile faded into a deep thought. "The funeral... you were at the riverboat captain's funeral."

"Yeah, Augie. He was like a Grandfather to me."

"Mum wouldn't approve if word ever got back to her that I was fraternizing with riverboat rousters."

"I'm not a rouster... I—"

"I know, Will, you and your brother *own* the boat. And now that Mum has seen you at church a few times, she *might* think it's okay."

The idea, that going to church would deliver me into social circles, had occurred to me, and now Andrew and I had finally cut through the mysterious fog between us; we were no longer strangers, merely exchanging glances. A feeling of satisfaction came over me, knowing that my efforts had gained another good friend.

"What time is it?" Andrew asked, a bit startled, and perhaps, a little desperate.

I pulled out my pocket watch. "Almost four-thirty," I told him.

"I have to get back home now. Let's go." His eyes saddened and the corners of his mouth turned down; his freedom, for the day, neared the end.

Andrew led the way again, at a very brisk pace. At the levee, he stopped.

"Will you meet me again tomorrow?" he asked.

"Sure," I said. "Where?"

"Right here."

"What time?"

"Three o'clock. Mum has students. I'll be here at three."

Before I could ask him what we would do then, he was gone, just as usual.

39

I was holding a full house, jacks and fours; all eyes were trained on me, as I practiced the blank stare that Morgan had taught me, while my opponents awaited my bet. Jesse had returned from St. Louis, late that afternoon; I could tell he had other things on his mind. Luke kept perking his ears toward every bit of noise outside, still a little edgy over the malicious prank that had sent the Madison dangerously adrift on Thursday night. Reggie seemed content in just enjoying a friendly poker game.

I was just about to drop ten pennies into the pot, when we heard a timid but panic-stricken voice call out from the cargo deck.

"Will! Are you here? Will! I need help! Where are you?"

Luke jumped up from of his chair, and then Jesse stood up; they both wrinkled their brows in puzzlement. I pushed my chair away from the table and started for the open saloon door. I recognized the voice, but I couldn't imagine why Andrew was on the cargo deck looking for me, or why he sounded so desperate.

"Will?" he called out again.

My footsteps on the stairway echoed through the empty cargo bay, and right behind me I heard Jesse, Luke and Reggie following; a herd of stampeding buffalo would have made less noise. It must have startled Andrew. Probably not expecting to see the four of us come charging down, he stood in the dim light, panting, stiff with the fear of being confronted by strangers.

"Andrew," I said to him. "What's wrong?"

He just stared toward Jesse, Luke and Reggie as if he were facing death itself.

"It's okay, Andrew," I said. "What kind of help do you need?"

Andrew glanced at me, and then returned his stare toward Jesse, Luke and Reggie. "It's Mum," he said between deep breaths.

"What happened?"

"She was on a stepladder washing a window... and she fell. I think her leg is broken."

"Where is she?" Jesse asked.

Jesse's voice worked its magical spell on Andrew, just as it had on me, many times. His concern seemed to ease the pressure from Andrew's anxiety; I think he sensed, right then, that his intrusion was not being looked upon with hostility. "On our back porch," he said.

"Where's your house?"

"Near the end of Fourth Street."

"Will and I'll go with you," Jesse said. "We'll take my truck." Then he turned to Luke. "You and Reggie stay with the boat."

We found Mrs. Lorado perched on the top step of the porch, her hands clutching her right ankle, and her face, drawn in agony. She looked at me with a tearful smile, struggling to combat the pain. "You're the boy I saw at the church," she said.

"Yes, Ma'am," I replied.

"This is Will Madison and his brother Jesse," Andrew said, trying to comfort his mother. He sat down on the step beside her. "They'll help get you to the doctor."

"Our telephone isn't working," Mrs. Lorado blurted, among the sobs that she couldn't hold back, as if she were apologizing for our inconvenience. "Otherwise, we could've called someone, but Andrew said he knew where he could find some help."

"Don't worry, Ma'am," Jesse reassured her. "We'll take care of you."

All the while that we carefully assisted Mrs. Lorado into the passenger seat of Jesse's truck, I noticed Jesse curiously eyeing Andrew. It would be just a matter of time; Jesse would certainly make the connection. He would recognize Andrew as the body we pulled out of the river, and because he wasn't aware of the secrecy of that event that Andrew guarded from his mother's knowledge, there was a good chance he might say something that would destroy Andrew's freedom. I knew I had to be ready with some sort of diversion.

Mrs. Lorado let out a few pitiful moans of pain as we gently lifted her swollen leg up into the truck cab.

"Now I know where I remember you from," Jesse said to Andrew. "You're—"

"Andrew plays the organ at the church," I said.

Jesse looked at me, a little disgusted that I had interrupted. He looked back at Andrew. "You're the fellow we—"

"Andrew played at Augie's funeral," I interrupted again, pleading with my eyes for him to abandon the issue. "I'm sure that's where you remember him."

"Well, no, actually I—"

"C'mon... let's get Mrs. Lorado to the hospital," I interrupted again.

That time, Jesse took the hint; his devilish little smile told me that he understood that the rescue should not be discussed in Mrs. Lorado's presence.

Once Mrs. Lorado was safely delivered to an examination room at the hospital, I explained everything to Jesse while we sat in the waiting lounge. Andrew sat next to me, nervously flipping the pages of a magazine, pretending not to listen, but I knew that he heard every word about how I had seen "Golden Boy" several times along the levee, thinking he was homeless and lost, and how surprised I was when I saw him playing the church organ at Augie's funeral, and how I had gone to church every Sunday morning, hoping to talk to him. I even told Jesse of Andrew's sly method of signaling me to meet him at the church, and about the haunted house we hiked to out in the country. But I didn't mention anything about the ring.

A doctor in a long, white coat strolled across the room toward us, and addressed Andrew: "It's just a bad sprain," he said. "Your mother can go home now, and I've instructed her to keep an ice pack on her ankle for a while. She'll have to stay off her feet for a few days."

Just then, I saw a nurse helping Mrs. Lorado maneuver across the room, hobbling along with a pair of crutches, her right knee bent, suspending her bandage-wrapped foot above the floor. The nurse handed a shoe to Andrew. "Now, you take care of your mother," the nurse said to Andrew, "and don't let her climb any more ladders for a while."

We all chuckled a bit, and then started for the front entrance.

"And Beth," the doctor added. "I'll stop by your house in a few days, so I can check that ankle after the swelling has gone down."

On the way out to the truck, Jesse asked Mrs. Lorado, "Where's your husband?"

"Oh, he's somewhere down in Louisiana, building a bridge across a swamp."

"Will he be back soon?"

"No, he's not due back for at least a month."

"Well, I'm sure Will won't mind coming by your house once in a while to see how you're getting along."

"That's very kind, but you really don't have to go to the trouble."

"It's no trouble," I said. "I'd be glad to look in on you. I'll stop by tomorrow afternoon."

Andrew seemed pleased with that idea too.

Bad moods aboard the Madison were about as thick as river mud; with all the crazy occurrences lately, no one got to rest properly. Just about the time one of us could manage to fall asleep, it was time to wake up for a two-hour shift as watchman. Jesse would have much rather been spending his free time in St. Louis with Sadie and Philip, but he thought that it was only fair to do his share of the guard duty. Luke was getting restless from staying in one place too long; Reggie was grouchy just because Luke was. We hadn't seen much of Mildred for a while; she was staying with a friend in town and helping out as a waitress at a local café. Lester would show up about every other day, go through the mail he had picked up at the Post Office, and then disappear again.

Because Jesse had volunteered me to go to Andrew's house every day, to check on Mrs. Lorado, he eased up on my daytime schedule, and we didn't worry too much about anything happening during the daylight hours, anyway.

After three days, Andrew and I had become good friends, and Mrs. Lorado took a liking to me, too. I knew by her smile, and the way she would say "are not," correcting me when I'd use the word "ain't," and how she always called me "William." I couldn't help but like her. She painted the perfect picture of a person, a homemaker, and a mother, who had nice things, a loveable personality, and plenty of redeeming features for her children to inherit.

When she found out that my home was on a riverboat, she seemed a little concerned. I asked her why that bothered her.

"Oh, it doesn't bother me," she said. "Just don't let Marion hear you say anything about riverboats... he hates them."

"Who's Marion?" I asked.

"He's my husband."

"Why does he hate riverboats?"

"Because they run into his railroad bridges."

"Well, *we've* never run into one, or anything else for that matter."

"William, you just have to understand Marion. He doesn't think Andrew should be playing the piano, either."

"Why not?"

"Because young boys should be out playing football and riding horses."

I listened for a moment to the magnificent piano music coming from the parlor. "Sounds to me like Andrew's better at the piano."

"Yes, I knew from the very first day he was in our home that someday he'd be a good musician. I couldn't keep him from climbing up on the piano bench and banging on the keys. I started giving him lessons when he was only six."

"Yeah, he told me."

"In fact, I teach him all his studies, now that the school doesn't have enough teachers."

"Must keep you pretty busy."

"Yes, it—"

Just then we heard a meek little knock on the kitchen door.

"Oh my," Mrs. Lorado said. "It's three o'clock. There's my first student for piano lessons." She reached for her crutches, got up from the chair at the kitchen table, and called out, "Andrew... it's three o'clock."

The music stopped, Andrew came into the kitchen, and Mrs. Lorado escorted the little girl across the room and into the parlor. When we heard *Twinkle, Twinkle Little Star*, in less than harmonious form, we knew that Andrew's mother would be preoccupied for a while; it was our cue to sneak out the back door.

I always knew we were in for an adventurous hike, somewhere, when Andrew abandoned his white shirt on a nail on the back wall of their garage. He seemed so eager to experience the world around him, yet timid to make contact with its inhabitants. We'd soon be prowling the little-traveled back streets and alleys, or wandering the hills and forests. It didn't take me long to learn how Golden Boy had been so elusive before, and I understood why, as well.

"Listen," he would say softly, tilting his head toward a meadow. "That bird is singing in the key of D-Minor."

I didn't know the key of D-Minor from the key of D-anything, but I'd listen. Soon, I was noticing all the orchestral sounds of nature: the birds and creatures of the wild, the babbling brooks, and even the wind seemed to hum a tune. The world could make wonderful music.

On the third day of our two-hour expeditions, Andrew led the way, once again, to the abandoned house that he deemed haunted, but that time, we approached it from a different direction, along the bank of the river. I hadn't seen this side of the house on our first visit there; I didn't realize that it was so close to the riverbank, nor had I seen that broken-down old boathouse, camouflaged by a growth of brush and weeds, and its rotted pilings wading at the edge of the small cove.

"This is where the pirates hide their ship," Andrew said, almost whispering. "Late at night they sail out to the Mississippi, rob and pillage unsuspecting riverboats, then sneak back here before anyone sees where they went."

Obviously, he had quite an imagination. The boathouse was barely big enough for a small fishing skiff, much less a pirate ship.

"There ain't no pirates or pirate ships on the Mississippi," I said.

"Are so!"

"Well, I never saw any, and I live on the river. How come I never saw any?"

"That's because they're only out in the dark of night so's nobody sees them."

"Then how come there ain't no ship here now? It's broad daylight."

"They're probably out in the backwaters fishing, where nobody will see them." Andrew looked at me, all serious-like, and then he laughed.

Then he gazed over the top of my head, toward the house, and he stopped laughing; his expression turned abruptly solemn. "I can hear the voices," he whispered, "and look... smoke from the chimney."

I spun around to look, certain that Andrew's imagination ran rampant again. It wasn't. I saw it too, a gray column, rising to the treetops, where the breeze whisked it away, but I couldn't hear the voices.

"They're in there," Andrew whispered.

"Who?" I asked.

"A tyrant once lived here, and they say he murdered his wife and children, and their ghosts are still in there."

"Let's look inside," I said.

It seemed that Andrew was neither for, nor against my suggestion, although, his usual enthusiasm for freewheeling adventure had certainly run off without him. "You're not going to see anything in there but empty rooms and a cold fireplace."

"That smoke means a fire, and a fire means somebody is in there," I said.

"Yeah... the ghosts."

"Ghosts ain't so bad. C'mon. We'll just look in the windows."

"Okay, but don't make any noise. We don't want to scare them. Hard telling what they might do."

"Which window can we see the fireplace?"

"The one on the right," Andrew said.

"Okay. Let's take a look." I had already convinced myself that a fire blazed in the fireplace; Andrew was just playing another trick on me.

Crouched down in the weeds, we slowly made our way toward the house, like a pair of wildcats stalking prey. I thought of the times, back in Wisconsin, when I had performed this very maneuver, to snatch a loaf of bread cooling on the back porch of a farmhouse. Now all I was after, was a glimpse of glowing embers in a fireplace.

We sat with our backs pressed to the wall under the window; Andrew whispered, "The fireplace is against the back wall. It's kind of dark in there... hard to see, but it's there."

I raised up, just high enough so I could peek through the bottom windowpanes. Very little light penetrated, but I could see the bare wood floor of a room, completely void of any furnishings, and just as Andrew had said, there, along the back wall, a huge stone hearth with not even a spark of fire in it.

"Do you hear that?" Andrew whispered. "I can hear the voices."

I sat down again and listened. Now I heard the voices, too, but they didn't sound like the voices of children, that Andrew had described.

"The other windows," I whispered. "Have you looked in the other windows?"

"All of them. Nothing."

"Well, I wanna look," I said.

"Suit yourself, but you won't see anything in there."

I crept from window to window, with Andrew shadowing my every step. He was right – nothing but bare floors and cracked plaster. And yet, the muffled voices still boiled from within those walls.

Then I happened to notice a small window that we had missed before – one at ground level in the stone foundation, nearly hidden by weeds. Cautiously, I stepped closer to it and stooped down to peer in. I knew immediately that I had found the answer. I saw the dim glow of light in the depths of the cellar, but the window was so dirty that I could see nothing more.

"Andrew!" I whispered.

"What do you see?"

"There's a light in the cellar."

He crouched beside me to look. I reached toward the glass to brush away some of the dirt. But as my hand slid across the pane, the pressure dislodged the whole window frame, and it fell inside, crashing on the floor below. There was a clear view of four slovenly men, slouched on wooden chairs around a small table next to a cook stove, and a kerosene lantern hanging above them from a ceiling beam. The sound of the breaking glass startled them; they all turned their heads toward the noise, and then two of them quickly rose from their chairs. Like charging elephants, and growling profanely, they started for the open window. By the expressions on their faces, I could tell they weren't coming over to invite us in for coffee.

Andrew and I ducked out of their sight to each side of the opening; neither of us had to suggest to the other of making a quick getaway. Driven by instinctive fear, within seconds, we ran, crashing through the brush, wasting no time to distant ourselves from that old house, and for once, I had no trouble keeping pace with Andrew.

We didn't stop running until we reached the edge of town; we slowed the pace to a fast walk to the garage behind Andrew's house. We both collapsed to the ground, and just sat there for a few minutes, until we were breathing normally.

"Two of them didn't look much older than us," Andrew finally said.

"Ever seen 'em before?" I asked.

"Never."

"Well, I have. The two older ones... I've seen them before."

"Where?"

"I can't remember... but I know I've seen 'em."

"Do you think they saw us?"

"Prob'ly... but it all happened so fast."

We faintly heard a miserable rendition of *Mary Had A Little Lamb* from the piano inside the house.

"What time is it?" Andrew asked.

I pulled out my pocket watch. "Ten to five."

"Mum will be done with the lessons soon." Andrew retrieved his shirt from the garage wall. "Are you coming over tomorrow?"

"I guess so," I said.

"Okay. See you tomorrow, then." Andrew buttoned his shirt and headed for the back door, doing his best to look as though nothing had happened.

40

Six o'clock Friday morning didn't come any too soon. Just as I was about to refill my coffee cup in the galley, Reggie came stumbling out to relieve me on watch; he was barefoot, rubbing his eyes with one hand and carrying his shoes with the other. Even though I could have slept until four o'clock when my shift began, I had been awake most of the night, thrashing my blanket, trying to rid the visions of those raging degenerates residing in the cellar of that old house.

They were just hobos, I thought, and nowadays, there were certainly plenty of them around. But why had those four taken refuge in a dark, dirty cellar, when the rest of the house, as dilapidated as it was, would serve as much more pleasant accommodations? And why did they display such anger when they realized that a couple of curious kids discovered their presence? Were they going to hunt me down and kill me because I had seen them? And why hadn't we noticed any signs of their coming and going outside the house? Not a single weed had been disturbed or a single footprint anywhere, before Andrew and I circled the building. Maybe they *were* the ghosts that everyone feared.

No. I knew that I had seen two of those men before. But I had seen so many strangers' faces during the last couple of years: passengers, stevedores, supply runners, fishermen, shipping clerks – and lots of hobos. I just couldn't associate the two faces with any particular time or place.

The dawn was creeping up, and now that I knew Reggie was up, I decided to abandon the coffee idea and go to bed. I was so exhausted from the mental rampage all night; surely I could fall asleep. "Wake me up by two," I said to Reggie. "I have to check on Mrs. Lorado."

Reggie nodded, rubbed his eyes again, and yawned.

"Do you, William Madison, swear to tell the truth, the whole truth, and nothing but the truth?"

I scanned the courtroom, filled to capacity with strange faces; everyone stared at me, and it was so quiet; you could have heard ice melting. To my right, the round-faced, gray-haired, black-robed Judge stared down at me from behind the bench, as tall as a Wisconsin barn. Ten feet away, the accused man sat behind a table. His black-and-white striped prison uniform screamed out a contrast with all the surroundings; a razor had not touched his face in a week; the hot stare from his black, beady eyes jabbed at me like a searing poker. I knew that face, and the mere sight of it frightened me.

I turned to the man holding the Bible where my left hand rested. "I swear," I said.

Then, instantly, another man wearing a shiny, silk suit stood before me. "Where were you at four o'clock, Thursday?" he blurted.

"At the haunted house, down by the river," I said.

"And did you see anyone else there?"

"Yes, the man in the striped shirt," I answered.

"And you witnessed the sight of that man as he murdered his own children in cold blood?"

I could almost feel the striped-shirted man's eyes trying to strangle me where I sat. "Y-yes, I saw it *all*," I said.

Just then, with a lunge so quick it would have made a greyhound racer look like a turtle, the defendant leaped from behind the table; his huge hands clenched the front of my shirt and hoisted me up out of my chair. Growling and snarling like a rabid mongrel, he slung me from side to side. I tried to fight back, but my strength was no match to the deathly grip he had on me.

"Isn't *somebody* going to help me?" I yelled. But no one came to my aid. I heard the Judge, furiously hammering his gavel on the bench, while everyone else just stared in awe at the bizarre outrage. I closed my eyes, certain that the next thing I saw would be the Pearly Gates swinging open.

"Will. Will!" Jesse's voice cut through the mayhem; at last, Big Brother was there to save me from this brutal attack.

"Will, are you going to check on Mrs. Lorado?"

The motley beast in the striped shirt evaporated. I opened my eyes. Jesse was there, standing over me; his hand prodded my chest, but we weren't in a courtroom, and there weren't hundreds of people staring at me, and there wasn't a Judge pounding his gavel. We were in my cabin, and

I was in my bed; I was exhausted, but I was relieved to know that it had been only a nightmare.

"It's quarter past two," Jesse said.

I sat up.

Jesse sat on the edge of my bunk. "We got the letter from the insurance company this morning," he said, but his voice didn't sound at all happy over the long awaited news.

"So, we'll be back on the river soon," I said, trying to prod a smile from Jesse.

"No, I'm afraid not for a while."

"Why?"

"The Mississippi is low. They've suspended their offer 'till spring, when the river comes back up."

"So what are we gonna do now?"

"Luke and I have been talking it over all day," Jesse said. "We'll take the Madison up to Alton Slough and tie her up there for the winter, where she'll be safe from the ice flows in the spring... just like we did last year, during the spring floods. Luke and Reggie are going to stay with her."

"And I s'pose you're going back to St. Louis."

"Yes, and you'll come too."

It appeared as though all the plans were cut and dried without allowing me to make a choice. I was being exiled to St. Louis – a big city – the *last* place I wanted spend a whole winter. But Alton Slough wouldn't be a picnic, either; I didn't envy Luke and Reggie.

"I'll drive you over to Andrew's house if you want," Jesse said.

"No... that's okay. I'll walk."

"Why the long face, William?" Mrs. Lorado set a cup of coffee on the table in front of me.

"We won't have insurance on the boat 'till spring, and Jesse says I have to go live with him and Sadie all winter in St. Louis."

"Well, that doesn't sound so bad."

"But I don't *want* to go to St. Louis. I *hate* the big city."

"Well I don't blame you one bit. I don't like big cities either."

"I'd rather just stay on the boat up in Alton Slough."

"Oh my. That doesn't sound very pleasant."

"Well I sure don't want to go to St. Louis."

Mrs. Lorado just stared at me, and the puddle of disappointment I was spilling all over her table.

I stared at my coffee cup.

"If it weren't for the cost of groceries, you could stay here with us this winter," she said, sighing, as if she were sharing my gloom. Her statement sounded like an invitation; it sang out a song of deliverance.

I would be willing to spend all that I had to avoid moving to St. Louis; Jesse would surely understand – he knew my dislike for the city. Without giving it any more thought, I asked Mrs. Lorado, "How much?"

Her brows lifted. I could tell she was a little surprised with my response.

"How much would it cost me to stay here?" I asked again.

"Well, I don't know. Let me think... perhaps three dollars a week should be enough," she said.

"And I could help with chores around the house too."

"Don't you think you should talk it over with your brother first?"

"I will. I'll talk to him tonight."

Andrew had stopped playing the piano. He must have heard our conversation, and he joined us at the kitchen table. "Is Will going to be staying here?" he asked.

"We *do* have an extra bedroom," Mrs. Lorado said.

An obvious look of concern came to Andrew's face. "But what about Marion?" he said.

"Let's not worry about that now," Mrs. Lorado replied. "I'll take care of him when the time comes. William has to get his brother's blessing first."

"Is there going to be a problem?" I asked.

"Not at all. I'll figure something out," she said.

At that moment, I recalled what had been said about Mr. Lorado hating riverboats. "If there's a problem, I'll—"

"Don't worry about it, William. Now, go talk to your brother."

A knock sounded at the door. Mrs. Lorado hobbled on her crutches, following the little girl to the piano; minutes later, *Twinkle, Twinkle Little Star* showed little improvement. Andrew and I snuck out the back door.

We sat on the lawn behind the garage, shielded from the painful sounds produced by Mrs. Lorado's student.

"Sorry to hear about the problem with the boat," Andrew said.

"Yeah, I was looking forward to goin' back on the river. I'm learning to be a pilot, but I guess, now that'll have to wait 'till spring."

"Look on the bright side... you'll be staying here all winter."

"Yeah, if Jesse says it's okay."

"Well, if you do stay here, just remember, don't say *anything* about riverboats to Marion."

"Why do you call your father by his first name?"

"Oh, he's not my real father. Mum isn't my real mother, either... they adopted me."

"Sorry... I didn't know that."

"When are you going to talk to your brother about staying here?"

"Tonight, after supper."

Jesse and Luke had rounded up most of the crew; they were gathered in the Madison's saloon when I returned. I figured that the crew didn't know, yet, that the meeting would deliver the bad news; everyone seemed cheerful, eagerly expecting to get back to work. I could only imagine their distress with the announcement; they were about to join the millions of other unemployed people. I felt bad for them.

I found Luke and Jesse in the pilothouse, discussing the preparations to ready the Madison for her winter nap in Alton Slough. Ample supplies of firewood and coal would be loaded on the cargo deck, so Luke and Reggie could keep warm, and Jesse said that he would bring them food and any other supplies they needed every couple of weeks throughout the winter.

"We're gonna get through this," Jesse said. "We just have to think positive."

"And how will we keep the crew thinking positive?" Luke said.

"We can only hope they'll come back in the spring."

Jesse tried to appear callous to our situation, but I knew him too well. The circumstances surrounding Augie's death had taken its toll; the insurance crisis had taken another vicious bite. And now, informing the crew that they would be without jobs until spring, had hung an albatross around his neck. But I also knew that he was emotionally strong; he had proved that, more times than I could count.

"I know you've got a lot of problems right now," I said to Jesse privately that night. "And I don't want to be a burden to you."

"What do you mean by that?" he said.

"Well... I really don't want to go to St. Louis."

"But where else would you—"

"Mrs. Lorado said I could stay there... for three dollars a week... to cover groceries."

"That seems fair, but are you sure that's what you want to do?"

"Yeah, I think so."

"Well, I guess it's okay with me, but if you ever change your mind—"

"I know. I'm always welcome at your place."

41

It was a few days before Thanksgiving. The Nation had elected a new President; we could only wait until next March for Mr. Roosevelt to start making good his promises of a New Deal. The Madison had been tied up in Alton Slough for two weeks, with Luke and Reggie aboard, like hermits, enduring the long winter, and I was settled in my room at the Lorado house. By then, I had been introduced to a different lifestyle. I soon realized how much I missed the creaking noises that the Madison made during the still nights, and all the other nighttime river sounds that usually lulled me into slumber. I missed the smells of the river and coal. I missed the solidarity of the tightly knit union of friends aboard the Madison.

Andrew and I huddled around the radio during the evening hours; we'd chuckle with the silly performances of George Burns and Gracie Allen, or break out in uncontrollable laughter with the antics of Amos and Andy, and we were awed by the unbelievable adventures of Buck Rogers. Then, it was off to bed, in the silence of a solid house that did not creak or gently rock in the waves of a passing boat. It wasn't a *bad* way to spend the winter; it was quite comfortable, actually. I was among friends, Beth Lorado was a pretty good cook, I had a warm bed to sleep in, *and I wasn't in St. Louis.*

Every morning after breakfast, Mrs. Lorado marched Andrew and me into a den that resembled a school classroom, filled with books, and maps on the wall, and even a chalkboard. Sometimes, she would read to us from a classic novel, and then encourage us to read the rest of it. Sometimes, she plodded us through mathematical equations, or explained the theories of science; sometimes the instruction centered on the proper use of the English language. She'd pose questions and expect answers, just like a real teacher in a real school.

In time, I began to enjoy those four hours every day; never before had learning seemed so satisfying, or had it ever been so much fun. And I could see the beam of delight in Mrs. Lorado's eyes with each academic accomplishment Andrew and I made.

Every day at one o'clock, Andrew began his two-hour piano practice, and I spent that time devouring the pages of *Robin Hood, Treasure Island*, and my favorite, *Huckleberry Finn*. Then, at three o'clock, *Twinkle, Twinkle* signaled the time for Andrew and I to escape out the back door. We'd engage in a ply to explore and to discover the season's change. We'd walk along the river levee, now nearly void of boats; even the Silverado had gone south to a warmer port. One day, I coaxed Andrew into visiting the café in town where Mildred worked; Mildred bought us coffee, and I bought us ice cream.

We roamed the sleepy streets of St. Charles, and took pity on hobos huddled around trash fires along the railroad tracks. We laughed at each other's jokes, and cried with each other's sorrows. We shared our hopes and dreams as we trod down country roads. But we didn't go back to the haunted house by the Missouri River.

The days were getting shorter, and the north wind chilled the air, keeping us closer to home. Eventually, our daily retreat led us to either Andrew's room, or mine. Andrew's room was more interesting: pictures, clipped from magazines, nearly covered the walls – everything from movie stars to automobile ads. On a table in one corner, sat a half-built wooden model of a schooner ship, and on another table, a half-finished giant jigsaw puzzle, with hundreds of pieces left scattered, waiting to be put in place to complete the picture of a medieval castle. Books lined a four-shelf bookcase, interrupted by a few surviving childhood toys – a scratched and worn fire engine, a locomotive, and a stuffed rabbit, faded and frazzled, with one ear and one eye missing.

We were sitting at the table with the puzzle, trying to fit a few more pieces together, and discussing that day's history lesson about Lewis and Clark starting their journey up the Missouri River from right there at St. Charles. Mrs. Lorado's last piano student had left a few minutes earlier, and we heard pots and pans rattling in the kitchen; supper was in the making.

The back door opened and closed, and then a man's voice mingled with the noises from the kitchen.

"Marion's home," Andrew said. He jumped up from his chair and ran to the stairway.

I wasn't invited to the homecoming, and although I was curious to see the man who hated riverboats, I thought it was best to just return to my room, and wait until the family had time to reunite, without me getting in the way. Their voices drifted through the heat register in the floor; what should have been a happy time for them sounded less than joyous.

"They laid off the whole crew," I heard Mr. Lorado say.

"For how long?" Mrs. Lorado asked.

"I don't know. Probably 'till next spring."

"Well, anyway, it's good to have you home."

There was a pause in the conversation, and then Marion said, "Why are you setting four places at the table? Are you expecting company for supper?"

"Oh... no." Mrs. Lorado replied. "I rented the spare room to a nice young man for the winter... his name is William... he'll be my student with Andrew."

"Beth, you'd take in a stray dog if you thought you could teach him something."

"Well, it's not like I *took him in*... he paid in advance, so you be nice to him."

Right then, I understood Mrs. Lorado's method to justify my presence. I *was* her student, and I *had* paid in advance, and the money was certainly important to them. There was only one issue left: how would I ever keep the Madison a secret? Mr. Lorado would surely ask questions, and I wasn't a very good liar.

"Well, you must be Beth's new student," Mr. Lorado said to me, as we took our places around the supper table. He was a big man with hair black as the night, and eyes bright as searchlights. Unmistakably, he was a man of industrial fortitude, and not one to follow any line of bull, just for the sake of having something to believe in.

Mrs. Lorado put her hand on my shoulder and said, "This is William Madison. His brother and sister-in-law live in St. Louis."

"St. Louie," Marion said. "You grow up there?"

"No sir," I replied. "Milwaukee."

Marion sipped a spoonful of his vegetable soup. "What brings you to St. Charles?"

"My brother, Jesse, met this lady friend from St. Louis a couple of years ago... they got married, and now they live there, but I didn't want to live in St. Louis."

Beth Lorado nervously stirred her bowl of soup and just listened; I think she was more worried of my secret getting out than I was.

"Where's your folks?" Marion asked.

I stared down at my soup bowl. "They're both gone."

"Oh. Sorry to hear that."

So far, I was in the clear. I hadn't lied about anything, yet, and I thought that Mr. Lorado was satisfied with the answers. He kept sipping his soup until the bowl was nearly empty, but he appeared to be deep in thought. Then, he calmly rested the spoon in the bowl; his searchlight eyes stared across the table at me. "There's a boat been tied up near the railhead down by the levee... the Madison... Captain's name is *Jesse Madison*. That wouldn't be your brother, now, would it?"

So much for keeping the secret. I felt my face turn redder than the tomatoes in the soup. Andrew quit eating and stared, astonished.

"Marion, dear," Beth said, trying to divert her husband's attention. "Would you like some more soup?"

Marion ignored her, and continued his interrogating stare at me. *"Well?"* he said. "Is that the *same Jesse Madison?"*

"Yes, sir. It is," I said, before anyone else could speak. I knew that I had to stand up to Marion, and defend my own pride.

"Dammit, Beth. You took in river trash."

"Will isn't river trash," Andrew piped up. "He goes to church every Sunday."

Beth stepped behind my chair and rested her hands on my shoulders. "Marion. You promised me you would be nice to the boy."

"He's *still* river trash," Marion said in a tone of disgust.

"He is not," Andrew said again.

Marion glared at Andrew. "Your father was no good river trash. We took you in when he couldn't do better than ride up and down the river and gamble his life away."

"But Will saved my life," Andrew said.

Beth looked at Andrew with a bit of surprise. "What on earth are you talking about, Andrew?"

"This summer... I was swimming in the river and I got cramps. I guess I passed out and Will pulled me out."

So much for Andrew keeping *his* secret, too.

"Andrew!" Beth stared daggers into him. "Your nanny drowned in that river. How many times have I told you to stay away from --?"

"Oh Beth," Mr. Lorado interrupted. "Ain't no harm in the boy going for a swim on a hot summer day."

"Isn't any harm?" Mrs. Lorado retaliated. "You heard him. He cramped up and almost drowned."

At least, I wasn't in the crossfire anymore; Andrew had become the target. It seemed that Marion had jumped sides, and was defending Andrew's actions now. It must have been because he thought young boys should be swimming or riding horses, instead of playing the piano.

Outnumbered, Mr. Lorado got up from the table and sauntered to an easy chair in the sitting room. "Hmf, river trash," I heard him mumble under his breath.

Mrs. Lorado must have decided she didn't want to hear any more about Andrew's mishap. She started gathering the dirty dishes from the table.

Andrew and I retreated quietly up the stairs.

"I told you he didn't like riverboats," Andrew whispered. "Why did you say --?"

"I couldn't help it," I said, staring at Andrew's raggedy stuffed rabbit. "He asked, and I couldn't lie."

"I suppose he would've found out sooner or later."

"And what about you?" I said. "You're the one that blabbed about you almost drowning."

"I was only trying to make you look good."

It occurred to me that Andrew had sacrificed his guarded secrecy, in an attempt to save me from Marion's scorn. This was the first time that he had ever spoken openly about the river incident; there was a chance it would threaten his relationship with Beth. Perhaps he was a better friend than I already thought.

After about two hours with the puzzle, we had barely fitted a dozen pieces, and we began tiring of it quickly. I returned to my room and settled in for the night; thoughts of the supper table skirmish kept rattling in my head. Mr. Lorado and I had gotten off to a very bad start; our confrontation had even caused a certain amount of unrest in his family. The timing was incredibly bad – it would be a long winter.

If I could only talk to him, I thought. If he would listen, maybe I could reconcile our differences. I lay awake for two hours rehearsing what I would say to him in the morning.

Marion sat quietly at the kitchen table with a newspaper spread out flat in front of him, and a coffee cup in hand. He didn't look up when I entered the room. I could see he was reading an article about the newly elected President, Franklin Roosevelt.

Beth stood at the kitchen sink, wiping her hands with a dishtowel; she looked as though she were just daydreaming.

"Well, good morning, William," Mrs. Lorado said. "You're up early."

"Good morning," I said, and sat down across the table from Marion. He still didn't look up.

Beth poured another cup of coffee and set it in front of me. I sat there nervously about two or three minutes, hoping Marion would at least acknowledge my presence. He didn't.

"Mr. Lorado?" I said.

He raised his brows and his bright eyes glanced my way for just an instant, but he said nothing.

"I know you don't like riverboats, because you work for the railroad. But me and Jesse own one, and we've worked hard for the last two years to earn an honest living on that boat, and we've kept a lot of other good men and their families fed, too. We're good people. We're not river trash, and I just want us to be friends."

Marion leaned back in his chair and just stared at me.

"He's right, dear," Beth said. "William and his brother were the good Samaritans who came to help, the night I sprained my ankle. Why, we didn't even know them then."

Marion folded the newspaper, stood up without saying a word, took his plaid wool coat from a hook, and put it on. "I'm goin' downtown," he said to Beth, and went out the door.

"Don't worry, William. He'll come around. He'll get over it in time," Beth said.

It was the day before Thanksgiving. I had not yet heard any mention of a special dinner, like Henry would prepare for the Madison's crew on Thanksgiving Day.

"Will you be needing any help to fix the Thanksgiving dinner?" I asked Beth. I thought I'd pose a question like that, just in case she had forgotten.

"I'm afraid there won't be a big dinner this year," Beth said. She sighed with sadness. "We'll just have to be satisfied with vegetable stew, and maybe some cornbread."

Just then, Andrew came into the kitchen, rubbing his eyes and yawning.

"Boys," Beth said. "We'll skip the lessons today. Now, sit down and have your breakfast, and Andrew, if you're going to practice, do it now while Marion is gone."

We ate our bread and jam. Andrew ambled into the front room and began playing. Beth busied herself at the kitchen sink. I slipped out the back door.

Jesse, Luke, and I were the fortunate ones. In a time when most people were barely getting by, out of work and with only a hope of an improved future to keep them going, we had done all right, although, we were beginning to feel the Depression's effects. We could not deny that luck had attributed our success, and if it had not been for a few foolish risks taken over two years before, we might not be so well off.

Surrounding me now, though, were the difficult times. Hardship seemed abundant. Nowhere, did I see the signs of our success, and likely, no one else did, either. As I walked along the lonely levee, I thought about Jesse and Sadie and young Philip, and I wondered how Reggie and Luke were getting along. I thought about our future, and about where we might find new adventure, farther down the Mississippi. I dreamed of the day that I would be a capable pilot at the wheel of the Madison, with the gentle river breeze whisking at my face through the open pilothouse windows. I wondered how long it would take Mr. Lorado to accept me as something other than river trash.

But with all those things to think about, another puzzle kept poking at me, like a pin left in a new shirt. During the few weeks that I had been living with the Lorados, something about Andrew nagged me, but I could never quite put my finger on it. He was smart, talented, and he had proven to be a very good friend, but there still seemed to be something rather mysterious about him.

Right then, though, I needed to concentrate on Thanksgiving dinner; the Lorados could not afford to buy anything special, but I could. Jesse had left some extra money with me; this seemed to be a good reason to spend some of it.

Beth was overjoyed and most grateful for the turkey – the last one left at the grocer's – and perhaps this act of thoughtfulness might earn some extra credit with Mr. Lorado, too.

Without a word of appreciation, except to his wife, for cooking such a wonderful meal, Marion retired to his easy chair in the sitting room and quickly dozed off into a nap. Being Thanksgiving Day, there wasn't much point in doing anything else. Andrew and I were helping Mrs. Lorado clear the table and wash the dishes when I heard a car stopping in the street. I stretched to see out the window. It was Jesse's Model A. I threw down my towel and ran to the front porch. Jesse met me half way up the lawn with one of his Big Brother bear hugs. We didn't have to speak any greetings.

"I'm on my way up to the boat... to take Luke and Reggie some supplies," Jesse said. "Thought I'd better stop in and see how Little Brother is doing."

"We just got done eating our Thanksgiving dinner. I bought a turkey... there's some left. Do you want some turkey?"

Jesse seemed a little startled. "*You* bought a turkey?"

"Yeah. Mr. Lorado lost his job for the winter, and they couldn't afford one."

"Couldn't afford a turkey? Maybe I should be bringing *you* a load of supplies, too."

"Oh... no. Mrs. Lorado has a whole root cellar full of canned vegetables and stuff. We'll be fine."

Just then, Beth called out from the porch, "Jesse, come on in out of the cold. I'm brewing a fresh pot of coffee."

We all sat down around the kitchen table – everyone, except Marion.

Beth poured the coffee. "Marion," she directed a louder voice toward the sitting room. "Come meet William's brother, Jesse."

"Don't need to meet no more river trash... one's enough," came the reply.

Beth looked at Jesse. I could tell she was embarrassed. "Don't mind him," she said. "He's just a little grumpy because there's no work right now."

"Is there anything I can do to help?" Jesse said.

Beth just shook her head. "No... not unless you have a job in your back pocket."

"As a matter of fact," Jesse said. He smiled and pulled several sheets of folded paper from inside his jacket. He laid them in front of me. "Mr. Lorado is a carpenter, isn't he?"

I unfolded the papers and eyed Jesse with smoldering curiosity. "What's this?" I asked.

"It's the plans for addin' more staterooms on the Madison."

With Andrew looking over my shoulder, I stared at the drawings spread out on the table.

"Will," Jesse said, "Me and Lester have been goin' over the books, and we figured now would be a good time to convert the cargo deck into more passenger rooms... before the heavy travelin' season starts."

"But how are we gonna manage all this?" I said.

"We'll have to hire a good carpenter." Jesse looked at Beth. "And if Mr. Lorado is out of work, maybe he'd take the job."

Beth's eyes lit up. "Marion! Come in here... right now!"

Mr. Lorado came stumbling into the kitchen, obviously irritated with being disturbed from his nap. "What do you want now?" he grumbled.

"I understand you're a pretty good builder," Jesse said.

"Pretty good?" Marion glared at Jesse. "I built eleven houses in St. Charles before I went to work for the railroad, including this one."

"And it's a nice house too," I said, pouring on the charm. "Don't you think so, Jesse?"

"What? You want me to build a house for you?" Marion sneered.

"No," Jesse said. "I already have a house in St. Louis. Actually, we're gonna add some more staterooms on our riverboat. We need a good carpenter... like you."

I held my breath. I knew Jesse wasn't totally aware of Marion's adamant dislike for riverboats, or the people associated with them.

Marion stepped closer to the table; his search light eyes scanned the drawings and then he stepped back again. "I wouldn't set foot on a riverboat. It'd have to be the last job left on the face of the earth."

Beth's smile turned into scowling anger. "Marion. You should be ashamed. This might very well *be* the last job on the face of the earth. Put aside your pride and think of your family. You *need* this job."

Marion looked at Beth, knowing he had been duly scolded. He turned and started back toward the easy chair. "I'll think about it," he said, sat down, and closed his eyes.

Jesse didn't seem nearly as disturbed with the insult that he had just received, as I thought he would. He sipped his coffee and proceeded to explain all the changes and additions, pointing them out to me on the papers as he went along. Andrew quietly looked on. Beth left the room with tears streaming.

"I have to be going now," Jesse finally said. "Luke and Reggie are waiting for me, and I have to get some more measurements."

"When will you be back again," I asked.

"The day before Christmas. And I'll leave those drawings here with you... I have more copies."

We walked slowly out to Jesse's truck. All the while, I thought about how long it would be until he returned; I felt a quiver in my throat when I said, "Tell Luke and Reggie Hi for me, and say Hello to Sadie and Philip, too."

Jesse gave me another bear hug, smiled a sad sort of smile, got in his truck and drove away.

That night, after Andrew and I had our fill of radio programs, I noticed Mr. Lorado sitting at the kitchen table as I started up the stairway. He was only a dark silhouette against the dim light of a small lamp. He was studying Jesse's drawings.

42

The weeks passed by at a glacier's pace until Christmas. Andrew spent a lot of time at the church practicing, and I spent a lot of time avoiding unnecessary contact with Mr. Lorado. I heard *Twinkle, Twinkle Little Star* so many times that I wanted to scream; I began having nightmares about Mary and a whole flock of little lambs.

There were some good times, too. On Saturday afternoons, Andrew and I would go to the downtown theater for a matinee; ten cents treated us to a couple of hours in a world somewhere beyond our simple existence. Chaplin made us laugh; Barrymore kept us in suspense; Garbo summoned a tear or two. Then there was Will Rogers, who could do all that, and then some. As for all the actors that appeared on that big screen, I liked him best; he always seemed so natural, and I had heard his name mentioned by so many people. It almost seemed like I knew him personally. Charles Lindbergh had held the top spot on my list of heroes since that day in 1927, but now, I thought Will Rogers challenged for that honor.

As Christmas drew nearer, I became more anxious – not because I expected gifts; I knew that there would be few, if any at all. I was anxious because Big Brother would be back. Our visit at Thanksgiving had been quite brief; we hadn't afforded ourselves enough time to connect on that personal level that always kept my compass needle pointing in the right direction. It had seemed more like a business meeting.

Beth did a good job of keeping Marion at bay whenever his inner army of anti-riverboat soldiers appeared to be mustering for an attack on my integrity. She'd send him on an errand, or draw from her mental list of fix-it jobs, that she knew would keep him busy for a while and get his mind off the resentment he held for me. At the supper table was her toughest task of defense, when she could not justify sending him away from my presence. She'd calmly remind him of the pending work that Jesse had offered – the work that he desperately needed to sustain his family through the winter. I think she was finally softening him a little, because I hadn't heard him use the term *river trash* since Thanksgiving, although, I wasn't sure if he would ever accept Jesse's proposition. When Mr. Lorado's army retreated, Beth would throw me one of her velvet smiles, and I knew that I was safe from imminent assault.

Marion's resentment didn't seem to end with me. Ever since that first night, when he discovered my true identity, and how Andrew and I had become associated, I noticed his lack of interest in Andrew. I didn't know if it had always been that way; Andrew paid little attention to he-man sports like football or baseball, and he didn't possess the desire to bivouac in the wild, to engage in the brutal assault on an innocent flock of geese or a graceful buck deer. Maybe Marion's resentment stemmed from Beth's successful capture of Andrew's interest in music; to her, Andrew's musical talent was a sacred cow, not to be questioned or criticized, but instead, to be guarded and nurtured, and Marion knew that he could do little to sway his son's interest to pursue a more manly lifestyle.

But I knew Andrew differently; I had witnessed his athletic ability; I knew that he had the stamina to outrun an antelope.

I recalled the day that he had described to me the radio broadcast of the World Series game, when Babe Ruth pointed to the bleachers, indicating his intentions of an out-of-here homerun hit, and then did it. Andrew's focus on that event captivated me, and I didn't know why he hadn't displayed that enthusiasm to Marion.

I knew Andrew loved the outdoors, and he always craved to be next to nature, shirtless and uninhibited by male instincts.

He could stick a knife blade into a tree trunk from ten yards, as good as any circus performer, and he could climb a tree quicker than a Minnesota lumberjack.

When we went to the movies, I would see Andrew's eyes falling on the pretty young girls waiting in line, and I would see their eyes flirting with him, the handsomest young man in St. Charles. Afterwards, when we returned to the privacy of his room, Andrew would tell me about his carnal fantasies.

I was very aware, too, of Andrew's love for the feel of the ivories at his fingertips, and the wonderful music that he could produce, but to me, that was no reason to warrant the label Marion seemed to be pasting on Andrew's forehead. There was nothing outwardly abnormal about Andrew; he was a red-blooded American boy, as much as I was, just a little different, and for some reason, he guarded his true character from Marion.

I thought that Marion might be confused by his own definition of *different.*

A couple of days before Christmas, Marion went off somewhere with a hatchet, to rid the forest of at least one small Christmas tree; Andrew and I had retreated to his upstairs room, to escape the torture from one of Mrs. Lorado's Twinkle, Twinkle students. Andrew had gathered together the ingredients for a recipe that he found in a book, for a clear, gooey substance. He started stirring it up in an old mixing bowl that Beth had stashed in the cellar.

"What's that for?" I asked.

"The book says you can smear this stuff on a jigsaw puzzle like paint. When it dries, all the pieces of the puzzle will be stuck together, and you can hang it up on the wall."

"Why would you want to hang a jigsaw puzzle on the wall?"

"It's going to be Mum's Christmas present... she likes pretty pictures."

"What about your dad? What are you giving Marion?"

Andrew pointed to the wooden ship model that was complete, with real cloth sails and a tiny American Flag, starched into a permanent wave, like it was blowing in the wind.

"But I thought your dad hates boats," I said.

"Just riverboats that crash into his railroad bridges. Sailing ships are different."

"Oh. I guess he'll like it then."

"Yeah. He used to be in the Navy before he married Mum."

I filed that bit of information away into my memory, in case I needed it later; I thought it might come in handy some time. Then I asked Andrew if I could help with the invisible paint project.

"Sure," he said, without any hesitation.

As usual, my painting experience produced the same results then, as it had aboard the Madison. By the time the castle was covered with a coat of the clear goop, so was the front of my shirt. It kind of reminded me of something personal that I didn't want to talk about – not even to Andrew.

He giggled when he saw it. "Better get that shirt off or it will be stuck to you permanently." He giggled some more.

It *was* rather humorous, but I didn't like the idea of wearing the same shirt for the rest of my life. I started to take it off.

"Don't worry," Andrew said. "It's mostly cornstarch... it'll wash out."

Whether it would wash out or not, I could still imagine myself stuck inside that shirt; I didn't waste any time getting out of it. I didn't worry about exposing my bare torso, and I didn't think about it until my shirt was completely off, and I noticed Andrew's stare, like a little kid eyeing a cookie jar that he knew he couldn't reach. At first, I thought he was staring at my scar collection. It wouldn't have been the first time that someone gawked at those scars. But then I realized that Andrew wasn't staring at my scars. The chain around my neck, with that silver ring dangling from it, had become about as natural a part of me as a fingernail; it never occurred to me, until that very moment, that I had just exposed another secret; I didn't have a clue how to explain why I had kept it from him.

I just stood there, feeling the warm sensation of my face turning the shade of a field-ripened strawberry, while Andrew stared blankly at my chest for a few moments. Then, like he snapped out of a hypnotic trance, he blinked two or three times, and his whole face turned into a grin as big as Missouri. "Better get another shirt... you'll get cold," he said.

I went to my room and found another shirt, arming myself with an explanation, should Andrew ask about the ring. He didn't.

"Are you gonna give us a concert on Christmas Eve?" I asked him.

Andrew threw me a surprised look. "Why?"

"Well, I thought it might be nice. I haven't heard you play since your Dad came home, except at church on Sundays. I just thought it would be nice to hear you play again... that's all."

Andrew's face fell solemn. "Marion hasn't heard me play in years."

"Why not?"

"Because he doesn't go with us to church, and he doesn't like me playing the piano at home."

"Why? Because he thinks playing the piano is for sissies?"

"Yeah, I guess."

"But if he hasn't heard you play in years, then he doesn't know how *good* you are now."

"I don't know, Will—"

"Well I *do* know, and I think you should give him a sample, no, a full-fledged concert... on Christmas Eve."

"But what if he gets mad and starts throwing one of his temper tantrums?"

"He won't. Didn't you see how he backed down when I stood up to him?"

"What do you mean?"

"He hates riverboats, and he probably hates me, too, but I stood up to him with the truth, and he has the decency not to kill me."

"That's different. *You* can walk away from here anytime you want. I can't. I have to live here."

"That's exactly why you *should* play for him now... because you have to live here. Why should you have to live in fear that your dad doesn't like your music?"

"I'd make more headway if I walked into the room wearing a football uniform, carrying a baseball bat on one shoulder and a shotgun on the other... and then asking him if he wants to go downtown to shoot pool after supper, or maybe go out in the woods and kill something. I don't know, Will—"

"Like I said... I *do know*... I just think you should play for him. It might be the best Christmas present you could give him. And maybe the best one you could give yourself, too."

I lay in bed that night, staring up into the charcoal gray where the ceiling should be. I didn't think about how I missed the Madison's creaks and groans. Instead, I worried that I might have enticed Andrew into firing the first shot that would begin another Civil War. I thought about the gifts, that he had spent months making, for Beth and Marion. I suspected that Andrew would have a gift for me too, as thoughtful as he was, and how there wasn't enough time left until Christmas for me to make something nice for all of them. But I did have one day, and I did have some money left, and I didn't care if I couldn't go to another Will Rogers movie all winter. I would spend my money on Christmas presents for the Lorado family.

Then I thought about Jesse... and Sadie... and little Philip, who I'd never met. They were important people, too; I couldn't leave them off my list. And what about Luke and Reggie? They were sacrificing their Christmas so we all would still have a boat to go back to next spring. And how could I forget Mildred? She'd been like a Mom to me for the last two years.

Nine people. Nine presents. One day.

I got out of bed, turned on the light, slid open the top dresser drawer, dug down under my socks where I stashed my money, and counted twenty-two dollars and fifty-eight cents. I turned off the light and went back to bed, happy. If I spent two dollars on each present, I'd still have enough left to see some more Will Rogers movies.

The smell of freshly baked cookies and pine trees met me at the top of the stairs. Beth had been up since dawn, baking the cookies, and Marion displayed his carpentry skills, building a Christmas tree stand in the sitting room. I remembered those same smells from Christmases when I was little, but now they seemed more significant and meaningful. Christmas. This was the first one ever, when I would go out on my own, with my own money, and shop for presents; it made me feel good.

Some of the stores were just opening as I marched proudly and curiously through the crisp early morning. I was a novice at this, but I tried not to let it show. After an hour, or so, of just peering into the many shop windows lining the brick-paved Main Street, I thought that I had made most of my selections, and it was just a matter of going in to buy them.

Luke and Reggie would get Chicago Cubs baseball caps – Luke, because I knew that he was a Cubs fan, and Reggie, because he was a fan of anything Luke was. Leather gloves for Jesse. Silky scarves for Sadie and Beth, red for Sadie, because she was a little on the bold side, and light blue for Beth, because I remembered her favorite powder blue dress she always wore to church. Mildred was easy – a bottle of her favorite lilac perfume. I had seen Marion's broken, numbers-worn-off, folding carpenter's ruler; he definitely needed a new one. I had a choice of a stuffed dog or a cute little stuffed rabbit for Philip; all the Teddy Bears were gone. I chose the floppy-eared blue rabbit.

That left Andrew, and I already had a very special gift in mind for him. It wouldn't come from any store in town.

I dropped off Mildred's present at the café. It was her day off, and I didn't know where she lived. As I hurried along to the end of Fourth Street with my arms laden with all the packages nicely-wrapped in mostly red and green, I couldn't get my mind off that stupid rabbit. Why had I picked a stupid *blue rabbit?* This was Christmas – not Easter.

From the upstairs window, I saw that the back of Jesse's truck was loaded with all sorts of stuff, covered by an old faded canvas tarp, the color of dried-up mustard. Supplies for Luke and Reggie, I thought. Once again, Jesse was alone.

I raced down the stairs and was on the front porch by the time Jesse reached the steps. Even though I was sixteen, going on thirty-five, at that moment, I felt like a little kid again, anxiously awaiting the arrival of Santa Claus, and there he was. I didn't care about any presents; I was just glad that Jesse was there. That's all that seemed to matter to me right then.

"Merry Christmas, Little Brother," he said with one of his bear hugs.

"Merry Christmas, Big Brother," I said back, duplicating the hug.

"Put your coat on and help me carry some stuff into the house," he said.

"I'm not cold," I replied. "What is it?"

We walked to the truck and Jesse threw a corner of the tarp back, uncovering several brown paper bags filled with groceries. He lifted one out and handed it to me, and then grabbed another one. "These two are for you and the Lorados," he said. "The others are for Luke and Reggie."

We started walking toward the house. I wasn't surprised to see Beth at the front door; she was all smile from head to toe, mixed with a few baking flour handprints on the front of her apron. But I *was* surprised to see Marion standing there with her. He wasn't exactly smiling.

"What's all this?" Beth asked. Her voice oozed with astonished enthusiasm, like a jellyroll with too much jelly in it.

"Look," I said. "It's groceries." I held the bag so she could see inside.

"We probably have a better selection in St. Louis," Jesse said, beaming with satisfaction.

Mr. Lorado glared at Jesse. "We don't need your charity."

"It's not charity," Jesse said, still smiling. "It's a Christmas present... for all of you."

I knew differently. But if Jesse's charm worked on Marion like it did on most everyone else, there was no way that Mr. Lorado could refuse a kind gesture that went with the Season.

I looked at Marion with a pair of puppy dog eyes, mentally begging him to accept the gift, and then ruffle the fur on the top of my head.

It worked. Marion reached out toward Jesse to take the bag from him. I could tell he wanted to accept it then, just as much as Jesse wanted to give it. Beth took the bag from me.

"Thank you," they both said, but Jesse did my fur ruffling part.

"We're having our Christmas dinner tomorrow," Beth said. She fondled and admired a can of pink salmon from the grocery bag. "Can you stay?"

"No, I'm sorry, I can't," Jesse answered. "My wife is cooking, and I have a little boy waiting for Santa Claus."

Mr. Lorado leaned against the kitchen counter next to Beth. "How old?" he said.

"Almost a year and a half."

That got Marion and Jesse started, and I was glad that Marion had decided that talking to river trash wasn't so bad, after all. I slipped away up to my room and returned, a few minutes later, carrying five festively wrapped packages. By then, Marion and Jesse were scanning the drawings that Jesse left on Thanksgiving; Marion pointed out several design flaws, and how to improve on them. Jesse nodded his approval.

An hour, and several cups of coffee later, it appeared as though Jesse and Marion had reached an agreement: by April, the Madison would be fitted with fourteen more staterooms.

My life would be much less stressful, now that Marion had miraculously shed his pit bull attitude toward riverboats and river people. But then I worried that he would turn his fury on Andrew again, as a result of the Christmas Eve concert that I had talked Andrew into, and maybe the pit bull would just take on a different snarl.

I tried not to think anymore about the impending battle, while Jesse and I spent another too brief visit alone. We walked to his truck, and once again, I realized our parting marked the beginning of another long period without Big Brother.

"Be sure to give Luke and Reggie my presents," I said.

Jesse nodded, and retrieved a bright red package from the seat of the truck; he handed it to me.

"This is from all of us. Sadie made it... might be a little big, but you'll grow into it. Merry Christmas."

"Thank you, Jesse," I said, and that time, I initiated the bear hug.

At the Christmas Eve supper table, Beth announced that no presents would be opened until the dishes were washed, dried, and put away. She only said that to ensure plenty of help. It worked.

We gathered in the sitting room around the tree that we had all taken a part in trimming. Not the most attractive Christmas tree I had ever seen, it was a little lop-sided and a bare spot here and there, but the lights, shiny balls, a few strands of sparkly tinsel, left over from the previous year, and a silver star at the top, made up for its shortcomings, and it was *our* Christmas tree. Beth had lined the floor around the bottom with white tissue paper, giving it the appearance of standing in an isolated little patch of snow. Very few packages lay under it, and that didn't surprise me.

Beth was thrilled with the silky blue scarf; she said it would go perfectly with her favorite Sunday dress. Marion said nothing more than "Thank you, Will," to the folding ruler, but I knew that he liked it.

Andrew and I got matching mittens and stocking caps that Mrs. Lorado had knitted: Andrew's were dark red and mine, dark blue.

Then Andrew handed his present to me. I tore the paper away to expose a Blue Tip matchbox, but by the way it rattled, I knew the box didn't contain matches. I slid the outer cover off. A compass, about the size of a silver dollar, stared up at me.

"It's so you don't get lost," Andrew said to me. He beamed a smile.

We laughed, but we were the only ones in the room to understand why.

"Thank you, Andrew," I said, and then I reached for a small white box under the tree. I held it out in front of him.

"Wait," he said. A look of urgency came to him. "I'll be right back." He jumped up and ran to the stairway.

"Aren't you going to open your present from your brother?" Beth said to me.

I'd been saving that one for last. I ripped off the barn red paper, opened the box, and pulled out a sweater. The rusty brown color reminded me of oak trees in the fall. I held it up for everyone to see, but by then, Marion was leaned back in his easy chair with a newspaper hiding him from the rest of the world.

"It's lovely," Beth said.

Jesse wasn't kidding when he said it might be a little large, but I liked it anyway.

"Close your eyes Mum," we heard Andrew call out.

Beth closed her eyes, and when Andrew stood before her with the glued-together jigsaw puzzle, she opened them again on command.

"Oh! It's beautiful!" she said, all surprised, as if she hadn't already seen it a hundred times.

"It's all stuck together so you can hang it up on the kitchen wall," Andrew said.

Mrs. Lorado admired the castle picture at arm's length, while Andrew ran up the stairs again, and moments later, he repeated the "close your eyes" request to Marion.

I never saw a grown man, so intrigued with a toy boat, as I did that night. He actually carried on a conversation with Andrew about sails and masts, poop decks and crow's nests. I'd never seen or heard them talk like that before.

Eventually the wooden boat was set aside, and Marion went back to his newspaper. Once again, I offered the tiny white box to Andrew. He said "Thank you" in advance of opening it. I expected his eyes to get the size of my compass, but instead, his cheerful face twisted into a bit of a frown; he stared blankly into the box a long moment, and then looked at me.

"I can't take this," he said. He plucked the silver ring from the box and held it toward me, as if he wanted me to take it from him. "It's *yours*."

"No," I said. "You lost it, and now I want to give it back to you."

Andrew shook his head. "I didn't *loose* it... I *gave* it to you... it belongs to *you*."

"But why?"

"Because some day you'll go away from here, and we may never see each other again. It'll remind you of our friendship."

"I don't need anything to remind me, Andrew. I'll remember our friendship without it. Please... put it on your finger."

He slipped it on, but I thought his expression was more of disappointment than pleasure.

Marion's newspaper rattled as he turned the page. Beth headed for the kitchen. I started struggling my way into the too large sweater for a test fit. Andrew disappeared up the stairway. I wondered if he would change into the football uniform.

A few minutes passed – long enough for me to push the sweater sleeves into a big bunch at my elbows, and determine that, even though it was too big, it was a gift I would treasure.

Andrew appeared again; I hadn't noticed his footsteps on the stairs. He *wasn't* wearing a football uniform. He paused just briefly, and gave me a worried glance as he stepped quietly toward the piano, and turned toward Marion, still buried behind a curtain of newspaper. Andrew lifted the cover off the keyboard; it made a moderate clunk. Marion didn't move. With his eyes focused intently on Marion, Andrew kicked off his shoes, and they made clunks on the hardwood floor, but Mr. Lorado still didn't stir. Then Andrew sat down on the bench and put his trembling hands up to the keys.

I felt beads of sweat trickling down my chest; I wasn't sure if it was because the sweater was too warm, or if my nerves were anticipating canon fire.

The first bass notes rumbled like thunder from a distant horizon; Andrew's fingers danced across the keyboard from left to right, performing an arpeggio that I thought, in itself, was a masterpiece, and then the tinkling high notes cascaded gracefully, like a majestic waterfall. I heard the newspaper rattle, and then I saw Marion slam it to his lap. Beth came from the kitchen, wiping her hands on a dishtowel. She fixed a worried stare on her husband.

Before anyone could say anything, Andrew began playing a familiar tune – *I've Been Working On The Railroad* – but in a classical style that made it sound like a great anthem. It was magnificent.

I kept one eye on Marion; I was ready to make a run for the door, should the shooting start, but Marion just sat there, still, gawking toward the piano. A trace of a smile began to form on his face, and it slowly flowered into a full-fledged pleasant grin. Andrew played, nonstop, into a medley of carols, beginning with *I Wish You A Merry Christmas,* with the same, elegant orchestral flare. Tiny droplets of perspiration painted wet lines down his golden cheeks, but he wasn't wearing a heavy sweater.

When Andrew finally stopped playing, about a half-hour later, he dropped his hands to his sides, closed his eyes, and just sat there in the silence, waiting for the condemnation from across the room. He slowly started to turn, to face his executioner, but instead of hearing anger and rage, he heard Marion's hands come together with complimenting applause.

Beth smiled with relief.

Andrew smiled with his accomplishment.

I smiled with the thought that this was a Christmas I would never forget. No one would.

Morning sifted through my bedroom curtains; I wondered if the sparrows, chirping outside the window, knew it was Christmas. I wondered if Jesse's gloves fit him okay, and I hoped that Sadie's red scarf wasn't too bold. *And that rabbit.* Why did I pick a stuffed rabbit?

Andrew was already up and getting ready for church; he always left earlier than Beth and me, so he could be playing the prelude when the first parishioners started arriving. And on that day, the church would be full – it was Christmas Day.

A glitter on the table next to my bed caught my eye; I studied it a few moments. It was a familiar sight – my silver neck chain, and Andrew's ring. *Andrew's ring.* I imagined Golden Boy slipping through the darkness, peeking through a cracked door to make sure I was asleep, and then tiptoeing to the table to replace the ring on my chain. I didn't have to wonder *why* he had done it, and I wouldn't question him about it, but I did feel sort of bad, now that I hadn't really given him a Christmas gift.

All decked out in my new, oak leaf brown sweater, I trotted down the stairs, expecting to see Beth waiting for me to join her on the usual walk to the church. That day, it was different. Marion was waiting, too.

We sat near the front, and for the next hour, I rubbed elbows with the new Marion Lorado, while *his* Golden Boy played better than I had ever heard him play before.

Yes, it was a Christmas I would not soon forget.

43

S ometimes at night, when Andrew and I leaned into the scratchy sounds from the radio, the news reports made me feel like a peeping Tom, peering into the front window of America. It was a time of profound trial – not just on a level of personal survival, but of democracy, the fundamental system of the American way. Hardship bred despair throughout the country. Everything had fallen apart: industrial output, employment, wages, prices, and worst of all, human spirits.

We heard about failed businessmen, selling apples on the street corners, and about breadlines at soup kitchens in the bigger cities. Large numbers of homeless people wandered from city to city, state to state, hoping to find the slightest crumb of prosperity, only to find more of the same impoverished life they had left behind.

Franklin Roosevelt seemed to understand what the Nation needed. He had lifted the American spirit with his pledge of a new deal; the country had listened, and it had trusted. Now, we could only wait.

Winter dragged on. Marion was away most of the time, working on the Madison at Alton Slough. Nothing changed much at the Lorado home; morning classes continued, Andrew resumed his daily practice, and the Twinkle, Twinkle kids began showing some improvement. Saturday afternoon matinees and coffee with Mildred highlighted the weeks. Then Marion would come home, Beth would cook a wonderful Saturday night supper, and we'd all go to church on Sunday mornings.

Jesse stopped by, now and again, on his way to and from the Madison's renovation progress, and sometimes, his truck looked like a portable lumberyard, loaded down with boards of all sizes and lengths, or window frames and doors, or big rolls of carpet. He never had much time to visit, but I knew that he had come out of his way, just to see me. That made it okay.

But sometimes, after he left, waves of anxiety crashed against me with tsunami force. Months had passed since our last journey on the mighty river; April seemed a lifetime away.

Andrew understood my yearning to be at the helm of the Madison. He understood my love for the river. He understood my craving to explore the far reaches of a world that I did not yet know. He'd look at me and recognize the glaze in my eyes, as my imagination floated me down the Mississippi to unfamiliar destinations. He'd ride along for a while, getting lost with me in the reverie, and then with the snap of his fingers, he'd calm the breakers beating against my shore, reducing them to a flat layer of foam that drifted back out into my ocean of impatience.

He did a good job of keeping me occupied at times like that. One unsuccessful attempt after another, to teach me chords and simple tunes, rendered nothing more than confirmation of my total inability to play the piano with more than one finger at a time. But even with my one finger technique, Andrew could transform some mindless melody into a symphony. "No matter what I play, just keep playing your tune," he'd say. I'd struggle along, plunking out *Down By the Riverside* on the upper register keys with one finger, while he accompanied the tune with some classical toccata on the lower keys. When we finished, Mrs. Lorado would stroll from the kitchen, giving us a standing ovation, but somehow, I knew we'd never make it in vaudeville.

Andrew and I spent several days engineering and constructing a picture frame for the castle jigsaw puzzle. Mrs. Lorado was quite pleased, particularly when we told her that we put to use the Geometry lessons she had pounded into us a couple of weeks earlier. Even Marion paid us a compliment on the handiwork – in a sandpapery sort of way -- when he came home that weekend and saw it hanging on the kitchen wall.

By late February, another ship building project was well under way on Andrew's bedroom table. That time, though, it was a riverboat; it kind of looked like the Madison. We'd spend hours on end with knife and paintbrush in hand, crafting the detail to the best degree, with the materials we had. String from the butcher shop, dipped in brown paint, became the mooring lines, heaped up in tiny coils on the Main deck; straightened-out paper clips and matchsticks made the railings; whittled-down tongue depressors from the medicine cabinet worked perfectly for the paddlewheel planks; the dowel from a wooden coat hanger, miraculously took on the form of majestic smokestacks. The blue paint wasn't quite the right shade, and the paddlewheel red seemed a bit too orange, but we were proud of our creation, anyway.

We'd sit back to admire and evaluate our miniature shipyard talent, and often, I would catch myself gazing at Andrew's one-eyed, one-eared, faded rabbit.

Then, March 4th rolled around, the day so many people had been waiting for. It was a Saturday. Marion came home early to sit in his easy chair and listen to the radio broadcast of Franklin Roosevelt's inauguration speech. Andrew and I skipped the matinee. I guess the whole country stopped what it was doing that day, tied up next to the nearest radio, and fixed an ear on the new President as he proclaimed, "The only thing we have to fear is fear itself."

Eight days later, the Nation stopped to listen again, that time, to the first of many to come Presidential radio addresses he called the "Fireside Chats." Mr. Roosevelt had captured everybody's attention.

Will Rogers had said, "If he burned down the capitol we would cheer and say, 'Well, we at least got a fire started, anyhow.'" But the new President and his new deal lit the fire of optimism at a time when we desperately needed a leader; he did it without burning down Washington.

I could feel the warmth and caring concern in that odd Eastern accent; coming from anyone else, it might have been irritating. The President explained how the banking system worked: when you deposit your money in a bank, they don't just put it in a vault; it is invested in new homes and businesses in the form of credit, constantly working to help improve the economy. He went on to announce that the banks would reopen the next day, and that those who chose to participate, would have their deposits guaranteed by the federal government. This was not the end of the depression, the President said, but surely the end of the downward spiral that had brought the economy to a standstill.

We listened to his words, but more to the rightness of his tone that suggested assurance everything would be okay.

I thought that he might have already taken a hint from Mr. Rogers – to leave all the big fifty-cent words at home, in the dictionary.

44

Lines of Canadian geese soared northward, like giant airborne zippers, parting winter from spring; their church social chatter punctuated the new season with secretive laughter, as if they knew something that we didn't. The poplars, maples and oaks had stood stark and black against the sky; now a delicate green veil seemed to float on their branches. Each day, the sunlight burned warmer, coaxing the dainty wild violets and the bolder trilliums to splotches of vivid color that sprinkled the countryside. The brown, drab winter was giving way to the freshness of spring.

But with the gentle caress of springtime, came the silent fierceness of the rising river. Every year at that time, the river transformed into a coffee brown monster, clawing at the banks, as if it were searching for an escape from its muddy confines. Sometimes it succeeded, and then after a week or two of rampant, defiant wandering, it slithered back to its comfortable bed, leaving behind a belligerent, mud-caked reminder on everything it had touched: it would repeat its mischief, again next year.

It was a great day when Jesse showed up, just after breakfast, and said that we would bring the Madison back to St. Charles. We could round up only a skeleton crew on such short notice – one fireman and two deckhands -- but that's all we needed. Charlie, the engineer, had been on board checking all the machinery since the day before; he was already building a head of steam by the time we arrived.

I expected to see changes; the Madison looked a little different with the cargo deck, not a cargo deck, but all of it enclosed, with stateroom doors and windows facing each side. The stairway to the Saloon deck was moved to the bow, and Lester would certainly be pleased that his tiny office had nearly doubled in size.

The biggest surprise hit me as I stepped into the saloon. New carpet that looked like a huge pool of swirling spaghetti sauce, with big cranberry-colored roses floating in it, covered the once naked wood floor; a parade of rich, gold velvet drapes lined up against the walls, like the brass section of a marching band; in one corner of the room, a raised platform, and on it, a baby grand piano glistened like the hood of a shiny new Buick. The opposite corner boasted a ten-foot long glossy mahogany bar with a brass foot rail. Our quaint saloon had mutated into an elegant palace ballroom.

"Sadie picked out the colors. What do you think?" Jesse asked me.

"It's... it's... *nice*," I said, smothered by the luxury. I wondered if we were expecting Mr. Roosevelt.

"The piano," Jesse added, "was Marion's idea."

"Who's gonna play it?" I asked.

Jesse grinned. "Oh, I think we'll find someone."

I recognized Reggie's Brit voice, long before I recognized Reggie; his boyish grin came from behind a mask of black fuzz. I thought Jesse had hired a new deck hand when I first saw him. With his book print black hair and eyebrows, he looked rather dashing.

Luke's sandy growth wasn't quite as noticeable from a distance, because it blended with the color of his skin. "Jesse kept forgetting to bring us new razor blades," he told me, and he seemed eager to dispose of the itchy mess.

But they were still the same Luke and Reggie, and they wore the Cubs baseball caps that I had given them for Christmas.

"How was your winter?" I asked.

"Oh! Was it winter?" Luke said. "We were so busy, we didn't notice."

It was just like Luke to express some benign comment, but I surmised that he and Reggie were anxious to say adios to Alton Slough, and to return to civilization.

A welcoming party waited for us on the mud-encrusted St. Charles levee. Since there was no cargo deck on the Madison anymore, Jesse drove his truck back to town; he was among them. Mildred waved; I could almost smell the lilacs. Dollar signs and numbers reflected from Lester's wire-rimmed spectacles; Henry just stood there with his arms folded, and leaning on a big smile.

Three people that I didn't expect to see right then -- the Lorado family -- seemed more enthusiastic about our arrival; Marion's barbed wire charisma appeared to be carrying on a conversation with the clerk. Beth and Mildred were hitting it off like old friends. Andrew gazed and nodded to Jesse's hand gestures, as if he were learning the secrets of the world.

Reggie lowered the gangplank; he and the other deckhand started wrestling the mooring lines, and by then, the whole welcoming committee had scrambled aboard for the grand tour. I could see Marion's pride bubbling.

I stayed with Luke in the pilothouse while he jotted an entry in the log and offered me some pointers. But when we heard the piano rip loose a jazzy version of *I've Got Rhythm*, I knew that there was only one person among the group who could play like that. Luke and I hustled down to the saloon. Everybody was whooping and cheering, dancing and clapping. Andrew played his heart out; I never saw such a happier bunch of people.

Lying on my bunk that night, I listened to all the creaks and moans. The

Lorado home had been quite comfortable, but it felt good to be back on the Madison. There was a certain sort of security there that I felt nowhere else.

I thought about all the work still left to be done before the Madison was ready for its next trip. No doubt I'd be spending the next several days with paintbrush in hand, but that was okay. Marion Lorado would still be with us for a while, finishing the two staterooms that weren't quite done yet, and that was okay too. I'd just stay out of his way. I wondered about the rest of the crew – if we'd see any of the same faces again. And what would they all do, now that we weren't hauling freight? I thought about how thrilled Lester must be with his new office, and how Mildred would never complain about her aching feet, now that she would be waltzing around on plush carpet. I imagined the nearing day, when most of my time would be spent in the pilothouse, and then I thought of Andrew, left behind to wander alone, while the Twinkle, Twinkle kids took over his space every afternoon. I thought about the blue rabbit.

All that new wood sucked up paint like a camel sucking water at a well in the middle of a desert. By the third day, my T-shirt and jeans were perfect. Reggie and Luke painted, too, but every couple of hours, we'd have to stop and help Jesse with another load of furniture for the new staterooms.

Mr. Lorado had been spending a lot of time with Charlie in the engine room; that didn't seem unusual, as Marion was quite mechanically inclined, and Charlie seemed to appreciate his help, and it didn't seem to bother Jesse that the last stateroom wasn't getting finished.

It was almost noon; the aroma from the galley overpowered the fresh paint, and it was having about the same effect on me as the smell of movie theater popcorn. I was just finishing the second coat around a window when I heard Jesse and Marion talking inside.

"Have you considered my offer?" Jesse said.

"Got a letter from the railroad yesterday," Marion replied. "They want me to come back to work now."

"So when do you have to leave?"

"Not gonna... I'm turning 'em down."

"Why?"

"'Cause your pay is better."

"Then you'll stay on with us?"

"I reckon so."

I couldn't believe what I had just heard. I knew that we had lost one engineer to the Silverado in the fall, and that we had to hire a second. But Marion? The man who considered us river trash? The man who detested riverboats? The man who set foot on our decks, only to feed his family through the winter? It hardly seemed possible that Marion Lorado would lower himself to river trash status. One thing was certain: I wouldn't ever hear him use that term again, now that Jesse had made him one of us.

Captain Jesse was full of surprises that night, as he, Luke and I conducted our little meeting in the pilothouse. Reggie, the new First Mate, was invited too.

"The Madison is booked solid for a pleasure cruise to Cairo and back," Jesse told us. "They're all wealthy businessmen and their wives from St. Louis... and they all paid in advance."

That didn't sound so bad. I just hoped they were all Democrats, who wouldn't whine about President Roosevelt.

"As you know," he went on, "we're a little short-handed since most of the crew lit out last fall, so we'll be training a new staff."

That was different, I thought. Now that the Madison turned pleasure cruiser, our crew would be known as the *staff*. I liked it.

"Lester took applications all week, Jesse continued. "Reggie, you'll have three new deckhands starting Saturday."

"Aye, Captain," Reggie said with confidence.

"Mildred will have an assistant, and Henry will have two in the galley. More people to feed, you know."

I anxiously awaited my official pilothouse assignment; this was the moment I had dreamed about for months – when I could gladly surrender my white shirts and black bowties, pawn the feel of a coffee pitcher handle for a steering wheel, read river charts instead of crooked political smiles, and breathe in the fresh virgin air blowing through the open pilothouse windows, instead of the dragon breath of the saloon.

The Captain still had more surprises. "And now that Prohibition has ended," he continued, "I have two barrels of beer, and a bartender to serve it, on the way from St. Louis." He peered into our somewhat bolted-from-the-blue faces and added, "Our passengers will expect it now." His expression turned, as if he demanded our approval.

Alcohol had never been an option on the Madison, other than the times when Henry snuck in a few bottles of home brew for our own private crew parties. We had always known that a majority of the passengers boarding our boat had a bottle tucked in their suitcase, or a flask hidden under their bulky coat. We'd look the other way, perhaps, but serve it? Not on a bet. Now, I understood the purpose of the shiny new bar in the saloon – our saloon would *really be a saloon*.

Then Jesse turned to me. "Will, you'll be training the new cabin boy."

"But I thought I was gonna cub with Luke."

"You will, but for a few days, you're going to show the new kid how it's done. *Nobody* knows that job better than you."

I liked the thought of that job about as much as I treasured peeling onions, and now that there would be beer, I worried about dealing with drunkards discussing politics; I couldn't think of any worse combination. But as long as Jesse put it that way, it didn't hurt much. "Who is it?" I asked.

Jesse grinned. "Andrew Lorado... you know him?"

My chin bounced off the pilothouse floor. "Mr. Lorado is the new second engineer, Andrew is the cabin boy, and I suppose Beth is one of the new cooks," I said.

"No," Jesse came back, "she's Mildred's assistant."

I was letting all that sink in when Luke asked, "When do we leave?"

"Next Monday, at two o'clock," Jesse said.

By Saturday morning, the white paint was dry and ready for the blue trim. Finally, I could add some Madison blue character to my T-shirt.

Mildred and Beth strolled by, assessing the appearance of the window curtains.

"Good morning Mildred, Beth," I said. "Where's Andrew?"

Mildred stared at my shirt. "Another one for the garbage bin, I see."

"No, not this one... I kinda like this one."

"Andrew's at the church, practicing," Beth said, "and going over the service routine with the new organist. He'll be here later."

They moved on to the next windows; I went back to painting. The church was losing its best organist ever... to river trash, I thought.

"And this is Will Madison," I heard Reggie say behind me, "part owner of the boat, and the Captain's brother."

I turned around. Standing before me were three new faces. I was glad that Reggie got the "owner and Captain's brother" stuff out of the way, so I wouldn't have to.

The First Mate introduced John, Sidney and Sparrow, the new deckhands. I shook their hands, and managed to get blue paint on every one.

John was built kind of like a bulldog and appeared to have a personality to match; Sidney was tall and lanky, grinned like a hayseed on his first trip to town, but his handshake grip -- that of a professional wrestler; and Sparrow seemed a bit shy – I thought the nickname fit him quite well. At last, someone on this boat who was shorter than me.

The hours ticked away. Everyone stayed busy. Charlie and Marion finished installing the gasoline engine to run the electric generator, so we wouldn't have to keep the boilers hot when we were tied up. Henry must have cleaned out the grocery store, stocking the galley pantry. Beth and

Mildred made up beds and cleaned and dusted till I thought they might wear the varnish off the furniture. Lester rearranged his office.

Sparrow helped me finish painting while the bulldog and Sidney helped the firemen load coal from the barge. Sparrow was a likeable enough fellow, but a little odd, too.

"Reggie said I should..." Sparrow said to me, and then his eyes wandered around until they found their mark on the extra brushes, picked one up, and started stroking the blue onto a window frame.

From that point on, I never heard him finish a complete sentence.

"There, that one is..." and then he'd move on to the next window.

I thought the name really did fit – just like a little brown bird that chirped once, and then flitted away.

I worried about Andrew; he seemed a bit nervous. I thought it might be his fear of being in contact with so many strangers. He'd gaze around the room while we dressed each dining table with the white linens, as if he were imagining the saloon full of strange faces.

"Just think of this as the forest, and all those people are the trees," I told him. "And when you hear them talking and laughing, just pretend it's the sound of birds singing."

He frowned a little harder, and stared at the baby grand.

"And if you start feeling too uneasy," I said, "just go over to the piano and play a tune. I think that's what Jesse has in mind."

Marion drove in the last nail holding the door trim of the just-finished stateroom on Monday, when the first of our weeklong guests started coming aboard. Unlike the passengers that I usually escorted to the staterooms, these people seemed a cut above the average traveler. Their clothes spoke clearly: blue, gray, and brown pinstriped three-pieces escorted fashionable silky gowns of more colors than a rainbow could paint. At times, the staircase to the Saloon deck was a porcelain doll parade of imitation Garbos, Barrymores, and Dietrichs.

The most interesting concept of the array of feathered pillboxes, canted berets, and white Panamas, was that those people weren't going anywhere in particular; their only destination was a seven-day escape from reality, a crusade against boredom and stress. Those crusaders were wealthy, and they were paying us handsomely, just for a relaxing ride down the Mississippi, and back.

I was standing at the top of the stairs; I concentrated on the cherry red scarf tied loosely around the collar of a conservatively blue dress coming up toward me. Sadie was exactly how I remembered her, except now, instead of a parasol and a camera tripod, she toted a little boy on her hip –

a miniature Jesse, I thought.

"Will!" Sadie said to me. "So good to see you again... and my! How you've grown." She leaned in to plant a little kiss on my cheek.

"Hi, Sadie," I said. "And this must be Philip."

The little guy buried his giggling, bashful Jesse dimples into his mother's shoulder.

Sadie bounced him a couple of times and said, "Philip, say hello to your Uncle Will."

Philip seemed more interested in keeping an armful of blue rabbit from hopping off into strange territory.

"He loves his bunny rabbit," Sadie remarked. "Won't go anywhere without it."

I stared at the blue rabbit for a long moment; now I didn't feel so bad about the choice, and then Sparrow broke my concentration.

"Where would you like...?" He glanced down at the two brown leather suitcases in his grip.

"The Captain's quarters," I answered.

Sparrow looked at me, puzzled.

"This is the Captain's wife," I said to Sparrow.

"Oh! Well, I'll take them right..." he said, and then trotted off to the Texas deck.

"I'm so anxious to see what you've done to the boat," Sadie said. "But right now, I think I'd better get Philip up to our room for a nap. He's been a little crabby. I'll talk to you later... okay?"

"Okay... I'll be around."

It was so good to be back on the river; the only thing that could have made it better, would have been the breeze blowing in my face through the *pilothouse* windows. But at least, the Madison was back to work, and with the most valuable payload she'd ever carried. Just sixty-eight passengers – but *wealthy* passengers, out for a pleasure cruise, and all we had to do was to keep them comfortable and happy.

Look at them, I thought. The women gathered on one side of the saloon, sitting there in their *Revlon* faces and rayon Cinderella innocence, jabbering about *Glo-Coat* floor wax, Tarzan's gluteus maximus, and winging off to the Big Apple for a $2.50 Ethel Merman Broadway show. Their pinstriped, double-breasted husbands, on the other side, sipped at their beer mugs, as if they'd never missed it, spewed fond memories of a 1931 St. Louis World Series title, driving their Cadillacs all the way to California on Route 66, and the sweet patooties adorning the pages of the new *Esquire Magazine*.

It was better than listening to politics. They must have been Democrats.

45

St. Louis was miles behind us. Dusk lowered its curtain, and the Madison started lighting up like a telephone switchboard on Mother's Day. For the most part, all of the passengers seemed to be quite content; a few had wandered out onto the open deck, soaking up the fresh evening air. Jesse was out there too, hobnobbing with several stuffed shirts.

I always knew that Jesse had a shrewd view on human nature; there was something about him – some divine savoir-faire that seemed to always let him land on his feet, with the right decisions in his head. He had certainly done it that time, and we were all pretty lucky to have him leading the way, with such finesse, through those difficult times.

Although everything seemed to be going smoothly, I felt a strange sensation that something was wrong, like trouble was lurking around just waiting for a vulnerable victim – that premonition like I knew a wet dog was about to gallop into the middle of the room and shake all over the new carpet. I tried to convince myself that it was only my imagination; the Madison was in perfect condition, with a competent, sensible pilot at the wheel; the new staff had been carefully handpicked; meticulous preparations ensured that glazed donut bunch of vacationers a comfortable, pleasant journey. So far, none of them had flaunted any irascible tendencies, but somehow, I still sensed a wet dog panting, prowling, somewhere.

The saloon crowd had thinned. I noticed Sadie, sitting at the Captain's table with Philip and a blue stuffed rabbit perched on her knee. It was still a half-hour before we started serving supper, and Andrew appeared not to need my shadow for the time being, so I decided to visit with Sadie for a few minutes.

I pulled back a chair and sat down beside her. Little Philip kept a protective grip on the rabbit; he seemed overwhelmed by the surroundings, and not too talkative.

"Jesse tells me you're the new cub pilot," Sadie said to me.

"Yeah, but I have to help out here for a while... 'till the new guy can handle it on his own."

"And how's he doing? He seems a little shy."

"He'll be okay... and I'll be in the pilothouse by tomorrow night."

All the while we talked, I realized that I gave more visual attention to the blue rabbit than I did to Sadie. I spoke other small talk words, but my mind saw images far removed from the immediate conversation. It was the rabbit – *that blue rabbit.* I recalled staring at the stuffed rabbit in Andrew's bedroom, puzzled, at the time, with my own fascination. But it wasn't until then, seeing Philip holding his rabbit, that I was reminded of the photograph in Spades Morgan's stateroom on the Silverado. A barrage of visions hit me like a sudden hailstorm, each one, vivid and supportive of the others. But it was the rabbit – Andrew's frazzled, faded, one-eyed, one-eared rabbit, that collected it all into one heap; I understood why Andrew had been the subject of the subconscious mystery, flitting around in my brain for months. I had finally answered the question, but now I had to question the answer.

"Will," I heard Mildred saying to me. "It's time to start with the supper."

I shook loose from the daydream that I had fallen into, apologized to Sadie for being unsociable, and gave a gentle ruffling to Philip's head of thick, blonde hair. A mouthful of baby teeth and the Jesse dimples grinned; he jabbered something that made no sense to me at all.

The saloon rapidly filled with hungry faces. I could see Andrew was nervous, catering that collection of high society stuffed shirts. He had already dropped three sets of silverware, spilled two cups of coffee, and knocked over a water flask.

I laid a hand on his shoulder. "Remember," I said, almost whispering. "Forest. Trees. Birds. *Piano.*"

He glanced at the baby grand and casually walked to it, kicked off his shoes, and gazed around the room. Hardly anyone noticed him there. He sat down and began playing a spicy rendition of *Happy Days Are Here Again*, the theme song that had accompanied Franklin Roosevelt into the White House. I desperately hoped that those people were Democrats.

At first, it was barely audible over the noisy chatter and clinking glasses. Then, one by one, the voices dropped off, and heads turned toward the corner stage; the babble trailed off to murmurs, and then to nothing; every head in the room pointed in Andrew's direction. From where I stood, at the opposite corner, I saw some smiles and a few heads nodding, but scantly any other immediate reactions. I feared Andrew's audience felt captive, forced to listen to the interruption of their supper.

After three or four minutes, Andrew played to a big, classical shave-and-a-haircut-six-bits finish; the last chord's resonance reverberated about the saloon, and died to silence.

One pair of hands, somewhere in the crowd, started clapping. Then two more. Then six more. Then ten, growing to a thunderous roar of applause, accented with cheers and whistles.

Andrew stood and gave a humble little bow. He almost looked embarrassed, but the more I thought about it, his expression was probably from shock – he'd never been applauded like that before.

"More, more," I heard a voice cut through the clamor. "Bravo," cheered another.

Andrew slipped into his shoes again, his cheeks flushed red, but with a smile that lit up the whole room. "I'll play more later... after supper," he said quietly to the people at the nearest table, and then went back to serving the guests.

He didn't drop a single fork.

I thought I saw a peacock strutting around the room, but it was only Mrs. Lorado pouring coffee.

"Where did you find that talented young man?" I overheard a stuffed shirt ask Jesse.

The Captain grinned and replied, "Floating in the Missouri River, actually."

After the supper was served, Andrew did play some more, losing himself in the solitude that his music provided for him. At the keyboard, he seemed more relaxed, as if all the strange faces in the room disappeared behind a curtain of rhapsody. He had quickly discovered his means of escape from his nemesis – the crowd – by taking his shirtless walks through the countryside in his mind, alone, and listening to the wonderful music the world made, and seeing the beauty of nature, in a way that only he could see.

I sat back, lost, too, in another realm, sorting out a slew of images that had overpowered me earlier. But they weren't of clouds, or trees, or birds singing in the key of D-minor; they weren't of my grandest dreams of a handful of cherry wood steering wheel up in the pilothouse. Of all the things I could have been thinking about, my thought gremlins scurried about, carrying to me one recollection after another, dumping them in front of me for careful consideration.

"We lived in New Orleans a long time ago," Andrew had once said to me, and "Marion and Beth aren't my real parents – they adopted me." That, in itself, didn't seem so incredible or difficult to accept, but then Marion's thorn bush voice popped in with, "Your father was no good river trash... riding the river... gambling his life away." Then Beth's stern proclamation jabbed, "Your nanny drowned in that river," and chills went through me, like someone had dumped a bucket of ice chips down the back of my shirt. And then I envisioned Andrew's stuffed rabbit sitting on the bookcase shelf. That rabbit brought it all together.

I recalled the many times that I had glanced at the photographs on Spades Morgan's bureau; one of a beautiful young woman, and one of a blonde-haired toddler clutching a stuffed rabbit. Given back its missing eye and floppy ear, the bunny on Andrew's bookshelf was one and the same.

I remembered Spades' painful account of giving up his only son for adoption to a family in New Orleans, after the nanny who had cared for his son – Jenny Dupree – threw herself into the river, off the deck of this very boat, and drown. "...And you never saw him again?" I had asked Morgan, and then Morgan abruptly let me know that he didn't want to talk about the subject any more.

I saw Morgan and me sitting in the church at Augie's funeral. I remembered the rare emotional tear forming in the corner of Morgan's eye, but I realized now, months later, that it wasn't a tear of sorrow for Augie; it was a tear of anguish, and the gentle squeeze on my hand was his touching the lost son, through me.

It was no coincidence that Spades Morgan had made his home on the Missouri River at St. Charles; there, he was close to his only flesh and blood, and perhaps just being there, viewing from afar, superficially satisfied his wish that things might have turned out differently. Even changing Mathew's name to Andrew hadn't prevented Morgan from finding the boy that meant so much to him.

I stared across the room full of mumbling joviality, clinking glasses, shuffling cards and rattling dice. Andrew, still lost in a melody, still wrangling the wind on some faraway hilltop odyssey, seemed oblivious to the occasional round of applause, as he ended one tune, and began another. I wondered if he knew. I wondered if Marion had been successful in brainwashing him into believing the vulgar lies about his real father. Morgan is a good and decent man, I thought, and he doesn't deserve the tongue-lashings Marion Lorado delivered.

I scanned the saloon, looking for a wet dog.

We were over halfway to the Cape; with Luke as the only pilot, we tied up overnight at Chester on the Illinois side, so he could get some rest. By the time we coaled up, and got under way the next day, the sun was high and hot. I spent most of the morning entertaining Philip, so Jesse and Sadie could socialize with their St. Louis cronies. It was sort of a vacation trip for them too, and I welcomed the opportunity to stay in my jeans and paint-spattered T-shirt, playing with Philip until noon. He wore me out, though, up and down the stairs, forward and aft a dozen times or more; he was an inquisitive little bundle of energy with a strange vocabulary, all his own, and he kept a Herculean grip on that blue rabbit. "Abba," he called it, and by noon, Abba was a very well educated blue rabbit.

I was "Unka Wiw," Luke came out "Ook," Reggie, "Eeggie," and Andrew, simply "Doo." But I think he was just playing games with us, because some words came out quite clear: "Mommy" and "Daddy," "up" and "down," "drink" and "potty." He uttered "hot" several times, when we came near the boilers, and he squealed his favorite -- "birdie"-- whenever gulls made a swooping dive past the upper decks. Abba received a tighter grip, though, sometimes with both hands, when Philip thought the gulls were getting too close.

Philip and I were real buddies by the time Sadie rescued me from the rabbit-toting little machine at noon, and I looked forward to doing it all again. He was a handful – but a fun handful.

Mid-day molesting heat didn't seem to disturb the passengers. Most of them had traded their formal gowns and pinstripes for cooler, casual cotton blouses and golf shirts, and only an isolated few irritable egos, were crushed and lost in the rapturous jungle.

Back in my white shirt and bowtie, I tackled the burden of helping Mildred, Beth, and Andrew serve the noon meal. It wasn't so bad, really; the conversations around the saloon still lacked the crooked smiles of politics, and some of them were actually quite interesting. "I can tell a man's morals by the way he plays golf," I heard one fellow say. And the gentlemen who spoke the previous day about road trips to California, had abandoned their Cadillacs somewhere on Route 66, and were now skimming the clouds in a twin engine Curtis Condor airplane, at 150 miles per hour. The women at the next table were still hung up on Tarzan's physique; obviously, they hadn't caught a glimpse of Reggie with his shirt off – or maybe they had, and that's what got them going again.

Andrew was still a bit nervous; I could see the butterflies fluttering about him. Beth watched him constantly, and came to his aid much too often. Finally, Mildred stepped in. "Let the boy make his mistakes," she told Beth. "He'll learn from them."

It was just like Beth to be the protective mother she had always been, and it was just like Mildred to show concern too, always knowing, always wise, always realizing that a little emotional pain must accompany growth, and I thought Mildred's tactics, in this case, would work better. But Andrew preferred the advice that I had given him. It didn't get the guests served any quicker, but it kept them entertained – they loved his musical interlude between the Swedish meatballs and the apple pie.

Jesse fancied it too; he was busy at the Captain's table, being a family man, trying to convince Philip that blue rabbits don't like Swedish meatballs, but not too busy to take notice of the pleasure Andrew dispatched to our guests.

Andrew continued to serenade the passengers on the Saloon deck into the mid-afternoon hours. There wasn't much that Beth and Mildred couldn't handle; many of the porcelain dolls had retired to their staterooms for an afternoon siesta, while some lounged in a subdued daze on the observation deck, watching Missouri slide by on the right, Illinois on the left. Jesse took Philip and Abba for a stroll around the decks, attempting to tire them out for a nap. Sadie melted into the woodwork somewhere. I still hadn't seen any wet dogs, so I decided to sneak up to the pilothouse with a meatball sandwich and a glass of lemonade for Luke. I knew he'd let me take the wheel while he ate his sandwich.

Luke perched on the bench behind me, appreciating the sandwich and the break; I studied the river ahead, appreciating the wheel in my hands.

"How's Doo getting along?" Luke asked.

"He's still a little jittery... but he'll be okay." I tugged at my bowtie and unbuttoned my shirt collar.

"See that patch of darker, smoother water?" Luke stood up; a calm sort of urgency flowed in his voice.

"Yeah, I see it," I said.

"Sandbar under the surface... steer left ten degrees."

Silently, I thanked Beth Lorado for teaching me some basic Geometry. We glided past the sandbar; Luke sat down again.

"Now point the bow straight for that white marker on the Missouri bank. Keep the jackstaff right on it 'till you see the next one down around the bend."

"Then what?"

"Steer toward that one."

I had just received my first official lesson; Will Madison was actually at the controls, *navigating* – and this time it wasn't a daydream – *it was real.* At that moment, I felt so invigorated; I wanted to learn everything, but for that to happen, right then, we'd be here long enough to grow a good crop of cotton; I didn't have that much time until I would be needed in the saloon again. Feeding time, for the porcelain dolls, was only an hour away.

I was in my glory, doing what I really wanted to do, but the thought of Morgan and Andrew – separated father and son – kept floating around in my head. Just barely within my view, down on the bow deck, I saw Reggie and Andrew, their elbows on the rail, their stares focused on the passing Missouri shoreline. They were talking some, and I was glad that Andrew had taken a break, and was socializing with someone other than Beth. It occurred to me that, there, shoulder-to-shoulder, stood two fellows so different, yet, with so much in common; both were severed from fathers and cast out into the same, cruel world. I had not given it any thought before, but I realized that Jesse, Luke, and I, all fit into that same category, too, but each for different reasons – some by choice, and some not. My real father disappeared when I was just a tike – I barely remembered him, and I jumped a freight train to get away from my stepfather, because he beat me up all the time; Jesse's father was killed in an accident when Jesse was only

10; Luke walked away from his home because he didn't want to grow taters all his life; Reggie ran away because he feared humiliation; and Andrew was never given any choices at all.

"Luke? Do you miss your dad?" I didn't turn to see his expression.

"Sometimes... a little," he answered, after a slight hesitation.

"Do you think he misses you?"

There was another pause before the answer came. "From the letters I get from Ma, he only misses me for the work I did on the farm, but I don't think he misses *me*."

I spotted the next white marker and started to turn the wheel. "Am I doin' this right?"

"You're doin' just fine," Luke said. "There's a crossing just past that one... watch for another marker on the Illinois side."

I fixed the jackstaff on the white cross and pointed my eyes to the Illinois bank, patiently waiting for the next one to appear. This was the greatest sensation that I had felt since Jesse pulled me out of the flood.

"Does Reggie miss his dad?"

"I think he's gotten over it," Luke said.

"Do you think Reggie's dad misses him?"

"After three years... hard to say." Luke stood beside me again. "Why all the questions about Dads?"

The white marker on the Illinois bank came into view; I started turning the Madison toward it, at the same time, trying to think of how to approach a delicate subject. I trusted Luke, and I knew that he was good at keeping secrets. "What would you do if you had a friend who is adopted," I began, not looking at Luke, but straight ahead at the marker, "and you found out who his real father is, but you didn't know if your friend knew?"

"Depends on who the friend is," Luke said. "Who are you talking about?"

"If I tell you, will you promise to keep it just between us?"

"I reckon so... sure."

"It's... it's..." Second thoughts tied my tongue in a knot.

"Look," Luke said, "if you don't want to talk about it –"

"Andrew," I blurted out. "And Morgan is his real father."

"*Doo?* The new cabin boy?"

"Yeah."

"Morgan? *Spades* Morgan?"

"Yeah."

"How do you know all this?"

"The rabbit... Andrew's rabbit."

Luke gave me a peculiar stare, like I had eaten a bowl of ice cream too fast, and my brain was frozen.

"It's been buggin' me all winter, and yesterday when I saw Philip with

Abba, I remembered the photograph in Morgan's stateroom."

Luke must have thought I was upset. "Maybe I should take the wheel again," he said.

"No. I'm okay. *Really.*"

"What photograph?" He pointed downriver. "There's your next marker... steer for it."

I started turning the wheel. "Morgan has this picture of a little boy, his son, holding a stuffed rabbit, and..."

I proceeded to tell Luke the whole story, about how I had pieced together all the facts – even the part about it being Andrew that he and Reggie tried to rescue from the Missouri River. Luke listened to every word, and then he interrupted when another boat coming upstream sounded one long whistle.

"Give one long whistle," Luke instructed. "That's tellin' the other pilot that it's okay to pass on that side, and you're gonna stay on this side... and then steer five degrees starboard... give 'er room to pass on your port."

I shuffled the Andrew/Morgan issue aside for the moment, concentrated on Luke's directions, and stepped on the whistle pedal. In the corner of my eye, I noticed Reggie and Andrew crossing over the bow to the port side, exchanging waves with the crew lined up on the bow of the other riverboat as we came closer.

My eyes focused on the pilothouse atop the other vessel, only thirty feet away, directly alongside. That pilot was waving, too, and I mimicked Luke's nonchalant return greeting, as if I had been doing this all my life. Within seconds, the other boat was behind us; only the frothy wake left behind, and a trail of lingering black smoke remained, swirling in the breeze like a Halloween witch searching for a dry place to land a broom.

I saw Reggie and Andrew looking up at the pilothouse as I pointed the Madison's bow toward the next marker. For a few moments, I felt like a king.

For me, this had been a great accomplishment, a milestone, a monumental experience; to Luke, it was just routine.

"I don't know, Will," he said, picking up where I had left off. "Guess I wouldn't say anything, unless I knew if Doo really *wanted* to know his father."

I thought about that while I scanned for the next marker.

"Look at it this way," Luke went on. "Would you want some butt-in-ski tryin' to force you back to your stepfather?"

I didn't reply; we both knew that answer was "no."

I glanced at the clock. The sun was going down, and we were still four hours from the Cape. It was almost time to feed the porcelain dolls.

46

Marion's bristly manner usually grated against my backbone, but as I neared the staff's dining room, his words, coming from inside, didn't seem so harsh.

"We'll go see the sights in Cape Girardeau tomorrow," I heard him tell Beth, just as I entered the room. Nearly half of the entire staff sat around the long table, enjoying the leftover meatballs and mashed potatoes.

"Please pass the..." Sparrow chirped, and Bulldog handed over the gravy bowl. Jack, the new bartender, and Lester sat at the far end, discussing the bar profits of the day, so far. Reggie and Sidney were too busy eating to talk; Andrew was too busy listening to eat.

"And then," Marion continued, "We'll find a nice store where you can buy a new dress."

I sat down between Andrew and Sparrow. Usually, I would eat at the Captain's table in the saloon, but the meatball aroma overruled my resistance.

Sparrow nudged my elbow. "Could you please..." He gestured toward the salt and pepper; I slid them over within his reach.

"But Andrew needs new shirts more than I need a new dress," Beth told Marion.

"Well, then we'll get *both*," Marion answered.

"Can I have some colored T-shirts? Like Will and Reggie?" Andrew spouted.

Before Beth could voice an opinion, Mr. Lorado chuckled; his searchlight eyes found me, momentarily, and then he nodded his approval: "Sure... why not?"

Beth shook her head methodically and curled her mouth to one side. She knew her little boy was finally reaching out for his own identity.

I smiled inside. Marion Lorado was finally accepting mine.

It didn't surprise me that Marion had softened from the keg of nails that I first met, to the wad of cookie dough that he seemed to be now. His whole family was there, aboard the Madison, all earning wages, and at a time like that, that had to be a reassuring thought for him; comforting too, that they were together, as he had spent so many years away from them, most of the time.

That first night in November that I saw him, gave me an impression much different from the man I got to know. In those first few minutes, he had seemed to me like a loving husband, a caring father and a likeable human being. Of course, all that changed in the time it took us to eat a bowl of soup.

I guess any one of us – Jesse, Luke, even me – could have turned out to be made of that same shoe leather toughness, had we not fallen into the graces of someone willing to give us a chance; that trunk full of money certainly didn't hurt, either. But I think it was the river getting in our blood that kept our heads screwed on straight. It gave us a purpose for existing, and no matter how desperate the world around us appeared, we knew that we always had a friend in Old Man River. He'd rock us to sleep at night, and carry us anywhere he was going the next day. He never complained, and he was always there for us.

Whether it was the money and dumb luck, or hard work and love for the river that got us there, we were offering that same opportunity to Marion Lorado, a man like so many others, angered and beaten by the Depression, and it seemed like he was graciously accepting the offer. He would no longer face the fear, or feel the pain of watching his family be hungry or cold. He could buy his wife a new dress, and his son, colored T-shirts, and it was all because of a boy – *his* Golden Boy – floating helplessly in the river, and rescued by river trash.

All through supper, the porcelain dolls, so carefree and willing to evade the vapors of economic doldrums, seemed collected up in faraway places and times; their bodies were right there, nibbling at the roast pork, but their imaginations soared elsewhere. Some of the men were in Pasadena, at the Rose Bowl, cheering for the Pittsburgh team that never got on the scoreboard, while others were in the bleachers at Wriggly Field, hoping to capture the ball that Babe Ruth slammed there in the fifth inning. The women were either riding the escalator at Gimbel's Department Store, shopping for the latest *Chanel* evening dress, or at the Ritz Theater, raving Greta Garbo's haughty wardrobe in *Grand Hotel*. I saw that movie in St. Charles, and personally, I got a bigger kick out of Will Rogers' apron in *Too Busy to Work*.

Andrew, though, appeared bogged down in an emotional quagmire – not with the platters of roast pork or the foam-topped beer mugs; he had all but mastered that art in the short time -- not a single fork on the floor, or a drop of coffee spilled. Something else bothered him. I thought that he might be worried that Marion would change his mind about the T-shirts, or that he might have hurt Beth's feelings with his desire to wear something other than formal white. Or maybe, all the trees in his forest had sprouted intimidating faces again. If that were the case, I figured that we'd soon be hearing *Lady of Spain, Dancing In the Dark*, and *Life Is Just a Bowl of Cherries* pouring out of the baby grand, not necessarily in that order.

Whatever troubled Andrew, didn't drive him to the piano right away. I continued to serve the guests on my side of the saloon, but I kept one eye on him, waiting for his empty shoes to appear behind the piano bench. That didn't happen until everyone had a peach cobbler, and blue pipe smoke curled around the saloon lights.

Andrew was at the keyboard again, riding the notes of *Georgia On My Mind,* when I slipped out of the saloon. His facial expressions were still as elusive as sunspots; something besides Georgia was on his mind, but I thought that he just needed some time at the baby grand to settle his nerves.

Still two hours from the Cape. Dirty supper dishes all shipped back to the kitchen. Porcelain dolls, happy and cooing. It had been a rather eventful day, and it wasn't over, yet. When we reached Cape Girardeau, many of the passengers would opt for a hotel there, and most of the others, as well, would seek the nightlife that the city had to offer; there was bound to be some scurrying when the gangplank hit the dock. I needed a little fresh air, and it was a good time for a stroll around the decks. Reggie, Bulldog, Sidney and Sparrow were congregated at the bow. I headed for the stern – I wanted to be alone for a while.

I leaned against the rail, gazing over my left shoulder at the paddlewheel, churning up the black water into a foamy wake that disappeared into a tunnel of black nothingness. A gentle breeze wafted the smell of coal smoke to my nostrils. Off in the dark distance, the trill of a boat whistle sliced through the paddlewheel sloshing, and then, the Madison's whistle answered, echoing from Illinois to Missouri, and back again. A hazy blue searchlight beam, from the oncoming vessel, darted across the river's surface alongside, finally hitting its white marker target on the Illinois bank. Two minutes later, a mammoth white wedding cake, the *Natchez,* labored by; her engines chuffed, black smoke billowed from her stacks into a blacker sky, and her side wheels gouged against the Mississippi current. All her windows glowed a bright yellow excitement as they filed by like a Mardi gras parade, while two hundred travelers inside her celebrated the night, laughing and dancing to the syncopated ragtime of a Dixieland band.

And then she vanished into the black tunnel.

It was great to be back on the river.

Full beer glasses on nearly every table indicated that Jack was doing a land office business. There was little sign that any of the passengers were tiring of conversation, cold beer, or the entertainment, but Andrew was beginning to look tired; he needed a break, too.

I stepped up onto the riser and sat on the end of the piano bench beside him, as he stretched his arms and arched his back.

"They really like you," I said, as if he didn't already know.

"But I'm running out of songs," he said. He spun around with his back to the keyboard, and just sat there with that worried look again.

"That's okay," I said, trying to instill a bit of encouragement. "Just play the same ones over... they'll never notice."

The chicken coop cackling noise level increased, fifty different voices blending together. I watched Mildred set some cold drinks on the table next to the stage, and slide the loose change onto her tray. She glanced my way and winked.

Then Andrew mumbled two words that didn't register: *"They're here."*

For no particular reason, I plunked a couple of the piano keys, that just happened to be the first notes of *Down By the Riverside,* and because the room was so noisy by then, I knew no one was listening, and I continued to pick out the tune. Andrew stared at me a long moment, and then swung his bare feet under the piano, positioning his hands over the keyboard. I stopped my one-finger concerto, thinking he had decided to resume with another round of entertainment.

"No, don't stop," he said. "Keep playing... and louder. No matter what I play, just keep going... like we did at home."

I looked around the room; it didn't appear that anyone was paying much attention to the piano at the moment, so I started again, banging out the only tune I knew. At the same time, Andrew started playing a dreamy bass rendering of *April In Paris*, and somehow, he mated the two melodies together.

It was great fun – my less-than-amateur one-finger technique, melding with his virtuoso style. For those few minutes, I forgot about the porcelain dolls, and colored T-shirts, and blue rabbits. I was off, somewhere, traipsing through the woods, listening to the birds singing in the key of D-minor.

We neared the finale, and reality started setting in again. I noticed the absence of chatter, and I could feel sixty-eight pairs of eyes poking at me, and then the silence exploded into cheers and whistles and clapping; Andrew and I brought the house down. Maybe we *could* make it in vaudeville, I thought, and then quickly dismissed the idea.

Andrew's face beamed a grin. "We need to teach you more songs," he said. I could hardly hear him for the applauding, and I knew that my face was as red as a bottle of ketchup.

The commotion subsided; the porcelain dolls went back to their babbling and drinking, while Andrew resumed with some soft atmosphere background; that troubled look hung on his face again. I got up, and feeling a little embarrassed, I slithered through the crowd toward the observation deck. When I passed the Captain's table, Jesse stuck his arm out, stopping me in mid-stride.

"That was quite a performance, Little Brother," he said.

"Just a thing we did last winter to pass the time." I could feel my cheeks blushing again.

Sadie threw me a rose petal smile. "I didn't know you could play the piano."

"I can't," I blurted, and then I thought about the words Andrew that had spoken, just before we started playing.

"They're here," he'd said. Andrew was trying to tell me something, perhaps, why he was feeling so down, and I had ignored him.

"Excuse me, but I have to go talk to Andrew."

I sat on the bench beside Andrew again.

A half grin glanced my way. "Come back for an encore?" He kept playing softly.

"No. What did you mean, *'They're here?'*"

His expression went somber again, whispering, "They're here."

"Who? Who's here?" I lowered my voice to a raspy whisper, too.

"The pirates, from the haunted house."

I was challenged by yet another of Andrew's mysterious ways. "What are you talking about?"

"Don't you remember? Those men we saw in the cellar... the haunted house... down by the river."

I jerked my head up, quickly scanning the room, expecting to lay my eyes on some absurdly out-of-place, gristly creatures, but I only saw a room full of pastel cotton evening dresses, pinstripes, and at worst, a few five o'clock shadows wearing golf shirts.

"The two men at the corner table," Andrew whispered. "It's them."

My search focused on the far corner table and the two men sitting there; they weren't gristly creatures. "Those are businessmen from St. Louis," I whispered, sort of criticizing Andrew's assumption.

"No... it's them," Andrew said again. "They always sit at that same table, and I've served them almost every meal... I know it's them."

"But they don't look anything like—"

"It's them... the river pirates."

Again, ridiculing his statement, I said, "River pirates."

Andrew seemed quite convinced, but I had my doubts. "I'm gonna get a closer look," I said, and headed for the coffee pitchers next to the dumbwaiter. I realized the coffee idea was next to brainless, when I remembered that nearly everyone there was drinking beer, but by the time that thought arrived, I had arrived at the corner table.

"Would you fellows like some coffee?"

The older of the two men glared at me with black, beady eyes. His lips tried to form a smile, but those eyes snarled. "Beers... two beers," he growled. Just the way he spoke, and the way he slammed his open hand onto some loose change on the table, dragging it across to me, it was easy to see this guy had the personality of road gravel.

"And peanuts... I want some peanuts," his partner snapped.

A wire brush, I thought.

I stared, for a moment, into their souls. Andrew was right. I *had* seen those faces before – in the cellar of the haunted house by the Missouri River – but then, they wore mangy beards and filthy, ragged clothes; no wonder I hadn't noticed them.

Andrew's words echoed in my head: "River Pirates." For just a second or two, I imagined them, as I had seen them that day, and then, black three-cornered hats formed on their heads; then, eye patches; then, dagger blades clenched between blackened teeth; sculls and crossbones danced on the table.

I picked up the change and hurried away to the bar. While Jack drew the beer, I thought about those two impostors, hiding behind a flimsy veneer of lies. How had those phonies shammed their way onto our boat among all those – those -- porcelain dolls? Those wealthy businessmen, who could probably buy and sell the whole city of St. Louis in two jerks of a goat's tail?

I carried the beer mugs and peanuts back to the corner table, trying not to look into its occupants' eyes. Instead, I fixed a stare on the younger man's jacket and its shiny gold buttons. One was missing. Typical, I thought. Of what, I wasn't sure.

"Would you gentlemen care for anything else," I said, making a horrible attempt at being polite.

"Yeah... for you to be gone," Road Gravel snarled.

I backed away. I didn't say thank you.

47

Umpteen thoughts crashed into my head, like a crowd of crazed women at a half-price hat sale. The Texas deck was the only place where I could be alone, without any distraction, to sort this all out.

Why were these gritty scraps of humanity faking to be wealthy businessmen? And why were they on our boat? Even a down-on-his-luck hobo was entitled to a little dignity, but something didn't add up with these two characters.

I couldn't recall seeing them socializing with any other passengers on the entire trip, so far. No one else seemed to have any interest in them, which could only mean that no one else knew them – or even *wanted* to know them. And I knew, first-hand; they weren't exactly the sociable type, and I was quite certain that they weren't St. Louis businessmen.

I concentrated on the indelible vision of their faces. Another flash hit me; after Andrew and I had discovered their hideaway in the cellar of the old house, I struggled with trying to remember where I had seen them before – and now I knew. Those were the same two men who were on board the Madison, the day before the Santo Domingo was burgled and robbed at Cape Girardeau. Yes, I remembered them well, now that I could put the faces with a time and place.

Maybe Andrew was right by calling them pirates. Maybe they were the culprits responsible for the Santo Domingo heist; it had been nearly a year, and as far as I knew, those rogues were never caught, and the crime was never solved.

Then another vision charged at me. But with this one, I thought, I had physical evidence; I hurried to my quarters, pulled my box of riverbank junk out from under my bed, and started digging through its contents. I found it there, among the rusty jackknives, broken fishing lures, a tarnished skeleton key, and numerous other unidentifiable objects – the button – the one that I had picked out of the dirt on the levee, the day after the Madison was cut loose from its moorings.

I studied it. I envisioned the buttons on the jacket in the saloon. They were unique – an embossed crescent moon and star – so unique, that it would be difficult to find a replacement. I was holding *the missing button*.

This was *proof* that they had been there. *They* had cut the Madison loose that night. But why? Were they attempting to steal the Madison? Had they been on board, trying to commandeer a vacant-looking boat, until they heard me yelling? It was so dark that night; they could have escaped in a rowboat, without us noticing them. Or were they just waiting for her to crash downriver, so they could pillage the wreck before anyone else discovered it? *Lucky for us*, I thought, that I drank too much sarsaparilla, and had to get up to use the privy.

On the Madison, they were like foxes in a hen house, and this hen house was only an hour away from arriving at Cape Girardeau with sixty-eight very wealthy chickens aboard – a perfect target. Andrew's keen senses had spotted the wet dog.

As long as I knew – or at least suspected – when and where the varmints would strike, it seemed quite simple to alert Jesse and all the staff before the Madison docked at the Cape, hide in the shadows, and then capture the thieves, red-handed. Convincing Jesse that two of his porcelain dolls were really river pirates in doll's clothing would be my biggest problem.

Wrong.

My biggest problem would be *getting to Jesse* – I noticed that as soon as I opened my cabin door, and plowed into a wall of button-missing jacket, and road gravel. They towered over me like skyscrapers with bad breath. I was no match against the two of them. They grabbed my arms and dragged me back into my room, slammed and locked the door. The older man, Road Gravel, thrust his palm over my mouth before I could utter a single sound.

"We can kill you right now and feed you to the catfish," he said in a low-pitched snarl, "Or you can keep your mouth shut and live to see the next sunrise."

By then, the other man had backed off, pulled the curtains across the window, and stood at arm's length away, pointing a steely revolver in my face.

"What'll it be? You gonna keep quiet?"

I nodded my head, still in the grip of a hand that smelled of stale beer. Squinting, I peered into his eyes that were overflowing with demons.

He slowly pulled his hand away. I wanted to take a deep breath, but I couldn't.

"That's a good boy. I thought you'd see it my way." He sneered.

So much for alerting Jesse and the rest of the staff, I thought.

"Allow me to introduce myself." His voice took on a calmer tone. "I am Thaddeus Bleaker, and this is my loyal assistant, Mr. Dudley Bismarck."

I stood silent. Terror gripped at my throat.

Bleaker came at me again, and with a forceful shove, he knocked me down into the wooden chair behind me. "Whatever I tell Mr. Bismarck to do, he does, and he's a very good marksman... understand?"

I nodded.

"I say we get rid of him right now," Bismarck blurted out. He appeared more nervous, shifting his weight back and forth, periodically throwing a suspicious glance toward the door, but never altering the aim of the pistol at the end of his outstretched arm.

"Now, now, Dudley. Let's not be hasty," Bleaker said. "I think the cabin boy, here, can be of service to us... now that I think of it."

Dudley's arm bent at the elbow and dropped to his side, keeping the gun, that started looking to me more like a cannon, leveled in my direction. A curious smirk came to his face.

Then Bleaker threw open his jacket, unbuckled his belt, and pulled it from around his waist. He stepped behind me and wrapped the belt around my belly, pinning my arms to my ribs, and cinched it tightly behind the chair.

"Give me your belt," he said to Bismarck.

When Dudley didn't react immediately, Thaddeus barked, "Well, come on... I have to tie his feet, too."

Bismarck pulled off his belt and handed it over. A minute later, my ankles were bound to the chair legs. Even though my hands were free, I couldn't move.

"There. That ought hold you for a while," Bleaker said.

Bismarck finally lowered his weapon. He and Bleaker sat down on the edge of my bunk.

"What's your name, boy?" Bleaker stared a hole through me.

"W-Will." My throat was dry; I could hardly speak.

"Now, Will... I just hate it when someone interferes with my plans." An obnoxious politeness drenched his words. "When I saw you starin' at us down in the saloon... well, I just knew you were apt to do just that. That's why we had to come have a little chat with you before we arrived at Cape Girardeau."

I just listened, and hoped the cavalry would come charging in.

"You see, we have this little job to do after all the passengers and crew have gone into town, and we certainly don't need any interference."

"And what makes you think you wouldn't have any?" I said.

"Well, *certainly* none of the deckhands would question a lingering passenger strolling the decks, now, would they?"

Dudley gave a deceitful grin.

"And besides," Thaddeus went on. "They'd be *much* too busy with their chores to watch all those staterooms, full of valuables, left behind by such careless travelers."

"You won't get away with it, you know," I said.

"Oh, but I think we *will*. We've had an ample amount of practice."

"Like the Santo Domingo? Last summer?" I said.

Bleaker's voice sang, "The Santo Domingo... Ahhhh, yes." He turned to Bismarck. "You remember *that* one, don't you, Dudley? The fog made it *so easy* to get away in that rowboat."

"Yeah," Dudley said. "And they left the safe wide open... like candy from a baby."

Just then I heard the Madison's whistle. We were nearing the port of Cape Girardeau.

"Now if anyone should come looking for you," Bleaker said, "You send them away. Understand?"

I stared at the iron in Bismarck's lap. "Yes, sir."

"Good boy. We'll just wait right here until all the other passengers are off the boat... and by the way. Where might I find the master keys to all the staterooms? It would make our job *so much easier.*"

"I don't know where they are."

"Surely the cabin boy would know where the keys are kept."

"I don't know."

Bleaker's obnoxious grin melted into an obnoxious frown. "Mr. Bismarck?"

Bismarck's arm instantly reacted to the command, and once more, I was staring down the barrel of his artillery.

"Lower right-hand drawer in the clerk's desk," I said spontaneously.

"Good boy, Will. I thought a little persuasion might jog your memory."

We sat there in silence. I could feel the boat making the turn as I watched the lights of Cape Girardeau brighten my cabin window. Within a short while, there would be the commotion, and the porcelain dolls would parade off the Madison to meet the city night. I wondered if I'd be missed.

I heard muffled talking. "I'm going to put Philip to bed," Sadie's voice said. "And I'm pretty tired, too."

"Okay," I heard Jesse say. "Everybody's going into town, but the deckhands will be down on the Main deck if you need them." Then, I heard their door closing, and Jesse tromping back down the stairs.

Upon hearing that, Bleaker and Bismarck smiled mischievously with that *'I told you so'* look in their eyes, and I wished that Jesse hadn't said that.

I felt the boat nudge the levee, and I could hear Reggie calling out the tie-up commands to the other deckhands. Then Luke's footsteps clamored from the pilothouse, and I hoped that he would come looking for me. He didn't.

Bleaker and Bismarck sat patiently, with their ears perked to the diminishing noise. It was just a matter of time; they would have their way, like two fiendish kids at an unguarded candy counter, and there was nothing I could do to prevent it.

Several minutes went by. Near silence claimed the deck below, and then, all I heard were footfalls past my door, as the staff members hurried to catch up with the rest of the crowd, well on their way to celebrate the Madison's return to the river.

"Will?" A voice called out from somewhere outside. It was Andrew. His footsteps came toward my door. "Will?" he called out again, and the doorknob rattled, and the door clunked as it pressed against the deadbolt.

Dudley's split-second reaction flashed the gun to my face. Bleaker spun his head to the door, and then to me; the demons in his eyes had returned, and they were saying, "Send him away."

"Will? Are you in there?" Andrew knocked gently on the door.

I stared at Dudley's nervous hand and the determined executioner glare in his eyes. "I'm busy," I managed to squeeze out.

"But everybody is going into town. Aren't you coming?" Andrew sounded pleadingly desperate.

"No," I answered, not too convincing. "I'll see you at church... tomorrow at three."

There was silence for a moment, and then Andrew's footsteps pattered away.

Dudley lowered the gun and I started breathing again.

"Very good, Will," Bleaker muttered. "I'm *so* glad you've decided to cooperate."

We sat there in the eerie silence again, while Bleaker twirled the T-shirt that he'd picked up from my bed into a rope. It was my favorite one with the paint splotches.

"One more thing, before we leave you," he said. "Where might we find the ship's safe?"

"There ain't one," I snapped back.

Dudley was instantly in my face with the gun again. "I'm getting sick and tired of your sass, boy. Thaddeus asked you a question... *where's the safe?*"

"It's in the Captain's quarters."

"That's better," Dudley snarled. He lowered the gun.

Anger began raging inside me at the thought of the harm these pagan brutes could inflict on Sadie and Philip. "But Sadie's in there, and she has the lungs of an opera singer... her screams would alert the whole state of Missouri."

"Who's Sadie?"

"The Captain's wife," I answered.

Bleaker stepped behind me. The next thing I knew, I had a mouthful of T-shirt, as he tied the ends tightly in a double knot behind my head. Then, what appeared to be an afterthought, he pulled off his necktie and bound my wrists behind the chair. While he was doing that, he said to Dudley, "The boy's right ... perhaps we *should* skip the safe on this one. With all the rich folks riding this boat, we'll get plenty without it." He leaned in close to me. His hot beer breath splashed into my face. "And we wouldn't want to disturb the Captain's wife, now, would we?"

Dudley unlocked the deadbolt, cracked open the door, and peeked out. "All clear," he whispered.

Bleaker started for the door, stopped, and turned toward me. In his singsong repulsive tone, he spoke quietly, "It's been *so* nice chatting with you, Will. Thank you for your... *hospitality*, and do have a nice trip to Cairo."

Then with the urgency of vampires avoiding sunlight, they slid out the door and closed it behind them.

I listened for their footsteps, but I heard nothing. Beads of sweat stung my eyes, and my heart pounded like a ten-pound mall on an anvil. I struggled against the bonds, but the knots only tightened. My whole body ached, and worse was the mental torture, stabbing at my very soul; the Madison and its passengers were being violated, as I sat there, bound and helpless. Our reputation was being destroyed, and all because of me. Had I not confronted those men in the saloon, they would never have noticed my suspicion, and I wouldn't be sitting there restrained, unable to defend in our battle to survive.

I sat there in my pool of anguish for five – maybe ten minutes – I had lost track of the time. My fingertips tingled with numbness, and my mind tingled as well. I could imagine sixty-eight porcelain dolls, and most of the Madison staff, laughing, dancing, drinking, and reaping the joy of a festive occasion, while two bandits – *pirates* – robbed them of their money and belongings. And I could do nothing but wait.

A faint knock on the door pierced the silence. "Will?" somebody whispered on the other side.

I tried to yell, but all that came out was a muffled groan.

The doorknob turned. The door cracked open. Andrew's blonde hair poked in. "Will? Are you okay?"

Not *exactly* the cavalry, but Andrew would certainly do.

His eyes first fell on my empty bunk, and then they found me. He scooted through the door, closed it behind him, and rushed to my side, tearing at the knotted gag. When it was off, all I could do was breathe.

He dug a jackknife from his pocket and began cutting at the necktie binding my wrists. "I sent Sparrow for the police," he said, frantically struggling with the belt buckle behind me.

Sparrow. Great. He couldn't finish a complete sentence. I could just hear Sparrow approaching a stranger on the street, and asking, " Where is the..." and never getting out "Police Station."

"Are you okay?" Andrew asked. "Did they hurt you?" He was genuinely concerned.

"I'm okay," I replied, once I caught my breath. "But how did you know?"

Andrew grinned. "When I heard you say you'd meet me at the church tomorrow at three, I knew something was up. I saw those two men leaving the saloon, not long after you did, and I didn't see them getting off the boat. That's when I got worried and came looking for you."

"But how did you know you should send somebody after the police?"

"I saw one of the men coming out of Lester's office with a bunch of keys, and Lester was already gone."

"Did he see you?"

"No... I hid under the stairs to the Texas."

I rubbed my wrists and shook some feeling back into my fingers.

"What should we do now? Wait for the Cops?" Andrew asked.

"Knowing Sparrow, that could take all night," I said. "You saw one of the men with the master keys?"

The blonde hair just nodded.

"Then that means they're already getting into the staterooms." I stood up quickly and started for the door.

"No, they're not." He paused.

I waited for an explanation.

"Reggie and Bulldog have them cornered in the coal bin. They never got into a single--"

"At least one of those guys has a gun! And I don't think he's afraid to use it."

"Reggie knows that... he saw it."

"Where's Sidney?"

"He's in town, trying to find the Captain."

"C'mon," I said. "Lead the way to Reggie."

The coal bins faced the outer walkway, alongside of the boiler room, and were open to the elements for easy coal loading. The floors slanted downward from the outside, so the coal would slide into a chute, where the firemen shoveled it into the fireboxes under the boilers. The top of the outside wall, next to the walkway, was about five feet from the deck, and the inside wall at the boiler room, about six feet. Anyone inside the bin, had only two ways out: over the wall to the outside walkway, or over the wall into the boiler room. We hadn't coaled up since early that morning, at Chester, Illinois, about 150 miles. The bins were nearly empty, so it would be a tall wall to get over the back into the boiler room.

A chain hung across the walkway from the wall to the outside railing, just beyond the last stateroom door. It was there to keep the passengers from meandering to the stern, near all the machinery, and out of the engine room, and it was about as effective as a screen door on a gorilla cage.

Reggie crouched along the wall just past the chain, just below the end of the coal bin opening. Bulldog crouched beside him. A bright yellow glow from the streetlights cast their black shadows on the wall. They looked like four.

I could see shadows moving about inside the coal bin, and every now and then I saw the figures making the shadows, smudged with coal dust, and almost as black as the shadows they cast. With the streetlights behind us, shining into the bin, Bleaker and Bismarck must have been somewhat blinded by them, and couldn't see us very easily, but they must have known we were out there. We still had a definite advantage, I thought.

"Where did Sparrow go to find the bloody Bobbies?" Reggie whispered. "Back to St. Charles?"

"You know Sparrow," I whispered. "It'll probably take him all night just to get out the whole sentence."

"Blimey! He'll probably come back with the midnight crew at the bloody crumpet factory."

We waited there for quite some time. Apparently, Sidney was having as much luck finding Jesse, as Sparrow locating the Police Station. The Madison being the only big boat tied up there, the levee rendered not even a passer-by. I had plenty of time to explain to Reggie and Bulldog what had happened to me earlier. Bulldog's temperament steadily heated; Reggie steadily lost his patience.

When it appeared that neither Jesse nor the cops would arrive anytime soon, Reggie was down to his last thread of patience. We all feared Bleaker and Bismarck were preparing to come out shooting, but we couldn't risk leaving them unguarded, and just let them walk away.

"I'm goin' into the bloody boiler room," Reggie whispered. "Maybe I can catch them off-guard from behind. You stay here and distract them."

Now it was only Andrew, Bulldog and I to take the brunt of a charge, should Bleaker and Bismarck come over the wall. Bulldog was the only one of us big enough, strong enough, to meet that challenge, but even he wouldn't stand a chance against bullets.

We waited, and watched the top of the back wall. I knew Reggie would be proceeding slowly, carefully, and quietly. Bulldog flexed his hands in and out of fists, as if he anticipated a fight; Andrew maintained a constant vigil on the back wall; my innards were dancing the boogie-woogie.

Then I saw the slow, deliberate movement, as Reggie's head cautiously rose above the back wall. Andrew saw it too; Bulldog's fists remained rigid. I slapped my hand on the deck – noise to attract the outlaws' attention away from Reggie. The sound of coal chunks rattling came from inside the bin. Reggie's broad shoulders rose up over the top of the wall, and then his hands appeared, delicately transporting a coal shovel. I rose up slowly to attempt a peek into the bin. Andrew and Bulldog peeked, too, and I hoped they were as ready as I was to duck from flying lead.

Reggie must have made an uncalculated sound. Bismarck heard it and looked up at Reggie. At the very same moment, Bleaker must have noticed our presence at the front wall. His arm extended toward us – he too wielded a firearm. Bismarck raised his hand, aiming a pistol toward Reggie. Muzzle flashes and two shots fired, almost simultaneously. Bismarck's ricocheted off the shovel; Bleaker's zinged off harmlessly into the night.

What happened next came so quickly, so precisely – as if it were carefully planned. I saw Andrew's swift hand movement, and then I saw the sparkle of a knife, tumbling, hurtling at remarkable speed, and stopping abruptly, as it sank into Bismarck's right arm. The gun ejected from his hand, and he gave out a blood-curdling scream. Bleaker fired another harmless shot, as the shovel swooped down from above and knocked him off balance. Bulldog went over the wall like a jackrabbit, charging at Bleaker with the force of a bull moose, and Reggie descended on all of them, like a hawk descending on a field mouse. Andrew scaled the wall, and I followed, diving into the sooty black madness. Fists flew, connecting with whatever body parts got in their way. Heads banged against walls and feet stumbled in the coal. It was a four-against-two mayhem, about as friendly as a Mexican cockfight, and I liked the odds.

We had all but kicked those bums into next week, when I heard the thunder of boot heels on the deck, outside the bin. Flashlight beams lit up the coal like diamonds, and then it seemed like a dozen pairs of hands were pulling us apart. The only way I could tell the newcomers from the rest of us, was that they weren't as black with coal soot.

Jesse, Luke, and Sidney were among six uniformed officers that put it all to an end. One by one, black as the bottom of a well, we jumped down to the walkway. The cops drug Bleaker and Bismarck out, unable to make it under their own power. Blood streamed from Dudley Bismarck's arm, as the cops propped him up, sitting against the wall. Thaddeus Bleaker lay limp on the deck, rolling his head from side to side, groaning.

As for Reggie, Bulldog, Andrew and me – our battle was over, and won. As for the cops – theirs was just beginning.

48

"Would somebody care to tell me what's goin' on here?" one of the cops asked. He must have been the senior officer, because he had stripes on his sleeves, and the others didn't. He was a little on the pudgy side, and not much taller than me. I remembered him from the previous summer, but I couldn't think of his name.

Everybody started talking at once, like a line of squawking black crows on a telephone wire. We all had stories to tell.

"Quiet! Quiet! One at a time!" the pudgy cop with the stripes commanded.

We stood in silence again; the only sound was Bleaker's moaning.

"I can only listen to one at a time." Stripes stepped in front of Bulldog. "You... what's your name?"

"John Emmet... I'm a deckhand here on the Madison." A bit of a growl sounded in Bulldog's voice.

Stripes turned his head to Reggie, and stepped sideways to line himself up with his next subject. "And you?"

"Reginald Pierce... First Mate."

Then the cop took another step sideways in front of Andrew – at least I thought it was Andrew; it was hard to tell. "How about you?" the cop said.

"Andrew Lorado... cabin boy and piano player."

Yep. It was Andrew.

Stripes sidestepped again to me.

I answered before he asked, "Will Madison... cub pilot." I had to throw that in.

Stripes gave me a peculiar stare. "Any relation to the Captain?"

"Yes, sir. Brothers."

The officer peered at Jesse. "Captain Madison? Would you concur that these four are who they say they are?"

"Yes, sir. They are."

"That's good," Stripes said. He turned to take a couple of steps, mumbling, "I'm glad I don't have to take *all* these filthy bums to my clean jail."

Then he directed Jesse's attention to Bleaker and Bismarck, laid out and guarded by two other policemen, like they were the trophies of a deer hunt. "And who would *those two* be?"

"It's kinda hard to say," Jesse said.

"Well go on over there and take a good look. Tell me if you recognize them."

Jesse paced off five or six long, official strides toward the two men.

I couldn't hold back any longer. "Thaddeus Bleaker, and the one with the bloody arm is Dudley Bismarck... *river pirates,*" spewed out of me like a mouthful of sour milk.

Stripes jerked his head around to me, but he spoke to Jesse. "Well, Captain? Do you know those men?"

Jesse looked at each of them and turned back toward the officer. "They would appear to be a couple of passengers on this cruise, but I don't know them personally."

Stripes stood by Bulldog. Bulldog started volunteering his story: "I was getting a cold drink when I saw them trying to break into a stateroom, up on the Saloon deck... that's when I went to find the First Mate down in the engine room."

Stripes stared at Bulldog suspiciously. "How did you know they were *breaking* in? That might have been their room."

"No sir," Bulldog continued. *"Their* room is on *this* deck... and they had this big ring of keys – that just didn't look right."

"What big ring of keys? I don't see any big ring of keys."

Andrew jumped in. "The ring of master keys ... I saw them steal it from the clerk's office."

Stripes turned his attention to Andrew. "You *saw* them take the keys?"

"Yes sir," Andrew said.

The cop turned back to Bulldog. "So where's the ring of keys now? I need some evidence."

"Well, you see, sir, when me and Reggie finally caught up to 'em, they was tryin' to get into another room – that one." Bulldog pointed.

"But you said their room is on this deck. They were going in *their room?*"

"No sir. Their room is over on the starboard. This is the port side."

"Hmmm. Go on... I'm listening," Stripes said.

"Well, like I said, they was fumblin' with the keys at the door when me and Reggie caught 'em by surprise. They dropped 'em... the keys sorta went overboard."

"Hmmm... overboard," Stripes mumbled. "So then what happened?"

"They pulled out guns and—"

"Guns? Where are the guns? I didn't see any guns."

"Prob'ly buried in the coal bin now."

"Hmmm... we'll find them later."

"Me and Reggie ducked around the corner. Guess that's when they made it for the coal bin, to hide."

Reggie joined in. "That's when Andrew found us and told us what the bloody mess was all about, and then we sent Sparrow to fetch the Bobbies."

"Sparrow? Now who in tar nation is Sparrow?" A cauldron of frustration boiled in Stripes' voice. Lost keys, lost guns, an Englishman calling him a 'Bobbie,' and now a Sparrow was suddenly involved.

"Another deckhand," Reggie said. He glanced around the group. "Has anybody seen Sparrow?"

Stripes said, "Well, if he's lookin' for us in town, he'll be lookin' for a while... we're all here."

Stripes finally got to me. "And how is it *you* seem to know their names so well?"

"We kinda got to know each other up in my quarters," I said, and proceeded to tell about the ambush, and how Bleaker and Bismarck tied me up, and then everybody started to listen as they gathered around me.

Somewhere during my story, I took the liberty of wiping a smudge of coal dust from the cop's nametag, so I could see his real name – Homer Appleton – I certainly couldn't call him Stripes if I had to address him by name. Of course, I made it look like I was doing Homer an honorable favor.

When I got to the part about Bleaker and Bismarck admitting to the

Santo Domingo robbery the summer before, and how they had escaped in a rowboat in the fog, Homer's ears perked, and his eyes lit up.

"Well, well." Homer rubbed his double chin, his eyes narrowed to just slits. "I suppose we have enough eye-witness accounts to make an arrest." He scanned the group some more. "They didn't actually break into any rooms, but I guess we *could* hold them on key theft and kidnapping."

He gave the order. Four other officers hauled Thaddeus Bleaker and Dudley Bismarck off in handcuffs; a blood-soaked white handkerchief tied around Bismarck's arm contrasted dramatically with all the black. In their condition, they couldn't offer much resistance.

"Oh, and one other thing, Homer," I said.

He turned to me. "Yes? What is it?"

"Last fall, the Madison got cut loose from her moorings... up at St. Charles... Bleaker and Bismarck are the ones who done it."

Jesse and Luke stepped closer to hear, because we'd kept that secret tighter than the formula for *Coca-Cola.*

"And how do you know that?" Homer asked.

"I found a gold button on the levee where the ropes were cut... Bismarck's coat is missing a button, exactly like the one I found."

"And this button. I suppose *it went overboard too."*

"No sir. It's in a junk box up in my quarters."

"Hmmm." Homer rubbed his chin some more. "St. Charles is a little out of my jurisdiction, and a button doesn't exactly prove they did it. I'm afraid I can't do much about that one."

A few of the porcelain dolls returned to the Madison that night, but by that time, the cops had retrieved the guns from the coal bin, and they were gone. Reggie, Bulldog, Andrew and I stayed out of sight, and took our turns scrubbing in the bathtub up on the Texas, so none of the passengers saw the sooty mess we were in. Andrew's blonde hair was still tainted with gray blotches, his cheek was bruised, and he complained of a stinging sensation on his back. We all discovered cuts and bruises; Bulldog and Reggie sported dandy shiners, fat lips and skinned knuckles; the skin on my left shoulder and right knee felt like it was on fire. But we laughed, anyway – we knew that we had delivered worse havoc on our opponents.

Jesse instructed the staff to keep the whole incident hush-hush; he didn't want to alarm the passengers, and no one would miss Bleaker and Bismarck. But it didn't take long for the word to get out, the next day, when the morning newspaper hit the street, and copies started showing up on the Madison. I guess Homer was anxious to publicly announce that he and his Department had captured the two criminals responsible for the Santo Domingo heist, and that he had them behind bars. He gave credit to the Madison crew for their "cooperation" in the apprehension effort.

Beth Lorado fussed over Andrew like a mother cow over a newborn calf. She must have shampooed his hair six times, trying to get all the black out. Marion, though, seemed quite proud of Andrew's heroic deed, especially when I told him about the knife throw – confidentially, so Beth wouldn't hear -- and there was no question, now, whether or not we would see Andrew strutting around in color, instead of black and white, by the time the noon whistle blew.

Mildred just shook her head in disgust when she discovered my blackened white shirt in the laundry room, and quickly disposed of it down the garbage chute. I sure was glad that I hadn't been wearing my favorite paint-splotched T-shirt. Mildred probably wished that I had.

Jesse was concerned. An incident like this could certainly put a crimp on future cruises, if we wanted to keep attracting the upper crust. Sadie didn't help matters, by reminding him that this boat had already attracted the likes of diamond thieves, murderous gamblers, and, now, a pair of riverboat burglars. How much more could time absorb?

"Don't worry," I told Jesse. "Everyone will forget about this in no time. And if they don't, we could always hang a sign on the coal bin: *Sight of the Bleaker Gang Shootout.* People would flock on our decks to see it."

Big Brother didn't think too much of the *Shootout* sign idea, but it did make him think of another way to put our double-edged reputation to advantage: "We can call the Madison *the safest boat on the Mississippi.*" He seemed encouraged with the notion of a new advertising campaign.

The Madison *would* be the safest boat on the river, I thought, as long as Reggie, Bulldog, Andrew, and I were on board.

Everything stayed calm aboard the Madison for the remainder of the day. Most of the passengers, seemingly not too concerned with the previous night's skirmish, wandered off again, this time to admire Cape Girardeau in daylight. The Lorado family trekked off on their sightseeing journey as planned; Henry and his assistants headed for the market to pick up a few needed provisions; Jesse, Luke, and the bartender, went in search for another keg of beer. Sadie pitched in, giving Mildred a homemaker hand with the laundry and carpet sweeping, while I walked the well rested, rabbit-clutching Philip, and Abba, up and down, forward and aft.

"Where's Doo?" he'd ask, and then his short attention span would be disrupted with, "Birdie!" as a flock of gulls hovered and swooped and squawked near by.

Down on the Main deck, I overheard Reggie tutoring Sparrow, trying desperately to get him to produce a complete sentence. "Go ahead... say it," Reggie pleaded with patience and compassion, "*I couldn't find the bloody*

Bobbies," and then he'd wait for Sparrow to duplicate. Sparrow wrinkled his forehead, and after a few seconds, replied, *"...Bobbies?"*

Of all the people to give speech lessons, I thought. By the time we got back to St. Charles, Sparrow would be gracing the dinner table with, *"Blimey! Pass the bloody crumpets."*

Our scheduled departure time from Cape Girardeau, 7:00 o'clock, was still three hours away; we didn't expect any of the passengers back on board until 6:30, so most of the staff were taking advantage of a little leisure time – all except Henry and his helpers, who were busy preparing for the evening supper. And Mildred; she was always busy with something.

I was in the pilothouse, taking a few lessons on river chart reading from Luke, frequently distracted by the splashing and joyous commotion down on the port side, created by four deckhands, two firemen and one bartender, having quite the time, diving off the Main deck into the Mississippi coolness. Luke would push his Cubs baseball cap back on his head, watch them a while, glance at the clock on the pilothouse wall, and then go back to the charts. I wiped the sweat from my forehead with the bottom of my painted T-shirt.

Luke navigated me around the sharp bend just before Cairo, when I noticed several people, ambling across the levee toward the Madison's gangplank. The heat had peeled off the men's jackets, and the women shaded themselves with parasols. A few porcelain dolls were returning early.

Then, I noticed a threesome, following a short ways behind – in the middle, a very blonde head, on top of a T-shirt, green as a seasick tourist.

Andrew waved triumphantly when he spotted me. Beth shook her dark hair, disgusted, and maybe fearful, at the sight of the swimmers; Marion's expression suggested that he might like to *join* them.

"That's enough for right now," Luke told me. "I'd better fish our crew out of the river, and get 'em back to work." He leaned out the open window and directed a loud voice with cupped hands around his mouth, "Okay, pool party's over... let's start looking like a riverboat crew again."

I trotted down the steps to the Texas, and then, on to the Saloon deck. By then, Andrew was far ahead of Marion and Beth, and met me at the top of the stairs.

"Well, look at you," I said. Never before, had I seen Andrew in anything but white, except for no shirt at all. He looked different, but I thought the pale green went well with his blonde hair and the light purple raspberry on his cheekbone.

"I got another one too... Madison blue," he announced rather proudly. "But I'm saving that one for later."

Whether it was the color, or the stroll around town among strangers, or the rage-venting encounter the previous night that did it, the character in the green shirt, the once-timid individual, who loved the world but feared its inhabitants – now, emanated a calmness, a contentedness, that I had yet to notice, for as long as I had known him. The gray cloud of doubt that always haloed him had given way to one of quiet confidence; Andrew had made a truce with the inhabited world.

"C'mon," he said to me. "I want to teach you another song... it's easy... and it was Mum's idea."

I glanced through the open saloon door at a lonely baby grand; it was at least an hour before anyone would gather there. Learning a new song only propelled me one step closer to vaudeville, I thought, but maybe it would be okay, to have a backup career, just in case this high class river cruise thing didn't work out.

We just made it to the door when I heard wet, bare feet slapping the deck at the top of the stairs. I turned to look.

Reggie and Sparrow stood at Lester's door, both with smiles as broad as a coal barge, their hair, water-slicked and pasted to their heads, jeans sopped, and a portion of the Mississippi dripping from their noses, elbows and just about everywhere else. Lester appeared more concerned with the wet mess they made on the floor, than he was with their jubilant grins.

"Go ahead, Sparrow... tell 'im," Reggie said.

Sparrow extended his hand toward Lester. In it, he held a lost treasure. "I found the... bloody keys!"

49

Coal bins loaded, pantry restocked, and one vacant stateroom, we steamed on to Cairo that night. The porcelain dolls were worn out from all the sightseeing and shopping in Cape Girardeau, so there wasn't as much activity in the saloon. But Jesse thought that I should spend one more night there, with Andrew, and assured me that I could be in the pilothouse, with Luke, during the entire return trip back to St. Charles.

Andrew played to a smaller audience after supper that night – mostly the men, who were too busy playing poker and pinochle, to notice Beth, delivering sheet music to the piano, and Andrew's switch from Benny Goodman and Duke Ellington, to Bach and Beethoven. It didn't seem to really matter to them.

I watched them puff their Cuban cigars, and sip their Missouri beer, exchanging stacks of dollars instead of pennies. I thought, what if Spades

Morgan were here? He'd show them a thing or two.

Spades Morgan. What if he *were* here? Would Andrew still be *Puttin' On the Ritz* and walking *On the Sunny Side of the Street?* Or would Beth and Marion have him locked away in his quarters, protecting him, depriving him of coming face-to-face with the man who gave him life? The man that they considered river trash? The man that I considered one of the most respectable people I had ever met.

I wanted to think that Andrew deserved to know his real father; Morgan was a good man, despite his occupation. With nothing to gain for himself, he had helped Jesse, Luke and me save Augie's boat, when he could've just walked away. He had handled evil with justice – he could have killed McDermott, that night up on the Texas, but he didn't. When he could have sat idly by, Morgan had searched St. Louis and found Jesse, so Jesse could be present at Augie's funeral, and then, Morgan comforted me during a time of my greatest need. Behind that stone cold face was a soul so rich with warm compassion; anyone could benefit from his alliance.

But maybe Luke was right; maybe it wasn't for me to decide. Perhaps, my stepfather had changed, too, by now, but I still wouldn't want him back – I carried around a collection of scars to remind me of that. The scars would eventually fade, and so would my memory of them. Maybe Andrew had scars, too – a different kind of scar, that wouldn't fade at all.

No. I could not – I *would* not interfere.

Our stay at Cairo, the next morning, lasted only long enough to take on coal, while Philip and Abba got acquainted with a whole new flock of birdies. Some of the more adventurous passengers scuttled about the town, in search of mementos they probably didn't need, or to mail picture post cards, that would probably arrive back in St. Louis long after they did. By noon, we had long since waved good-bye to Cairo, and started the four-day journey home.

Finally. I was right where I wanted to be; that was the day I had so longed for. No more white shirt. No more black bowtie. No more "Would you like another bowl of soup, sir?" I was a pilot – not a full-fledged one, yet, but at least, I could view the river, all that it touched, and beyond – and from the best seat in the house.

Luke and I made a good team. We took one-hour shifts at the helm, although, Luke was never very far away during my time at the wheel. Sometimes I'd get a little nervous about pointing the bow in the wrong direction, and he'd reassure me: "It's kinda hard to get lost out here... the river only goes two ways – upstream, and downstream." Then I'd pick out the next white marker, and I'd be right on course.

We tied up at Cape Girardeau that first night, long after the porcelain dolls had gone to bed. The firemen loaded us up with coal during the night, while Luke and I slept, and we were under way again, early the next morning, before any of the passengers knew that we had even stopped.

The next night, though, Luke insisted that I take a longer break; he thought I looked tired. I went to the saloon, to soak up some atmosphere, and maybe sneak a small sip of cold beer. The scene hadn't changed much; the men still played poker and pinochle under a haze of blue smoke, and the women still gathered in their little bridge groups; everyone seemed to be enjoying Andrew's music. But the conversations had shifted to other, heavier topics. Though they had suffered no bitter hurt, themselves, they realized that something bizarre, something unthinkable, had happened, and they found safe refuge in their numbers.

"Capone's been in prison for only two years," I heard one gentleman say. "And already there's a dozen or more right in his shadow."

Another man added, "Yeah, that list of public enemies the FBI put out..." and then I started hearing names like Dillinger, Baby Face Nelson, Machine Gun Kelly, and Pretty Boy Floyd – all the new names associated with a new wave of crime.

"And just think about that heathen that kidnapped and murdered the Lindbergh baby last year..." another man said. "Kind of makes you wonder how safe you are right in your own home."

"To think we had a couple of gangsters right here on this boat with us... and we didn't even know it."

"Personally, I worry about my business these days, too. Why, any one of us could be ruined in a heartbeat."

I gathered, from this rambling pow-wow that their subject matter stemmed from the near disaster just a couple of nights earlier, and that they had probably learned more about it. Hopes rode high, but through their shifting moods ran an undercurrent of fear. They seemed disillusioned with the worship of business, but they shared a remarkable solidarity and sense of community as Americans; their observations of the troubled times seemed less political than practical. Something had gone wrong with the country, but they didn't know what, couldn't figure it out, and wondered if anyone could. If moving up the business and social ladders had been their common goal in previous years, survival was their main hope now.

That sunny Sunday afternoon, I sounded the whistle as the Madison proudly steamed into the St. Charles port. Several other boats were moored at the levee, among them, the gallant Silverado, poised in its usual berth along the pier.

Luke and I joined Jesse at the head of the gangplank, smiling, and shaking hands with the departing porcelain doll parade, making its way to waiting cars on the levee. Some of the faces rained sorrow, now that their vacation was ending, but at the same time, the voices sang eagerness to reclaim their dollhouse mansions, and to resume their fragile, complex lives.

"Thank you for a *wonderful* week," one of them said.

"Quite an enjoyable cruise," another discharged.

"I thoroughly loved the entertainment," one lady poured out. "Do give that boy a raise."

Jesse grinned and nodded.

Then a distinguished-looking gentleman paused in front of Jesse. "Most enjoyable," he said. "And don't worry about that little incident the other night. It could've happened anywhere."

Another pinstripe stepped up beside the first. "And we're all going to recommend the Madison to *all* our business associates... they'll flock here once we tell them about it."

"Thank you," Jesse beamed, and extended his hand in a cordial, appreciative farewell.

Maybe we wouldn't need the *Shootout sign* after all, I thought.

Boiling black smoke from the stacks faded to a simmering gray. The bustling horde withered, and then dissolved. Only the sounds of the crew rattled around, readying the Madison for a bed down. To most of them, it was just another busy day, but to Jesse, Luke, and me, it was a day of triumphant victory. Few people could enjoy the satisfaction that we felt. We had battled the Depression's odds – and we had won.

50

I had taken the last overnight watchman shift again. I didn't mind getting up at 4:00 o'clock. Although Bleaker and Bismarck were behind bars, two hundred miles downriver, Jesse and Luke weren't thoroughly convinced of my button theory, and there could be plenty of others, just like Bleaker and Bismarck, lurking around in the night shadows. I couldn't disagree with logic like that.

Jesse was already in the galley, rounding up a few leftovers for breakfast, when I went up there at 6:00 to refill my coffee cup.

"Everything quiet out there?" Jesse asked.

I nodded, filled my cup, and found a biscuit and some strawberry jam. "Only thing I saw all night was an ol' tomcat prowlin'."

We took the delicacies into the staff's dining room, and sat at one end of the long table.

"So... where to next?" I said, wiping a glob of red goo off my chin. "New Orleans?"

"Whoa... not so fast, there, Little Brother. Let's take a couple of days off... and then we'll talk about it."

I heard cups rattling in the kitchen, and then Luke stumbled in, no shirt, no shoes, hair sprawling in all directions, and squinting his way into daylight.

"You're looking rather stunning this morning," Jesse said.

Luke just groaned, sat down beside me, and sipped his coffee.

There we were: the most unlikely trio to be in our positions. A small town baggage handler, a back woods country bumpkin, and a Milwaukee street kid, three years prior, and that day, we were among the ranks of successful businessmen. Back when I was still in Milwaukee, I would have had a hard time spelling riverboat, and now, I was the part owner of one.

"What's on the agenda today?" Luke's scratchy voice mumbled.

"Well," Jesse responded. He pushed his empty plate away, and hooked an index finger in the coffee cup handle. "You guys take it easy today. Soon as I get Sadie and Philip awake, I'm takin' them back to St. Louis. She has to get back to her studio -- made six appointments last week for portrait photographs."

"The cruise must've been good for her business, too," Luke said.

Jesse just nodded.

"How long are *you* gonna be there?"

"Maybe a couple of days," Jesse said. "I think I'm gonna trade the Model A for a new truck."

"Let me guess. One of our passengers last week is a dealer."

Jesse grinned, nodded again, and sipped his coffee.

Sunlight peeked through the port side windows. We heard footfalls on the stairway.

"That's Lester," Jesse said, as if to satisfy Luke's and my curious, wrinkled foreheads, aimed at the open door. "He said he'd be here early to get the bank deposit ready."

I knew that we had done quite well on this trip, and I could see Jesse's eyes, mentally counting the profits.

The sun quickly burned away dawn's hazy fog. I sat on the open observation deck, watching some of the other boats paddling away toward the Mississippi, like huge white swans, out for an early morning swim. The smell of coal smoke spiked the air, and the chuffing steam engines and whistles were like an alarm clock, waking the sleepy town. Everything seemed to be just as it was supposed to be.

Footsteps on the deck above started down the stairs. "Birdie!" I heard Philip squeal, and then Jesse appeared, carrying Philip and Abba, and Sadie at his side. Luke and Reggie followed close behind, each lugging a suitcase. The swelling had gone down on Reggie's lip, the black eye, barely noticeable.

Jesse's Model A waited on the levee, so we didn't have far to walk. When we got to it, Jesse turned to Luke, Reggie and me. "I'll see you guys in a couple o' days." He stood Philip on the ground, and took the suitcases from Luke and Reggie, swinging them, one at a time, into the truck bed.

Sadie leaned toward me and gave a little kiss on my cheek. "It was *so* good to spend this week with you," she said, and then she gave Luke and Reggie little smooches too.

"Bye-bye Philip," I said, giving a pint-sized wave.

"Ba-ba Unka Wiw. Ba-ba Ook. Ba-ba Eeggie," he returned, and then, he started looking all around, with a worried face that only a child could make; "Where's Doo?"

Lester sat in his office, juggling numbers, the world around him, faded into oblivion. Mildred stayed busy trying to polish the varnish off the furniture again; I wondered if she knew how to take a day off. The rest of the staff were gone, except for Sparrow, who was just hanging around, and drowning some worms with the cane pole, for the lack of anything better to do.

It wasn't even noon yet, and I was bored. I climbed the stairs to the pilothouse, stood with my hands loosely gripping the wheel, and closed my eyes. I imagined the Madison, stealing its way down the Mississippi in the dead of night, with just the stars and moon to guide the way. I swung wide around a bend, hoping to find enough water, and that there wasn't a menacing shoal lying beneath the surface. Up ahead, a flock of mallards fluttered out of the reeds and flew recklessly across the moonlit sky. Only an isolated flickering light or two betrayed the secrecy of a slumbering little town, hiding in the darkness.

I opened my eyes; the sunlight stole my night. Realizing, then, that I no longer had to dream about what was reality, the pilothouse, and everything in it, vanished behind me as I made my way down to the Main. I took a stance at the railing beside Sparrow. He acknowledged my presence with a nod.

"Catchin' anything?" I asked.

"No," he replied, but his eyes anticipated a bite at any second.

No, could probably qualify as a complete sentence, I thought, but it was plain to see that Sparrow wasn't in the mood for company; I headed back up to the observation deck.

A thought tornado struck, whirling fragments of images around in my head. One by one, I snatched hold of them, examining each one, until another came whisking by.

The past year was packed with events. I thought about how the Madison looked before the new staterooms were added, and how another daring decision had hauled us out of the slough, when there seemed to be no tomorrow. I thought about the intellect that Beth Lorado had bestowed upon me. And then there was the new President, Franklin Roosevelt, and his new deal, and the end to prohibition. Certainly, the country and the economy were on an upswing.

I thought about Augie, and the day that I lost one of the best companions a boy could ever hope for. And then I thought about the day that gave me a new friend – Golden Boy; Andrew had helped me to understand how small my world was, there on the Madison, and how large it was, everywhere else. I thought about how I had helped Andrew expand his world, too, and how we shared an unforgettable Christmas experience.

I recalled the day that I stood, naked, before a mirror, and discovered that I wasn't a scrawny kid anymore, but that somehow, I wished that I were, again.

I remembered all the nights, sitting with ear to the radio, introduced to the voices of entertainment – Jack Benny, George Burns, Gracie Allen, Amos and Andy, Buck Rogers, and Will Rogers...

Will Rogers. It occurred to me that I hadn't heard one of his Sunday night radio speeches since April, when he talked about Washington committees gathering useless information: "It's kinda like garbage," he'd said. "What's the use of collecting it if you ain't got nowhere to put it?"

I wondered if I was doing the same thing – collecting all those thoughts, with nowhere to put them.

So deep in that mineshaft of memories, the voice speaking my name didn't register as one of reality. "Will?" it echoed. It was a familiar voice – one I hadn't heard in quite some time. Spades Morgan sat down beside me; I snapped back to the present.

"Spades!" I said, adjusting my concentration. "I was just thinking about coming over to see if you were back on the Silverado."

"Got back last week," he said, in his usual granite statue manner. "Arrived on the *Natchez*... Wednesday."

"Then, we just missed you at Cape Girardeau. We met the *Natchez* a few miles north."

"Yes, and I hear y'all've been catching criminals again."

"But how did you know about--?"

"It's been in all the papers... and when I saw the Madison's crew was involved, I knew that you and Jesse must've been who they were talking about."

"Well, actually, Jesse didn't have much to do with it, this time, but I guess I was in the thick of things."

"I was wondering how long it would take the law to outsmart those two scoundrels," Morgan pondered, without showing a trace of emotion. "Guess it took the likes of Will Madison to do it."

Morgan seemed to know the crooks, and he was astonishingly well informed about their capture. There was no need to dwell on it.

"D'ya like the new additions to the Madison?" I said, eluding to something closer at hand. "Did you see the saloon?"

"Yep. I noticed all the new staterooms on the Main... and I ducked in to say hello to Mildred. Mighty impressive."

I heard the patter of feet on the stairs from the Main; another voice called out, "Will? Where are you?"

That voice was familiar, too – Andrew's. Another bucket of ice chips went sliding down my back. About twenty miles south of Cape Girardeau, I had all but dismissed the possibility of introducing Andrew to the father he didn't know. Never, in all of my mental meandering, had I imagined such an occurrence. What would I say? What would I do? I felt like I was sitting on a broken beer bottle.

I jumped to my feet, thinking that I would meet Andrew, halfway down the stairs, but running off, leaving Morgan, seemed awkward and impolite, and by that time, Andrew's Madison blue T-shirt walked toward me from the top of the stairway.

"Hey Will! Wanna go... for a hike?" Andrew's words trailed off into nowhere, as his eyes collided with Morgan.

I felt like I was standing in pail of wet cement. I could see a whole universe of stars, twinkling in Andrew's eyes, but the weight of a baby grand piano pressed on his shoulders, as if the secret of the century had blabbed his clandestine identity. His eyes prodded at me with worry, and then he turned to Morgan.

"Hi Dad," he said. Never had I heard him say that word, and it sounded so natural, so nonchalant.

"Hi Son," Morgan replied, as if they had lived under the same roof since the beginning of time.

"Sorry I haven't stopped over to see you," Andrew said to Morgan. "I've been kind of busy."

Morgan nodded his acknowledgement. "I understand you've become quite the entertainer."

Just then, Reggie and Luke rumbled down the stairs from the Texas.

"Hey Will... wanna go for ice cream?"

PART 3

THE
GASLIGHT
KNIGHTS

51

The night they pulled Johnny Dempsey's body out of the Mississippi River is when Andy and I, Will Madison, decided to get out of town while the gettin' was good, no matter what it took. We hadn't known Johnny a long time, but long enough. That went for some of his other friends, too. At one time we thought they were all a bunch of great guys, but as the weeks and months passed by, it became clear to us that we had jumped off a perfectly good boat into a cesspool of trouble. If we hadn't been using our heads, we might've gotten tangled in a mess we didn't want.

And speaking of perfectly good boats, that's why Andy and I were in the middle of that mess. We had had three good seasons aboard the Madison, an elegant old lady of a steamboat, of which I was a part owner, with my big brother Jesse Madison and our good friend Luke Jackson. We'd owned that old boat for six years, and she made us a good living hauling rich folks up and down the Mississippi on vacation excursions. Oh, we had our share of headaches, too, but for the most part, we had it better than most people, considering the Depression and all that went with it. And then one night while we were tied up at the St. Louis levee, a fire broke out on the boat next to the Madison. That fire spread so rapidly that by the time anybody could do anything it had raged across five more boats. The Madison was a total loss.

Jesse, Luke, and I came out of it okay. All the staff was off duty between excursions so nobody was injured. The insurance company paid us off, but we were all out of work kinda sudden like. Wasn't long, though, until Jesse got hooked up with the captain of a barge tow—the Bill Horne—he and Luke signed on with the condition that once they had a little experience with pushing barges, they would be in line for Captain and Pilot of the next available boat in the company.

Barge tows don't have pianos or piano players, so Andy was officially an unemployed piano player, and Jesse told me that as soon as he became the captain of another boat, I would be back on the river again. And if Andrew was willing to work as a deckhand, he'd have a job, too. So, in the meantime, Andy and I went back to St. Charles with his mom, Beth Lorado, who was one of our chambermaids, to their house at the end of Third Street, where I had spent the winter when Andy and I first met. Andy's dad, Marion Lorado, who was one of our engineers, was already hired as the second engineer on another barge tug, so we didn't see much of him. Beth went back to teaching piano lessons, and Mildred, the other chambermaid on the Madison, got Beth a part-time job at the hotel where she worked.

Luke was our pilot. He could afford most anything he wanted, and he made sure Reggie had a nice place to live in St. Louis until he could get him back on a riverboat crew again. Reggie had eventually become the Captain's First Mate after he worked as a deckhand for a while. He and Luke, of course, had been sharing quarters since our first day on the river aboard the Madison. We all learned in time what was going on between them, but it didn't seem to bother anybody, so it really didn't matter.

So everything worked out alright for all of us.

Andy was the best piano player I'd ever heard tickle the ivories. He played the church organ in St. Charles, too. That's how I happened to first meet Andy. I'd seen him many times before, and I had thought that he was a homeless kid without good clothes or food. But then I saw him playing the church organ, and I finally got to meet him—well, he actually found me lost in the woods one day and he showed me the way back to town. After that, we got to be really good friends, and I lived with his family while the Madison was tied up in Alton Slough one winter. That's when the Madison was remodeled into a luxury excursion boat, and Jesse hired Andy as cabin boy and the live entertainment. He hired Andy's mom and dad, too, as chambermaid and second engineer.

We called him *Andrew* back then, and he was a bit shy about performing in front of all those people, but after about a year or so, "Andy" Lorado had become quite popular with the vacationers, and some of them came back for another trip... "Just to hear Andy play their favorite tunes." On every trip, at least once or twice, Andy would always get me to the piano to play a duet with him. I couldn't play the piano except to pick out a melody, *Down by the Riverside*, with one finger, and   Andy would play a dreamy rendition of *April in Paris* at the same time, and somehow he could make me sound like a real professional. Of course, we always hammed it up a bit, too. It never failed to bring the house down. He taught me some more tunes later on, and eventually we played together more often, but I knew it was Andy that the crowd loved.

Ever since I ran away from home in Milwaukee to escape the daily beatings by my usually drunken stepfather, I had learned to hate the big city. I was only fourteen then, when I jumped a freight train headed west and landed someplace near a big river. I had no idea where I was or what to do next, but I managed to learn how to take care of myself, stealing clothes off a line in a back yard when I needed some, and swiping a loaf of bread cooling on a back porch, and raiding gardens late at night. I found places to sleep in haylofts, and in general, I was getting along pretty good. But it was lonely.

Then one night a bad storm hit—took the roof off the barn I was sleeping in! I ran into the woods so I wouldn't be found and stayed the rest of the night in a little cave. By then I had wandered so far I wasn't sure if I was still in the same country. The next morning a flood filled the valley because of all the heavy rain the night before, and as I sat there watching it, I noticed a young man chasing after something floating away in the floodwater. I saw the top of a trunk coming toward me and when I thought I could grab it for him, I went head-first into the swift, muddy stream, too. Guess I would've drowned if Jesse Madison hadn't found me and pulled me out. Now Jesse could've hauled me right to the nearest police station and turned me in for the runaway that I was. But he didn't. Guess he felt sorry for me. He even lied to the clerk when he bought me some new clothes— said I was his "little brother," I guess so nobody would ask any questions. He sort of took me in, and it wasn't long until I changed my last name to Madison, and Jesse and I *were* brothers. It was the greatest thing that ever happened to me.

Jesse met a lady friend on our first trip down the river on our new boat. Oh, yeah... the boat. Another guy, Luke Jackson, had joined up with us, and we met an old riverboat captain named Augie on the riverfront at La Crosse. He owned the boat, and he invited us aboard to take a look. We became good friends with Augie, and he let us stay there for a while. But old Augie was sort of down on his luck, and he lost the boat in a poker game one night. We felt awful. Jesse, Luke, and I had planned to work as crewmen for Augie on his boat.

Just about the time we thought all was lost, along came Spades Morgan struttin' off another steamboat that came in from St. Paul. Jesse and I had met him before, up in Alma, and we knew he was a professional gambler. He was a great guy, though, but we didn't know how important he would become to us. He agreed to help us get Augie's boat back from the swamp scum gambler J.D. McDermott. He did win it back, but by then Augie had decided to retire, and he didn't want it. That's how Jesse became its official owner, and of course, later on, he made me and Luke partners. Luckily, Augie consented to stay with us as the pilot for a while and teach us all how to run a riverboat. He was a good teacher. Luke learned piloting and a year or so later, he got his pilot's license. Jesse became a first-class Captain and entrepreneur. And I was the most popular cabin boy on the river.

Sadly, though, we laid Augie to rest in St. Charles the next year when he died of a heart attack. But I think he died a happy man.

Like I started before, the lady friend Jesse met, Sadie Perkins, eventually became his wife and the mother of their son, Philip. Sadie was a top-notch photographer, and just moving to St. Louis where she was starting a photography and art studio. She booked passage on our boat from La Crosse to St. Louis, and it must've been love at first sight for her and Jesse, because they spent the first night in a hotel while the boat was tied up overnight at Prairie du Chien.

They had to part when we reached St. Louis, and it was more than two years later when Jesse found her again; Philip was almost two. They married and lived in Sadie's house in St. Louis.

They invited me to stay with them, too. But I hated the big city—any big city—and St. Louis was a *very* big city. That's why I chose to stay in St. Charles with Andrew's family that next winter.

As time went on, though, I visited them more often and stayed there frequently when the boat was not busy or was in harbor for repairs. Gradually, I disliked the city less and learned to tolerate the rows of tall buildings towering over my head, and the noisy traffic and pedestrians at ground level. I learned my way around, although I didn't bother trying to remember street names, just familiar buildings and other things at the corners. I had learned my lesson about getting lost out in the woods, and so I paid closer attention to landmarks starting the very first time I decided to explore the streets of St. Louis.

52

When the Madison burned in September of 1934, my world sort of turned upside down, as I'm sure it did for the others, too. One thing I could be thankful for was that Big Brother Jesse had always insisted that we keep all of our valuables and money in the safe instead of hiding it in our cabins. That safe must've weighed a ton and the walls and door were a foot thick. When we finally found the safe and got it opened the day after the fire, everything was still intact; we hadn't lost a thing. All the important business papers and books were unharmed, and just about everyone on the staff retrieved their canvas bags containing personal valuables and money. A gold pocket watch that Spades Morgan gave me five years ago and about eight hundred dollars were in my bag. I think I hugged Jesse and kissed him on the cheek for always making me keep it there. Even Andy hugged Jesse out of pure joy when he got out the bag with his name on it. All that helped ease the pain of seeing our beloved boat, the Madison, lying there in a charred heap of rubble. A salvage company towed away the hull, said they would try to save some of the machinery and boilers, but the rest was simply worthless junk.

Captain Brooks from the towboat Bill Horne was there when Jesse, Luke and I watched the salvage tug haul away what remained of the Madison. He knew Jesse and Luke, as many of the riverboat captains and pilots were acquainted. He shook our hands, offered his sympathy. And then he offered Jesse and Luke jobs on his boat. "Once you get a little experience towin' barges," he said, "Continental will put you in command of one of their other boats."

It didn't take Jesse long to accept the offer, and Luke seemed pretty excited about it, too. They all shook hands again, after they had set a time later that day for an official meeting at the Continental Shipping Company's office, and then Captain Brooks left.

Jesse looked up and down the levee, and then he looked at me. "Will, as soon as I'm on another boat of my own, you'll be there on my crew... I promise."

Tears were burning my eyes, and I wasn't sure if they were tears of joy for Jesse, or tears of sorrow that we wouldn't be together for quite some time. "What about Andy?" I said, for the lack of anything better to say.

"I really like Andy," Jesse replied. "If he's willing to work as a deckhand, or maybe a cook's assistant, you can tell him he has a job waiting for him, too."

"Yeah," I said. "I guess barge tows don't need a piano player, do they?"

We all laughed a little. At least, I had *something* to look forward to. "I think I'll go with Andy and Beth back to St. Charles this afternoon. Mildred is going, too. She checked the bus schedules. There's one at three fifteen.

"You know, Will, you can stay with me and Sadie."

"I know. But Andy's a little down in the dumps about all this, and I think he could use a little company for a while."

"Guess that's a good enough reason to go to St. Charles. But just remember... you can come to our house anytime."

He gave me one of those sincere Big Brother bear hugs that had never lost their effectiveness. I returned the gesture, thinking about all the good times we had, and all the good things Jesse had done for me. I had a lot of faith in my big brother, and I knew he'd never let me down. I detected tears in his eyes, too, but I wasn't sure if they were tears for me, or for the boat. I wanted to think they were for me.

The bus to St. Charles was late. It was nearly five o'clock when it left the St. Louis station, and quite crowded. Beth and Mildred found seats across the aisle from each other near the front, but Andy and I had to share the seat across the back of the bus with an old couple who could barely keep awake. The old man kept tipping over onto me, and he'd wake up when I pushed him back. "Oh, excuse me," he'd say every time. "Guess I must've dozed off."

At least it kept Andy amused. It was the first time I had seen him smile all day.

We arrived in St. Charles a little after six. I hugged Mildred when Andy and I finally struggled our way through the crowd gathered to meet other disembarking passengers. Mildred seemed so worried, but I sensed that she was more worried about me than she was about herself. "Everything will be okay," she said to me. "You just keep smiling, and everything will turn out just fine."

"Will you be okay?" I asked her. I knew she was headed off to her little apartment downtown, and she would be alone.

"Oh, heavens, yes! Don't you worry about me. I'll be just fine."

I didn't worry about her, but I *was* concerned. Mildred was like a mom to me. She had seen me through my adolescence, and I knew she truly cared about me. I loved her very dearly.

"We'll be in touch," she said, and then she pushed me away from our embrace, turned, and briskly strutted down the sidewalk toward Main Street.

"Stop over for coffee tomorrow if you can," Beth called out to her.

Mildred turned and waved. "Thank you. I will."

Beth, Andy, and I walked casually out to their house at the end of Third Street. Beth had already been home a couple of days after the last excursion, and she had just left there that morning on the bus back to St.

Louis when she got word about the Madison fire. Her husband, Marion, had stayed in St. Louis to help with some maintenance on the boat, and Andy decided to stay there with me, so she had come alone. When she unlocked the back door into the kitchen, I could tell she was glad to be home again. "I'll make a pot of coffee, and then we'll have some supper," she said.

As we sat at the kitchen table eating the pancakes and bacon that Andy suggested, Beth asked: "What are your plans, now, Will? You'll need some new clothes, won't you?"

"I guess so," I replied. "I have a few things at Jesse's place, but I s'pose I'll be needing some more."

"And what would you like for your birthday supper next week?"

I had almost forgotten. Next week, Monday, the 24th of September was my eighteenth birthday. It was just like Beth Lorado to remember. "Oh, you don't have to bother," I said modestly.

"It's no bother. I have to make supper anyway, and you can make your request."

I thought for a long moment. "Well... how 'bout biscuits and your delicious chicken stew?"

"If that's what you want, that's what you'll get."

Andy piped up. "Can you bake a cake, too?"

"Sure," Beth replied with a big smile. "We can have cake, too."

It was a pretty fantastic birthday, considering the catastrophic turn of events that preceded it. The Madison's destruction was still quite heavy on everybody's thoughts, but that didn't stop Jesse, Luke, Reggie, and Mildred from showing up Monday afternoon for the best birthday party ever. They all carried in brightly wrapped packages and Jesse had a tub of strawberry ice cream—he knew how I loved ice cream.

When the day was over, I no longer had a clothing shortage problem, as all the packages contained shirts, trousers, and Luke and Reggie gave me socks and underwear. But Jesse didn't have a package; instead, he handed me a paper envelope. When I opened it and looked inside, I couldn't believe my eyes. Baseball tickets. In just a few days the St. Louis Cardinals and the Detroit Tigers would face off for the 1934 World Series, and I had two tickets for the games that would be played in St. Louis. "Didn't want you to go alone," Jesse said, "so I got tickets for Andy, too."

Jesse was the greatest.

53

It was the middle of October. I was getting restless, and so was Andy. We'd taken a bus to St. Louis and watched Dizzy Dean and the "Gashouse Gang" Cardinals whip the Detroit Tigers, and listened to the radio broadcast from Detroit of the last game of the Series when they massacred the Tigers eleven to nothing. Now the excitement was over. Beth was teaching piano lessons to less-than-talented little kids again, and Mildred had coaxed her into a part-time job at the hotel where she worked. Andy practiced at the piano every day, and I read a lot of books when we weren't trying to escape the painful renditions of *Twinkle, Twinkle Little Star* and *Mary Had a Little Lamb* from Beth's students.

Then one day the telephone rang, and when Beth told me it was Sadie calling for me, I thought for sure that Jesse was ready to get me and Andy on a riverboat crew.

"Hello?" I spoke with enthusiasm.

"Will?" Sadie sounded tired or distressed, I couldn't tell which.

"How are you doing, Will?"

"Good, Sadie. How are you?"

"I'm okay, but I was wondering if you could come to St. Louis and stay here for a while. My babysitter has fallen and broken her leg, and Philip just doesn't like any of the others I can get on such short notice. I'm really busy in the studio these days, and I sure could use your help. Philip would love to see you again, too."

"Well, I s'pose. Where's Jesse?"

"Jesse is on the way to New Orleans. I don't expect him back for at least two weeks."

"New Orleans! Well, that lucky son of a gun."

"How about it, Will? Can you come?"

"Sure, Sadie. I'll see what time the bus goes tomorrow, okay?"

"Okay! That would be great! I'll see you tomorrow, then."

"Okay. Good-bye Sadie."

"Good-bye Will."

In a way, I was glad to have a change of scenery, but I also hated to leave Andy all alone with just his piano and having to dodge the Twinkle, Twinkle kids all by himself. Then it occurred to me that Andy could come to St. Louis with me.

"Sadie has a piano in her parlor," I told Andy. "You can still practice every day if you want to."

"But where will I sleep?"

"There's a big double bed in my room."

"How do you know it's okay with Sadie?"

"I'll call her back right now."

I knew Sadie wouldn't say no. She needed my help, and she knew how close me and Andy were. And besides... she liked Andy, and Philip adored him. It would be perfect.

"Of course, Andy can come with you," Sadie said. "It'll be good for both of you."

When I knew Andy was convinced that he should come to St. Louis with me, Beth was my next obstacle. But she wasn't as difficult to persuade as I had expected. She was actually glad that Andy wanted to get out and explore his options. "As long as he's going with you, Will," she said, "I shouldn't have to worry at all. And I know you'll both be in good hands with Sadie."

Beth loaned us a spare satchel to put our clothes in; both Andy's and mine were lost in the fire. We jumped on the bus to St. Louis the next morning.

Jesse and Sadie's house on Fulton Street hadn't changed much in all the time I had been going there. It was a quite large two story Victorian style, painted white with blue trim, just like the Madison had been. Even Andy remarked about the resemblance when he saw it. The huge front parlor had been converted into the business end of Sadie's studio; one side was partitioned off with floor-to-ceiling drapes that parted in the middle, behind which were cameras on tripods, chairs, and several different backdrop screens. This is where close-up portrait photographs were taken. In the far corner on the other side stood a dressing table and mirror, where the women could apply make-up and restore hair-dos that might have been disturbed by the wind. Plenty of comfortable chairs offered a congenial atmosphere among several easels holding paintings and photographs that aptly displayed Sadie's talents. Right in the center sat a large desk where Sadie conducted business.

Sadie was happy to see us when we came in the front door. She sat at her desk, busy with a stack of paperwork, and 3½-year-old Philip was busy beside her on the floor with a pile of wooden building blocks. His blue stuffed rabbit, "Abba," that I had given to him for Christmas a couple of years before, wasn't far away.

"Hi, Will. Hi Andy," Sadie said with her usual smile. "It's so good to see you again."

I hadn't seen Sadie since before the fire. I gave her a hug when she got up from behind the desk. Philip left his blocks and came running. I scooped him up and he hugged my neck. Then he noticed Andy. "Doo!" he squealed, and reached out for Andy's turn to be coddled and hugged. Philip had called Andy "Doo" when he first started talking, because he couldn't pronounce "Andrew." The name just stuck. He liked Andy as much as he liked me, and he seemed pretty excited to have us both there.

Sadie glanced at the clock. "Some customers will be here soon," she said. "You can take your things upstairs... and there are some fresh cookies just out of the oven in the kitchen if you're hungry."

With Philip riding on Andy's shoulders and clutching Abba, they followed me up the stairs to the bedroom where I always slept when I stayed there. I was so glad to see that Sadie had been thoughtful enough to replace the pink-and-white bedspread with a blue one.

While Sadie conducted usual business with several clients throughout the afternoon, Andy and I kept Philip amused until he tired, ready for a long nap. That routine lasted all week while we took turns playing with Philip, and Andy spent about an hour each day at the piano in Sadie's parlor. Sometimes he'd coax me to the piano bench so we could play our *"Down by the Riverside/April in Paris"* duet. Whenever I had the chance, I spent time in the studio with Sadie when she wasn't busy with customers, and I suppose she got tired of me asking all sorts of questions about cameras and picture-taking. But in a way, she seemed pleased, too, that I was taking an interest. When I asked her if I could try my hand at taking a picture, she opened a cupboard, pulled out a black case, and then took a small camera out of the case. "I've had this for three or four years," she told me, "but I hardly ever use it anymore." She turned it over, examining all sides, and then held it up to her eyes, panning around, viewing various portions of the room through the lens. Then she offered to let me hold it. "This is a thirty-five millimeter Leica... uses roll film, easy to operate. It would be a good camera for you to try," she said.

I took the camera from her with a little hesitation, fearful that I might damage it just by touching it.

"Don't be afraid of it, Will. It won't bite you."

Carefully, I imitated Sadie's earlier actions by holding it up to my eye and looking through the lens. I saw the world differently and I immediately became fascinated.

"This is the kind of camera that a lot of newspaper and magazine journalists use," Sadie explained. "You can take it just about anywhere but underwater. I was thinking of giving journalism photography a try, but it's men that dominate all the newspaper and magazine photographer jobs so I decided to just stick with what I do."

I had seen hundreds of people vacationing aboard the Madison, and many of them carried cameras much like this one. Seemed like there was always someone taking pictures of the scenery along the Mississippi from our decks, and sometimes they would take pictures of their family, and occasionally they would take pictures of me and some of the rest of the crew. The pilothouse and Luke were always popular subjects, too.

Sadie retrieved from the black case a thin book and offered it to me. "Here... read this manual first so you understand a little more about it, and then tomorrow I'll help you load some film and you can take a few pictures. I'll develop the film for you, and we'll see how you did."

I studied that manual from cover to cover, several times. The next day while Philip was napping and Andy was practicing on the piano, Sadie gave me a crash course in photography—how to hold the camera and keep it steady, how to always try to keep the sun at my back and to avoid shadows, how to "compose" the subject in the viewfinder, and all sorts of other little tricks she had learned from experience. I absorbed as much as I could. She showed me how to put the film in; I was ready to take pictures.

Choosing the subjects to photograph was tough. I don't know why I wasted so much effort on making that decision; I would have many more opportunities. I finally decided on Jesse's house, one of Andy, a couple of shiny new cars in the street, and various street scenes downtown. When I came back to the house, Sadie showed me how to remove the film safely, and said she would develop the pictures in a day or so.

I'd had plenty of time to think about what Sadie said about journalism photography, and I had really enjoyed seeking my subjects and composing the scene in the viewfinder. Hearing the click of the shutter made me feel like I had recorded a piece of time for all eternity. If Jesse wasn't successful in getting me back on the river soon, I thought I'd like to try this photography business.

54

Saturday, Sadie must've felt sorry for us and told Andy and me to get out for a while and enjoy ourselves... maybe see a matinee. We hadn't done that for a long time, and it sounded like a good idea. There were several theaters to choose, and one of them was bound to be playing something we would like. We took a trolley car to Grand Boulevard and Olive Street, the center of the midtown theater district.

When we came out of the Fox movie theater that afternoon, we stood on the sidewalk next to Grand Boulevard for a while watching all the people scurrying by. We weren't looking for anyone in particular, or attempting to make any new acquaintances. That's when another young fellow who looked to be about our age casually walked up to us and said "Hi."

Andy and I acknowledged his greeting.

"Saw you goin' in the theater earlier," he said. "Thought I should know you from somewhere."

Andy and I exchanged glances and shrugged our shoulders. The handsome young face didn't seem familiar, but we had seen so many faces over the past few years, it was nearly impossible to remember them all.

"We were on a riverboat crew until a month ago," Andy offered. "The Madison. Were you ever on it?"

The stranger thought a long moment, and then shook his head. "No, but isn't that one of the boats that burned about a month ago?"

"That's right," Andy replied. "But if you were never on it, then I don't know why you think you know us."

"Well... maybe I've just seen you along the waterfront. I spend quite a bit of time there."

"What d'ya do there?" Andy asked.

"Write my poetry."

"You write poetry?" I blurted out, not intending to sound rude, but it may have seemed that way. I think I must've struck a sensitive nerve. "I'm sorry," I added. "I didn't mean it the way it sounded."

"That's okay," the stranger replied. "I'm getting used to that response from people." Then he stuck out his right hand toward Andy. "I'm Marty Genshaw."

Andy accepted his brief handshake, and then Marty offered the same to me.

"I'm Will Madison, and my friend is Andy Lorado."

Marty eyed me with suspicion. "Madison. Any relation to the boat?"

"Well... yeah... me and my brother Jesse owned it."

The breezy October air was getting just a little chilly as the sun dipped behind the tall buildings leaving us in the shadows. Marty wore only a T-shirt and jeans, and I could see the goose bumps flourishing on his arms. "There's a coffee shop just around the corner," I suggested. "We can get in out of this wind. I'll buy the coffee."

The others agreed and we all headed around the corner.

Marty asked a lot of questions about the Madison, and what it was like to work on a riverboat. He seemed to turn his interest mostly to Andy when he found out Andy was a musician. Watching people aboard the Madison, I had noticed that people of the arts tend to be attracted to one another.

"Have any of your poems been published?" Andy asked.

"No," Marty replied. "I'm kinda new at poetry. I switched from prose to poetry only about a year ago while I was..." His face turned strawberry red as he abruptly cut off.

"While you were... what?" Andy asked.

After a long pause staring down into his coffee cup, Marty hesitantly finished the statement. "Okay... I guess you would've found out sooner or later... while I was in jail."

"Why were you in jail?" I asked.

"For stealing a typewriter... but I was just borrowing it... I was going to bring it back... honest!"

"But you got caught taking it without permission, so you got thrown in the slammer for theft."

"Yeah, something like that."

I wasn't sure if I should believe he was truly sincere. Marty was a dynamo, a ball of energy with legs and arms, and probably a hustler for any kind of action. My first impulse was to beware. But Andy seemed quite comfortable with our new acquaintance.

"I quit school when I was sixteen and got a job as an office boy in a New York publishing house," Marty went on.

"You're from New York?" Andy asked.

"Yeah... and that's when I decided I wanted to be a writer." His eyes quickly jerked back and forth from Andy to me; his expression appeared as if he was concerned about losing our attention.

"Then, why did you come to St. Louis?" Andy said.

"After almost a year in prison, I just wanted to get away from New York. I'd educated myself quite well by reading *everything* in the prison library— that's when I became fond of poetry, and even started writing some. But when I was released, I met a man from St. Louis in a tea pad, there in New York. He told me about St. Louie, and so I decided to come here."

"Whoa! Whoa!" Andy said. "A tea... what?"

I was curious, too.

Marty looked at us like we must've been from another planet. "*Tea pad*... you know... like an opium den, where you can go to smoke marihuana and hashish. There's hundreds of 'em in New York. They're here in St. Louis, too."

We'd heard about marihuana and hashish becoming popular as substitutes for alcohol during prohibition days, but we'd never been exposed to it. Neither Andy nor I had spent enough time in the big city to be familiar with "tea pads." Marty explained that they were similar to the speakeasies of prohibition, where illegal booze was available, but only if you were a member of the "private club." But apparently, tea pads were more acceptable and not necessarily under scrutiny of the law.

I decided to ease up on my torrid feelings toward Marty, primarily because Andy really seemed to like him; if prison had rehabilitated him and turned him into an intellect, then I guess I couldn't think of any reason to dislike him.

While Andy and Marty conversed about music and poetry, I thought some more about the Leica camera and all the other things I would like to put into pictures. I certainly hoped that Sadie would let me use it again, or maybe even sell it to me. I'd go to the levee and wait for some really good riverboat scenes, and... and... maybe I'd see Marty there, and then I could show him that I was eligible to be called an "artist." But I decided right then that I wouldn't wait for that. "I'm learning photography," I said when the opportunity came. "Maybe I'll be a journalism photographer someday."

"Well," Marty said, as if he were finally accepting me into an exclusive group. "I have a friend who works at the *Post*. He's just a copy boy now, but he's studying to be a journalist, too. You should meet him sometime."

"Okay... sure," I said, hoping that I hadn't overstepped the boundaries. I knew scarcely little about photography, and I knew absolutely nothing about journalism. But it certainly couldn't hurt to meet Marty's friend.

I pulled out my pocket watch. It was nearly five o'clock. "We should be going," I said to Andy. "Sadie will be waiting supper on us."

We agreed to meet Marty again the following Friday night. He'd take us to a place called the Lion's Den, a bar at North Sixth and Olive Street. That was only about three blocks from the river.

55

Only half of the pictures I took with the *Leica* camera were worth keeping. Sadie explained the reasons—I didn't hold the camera steady, overexposed, underexposed—it was clear that I had a long way to go to become a good photographer, or even a mediocre one.

"Don't be discouraged," Sadie told me. "You actually did pretty good for your first try."

"You really think so, or are you just saying that to make me feel better?"

"Really. You did better than I did on my first try."

Whether it was the truth or not, it did make me feel better, and I wanted to try again. "Can I try some more? I'll pay you for the film and the developing."

"Sure, you can try some more, but you don't have to pay me for the film. I owe you that much for helping me take care of Philip."

Every day that week, I took more pictures, and Sadie helped me with a few of them to get the camera settings just right. The next picture I took of Andy turned out nice, but I thought he looked a lot younger in the picture. By Friday I had a collection of photographs, and even Sadie was impressed with some of them. "You'll make a good photographer, Will. You should keep at it."

Somehow, I knew this is what I wanted to do. I still loved the river, too, and I would go back to a riverboat in a heartbeat if Jesse offered. But photography would allow me to express myself creatively, something that had not occurred to me until now. The whole idea of it was exciting. Andy gave me plenty of encouragement, too. "Some of your pictures are just as good as any in the newspaper," he said.

Now I wasn't afraid to meet Marty's friend and talk about photography. Of course, I still knew nothing about journalism, but I could learn that, too, with a little help.

Andy and I rode a bus again Friday night destined for the midtown theater district. Just as he said he would, Marty was there to meet us. We boarded a street car that went all the way down Olive Street toward the Mississippi River. We got off at 6th Street. I recognized the neighborhood, because just one block away—6th & Pine—there was a sandwich shop within walking distance from the St. Louis levee where Luke, Reggie and I used to go when the Madison tied up overnight. Andy had been with us a few times, too.

The crowd in the Lion's Den was rather subdued, mellow, when we arrived, but I guess that was because it was still early. As the night wore on, though, voices got bolder, the music played louder, and the beer flowed more freely. Marty led us to a table in the back corner area that was sectioned off from the main floor with a half-wall. From the top of the wall to the ceiling grew ivy vines on white painted lattice. Gas lights gently illuminated the room. Five more tables took up the secluded space where four of them were occupied by poker games. The partition was evidently there to provide a little protection from the crowd for such purposes. The table where Marty's friends sat seemed to be more of a social gathering with no gaming. They all greeted Marty, happy that he could join the party. And then they all took notice of me and Andy. "Who are your friends?" one of them asked. He didn't appear to be irritated with our intrusion, but instead, he seemed eager to have us join the party, too.

"Knights of the Square Table," Marty addressed the group. "I'd like you to meet Andy Lorado, unemployed musician." He put his arm across Andy's shoulders. "Andy was the entertainer on the steamboat Madison that burned a while back." Then he put his hand on my shoulder. "This is Will Madison, ex-steamboat owner. He's studying photography."

"Knights of the *Square* Table?" I chuckled.

Marty eyed me with pseudo seriousness. "Well... yeah... Knights of the *Round* Table was already taken."

Everyone sitting there laughed, and then Andy and I were invited to pull up chairs from the vacant table. They all shifted one way or the other to make a couple of open spaces.

At first, I got the impression that these guys were upper class in social circles; they all wore nice clothes, their speech was correct and polite, and they weren't loud or boisterous. I had been among a large number of high standards people on the Madison; those were the people we catered to—the wealthy businessmen and their families—and the young men sitting around this table, although they were much younger than most of our passengers had been, seemed to possess similar qualities.

As with almost any group, newcomers are always the center attraction. Marty had disappeared while the others were fussing over making Andy and me comfortable, but he soon returned with three glass beer mugs and a pitcher filled with golden brew topped with a mound of white foam. He poured the mugs full, slid one across the table to Andy and one to me, and then set the pitcher in the middle of the table where there was another one nearly empty. "I hope you like beer," he said. "Guess I should've asked first."

Andy and I both assured him his choice was okay, and we sampled the cold brew.

The guy sitting to my left offered a handshake. "I'm Curtis," he said. And then the guy sitting next to him reached across for a handshake. "I'm Frank."

I noticed that on the other side of the table Andy was receiving the same treatment. "They call me Cheechee," the fellow next to him said. "Real name is Christopher Chapman." He reached across the table to shake my hand, too, and that's when I took notice of his extremely good looks and that he seemed a little younger than the rest.

The others introduced themselves with handshakes, too; Leo Majors and Johnny Dempsey offered pleasant greetings. They seemed much older than the rest by at least four or five years.

I gathered from listening to the various conversations that evening that this circle of friends was much larger than what was present here; many of the "Knights" were aspiring writers; some of them were off to various parts of the country seeking education or employment, or in some cases pleasure, because they hadn't yet found their sense of direction. Someone by the name of Milo Lipinski was in New York trying to get into Columbia University, and there was a Tony Delaware, who had gone to San Francisco, living with other members of the group hoping to find a job.

It turned out that Leo Majors worked at the *St. Louis Post Dispatch* and was enrolled in some night classes at the University. "When I get enough money saved up," he told me, "I'm going to college full-time." But for now, it sounded like Leo was just barely making ends meet.

Johnny Dempsey was the only one who didn't seem to fit in with the rest of this crowd. Besides appearing much older, there was something else that made him less conforming, but I couldn't quite figure what it was. He smiled a lot and laughed with the others, but he was less talkative, and more cautious, and even though everyone included him in conversation, his input was always short and to the point.

I learned, though, as the evening went on, that Johnny was a different kind of artist, and why he was accepted by this group where he seemed so out of place. Johnny had connections; he could obtain almost anything illegal or immoral, including morphine, cocaine, heroin, Benzedrine, marihuana hashish, or any other drug not readily available at the local pharmacy. If somebody wanted a gun, Johnny had a ready supplier for that too. I hoped there wasn't too much demand for firearms among this group.

"How long have you been a photographer?" Christopher asked me. He had temporarily broken away from his lengthy conversation with Andy.

"Not very long," I replied. "I'm still learning." That was better than telling the whole group that I had taken my first picture only a week ago.

"So, do you have pictures of your riverboat?"

"Oh, no. I didn't have a camera then."

"I wish I knew how to use a camera. Where I'm from in Colorado there are so many great things to photograph. We have the Rocky Mountains, you know..."

Christopher was a pleasant conversationalist, and I felt myself drawn toward his charming personality, just as Andy must have been. I had been noticing, too, that Marty was paying more attention to Christopher, as was Curtis who sat right next to him. When the two attractive young women appeared, and one of them sat in Christopher's lap—for the lack of any more available chairs—Marty and Curtis seemed a little put out and disappointed.

The other girl stood behind Leo, wrapped her arms around his neck and gave him a little kiss on the cheek. "How much longer are you gonna be here?" she asked Leo.

Leo glanced at his watch. "I don't know. Why?"

"Let's go over to the Liberty House. There's a good jazz band playing. Marcy and I feel like dancing."

The girls were certainly ready for dancing, in silky party dresses with low-cut necklines, and multiple strings of colorful beads and baubles dangling from around their necks.

Leo looked at me. "This is Sandy, my fiancé." Then he nodded toward the other girl who was heavily flirting with Cheechee. "And that's Sandy's friend, Marcy."

"How 'bout it, Sweetie?" Marcy enticed Christopher. It sounded more seductive than just a request to go dancing. He glanced over to Leo and winked. "If Leo and Sandy are going, then let's go."

Leo and Cheechee excused themselves, and then the four of them left.

Now that Leo was gone, I asked Frank, "Are they a couple, too?" I was referring to Christopher and Marcy.

Frank grinned a little, and then everyone but me and Andy expressed amusement with the question.

"No, not exactly," Frank said. "Cheechee plays around a lot, and it would surprise me if he ever settled down."

There was a lot yet to learn about Cheechee, but it was easy to determine that both women *and* men were attracted to Christopher Chapman's charisma. Cheechee had certainly added life to the party.

Johnny Dempsey got up from his chair. "Anyone needs anything," he said, "...you know where to find me." He made a quiet and unceremonious exit.

"Good night, Johnny," Marty said as Johnny walked by. "I'll catch up with you tomorrow." He reached for the beer pitcher and poured what was left in the glasses of those who remained. Only one poker game was still in progress three tables away. I could hear billiard balls clicking from some other corner of the establishment, and there was still plenty of music and vocal activity spewing out from the barroom, but this party, for all practical purposes, was over. Andy and I had experienced our first encounter with the "Knights."

56

During the bus ride back to Sadie's house, Andy told me all that I had missed in his conversation with Christopher. "He was born poor," Andy began. "His father is a part-time janitor and a full-time alcoholic. Sounds like he stumbles around from one flophouse to another."

"What about his mother?" I asked.

"She tried to protect Chris and his brother from their dad, but she died when Chris was ten. So Chris didn't have any choice but to live with him."

"They lived in Colorado?"

"Yeah, Denver. Chris's brother was older and he'd left, and Chris said that by the time he was sixteen, he'd stolen no less than twenty cars."

"His brother stole twenty cars?"

"No. Chris did," Andy continued. "He dropped out of school, and then he got sent to a reformatory for a couple of years. And when he got out of there, he didn't have a home to go to, so he lived on the streets."

"So, how did he end up here?" I asked.

"He stole another car and drove it here to St. Louis."

"What an idiot!" I said.

"He's not an idiot," Andy corrected me in Christopher's defense. "When he was in the reform school they gave him IQ tests. He scored one-twenty."

With an IQ of 120, he was apparently as intelligent as he was charming, and I found it difficult to associate Cheechee as a car thief. He seemed much too refined for that. Obviously, he didn't have much going for him other than his astonishing good looks and an uninhibited personality, and he certainly knew how to play his charm for all it was worth.

"So, what does he do here? Steal cars? How does he make a living?"

"Says he hasn't stolen a single car since he's been here. He shares an apartment with Marty, and he actually has a job in a warehouse down on Walnut Street... oh... and he's writing a book."

Now it made sense to me why a car thief was admitted into the social clique we had just met. Marty had a rather tarnished background, too, and their personalities *did* seem compatible, and they both *did* have something in common with others in the group—they desired to be authors.

Andy had talked with Christopher at length and had gotten to know him better than I had. He liked Cheechee, and I was not going to disagree with him. Maybe Cheechee was trying to straighten himself out, but his recent past was still the makings of a juvenile delinquent.

I thought I should inform Andy of what I learned about Johnny Dempsey, the older man in the group. "Did you hear about Johnny?" I said.

"Well, Cheechee told me he gets Benzedrine from him, and they go to a tea pad together sometimes. He invited us to go with them sometime."

"And what did you say?"

"I told him maybe... we'd see."

"Kinda looks like we've been accepted into the group, eh?"

"Kinda looks that way," Andy replied. I sensed that he was just a little intrigued by it. And in a curious sort of way, so was I.

The next morning Sadie made us breakfast. "What did you do last night?" she asked while we ate our oatmeal. "It wasn't so very late when I heard you come in."

"Oh, we met some friends and had a few beers downtown," I said. At first I thought I had said too much, and now we would have to start answering all sorts of questions that we might not want to answer.

"Well, good for you," Sadie said. "You've made some new friends here. Did you have a good time?"

"Yes, ma'am," Andy said.

"Where did you meet these friends of yours?"

"In the theater district, on Grand Boulevard." I wasn't exactly lying; we did meet Marty there.

Sadie seemed impressed that we were frequenting the more intellectual sector of the city.

Then Andy reinforced the idea. "They're all writers, journalists, musicians. They have a little get-together every week, and they invited us to join them."

"Musicians?" I said frowning. "Who else besides you in that group is a musician?"

"Curtis plays the saxophone, and Cheechee sings."

"Cheechee?" Sadie quizzed.

"His name is Christopher Chapman... first and last name begin with C-H... so they nicknamed him Cheechee."

Sadie wrinkled her brow in thought. "Well... I guess that makes perfect sense."

I knew then that Andy had learned a lot more good things about the members of the "Knights," while I learned about all the dark sides. But I was glad that Andy had steered the conversation away from dope peddlers and car thieves.

"Sadie," I said. "Everybody in the group is an artist of some sort. Andy fits right in. So I have to get to be a good photographer. They might kick me out if I'm not *something*. So can you help me?"

"Well, sure," Sadie said. "We wouldn't want you to get kicked out of a club like that, now, would we?"

I smiled and frowned at the same time. I knew Sadie was able and willing to teach me more. I only hoped that I would have the right stuff in me to learn it.

It was Saturday and Sadie only had two appointments for portraits that morning. She was finished with them by 10:30. I had given Philip a bath, got him dressed and helped him with his breakfast, so Andy took him for a long walk and played with him while I received some more tutoring from Sadie. She taught me how to use flash bulbs when the natural light wasn't adequate, and how to make things appear differently by shooting the subject from different angles. "A fat man isn't so fat if he is facing the camera, but if his picture is made from his side profile... well, then he's fat."

She had me practice with several objects from around the house—a stack of pillows, Philip's stuffed blue rabbit, a potted plant from Sadie's porch, an ugly green pitcher from the kitchen cupboard—and when she developed the film later that afternoon, she could only give me praise. "It took me three months to learn what you've accomplished in a week," she told me. "Of course," she added, "I didn't have nearly as good a teacher," and then we both laughed.

But it was probably true. Much advancement in cameras and picture taking in general had occurred since Sadie learned the trade back in

Philadelphia. She hadn't used a glass plate negative in nearly three years, and now she was eagerly looking forward to color photos, a process that was soon to be made practical. Sadie kept up with every new technique that came along. No, I couldn't have asked for a better teacher.

57

Andy took the bus to St. Charles occasionally to visit his mom. He'd be gone for a few days, and sometimes I thought maybe he wouldn't come back to St. Louis. But he always did, and every Friday night we'd sit in the dim gas light at the Lion's Den drinking beer with the Knights. Andy's friendship with Cheechee grew stronger, and Cheechee even went with Andy to St. Charles a couple of times. I was glad that Andy was establishing new friendships—if anyone deserved to have friends, it was Andy. My relationship with the Knights elevated quickly, too, as I brought some of my "masterpiece" photographs for them to see.

By the end of November I had received my share of the insurance money for the loss of the Madison—$2,160.65—and I had discussed with Jesse on several occasions about combining our money to buy another boat, but Jesse was reluctant, said he'd rather work for Continental for a while before he made any decisions. It would be many more months until Luke could obtain his pilot's license for barge tows, and that seemed to be the most lucrative business on the river.

So as long as we had a place to live, and I could pitch in a little for groceries now and then, we decided to stay at Jesse's house and wait for the right opportunity, even after Sadie's regular babysitter got the cast off her leg. Andy didn't particularly want to move back to St. Charles; Mildred was staying with his mom, and even though he loved them both dearly, he thought living in a house with two "older" women would not be a good environment for him. I had to agree with his thinking, although I knew there were other reasons he wanted to stay in St. Louis. Cheechee was there, and his association with Curtis was getting him in line for an audition with a night club owner. But most of all, I think Andy was getting hooked on the new lifestyle he had tasted in the big city.

December brought chilly temperatures, but very little snow. It had been quite dry all over the Midwest for a couple of years, and farmers were plagued with drought conditions. Another year of the same would surely bring failure to many.

But there in St. Louis, we continued our association with the Knights; invitations to private parties started coming our way, and one night Johnny

Dempsey and Cheechee took us to a tea pad in North St. Louis. Our first experience with marihuana was in a seedy neighborhood in a run-down brick building that should have been condemned. Cheechee said he knew some better places, and he'd take us to them sometime.

Expecting something a little more sophisticated, I might have been somewhat disappointed with some of the parties we attended at private homes in various parts of the city. When Marty invited us to a weekend soiree at George Sissel's place, I anticipated a dwelling of luxury to some degree. George wasn't a regular participant of the group, but he had showed up at the Lion's Den a few times. He had gone to law school a couple of years, but his life centered on parties and taverns more than on the fine points of the law. He had proven himself as the ultimate carouser, and his house parties were already legendary.

But instead of the deluxe *manor* that I expected, George's place was a deluxe *shack* with sagging porch and peeling paint. It was certainly large enough to accommodate a crowd, and despite its shabby appearance, there was certain splendor that had nothing to do with elegant rooms and plush furnishings. It was the people. This gathering could've been in a back alley and the atmosphere would be the same.

Andy and I had just arrived when Marty found us and led us to the kitchen where beer was being dispensed from a keg. We each got a glassful, and then Marty pushed our way through the mob into the parlor. Many of the people there we had seen and met before, but there were a few unfamiliar faces, too. A blue haze hung in the air, and since we had recently visited a tea pad, I recognized the hint of marihuana odor mingled with the cigarette smoke. Music wailed from the far side of the room, but it didn't come from a Victrola. I saw Curtis with his saxophone but I couldn't see who was *trying* to play the piano; whoever it was could have used a few lessons from Beth Lorado. When Curtis spotted us, he abruptly ended the tune and called out to Andy. Without any hesitation, Andy threaded his way across the room, and by the time he reached the piano, Curtis had leaned close to the piano player's ear and whispered something. There was an immediate vacancy on the piano bench.

It wasn't surprising that Andy was so willing to play; he hadn't entertained a crowd since the Madison burned. I could tell that he seemed eager, and when he started hammering out the tune that had sort of become his theme song—*Happy Days Are Here Again*—the crowd began cheering and dancing, as if they had been waiting for the main attraction. I thought back about the time when "Andrew" first took to the piano on our riverboat, nervous and uneasy, playing that very same song for a highly sophisticated audience. They had loved him and his music, as had every group of excursionists since.

It was no different here. The mood of the crowd seemed to change, and there could be little doubt that Andy was suddenly in control. He picked the songs, and Curtis followed his lead. I couldn't help but think that Curtis was as good on the saxophone as Andy on the piano. They made a good team. It didn't take long for Cheechee to appear at the piano, and as if it had been rehearsed, he started vocalizing and soon led a sing-along with a large number of partiers gathered around.

Another mood changed, too. I was chatting with Marty while Andy and Curtis were getting really warmed up, and he seemed to enjoy their sounds as much as anyone did. But when Cheechee became part of the act, Marty stiffened and sneered toward the musicians. Whatever problem there was, it must have had something to do with Cheechee. I knew he and Marty shared an apartment; Cheechee had been avoiding any close encounters with Marty for some time; there must have been some sort of conflict.

"What's wrong?" I asked Marty.

"Oh, nothing," he said, but he looked at me as if to say *mind your own business,* and so I didn't ask any more questions.

A long while later Andy, Curtis and Cheechee must have decided to end the show, or else they were just taking a break. When I realized the music was absent from all the other noise, I noticed only Curtis coming out of the kitchen with a tall glass of beer.

"You and Andy sound real good together," I complimented him.

"Thanks," Curtis replied. "It's fun to play with a *good* piano player for a change... and Andy is *really good."*

"Yeah, I know. I hear you're setting up an audition for him."

"Actually, he just *had* his audition."

"He did? But I thought—"

"I told Harry we'd be playing here tonight and that he should stop by to hear Andy play."

"Who's Harry?"

"He books acts for the theaters and night clubs."

"Why here?"

"So Andy wouldn't be nervous. He told me he might be a little jittery in a place like the *Empress* or the *Arcadia,* especially for a formal audition. He didn't even know Harry was here watching and listening."

"So, how do you think it went?"

"Harry liked him. He gave me a wink and thumbs up just before he left."

"Does Andy know?"

"Not yet. I haven't talked to him."

"So... what will Harry do for Andy?"

Curtis put his hand on my shoulder, a serious expression on his face. "Whatever you do, don't tell Andy that this could turn into something big.

It prob'ly won't. Harry just looks for people like Andy and me to fill in on off nights for maybe an hour... maybe just fifteen minutes. But I usually make enough to pay the rent and buy groceries."

"Well... you get paid to play music. Then you're a professional musician."

"I don't consider myself a professional... yet. But I wanna be someday, and this is a good way to get started. Actually, Andy is more professional than I am. He had a full-time job as an entertainer... on your riverboat, didn't he?"

"Well, yeah, sort of... but he did other things, too."

"Yeah, I know... he told me he was just a cabin boy. But I know the real reason he was there... to be the entertainment."

"Sure. I guess you're right, Curtis." I looked around. "Where *is* Andy? Did you see where he went?"

"He and Cheechee went off somewhere."

"You mean... they left?"

"No. They're prob'ly upstairs... said they had something important to talk about."

By the time Andy and Cheechee showed up again, the party had progressed from the earlier joyous feel to drunken disorder. Too many people had consumed too much alcohol; temperaments began to clash as voices raised and punches were thrown. Then the fighting seemed contagious, and when blood started to spill, Curtis suggested that we should leave.

"Let's get outa here," he said. "My car is just around the corner." He dodged a couple of swinging fists getting to the piano to grab his saxophone case, and then Andy, Cheechee and I followed him out the front door and down the sidewalk to the end of the block. Andy and Cheechee piled into the rear seat of the old Ford sedan, and I sat in the front with Curtis. That car was like an oasis, a safe haven from the brawl that had developed in George's house. I was so thankful to escape that I barely noticed the freezing cold night.

58

It had been nearly 2 a.m. when Curtis dropped off me and Andy at Jesse's house. An exciting night had us both exhausted; we went right to bed without hardly talking. I think I was asleep before my head hit the pillow, and I think Andy was sleeping by the time we reached the top of the stairs.

I sensed the bright sunshine without opening my eyes. The night had seemed to pass by so quickly. Philip was patting my chest. "Unca Will! Doo! Wake up! Time for brefus!" He had climbed up on the bed and sat between me and Andy.

"Okay, okay," Andy grumbled. "We're getting up."

I squinted at the clock on the nightstand. It was almost 9:00. I couldn't remember when I had slept that late. Philip bounced on the mattress a few times, then jumped to the floor and scurried out of the room babbling something that I couldn't understand. His footfalls on the steps were quite distinct, and then I heard Sadie downstairs. "Did you wake up those two sleepy heads?" "Yeah!" Philip giggled. "Good boy," Sadie said. "Their breakfast will get cold." And then their voices trailed away into the kitchen.

I could smell pancakes and fresh coffee.

Sadie had become less inquisitive about our nighttime activities; she knew we were usually at the Lion's Den with the Knights on Friday evenings, and carousing on Saturdays. Maybe she didn't want to make any fuss about it, or perhaps she was respecting our privacy, or maybe she just didn't care.

"Have you heard from Jesse?" I asked at the breakfast table.

Philip looked sad and shook his little head. "Daddy's not coming home today."

"Yes, as a matter of fact," Sadie replied. "I heard from him day before yesterday... they're in Baton Rouge."

"Coming this way?" I asked.

"No... they're headed back to New Orleans... maybe two weeks until they're back here again. But at least he'll make it home for Christmas."

It seemed strange not to be around Jesse all the time like it had been when we still had the boat. Those years had given me the best sense of security in my entire life. But perhaps this was a good challenge for me, too; to not rely on Big Brother all the time; to experience independence; to see what else life had to offer away from the river. I had to admit that I had overcome my fear of venturing alone too far from the Madison. I had overcome my hatred for the big city. I had made a lot of new friends. I had learned photography, and I was eager to master it.

This had been a good experience for Andy, too. He had finally severed his mother's apron strings that kept him somewhat restricted. He seemed content with his new lifestyle and comfortable with his new friends. Until now, Andy had been a bit shy, but spending so much time with Cheechee and his uninhibited personality had opened a release valve, and now the real Andy was pouring out like an overturned syrup bottle. Whether he knew it or not, last night might have been a new beginning.

"Andy had an audition last night," I blurted out. I couldn't help myself.

"I did not," Andy said.

"Did so," I retaliated. "Curtis told me all about it when you and Cheechee went off somewhere."

"What are you talking about? I didn't have an audition last night."

"Sure you did. Harry was there at the party. He heard you play... and he liked you."

"Harry was there? How do you know that?"

"Curtis told me... he had Harry come because you'd be nervous for an audition at one of the big night clubs, and you'd play better if you didn't know he was there." I turned to Sadie. "You should've seen it, Sadie. Andy at the piano, Curtis on the saxophone, and Cheechee sang. They had that house jumpin'!" I bobbed my head and waved my arms as I spoke for a little more effect.

Philip laughed loudly and banged his spoon on the table.

"Doesn't surprise me," Sadie said. "I've heard Andy play."

"Yeah. When he started playin' his theme song, it was like everybody in the place recognized it and they all started cheerin' and dancin'."

Sadie eyed Andy. "You know, don't you, that you stole that song from *President Franklin D. Roosevelt?*"

Andy beamed a smile wider than Grand Boulevard. "Yeah, but I don't think he'll mind." Then he turned to me. "What else did Curtis tell you?"

"Just that you'd be filling in sometimes... with Curtis, I think... but I wasn't supposed to tell you any of this."

"Will!" Sadie scolded.

"I couldn't help it," I pleaded. "Andy deserves to know about it." Then I looked Andy square in the eyes. "And don't you tell Curtis that you heard it from me."

"Okay..." Andy laughed. "I won't tell him... blabber mouth."

"Well, congratulations, Andy!" Sadie said. "Even if Will *wasn't* supposed to tell you... I'm glad for you."

"Better not congratulate me yet," Andy said. "I haven't played a single note anywhere, yet."

"No, but you will," Sadie assured him.

"And I'll be there to take your picture!" I added.

Andy seemed quite pleased, but I sensed that something was troubling him, too. After we finished breakfast, he said to me: "Will, let's go in the parlor and play our song." And then in a low whisper he added, "We gotta talk."

"If it's about the audition last night—"

"No... something else."

351

Whatever Andy wanted to talk about, he was guarding it from Sadie. He pushed me into the parlor, we sat on the piano bench, and as usual, I started playing *Down by the Riverside* with my one-finger style. He joined in with *April in Paris*. While we played, he said in a low voice, "We should move out of here."

"Why?" I said.

"We're probably a bother to Sadie."

"No we're not. Sadie doesn't mind us being here." There was some other reason for Andy's suggestion. I stopped playing and stared at him, waiting for further explanation.

"Cheechee is having some problems," Andy continued. He saw that I wasn't buying the bother-to-Sadie reason. "He's found a place to move to, and he wants *us* to move in with him."

"What kind of trouble is he in? Steal another car?"

"No, he's not in *any trouble,*" Andy corrected me. "He has *problems.*"

"Okay... so what kind of problems?"

"Cheechee is staying with Johnny Dempsey now... for the time being. It was the one place he knew he could go without an invitation. And actually, I think he stayed at Curtis's place last night."

"I thought he was sharing an apartment with Marty."

"He is... or maybe I should say he *was.*"

"What happened?"

"Marty wanted Cheechee to get him a car, and Cheechee said no, he didn't want to do that anymore."

"So that's why Marty was acting a little strange last night."

"Well, that's not all. When Cheechee wouldn't get him a car, Marty demanded some other favors if he wanted to keep staying in Marty's apartment."

"What... oh... you mean..."

"Yeah, and when Cheechee refused, things started getting ugly. That's when he packed his bags and went to Johnny's."

"So... why doesn't he just stay at Johnny's place?"

"Well, that's the problem. He's having almost the same thing happening there, too."

"Johnny wants him to steal cars?"

"No."

I went back to playing *Down by the Riverside* again; Andy played the usual backup. It gave me some time to think. All this information was piling up too quickly.

"Okay," I finally said. "Marty's dirty looks weren't intended for Cheechee last night... they were intended for *you,* 'cause you and Cheechee have been spending a lot of time together lately."

Andy nodded. "That's probably right."

"You and Cheechee..."

Andy's face turned a mild red. "We're friends, Will."

"Well, I thought he and Marty were friends; and Johnny, too."

"They are."

"Then, why you?"

"I guess I'm different."

"How?"

"I didn't stumble and trip over my own feet running to him, or drool all over him. That happens to him a lot. He's a pretty handsome guy, in case you haven't noticed."

I had noticed. The very first time we met at the Lion's Den.

"Cheechee is trying really hard to straighten out his life," Andy went on. There was certain compassion in his voice. "He's really a good person... not like some of the others."

"But he drinks and he smokes dope."

"Will. Listen to yourself. So have we. I s'pose that's water you drink at the Lion's Den every Friday night, and how many tea pads have we been to lately?"

"A few. But I haven't stolen twenty cars or been in jail."

"That's all behind him, now. Will, you've told me about *your* life in Milwaukee. You jumped a freight train and ran away when you were fourteen. You stole shirts and jeans from backyard clotheslines and you raided gardens and porches for food. How do you think your life would've turned out if you hadn't met up with Jesse?"

Andy made a solid point. It was true. I could have easily turned into a hardened criminal if Jesse hadn't taken me in and steered me away from my life of petty theft. I hadn't thought about it for a long time, but I used to think about it a lot. Now, Andy was showing me, once again, how important Jesse's companionship and brotherly love had always been to me, and I could clearly understand what he was trying to do for Cheechee. I think I was beginning to soften.

"The place Cheechee found is just four or five blocks from Grand Boulevard, fully furnished, ready to move in. You can have your own room if you want. And Will, there's a piano! Twenty-five bucks a month. We can split it three ways. I know you can afford it, Will. You've got more money than most banks. I've got some money saved, and it sounds like I'll be working again soon. Cheechee makes enough to pay his share, too, so how 'bout it? What d'ya think? We can go see the place tomorrow."

"You see it yet? I hope it's not a shack like George's place."

"No, I haven't seen it yet, but Cheechee says it's real nice."

There was no doubt in my mind; Andy was sincere, and from that first time we met face to face in the woods and I touched him to make sure he was real I had always known that his heart was in the right place. Now he was trying to be convincing, and it was working quite well.

"You really like Cheechee, don't you?"

"Yes. He's a good person inside, and he deserves my—*our*—friendship."

59

T hanks to Curtis and his old car, the move to our new place went quite smoothly. I was afraid that Sadie and Jesse would pressure me and Andy with some opposition to our moving into our own house, but they were actually quite supportive. We would have waited until after the holidays, but Cheechee's situation was more urgent, and Andy and I were feeling awful about him being all alone with no place to go on Christmas.

Good old Jesse, the thoughtful and caring soul that he is, didn't hesitate to invite us all to their house for Christmas Eve supper. When we arrived, another pleasant surprise awaited us: Andy's mom and dad, Beth and Marion Lorado were there, too, and shortly after we arrived, Luke and Reggie showed up. I hadn't seen them since the Madison fire, although Andy said he had bumped into Reggie one day somewhere in town. So that Christmas turned into a grand reunion. Mildred would have been there, but she had gone to visit her sister in Kansas City for the holidays.

Cheechee was the only "stranger" in the entire group. Beth Lorado had met him when he went to St. Charles with Andy, but he was a new face to everyone else. Of course, his charming personality had no difficulty to quickly develop nothing less than stellar relationships with everyone there, including Marion Lorado, who usually warmed up to anyone slower than grass grows. Perhaps Beth had prompted him to be civil to Andy's new friend, but it seemed that Marion's acceptance of Cheechee was sincere. Either Cheechee did possess some magical power, or I had witnessed an amazing change in the man who had once considered me and Jesse "river trash."

Although I didn't consider any of our riverboat family high-class snobs, we had become a more sophisticated lot while catering to the upper class patrons who traveled on the Madison. Naturally, I was concerned about the questions that might be asked of Cheechee. His background was a little stained, and I knew for sure that the purification process was not yet absolute. Christopher Chapman was still the makings of a juvenile delinquent.

"Where are you originally from?" Jesse asked Cheechee.

"I was born and grew up in Denver, Colorado."

"Your family is still there?"

"My mother passed away when I was ten years old. My older brother moved on to bigger and better things, and my father suffered from mental and physical depression, and he has been institutionalized."

"Oh," Jesse replied. "Sorry to hear that."

"There was little I could do to help the situation. The state looked after me until I was old enough to be on my own, and when I realized that I couldn't be of any help to my father, I scraped together my resources and came to St. Louis."

Oh boy! Cheechee could charm! But that's what I liked about him. He carried himself with such confidence, and he could express himself so eloquently, and he did it all in such admirably pleasant style. I kept thinking all the while he chatted with Jesse: *How could've this prince of a guy stolen even* one *car?*

Sadie and Beth had been working nearly all day preparing a magnificent feast—roast turkey and all the trimmings. The wonderful aroma that filled the entire house was nearly indescribable, and all the food tasted even better. Perhaps, by force of habit, when the meal was finished Andy and I dug into the clean-up chores, helping Sadie and Beth with clearing the table and washing dishes. When the kitchen and dining room were in riverboat spotless condition, we all joined the others in the parlor around a festive Christmas tree. Little Philip was so excited. He was old enough now to remember past Christmases, and he had a pretty good idea of what to expect.

Everyone received gifts; even Cheechee got a stocking cap and mittens that Beth had knitted, just like she had given me the winter that I stayed at the Lorado home. This year, she and Marion gave both me and Andy gentleman's walking sticks—something we had noticed and commented about many times when we saw the wealthy men aboard the Madison using them. They remembered.

Andy and I had gifts for everyone, too. We had been thinking ahead in October when we got the *St. Louis Cardinals—1934 World Series Champions* baseball caps for Reggie and Luke. They were both Chicago Cubs fans, but they liked the caps anyway. Philip loved his big yellow teddy bear that he immediately named *"Cuddles."*

I would cherish my gift from Sadie and Jesse for years. When I opened it, I think my heart nearly stopped; I was totally speechless as I held the 35mm *Leica* camera and stared at Sadie with my lower jaw hanging like a porch swing.

"It's just like mine," Sadie said. "It's the newest model. Do you like it?"

"I... I..." I still couldn't say anything. Words just wouldn't come out of my mouth. I jumped up and bounded to where Sadie and Jesse sat together on the couch. I threw my arms around them both and squeezed out the most sincere hug of my life. When I finally gained my composure again, all I could say was "Thank you." I felt rather foolish for not saying more, but the look in their eyes told me I didn't need to say anything more.

I remained in awe for quite some time as I closely examined the *Leica*. Sadie had included six rolls of film and two dozen flash bulbs. By the time I loaded some film, Philip was yawning and ready for bed; he and Cuddles were my first subject with my brand new *Leica*.

We had already finished off a couple of bottles of excellent local wine that Marion brought from a St. Charles winery when Jesse carried in from the back porch a case of imported ale. He'd purchased it in New Orleans. Andy serenaded us for a while, and Cheechee even sang three or four songs and as usual, no one would let the evening end without hearing Andy and I play our *Down by the Riverside/April in Paris* duet. It was certainly a joyous night.

I had plenty of time to reflect on the past as I shot a few more pictures of everyone enjoying the Christmas holiday. In my entire lifetime, I would never be able to repay Jesse for all he had done for me; I still admired Luke and Reggie for putting up with me and being my friends.

As I listened to Andy play, I watched Marion Lorado and Cheechee converse as if they had known each other for years. I thought about that Christmas Eve when Marion finally took notice of Andrew's talent and accepted him for who he is.

I smiled inside.

60

The house on Prairie Avenue was a modest, two-story affair, nicely furnished with the basic needs—nothing fancy or extravagant, but adequate.

Andy and I were accustomed to housekeeping—skills we learned aboard the riverboat. As cabin boys we had been involved with everything from galley work and serving meals for sixty or seventy people, to sweeping floors and putting clean sheets on beds. Of course, in this house there were fewer people to clean up after—just us—so it was a lot less work.

But Cheechee, on the other hand, was not accustomed to such chores, and he required a little "training" to conform to our standards. Anything he might have learned from his mother was so long ago that he'd forgotten it all. And living with an incompetent, drunken father certainly taught him nothing but bad habits, which soon surfaced. But Cheechee was such a pleasant person to be with, polite and considerate of others. Andy and I tolerated his shortcomings until we got him "trained." Perhaps we were a little hard on him at times; we had just come from an environment on the excursion boat where tidiness was mandatory, and our good habits followed us here.

He didn't know how to cook, so whenever the opportunity presented itself, we conducted cooking class. Within a few weeks he was doing his fair share of the meal preparation, and he even seemed to enjoy it. Naturally, his entrées sometimes weren't what we would expect from the Madison's chef, but at least it was edible, and he *was* trying, and he *was* getting better with practice.

Cheechee went off to work every morning, Monday to Friday. He walked half a block to the bus stop where he boarded a *St. Louis Public Service Company* bus, and he said he had to change buses only once to get to the warehouse where he worked on Walnut Street. I had expected that he would be out late partying almost every night, and I feared that he would be influencing me and Andy to do the same. But I was surprised to see Cheechee at home most of the time. Every night he sat diligently at a writing desk, or sometimes at the kitchen table, or sometimes in his room, with pencil and notebook. He was working on something he called *"If I Could Steal the Stars."* He kept telling us that he would let us read it when he had more of it written. But for now he said it was a story about a young man and his destiny. I was never one to pry into another person's private affairs if I hadn't been invited. It was clearly obvious that Cheechee wasn't ready to share the story just yet, so I certainly wasn't about to invade his privacy. I remained curious, though, and I continued to let him know that I was still interested.

"Will," he told me. "Believe me, I will want you and Andy to be the first to see it... when it's ready."

Curtis Owens was the only one of the Knights who knew exactly where we lived, and in no uncertain terms we made it clear that we wanted to keep it that way. He kind of understood the problems Cheechee had with Marty and Johnny, but Cheechee hadn't been quite as explicit with Curtis as he had been with Andy and me. Even though we still considered them our friends, and they didn't ever pose any difficulties at the Friday night gatherings at the Lion's Den, we didn't need them stalking our house waiting for the first opportunity to confront Cheechee alone. But we trusted Curtis—we had to—he had helped us move to our new place, and he came over to practice with Andy a couple times a week. I think, too, that he was beginning to enjoy the solitude, the privacy, the safety that our place offered. His place, not much more than a single room with a closet, a hot plate, and a shared bathroom on the second floor over a hardware store, didn't provide much in the line of hominess or cozy comfort. Andy and I had been there a couple of times, and although we had grown to like Curtis, we had little desire to return to his bachelor pad for frequently repeated visits. I could easily understand why he took pleasure in our place so much.

About the middle of January, Curtis appeared at our door one night. He seemed all keyed up about something, and I was sure it wasn't "Bennies" or marihuana that had him bouncing off the walls.

"Where's Andy?" he asked. He almost ran me over getting into the parlor. "Hi, Cheechee!" he sang out when he saw Cheechee sitting at the writing desk. "ANDY! WHERE ARE YOU?" he called out. His excitement caught us all off-guard.

Andy came trotting down the stairs. "Curtis! What's goin' on?"

Curtis had good reason to be excited. "You and me are in the line-up at the *Arcadia* three nights next week! Half-hour pre-show for Benny Goodman!"

Andy's jaw dropped and he stopped dead in his tracks on the bottom step.

"Harry just told me tonight... said we're a perfect opener."

Andy still stood there speechless.

Cheechee rushed over and put an arm around each of them. "Congratulations, you two! This is great!" Then he threw both arms around Andy, engulfing him in an enthusiastic hug. "I'm so happy for you, Andy. This is what you've been waiting for."

I had to get in on the hugging and handshaking, too. I was truly happy for both of them.

"It's a sell-out crowd," Curtis continued. "Harry's gettin' us a hundred and fifty bucks for the three nights... that's seventy-five each. Not bad for three nights."

Now I was really happy for Andy. That was more money than he had made on the Madison. Of course, his tip jar always filled there every night, too, and I didn't know how much that amounted to, but this sounded pretty darn good!

Andy and Curtis practiced at least two hours every afternoon at our house for the rest of the week. I was usually at Sadie's studio learning and helping her as much as I could. By then Sadie had taught me how to develop film and how to operate the apparatus that enlarges and transfers the image onto paper. So there were always plenty of things for me to do, and it helped sharpen my abilities. I was well on my way towards a new career, and all because Philip's babysitter broke her leg.

61

We didn't have to ride a bus or street car to the Lion's Den Friday night; Curtis was already at our house for the afternoon practice with Andy. We all went together in his car. Friday night at the Lion's Den wasn't a lot different than any other Friday night had been there, except for a couple of new faces that Andy or I didn't recognize. Everyone else seemed to know them, though. Milo Lipinski had just returned from New York, and Tony Delaware had been on the west coast. Because both had been away for several months, they were receiving a good share of the attention. Milo was here for just a short visit during a semester break at Columbia University, but Tony seemed unsure about his next move. He had worked for a short time in California; it didn't last.

After the initial chatter among just about everyone over where Milo and Tony had been and what they had been doing, Milo and Marty settled into a conversation about poetry; Milo had given Marty a copy of *The Vision* by William Butler Yeats, and they were discussing its contents, Milo convinced that "this is what poetry should be." I had never heard of Yeats, so I had no idea what they were talking about.

Tony and Cheechee talked about Denver; apparently Tony had stopped there for a while on his way back from San Francisco.

Frank and Johnny were talking about some parties they had recently attended, and I told Leo about my new camera; he was interested in my progress with photography.

Curtis and Andy were just waiting for the right moment to announce their first gig together on stage. It would be a big night for them; certainly they would want everyone to know. But Curtis's declaration came with little fanfare. "Andy and I won't be here next Friday night. We'll be performing."

It only took a few seconds for that to sink in. "Who's having a party?" Milo asked.

"It's not a party," Curtis returned. "We're playing at the *Arcadia* Thursday, Friday and Saturday."

"Yeah, right," Marty said sarcastically. "I saw in the newspaper that Benny Goodman is playing there next weekend."

"He is," Curtis replied. "We're the opener."

"You... are gonna be the warm-up for Benny Goodman?"

Everyone at the table had taken notice of the banter, and all eyes shifted to Curtis as he just nodded and smiled. Andy was grinning, too, and in the few moments of silence while everyone digested the news, he looked around to each face, as if expecting reactions other than dropped jaws and silence.

Nearly everyone had heard Andy and Curtis making music at George's party, so they were very much aware of the talent and showmanship they commanded. There was no question that they were both capable. That an opportunity like this should come to members of our little group was the real surprise. Local radio stations were airing the new Benny Goodman "swing" music, and even though it was 11:30 at night, the syndicated radio program *"Let's Dance"* with Goodman and his band as one of the regular performers had become quite popular in St. Louis. People were excited about the new kind of music and they were eager to see and hear the clarinet-playing band leader, Benny Goodman in person.

Then the reactions came. "That's great!" "Wonderful!" "Fantastic!" "Can we still get tickets?"

"From what I've been told," Curtis said, "It's standing room only."

"Well... that's okay. I'll be there!" "Me too." "We'll all be there, for sure."

After all the congratulatory remarks were delivered there was a new wave of chatter going around the table about which night to go to the *Arcadia Ballroom*, who was going with who, and transportation arrangements. It seemed that everyone favored Friday night; the Lion's Den would be without the Knights of the Square Table the next week.

Milo seemed a bit standoffish to me, and even though he had said that he would go to the *Arcadia* next Friday night, his sole focus otherwise was Marty and poetry. He and Marty did have New York in common, so I guess they had plenty to talk about.

But I liked Tony Delaware. Much like Cheechee, he was attracting attention from more than one person there. He had apparently been quite popular before he left for California, and it wasn't difficult to tell why. Good-humored and talkative, his smile must've been permanently molded on his face; I didn't see him without it all evening. His teeth weren't perfectly straight and his hair looked like he'd just climbed out of bed, but it was those things that helped make him the unique character that he was.

62

Just a block off Grand Boulevard on Olive, the *Arcadia* packed in a crowd—even for a Thursday night. Young and old alike were there to see the band they had been hearing on the radio. The "King of Swing" was there in flesh and blood, and no one thought the seventy-five cents admission was too much to pay to have Benny Goodman set their feet to dancing. Spirits were high, and it promised to be an enjoyable evening. I was excited for Andy and Curtis; that afternoon while they were getting ready (Curtis was spending most of his time at our house now) I could sense their energized emotion, although they were trying very hard to conceal it. Harry had outfitted them with tuxedos from a theater's stage wardrobe. Curtis wore black, and Andy wore white, and I have to admit they looked quite stunning. But they chose to carry their tuxes with them on the ride to the ballroom where they would change in a back-stage dressing room that they had been assigned.

Armed with my new *Leica* 35mm camera, I parted with Curtis and Andy in the parking lot; they headed for a side entrance that led to the back-stage dressing rooms, while Cheechee and I made our way toward the front entrance where I was supposed to meet Leo. He had arranged for me to hook up with a reporter/photographer from the *Post Dispatch,* the newspaper where Leo worked. Not only would I get some front-and-center pictures of Andy and Curtis—*and Benny Goodman*—but perhaps I would learn a few pointers, too.

Keith Blake was tall and slender, thirtyish, high cheek bones and square chin that were covered with a day's growth of black stubble. His pinstriped suit was far from being fresh, like he'd been in it all day. A narrow brimmed hat sat cocked back on his closely-cropped black head of hair.

Leo introduced us. "Keith Blake... this is Will Madison." He had already filled in Mr. Blake about who I was and why I was there. Cheechee was already headed for the entrance in the line for people who didn't yet have a ticket.

"You're the riverboat guy," Blake said as he shook my hand.

"Yes, sir, Mr. Blake, I am... but how—?"

"I'm a newspaper reporter. It's my job to remember stuff like that. I took pictures of your burning boat... and please call me *Blake."*

I thought back to that night and recalled the many reporters and photographers lined up on the levee, flashbulbs exploding every three or four seconds. With all the smoke and the flashes and the chaos, it might have been a war zone.

"So it was *your* pictures of the fire that I saw in the newspaper?"

"If you saw the front page of the *Post* the next day... yeah, you saw my pictures." He eyed me suspiciously. "You're kind of young to own a riverboat."

"Actually, I was just a junior partner with my older brother, Jesse Madison."

Blake squinted a little. "Oh, yeah, now I remember... there were three of you."

"Yeah. The third partner was Luke Jackson. He and Jesse are on a barge towboat now."

Blake stared for a moment at my camera suspended on a strap around my neck. *"Leica,"* he said. "That's a fine camera." Then he held his up where I could see it better. Same camera.

"Okay," Blake said as he peered over the people scrambling to get into the Arcadia. "You got a ticket?" he asked.

"No, not yet," I replied.

"That's good. You don't need one. If you had one, you could give it to your friend. Just let me do the talking when we get to the ticket taker inside."

"I'll see ya later," I told Leo, and then we pushed toward the entrance.

"Hi Blake," the ticket collector said.

"Hi, Tommy. This is Will Madison," Blake said as he laid a hand on my shoulder. "He's with me... a new trainee... and if you ever see him here alone, you treat him just like you'd treat me... got it?"

Tommy gave me a thorough inspection, as if memorizing every detail of my image. "Glad to meet you, Will," he said as he briefly shook my hand. "Enjoy the show, and I hope you get some good pictures. Blake will show you where to go."

Apparently, Blake was on first name basis with the ticket taker, and his position with the newspaper obviously gave him an inside edge at the *Arcadia*—perhaps any theater in the whole city where well-known performers attracted reporters and photographers.

Blake led me through the inner doors into the ballroom and then down along an outer wall behind a large seating area toward the right end of the stage. From there we went directly to stage center, only ten feet back from the footlights. Several other photographers were seated on folding chairs there, too, in a reserved little area just for them.

"You'll never need to pay your way in here, Will," Blake whispered to me. "...As long as you have that dandy camera hangin' 'round your neck."

The next ten minutes seemed like hours. I could hear scuffing noises and muffled voices from behind the stage curtain, obviously some last-minute preparations. Then the house lights dimmed and a big, bright, round circle of light projected against the curtain from a balcony. A distinguished-looking, silver-haired man in a black tuxedo and top hat stepped into the spotlight in front of a microphone. "Ladies and gentlemen," he began, as if he were announcing the opening act at a three-ring circus. "With great pleasure," he continued, "the Arcadia proudly presents to you... the King of Swing himself, Benny Goodman."

The crowd hushed from its anxious rumbling, mingling voices.

"But first, please welcome and enjoy Saint Louis's newest jazz duo... The Gaslight Knights!"

I was taken by complete surprise as the spotlight faded to nothing and the curtain rose. I had expected to see Andy and Curtis open the show. But then I heard the familiar sounds of Andy's theme song, *Happy Days Are Here Again*, and then a blue-tinted spotlight beam splashed on the stage, exposing a brilliantly shining baby grand piano, white tuxedo, and Andy's big grin. Just as I had heard them practice at the house, Curtis joined in with his saxophone, and another blue spotlight found its mark on him. In this great hall, with the help of amplifiers, they sounded fantastic!

A few seconds went by and the crowd was still silent, waiting patiently to decide on cheering or booing of this new duo, "The Gaslight Knights." I held my breath in anticipation, and then I felt the joy of relief as the hoots and cheers and whistles and claps rose to a brief roar, and then descended to a rhythmic clapping and shuffling of dancing shoes.

Blake leaned toward me and spoke in my ear: "Aren't you going to record this first moment? It's the important one, you know. Never comes again."

I was so excited for Andy and Curtis and so wrapped up in the reactions from the audience that I had nearly forgotten why I wanted to be so close to the stage. I was so glad that Sadie had coached me on taking pictures in this type of light. I got my camera set, focused, and clicked off several shots.

They played six more lively numbers in their allotted time, and when they ended, Andy and Curtis joined together at center stage, bowing and waving to a pumped-up, cheering crowd. All I remember of Benny Goodman saying when he was introduced was, "Good evening ladies and gentlemen... what an act to follow!"

63

H arry, the booking agent, had been so impressed by the performance and the crowd's reaction to Andy and Curtis that he lined them up with more appearances right away. It seemed that every week he was calling on them with another date at another night club, hotel, or dance hall. Cheechee and I tagged along a few times, but eventually, the thrill lessened for us. We resumed our regular routine on Friday nights at the Lion's Den, and sometimes, depending on what time Andy and Curtis performed, they would show up a little later, too.

Now that Curtis and Andy were established in the entertainment scene, Cheechee and I had more time together. Not that our relationship with Andy ever diminished—if anything, it became stronger. But Andy needed his time for arranging and practicing new music with Curtis. Both of them took performing quite seriously, and why shouldn't they? They were making good money. Not all the engagements paid as well as that first one opening for Benny Goodman, but they were still fairing quite well.

In spite of our differences in character, I couldn't help but feel a strange closeness to Cheechee; he reminded me, somehow, of a long-lost brother. It wasn't the same kind of feelings I had toward Big Brother Jesse—there could be nothing that would ever compare to that. Perhaps it was just Cheechee's magical, mysterious charm that drew me in, or maybe it was because I could relate so well to his broken family history that was so similar to my own. Whatever it was, I found my admiration for him growing, and as the weeks passed, I sensed that he began to consider me an important part of his life, too.

He'd come home from his workday about the same time in the afternoon that I would arrive after working a few hours at Sadie's studio. Cheechee's dirty work clothes clung to his muscular form so gracefully, as if you couldn't buy a better fit from a custom tailor.

Andy and Curtis would either be deeply involved with a practice session, or they would be away searching the music stores for sheet music, or off for the evening playing a gig somewhere. So supper, much of the time, was just the two of us, and quite frequently a hamburger at the *Dixie Sandwich Shop* seemed more appealing than cooking. We'd hop on a bus down to Olive Street, and then catch a streetcar toward the river to Sixth and Pine. There were probably closer places to get a hamburger, but we favored the *Dixie*. Many hours were spent there eating and talking, learning about each other, and swapping information about all our mutual friends.

It seemed that all my current acquaintances were intellectuals, or, they were casting a shadow on that very fine line, on the other side of which lurked slinking criminals. Regardless of his tainted past, Cheechee's intelligence was genuine and impressive for someone who had spent a good share of his early life on skid row with an alcoholic father among vagrants and bums, and another good share in jail, leaving little time for education. But his criminal side was not that of a sneering and threatening type; he'd made some foolish mistakes, and his youthful inexperience had gotten him caught a time or two. Now he was simply a kid tremendously excited with life. He was a wild outburst of American joy that blew in on the West wind, seeking something new. In Denver, he'd spent a lot of time in the public library—when he wasn't in jail. He'd carry stacks of books to the pool hall or climb fire escapes of abandoned buildings to the attics where he spent days reading and hiding from the law. Here, now, he was applying his knowledge, trying to make a better life.

"I really don't regret all that I've done in the past," Cheechee told me. "It's true... I did steal a bunch of cars back in Denver, but only for joy rides, never for financial gains. The rightful owners got their cars back. And yeah, I did some jail time, and a couple of years in reform school. No, I didn't have much of a home life. But it's all helped me learn about the real world, and all that reading helped me understand who I am."

I had listened to all this sort of information trickle into our conversations over a period of time; there was ever-present consistency and the "facts" didn't ever change, so it didn't appear that he was inventing the stories as he went along. It seemed like he was feeding me a lot of guarded details about his life that he had not shared with the rest of the Knights of the Square Table—with Andy, perhaps, but not the others—and I began to associate his verbal offerings with his secretive writing. "So the book you're writing... it's about you, ain't it?"

Cheechee took a bite of his hamburger, smiling while he chewed. "I'll let you read some of it soon, Will... I promise."

64

One rainy March Saturday evening Cheechee and I had just settled into a corner table by the window at the *Dixie* with our hamburgers and beer. Andy and Curtis were playing at the *Chicago Dance Palace* way down on South Jefferson Street. Because of the weather, more than any other reason, we had decided not to go there, and so we weren't in any hurry to finish our supper.

I noticed Cheechee peering out the window with a concerned stare, his entire body tense. Then I noticed the two people out on the sidewalk that had caught his attention; I could understand his concern. Johnny Dempsey and Tony Delaware paused in the entryway where the front door was recessed into the corner of the building, affording them some shelter from the light rainfall. I knew Tony had spotted us because we made direct eye contact as they passed by the window, but I wasn't certain that Johnny had noticed us. They talked for a bit, and then Tony patted his belly and pointed to the general direction of inside the *Dixie*. I supposed Tony was trying to convince Johnny that satisfying his hunger was top priority at the moment, but Johnny seemed more interested in moving on. Finally, Johnny walked off into the rainy night, and Tony pulled open the door. Cheechee relaxed and I saw relief in his eyes.

Tony invited himself to sit down at our table, and then as an afterthought he said, "You don't mind if I join you, do you?"

"Of course not," Cheechee instantly replied.

Despite a baseball cap and a light jacket, Tony was dripping from the rain. He took off his jacket and cap, leaned away from the table and ruffled his hair with both hands, shedding most of the wetness onto the floor. His hair stood out in all directions, but that's usually the way it was; I had never seen it neatly combed. After he ordered a hamburger and a beer, I sensed that there was something different about Tony that night. He was usually happy-go-lucky, always smiling, always ready for snappy conversation and willing to consider some suggested spring for a thrill. He was much like Cheechee except that he wasn't quite ready to give up his youthful, fun-loving ways; he wasn't yet ready to settle down or make any commitments.

That night, though, his spirit seemed dampened, but not from the rain. His perpetual smile was only half there and his usual vibrancy did not radiate as I had always seen before. I knew he had been hanging out with Johnny Dempsey a great deal, and I had even heard that since he came back from California he had been hanging his baseball cap at Johnny's place. I suspected he was experiencing the same kind of conflicts that Cheechee had, but I didn't know him all that well yet; I decided I would wait for him to volunteer whatever he wanted to tell.

"You still living with your Aunt?" Cheechee asked Tony.

Now, *that* was a brilliant question. Cheechee must've been reading my mind. He was probably just as curious as me, but he didn't want to probe too sharply into a personal matter.

"Yeah... well... no..." Tony was a little indecisive. "I've been stayin' at Johnny's place for a while."

"Oh," Cheechee said. "I stayed there for a while, too, but I didn't care for the neighborhood. Now I live with Andy and Will."

"I don't care much for the neighborhood, either," Tony responded. He winked at Cheechee and gave a little smirk, as if he thought he was hiding a personal joke between them.

"It's okay," Cheechee said. "Will knows."

From there, the conversation became a little more open. This was actually the first time I had ever talked to Tony outside the Lion's Den get-togethers. Here, away from that crowd of peers he seemed slightly more tranquil, although there was the possibility that he could've been under the influence of some drug that Johnny had provided.

"I had to get out of my Aunt's house... at least for a while," Tony explained. "Gertrude was just getting too damned controlling."

"Why do you live with your Aunt?" I asked. "Where are your folks?"

"They're both dead... in the graveyard at Bisbee, Arizona."

"Sorry," I said. "What happened?"

"They were prospectors... worked a little silver mine out in the desert hills where we lived. One day the rocks gave way and the mineshaft caved in on them. I was only nine. I rode our burrow twenty miles into Bisbee for help. But by the time anybody could dig them out, they were both goners.

"About a week after the funeral, the sheriff located my Aunt Gertrude in St. Louis, and she came out and took me back here. I guess if there is such a thing as culture shock for a kid of nine, it happened to me. I was used to the outdoor open air and the hot sun and the solitude of the desert, living in a two-room adobe. We went into town once a month for supplies. All of a sudden, I'm living in a big plush house in city environment, getting schooled by private tutors until I was ready to enter public school. It was quite an adjustment."

"Must've been a little overwhelming," I said.

"Especially at first," Tony went on. "I slowly got accustomed to the city life, but I still long for the outdoors. Now, Aunt Gertrude insists that I'm going to University."

"So, why did you go to Johnny's?" Cheechee asked.

"Aunt Gertrude knows all my other friends. It was the only place where I figured she wouldn't find me."

"And now you're not exactly happy at Johnny's?"

"He's smothering me, Cheechee. Johnny follows me every place I go. I can't go to the bathroom without him being right outside the door. He thinks I should be by his side night and day."

"What about tonight?"

"He had some *business* to do... you know... and I told him I'd meet him later."

"Why don't you just go back to your Aunt's house?"

"I talked to her, but now she's gettin' all pissy with me... said the next time I come to her house, it should only be to get my stuff out. Thinks I'm acting ungrateful."

I could see that an emotional disaster of some sort was inevitable, given the volatile atmosphere. "D'ya have any plans?" I asked.

Tony gazed at a far wall. "Farther than next Friday night... no. Got any suggestions?"

"D'ya have a job?"

He looked at me with sad eyes and shook his head.

"If you like the outdoors, you could try to get a job on the river."

Tony looked at me again, this time with curiosity. "What do you mean?"

"Riverboats. You might be able to get a job on a riverboat. Travel up and down the Mississippi. See lots of places. Find one you like, move there, and viola, you've solved all your problems."

"You make it sound so simple," Tony said. "I don't think it'll be that easy."

"Listen," Cheechee said. "That's a great idea. Will knows what he's talking about when it comes to riverboats. He and his brother owned one, and he lived and worked on the river for many years."

"Are you at least interested?" I asked Tony.

"Well... I don't know... maybe... sure, I'd give it a shot... but I really don't want to go back to Johnny's place tonight."

My eyes met Cheechee's, and I knew we were thinking the same thoughts. If we allowed Tony to come to our house, we could be compromising the security of our sanctuary—that place where we had been safe from the people we didn't want to find us. But it wouldn't be right to turn our backs on a friend, either.

65

Since Andy had recently moved into the bigger bedroom with Cheechee so Curtis could move from his downtown cracker box apartment into Andy's old room, Curtis was now an official member of our household; it seemed only fair that he should have a vote in the decision to offer Tony safe haven in our house. Neither he nor Andy displayed any objections. But Monday morning was the last morning that Tony ate breakfast with us. He understood our desire for our street address to remain unknown to Johnny Dempsey. Most grateful for our concern with his current situation, he knew, too, that if he accepted our offer of a *temporary* place to stay, Johnny might follow him here, and he sincerely didn't want to jeopardize our friendship in that way. He'd try to somehow work things out.

Tony bid us a farewell with the promise that no one would know where he had been for two nights. We wished him luck and assured him that we would still honor our offer to help if it became necessary.

After he left for the bus stop, everything seemed to be back to normal.

"Now that we have a little break in our schedule," Andy announced, "I'm gonna take a bus to St. Charles to visit Mom for a few days. Wanna come along, Cheechee?"

"Not this time," Cheechee replied. "I've got a lot of writing to do. Will has stirred up some ideas in my head, and I want to write it down before I forget it."

"And I'm going to an estate sale over on the west end of town," Curtis said. "Will... d'ya wanna come with me?"

I wasn't exactly excited about going to look at some old dead guy's furniture and dishes. "No, but you can drop me off at Sadie's house. I promised her I'd work at the studio today for a few hours."

"It's a deal," Curtis said. "I can pick you up again on my way back."

We dropped Andy off at the bus depot to catch the 9:45 to St. Charles. Then Curtis drove me to Sadie's house. "I'll pick you up around three o'clock," he informed me.

"You really don't have to, y' know... I can catch a bus."

"Nonsense," Curtis scolded. "I'll be here about three."

Before I could say any more, he rattled away in his rusty old blue Ford sedan.

Sadie's studio was quite busy at this time of year with all the school graduations coming soon, confirmations, bar mitzvahs and June wedding announcements. There was plenty of work to keep me busy, and the day went by so quickly that I was surprised to see Curtis standing just inside the front entrance. I glanced at the clock; it was 3:15.

"If you're not ready to go, I can come back later," he said.

Sadie intervened. She was just finishing with her last client of the day. "You're already fifteen minutes past the time you said you would leave," she said with a big smile. "I'm almost done anyway." She insisted that Curtis should not have to make another trip.

I ran up the stairs to say goodbye to Philip, but the nanny winked and said she would be happy to relay the message when Master Philip awoke from his afternoon nap.

When we walked down the sidewalk to the street, I didn't see Curtis's car. "Where did you park?" I asked.

Curtis beamed a big toothy grin and pointed at the shiny two-tone red and maroon sedan parked right in front of me. "I bought it at the estate sale today," he said. "Saw it listed on the sale bill, so I thought I'd check it out. Guess I got lucky, 'cause nobody else was interested. And I needed a better car."

He was right about that; there were times that he and Andy walked part way home from a late night gig because the old car broke down. I sauntered around the shiny new machine as Curtis told me all about it. "1934 Pontiac... barely ever out of the garage, so it's practically still like new. The old guy croaked just after he bought it, and his wife couldn't drive, so it sat in the garage all this time until she died."

I opened the door and peered inside. The chrome-ringed gauges on the wood-grain dash sparkled in the sunlight. Rich brown mohair covered the seats that appeared as if they had never been sat on; even the floor mats looked as though they had never seen the sole of a dirty shoe. I was impressed. "Looks expensive," I said. But, of course, I knew Curtis and

Andy were making a lot of money, and he could afford it.

"I paid half of what I expected... three hundred and twenty-five dollars for a car that sold new for eight seventy-five."

"What'd you do with your old car?"

"Sold it for ten dollars to a junk man who happened to be there."

"So," I said, grinning. "Are you gonna take me for a ride?"

"Hop in!"

66

Andy was still in St. Charles on Wednesday and Cheechee was so busy writing that I think he forgot he needed to eat. He passed on a hamburger at the *Dixie*, seemingly happy with his box of crackers and cheese. Curtis and I went without him.

As the proud owner of a new car, Curtis wanted to take a little ride in the country before dark, so he headed across Eads Bridge to East St. Louis on the Illinois side of the river. We were all the way to Collinsville when he decided we should head back to our favorite supper spot. Curtis was an excellent driver, and I could tell he was in love with his new Pontiac... and for good reason; it was like riding in a dream compared to that rickety old jalopy he had before.

Dusk shrouded St. Louis when Curtis parked his snazzy new car in front of the *Dixie*. Darkness would soon gobble up everything and bright lights would electrify the city. We made ourselves comfortable at our usual table in the corner by the window, and now it served a double purpose: Curtis could stare out the window at his new love, *his* Pontiac.

We had been there a while when Tony showed up. He'd checked here often hoping to find us. "Where's Cheechee?" he asked, as if he was surprised that I was there without him.

"He's at home working on his book," I said.

"Oh. Well, it's you I wanted to talk to, anyway." Tony appeared in better spirits now than when we had last seen him. His energetic smile was back. His clothes were fresh and clean. His hair still stood out in all directions, but that was to be expected; that's what made him *Tony*.

"I managed to talk to Aunt Gertrude," he began. "I spent all day after I left your place planning what I would say to her, and I practiced saying it over and over to a tree in the park."

"And how did that turn out?"

"I gave her my deepest regrets and most sincere apologies for appearing disrespectful, but I also explained that the University stuff was just too overwhelming right now... that I wasn't ready for that yet."

"Did she understand?"

"I think so... at least she's letting me come back to live in her house again... for the time being, anyway."

"Well, that's great, Tony," I said, showing as much encouragement as I could muster. "Sounds like you've licked the problem."

"That's not all," Tony added. "I worked things out with Johnny, too."

"Oh? What did you work out with him?"

"I told him that we could still be friends, but that I couldn't be with him twenty-four hours a day, every day. I told him that I have my own life to live, that I was moving back to my Aunt's house, and if he promised not to follow me around everywhere I went, or make trouble for me when I'm with other friends, I would still come to see him once in a while."

"And will you?"

"Yeah... well... maybe."

Curtis joined in. "Think that's a good idea? Johnny is—"

"Johnny's okay... he's just a little overbearing sometimes."

To me it sounded as if Tony might be headed in the right direction, but he was still indecisive on his opinion of Johnny Dempsey. He could still be lured by a bad influence, but I didn't think it was my place to tell him that I thought Johnny was a bad influence.

"There's something else that I wanted to talk to you about, Will," Tony continued.

"What about?" I said.

"The other night you said I could get a job on a riverboat."

"Yeah, I think you prob'ly could."

"Would you help me with that?"

If there was any one subject that I could coach, it would be life aboard a riverboat. In the last five years, I had spent more time afloat with wooden decks beneath my feet than I had on solid, dry earth. Although the times were changing—diesel engine power was slowly replacing steam—from what I had gathered from Jesse on his not-so-frequent days at home, the protocol had not changed. Navigation on the big river was the same now as it had been for many years, except on the Upper Mississippi the Army Corp of Engineers had built several dams and locks, and construction of more was in progress. As far as the crew was concerned, their duties were still the same; only one job would have been eliminated on a diesel powered boat—the fireman. No one would be shoveling coal into a boiler firebox. But deckhands are still deckhands; engineers still run the engine room; cabin boys are still cabin boys; cooks and their helpers still prepare the food; the pilot still steers the boat, and the Captain and his Mate still oversee the whole operation. No, not much had changed since I stepped off the Madison.

I sensed that Tony might be serious about working on the river, and I could think of no reason to discourage him.

"Meet me here tomorrow at ten o'clock," I told Tony. "We'll talk about it, and then we'll go down to the levee."

67

I spent the entire next day with Tony acclimating him to the river and the big boats, explaining protocol and teaching him the terminology, the "river lingo" he needed to know. We even came across a couple of Captains who remembered me, and they allowed me to take Tony aboard their vessels to show him around. By late afternoon I had put him in contact with several Captains and First Mates, plus a list of others that weren't in port but would be within the next week or so. Tony seemed enthusiastic, and when Aaron Tyler, the First Mate on the Hercules asked if I was interested in joining his crew, because he was quite familiar with the Madison, I thought Tony would throw me overboard when I replied, "I don't think I'm quite ready to go back on the river yet. Let me think it over."

I know Tony would've felt more comfortable working with me there, and maybe I shouldn't have acted so selfishly. Maybe I should have taken Mr. Tyler up on his offer, and Tony would've been hired on the spot, too.

But I *wasn't* ready. I had dabbled in photography and I wanted to see where it might take me. I was still young enough to try new things, and then return to the river at my choosing. And besides, I had made my commitment to Big Brother Jesse the day we lost our boat, and I owed my loyalty to him. In the deep, dark reaches of my mind, I knew it was doubtful that our old crew—Jesse, Luke, Reggie, Andy and me—would ever be back together again, but I wanted to hold onto that hope for all it was worth. Although I had made many new friends in St. Louis, I missed the old ones.

Cheechee was already home when I got there, bathed squeaky clean and clad in a freshly-laundered white *Arrow* dress shirt, tailored so nicely that it made him look like a young executive. But his emotion didn't match the stunning attire as he sat at the writing desk staring blankly into his notebook.

"Curtis is gonna drive me to the bus station," he said, but there was little of the usual cheerfulness in his voice. "Andy is coming back from St. Charles on the six-fifteen."

I knew immediately that something was troubling him. "What's wrong?" I said. "Aren't you happy that Andy's back?"

"Of course I'm happy he's back... but I have some bad news."

"What—?"

"The warehouse supervisor cut my hours down to just two days a week."

Although it did sound rather devastating, I tried to ease the pain. "Well, that's not so terrible... at least you still *have* a job. That's better than a lot of people these days."

"I guess so," he replied. "But now I'll be making less than half of what I was... and that's not much."

Of all of us, Cheechee was categorically the least prepared to lose his income, although he had not totally lost it yet. It would certainly put a strain on his expendable cash, but I knew that Andy would never let him starve or sleep on a park bench under a newspaper salvaged from the trash barrel. Nor would I. Cheechee was a part of *my* family now, too, just as equally as Andy, Jesse, Luke, Reggie, Sadie, Philip... and I'd put Curtis in the circle, too, even though he could be a bit eccentric at times, wildly extravagant—like buying a flashy red car—but he, too, was focused on camaraderie, and I'd bet that he'd go down fighting for any one of us. I felt confident that Cheechee was in good company, and he had nothing to fear.

I put a hand on his shoulder. "Don't worry, Cheechee," I said. "You're among brothers that aren't going to let anything happen. We'll all get through it together."

He jumped up from the chair and threw his arms around me in an affectionate bear hug like Big Brother Jesse always did. "Thanks, Will," is all he said right then, and I knew he meant it. Nothing else was necessary.

"Who wants to come along to the bus station?" Curtis called out as he came in from the back yard. He'd been washing his car. Cheechee had gained his composure by then and we were sitting on the parlor couch. When Curtis saw the solemn mood he said, "Did Cheechee tell you about his job?"

We both nodded.

"I told him not to worry," Curtis said. "We're all here to help each other."

"See?" I said to Cheechee, and I caught a fraction of a grin creep onto his gloomy face. "Everything will be okay here."

Sorrow had sort of ruined Cheechee's excitement for the grand surprise he had planned for me. Little had I known earlier in the week that he was feverishly preparing a fresh, clean copy of the manuscript—or as much of it as he wanted me to see now—that he had been working on all winter. He stepped over to the writing desk, picked up the notebook, and then gingerly handed it to me. Neatly printed in big, bold letters on the front cover was:

IF I COULD STEAL THE STARS
by Christopher Chapman

"I know you read a lot," he told me. "So... you can tell me if it's any good. Read it at your leisure, but *please* don't give it to anyone else... and for God's sake don't discuss it with anybody, okay?"

It was true. I did read a lot. Cheechee had seen the accumulation of books lining the shelves in my room, and he'd even borrowed a few.

"You have my word," I assured him.

I would have let Curtis and Cheechee go to the bus station while I prepared a good supper for all of us, but they insisted that I come along, and then we could all go to the *Dixie* for hamburgers and beer. In light of Cheechee's situation, it was probably a good idea. In light of Curtis celebrating his new car, it was a *very* good idea. In light of the fact that I didn't really feel like cooking, anyway, it was a *great* idea.

Andy was just as surprised with the new red Pontiac as any of us. He stared at Cheechee with a devious, questioning grin.

"I didn't have a thing to do with it!" Cheechee said. "Curtis bought and *paid* for this car himself!"

We all had a good laugh, and then we climbed into the new red Pontiac; Curtis drove us to the best hamburgers in all of St. Louis. Andy was glad to be back, and he was quite pleased with the new car; no more walking home in the middle of the night from a broken down jalopy.

He told me about his visit in St. Charles, and in particular, about his visit to Spades Morgan. "He has a stateroom on the *Goldenrod* now, and I just caught him before he left for New Orleans." Cheechee knew about Spades, but Curtis didn't, so there followed a brief explanation about Andy's real father, and my connection to him, as well.

I told Andy about Tony and how I set him up with contacts to hire on with riverboat crews. "I got a job offer, too, from First Mate Aaron Tyler on the Hercules."

"You gonna take it?" Andy asked.

"No."

"Will! Why not? The Hercules is a *great* boat."

"I know. I'm just not ready yet. I wanna wait to see what Jesse does."

"But that could be months—"

"I know... but I'll wait."

Then the conversation turned to Curtis. "Hear anything from Harry?" Andy asked him.

"Not a word, so far. Looks like we've got the weekend off."

68

During the next few weeks, Andy and Curtis played a pretty light schedule at the theaters and clubs. I thought they were lowering their standards when they started performing at neighborhood bars, but as they kept telling me, it didn't matter *where* they played as long as the money kept coming in.

Because Cheechee was only working two days a week, he started singing along at their practice sessions. He knew the words to many of the songs they played only instrumentally. At first they were just having fun, but then it seemed as though they had discovered a wild card in Cheechee's voice; the *trio* began working in earnest, and before long there was a whole new versatility in their music. I had always known of Andy's talent, and practically the entire city of St. Louis had confirmed that he and Curtis, together, were quite sensational. Now, with Cheechee's rich tenor voice added, St. Louis was in for another new treat. Even *my* limited knowledge of music skills could identify the potential.

Cheechee was a little nervous about performing in front of a real audience; Curtis suggested that for the first couple appearances, scheduled weeks earlier, Cheechee could join them on stage part-way into the show after the audience was "warmed up." He could sing one song, or as many as he felt comfortable with. "But you'll be fine once you get started... you'll see," Curtis said.

"Maybe," Cheechee replied. "But I always sang with a group, y' know, the school choir and such. Never sang solo before... not for a big audience."

"You won't be alone," Andy assured him. "Curtis and I will be right there with you."

Sadie's studio had remained fairly busy all along, so naturally I stayed busy, too. I went to bed every night at a reason-able hour so that I might be fresh and alert at the studio, but the night that Cheechee made his debut as the new voice of The Gaslight Knights, I couldn't just stay at home. They were playing at a place called Charlie's, a combination bar and dance hall, way out on the west end of the city. The warm April weather enticed people out of their houses, and Charlie's Place certainly did a good job of luring them in. When we arrived a little before nine that Friday night, the parking lot was nearly full. The crowd inside was already primed with alcohol, and I could feel the pent-up energy among them waiting to be unleashed.

Andy and Curtis started playing while Cheechee stayed with me for a while, perhaps to build his courage after seeing the enormous crowd he would have to face. We sipped cold beers, mingled with the noisy horde and looked for any familiar faces, to no avail. There were plenty of people seemingly more interested in getting intoxicated than they were in music and dancing, but the dance floor was full of bodies, too, all moving in one big mass. The Gaslight Knights were sufficiently satisfying.

About a half-hour into their show I saw Curtis waving and motioning for Cheechee to come up onto the stage. "Ladies and gentlemen," he spoke into the microphone. "We have a surprise for you tonight."

The crowd quieted a little with curious stares as the crisp white shirt approached the microphone and came to rest beside Curtis. "Making his first public singing appearance tonight, please welcome Cheechee..." He stepped back, and on cue, he and Andy began the introduction to Cheechee's first number, *I Get a Kick Out of You,* a song that had been made quite popular by Paul Whiteman last December. A few hands clapped, a couple of whoops were heard, and a whistle or two sounded.

It wasn't difficult to see that Cheechee was jittery, but he started singing to the now subdued audience in his vibrant style. As the crowd gradually gained its momentum once again, apparently in approval and acceptance of the new voice singing one of their favorite songs, I could see Cheechee's tension dissolving. By the time he sang his second and third songs, the audience had decided they liked this dazzling new talent. Later, when he finished his night with *My Little Grass Shack in Kealakekua, Hawaii* they were chanting *"Chee-Chee, Chee-Chee, Chee-Chee."* Thanks to Andy and Curtis, Christopher Chapman had taken his first step into show business, and I had recorded it on film.

This was a less sophisticated crowd than I had seen at the *Arcadia*, and I sincerely hoped all the energy would be contained on the dance floor. But typical of any large gathering where the liquor took control of a few who didn't know when they'd had enough, about midnight the place turned into a brawling pandemonium. It started among a group near the bar, and at first I thought that's where it would stay. Next thing I knew, though, like an infectious disease it spread quickly throughout the barroom. Try as I might to avoid any contact, the side of my face caught a wild flying fist that I doubt was intended for me. A fighter, I was not. Without mounting any retaliation, I just scrambled to get away and managed to find the exit before any more violence found me, or my *Leica* got smashed. Curtis's Pontiac was across the parking lot, and I thought that would be the safest place to wait out the mayhem. I sat on the running board of the locked car until Curtis, Andy, and Cheechee showed up a half-hour later. Apparently, Cheechee had been accosted as well; the sleeve of his new $2.50 *Arrow* white shirt was nearly ripped off, but otherwise they all seemed to have escaped unscathed.

"We were worried about you," Cheechee said. "I went out looking for you... that's when some roughneck grabbed me and tore my shirt." Then he caught a glimpse of the dandy bruise on the side of my face. "What happened to you?" he said. In the dark parking lot I hadn't been able to see my reflection in the car window well enough, but the wound obviously looked worse than I had imagined. Andy and Cheechee fussed over me while Curtis unlocked the doors and put his saxophone case in the back.

"I'm okay!" I insisted. "It's not like I'm crippled or something." Their concern and attention, though, did make me feel good.

On the ride home Curtis nudged my arm. "Y' know the best part?" he said. "When the owner of the place came to pay us our forty bucks by the back door, he gave us an extra ten bucks... said he hadn't seen such a rambunctious crowd all winter... said we could come back anytime we wanted."

That was the first of many engagements at various neighborhood bars and taverns that ended in a late-night free-for-all or a parking lot rumble that often entailed bloodshed. I didn't see them all, but I heard about them. What a way for Cheechee to start his show biz career!

69

Too embarrassed about the unsightly contusion on my face to let Sadie see it, I begged off work for a few days, telling her on the telephone that I wasn't feeling well. I hoped that the swelling and the brilliant purple color would dissipate soon.

"Should I come over to look in on you?" she asked.

"NO!" I responded hastily, and then I restated my answer in a calmer tone, to make her not believe that I was trying to hide something. "No, there's no need for that. You're busy, and besides... Curtis and Andy and Cheechee are here... they won't let me die."

"Should I send my doctor over to see you?"

"No, Sadie. That won't be necessary. I just have a little stomach flu, that's all. I'll be fine in a few days."

She knew how close Jesse and I were and I was afraid that she would come anyway. I thought the world of her, just as I did Jesse, but this was one time when I wished she would stay away, so that I wouldn't have to explain that I got in the middle of a barroom brawl.

Monday afternoon I settled down on the parlor couch with Cheechee's manuscript, *If I Could Steal the Stars*, and I read a couple of pages. It began:

> *Sometimes my mind drifts back to a time that perhaps went by too quickly. Then, I was wishing to grow older. Now, I live to stay young and not to die. If I could just steal all the stars from the sky, time would stop, and I could stay a kid forever.*

I thought about that for a few moments; what a profound statement! It had the ring of a seasoned philosopher, yet it sounded like the voice of an innocent child. If I didn't already know the author, I wouldn't have pictured Cheechee.

I read on, discovering that the first part was a brief summary of someone's early life, progressing quickly into his teen years. I could only assume that Cheechee was describing his own existence, as I had suspected this would be. But then I read the passage that said he really liked his dad, and that he had so many fond memories of him. To me, this seemed odd, because I had been given the impression that Cheechee's father was a disgusting drunkard that couldn't take care of his family. But then I read some more. The summary raced from grammar school and playing baseball in a sandlot, to stealing a car and reform school. Now, that sounded more like Cheechee.

> *There came a point in my life that I was not comfortable with the restrictions that society placed on me... I played beyond the limits that were socially accepted...*

I heard a knock on the front door, abruptly closed the notebook and thought of running upstairs to lock myself in my room. But Andy's footsteps rushed to the door too quickly. There was no time. I was caught. Sadie was going to see my black-and-blue face.

"Yeah, he's in the parlor," I heard Andy say cheerfully. "He'll be glad to see you."

I wouldn't have been happy to see *Will Rogers* right then, but I got up to bravely face... "JESSE!" Suddenly I forgot about my bruised cheek and dashed to the door.

"I just got home this morning," Jesse said. "Sadie told me to come over here, that you were sick..." He studied my face for a long moment. "Good heavens, Little Brother! What happened to you?"

It never crossed my mind that I should be ashamed to tell Jesse the truth about what had really happened. We'd never kept secrets from each other, and I certainly wasn't shy about admitting to him that I was at a rowdy bar and got clobbered by some drunk who missed his intended target and hit me instead. "I didn't want to tell Sadie... thought she'd think badly of me... and I didn't want to show up at the studio looking like this."

"I wouldn't worry about that," Jesse said laughing. He seemed to be amused by the whole situation. "Why were you at a roughneck bar like that, anyhow?"

"Andy and Curtis were playing there... and Cheechee sings with them now, too. It was his first time on stage, so I *had* to go... to take pictures."

"You should've seen it, Jesse," Andy bragged. "Will flattened that guy with one punch!"

Jesse ruffled my hair like he always did. "Way to go, Little Brother."

"No, no, no, Jesse," I said laughing. "It didn't happen that way. I cleared outa there before I got clobbered again. Those guys were more than *twice* my size."

"Well, I guess that was the smart thing to do," Jesse said.

By then, Curtis and Cheechee had joined us, too. Even though they had only met Jesse at Christmastime, they considered him a close friend, and they were glad to see him.

"Hey, Cheechee," Jesse said. "Will tells me you're singing with Andy and Curtis now."

"Yeah," Cheechee replied. "Came at the right time, too, 'cause I'm losing my job at the warehouse."

"Sorry to hear that."

"It's okay... I like show biz better. It pays more."

"Say..." Jesse turned to me again. "You'll never guess who I ran into down in Natchez last week," he said. I could tell he was quite amused with this bit of information, too.

"Spades Morgan?" I said. It was a good guess, because Andy had told me Spades was traveling south.

"Well, I saw him, too, down in Baton Rouge a couple of weeks ago."

"So who did you see in Natchez?" Andy asked.

"J.D. McDermott."

My lower jaw bounced off my breastbone. "Then, he didn't drown," I mumbled.

Jesse eyed me suspiciously.

"Did he remember you?" I asked.

"He did," Jesse replied. "Said he fell overboard off our boat that night the band was playing so loud. No one heard him yelling for help. He was stranded on a sandbar 'til the next morning when another boat picked him up and took him all the way to New Orleans."

Curtis and Cheechee didn't have a clue about what we were discussing, but Andy had been filled in on the whole story about McDermott winning our riverboat in a poker game—before it was *our* boat—and Spades Morgan winning it back. Andy also knew about McDermott and Spades facing off on the Texas deck of the Madison that night, with me watching, in a confrontation over a murder that Spades saw McDermott commit ten years prior. McDermott fell overboard as a result of his own guilty conscience. But there was so much hatred toward McDermott that Morgan and I pretended we knew nothing about it when McDermott turned up missing.

"Did you know he fell overboard?" Jesse asked.

"N-no... Spades said something about... um... no I didn't."

I guess, now, I should retract my statement about *never* keeping a secret from my Big Brother Jesse. But I think that's the *only* one.

We all talked and had a grand time the rest of the afternoon, and, of course, Curtis had to show Jesse his new Pontiac.

"Luke should see it," Jesse said. "He's thinking about a car."

"What about Reggie?" I asked. "What's he doing now?"

"Reggie got a job as a salesman at a clothing store downtown... the Top Hat. You should stop in and see him."

"I will." I couldn't imagine Reggie dressed in a salesman's suit and tie in a fancy store like the Top Hat, but his British accent and his flair of sophistication would fit right in.

About four o'clock, Jesse indicated that he should be going. "Our boat is getting some repairs, and Luke and I have some classes to attend, so we'll be in town for a few days."

"Classes?"

"Yeah... I'm getting my pilot's license, too," Jesse said.

"That's great! How long 'til you get your command?"

"Could be as far off as next year, Will. They're a lot more stringent about training pilots now."

Maybe some things on the river *had* changed.

70

After a couple of days the swelling was gone from my cheek, but there still remained a little discoloration of the skin. Although I still didn't want to go to the studio in that condition, it wasn't so bad that I couldn't go downtown.

"I'm gonna take the bus downtown," I announced. "Wanna come with me, Andy?"

"What are you going to do?" Andy asked.

"Look up Reggie."

"Sure, I'll come. I'd like to see Reggie again, too."

Cheechee overheard our conversation and popped his head around the corner. "Are you going to that Top Hat clothing store?"

"Yeah, if we can find it."

"I know right where it is," Cheechee said. "That's where I bought my new white shirt that got wrecked. I need a new one, so I'll go too... if you don't mind."

Curtis called out from the kitchen, "What's this I hear about you taking the bus downtown?"

"We're going down to the Top Hat Clothier," Andy replied.

"On the bus?"

"Yeah."

"Nonsense! I'll drive you downtown in the car."

Curtis was always ready and willing to play chauffeur with his new red Pontiac. And the rest of us were always ready and willing to let him.

On the way into town, we were all in agreement that certain articles of clothing were needed by each of us, and because Reggie was probably earning some sort of commission on his sales, we would all purchase something from him. I certainly needed a new pair of trousers; Cheechee needed a shirt; Andy said he could use some new socks and underwear; and Curtis was in the market for a new hat *and* trousers. There would be no better place to get them.

Curtis parked his car in the nearest parking lot about four blocks away from the Top Hat. We didn't mind the walk on that pleasantly warm spring day. We passed more than a dozen out-of-work men selling apples on the street corners, and I could only imagine that come nightfall, they would all be standing in some breadline. My heart went out to them as I stopped to buy an apple, not from just one, but three different men. Their expressions were so grateful when I handed over the nickels; it was quite gratifying to me. Then Curtis and Andy followed my lead, and they purchased a couple of apples each, and finally Cheechee decided that he should afford himself just one. But his heart was in the right place.

We noticed that there appeared to be more people just walking aimlessly about; farmers had lost their land to fore-closure; city dwellers were unable to find jobs when factories shut down all production. Few businesses remained flush, some had closed their doors, and many more were merely operating on a shoestring. President Franklin D. Roosevelt had improved the nation's condition   after entering the White House in 1933 with his "New Deal" that created government work forces, providing jobs for some. But there were mixed emotions among the people; some still supported him strongly, while others opposed. He was up for re-election, and only time would tell the rest of the story.

We walked the remaining distance slowly, eating our apples while we contemplated our fortunate position in this ailing society. *Where would it all end?* we wondered, and we recognized that we could only live day-by-day, keeping ourselves focused on survival.

But so far, we *had* survived the Depression's revolting blows. Perhaps we *were* lucky. Perhaps we *had* fallen into the right hands at the right time. But it wasn't *all luck.* We had faced the adversities with strong will and healthy body, and we had persevered and maintained our hold on whatever we had. No, it wasn't *all* just luck.

We entered the Top Hat, a large, classy, men's clothier, expecting to find a rampantly busy atmosphere. But it was something less than rampant. At the very center of the store, an escalator made its silent, resolute movement upward, and likewise, beside it a column of steps came steadily, silently down. Neither column carried a single soul. Row upon row of racks and aisle after aisle of gondolas contained every piece of men's clothing and accessories imaginable, being scrutinized by only a very few potential customers.

Just inside the door we were greeted by a distinguished gentleman, dark blue business suit, starched white shirt and tie. "May I be of assistance?" he said politely.

"Yes, actually," I replied. "I would like to see the salesman named Reginald Peirce. Is he here today?"

"Certainly," the suited man said. "I'll get him for you." He turned and walked toward the back of the store.

A couple of minutes later, our foursome had dispersed into the immediate area viewing various textile items. When Reggie saw us, he practically ran up the aisle to meet us, grinning.

"Will, Andy," he said, seemingly overwhelmed by our presence. "It's so bloody great to see you." He looked rather stunning in his blue suit, starched shirt and tie. He gave us all hearty handshakes. "What brings you here?"

"Well, actually, we came to see you," I started. "But we came to buy some clothes, too."

"You came to the right place..."

We chatted briefly about our present situations, and then, because Reggie's supervisor was apparently monitoring his activity, he shifted into salesman high gear. "So, what can I help you find?"

We expressed our needs and Reggie guided each of us to the various departments of goods. He expertly measured across Cheechee's broad shoulders, and then stretched the tape down the length of his arm to determine proper shirt size, pointing out the racks with the "perfect fit" shirts for Cheechee.

Then he put his tape around my waist and measured my inseam. "Will... looks like you've put on a little weight since I saw you last," he said smiling, and proceeded to show me dozens of trousers in my size.

When he was finished with all of us, we couldn't have been more satisfied. Everything was of perfect fit and color.

"I wish we had more time to talk," I told Reggie when we were about to leave. "Maybe you could meet us some night at the *Dixie*. You remember that place?"

"Sure," Reggie said. "Jesse used to take us there. It's on Pine Street, is it not?"

"That's the place. We'll have supper there some night. I'll let you know when."

71

We made good our promise to Reggie the following week. I had gone back to work at Sadie's studio when the black-and-blue was hardly noticeable. (Sadie only asked if I was feeling better, so I trust that Jesse didn't tell her about the bar fight.) When I knew that Jesse and Luke were back on the river again, there seemed little chance that Reggie would be preoccupied, so we arranged to meet at the *Dixie* Thursday evening after he was through with work.

Andy and I had a ball reminiscing the good old times on the Madison with Reggie. He'd get us going with "Remember that time when..." and we'd recall incidents like the time the new pilot ran us aground in the fog; or the time we captured the "river pirates" in the coal bin; or the time someone cut our mooring lines and we were adrift alone down the Missouri River in the middle of the night. We carried on for several hours, every once in a while stopping to explain something that Cheechee and

Curtis couldn't understand without explanation. I think Cheechee was taking mental notes for his next book; Curtis was just plain entertained.

I got the impression that Reggie wasn't enjoying his stay in St. Louis to its fullest, that he was spending much of his time alone. So I was glad that Reggie, Curtis, and Cheechee had the chance to spend some time together and get to know one another better. It helped broaden the scope of our circle, and it offered Reggie some needed companionship. He welcomed the idea that we should do this every week. And we did.

Summer burst into full bloom during May; even the nights were warm enough for outdoor activities. But I had been interrupted during several attempts to read Cheechee's manuscript, and I was determined to finish it—not only to satisfy his desire for feedback, but to satisfy my curiosity about his history, if this was in fact a true accounting of his life experiences. So one Saturday night when Andy, Curtis and Cheechee were out being The Gaslight Knights at some club, I settled in with Cheechee's notebook.

If I Could Steal the Stars was a touching story about a young boy growing up in Denver, Colorado. It didn't really have a plot, but there was so much feeling it didn't need one. It told of the boy's struggle, continually bullied by an older brother. His only escape, at times, was to slip away and hide under a railroad trestle. He played baseball in a sandlot with other neighborhood boys, but because he was younger and smaller than most of them, he was never able to score a run, much less, make it to first base.

His mother's passing seemed to be a turning point in his life. At age ten, his home became flophouses on Larimer Street because his father could afford no more. Dad had always liked the bottle, but losing his wife pushed him over the edge. His employer soon lost patience, and Dad soon lost his job.

It was after several months in a flophouse when the boy came to understand the reason for older brother Robert's animosity toward him: the younger boy was and always had been Dad's favorite son, and Big Brother's easy retaliation was mean treatment of Little Brother. But he eventually left to join a band of petty thieves in Greely.

No wonder the boy never stopped loving Dad; for the story went on to tell of walks in the mountain forest, fishing at a creek, and sometimes just a lazy Sunday in a park, all by Dad's side. There seemed to be so much love and affection between them.

And then there came the hobo trip to Texas one summer, riding box cars, working carnivals, picking cucumbers, meeting interesting people. But the most heart-wrenching episode was Dad and Son accidentally getting separated for a day and a night. Tears streamed down my cheeks as I read it, and joy filled my heart when they were reunited by a stroke of luck.

Back in Denver, as the boy grew older and stronger, he was tempted by peers with illicit "fun," and his days of innocent childhood play was over. After a generous taste of uninhibited sex, drugs, and wild adventure, he was no longer satisfied with what society deemed acceptable. He stole a car so he and his buddies could go for a joy ride. That led to another, and another… and then his life seemed to be tethered to a revolving door in and out of jail and reform school until he became an "adult."

Another turning point occurred: he recognized his intelligence and talents; he woke up to realize his life, at this point, was a moralistic wreck. His father had become an invalid in a state asylum and now the boy's life in Denver was headed nowhere. One last deviant act got him a car that afforded him quick escape, which he abandoned a few miles from the city where it would easily be found and returned to its rightful owner. From there he hitchhiked across country to St. Louis, taking the time to reflect on his past, and to find a new sense of direction. In St. Louis, he would start over, and maybe there he would find a way to steal all the stars.

The story ended there, but somehow I knew that Cheechee intended to continue; too many things were still left unsaid.

The Gaslight Knights returned home long after I had gone to bed; I didn't even hear them come in. The next morning they didn't wake up so early; they'd had a rough night at a dance hall in North St. Louis where several fights broke out at various times while they played. At the end of the dance, the final clash continued in the parking lot; Cheechee and Andy both had black eyes, and Curtis suffered some nasty bruises on his shoulders and one leg. They hadn't been able to avoid it, caught by surprise on their way to the car.

Although this was the first time they had suffered injuries, they had experienced other similar incidents; it was becoming discouraging. Harry hadn't gotten them into any of the respectable theaters for many weeks.

"Maybe we should just get out of St. Louis," Curtis suggested. "Try some other cities."

We all agreed that St. Louis was getting rough. Was it because the city was attracting so many out-of-work people? We didn't know, but there would be time to contemplate other options; Andy or Cheechee didn't want to perform in public with black eyes.

I sat on the back porch with Cheechee one afternoon while Andy and Curtis were practicing. "I've read your entire manuscript," I said. "I think it's very good, so far."

"Thanks, Will," Cheechee replied.

"But do you mind if I ask you one question?"

"Please, do."

"In your story, you say that you really liked your dad, but I thought you told us he was a drunk, and that he couldn't take care of you. Which is true?"

"Will, my father's an *alcoholic*... that's what I told you. It's true that he hasn't worked all the time. But I never said that I hate him."

"I'm sorry, Cheechee. Guess I must've misunderstood."

"Easy thing to do sometimes."

72

A few days later, near the end of May, we were all getting restless. Maybe it was just spring fever, but there seemed to be something else in the air, something unsettling that none of us recognized or could clarify. With the exception of—perhaps—Cheechee, we were all fairly financially secure, considering the economic times, and since he had started performing with Andy and Curtis, even Cheechee wasn't in any immediate danger of starvation. So, we knew money wasn't necessarily the issue. Curtis, Andy and Cheechee had discussed the possibility of playing at theaters and clubs in other cities, but so far there were no steadfast plans in place. The dread of finding more of the same violent audiences usually quenched the conversation.

While the black eyes and bruises healed, we needed some diversion to ease the anxiety. Andy and I had always enjoyed the cinema, so we drug Cheechee and Curtis to the movie theaters. Of course, they both admitted that they, too, were fans of the big screen, so it wasn't as if we were torturing them. We were thrilled with the high seas adventure of Captain Bligh and Fletcher Christian in *Mutiny on the Bounty;* we sat on the edge of our seats watching *The Bride of Franken-stein.* Curtis and Cheechee really enjoyed *Top Hat* starring Fred Astaire and Ginger Rogers, the song and dance musical that kept us laughing and smiling.

The Scarlet Empress was a tragedy and a farce all rolled into one baffling mess about a Russian princess, Sophia. We didn't know whether we should laugh or cry, and neither did the rest of the audience. No doubt, that movie was destined to be a box office flop. But we had no trouble laughing out loud at Clark Gable's gangster impression and Claudette Colbert's show-a-little-thigh hitch-hiking lesson in *It Happened One Night,* the motion picture that became the biggest hit of the year.

In the darkness of the theater we found reality in imagination, free from restrictions of real life. Ocean waves and spooky mansions, ten gallon hats and Colt .45s, flashy motorcars and raging stallions; they all passed through the screen from that wonderful world of cinema.

I awoke later than usual Monday morning after a late-night movie at the *Orpheum*. No one else was up yet, either. I stared at the calendar on the wall as I waited for the coffee to brew; it was June 3rd. I had informed Sadie that I planned to look up my friend, Keith Blake, the *St. Louis Post Dispatch* photographer who I had met the night Andy and Curtis opened for Benny Goodman at the Arcadia. Not that I expected to get a job with the newspaper, but Blake had told me to look him up sometime, and he would show me around, maybe put me in touch with the right people. It couldn't hurt.

I poured a cup of coffee to take to the back porch; that's where I most enjoyed my morning coffee now that the weather was warm. As I approached the door, I was startled by the sight of someone sitting on our back steps. He had his back to me, leaning against the railing, arms limp at his sides; he appeared to be asleep. I opened the door, thinking the noise would alert whoever it was of my presence, but it did not. I cautiously stepped closer to identify the sleeping stranger. But to my astonishment, it was not a stranger.

Tony Delaware's appearance was dismal, to say the least. His clothes were a mess—shirt stained and wrinkled; trousers caked with mud—his hair was dirty and mussed up more than usual, and his face was smeared and smudged from wiping it with soiled hands.

I stood there, gawking at Tony for a few moments, wondering what circumstance would have put him in that condition. A beating didn't seem likely because there appeared to be no cuts, scrapes or bruises. Likewise, he'd not fallen nor was he the victim of some accident. Physically he didn't look harmed.

I gently shook his shoulder. "Tony. Wake up," I said softly, as not to startle him.

His head jerked up and his whole body tensed, one hand grabbing for my wrist. His expression at first was that of fright, and then when he recognized who had wakened him, it turned to relief. "Will," he whispered.

"How long have you been out here?" I asked.

"Since dawn," he replied, his voice still raspy and weak. "I... I... I walked from the river last night... to the park... and I slept there for a while. Then just before sunup... I came here."

"What happened to you? Why are you so dirty?"

Tony gazed deeply, silently, into my eyes, and then tears spilled from his eyes, streaking down his dirty face. He buried his face in his hands, slumped, unable to speak.

I tried to coax some more out of him, but the only response from Tony was intense sobbing. I rubbed his shoulders and back, and it must have been comforting to him as it seemed to calm him a little, but I still couldn't get him to talk.

After some effort I finally helped him to stand. "Let's go inside," I said. "I've got fresh coffee in the pot. Would you like a cup of hot coffee?"

Tony nodded his approval, but still no words. Whatever happened to him had temporarily destroyed his ability to function wholly. Although I noticed no physical trauma, his endurance was nearly nonexistent as I assisted him into the kitchen and sat him down on a chair at the table. I poured another cup of coffee for him; his hand shook and he could barely raise the cup to his lips.

I just sat there with him, sipping my coffee, waiting for him to gain some strength. "Whenever you're ready to talk," I said as soothingly as I knew how, "I'm here to listen."

I heard Curtis stirring upstairs. I knew it was Curtis because his was the only room in the house that the floorboards squeaked when he walked across them. When he had made a brief visit to the bathroom, he came down to the kitchen. "I smell fresh coffee..." he said, and then he saw Tony in his miserable state. "Tony!" He obviously sensed that something was terribly wrong, and he just stared at me questioningly.

"I don't know," I said. "He's not saying anything. All I know is that he walked here from the river last night and slept in the park."

Tony continued his distant gaze and occasionally sipped his coffee. Nearly an hour later, he had not spoken a single word. Curtis suggested that we get him upstairs. "A warm bath and some clean clothes might help him feel better," he said.

I thought it sounded like an excellent idea. "How 'bout it, Tony? Does that sound agreeable to you?"

Tony glanced down at his filthy clothes and nodded.

He had stayed with us a couple of nights once before, so he was in familiar surroundings. That made it a simple matter to guide him up to the bathroom. I filled the tub while Curtis helped Tony get undressed. We both steadied him when he stepped into the bath and then stretched out in the warm, soothing water. Curtis soaped a washcloth and gently started scrubbing the grime from Tony's face and neck.

"You look like you've had some experience with that," I said to Curtis.

"When I was growing up," he replied, "I took care of three little brothers that knew how to get a lot dirtier than this. So this is nothing new to me."

I went to find some clothes while the bath continued. I figured mine would fit Tony fairly well. By the time we got him out of the tub, dried off, and dressed again, Tony was mumbling a few words of gratitude to us; it seemed as though the warm bath had been the therapy he needed to start the recovery process.

Andy and Cheechee hadn't seen the earlier, pitiful version of Tony, so naturally they were quite curious when they watched us escort Tony from the bathroom and down to the parlor. I discretely took them out on the back porch and explained the situation as I knew it. When we returned to the parlor, Tony spoke.

"Will," he said meekly, as if he were embarrassed to talk in front of everyone. "Now can *we* talk? *Alone?*"

73

"**A**ndy... Cheechee," Curtis said. "Let's go down to the Dixie and get some breakfast. We can bring something back for Will and Tony. Okay?" He wasn't asking. He was telling.

I had been Tony's confidant a couple of months ago; I knew he trusted me; that's probably why he was there. In the short time I'd known him, he seemed likeable enough, although I had questioned his close association with Johnny Dempsey.

After Andy, Cheechee, and Curtis had left, I sat on the couch beside Tony. I didn't know what to expect, and I didn't say anything, just waiting for Tony to begin.

"I... I... don't know where to start," he said. His voice was still weak, but sounding more normal now than it had earlier. No more tears streaked his face; it seemed that he had cried out all the anxiety, but I could still sense high levels of fear and emotional confusion.

"Try the beginning," I said. "That always seems to work for me."

Tony looked at me and tried to smile, as if he were grateful for my understanding. "Okay... I'll go back to... well... remember when you hooked me up with Aaron Tyler? The First Mate on the Hercules?"

"Sure," I replied. "I think he wanted to hire both of us that day."

"Yeah... he... I... I saw him again last week... and he... he asked about you..."

Tony was still having difficulty talking comprehensibly, but I thought I should just let him go at his pace until he found a comfort level.

"I told him... I told him that I hadn't talked to you much lately... but that I would... " Tony paused a few moments to gather his thoughts. "He wants you to get in touch with him again... "

"Maybe I will," I said. "Did he hire you?"

Tony nodded, and then he continued. "Yeah... he gave me some papers to fill out... said I could start next week... "

"That's great!" I encouraged.

"But... I'm afraid... it's not going to happen... "

"Why? What's wrong?"

"Well... Johnny and me were hangin' around together again some... and he... well... he was getting back to... his old tricks... following me around... y' know... obsessed, I guess is the right word... well... I thought if I hired on with Aaron on the Hercules... I could get away from him... Johnny... "

"Yes, you could."

"Well... Johnny somehow found out... that... that I would be working on the Hercules... found me at a bar last night... and we drank quite a bit."

My gut reaction was that this is where the story would take a bad turn. Johnny Dempsey and too much alcohol in Tony didn't seem like a good combination. I was still convinced that Johnny could be a bad influence on anyone, but the rest of the Knights of the Square Table seemed to like him well enough to welcome him to every Friday night gathering at the Lion's Den. I knew they were aware of his drug dealing because most of them were his customers. But they probably weren't aware of his warped sexual practices, among other criminal divergences that I had privately discovered from Cheechee and Tony.

"Johnny told me..." Tony continued. "... That he would get a stateroom... on the Hercules... so that we could still be together all the time."

"So, did you tell Johnny—*again*—that you didn't want to be with him all the time?"

"I... I tried to... but then he bought a six-pack of beer and took me out to a lonely spot along the river north of town... we... we drank some more... and I... I kept pushing him away... and then I was just going to scare him... I... I had my back to him and... I had... I had my open pocket knife in my hand... I didn't realize that he had stepped so close behind me... and I swung my hand around to scare him with the knife... and the blade must've went right between his ribs... stabbed his heart. He fell to the ground... and he never moved or breathed again." Tony paused and looked into my shocked eyes. "I killed Johnny," he said calmly. "I stabbed him with my knife, and now he's dead."

"Are you sure? Are you sure he's dead? Maybe you just wounded him."

"No, Will... he's dead. I dragged him down the riverbank and put him in the river. He sank out of sight. He's dead."

I quickly took inventory of all my senses to make certain that I wasn't dreaming. Now I understood why I had found Tony in that wretched condition that morning, but I was stunned by this ghastly account of how it occurred.

"I spent most of the night," Tony went on, "Walking... and finding my way to the park just up the street. All I could think of was trying to find you. By then I had sobered up some, but I was so exhausted and I fell asleep for a while under some trees."

He leaned against the sofa backrest, closed his eyes, and took a deep breath. "And now I am so tired, Will. I am so very, very tired."

Exhaustion from re-living that whole scary episode in his mind again had overcome him. Perhaps some sleep would do him good, and help him to think more clearly. "You can go up to my room and sleep for a while if you want," I suggested. "You know where it is." I didn't know what else to say.

Tony opened his eyes. "I think I will. But please tell me you'll help me... I don't know what to do."

"Get some sleep, and let me think about it."

"Thanks Will." He slowly navigated up the stairs to my room.

More than two hours later I heard Curtis's Pontiac pull up into the back yard while I sat at the kitchen table nursing a cup of coffee. They didn't waste any time coming in, but they came in quietly. Andy set a paper bag on the table in front of me. "We brought you doughnuts. Eggs and toast would've been soggy and cold by the time we got it here."

"Where's Tony?" Curtis asked.

"He's sleeping up in my room."

"So, did you find out what happened?"

"Yeah, I found out."

"So, are you gonna tell us?"

"All of you," I said. "Sit down. This is serious."

They all sat down around the table, eyes on me as I tore open the bag of doughnuts.

"Did he get into a fight?" Andy asked.

"A rough-ass dance hall, I bet," Cheechee added.

Curtis just sat there patiently waiting for me to swallow my doughnut.

"No, he didn't get into a fight... not like that," I responded.

"Well, what then?"

I took a deep breath, exhaled, and looked each one of my best friends in their eyes. "Tony killed Johnny Dempsey last night."

Just a few seconds passed silently while the statement registered with all of them.

"What?" "Are you serious?" "He killed Johnny?" came from around the table.

I well expected this to be difficult, one way or another. "Yes, I'm serious," I said.

"Great! We're harboring a murderer—"

"It was an accident!" I said, before the conversation got out of hand. "He only meant to put a scare in Johnny, and he accidently stabbed him. And I believe him. I don't think he's making it up."

I retold the story just as Tony had told it to me. Cheechee fully grasped the concept—he knew Johnny better than the rest of us—and I think Andy and Curtis accepted my logic, too.

"So, what are we gonna do?"

"Other than convincing Tony to go to the police on his own, I don't think we should do anything," I said. "We weren't involved, and I think we should keep it that way."

"We could take him with us on tour... get him out of town," Cheechee suggested.

"No," I insisted. "Then we'd all be fugitives. Better for him, better for all of us if he just turns himself in. It was an accident... he'll get off easy."

74

I was beginning to hate this city again. Granted, some wonderful things happened while I had been here: I learned a new skill—photography; I gained some good friends; the city opened my eyes to a bigger world. But now it was starting to show me its mean side, and I was quite sure that I had only witnessed a meager sampling, so far. Uncertain that I could withstand the full impact of any more of its brutal tricks, I thought I was ready to make some changes, and I suspected that Andy, Cheechee, and Curtis were feeling the same way. Since their encounter with that drunken dance hall mob, I'd heard them make mention of a Gaslight Knights "tour" several times but I didn't know if I would be invited to join them. I never asked, and they never volunteered. Right now, though, we stared another serious problem in its ugly face: what to do about Tony.

"We've been talking this over," Curtis said to me. "We've been thinking for quite a while that we'd like to go somewhere else... get out of St. Louis for a while... play in some other towns."

"Where do you want to go?" I asked.

"Don't know for sure. Haven't really decided that."

"And you think now would be a good time to go?"

"Things aren't getting any better here."

"So, you're just gonna take off without a plan of where you're going, and leave me here alone to deal with all this."

Curtis looked at me as if I had lost my mind. "No... you'll go with us... won't you?"

Andy and Cheechee stared at me with expectation. Just moments ago I had felt like I was being abandoned; now, suddenly it seemed like I was being shanghaied.

"But I'm not a Gaslight Knight."

"Sure you are, Will. You're one of us."

I was quite relieved to know they had assumed all along that I would accompany them, wherever they intended to go. I had even talked to Sadie a few days ago about leaving St. Louis, but, of course, then, I didn't have a plan, either. She was just a little disappointed—at first—that I would not be there to help her in the studio, but then she realized that the busy time was nearly over, and she thought it was good that I had decided to explore my horizons.

But before I could leave town, now, I had to resolve my connection to Tony's predicament; I could imagine all sorts of reasons why the police would come snooping. They would eventually find Dempsey's body, and then they would associate him with Tony, and Tony with the rest of us. There were bound to be a lot of questions asked. If I could convince Tony to voluntarily go to the police, though, it might ease the pressure on those who had nothing to do with Dempsey's death. As far as I knew, that included everyone except Tony.

"He should get a good lawyer," Curtis suggested.

"But does he have any money to hire a lawyer?"

"His Aunt Gertrude has money, and she has a lawyer, too."

After Tony had slept another four hours, he seemed to be coherent again, although I could tell that he was still quite suppressed with his situation, and understandably so. At least he could think rationally and had control of all his functions. When I explained to him that I was optimistic about his fate, because Dempsey's death was the result of an accident and not a premeditated act, Tony realized that his chances were pretty good, even though the unavoidable experience with the police might not be the most pleasant.

"Do you know any lawyers?" I asked. "You should really talk to one before you go to the police."

"Yes," Tony replied. "Bob Turner... he handled all the legal custody stuff for Aunt Gertrude when I came here. I got to know him real good."

It was comforting to know that Tony was acquainted with Mr. Turner so well—he addressed him as "Bob" during the telephone call to the lawyer's office. I couldn't hear but one side of the conversation in which Tony expressed his urgent need to see Bob right away. "I'm in some serious trouble, Bob. I have to talk to you right now... No, it can't wait... No, I'd rather talk to you at your office. Can I come right over?"

We shared some late lunch with Tony, and then Curtis drove him away to the lawyer's office somewhere on the west side of town.

I worried about what Tony would say in regards to my connection with the recent chain of events. Curtis and I had given him a bath, clean clothes, and he slept for a few hours in my bed—that's all. But I envisioned that to evolve into providing shelter for a fleeing criminal, or whatever the legal language would call it. And I worried, too, about what would happen to Tony; I didn't think he deserved to spend the rest of his life behind bars. Johnny's death was an accident. I was convinced of that. But then Curtis— good old Curtis—convinced me that I shouldn't worry. He had known Tony the longest, since Tony started public school. He knew Tony's Aunt Gertrude, and he was familiar with Bob Turner, the attorney. "Aunt Gertrude will pay Bob well," Curtis said. "Bob will see to it that Tony gets fair treatment. None of us were involved, so don't worry."

I tried not to.

A couple of nights later Andy and I heard the news bulletin on the radio while we were waiting for *The Jack Benny Show*. The day before, someone had pulled a body out of the river. It had finally been identified as that of thirty-year-old John Dempsey, resident of North St. Louis. An autopsy revealed he had been fatally stabbed only once. In custody awaiting an arraignment hearing, the suspect, who had turned himself in, admitted to the stabbing, claiming it to be accidental. Police had already initiated an investigation.

"Hear that, Andy? An investigation. Wonder how long it will be before the cops are on *our* doorstep."

"Maybe we should get out of town... before that happens... no matter what it takes."

I thought about that for one, brief moment.

"CURTIS! CHEECHEE! START PACKING!"

75

None of us had much to pack. To conserve space, Andy and Cheechee managed to get all their clothes in one suitcase, and Curtis and I did the same. A third suitcase accommodated sheet music, notebooks, my camera and film, and other assorted miscellaneous items. All my books and the food in the ice box went to Jesse's house.

"Where are you headed?" Sadie asked. She already knew about our notion to leave St. Louis for a while, and I suppose she thought we had perhaps laid out a route with some sort of destination in mind.

Each of us blurted out a different compass point simultaneously, and then we confessed that we hadn't yet formulated a crystal-clear plan.

"Well," Sadie said. "This time of year, north would seem to be the most logical choice, don't you think?"

We all nodded in agreement.

"How long will you be away?"

"Can't say for sure," I said. "Guess we'll know that when we get there."

"So... you don't know where you're going, how to get there, or how long you'll stay?"

"No."

"Have you planned *anything*? I hope you at least packed some extra clothes."

Now, I thought Sadie was sounding like a mom. "Yes, Sadie. We have *all* our clothes... and everything else we need with us."

"Do you have money? It costs a lot to travel these days, y' know."

"Yes, Sadie. We all have plenty of money to travel."

"And you're going in Curtis's car?"

"Yes, Sadie. It's like new and it's in very good condition... and Curtis is an excellent driver."

"What if you get lost?"

"Sadie... I've been reading river charts for five years. I think I can follow a road map. We won't get lost." I could tell that Sadie had suddenly renewed her concern about us traveling into unknown territory on our own. But in reality, we were all seasoned travelers to some degree. Andy and I had been on the go, up and down the Mississippi River a hundred times, visiting and exploring towns we had never seen before. Cheechee had left Denver on his own, and traveled across the country to St. Louis. Curtis had told us of several vacation trips he made with his parents to many parts of the country. So it wasn't like we'd never left the neighborhood. We were young, adventurous... and we were anxious.

"And where will you stay at night? Hotels? You have to be mighty careful these days of flimflam men and—"

"Sadie!" I interrupted. "We're big boys. We'll be fine."

Sadie finally realized she couldn't talk us out of going. "Andy," she said. "Does your mother know about this yet?"

"I mentioned it last time I visited her," Andy replied. "We'll go there first before we leave."

I wished Jesse had been there; one of his brotherly bear hugs would have done me good right then. But he wouldn't be back in port for two weeks, so I t told Sadie to say good-bye to him for me.

Sadie wished us well. "Write," she said. "At least send post cards... let me know you're okay."

We all assured Sadie that an abundance of post cards would adorn her mailbox. We said our good-byes, and of course, there were four big hugs for little Philip.

With the four of us, three suitcases, a picnic basket, four blankets and a saxophone, the red Pontiac Touring Sedan was northbound, next stop, St. Charles. We couldn't leave without seeing Beth Lorado. She was shooing the last of the "Twinkle, Twinkle" kids out the door when we pulled up in front of the house at the end of Third Street. Beth was happy to see us all, but naturally, we went through the same line of questioning there as we had at Sadie's: "Where are you going?" "North." "How long will you be gone?" "Don't know." ... And so on...

Beth was proud of Andy, and glad that he was spreading his wings. But I could tell that she was concerned, too, for all of us. She had molded Andy into a fine musician, and now he had found his mark. That it had led him to St. Louis, just a few miles away, was one thing, but now, his travels would take him far beyond a half-hour bus ride. It was fortunate that Beth had been conditioned by Andy's being away—albeit a short distance away—for the last several months; that made his leaving now a little less abrupt. But there were still tears, and, of course the last efforts attempting to convince us all to postpone the departure. Even I had difficulty saying good-bye to Beth without shedding a few tears, as I had long ago established an endearing relationship with her when I lived in her house as a boarder, and as her student. She had unleashed that urge within me to read books and to learn. She had taught me so much about the world around me and how to live in it, and I was grateful for that.

"I'll expect letters," Beth said from behind the tears. She was directing the statement to both Andy and me.

"Of course we'll write you." What else could we say?

We hadn't mentioned to Sadie, nor did we tell Beth about Tony, the trouble he was in, or the real reason we decided to leave town at that particular time; it would only add to the concern, and to the list of questions. We just hoped that anything they heard on the radio news broadcasts or read in the newspapers about Johnny Dempsey and Tony Delaware wasn't associated with any of us.

76

And that's how it happened that we left St. Louis. By the time we checked into the Stoddard Hotel we had traveled over 400 miles, experienced—and survived—two flat tires, three million ants, ten thousand bees, a dozen raccoons, two hundred stray cows, a circus convoy, four hay wagons, and one very persistent fellow wanting us to join his carnival troupe. It had been an interesting journey of five days and nights, camping out under the stars mostly, not because we *had* to, but because we *wanted* to. Once we learned how to avoid the ants and bees, and how to combat the raccoons, the rest didn't seem so bad. Aside from the two flat tires, Curtis's Pontiac performed flawlessly. All considered, the trip, so far, had progressed quite enjoyably.

Andy and Curtis called the terrain "mountains" when we reached northeastern Iowa and southern Minnesota; they had never experienced the bluffs and hills of the Upper Mississippi River Valley, and they were quite amazed. But of course, Cheechee had grown up in Denver, accustomed to the towering, massive Rocky Mountains; to him, what he saw in Minnesota and across the river in Wisconsin were just big hills. Nonetheless, they were all impressed with the beauty of the region. Even I was a bit in awe, as it had been several years since our steamboat passed from here, never to return again. A certain anxious excitement simmered inside me as I anticipated the return to La Crosse, where Jesse, Luke and I had spent many weeks in the late summer of 1930. It was there that our steamboating career was born, and where my "new family" started to come together. It was where Spades Morgan (Andy's biological father) made a little magic happen, and it changed our dismal outlook into a prosperous business. (That's when he won the steamboat back in a poker game from the dastardly riverboat gambler, J.D. McDermott. That boat, of course, became the *Madison*. It might not have been magic, but I was only fourteen years old then, so a lot of things seemed magical to me.) Yes, I had some fond memories of La Crosse that were mine alone, and the others would have to experience some "magic" of their own.

Then how, you might ask, did it happen that La Crosse, Wisconsin became our destination? While we were northbound across Missouri, I officially became the navigator with the map in the front seat beside Curtis. Guiding him, keeping our course as close to the Mississippi River as possible, gave us many opportunities for little side trips into the river towns where I had once been, and thought Curtis, Andy and Cheechee would enjoy seeing, too. After all, we were on a trip of discovery, and our only urgency of getting out of St. Louis was already behind us, so we weren't in any hurry.

At a little country store just south of Hannibal, we bought some groceries to complement the contents of our picnic basket, found a secluded spot on a country road near the river and camped there for the night. It was the next day while we were roaming the streets of Hannibal on foot when Andy asked me about some details of my early encounters with Spades Morgan. After I told them the story of when Spades invited me and Jesse and Luke to supper at the Stoddard Hotel, where the plans were laid for the recovery of the lost steamboat, all three—Andy, Cheechee and Curtis—thought they might like to someday see the town where "it all began." During the next three days while we made our way upriver, their interest in La Crosse grew, and because it was the town where I had spent the most time since I left Milwaukee, I was able to answer most of their questions about it. "Just remember," I told them. "That was five years ago, and things are bound to have changed." But a decision was made; La Crosse was our target destination. Whether or not we'd stay for any length of time we could decide after we were there.

77

Five stories of brown brick, The *Stoddard Hotel* had seen some interior face-lifting since I last saw it. The new owner and manager, John Elliot, who had taken over the inn several years ago, was in better tune with making a large, luxury hotel more appealing. Many improvements were already completed, and many more were underway. The first thing I noticed was all the new furniture in the lobby, but the renovation went much further than skin-deep. My recollection of that one visit to the *Stoddard* nearly five years earlier left me only vaguely familiar. I remembered it as elegant in 1930, but now it was downright classy.

We took two adjacent rooms on the third floor, 315 and 317, for a week. Andy asked the desk clerk if he knew of a   piano anywhere near that he might have access to.

"Why, yes, there's a piano in the Crystal Room," the clerk replied with a mechanical smile.

"Would it be okay if I used it for a little practice?" Andy asked.

"I don't see why not," the clerk said. "Our guests play that piano quite frequently when it isn't being used by an entertainer."

"Great," Andy said. "We'll do a little practicing, then, if it's okay."

"Sure. Mornings are good... there's very few people in the Crystal Room in the morning."

I could see the wheels turning in Andy's head; he winked at Curtis, and I knew immediately that they would be performing some night, sometime soon, in the Crystal Room.

Even though we didn't really need any help with our luggage, a bellboy in his snazzy dark green uniform insisted that he would accompany us to our rooms. He wouldn't take 'no' for an answer as he managed to grasp the three suitcases and one saxophone case, directing us to the elevator at the north end of the lobby. The heels of his shiny black shoes clicked across the marble floor, and then he waited for us with a smile while we caught up to him and boarded the elevator. An older gentleman, the elevator operator, greeted us all. "What floor, Luther?" he asked the bellboy.

"Three," was the reply. "And Carl, you don't have to wait for me to go down. I'll take the stairs."

When we arrived at the two adjacent doors, Luther looked at us questioningly. "Which bags go in which rooms?" he asked.

"Doesn't matter," Curtis said. "We'll sort 'em out later."

"We get a lot of entertainers staying here," Luther said.

His youthful face didn't strike me as one of such wisdom as to determine that Curtis, Andy and Cheechee were entertainers; we had not indicated that fact to anyone here, yet. I threw the bellboy a curious glance.

As if he read my mind, as if the question were clearly printed on my forehead, he replied, "The saxophone... and I overheard you asking about a piano for practice."

I grinned and let out a little chuckle as I dug in my pocket for a tip. "You should be a detective," I said, and then I put the fifty cents in his hand.

"Thank you," he said appreciatively. "My name is Luther. You fellows need anything at all... you just call down to the desk and ask for me."

"We will, Luther," I replied, and then with a big smile on his face Luther turned and headed for the stairs. *Luther is alright* I thought. His friendliness wasn't faked like the desk clerk; it seemed quite genuine and energetic. I liked him already.

It was quite a change for us occupying hotel rooms among all those other people when we had been used to the seclusion and privacy of our house. But the transition from St. Louis to La Crosse had involved lesser accommodations during the last several days and nights, so the sight of comfortable beds was rather inviting.

"Do you miss St. Louis yet?" I asked Curtis while we were getting settled in our room.

"I was afraid that I would," Curtis said. "But I don't... not yet, anyway. Do you?"

I didn't have to think about that. "Not in the least," I re-plied. "I feel more at home here than I *ever* did in St. Louis."

"In a *hotel?*"

"Well... not in this hotel... but in this town is what I mean."

"How long did you live here?" Curtis asked.

"Jesse and Luke and I were here only for a few weeks, and the only home we knew here, then, was a couple of staterooms aboard the boat that we eventually owned. But I liked the town then."

"It does seem to be a nice town," Curtis said. "I'm anxious to see some more of it."

"Well, I hope you don't expect to find a city like St. Louis out there," I said. "It ain't nothin' like St. Louis."

"What's so different about it?"

"First of all, it's much smaller... ain't no thirty-story skyscrapers."

"But I saw streetcars," Curtis said. "Town's big enough for streetcars."

"Yeah, and you might even see a traffic jam now and then, too, but it still ain't like St. Louis."

"Well, it doesn't matter," Curtis conceded. "I think I'll still like it. It has a good feel."

"That's what I always thought, too."

"Then, why didn't you ever come back here 'til now?"

"The river," I said. "The Mississippi is a lot friendlier to boats south from St. Louis. Up here there's snags and sandbars and rapids and shallow water that make navigation more difficult. We didn't have enough experience running a boat on the Upper River... too dangerous... so we just kept running south."

"Oh. I guess that makes sense. So, now that you're here, what d'ya think you'll do?"

"Well, for starters, I'll be your tour guide and show the Gaslight Knights around town. You need to find places to play, don't you?"

"Sure. That's why we left St. Louis... to find new places."

There was a knock on our door. Curtis happened to be closer, so he opened the door to let in Andy and Cheechee.

"How's your room?" I asked.

"Just like this one... it's great," Cheechee said.

"Any good restaurants near?" Andy asked.

I looked at my watch. It was 4:30 and we hadn't eaten since mid morning. "There *was* a place just down the street from here... had a funny name that I can't remember... I think it starts with *B*."

"Well, let's go find the place that starts with *B*. I'm starved."

The *Bodega* was only a couple of blocks away on Fourth Street. Although we were all keyed up after traveling and finally arriving at our planned destination, we decided to postpone any further exploration until the next day. It felt good to sit and relax, eat hamburgers and drink beer, discussing things that were important, and some that were not, just like we had always done at the *Dixie* in St. Louis. Tomorrow we would find post cards to send to those we thought should know of our whereabouts and well-being; and maybe we should write a letter to Leo Majors at the *St. Louis Post Dispatch*, so that he might write back to let us know the outcome of the Tony Delaware situation. There were places to go and things to see and pictures to take, and the Gaslight Knights could begin their quest to determine if Shakespeare was correct in saying that the whole world is a stage.

After a couple of hours, several hamburgers, and a few more beers, we declared that the *Bodega* was our "*Dixie* of the North."

78

A ndy and Cheechee found another piano early the next morning that the desk clerk obviously had forgotten to mention. In one corner on the second floor was a sumptuous parlor for use by any and all hotel guests and visitors, and adjoining it was a music room. These rooms were large and elegantly furnished, and could have easily accommodated parties with live entertainment. Rich-looking original oil paintings graced the walls, fine carpet covered the floor, and velvet drapes adorned the windows.

"It was actually Luther who told us about it," Andy explained. "The desk clerk prob'ly didn't tell us about it because it's close to a suite that's rented to a permanent resident... didn't want us disturbing him at odd hours."

After we ate breakfast in the hotel dining room, I left Andy, Cheechee and Curtis to their practice session in the Crystal Room and went in search for Luther. He was the only acquaintance I had made, so far, and he seemed like he would willingly help me with a few questions. Though I had spent some time in La Crosse, it was five years ago, and I knew some things would have changed.

The hotel buzzed with activity that morning, people coming and going. Luther was busy helping several people with luggage, and what I gathered from their conversation, they were in a hurry to get to the train depot. But I had all the time in the world, so I found a comfy chair in the lobby and waited until the bellboy was free. When it appeared that the guests seeking the railroad station were safely on their way, and Luther was finally getting a breather, I sauntered over to him near the front entrance. "Excuse me... Luther?" I said.

He immediately turned toward me, acknowledged me with a genuine smile and a unique nod that included a casual two-fingered salute—nothing mechanical or rehearsed. Perhaps he had practiced it a million times, but he had mastered it so well, it looked nothing but natural. "Yes, sir," he said. "What can I do for you, Mr. Madison?"

I was impressed; he remembered my name. I wondered if that, too, was stamped on my forehead, but I finally conceded all the credit to Luther. "First of all," I replied. "You don't have to call me *Mr. Madison*. If I'm gonna call you Luther, then I'd prefer that you call me *Will*."

Luther grinned. "Sure, I'd like that." And then he leaned in closer to me and lowered his voice. "But if Mr. Elliot is anywhere near, please understand that I'll have to call you *Mr. Madison*. That's *his* rule."

"Okay," I said. "I can live with that."

"So, what else can I help you with, *Will*?"

"Well, maybe you can answer a few questions... if you have the time."

"Sure. I'll try."

"Do you, by any chance, know a fellow named Lester Collins? He worked in a bank here in La Crosse about five years ago. When the banks closed, he came to work as the clerk on our riverboat. But I think he came back to La Crosse last fall... said he'd try to get his old job back."

Luther thought a moment. "I was only thirteen years old five years ago... didn't know too many people in banks then. You worked on a riverboat?"

"Me and my brother *owned* one. It burned at the St. Louis harbor last fall. That's why Lester is back here, but I don't know which bank."

"Hmmm. There are several banks in this town, but the name doesn't ring any bells. But I could certainly try to find out for you... maybe someone else here knows him. Your boat burned?"

"Yeah... total loss. The boat tied up next to it caught on fire, and when it was all over, ours and four other boats were destroyed, too."

"Sounds terrible," Luther said sympathetically.

"Yeah, it was quite a shock to all of us."

"So you gave up on the riverboats?"

"My brother and our other partner—he was our pilot—got jobs right away on another boat, a barge tow. But I decided to wait a while."

"And you joined a band."

"Oh! No... I'm not in the band. That's Andy and Curtis and Cheechee... they're the musicians."

"So what do *you* do?"

"I got started in photography... my brother's wife taught me. She has a studio in St. Louis."

"And you're looking for a job here?"

Another of my questions that must have been emblazoned on my forehead; Luther was quite perceptive. "Well, sort of... I guess I wouldn't turn one down. I think we'll be in La Crosse for a while."

"I know a lot of people," Luther said. "I'll ask around for you... Mr. Madison." His gaze fell upon the front desk where a dignified gentleman beside the desk clerk scanned the hotel register. I assumed that he must be John Elliot, the hotel owner.

"Who are those musicians playing in the Crystal Room?" he asked the clerk.

"Hotel guests, Mr. Elliot. I gave them permission to use the piano. Are they disturbing the other guests?"

My heart sank. For the moment I feared that Andy, Curtis and Cheechee were off to a bad start.

"No," replied Mr. Elliot. "They're not bothering anyone. Have you heard them?"

"No, sir, I haven't."

"Well, you should go give a listen."

"Why, sir? Are they that bad?"

"Bad? Heavens! No! They're that good! Are they performing somewhere in town?"

"I don't know, sir. They never said."

"Well, find out what you can... and then let me know." Mr. Elliot strode away, apparently in a hurry to get somewhere. On his way out, he paused and cordially greeted the bellboy. "Good morning, Luther," he said, and then he brushed some lint from Luther's shoulder. "Everything okay this morning?"

"Good morning, Mr. Elliot. Yes, everything is just fine."

"How's your mother? She feeling better?"

"Yes, sir, much better. She just had a touch of flu, but she's much better now."

"That's good. You tell her hello from me, okay?"

"Thank you, sir... I will."

Mr. Elliot acknowledged my presence with a friendly smile and a nod. "Good morning," he said to me, and then he went out the door. As I saw it, he was not only in tune with running a successful hotel; he was very much in tune with his employees, as well. His interaction with Luther didn't appear as just a show for my benefit.

"Mr. Elliot runs a tight ship," Luther said to me. "But he's a really decent man, too."

"I could tell," I said. "But I hope he wasn't upset about Andy and Curtis practicing."

"I don't think so," Luther responded. "I think he liked what he heard, and he probably wants to go where they're performing so he can hear some more. They *are* playing somewhere in town, aren't they? That's why they're here, isn't it?"

"Well, yeah, that's why they're here, but they haven't actually booked any dates yet."

"Oh. You came all the way from St. Louis without—"

"Yeah, it's kind of a long story why we left St. Louis, and I'll be happy to tell you sometime, but for now, do you know any places where they could play?"

Luther pondered a moment. "Well, there's the *Rivoli Theater* across the street... and the *Avalon Ballroom*... yes, there's lots of places in the area."

"That's great," I replied. "They'll be glad to hear that."

Another wave of people checking out of the hotel started gathering in the lobby. Luther excused himself; "I'll see you again later," he said, and then he went to assist an elderly woman with her luggage.

79

A dozen picture post cards, a new notebook for Cheechee, envelopes, and a box of pencils were in the bag we carried from the *Woolworth's*. It was late enough in the afternoon that we thought hamburgers and beer were in order, and after all, we had to walk right past our *Dixie of the North* to get back to the hotel. We had covered most of the downtown blocks, looking in store windows, and browsing through some. I took pictures of Andy, Curtis and Cheechee in Riverside Park with the big, bronze Spanish-American War cannon behind them. Now it was time to sit down, rest our tired feet, and fill our bellies.

"What should we say in the letter to Leo?" Curtis asked as he took out a pencil and tore a sheet of paper from Cheechee's new notebook.

"Tell him the Gaslight Knights are on tour," Cheechee said.

"And we're having a wonderful time here in Wisconsin," Andy added.

"And then..." I said, "...ask him if he would please write back with any developments on Tony's situation."

By the time Curtis had finished the letter to Leo, he had written a whole page; he obviously had some of his own ideas to include, too. We all signed it at the bottom.

"I have his home address," Curtis said. "I'll send it there instead of the newspaper office. Then we know he'll get it."

While we were all in the letter-writing mood, we scribed messages on a few post cards, too, just as we had promised to do. Sadie and Beth, especially, would certainly enjoy getting four different picture post cards— one from each of us. We figured that would make up for the five-day, four-hundred-mile trip, during which time we sent none. A different desk clerk was on duty when we finally arrived back at the *Stoddard*; he cheerfully dispensed the necessary postage stamps and offered to put our cards and letters in the outgoing mail to be picked up the next morning.

This place made me feel so good; it was as if I had come home after a lengthy visit away. Even though this wasn't my actual hometown, it gave me a feeling of comfort and security, and for that I could not think of any explanation. Other than this is where my new life on the river began. Other than it was a long ways from St. Louis—where the police had probably, by now, knocked on the front door of our empty house several times. I didn't know why I was so concerned about that. Tony's trouble didn't involve any of us, besides him showing up on our doorstep while his trail was cooling off. Yet, it still made me nervous to think the cops would come asking questions and snooping through our house, aware that Tony had been there soon after he killed Johnny.

But there was more to it than that; for quite some time an apprehension was growing somewhere inside me that concerned the lifestyle Andy and I had fallen into. Andy's music career was important to him, not that it was the problem. It was the other activity that surrounded it. Our association with the Knights of the Square Table was where it all started, although some good things came from that as well—Cheechee and Curtis—without them, Andy might not be as far advanced in the entertainment world as he was now. And of course, Leo Majors had made it possible for me to rub elbows with Keith Blake, the *St. Louis Post* reporter/photographer, who had given me some good pointers. But we had been introduced to the temptations the underworld offered, too, and neither   Andy nor I could deny partaking of its pleasures. Fortunately, though, we recognized the rough waters we were sailing, and just in time we found a life boat, and paddled back to shore before the ship went down. It was clear to me, now, that the Tony Delaware incident was the catalyst that propelled us away— *our excuse to leave St. Louis*—and we managed to take Curtis and Cheechee with us.

The next morning after breakfast, I settled into the reading room just off to the side of the main lobby. Their library contained one of the old classics I had always intended to read but never did. So I made myself comfortable with *The Count of Monte Cristo* while the other guys practiced in the Crystal Room. I was just getting a vision of the three-mast sailing ship slowly coming into port when a voice speaking my name beckoned me back to reality. "Will? Excuse me. Sorry to interrupt your reading."

I glanced up from the book to find a snazzy green uniform standing there. "Oh! Hi, Luther," I said, glad to see him. "You ain't botherin' me a bit."

"Thought you might like to know... I found out where your Lester Collins works. The night desk clerk knows him."

"Great," I said. "Where?"

"The State Bank, over on Main. It's just a couple of blocks."

"Thanks, Luther! I'll go over there to see him."

Luther pulled out a pocket watch. "It's only eight o'clock," he said. "Bank doesn't open 'til nine." Then, as if something had jogged his memory he said, "Say, by the way, if you ran a boat on the Mississippi River, did you ever run across an old guy... Augie Bjornson? He had a boat... stayed here when he came to town. I met him when my mom used to work here."

I couldn't believe what Luther had just asked me. "Well, yeah, Luther. I knew Augie quite well. It was *his* boat my brother and I acquired."

"Really? Whatever happened to him? He hasn't been here for years."

"Augie died about three or four years ago," I said. "We buried him in St. Charles, Missouri. That was his home."

Luther's face turned somber. "Oh. I'm sorry to hear that. He was a nice old man."

"He got to be just like a grandfather to me," I said. "He stayed on with us for about a year as our pilot... taught us everything we needed to know."

"He used to tell me sailing stories," Luther said, far-away reminiscence in his tone. "I really liked that old guy."

"Yeah, Augie was special." For just a moment I felt the need to fight back a tear, and then I moved on. Perhaps Luther and I had another mutual acquaintance. "If you knew Augie," I said, "maybe you know another good friend from the river. He used to stay here, too, and he invited me and my brother to dinner here one night... a long time ago."

"What's his name?" Luther asked.

"He's a gambler... goes by Spades Morgan."

Now it was Luther's turn to be amazed. He smiled, almost in disbelief. "Sure, I know Mr. Morgan," he said. "He comes here several times every summer. I haven't yet seen him this year though."

"Last I heard," I replied, "He was headed to New Orleans on the *Goldenrod*."

"Sounds like Mr. Morgan. Then he should be here sometime soon. How do you know him?"

"Well," I said and leaned back in my chair. "Spades Morgan is the only reason me and Jesse became the owners of a riverboat, but that's a long story. D'ya really think he'll be here soon?"

"You can count on it. And I want to hear the story."

"I'll tell you sometime... when you have time. But there's one other thing I should tell you about Spades now."

Luther eyed me curiously. "What's that?"

"Andy? The piano player? Spades Morgan is his dad."

Just then, Cheechee came in carrying his new notebook and pencils. "Hi," he said to me, and then he acknowledged the bellboy. "Hi, Luther."

"Good morning, Mr. Chapman."

Wow, I thought. *Luther is good. He remembers everybody's names.* "Done practicing for today?" I asked Cheechee.

"No... Andy and Curtis are working out some new music, and they don't need me buggin' them right now." He sat down at a reading table and opened the notebook. "I'm gonna catch up on some writing."

"I'll see you gentlemen later," Luther said, and he hustled off to help someone with their luggage.

80

For the second time in one day I got that *"I can't believe it"* look. The last time I had seen Lester Collins was the day he completed all the paperwork for our insurance claim when the Madison burned in St. Louis last year. He took off his wire-rimmed glasses and stepped from behind his desk. "Will Madison!" he said. "What... why..." he stammered as he shook my hand.

"The bellboy at the hotel told me where to find you," I said.

"Is Jesse here, too?" Lester asked.

"No. He and Luke are on one of Continental's barge tows... they're prob'ly somewhere between St. Louis and New Orleans right now."

"And you? What are you doing now?" Lester asked.

I explained to Lester that Sadie had taught me photography and photo developing skills, and that I was trying to be a photographer, but so far, since I left Sadie's studio, I hadn't been working.

"Then, what brings you to La Crosse?" Lester asked.

"Andy has a jazz band now... well, it's just a trio, actually, and I'm traveling with them."

"Andy? Andy Lorado? He's here, too?" How long will you be in La Crosse?"

"If they can find plenty of places to play, we'll prob'ly stay all summer."

"Where are you staying?"

"For now, the Stoddard Hotel," I said. "How 'bout you, Lester? How've you been?"

"Oh, I'm just fine. Got my old job back and everything's just fine. I'll bet you miss that old boat. I sure do."

"Yeah, I do..." Lester and I talked for the better part of an hour reminiscing old times aboard the Madison, and catching up on events since. I told Lester about the mess in St. Louis involving Tony Delaware, that being one of the reasons we came north. I told him, too, about Andy and Curtis opening the show for Benny Goodman last January at the *Arcadia* in St. Louis.

"Benny Goodman! Wow!" Lester exclaimed. "They must be good!"

"They are, Lester. They're *very* good," I said. "St. Louis loved them. Now they just need someplace to get them started here."

"Do they have a name? They *must* have a name."

"They call themselves the Gaslight Knights."

Lester held up one index finger, indicating that he wanted me to wait for something, I did not know what. He returned to his desk and picked up the telephone receiver. A few moments later he spoke: "Mary, this is Lester Collins. Would you please get John Elliot at the Stoddard on the line for me? Thank you."

Apparently, Lester knew a few ins and outs around La Crosse, including influential people.

"Hello, John? Lester Collins here... Fine, thank you, and you?... Glad to hear it. John, the reason I'm calling, you have some young gentlemen staying at your hotel. Fine musicians. I happen to know one of them personally, Andy Lorado... oh... you've heard them practicing in the Crystal Room?... well, then you know what I'm talking about. Andy was the piano player on a Mississippi riverboat, and his group has been a show opener for Benny Goodman... yes, they *are* available... yes, I'll have their manager get in touch with you... Thank you, John. Good bye." Lester hung up the receiver. "There. Andy has his foot in the door with the owner of the Stoddard... and I'll call the managers of the *Rivoli* and the *Avalon*... and maybe *Carroll's Place* in La Crescent. I know them all."

"But you told him their manager would get in touch. They don't have a manager."

"Will..." Lester said leaning over his desk toward me with a sly smile. "*You* are their manager."

"Me? But I wouldn't know what to say."

"Just tell John that you represent the Gaslight Knights, and that they would like to negotiate for a night of entertainment at the hotel. Then John will ask you some questions, and all you do is answer them... simple."

"What if I don't know the answers?"

"You and Andy have been working and playing together for a long time,

Will. I think you know him better than his own mother knows him. Talk it over with him and his music partners first, and all the answers will come. And whatever their regular fee is for a night... double it when you talk to John. Trust me. He pays well for *good* entertainment."

Lester had a way of pumping up my confidence; I was eager to get back to the hotel to talk this over with Andy, Curtis, and Cheechee. I had never mentioned to them about the conversation between the desk clerk and Mr. Elliot I overheard the day before, but now it was a must. I had already experienced a very brief encounter with John Elliot, and I was confident that he was a person I could easily talk to... no different than any of the high-society people that traveled on the Madison.

I almost forgot the real reason for my visit to the bank. "Lester," I said. "I need someplace safe to keep my money."

Lester grinned. "Well, a bank is as safe as it gets," he said.

81

Just a little past noon I flew through the Stoddard Hotel front entrance. Luther was talking to the desk clerk. He saw me coming and met me half-way across the lobby. "Hi, Will. You're looking for Andy, Curtis and Cheechee," he said.

How could he possibly know everything I was going to ask, before I asked? I was definitely going to check my forehead in a mirror first chance I got. There *had* to be something printed on it! "Yeah, I am, Luther," I said. "D'ya know where they are?"

"They said if I saw you, to tell you they were going to the Dixie... said you'd know what I mean."

"Thanks, Luther," I said. "I hafta run right now, but can I talk to you later?"

"Sure... I'll be here 'til six."

The Bodega—our *Dixie* of the North—was moderately busy with noontime diners, but the Knights must have been lucky because they were sitting at our usual table by the window. "Okay," I said as I sat down. "I am your manager now."

They stared at me with weird and wonderful expressions; I wasn't sure if they were merely amused or if they thought I had fallen and bumped my head.

"I just talked to Lester Collins at the bank," I started to explain.

"You talked to Lester?" Andy said, surprised. "He's here?"

"Yeah... he came back to his old job at the bank."

"Who's Lester Collins?" Cheechee asked.

"He was our clerk on the riverboat," Andy explained.

"He handled all the money and the paperwork... and all the legal business for us," I added.

"And I would imagine," Andy said, "that it was Lester who got the insurance payoff for you, too."

"Yes, as a matter of fact," I replied. "He did that, too."

"So," Curtis joined in. "What does all this have to do with you suddenly becoming our manager? I don't mind, but five minutes ago we didn't have one."

"How much do you usually get for playing one night?" I asked Curtis.

"Thirty to forty-five... depending on the place."

"What would you say to *ninety* dollars for *one* night in the Crystal Room?"

"I'd say halleluiah!... manager."

"Ninety dollars!" Cheechee said. "When do we go on?"

"We have to talk to Mr. Elliot," I said. "But from what I heard of the telephone conversation Lester had with him a little while ago, you're as good as in."

"But he doesn't even know who we are," Andy said. "He's never heard us play."

"Yes, he has," I said. "He heard you practicing yesterday morning. I overheard him asking the desk clerk about you."

"When do we talk to Mr. Elliot?" Cheechee asked.

"Just as soon as I can arrange a meeting," I replied. "And I think Luther will help me with that."

Curtis stared at me with an evil eye and a quirky grin. "Does this mean we have to pay you?"

82

Feeling so satisfied, knowing that he had helped me locate Lester Collins, Luther was even more eager to arrange my meeting with Mr. Elliot. That meeting turned out to be a lot less formal than I had expected, and with pleasantly surprising results. John Elliot was truly impressed with the sampling he had heard while the Knights were practicing, and he liked the advertising opportunity of presenting a group that had opened the show for Benny Goodman. I laid out on the table several of my best pictures I took of them performing on various theater stages and dance halls in St. Louis. He said he would have *Inland Printing* make some advertising posters, using one of my photographs.

I went back up to my room where I was certain Andy, Cheechee and Curtis would be waiting. When I entered, Cheechee sat at the writing desk with pencil applied to notebook; Curtis and Andy sat in armchairs on either side of the window. All three jumped to their feet. "Well?" they all said in unison. The little devil sitting on my shoulder told me this would be a good time to have some fun. Without saying a word, I stepped over to the bed closest to them and sat down.

"Well?" Andy said again. "Did you get us the ninety dollars for one night?"

"No," I replied, shaking my head, trying to look serious. I saw how forlorn they all instantly appeared, as if they had been whipped. I almost felt bad for them, their feeling of rejection having such an impact. The little angel sitting on my other shoulder told me I couldn't let it go on.

"I got you one-seventy-five for *two* nights," I said calmly with a straight face.

It seemed like only a second or two had passed when all three pounced on top of me; I thought they were going to break the bed. Obviously, they were delighted.

When they finally eased up on the playful rough-housing, I continued with the full report. "Mr. Elliot is having handbills and posters printed advertising The Gaslight Knights from St. Louis, Missouri performing in the Crystal Room for your dining and dancing pleasure, Friday and Saturday night, June twenty-eighth and twenty-ninth, eight to midnight."

"He's printing posters?" Cheechee said.

"Yeah. He took one of my photos of you on stage in St. Louis... it'll be on the poster, too."

"Twenty-eighth," Curtis said. "That's *two weeks* from tonight. We'd better find a cheaper place to stay."

"Got that covered, too," I said. "If we all move into one room, he'll give us the monthly rate... which is about half of the regular price. And he'll arrange for you to use the music room on the second floor for rehearsals every afternoon if you want... it can be closed off, so it'll be private."

The three of them milled the information around and mumbled amongst themselves for about a minute.

"One other thing," I said.

They all stared at me with question marks in their eyes.

"John told me that if La Crosse likes your music, you can play in the Wisconsin Lounge one or two nights a week, thirty dollars a night... sort of like a house band... but that'll be after the twenty-ninth."

"How much better can it get?" Curtis said cheerfully.

"Does that mean you're going to pay me?" I said with a   devilish grin.

83

Within a few days a big, colorful, hand-painted poster on an easel sat at the front entrance of the Stoddard; it announced the two-night show of musical entertainment featuring The Gaslight Knights; dinner seating reservations were recommended. A couple of days later, smaller posters started appearing in windows all over town displaying my photo of the Knights on a St. Louis stage, and boasting "the opening act for St. Louis Benny Goodman Show; Dinner reservations recommended; dancing 8:00—midnight, Friday & Saturday, June 28th & 29th." John Elliot was certainly doing a fine job of promoting the upcoming performance. A week before the show, Luther told me that dinner reservations were sold out for both nights, and there had been three requests from other clubs for booking information. They turned out to be the places Lester Collins had mentioned to me; he must've called them like he said he would. Andy, Curtis and Cheechee were already becoming a hot number, and they hadn't even performed one show in La Crosse yet. The only music they had made was behind closed doors during their afternoon practice sessions. Of course, there had been a few curious people listening at that closed door from time to time.

When Curtis saw so many window posters, and then heard of the sell-out crowd, he suggested that they should find a good men's clothing store and get new matching shirts—"Something really nice," he said. Cheechee and Andy fully agreed without hesitation, and off they went. About two hours later, they returned to the hotel room, all smiles, carrying their bundles of new show wardrobe.

Everything was going along just great.

Almost too great, I thought.

I had experienced feelings like that before—like at any moment a wet, muddy dog would run into the room and shake itself dry all over the new carpet. But I didn't want to cause any concern for Andy, Cheechee and Curtis, so I just kept those thoughts to myself and hoped that I was wrong.

Cheechee and Andy had moved into our room because it was a little larger. We had shared our habitat long enough in St. Louis that the closer quarters here did not present any discomfort; there was nothing we needed to hide from each other. But within a couple of days we discovered the necessity to "spread out" once in a while—to flex our muscles in our own space.

I had found a good friend in Luther, the bellboy. Whenever he had time off—evenings, mostly—we would go to the *Bodega*, eat hamburgers, drink beer, and talk for hours on end. It was then that I explained why we called the *Bodega "our Dixie of the North."* Luther said he hoped to travel sometime and see the country, and if he ever made it to St. Louis, he would surely visit the *Dixie Sandwich Shop* at Sixth and Pine.

I told him, too, the story I had promised to tell about how Spades Morgan had saved Augie's riverboat, and how that boat came to be the legal property of Jesse and me. Naturally, one story led to another, and another. The more I told, the more Luther wanted to hear. So I kept telling him stories about life on a riverboat, about St. Charles, St. Louis, the adventures Andy and I had shared... until the *Bodega* waitresses kicked us out at closing time.

Curtis ventured out on his own, too, exploring La Crosse and the surrounding area in his red Pontiac. He'd tell me about places that even I didn't know. Of course, he had the advantage of reaching farther distances with his car, so he was able to become familiar with a much larger territory than I ever had. He found the *Avalon Ballroom* in La Crosse, and *Carroll's Place* across the river in La Crescent, both clubs having already booked the Gaslight Knights to perform for Saturday night dances. He'd been to North La Crosse, Onalaska, Holmen and West Salem, and found more dance halls and clubs, nearly every one picking a date for the Knights to play. Curtis was definitely not letting this trip go to waste.

Andy and Cheechee frequently wandered over the bridge to the beach on Barron's Island. For as long as I had known him, swimming had always been second nature to Andy, and it seemed Cheechee was rapidly adapting to that as well. Andy had always enjoyed hiking, listening to the "earth's music," as he called all the sounds of nature. Cheechee had been introduced to all of that by his father long ago, too. Their personal interests—far beyond that of performing their music—seemed to just blend together.

We were all content and happy in La Crosse. And so far, no wet, muddy dogs.

84

Thursday, June 27th. One day before the Gaslight Knights made their big debut in La Crosse. I'd guess I was more nervous about that appearance than they were. They were good musicians, an excellent combination of talent, well-rehearsed with a repertoire of popular old and new tunes that people loved. I admired their confidence in themselves that kept them in perfect step... and calm.

Late that afternoon the Knights were up in the music room on the second floor for the last practice session before the weekend shows. Once more, I got comfortable in the main lobby reading room with *The Count of Monte Cristo*. Once more, a few pages later, the snazzy green uniform stood beside me.

"Ah-hem," Luther got my attention. "Sorry to bother you."

"It's okay, Luther. Really."

"There's someone here to see you," Luther said.

"Who?" I asked. I expected it to be another club owner wanting to book the Knights for a performance; I had already talked to several.

"Well, he didn't' ask for you in particular, but I know you'll want to see him."

I put the book down on the table and followed Luther to the main lobby.

"Will!" I heard a familiar voice call out. "I'd never guess in a hundred years that I would see y'all here!"

Even though Luther had said Spades Morgan would show up soon, I wasn't expecting such a breathtaking surprise. "Spades!" I blurted out and hastened my step to accept a hug and a handshake. I hadn't seen Spades for nearly a year. He hadn't changed much, but Spades *never* seemed to change or age. The only thing that ever changed was the color of his suit; today it was blue.

"Luther said you'd be here sometime soon," I said. "It's so good to see you... I'm really glad you're here... how long will you stay?"

"Don't know. Never know how long I'll stay in one place. Y'all know that, Will. But I see Andrew and the boys are performing here this weekend." He pointed to the colorful sign just inside the front entrance. "That's quite a surprise...wasn't expecting that, either."

"It was a rather quick decision to leave St. Louis," I explained. "And this is where we decided to go."

"Well, I'm glad you did," Spades said. "Where's Andrew? Is he here now?"

"Yeah, they're up in the parlor on the second floor practicing. Have you heard them play yet?"

"I caught one of their shows in St. Louis this spring... if y'all could call that a *show*. It was at a saloon."

"*That* was one of the reasons they wanted to get out of St. Louis for a while." I went on to explain how the Knights had been accosted in the parking lot at a bar where they had just played. Spades' poker face, as usual, showed no emotion, but I could tell that he was concerned. "But we're here now, and their first big show is tomorrow night in the Crystal Room. "You'll be here, won't you?"

"I couldn't miss something that important," Spades said.

"Oh! But Luther told me both shows are sold out. You might not get a seat for dinner. *I don't even have one.*"

"Don't worry about that, Will." Spades winked. "I know the owner of the hotel... *and* I know someone in the band. I'll get a seat... for both of us. Now, let's go upstairs and pay Andrew a surprise visit." He retrieved something from his pocket and then extended his hand toward Luther. "Thank you, Luther, for bringing me such a pleasant welcoming gift."

I heard the money jingle as it changed hands.

"The pleasure is mine, Mr. Morgan," Luther responded. "I'll take your suitcase up to your room for you."

As Morgan and I strolled to the elevator, he said, "I like Luther. He always takes good care of me when I'm here."

"I like him, too," I said.

Spades had stayed at the *Stoddard* so many times over the years that he knew exactly where to find the second floor parlor and music room. Andy's eyes widened and the piano abruptly stopped producing sound; he sprang up from the bench and quickly met us at the door. Andy had visited his dad recently in St. Charles, but it was still clearly a joyous moment now, too. Curtis and Cheechee knew of Spades, but they had met him only once, just briefly in a dark, noisy barroom in St. Louis. I doubt that they recognized him, and they were somewhat baffled as to the affection Andy displayed toward him.

"I didn't mean to disrupt your rehearsal," Spades said. "I just wanted to let y'all know I'm here."

"You're not disrupting anything," Andy responded. "We do this every day, so it's kind of routine. Will you be here for our show tomorrow night?"

"Sure, I'll be here. It's quite an unexpected surprise that I should find y'all here, so far away from St. Louis."

"Well, Dad," Andy said. "It was Will's idea to come here, and now we have quite a few dates set to play at clubs and dance halls... so we like it here."

"That's good, Andrew. La Crosse is a nice place."

By then, Cheechee and Curtis had joined us at the door, too; they had finally realized Morgan's identity.

"Good to see you again, Mr. Morgan," Cheechee said with his charming smile and a handshake.

"Now I don't remember..." Spades said. "One of y'all is Curtis, and one is Christopher—"

"I'm Christopher; this is Curtis."

"Hello, Mr. Morgan," Curtis said as he offered his hand.

"Boys... I'm looking forward to your show."

"I'll guarantee you, sir," Curtis said, "that this will be a much better performance than you saw in St. Louis."

"I'm sure it will," Spades replied. "That was just a hole-in-the-wall saloon; the *Stoddard Crystal Room* is a pretty high-class place. Now, I'm going to leave y'all to your rehearsal and go up to my room. But I want y'all to join me for supper tonight. My treat. Seven o'clock okay?"

We all nodded our approval.

"Good," Morgan said. "I'll reserve a table. Meet me in the lobby at seven."

Out in the corridor I said to Spades: "I am supposed to meet Luther at the *Bodega* tonight for supper, but I'll see you tomorrow night. I don't want to disappoint Luther."

"Nonsense," Spades replied. "Have Luther join us, too... if that's okay with you."

"Sure, it's okay. I'll ask him."

When Spades and I parted, I immediately went down to the lobby to find Luther.

"You're here to tell me that you can't meet me at the *Bodega* tonight," he said before I could say anything.

How did he know that? I thought.

"*This time*, Luther, you are only *partly* right."

He seemed stunned—but pleased—that Spades had invited him to join us for supper, and I was glad that he accepted the invitation. Luther probably didn't realize, yet, that he had become one of those "very special friends" to Will Madison.

85

L uther always wore street clothes when we met at the *Bodega* several times, and that was usually faded blue jeans and a T-shirt, but I had never seen him in anything but his snazzy green bellboy uniform at the *Stoddard*. So he looked quite dapper in a crisp white shirt and pressed black trousers. But when we sat down at the reserved table for six in the dining room, Luther seemed a little uneasy.

"What's wrong?" I asked discretely. "You look nervous."

"I'm not nervous," he replied, glancing around the room. "It's just that I feel a little out of place... I've never been here as a regular customer before."

"Never?"

"Never."

"Well, just relax," I reassured him. "You're with us tonight. You're not at work, and I want you to enjoy every minute."

"Luther," Spades Morgan intervened. "Will y'all be working tomorrow night during the show?"

"No, sir. I get off at six tomorrow."

"Well, then," Spades said. "Would you and your mom like to join Will and me at our table for dinner and fine music?" He looked at me. "Y'all don't mind, do you, Will?"

"Heavens, no, I don't mind," I said. "In fact, I'd like that. Did you get a table reserved for tomorrow night?"

"Of course I got a table. I know the owner... remember?" Then he looked back to Luther. "How 'bout it, Luther?"

"Sure. I'd love to see the show, and I'm sure Mom would, too. I'll see if she wants to come."

"Y'all just tell her that I insist," Spades said.

"I'll tell her," Luther replied. "And I'm sure she'll be happy to see you again. It's been a long time... last year."

I had not yet met Luther's mom, so this meant that I would be sharing a dinner table with a total stranger. But Spades Morgan would not invite an undesirable person to dinner, and after all, this was Luther's mom.

It was good to visit with Spades again after all this time. He filled us in on his recent travels, which amounted to just a little more than the usual riverboat stops up and down the Mississippi. But steamboats carrying passengers on the Mississippi were on a drastic decline. Spades had arrived on the *St. Paul*, but because he would be staying in La Crosse for Andy's weekend show, he wouldn't be aboard when it departed the next morning. Waiting for another boat was nothing new to Spades, and he thought there would be nothing wrong with an extended stay in La Crosse. It was kind of reminiscent of five years ago, although now, we didn't have to make plans for Spades to win back a riverboat in a poker game.

He had all sorts of questions about Jesse and Luke, and about what I had been up to since the Madison fire. He was sad, of course, that the Madison was destroyed, and that another boat had not replaced it. That's where he thought we belonged, on an excursion boat, because our success had been so extraordinary, all things considered. Maybe Spades was right—and perhaps we would all still be together had I effectively convinced Jesse to pool our insurance money to buy another boat. But that didn't happen, so here I was, back in Wisconsin with some new friends, and with a new career lurking somewhere in the shadows.

Throughout the evening I couldn't help but notice that Cheechee associated with Spades so well. Perhaps the reason for it was simply his close relationship with Andy and he was seeking acceptance; or maybe he saw a father figure in Morgan, to fill that void in his life, just like I had done so long ago. But then again, Cheechee's charm was like a magnet to anyone he took a liking to, and he certainly seemed to know how to pick the right people. I was glad, too, that Spades was receptive, and there could be no doubt that he truly liked Cheechee.

"I've written a book," Cheechee told Spades amidst their conversation.

"A book?" Spades replied. "What's it about?"

Cheechee seemed so delighted that Spades displayed an interest. "A boy growing up in Denver, getting into a lot of trouble, and then running away to St. Louis to start a new life." But as he spoke, he gazed at Morgan with a little apprehension; he was not yet accustomed to Spades' poker face that seldom revealed any outward emotions.

"Well," Spades said. "Sounds like it might be about y'all."

Cheechee's face reddened a little. "Yes, sir, it might be."

"I like the idea," Spades said. "What's the title? Where can I get a copy?"

"Oh, it's never been made a book, yet, but I call it... *If I Could Steal the Stars.*"

"Not published? Well, I'd still like to read it anyway."

"I've read it," I said to Spades. I couldn't help myself from butting in. "I've read it, and it's very good. Cheechee is a good singer, but he's a good writer, too."

Cheechee seemed a little embarrassed by my observation. "I have the *only* copy up in our room," he said to Spades. "If you really want to read it..."

"Yes, by all means," Spades responded. "Get it to me tomorrow."

It seemed quite official; Spades had certainly accepted Cheechee. It remained to be seen, though, if he still felt the same way *after* he read *If I Could Steal the Stars*. But I couldn't think of a single reason why he wouldn't.

Luther had relaxed and was entirely at ease by the time we finished our meal. I knew he and Spades had been acquainted for quite some time, but I didn't know to what degree. It became more apparent to me as the evening went on—listening to their occasional conversation—that they were on a more personal level than I had realized. Luther had never let that show in the hotel lobby; there, when it came to the hotel guests, he was all business; but here, among friends, out of his snazzy green bellboy uniform, he could be himself.

It was Curtis who finally exercised good common sense and convinced us all that it was getting late; tomorrow would be a long day.

86

The Crystal Room would be a little different from many of the places the Knights had performed: no darkened theater atmosphere; no bright spotlights; no big stage—just a riser where the baby grand sat at one end of the ballroom, a large portion of which was populated with elegant white linen-covered tables. Suspended from the high ceiling by bronze chains, eight fabulous crystal chandeliers cast a comfortable glow evenly through the entire room.

They started serving dinner in the Crystal Room at six o'clock, but by seven-thirty no one was seated except those with eight o'clock reservations. Spades Morgan and I with my *Leica* camera hanging from my neck relaxed in a couple of comfy chairs in the hotel lobby when Luther and his mom arrived about 7:45. By then, there was quite a crowd gathered waiting to be seated in the Crystal Room, so in the congestion we didn't notice their entrance right away. Luther found us, and in no time at all, I understood why Spades had invited them. First of all, I saw an attractive, fortyish, dark-haired woman, who Spades spontaneously greeted: "Hello, Irene," and then initiated an affectionate embrace.

"Hi, Will," Luther said to me with a grin nearly as big as the lobby. "I'd like you to meet my mom. Mom?"

She turned toward us, still clinging to Morgan's arm.

"Mom, this is Will. Will, this is my mom, Irene."

I offered my hand. "Pleased to meet you, Ma'am."

"And I'm pleased to meet you, Will," she replied. "Luther has talked so much about you."

"I don't know why he would do that," I said jokingly. "I'm not much to talk about."

"Oh, quite the opposite," Irene said. "You and your brother owned a riverboat."

"Yes, ma'am. It was because of that riverboat that me and Mr. Morgan became such good friends."

"Oh, yes, I know," Irene said. "Spades told me all about the night he saved Augie's boat, and now I finally get to meet the young man he saved it for."

"Mom!" Luther said. "You never told me that you knew about that."

"You never asked... and besides, you were too young to be involved with such things as gambling."

"Mom! I was... I was..." Luther thought a moment. "I was thirteen!"

"Exactly," Irene said with a playful smile. "You were *only* thirteen."

Just then, another bellboy in an equally snazzy green uniform—just a smaller, younger version of Luther—approached Spades. "Mr. Morgan?" he said. "I'll be happy to show you to your table now."

"Well, thank you, Richie," Spades said. Apparently he was on a first name basis with everyone here. "Let's go."

Freckle-faced, red-haired Richie proudly led us to a table just to the left but near the riser with the piano. It looked as if the table had been added, and a few of the other tables had been squeezed together to make ample room. At the center of the table-for-four, beautifully set with silver, linen napkins, and crystal tumblers filled with ice water, sat a little sign that read: "V.I.P.—Morgan."

I looked around at the other tables to see what their little signs revealed; the ones I could see only had names, but no "V.I.P."

When Richie arrived at our table and turned to offer Spades and his guests their chairs, he curiously eyed Luther. "What are you doing here?" he whispered. "This is Mr. Morgan's table."

"I know," Luther said. "He invited me and my mom as his guests."

The redness didn't show so much among Richie's freckles, but I could sense the envy—his co-worker sitting at a table designated for *V.I.P.* But he cheerfully seated us, and went on his way to escort more diners to their tables.

We hadn't more than gotten comfortable when the blonde and brassy Minnie Woods, the very popular head waitress came to our table for our dinner order. A peroxide blonde long before it became fashionable to be one, Minnie was kind-hearted and well-liked by everyone, and she was familiarly known all around La Crosse as "Stoddard Minnie."

"Will, Luther," Spades said. "Order anything you want. This is my treat."

I ordered the roast beef, reminiscent of the dinner with Spades here five years ago. Luther ordered the same. Spades ordered the baked chicken for Irene and himself.

I was still somewhat in awe over the seemingly closeness of Spades and Irene, and then it dawned on me why Luther and Spades had seemed so closely acquainted the night before. Luther had not mentioned it in all of our conversation.

We were all engaged in small talk about the weather and the impressive turn-out for the show when an amplified voice filled the night. "Ladies and gentlemen, distinguished guests..."

I turned toward the stage to see John Elliott, the hotel owner at the microphone. I clicked off a picture. The room fell quiet; John continued. "Welcome to the Stoddard Hotel's Crystal Room. I hope you are enjoying your stay at the Stoddard, and your dinner as well. I hand-picked the musical entertainment you are about to hear... they were the opening performance for the Benny Goodman show in St. Louis earlier this year... and their music is truly magnificent. So, without further ado, please welcome Andy, Curtis, and Christopher... the *Gaslight Knights!*"

I was prepared to lead off the applause, to ensure there would be a warm welcome for the Knights, but seventy or eighty other people beat me to it. I watched as Andy, Curtis and Cheechee took their places. They had let me see their new outfits up in the hotel room, and I saw them again when Luther delivered them back from being pressed, but here, in this crystal light, their ruffle-fronted sapphire blue shirts and sharply-creased charcoal gray trousers gave them a striking air of royalty, the likes of which I had not seen before. I could tell by the gleam in their eyes and the way they glanced at each other that they were quite pleased with the friendly welcome they were receiving, and I couldn't help but think it would propel them into the greatest performance ever. I clicked off some more shots with my *Leica*. The applause hadn't yet stopped when Andy started playing his theme song, *Happy Days Are Here Again*. Curtis joined in with the tune, and because this was their usual opening instrumental only number, Cheechee briskly strolled among the tables, smiling and shaking hands with whoever offered one. Oh! What a charmer he was! I had never seen them open this way, but everyone loved it.

I'm not entirely sure that the applause had completely stopped by the time Andy and Curtis finished that first piece, and Cheechee came to the microphone. All I remember is the applause rising to a roar.

"Thank you, all," Cheechee said. When the applause finally died down, he continued. "We are the Gaslight Knights from St. Louis, Missouri... but tonight, we are going to make music for La Crosse, Wisconsin!"

More applause continued until Andy began the introduction bars for Cheechee's first song, *I Get a Kick Out of You*. Even after the plates of food started arriving at the tables, everyone took time out from eating to applaud at the end of each song. There could be no doubt; La Crosse had officially put its stamp of approval on the Gaslight Knights.

A couple of hours later, after the busboys had cleared the tables of dishes, and the waitresses were busy taking orders and delivering drinks around the room, the Knights returned to the stage after a short intermission. By then, the applause was more subdued, but still enthusiastic.

Andy addressed the crowd with the microphone this time. He introduced by name his musical partners and then himself. Then he continued: "There's a couple of *very special* people in the audience that I want to give some *very special* thanks."

The room became reasonably quiet; perhaps everyone was curious to see who would get the notable recognition.

"In the audience tonight," Andy said, "Is the man who put me on this earth. My father, Spades Morgan, is right over there." He pointed to our corner table. "I think he came all the way from New Orleans to see the show tonight. Wave to the people, Dad."

Spades rose from his chair, smiled and waved. The crowd clapped their recognition.

"And sitting right beside my dad," Andy went on, "Is one of the best friends I have ever known. He has stayed by me in good times and bad. He helped me launch my musical career aboard his riverboat, and if it wasn't for him, we wouldn't be here tonight. Will Madison ... wave to these fine people."

I was probably the most vivid shade of red that I could possibly imagine, but Andy had just made me feel about as good as I could ever remember, so I didn't care. I stood up and waved to the applauding crowd.

"I should mention, also..." Andy continued as the applause diminished. "... That Will was my very first music partner."

I could almost feel the curiosity bubbling up in the room.

"Will and I played piano duets together for the audiences on the riverboat excursions. They are quite entertaining. Would you like to hear one tonight... *La Crosse?*"

The room erupted instantly in clapping and cheering. It was easy to tell that this was a fun-loving crowd, and they were game for anything.

Andy coaxed me up to the piano, and even though we hadn't done this in a long time, much less, recently rehearsed, we went into our usual routine of me whining about the fact that I don't know how to play the piano, and him trying to convince me that it will be fun. We were already generating laughs and cheers from the audience.

I sat down on the bench, and Andy sat down beside me. I started picking out *Down By the Riverside* with one finger, the only way I knew how. Then Andy began his dreamy version of *April in Paris*. It would've been hard to mess it up—we had played that polyphony a thousand times.

Once again, as it had always done aboard the Madison, we brought the house down.

87

The second show on Saturday night was performed before another standing-room-only crowd. Spades and I looked in occasionally, but most of the time we sat in the lobby. Luther was on duty, and it had proved to be a rather busy night for him. The audience included some dignitaries—the Mayor, several city councilmen, and at least one State Representative. The word must've gotten out after Friday night's show, because several reporters and photographers shuffled in and out all evening. I was feeling pretty darn good for the Gaslight Knights.

That night, Spades and I had plenty of time to talk—just the two of us—without interruptions from anyone. By the time the Knights had played a fifteen-minute encore just a little past midnight, we had covered a lot of ground, catching up on the past, mostly, but projecting into the future just a little, too. He asked me several times about what I thought the future held in store for me, and what I planned to do *after this*.

"I guess I don't possess the wisdom—or a crystal ball—to see into the future," I responded.

"Wisdom is achieved to different degrees," Spades said. "And even though y'all don't have that crystal ball you *think* you need to see into your future, you can still make choices that will make the difference between success and failure."

"I still don't get it," I said, a little puzzled. "How can I know I'm making a right choice if I can't predict the future?"

"It's a judgment call, Will."

"Okay, but how—"

"One of the greatest benefits of wisdom," Morgan went on, "is accurate perception... the ability to immediately recognize right from wrong; good from evil; acceptable from unacceptable. It's a matter of understanding your gut feelings, sometimes. You see, most people can easily tell good from bad, but a truly wise person can see that very thin line between good and *best*. And *that* line is what separates a roll of the dice from a sure thing."

I thought about that for a moment. "Like when you won the boat back from Swamp Scum McDermott? You knew that was a *sure thing?*"

"I knew it was the *best thing* to do... the *right thing* to do... for the right people... and yes, I suppose y'all could say I was confident about it being a sure thing."

"But how could you be sure?"

"Will, y'all have to understand that gambling amounts to a psychological game. McDermott didn't realize that I had discovered how he cheats. Knowing that a man cheats at cards is one thing, but when you know *how he cheats*, he is easily defeated."

"So, why did you even bother with us, when you could've rather been building your own wealth?"

"But I *did* build my own wealth that night, Will... wealth that takes time to collect."

I wasn't entirely certain that I knew what Spades meant, exactly. I was still stuck on understanding how to make a judgment call that would let me see the future.

"If one can evaluate and weigh the future consequences of the choices that are available, y'all possess the right wisdom, Will. And sometimes you just have to listen to your heart."

So then I asked Spades what was in store in his future.

"Life on the river has changed, Will," he replied. "At least, *my life* on the river. I've seen it coming for a while, now... fewer boats out there... the kind I rely on, anyway."

"So, what will you do?" I asked.

"Think it's time for me to retire from professional gambling... as I know it. It's time for me to settle into something I can count on, for a few years, at least."

"And... let me guess. You've made a choice..."

"Sure... I've made several choices. Some are a sure thing, and some I'm still sorting out."

"And the sure thing?"

"I've decided to go into business. During my later years of gambling, I found the good sense to stash away some of my winnings now and then. It's become a rather substantial sum, and I've decided to invest it in... a business."

"What kind of business?"

"Well, as much as I'd like to tell y'all about it, Will, it must remain guarded information until I sort out a few details."

I knew Spades Morgan well enough to know that no matter how persistent my inquisitiveness, I would learn no more from him on the subject. Not now, at least. When he was ready, he would tell me.

88

A ndy, Cheechee and Curtis were all sound asleep. It must've been three A.M. and I was still wide awake thinking about what Spades had said about choices for a successful future. *Sometimes you have to listen to your heart,* he had said, and *learn to recognize the fine line between good and best.* Right then, though, my head was spinning. I could briefly imagine myself staying in La Crosse; Luther had introduced me to the owner of a photography studio who seemed interested in my abilities, limited as they were. Then my mind swooped me away with Andy, Curtis and Cheechee to other parts of the country; and then my heart led me back to the Mississippi and Big Brother Jesse. *Listen to my heart...* Spades said. But Jesse and the river weren't *available* options right now...

I think that's where I finally drifted off to sleep.

Despite the lack of sleep, I was wide awake again by 7:30. I knew the others probably wanted to sleep late—that they would be tired after two long shows—so I dressed quietly and headed down to the dining room for breakfast. It didn't surprise me that Spades Morgan was already there. He waved me over to his table when he noticed me at the door.

"G'mornin' Spades."

"G'mornin' Will."

We chatted over eggs and bacon about the weather, about La Crosse, and of course about the great success of the Gaslight Knights' two shows in the Crystal Room. I could tell that Spades was quite proud of Andy. It was the first time ever that Andy had been able to publicly acknowledge Spades Morgan as *his father*. I was never sure if Beth and Marion Lorado, Andy's adoptive parents, were aware of Andy's closeness to Morgan; I assumed not, because Andy never spoke of him around them, and I knew Marion's opinion of Spades was quite low. Since Marion had changed careers from the railroad to the river, and since he had eased up on calling me and Jesse "river trash," maybe his attitude toward Spades Morgan might have been altered, too.

"Did you read Cheechee's book yet?" I asked Spades.

"Cheechee?" he replied. "Oh, y'all mean Christopher, don't you?"

I nodded.

"Yes, I did read it... yesterday."

"What d'ya think?"

"I'm impressed."

"With the writing?"

"Yes, it's good... but more with the boy in the story." Spades paused, stared at me. "Is that really his true story?"

"As far as I know, it is. Before he started singing with Andy and Curtis, we spent a lot of time together when they were practicing and playing shows, and he told me a lot about his life in Denver before he came to St. Louis. Most everything in his book is consistent with what he told me."

"Do y'all think he *really* stole all those cars?"

"Prob'ly... but he didn't do it for financial gain... and y' know what, Spades? Since all of us have been living together under one roof, I've gotten to know him, and I think Cheechee is a pretty darn good guy."

Spades gazed at me with his usual poker face expression. "Andrew sure seems to like him. And he certainly has a lot of talent."

"Yeah... I sure was surprised when he started singing along with Andy and Curtis while they were practicing, and I was *really* surprised when I read his book. I just hope he finishes it."

"Something tells me he will," Spades said. He looked at the big clock on the wall. "Oh, my! I promised Irene that I would meet her for church this morning... I hope y'all don't mind, Will, but I really must run."

89

While the Knights conducted their usual afternoon jam session in the second floor parlor on Monday, I demonstrated my film developing and picture printing skills for John Jacob, the owner of Jacob's Photo Studio. He had a lot more equipment than Sadie had, but much of it was identical or similar to what I was familiar with, so I had no trouble in displaying my worthiness. I guess it was my experience in that specialized field that gave me the edge over several other people who wanted the job. Mr. Jacob seemed delighted that he would not be required to teach someone the procedures of film processing. So within a few days I had settled into a daily routine working at the studio, earning not as much as the Knights were earning, but they were sharing some of their take with me because I had arranged several of their engagements. Fifteen dollars a week, give or take, wasn't quite "riverboat" pay, but at least I was earning my keep.

Andy, Curtis and Cheechee performed a few hours a couple of nights a week in the Wisconsin Lounge, the Stoddard's cocktail bar. When people found out they were there, the place usually filled up. They continued to play at other clubs and dance halls on the weekends, too, so they maintained a rather busy schedule.

I usually spent part of my days off from the studio in the reading room trying to get through *The Count of Monte Cristo*; it was an intriguing story that kept me turning pages. *Edmond Dantès*, the main character had just been imprisoned when I noticed Spades Morgan enter the lobby through the front door; Irene was with him. They paid no attention to my side of the room, but went straight to the elevator where Luther joined them. I didn't hear any of their conversation, but nothing seemed out of the ordinary, so I continued to read after they disappeared behind the elevator door.

A little while later, Cheechee and Curtis came from the up-stairs parlor where they had been practicing.

"Luther said you were here," Curtis said.

"I've been here for over an hour," I replied.

"Mr. Morgan and Irene wanted to talk to Andy in private, so we left them in the parlor."

"I saw Luther going up in the elevator with them," I said.

"Yeah, he's in there with 'em, too."

"Is there trouble?"

"They all seemed quite happy, so I don't think there's trouble."

"I wonder what they're talking about."

"Don't know, but I'd bet we'll find out soon enough."

Curtis was absolutely right; we did find out soon, and we didn't have to threaten Andy with throwing him out the second story window to get the answer. Instead, Spades and Irene found us still in the reading room. I knew it must be good news, because Spades was actually smiling just a little. Irene was glowing.

"We have an announcement to make, boys," Spades said. "It wouldn't be fair to y'all for us to keep a secret from you... as long as you know about our private meeting with the other boys. We had to talk to them first... I think you'll understand why." Spades paused, took a deep breath, put an arm around Irene, and then went on. "I have asked Irene to be my wife."

"And I said yes," Irene added with a most joyous smile.

"Of course," Spades continued, "Andrew and Luther needed to be the first to know, and they seem to be quite comfortable with becoming stepbrothers."

A moment later when Spades' announcement registered in my head, a slight breeze might have tipped me over. Curtis and Cheechee rushed over to offer handshakes of congratulations to the couple while I spent a few seconds thinking about what I had just heard. I was indeed happy for them, but I didn't know what to say.

Spades stared at me, as if waiting for my reaction. "Will... say something."

"I... I... I think it's wonderful!" I said.

"When is the wedding?" Curtis asked.

"And where?" Cheechee added.

"Oh, we're just gonna get hitched by a Justice of the Peace," Spades replied. "Nothing fancy... no big wedding, no big parties..."

"When?" I asked as I shook his hand, and then Irene's.

"Twenty-sixth of July... a week from this Friday," Irene re-plied. "Now, if you boys will excuse me, I must do some shopping in town." She lovingly kissed Spades on the cheek, and then she was off with a song in her heart.

"Is this one of the choices you were sorting out?" I asked Spades.

"Honestly, Will, I have been planning to ask Irene's hand in marriage for over a year. Just been waiting for the right time."

"Is that why you got off the boat here in La Crosse?"

"Will, I never planned to go any farther. I'm not waiting for another northbound boat. The next boat I board will take me and Irene back to St. Louis on a honeymoon cruise."

"What about Luther? Is he going, too?"

"I've talked briefly with Luther," Spades said. "He'll stay here for a while, but then he's coming to join us in St. Louis."

"Oh," I said, and I must have frowned.

"What's the matter, Will?" Spades said.

"Oh... it's just that me and Luther have become such good friends..."

"Will," Spades said. He laid a hand on my shoulder. "Something tells me you'll be coming back to St. Louis soon, too."

"What makes you think that?"

"Let's just say... I know."

90

I had been waiting for the sixteenth of July, but not for any usual reason that most people would wait for a particular date. On the calendar it showed a full moon would appear in the sky on the sixteenth, and I had been watching the waxing moon for several nights. I wanted to try to take pictures of the moon at its fullest, and I had this dramatic picture in my mind with the full moon rising over the *Stoddard Hotel*. It would be great! I had mentioned my plan to Mr. Jacob, and he gave me a few pointers about the camera settings to use, and he loaned me a tripod on which to mount the camera, to make absolutely sure of a steady shot. I already had my spot across the street picked out, where I would be in shadow without any street light casting unwanted brightness on the camera lens, and where I would be in perfect position for a splendid view of the moon just above the roof of the *Stoddard*.

It's going to be a spectacular photograph... I thought.

I didn't work at the studio that day, so I had plenty of time to get ready for the moon pictures that would surely get me recognized as an accomplished photographer. The free day also gave me plenty of time to think about all the other things that were happening all around me, and how my life was apt to change—whether or not I *wanted* it to change.

Sitting alone at the *Bodega* with a cup of coffee as my only companion, I vividly recalled that day aboard the riverboat a few years ago when I gazed into a mirror. I had studied the fellow looking back at me, and realized then that I wasn't a kid anymore, but still somewhat unsure about adulthood, I thought that I would prefer reclaiming my youth and starting over. I knew that wasn't possible, so I accepted my position in the world for what it was worth.

That day, as I reflected on it, seemed a turning point in my life. As I accepted the responsibilities of growing—spiritually as well as physically—I merely stumbled onto the greatest lesson that every person should learn: change the things that need changing; accept the things I can't change; and possess the wisdom to know the difference.

Just a few days ago Spades Morgan had taken that lesson to the next level when he explained to me about wisdom being the ability to recognize *good* from *best*. He was referring to the choices that would change one's life. I understood that concept quite clearly. What *wasn't* clear to me, though, right then, was what my choices really were, for there seemed to be so many uncertainties looming in my future. Spades had even planted a few of them.

Now that Spades and Irene were getting married, it seemed unmistakably certain that they would return to St. Louis, and there didn't seem to be any question about Luther going, too. Whatever "business" Spades was intending to enter probably enticed Luther as well. Perhaps Spades was buying a hotel, and Luther would be the Head Bellboy. At any rate, my friend Luther would be leaving La Crosse...

Although I had not seriously considered my return to St. Louis since the day we left, Spades seemed to think I would. True, my Big Brother Jesse was there, and he had settled in there with his wife and child. To him, St. Louis was home. And because Jesse, Sadie, and Philip were *my family*, too...

What would Andy, Curtis, and Cheechee do in the near future? They had already tasted sweet success in the entertainment world, and by now, they were probably dreaming bigger and better dreams...

What of my career in photography? Had I found the profession that suited me? I still had a lot to learn, but I certainly enjoyed the business, and I savored the anticipation of advancing myself further—perhaps running my own studio someday... somewhere...

Luther wasn't on duty that day either, and he knew right where to find me. I had not seen much of him since the previous day, so I didn't know for sure how he was taking the big news.

"I've suspected for quite some time that it would happen sooner or later," Luther said. "Guess I wasn't expecting it right now, though."

"Are you... ?"

"Happy about it?" Luther finished asking my question. "Yeah, I'm happy for Mom. Spades is a decent man, and I know he cares about her, and I've seen them together enough to know they're right for each other."

"They must've been seeing each other for a long time... your mom knew about Spades winning our boat in a poker game. That was five years ago."

"They'd been spending time together, off and on, long before that... a couple of years, I think."

"What d'ya think about suddenly having a brother?"

"Andy? I like Andy. It'll be a little different not being the *"only child,"* but I think we'll get along just fine."

"So... you're going to St. Louis?" I said.

Luther frowned. "Yeah, and I wanna talk to you about that."

I saw in his eyes a look of doubt, as if he questioned his desire to go to an unfamiliar city. "You look worried," I said. "I thought you wanted to travel... to see the country..."

"Yes, I know I said all that, and I do wanna see the country."

"Then, what's the problem?"

"Well... I've never traveled much. Mom and I went to St. Paul once... on the train... but that was a long time ago. Mom and Spades are going on a boat to St. Louis... their honeymoon cruise, they're calling it. I'm supposed to go later, and I'm hoping you'll come with me."

"I don't know, Luther," I said. "I've got a job here now—"

"Spades gave me *two* fares to St. Louis."

"Two fares? What about Andy?"

"Andy won't leave Cheechee and Curtis... it wouldn't be fair to them. They're a team... you know that."

"Sure, I know that, but—"

"I think Spades meant the second fare to be yours."

I hesitated. I didn't know how I should react. I wanted the choice to be mine, but suddenly it seemed as though someone else was making the decision for me. "I'll have to think about it, Luther," I said.

His face drooped with rejection.

"It's not that I don't want to go with *you.*" I said. "It's more like... well... I don't know if there's any reason for me to go back to St. Louis, or actually, if I *really want* to go back to St. Louis. I'll just have to think about it."

91

It was well past midnight when the yellow moon started inching its way over the hills from the east. I was settled into my dark, shadowy spot across the street from the *Stoddard*, *Leica* on the tripod, aimed at the front of the hotel with plenty of sky above it, anxiously awaiting the right moment to start clicking the shutter. The night heat and humidity stuck my clothes to my skin, but I was so excited about my photographs that I didn't really notice the sweltering discomfort. All of La Crosse seemed to be sedated by the heat; not much stirred; only a distant barking dog and an occasional passing car or truck blemished the serenity. It seemed quite unusual.

Despite my anxious anticipation, I couldn't stop thinking about Luther's request. I had all but decided to stay in La Crosse and work for John Jacob for a while, knowing Andy, Cheechee, and Curtis would move on sooner or later. Not that I really wanted to part with their company; they didn't need me as extra baggage, and it was becoming more evident that I wouldn't fit in with their travel plans for much longer. I figured that I would eventually settle into a permanent home, somewhere, and that could always remain as a home base for them, for as long as they needed one. I hadn't mentioned any of this to them, yet, nor did I know their plans, for sure, but it would do no harm to prepare myself for the likely event.

In all its radiance, the moon was slowly approaching the very part of the sky where it would give the most spectacular effect. The stage was set. I double-checked the aim of the camera on the tripod, and made sure the flash bulb was secure. John Jacob had suggested using the flash so the photograph would reveal more detail of the front of the building. "Otherwise," he'd said, "The building will just be a black, square silhouette against a black sky and no one will know that it is even in the picture." It made sense to me, and I wanted to learn, so I had followed his advice.

There would only be a few minutes while the moon was in perfect position, and I wanted to get as many shots as possible, altering the camera settings ever-so-slightly to ensure at least one good picture. I squinted into the viewfinder. I held my breath.

Click. Flash.

Adjust camera. Insert new flash bulb.

Click. Flash.

"What was that?" I heard a voice in the darkness say in a loud whisper.

"Just heat lightning," another voice whispered in reply.

I managed to get about a dozen shots before the moon had slid away in its orbit just enough to diminish the quality of my composition. But I felt confident that the pictures would be as stunning as I had imagined. The next day at the studio I would process the film, and then I'd know.

I shouldered the tripod and camera, and ambled across the street to the hotel entrance. The lobby was deserted except for a bellboy and the night clerk, who were passing the quiet time with a game of five card draw poker at the front registration desk. They were about to hastily dispose of the cards, but when they saw it was only me, they waved with a sigh of relief and continued their game. They both had often seen me come and go with my camera, so they didn't even think to question my late-night activity.

92

E arly the next morning, while I was getting ready to go down for breakfast before heading to the studio, there seemed to be more than the usual activity in the hall. By the time I opened the door to leave, Curtis was awake, but Andy and Cheechee were still sound asleep.

"What's all the commotion out there?" Curtis asked, rubbing his eyes.

"Don't know..."

I was met at the door by a bellboy and a blue-uniformed police officer. "Hi, Roger," I said to the bellboy, who I had seen playing cards with Larry, the night clerk just hours earlier.

"This is Will Madison," Roger said to the cop. "He's the one we saw coming in about one-thirty this morning."

"What were you doing out at one-thirty in the morning?" the cop asked.

Taken by surprise, the first thought that came to my mind was that a wet, muddy dog had run into the room. "I... I was... I was out taking pictures."

The officer eyed me suspiciously. "In the middle of the night? In the dark?"

"Yes, sir. Roger saw me come in with my camera." I looked at Roger. Then the cop looked at Roger.

"Yes, sir," Roger said. "He did have his camera on a tripod."

"What were you taking pictures of in the middle of the night?" the cop asked.

"The full moon," I said. "It was a full moon last night."

"What time did you leave your room to go take pictures of the full moon?" he asked, as if mocking me.

I thought a moment. "I think it was about midnight. Am I in some kinda trouble for taking pictures of the moon?"

"I don't know yet," the officer said. "Did anyone else see you?"

"I don't know... it was rather hot and sticky last night and there weren't many people moving around at that time."

"So you didn't see anyone else... even *in* the hotel?"

"Only Roger and Larry. They were at the front desk when I came in."

"And what are you doing up so early this morning?" the officer asked.

"Breakfast," I said. "And then I'm going to work."

"Where do you work?"

"Jacob's Photography Studio."

The uniformed cop took out a notepad and pencil, scribbled a few notes, and then he said: "I'd like to look around in your room."

"There's three other people sleeping in there," I replied.

"Well, we'll just have to wake them up. I need to talk to them, too."

Curtis was already out of bed getting dressed. He had heard us talking. "What's the problem?" he said.

"ANDY! CHEECHEE!" I called out. "Get up. A policeman wants to talk to you."

They both sat up in bed, yawning and stretching. The cop stepped into the room, immediately examining all corners, behind the chairs, in the bathroom, and then he knelt down and peered under both beds. He stopped a moment when he discovered my camera still mounted on the tripod, scribbled some more notes, and then he stepped to the foot of the bed and faced Andy and Cheechee. Curtis was standing beside them, too.

He started to ask their names, but stopped short. "Hey," he said. "You're those musicians I saw at..." He cut himself short again.

"Yes, sir, we prob'ly are," Andy said. "Why are you in our room?"

"Just want to ask you a few questions, if you don't mind."

"What about?"

"About what you were doing last night."

"When last night?"

"All night."

"Well, after our practice, we went to the Dixie—I mean the *Bodega*—for supper. We met Will and Luther there."

The cop glanced at me.

I nodded.

"Then what did you do?" he asked.

"We went to see a movie at the *Rivoli*."

"What movie was playing?"

"Alfred Hitchcock... *The Thirty-nine Steps.*"

"Where do you practice?"

"In the music room next to the parlor on the second floor."

The cop's eyebrows raised. "What time did you leave there?"

"About five."

"Did you notice anything unusual in the parlor then?"

"What d'ya mean... unusual?"

"Did you see anything missing?"

Andy looked at Cheechee and then Curtis. They all seemed quite puzzled. "No... not that I know of... what's missing?"

The cop sighed a deep breath. "There are three very expensive paintings missing from the parlor."

"Well, they weren't missing at five. I would've noticed," Andy said.

"What did you do after the movie?"

"We came back here and went to bed."

"What time?"

"I think it was about eleven-thirty."

"Did you use the elevator or the stairs?"

"Elevator."

"So you weren't on the second floor at all at eleven-thirty?"

"No sir."

"Did you see anyone else in the hotel when you came in?"

"Just the night clerk... Larry. If someone carried those paintings out of the hotel, Larry and Roger are the ones who would have seen them do it."

"Well, they didn't," the cop said. "And so I think the paintings never left the building." He stepped to the door. "Thank you, gentlemen. Sorry to bother you." And then he left.

I think he was satisfied that none of us had taken the paintings, but something told me we hadn't seen the last of him.

93

The delay with the police officer had cut my breakfast time short, and I was still five minutes late getting to the studio. Mr. Jacob understood, though, when I explained the situation.

"Who would be bold enough to steal paintings from a hotel?" he asked. "And how could they get them out without someone seeing?"

"I don't know," I replied. "And neither do the police."

It was mid-afternoon when I had finished all my work. I told Mr. Jacob that I was off the clock, and that I wanted to stay a while longer to process my film of the moon pictures.

"Take all the time you want," he said. "I'm curious to see how they turned out, too."

Developing film had become one of those "second nature" tasks to me, so all day my thoughts had been bouncing back to Luther and *the extra fare to St. Louis*. I liked my job with Mr. Jacob, and he seemed quite willing to let me advance; there was little doubt in my mind that I would be shooting portrait photographs in his studio sometime in the future.

But Luther seemed so desperate. Then I recalled the comment from Spades; he seemed certain that I would return to St. Louis. He must've known something that I didn't.

All of my pictures developed quite nicely. I was a little disappointed that the moon wasn't nearly as spectacular as I had anticipated; it was merely a large white spot just above the roofline of the hotel. But the Stoddard was identifiable with much more detail than I had expected from a nighttime shot.

I printed most of the frames five by seven inches, but a couple of the ones I thought were the best I printed eight by ten. As I hung the finished photos on the drying clips I took a little time to admire my work. It was then that I noticed something in one of the eight by tens; there was something more in my pictures that I hadn't counted on.

"Mr. Jacob!" I called out to the studio owner. "Come and look at these photos."

While he studied the pictures, I pointed out the extra feature that I had noticed. "Oh my," he said. "I think you've accidentally solved a mystery."

The prints weren't dry yet, but I had to get back to the hotel immediately. "I'll come back for these later when they're dry," I said. I think Mr. Jacob understood the reason for my hasty exit when I took off my apron and tossed it aside. I ran the six blocks to the hotel. Luther met me in the lobby.

"You ran all the way here from work," he said.

This time it was quite obvious how he knew; I was sweating and nearly out of breath so I could hardly speak. "Yes... you're absolutely... right... can you... find... Mr. Elliott? I... need to see him... right away!"

"It's about the missing paintings, isn't it?" Luther quizzed.

I nodded. *Good guess*, I thought.

Luther grabbed my arm and guided me to the elevator where the operator stood at the open door. "Second floor, Carl," he said as he whisked me into the elevator car. "Mr. Elliott is up in the parlor with a detective and you're too out of breath for the stairs right now."

"Oh... you noticed... thank you."

Luther laughed as Carl shuttled us upward, and then he walked me slowly from the elevator to the parlor so that I might catch my breath. John Elliott stood with his arms folded across his chest, staring at a blank space on the parlor wall; another man dressed in a gray suit—the detective, I assumed—stood beside him.

"That was one of my favorite *Monet* originals," Mr. Elliott said. "I paid over a thousand dollars for it..."

Not so strange that I should know the painting that John was imagining on the empty wall, for I had examined all those paintings and admired them many times. I recalled a flowered patio setting overlooking an ocean harbor with sailboats and steamships. *A thousand dollars!* I thought. *No wonder why everyone was concerned about its disappearance.*

The gray-suited man noticed Luther in the open doorway; he nudged Mr. Elliott and pointed to the bellboy.

"Yes, Luther," John said. "Do you need me for something?"

"Excuse me, sir," Luther said. "One of our permanent residents would like to talk to you about the missing paintings."

"Who?"

"Mr. Madison, sir." He stepped aside to allow me through the door.

By then I had regained normal breathing, but I was still quite excited with my discovery. "Did you find the paintings yet?" I said.

"Why, no... we've searched every room, but the police seem to think—"

"I know how they left the building!" I interrupted.

Immediately the gray-suit was inches from me. "I'm Sam Anderson, Police Detective," the man said. "How do you know that?" he asked.

"I was out taking pictures of the full moon last night," I began to explain.

"Oh... so you're the young photographer the officer questioned this morning."

"Yes, sir, Mr. Anderson. You need to see my photos. They lowered the paintings with a rope from a second story window on the alley side of the building... where it's dark and no one saw them. It shows up quite clear in my pictures."

There was renewed excitement in both John Elliott and Detective Anderson. "Where are the pictures?"

"They're still drying at the studio where I work. I just developed them a little while ago."

"Well, let's go have a look."

Detective Anderson drove me and John Elliott to Jacob's Studio in his car. The hotel owner was extremely encouraged, but Anderson warned him: "This doesn't mean we found the paintings, John. It only means we know they're not in the building anymore."

When we arrived at the studio, Mr. Jacob was studying one of my photos. "Ah, Detective Anderson," he said. "I figured you'd be here soon."

94

For the fourth time in my young life, I had aided the police in rounding up dangerous criminals. The first was in Alma, Wisconsin, right after Jesse rescued me from the flood. A scoundrel drifter tried to kill Jesse and steal his valuables, but I beaned him with a rock before he could do the nasty deed. The police found him deliriously wandering about the next day. Turned out he was wanted in several states. The second was in Northern Wisconsin when Jesse and I tangled with a couple of crooks who robbed several country general stores and stole a car. The third was when me and Andy, Luke and some other deckhands captured a pair of river pirates in the coal bin aboard the Madison down in Cape Girardeau,

Missouri. All those times, I guess my life had been in danger, threatened with weapons by violent outlaws. I don't know how *dangerous* thieves of fine art can be, and considering all I did this time was take a few pictures, I can't say that I was threatened or in danger... that I am aware of, that is.

What I can say, though, is that my photography skills became rather well-known in La Crosse. John Elliott used my pictures to determine which room the man was leaning out of the window. The hotel guest register identified who occupied that room, and after the police tracked him down—and his accomplice—and recovered the stolen paintings, my pictorial account of the act (four photos that revealed one man in the second story window, his accomplice in the dark alley below, and the paintings suspended by a rope between them) appeared on the front page of the *La Crosse Tribune* along with a story about how I happened to capture the criminal act on film. You might say that I had taken the first step in becoming a photo journalist, but I doubt that the *La Crosse Tribune* was considering my employment just yet.

Friday July 26th was a day of mixed emotions for me; Edward "Spades" Morgan and Irene Holt were married at their private little ceremony that lasted only ten minutes in Irene's house on Market Street. Only Andy, Luther, Curtis, Cheechee, me, and a couple of Irene's closest friends were there. Because it was the middle of the afternoon, John Elliott gave Irene the use of the Crystal Room for a private dinner party, and he insisted that he would provide all the food and service—said it was his wedding gift to her, a friend and former employee of the hotel, and Spades, a long-loyal patron. The Crystal Room was about twenty times larger than was necessary for ten people, but the piano was there; Andy provided a pleasant musical atmosphere while we all enjoyed a few drinks and conversation after the dinner. It was a most joyous occasion.

For me, that day also meant a time when the departure of my good friend Luther was drawing near. Spades and Irene already had passage booked; they would check into their stateroom on the steamer *St. Paul* the next morning, and they would arrive at St. Louis in about four days. Luther's plan was to leave in about two or three weeks. It seemed odd that Spades had not mentioned to me anything more about my return to St. Louis... that he had been so sure of happening. Maybe he had changed his mind.

Andy, Cheechee and Curtis were playing a show that night at the hotel in Trempealeau, a small town about twenty miles upriver from La Crosse. The *Trempealeau Hotel* was a popular weekend night spot, and the Knights' growing popularity assured a full house. I hadn't been to any of their shows for a while, and neither had Luther, so I convinced him that we should go.

"How will we get there?" Luther asked.

"I checked the train schedule this morning," I replied. "There's a train to Trempealeau at eight p.m., and one that returns to La Crosse at midnight."

"Why don't we just go in the car with Curtis?"

"Because they're staying there overnight, and your mom and Spades are going, too."

95

Saturday was a day off for me, so there would be no need to get up early; I wasn't concerned about being out late. It would also afford me plenty of time for a farewell visit with Spades and Irene before they sailed off to St. Louis—Andy was saying his good-byes now, because he and Curtis and Cheechee would be staying in Trempealeau for another show Saturday night.

Right after our celebration dinner party broke up I went to the train depot to buy all the tickets so Spades couldn't. I knew he'd try to pay for everything again, like he usually did. I always appreciated his generosity, and he knew it. But this time, it was going to be *my* treat.

Spades, Irene, and Luther met me in the hotel lobby about seven-thirty; we walked to the train depot, and just as I suspected he would, Spades pulled out his wallet. I held up my hand to stop him, and then passed around the tickets. "My treat," I said with a big smile. "You didn't want any wedding gifts, so consider tonight a going-away party... on me."

"Will," Spades said. "That's mighty thoughtful of you."

We rode the train for about thirty minutes, and then it was a five minute walk to the *Trempealeau Hotel*. The Gaslight Knights were advertised on a sign at the entrance. They hadn't started playing yet, but when we found one of the last vacant tables at the perimeter of the dance floor, they were just getting ready. Their ruffled blue shirts—the ones they wore for their first show in the Crystal Room—glistened under the lights and Curtis's saxophone sparkled more than his new red Pontiac on a sunny day.

The crowded room broke out in cheers and whistles when Andy began his theme song. Curtis soon joined in, and there was Cheechee shuffling around among the people, smiling, shaking hands, pouring on the charm, just like he had done at that first show. This was *their* style, and the audience loved it.

The Knights had performed three or four numbers when a young gentleman sitting at the next table leaned over between me and Spades. "These guys are great, aren't they?"

I nodded and grinned.

Spades calmly said, "Well, of course they are. The piano player is my son."

The young man gave a pleasantly surprised smile. "Well, then you must be Mr. Morgan. Andy and I were talking at the bar a while ago... he said you got married today."

"I did indeed," Spades replied. He put his arm across Irene's shoulders. "And this is my lovely bride, Irene."

"Pleased to meet you both. I'm Fischer Blinn," he said as he offered his right hand. "I'm the resident engineer at the Trempealeau dam project."

Spades shook his hand, and then introduced Luther as his new stepson, and me, his "long-time riverboat friend."

Fischer threw me a puzzled stare.

"Me and my brother," I explained, "owned an excursion boat on the Mississippi. Mr. Morgan helped us acquire it in La Crosse a few years ago."

"Where's your homeport? La Crosse?" Fischer asked.

"St. Charles for a couple of years, and then St. Louis. We didn't have the experience to run the Upper Mississippi."

"The dams and locks we're building now will make it a better river to navigate."

"Yeah, I know. I've been reading about them."

"Where's your boat now?"

"Oh, the Madison burned at St. Louis last year."

"Sorry to hear that," Fischer said frowning. "So you're just here visiting?"

"I'm here with the band. Andy's my best friend. He was the entertainment on the Madison."

Fischer fit all the pieces together quite easily, and because we had a common interest—navigation on the Mississippi River—we talked a lot. He explained how the locks would work once they were operational, and how the dams controlled the water depth, making navigation for bigger boats possible. I told him of my experiences on the river, and about Jesse and Luke piloting barge tows on the Lower Mississippi. We had so much to talk about that the night slipped by rather quickly for me.

About eleven o'clock, Spades pointed to his open pocket watch. "I hate to cut this short," he said. "But we have to get to the depot."

I acknowledged, and then I said to Fischer, "I live at the *Stoddard Hotel* in La Crosse now. I go to the *Bodega* for supper a lot. Stop in and see me sometime."

"Sure, I will," Fischer replied. "My good friend Francis Landrieu lives on

Market Street. I go to La Crosse to see him often. In fact, Francis told me about the Gaslight Knights... he saw them at the *Avalon Ballroom* a couple of weeks ago."

"Well, next time you're in town, look me up."

96

Two hours after the *St. Paul* had steamed southbound out of La Crosse harbor with Spades and Irene aboard, Luther found me in the reading room with *The Count of Monte Cristo* laid open in front of me, but I wasn't focused much on reading that day. Luther had traded his Friday afternoon work hours for another bellboy's Saturday morning. It was a little past noon; he was off for the rest of the day, had already changed into a T-shirt and jeans, and he was hungry.

"Wanna go to the Dixie?" he said. "You're not concentrating on *Edmond Dantes*, so let's go eat."

"You've read *The Count of Monte Cristo?*"

"Yeah... about a year ago. It's a little hard to follow sometimes, but otherwise it's pretty good."

I couldn't disagree; at times I found myself confused with all the French names and keeping track of who they were, but how did Luther know my mind had wandered away from the book?

"So... are you interested in food?" he asked.

I closed the book. "Sure. I'm starved."

"Did you see them off this morning?" Luther asked while we walked to our favorite cafe.

"Yeah... I had a nice visit with them. They seemed very happy."

"Mom's been head-over-heels with Spades since the day she met him."

"Luther... I don't mean to be nosey, but what about your real father?"

"My father was killed in the World War. Mom was pregnant with me when he left for Europe, so I never knew him."

Luther didn't seem distraught about his real father, but I guessed there was a logical explanation: how could he miss someone he never knew? But he did appear to be quite content with his mother's marriage to Spades. He'd known Spades for longer than I had, and I wondered if I would ever hear him address Spades as "Dad."

With the noon-hour rush, the *Bodega* was crowded; our usual table by the window was occupied, so we found another in the far corner. When our waitress finally came to take our order, she apologized for the delay. "We've been really busy today."

"That's okay, Susan," I said smiling. "We're suffering from severe hunger pains and I'm sure we'll pass out any minute... but we've got plenty of time for recovery."

Susan laughed. "Yes, you *are* looking rather pale."

"So, could we get a couple orders of your roast beef special? Y'know... to prevent our premature demise?"

"Sure... mashed potatoes and gravy?"

"Yup... and a *Coke* for me."

"I'll have the same," Luther said.

A very short time later, Susan returned with our food and drinks. There was advantage in being a regular customer.

"Luther," I said as I dug into the mashed potatoes. "Has Spades told you about the business he's starting?"

He looked at me with surprise. "I... I'm sworn to secrecy," he said.

"So he *has* told you about it."

Luther only nodded and bit into his roast beef.

"What kind of business is it?"

"Can't tell you... I'm sworn to secrecy."

"Is that why you're going to St. Louis?"

Luther just smiled and chewed.

"Are you gonna work for him?"

Luther smiled some more and shrugged his shoulders.

"He's buying a hotel, isn't he?" I asked.

Luther smiled, swallowed, took a sip of his Coke.

"Come on, Luth... you can tell me. Is it a hotel?"

"There are some things he has to work out yet, and in the meantime... I'm sworn—"

"I know," I interrupted. *"You're sworn to secrecy."*

Quite obviously I wasn't going to get the answer I wanted from Luther, but his reaction to my line of questioning led me to believe that I was correct about the hotel. For any more than that, I would just have to wait.

"Have you thought about coming with me to St. Louis?" Luther asked.

"Yeah, I've thought about it," I said. "But I still haven't come up with any good reasons to go back there, and I like my job at Jacob's Studio. Unless Andy and Curtis and Cheechee decide they want to go back, I'll prob'ly stay here."

97

It was nearly four o'clock Sunday morning when Andy, Cheechee and Curtis came back from Trempealeau. I woke up as soon as the door opened, but they must've been so tired that they barely said a word between them, and within seconds, it seemed, they were undressed, in bed and sleeping.

They finally woke up about noon and when I was nowhere in the hotel, they came to the *Bodega* for some lunch. I had been there a while waiting for Luther.

"Thought we'd find you here," Andy said. They made themselves comfortable around our usual table by the window.

"I'm waiting for Luther," I said. "Didn't want to wake you. Why did you get home so late? It was four o'clock."

"We met a man at the *Trempealeau Hotel* last night, and he wanted to talk to us after the show."

"What did he want to talk about?"

"Will..." Andy said. I sensed a little reluctance in his hesitation. "I know you love your job at the studio."

I nodded. "Yeah, I do."

"And I know you like this town."

I nodded again.

"But what would you say if I told you we have *big* opportunities waiting for us elsewhere?"

You see? I told myself. *You knew this was coming.* "What do you mean?" I asked as if I had not given it a thought.

"Thomas Conrad, the guy we met last night, is an entertainment agent. He was passing through here on his way from Minneapolis. Somehow he heard about us and he showed up at the *Trempealeau Hotel* to see our show."

"So, is he *your* agent now?"

"No... we didn't make any deals or promises."

"But he wants you to come to Minneapolis."

"No..." Andy looked at Curtis and Cheechee for help.

Curtis answered. "Mr. Conrad wants us to come to New York."

"You see," Cheechee chimed in. "Conrad is to New York like Harry is to St. Louis."

"Oh," I replied. "Like the Harry that left you hanging out to dry after about a dozen shows."

"This will be different," Andy said.

"How?"

Curtis cut in again. "New York is bigger—much bigger—a hot spot for

442

entertainers..."

"And recording studios," Cheechee added.

"Do you trust this Mr. Conrad?"

"He seems like a straight-up guy," Curtis replied. "But like Andy said... we didn't make any deals. We told him we'd think about it... and that we'd contact him if we decide to go there."

"Have you thought about it?" I asked.

"We have two more weekends to play here," Andy said. "We'll make our decision by then."

"What about you, Will?" Cheechee said. "Are you going with us... if we go?"

I felt a lump in my throat. "I... I... I love you guys like brothers... I think you know that."

They all nodded.

"And you know that I'd prob'ly do anything to help you."

They all nodded again.

"But I'd just be extra baggage for you, and what would a guy like me do in New York? I hate big cities... *remember*? If you go, I think you'll be going without Will Madison."

"So, what will you do if we go?" Andy asked.

"Oh, I think I'll stay here in La Crosse for a while... keep working for Mr. Jacob... get a house... one you guys can come back to anytime you want."

"So..." Andy said. "Are you saying that you approve of us going to New York?"

"Do you *need* my approval?"

"As our best friend... yes."

"Well then, I guess you have it."

98

At about ten o'clock Tuesday morning there was a knock on our door. Cheechee and Andy had left for a late morning swim; Curtis and I relaxed in the room after an early morning hike on Grandad's Bluff.

We certainly weren't expecting company, and Andy or Cheechee wouldn't be knocking. I opened the door to see Luther's snazzy green uniform.

"G'mornin' Luther. C'mon in."

"Oh, I can't stay," he said. "I just brought this letter that came in the mail for Mr. Curtis Owens. It was addressed to the wrong room number. I wanted to make sure he got it."

"Well, thank you, Luther," Curtis said as he stepped over to the door.

Luther handed him the envelope. "I'll see you later," he said to me. "Tonight at the Dixie?"

"Tonight at the Dixie," I replied. "Seven o'clock."

"It's from Leo in St. Louis," Curtis said as I closed the door.

It had slipped my mind that we had written to Leo just after we arrived in La Crosse; I hadn't been thinking much about the Tony Delaware/Johnny Dempsey incident lately, but suddenly there was a spark of renewed interest. I patiently waited for Curtis to open and read the letter. "So, what does he have to say?" I asked.

"Well," Curtis said. "It's not terrifically good news, but I guess it's kinda what we expected."

"About Tony?"

"Yeah. Leo says that the Knights of the Square Table have dispersed: "With the four of you in Wisconsin," he read from the letter, "Marty and Milo gone back to New York, Johnny dead and Tony in jail, it's only me and Frank that show up at the Lion's Den on Friday nights."

"Marty went back to New York?"

"Sounds like it," Curtis replied, and read aloud some more of Leo's letter: "A week after Milo came back from college, they both left to go back to New York City."

"Hmmm. Marty must've gotten homesick," I said. "So Tony is in jail?"

Curtis continued to read aloud from the letter: "Court proceedings moved swiftly. Johnny's death was ruled accidental, and considering that Tony was acting in self-defense, he might have gone free without any jail time if he had not dumped the body in the river and had gone to the police right away that night. Even the fact that he had been drinking quite heavily and perhaps not thinking clearly did not sway the court's decision from a one-year prison sentence."

"Poor Tony," I sighed.

"You should be saying *lucky Tony*," Curtis replied. "Only one year... I'd say he got away with murder."

"But it was an accident," I protested.

"Think about it, Will. Why did he dump the body in the river if it was an accident? I'll go along with the self-defense idea... maybe... but I'm not so sure about the accidental part."

Maybe Curtis was right. Maybe I had been seeing only the black and white of the issue. Tony seemed to be a good fellow, but maybe I had trusted his word a little too far.

When Andy and Cheechee came back from the beach, Curtis read the letter to them, too. Their reaction was less sympathetic toward Tony than mine had been; time had obviously diluted their concern. But we all agreed that even though Tony was our friend, we had done the right thing by avoiding any involvement; leaving St. Louis had been our best option.

Little did it matter now. In all the letters I had received from Sadie during the summer, never once did she mention that the St. Louis Police came looking for me.

99

I sat at our regular table by the window at the *Bodega*, but I was alone— very alone. Me and the Knights had spent quite a summer in Wisconsin. They had taken their music career to another plateau, and now it seemed they would soon be off on an adventure that could take them around the world, perhaps. They had only one more scheduled engagement here, and there was little doubt in my mind that they would leave for New York soon after. It was all they had been talking about lately.

I reminded myself that it was Wednesday August 7th; one week from today, Luther would board the steamer *St. Paul*, bound for St. Louis, and I wondered if I would ever see him again. I wondered if I would ever see the Knights again. This separation could very well be the end of an era that I would not soon forget.

Even though all my closest friends were leaving soon, I felt good about my job with Mr. Jacob; *my* new career was off to a good start, too. A sense of security washed over me. I thought about the uncertainty I would face if I went with Andy and the boys to New York, and St. Louis was just that big city that I didn't much care for. Here, I had a good job, I had money in the bank, and I could still be close to the river that I loved. All things considered, I had justified my staying in La Crosse.

Right in the middle of my revelations, I noticed someone standing next to the table. "Hi, Will. Remember me?" he said.

I gazed up at the face; it was familiar, but it took me a few seconds to associate it with a name. "Oh! Hi, Fischer!" I said when I recalled our meeting at the *Trempealeau Hotel*. "Have a seat. I'm here alone."

"Thank you," Fischer said as he sat down. "I came to La Crosse to see my friend, Francis, and I thought I'd look you up, too."

"Well, I appreciate that," I replied.

"You weren't at the *Stoddard*, and I remembered you saying that you came here a lot."

"Yeah, this is my favorite place to eat... or to drink coffee... or to just think."

"I see you must be here drinking coffee tonight."

"And thinking."

"Oh... did I disturb you?"

"No, not at all. I'm glad you stopped."

"Where are your band friends playing this weekend?"

"They're playing their last shows here tomorrow, Friday and Saturday nights at the Road House in Winona."

"Their *last* shows?"

"Yeah... then they're headed for New York."

"You going with them?"

"No... I'm staying here."

"So that's why you're looking a little lonely."

"Maybe."

"Well, my girlfriend is coming to visit this weekend. She's arriving tomorrow afternoon from Minneapolis. I came here to make plans with Francis and his wife to go out to dinner. Maybe we'll go to Winona, and then we can stop at the Road House for some good music and dancing. Will you be there?"

"Prob'ly... if the Knights don't decide to stay in Winona all weekend, like they did at Trempealeau."

"Great! Fischer said. "Then maybe we'll see you there."

"Sure! I'll be watching for you," I said.

"Okay. Well, Francis should be home by now. He's the resident engineer at the Genoa Dam project. You'll meet him tomorrow night, and I'm sure you'll like him... he's a great guy."

"Okay... see you tomorrow night."

I was glad that I had met Fischer. He was at least ten or twelve years my senior and his friend probably was, too. But what did it matter. We had a lot in common, and I was certainly interested in learning more about the new locks and dams on the river. He'd kept his word to look me up when he came to La Crosse, so I assumed that he was interested in building a friendship. And right now, it would be wise for me to make some new friends.

Soon after Fischer left, Luther strolled in looking hungry.

"Must be six-fifteen," I mused.

"Yeah, and I'm hungry."

We ordered our burgers and beer.

"The Knights are playing at the Road House in Winona tomorrow night," I said. "Wanna go?"

Luther pondered a long moment. "Are they there all weekend?"

I nodded.

"Well, then I'll go Friday or Saturday. I have to work Friday morning early, so I'd better not be out late tomorrow night. Don't wanna oversleep and be late for my last day of work at the hotel!"

Friday would be a work day for me, too, but I wanted to spend as much time as possible with Andy, Cheechee and Curtis, because I knew they'd be gone soon, and I didn't want to pass up the opportunity to nurture a budding new friendship with Fischer.

Just then, the Knights arrived after their late afternoon practice. They were hungry, too.

"Andy," I said. "Will you be staying in Winona overnight tomorrow?"

"No, we're coming back here. "Why?"

"I'd like to go with you."

"Sure," he replied. "We'll have supper here, and we'll leave about seven-thirty."

Thursday was another sunny, hot day. Thundershowers were predicted for later that night, and the rain would certainly be welcome. But so far, the evening was still pleasantly warm and dry. After we ate our supper, we bid our farewells to Luther and headed to Winona, Minnesota in the shiny red Pontiac.

The Knights started their usual routine at nine o'clock—Andy and Curtis playing *Happy Days Are Here Again*, Cheechee jumping off the riser, wandering around the dance floor smiling, shaking hands, pouring on the charm—and as usual, the crowd loved it.

About ten o'clock I heard the thunder rumbling and saw the lightning flashes through the windows, and then the hiss of rain seemed to usher in a few gusts of cool, refreshing air. What a relief it was after so many hot, dry days.

A little while later, I waved to Fischer as he, his girlfriend, and another couple hustled in from the rain. By then there were no vacant tables, so we just stood off to the side and talked for a while. Fischer introduced his girlfriend, Marceline Patro, and his friends, Mr. and Mrs. Francis Landrieu. While the two women went off to the "powder room," Fischer, Francis and I talked about the much-needed rain. Francis wanted to know more about my riverboat background that Fischer had only briefly told him about. But then, the ladies came back and they wanted to dance. So our conversations after that were short and sometimes rather incomplete when the women dragged Fischer and Francis back on the dance floor as the Knights struck up another danceable tune. But we still had a good time.

The rain had diminished to merely sprinkles when I watched Fischer's 1932 Auburn sedan pull out of the parking lot. It was half past midnight, and I hoped Andy, Curtis and Cheechee wouldn't spend the rest of the night talking to someone again. I was tired, and I had to go to work in the morning. Fifteen minutes later, while I watched other people leaving, Curtis tapped me on the shoulder. "Ready to go?" he said, and then we dodged the few raindrops that were still falling.

A few miles south, the rain had stopped completely, but the road was wet and slick, so Curtis drove a little slower than usual. The storm had moved off to the east across the river; we could still see lightning bolts streaking through the distant clouds over Wisconsin.

There were no lights burning anywhere at La Crescent, just across the river from La Crosse. "Power must be out from the storm," Curtis said. His voice woke me; I had dozed off. Andy and Cheechee were sound asleep in the back seat.

As we approached the west end of the Mississippi Bridge at Pettibone Beach, Curtis slowed to a stop behind several other cars and what appeared to be a bus. I saw a lantern moving about in the darkness ahead, and then a man appeared. I judged him to be the bus driver by the hat he wore.

"What happened? Why are we stopped?" came sleepy voices from the back seat.

"I can't see anything," Curtis said. "Must be an accident."

We sat there for a few minutes without any movement of the traffic ahead. Then the man carrying the lantern came toward us. Curtis opened his door and got out. "The bridge has collapsed," I heard the man say. "You'll have to turn around... nothing can get through."

I could see the lights of La Crosse. We were so close. But I knew I wouldn't feel my pillow for a long time.

"We'll have to go back to Winona and cross the river there," Curtis said as he entered the car again.

"Why do you s'pose the bridge collapsed?" I asked.

"Prob'ly something with the storm," he replied.

Curtis turned his red Pontiac around in the road, as did the other drivers, and we all headed back to Winona. It was four o'clock when I laid my head down on my pillow.

100

My alarm clock jarred me awake at seven. I guess it was my young stamina that allowed me to get out of bed, splash some cold water in my face, and attack the day. But I was still very tired.

"Did you hear about the bridge?" Larry, the night clerk asked as I passed by the front desk in the lobby.

"Huh? Oh, yeah," I said. "I was there... stranded on the other side at two o'clock this morning."

"Oh, so you know about the car that went down with it and the people drowned."

"No! I didn't know that. We turned around and went back to Winona… crossed the river there."

It was the buzz everywhere, and rumors sizzled like steaks on a grill. Uninformed reports were saying that a bus carrying thirty passengers had plunged into the river. I knew that wasn't true, because I saw the bus *and* its driver on solid ground. I thought it unlikely that he drove the bus off the end of the bridge after we left.

Later that day, when the afternoon paper hit the streets, I learned the shocking news. Even seeing it in print, I had difficulty believing it—Fischer Blinn had skidded and lost control of his 1932 Auburn sedan and crashed into the concrete and steel support girder, causing a 131-foot-long span of the bridge to collapse and plunge into the Mississippi River, taking the car with it. He escaped through the car window as soon as it hit the water, and then he had pulled his girlfriend out. He swam with the hysterical Miss Patro to the nearest shore pier where they were later picked up by a small police boat. The car had sunk in twelve feet of water; occupying the rear seat, Francis Landrieu and his wife had both suffered skull fractures in the crash and were unconscious, unable to help themselves. They drowned.

Fischer Blinn and Miss Patro were examined at St. Francis Hospital; no serious injuries were discovered other than severe shock.

Little had I known at two o'clock that morning that my new friend, Fischer and his girlfriend were clinging to a bridge pier, desperately struggling for their lives, and that Francis Landrieu and his wife had lost theirs—only a few hundred feet from where we sat curiously in the car. I was the last person to see them alive.

I never saw Fischer again.

101

To say Monday August 12th, 1935 was a sad day in my life would be an understatement. While Fischer's accident was still heavy on my mind, Andy, Curtis and Cheechee had given me their official decision: they were going to New York. I realized that their choice held in store unlimited potential for their success as musicians; a multitude of opportunities as entertainers. But it also held in store danger and risk; I hoped they had counted those elements in their evaluation.

What made it a sad day for me, mostly, was that I would be parting company with my best friend of four years. Four years might not sound like a long time, but considering I ran away from home and all my friends and started life over only five and a half years ago, four years is a large portion. Andy had been the best friend anyone could have, and I knew I was gonna start missing him five minutes after he left.

Andy and I had breakfast together in the hotel dining room early that morning; Cheechee and Curtis were still sleeping. For over an hour we talked about our futures; I remained with a positive outlook on my job at the studio. The last thing I wanted was for Andy to be concerned about leaving me here alone. He was about to face plenty of his own concerns.

"Why don't you go back to St. Louis with Luther?" he asked.

"I'll tell you the same as I told Luther... I haven't thought of any good reasons to go back there... not right now."

Just then Cheechee and Curtis sat down with us. "G' morning, Will," they both greeted me. "Did we give you two enough time alone?"

"I guess so," I said.

"Are you sure you won't come with us?" Curtis pleaded. "It just won't seem the same without you."

I thought about all the good times the four of us had spent together... in St. Louis... traveling... in La Crosse... and for just one brief moment I was ready to pack my suitcase and venture out into the unknown. But then, just as quickly, reality set in, and the feeling of security with a sure thing put my clothes back in the bureau drawer. "Yeah, I'm sure," I said. "I think I've found my place in the world... and I think staying at the photo studio is the best choice for me right now."

"Well, we have a few things to do before we leave... get our money out of the bank, and get some traveling supplies, so if you change your mind in the next couple of hours..."

"I don't think I'll change my mind," I replied. "What time are you leaving? I'm going to work now, but I want to be here to see you off."

Curtis gazed at the big clock on the wall. "Ten o'clock... we should be ready to go by ten."

"Promise me that you won't leave 'til I get here."

"I promise."

I went to the studio and immediately told Mr. Jacob that my best friends were leaving town and that I needed a couple of hours off at ten o'clock.

"Take all the time you need," he said. "Where are they going?"

"New York," I replied. "I don't know when I'll ever see them again... if ever."

"Well, then... you'd better go say your goodbyes." He was so understanding; that was only one of the reasons why I liked working for him.

The shiny red Pontiac was parked at the curb, and Luther stood talking to the desk clerk when I returned to the hotel; Andy, Cheechee and Curtis stepped out of the elevator carrying luggage and a saxophone case. It was at that moment that their leaving seemed a reality. I had to fight back the tears.

As they approached the front desk, Luther said to the clerk, "I think I see a letter in their pigeon hole."

"Oh, yes," the clerk responded. "I almost forgot... it's for Andy Lorado." He retrieved the letter and handed it across the counter. With his free hand, Andy took the letter from him, folded it and stuck it in his hip pocket. "Thank you," he said.

"It's been a pleasure having you here," the clerk said. "Have a safe journey... and if you're in La Crosse again, please come and stay at the *Stoddard*."

Then we all walked across the lobby to the front door, out to the sidewalk, and I watched as the Knights piled their suitcases and the saxophone in the back seat. "You see?" I said. "There wouldn't have been room for all of us."

"We would have made room," Curtis said, and then he threw his arms around me and we hugged. "I'll miss you, Will," he said, sounding a little choked up. "I wish you were coming with us."

And then Cheechee took his turn for a tearful hug. "There's a notebook on the writing desk up in the room," he said. "I left it for you."

"Thanks, Cheechee," I said. "I hope you find a way to steal the stars in New York."

Andy was already wiping away the tears from his eyes. We embraced in a hug that I didn't want to end. "I'll miss you," he strained to say.

"Take good care of yourself," I said. My tears were streaming now, too.

"I'll write you a letter when we get..." He couldn't finish.

"Just remember me when you get rich and famous like Benny Goodman."

I watched them get in the car, and then the shiny red Pontiac slipped away around the corner.

A minute or so later, as I stood there alone staring at the street, I felt a hand on my shoulder. "I didn't just come here to talk to the desk clerk, you know," Luther said.

I wiped away tears from my cheeks. "Oh?" I replied.

He turned me toward the hotel entrance and guided me into the lobby. We sat in a couple of comfy chairs.

"I knew this would be a hard time for you," Luther said. "I thought I should be here with you."

"Thanks, Luther," I said. "Andy and I have been best friends for a long time... I miss him already."

"And I'm sure he'll miss you, too," Luther said. "But he has his career to pursue, and you have yours. Unfortunately, those careers aren't up the same road."

Luther was right. If for no other reason, I tried to make that the justification for Andy going to New York.

102

I managed to get through the rest of the day at the studio. Because of the Mississippi River Bridge collapse, many amateur photographers had dropped off film they wanted Mr. Jacob to develop. So I had plenty to do that afternoon. But by five o'clock, I was eager and ready to go back to my room at the hotel. Emotional distress was setting in again, not only because of Andy's departure, but because in a couple of days, I would experience yet another loss of companionship—Luther would be leaving Wednesday, and there would be no one else left to help ease the pain.

When I passed the hotel front desk, the clerk hailed me. "Mr. Madison, sir," he said. "There is some mail here for you."

He handed me a letter. I immediately recognized the handwriting; it was from Sadie. "Thank you," I said, and headed for the elevator. "Third floor, Carl."

I studied the envelope in my hand, wondering why Sadie had written when, in fact, it was my turn to write to her. I squelched the urge to rip it open, right there in the elevator, and decided to wait for the privacy of my room.

Just as Cheechee had said, a notebook—the same notebook he gave me to read in St. Louis—lay on the writing desk. I flipped it open to discover many more pages had been written since I last saw it. Tucked between the pages was a note:

Dear Will,
You have been such a good friend. I haven't stolen any stars yet, but your inspiration has kept my story alive.
Your friend,
Christopher "Cheechee" Chapman

I wanted to sit right down, right then, and read Cheechee's continuation of *If I Could Steal the Stars*, but then I remembered Sadie's letter. That should be my first priority.

Sitting on the edge of the bed, I kicked off my shoes and then carefully tore open the envelope. Sadie usually had plenty to say, but this letter was astonishingly short:

Dear Will,

    I hope all is well with you and the other boys.

    I have some really good news for you. Jesse wants you to come back to St. Louis as soon as would be possible. He says your future employer would like to talk to you. I know you hate to leave your job there in La Crosse, but Jesse thinks you will be very pleased with what is waiting for you here.

    Hope to see you soon.

Love,

Sadie

I checked the inside of the envelope to see if I had missed another page. It was extremely difficult to imagine that's all she would tell me! *My future employer wants to talk to me!* Suddenly my head was spinning with a hundred different thoughts all at once. Even though the letter was a bit mysterious, it could mean only one thing: Jesse must be the captain of his own boat now, and he is ready to get me back on the river! Yahoo!

I glanced at my watch. Ten minutes to six. I had time to relax in a bath before I met Luther for supper at the *Dixie of the North*.

At a quarter to seven, after the soothing bath, I felt as refreshed as if I had just slept for eight hours. I saw Luther already sitting at our usual table by the window in the *Bodega*. He waved as I walked by.

"You're looking mighty cheerful," he said when I sat down.

His comment reminded me of the events earlier that day. "I know I was almost in tears the last time you saw me—"

"*Almost?*" he said grinning.

"Okay. Maybe I *was*... and I'm still sad that Andy and the guys are gone. But I got a letter from Sadie today."

"And that made you happy again?"

I pulled the letter out of my shirt pocket and handed it across the table to Luther. "You read it and maybe you'll know why it makes me happy."

He unfolded the paper and read. A devilish little grin crept onto his face. He laid the letter on the table in front of me.

"So, when are you going to St. Louis?" he asked.

In all my ecstasy I had not yet thought about how and when. "I don't know," I said. "I'll hafta check... maybe the train..."

Luther held up his hand as if to stop me. He reached for his wallet, opened it, pulled out a green paper and handed it to me.

"What's this?" I asked.

"Look at it."

I unfolded the three-by-five inch card-like paper. It was a one-way ticket for a stateroom aboard the Passenger Steamer *St. Paul*, entitling occupancy by two persons; Departure time and date: 10:00 a. m., August 14, 1935 from La Crosse, Wisconsin; Destination: St. Louis, Missouri.

Recollection of the "fare for two" came to me. Luther had told me of the tickets Spades gave him before he and Irene left. "So, I s'pose this means I'm going with you to St. Louis?" I said.

"It would be a shame to let the ticket go to waste," Luther replied.

Then it occurred to me. "The fourteenth is the day after tomorrow!"

"Yes it is," Luther said. "You have a whole day to get ready."

"Only one day," I whined. "But—"

"Let's eat," Luther said. "And then we can plan all the things you need to do. We'll have plenty of time... you'll see."

I was like a kite in a tornado. Lucky for me that Luther stayed there to hold onto the string.

103

It seemed I was returning to St. Louis as abruptly as I had left, but for a better reason, and under much better circumstances; I wouldn't have to be looking over my shoulder for pursuing police. Now that I knew the Tony Delaware case had been closed, I could rest easier.

Mr. Jacob didn't put up any fuss when I told him why my brother wanted me to come back to St. Louis, although I knew he was a little disappointed with my leaving. "You have to follow your heart," he said, "and if you find that your heart misled you to St. Louis, my door will still be open to you."

Follow my heart. That's what Spades Morgan had told me, too, and I desperately hoped that my heart wasn't leading me astray.

Lester Collins at the bank thought my returning to St. Louis—and Jesse—was a wise choice. He had always looked out for our best interests, and I had learned to trust his judgment. "You'd be like a mushroom out in the sunlight here all alone, Will," he told me. "Now that Andrew is gone, you *should* go back to your brother."

Lester withdrew all the money from my account for me, and after he had counted out $3,859.75 in cash, he reminded me of a safety precaution:

"Get this cash into the ship's safe as soon as you board," he said. "You never know these days..."

"Thank you, Lester. You've been a great help."

"Say hello to Jesse and Sadie for me when you see them."

"I will, Lester. I will for sure."

Luther was like a little kid at a State Fair midway once we had boarded the *St. Paul*. I couldn't blame him—I was quite impressed, too. She was big and luxurious, and it was easy to see why Spades fancied this boat. Our stateroom was on the upper deck so we had a good view of the wrecked bridge as we passed through the open swing span. Construction crews were already at work on the temporary replacement span, but talk around town was that there would soon be a completely new, better bridge to connect La Crosse with Minnesota. For now, a ferry boat, called in from Prairie du Chien, was shuttling people and cars across the river.

The next four days seemed like a new adventure to me; even though I had travelled this river before, it had been so long ago. I remembered many of the towns we passed, because the Madison, unlike this much bigger boat, had stopped at nearly every one of them. But the hundreds of miles of shoreline were just vaguely familiar. It was a great experience, though, to ride as just a passenger, and to enjoy all the pleasures that the craft and crew provided.

There was plenty of time for me to read Cheechee's addition to his story. It continued with telling his experiences hitch-hiking across the country, enduring adverse weather conditions, begging for food when it was possible, stealing it when it was necessary. Then a miraculous ride with a trucker brought him the entire remaining distance to St. Louis. When he arrived there, he decided to stay. His experience of living on the streets of Denver gave him the knowledge to live on the streets of St. Louis; he soon learned where the soup kitchens and bread lines kept him nourished.

Then he made some acquaintances that became good friends, and they took him in and helped him find a job. But his life in St. Louis was becoming a repeat of what he had left behind in Denver—until he met a couple of new friends named *Andy and Will.*

The story went on with a familiar ring, because now I had become part of his story. It continued with Cheechee's eloquent writing style, telling of his rise into entertainment, to our journey into Wisconsin, where perhaps he could *steal all the stars.*

Once again, I was quite impressed.

I had plenty of time, too, to imagine what new adventure awaited me. I could be nearly certain that I would finally see New Orleans, and perhaps the ocean. Jesse went there often, and so would I. But my imagination left me with so many unanswered questions, as I was sure Luther's imagination had him curious about Spades' new hotel. Trying to get anything more from him, though, was like trying to break into Fort Knox. I eventually gave up, and just watched the scenery go by, shooting a few pictures now and then, until we docked at St. Louis.

104

T he St. Louis skyline was nothing new to me; I recalled my first arrival here and then it didn't seem so unusual that Luther appeared as if he were about to land on another planet. I had been wondering if anyone would be waiting at the levee for us; Luther assured me that Spades and Irene would be there. That seemed logical because Spades had purchased the tickets.

We stood at the railing on the upper deck, watching the St. Louis levee coming closer. Other passengers scurried by, toting bags, suitcases, and small children. Luther thought we should be among them.

"No hurry," I said. "The gangplank won't hit the ground for another fifteen minutes. There's already a mob of people gathered there... has been for the last half-hour."

"How do you know that?" Luther asked.

"I've seen it a thousand times," I replied.

"Oh, yeah. I suppose..."

As the huge craft gracefully floated to a stop, Luther raised his arm and pointed. "Look! There's Spades and Mom!"

I searched the crowd of people waiting in the hot sun on the levee. There they were, and beside them were Jesse and Sadie! What a pleasant surprise! Seeing them suddenly gave me the urge to hustle toward the gangplank. We retrieved our luggage from the stateroom and headed for the bow where a steward wished us a pleasant farewell.

My next pleasant surprise was seeing the rest of the welcoming party that had joined Spades and Jesse. Luke and Reggie were there, too, but my first priority was to receive one of Big Brother Jesse's bear hugs. I hadn't had one for months.

"Welcome home, Little Brother," Jesse whispered in my ear. Those were the most soothing words I had ever heard, not because I had returned to St. Louis, but because I had returned to my Big Brother.

Then there was a warm welcoming hug from Sadie. "I'm so glad you came back," she said. "You must've gotten my letter."

"Yes, I did," I said. "And just in the nick of time... another couple of days and I would've missed the boat."

"Good to have you back with us," Luke said, and then he and Reggie each gave me a hug.

I introduced Luther—who had been receiving an equally warm welcome from his mom and Spades. "He's been a great friend since the first day we arrived in La Crosse," I said.

"We've heard a lot about you from Spades," Luke said. "And we've been anxious to meet you." He and Luther shook hands, and then everyone else greeted him with sincere handshakes. Luther was already receiving acceptance, and in time, I knew everyone would like him as well as I did.

Luke and Reggie grabbed our luggage from the ground. "We'll take these to my car," Luke said.

"You have a car?" I said, a little surprised.

"Well sure! Didn't Sadie tell you in her letter?"

"I guess it slipped my mind," Sadie admitted.

After we had chatted for a while, and we had determined that everyone was in good health, Sadie excused herself; she had to go home because Philip's babysitter could only stay for a little while. Irene left with her.

Then Jesse commanded everyone's attention. I could easily tell that he was eager and anxious about something.

"Will," he said. "Shall we go see our new boat?"

This was the moment I had been anticipating for the last five days. He didn't have to ask twice. "Yes!" I responded instantly.

Shoulder to shoulder with Jesse we started down the levee; the others followed.

"Now, Will," Jesse said as we walked. "You know this won't be exactly the same as it was on the old Madison."

"Oh, I expected that much," I replied. "Are you and Luke captain and pilot?"

"We are."

"Will we be going to New Orleans?"

"Without a doubt."

After a hundred-yard walk, Jesse stopped me at the pointed bow of a freshly-painted blue and white, shined and polished, new-looking four deck excursion boat.

I gave Jesse a puzzled stare. I was expecting a squared bow with bumpers where the barges were attached. "This doesn't look like a barge towboat to me," I said.

"It's *not* a barge tow," he replied. By then, Spades was standing beside us. Jesse pointed to the front of the pilothouse; there, painted in gold and black letters was the boat's name, MADISON II. "Will?" Jesse said. "I'd like you to meet *our* new employer, Mr. Edward Morgan."

I glanced at Spades, and then quickly back to Jesse. He was grinning, and I suppose it was because of my utterly astonished expression. "Spades!" I said. "I thought you bought a hotel."

"You could say I did," Spades replied. "A *floating* hotel. Shall we go aboard for a tour?"

We stood on the bow admiring the beautifully-polished hardwood staircase that led to the next deck. "She's a very modern boat, Will," Jesse said. "Diesel power, propeller driven. No more coal shoveling, no more boiler fires, no more broken paddlewheel planks."

"Two hundred fifty feet long," Spades added. "Eighty staterooms, two dining rooms, two lounges, game room..."

I was in total awe. I couldn't believe my eyes. "And what's with the name?" I asked. I looked to Spades for the answer.

"Will," he said. "You and Jesse were my inspiration for undertaking such a project. I thought it was only fitting that my boat should be christened Madison II."

"Why didn't you tell me about it in La Crosse?"

"I couldn't. I had to get back to St. Louis first, and make sure Jesse would take command."

"He made me an offer I couldn't refuse," Jesse said smiling.

"So, how 'bout it, Will? Y'all gonna accept the position of the Official Photographer?"

"I... I..." I couldn't speak. I was standing on the main deck of the most attractive boat I had ever seen, my new adventure, and I couldn't utter a single word.

"Reggie will be my First Mate again," Jesse said. "Mildred and Beth will be the heads of housekeeping. I couldn't get Marion to leave his engineer job that he has, and I didn't think Lester would leave the bank in La Crosse, but I did find a few of our old deckhands. And I'm told that Luther will be an excellent steward."

I finally regained my composure. "Then our whole gang will be together again..." And then I remembered. "All except..." A lump formed in my throat. "All except Andy," I cried.

The next few moments were probably the most memorable ones of my entire life... for out of the shadows, down the polished staircase came the sound of footsteps.

"Did I hear someone say my name?" a very familiar voice called out.

I spun toward the voice. Andy's beaming smile made every other sight and sound disappear into oblivion. Once again, I became speechless.

"Hi, Dad," he said and gave a little wave. And then he gazed at me. "I was afraid you wouldn't make it."

I touched him to make sure he wasn't a mirage, and then we replayed the last hug at La Crosse. This time, it felt even better. Curtis and Cheechee took their turns, too.

"Did you know about this?" I asked when I came out of the clouds. Curtis and Cheechee smiled.

"Not until I remembered the letter from Dad that the desk clerk gave me just as we were leaving the *Stoddard*," Andy explained. "We were almost to Chicago. I forgot I had stuffed it in my pocket. I tried calling you on the telephone at the hotel that night, but Larry only said that you had checked out. He didn't know any more. So I could only hope that you went with Luther."

Curtis explained further. "We talked it over and we all agreed that New York was too far away... and the offer of House Band on a riverboat sounded more our style... you know, new audience every few days without having to go anywhere."

"So we drove straight back to St. Louis," Cheechee added.

"You have no idea how glad I am that you didn't go to New York," I said.

Jesse and Spades gave me a full tour of our new boat, starting with the spacious main lounge, complete with stage, spotlights, and a glistening baby grand piano. Andy, Cheechee and Curtis stayed there with Luke, Reggie and Luther while my guided tour continued.

I saw the elegant staterooms, the magnificent galley and dining rooms, the recreation area, and the observation deck. We climbed more stairs to see the staff's quarters, laundry and utility rooms, and finally the largest and most comfortably furnished pilothouse I had ever seen. It looked more like a parlor... equipped with all the gauges, controls, and of course, the brass and teakwood steering wheel. I could easily understand why Jesse and Luke would never turn down this command.

While I was admiring all the exquisite appointments of the pilothouse, Reggie appeared at the door. "Luther wants to go to the *Dixie*," he said. "We're all going. Wanna come along?"

ABOUT THE AUTHOR

Born into a farm family in the late 1940s, J.L. Fredrick lived his youth in rural Western Wisconsin, a modest but comfortable life not far from the Mississippi River. His father was a farmer, and his mother, an elementary school teacher. He attended a one-room country school for his first seven years of education.

Wisconsin has been home all his life, with exception of a few years in Minnesota and Florida. After college in La Crosse, Wisconsin and a stint with Uncle Sam during the Viet Nam era, the next few years were unsettled as he explored and experimented with life's options. He entered into the transportation industry in 1975.

Since 2001 he has fourteen published novels to his credit, and two history volumes, *Rivers, Roads, & Rails,* and *Ghostville.* He was a featured author during Grand Excursion 2004.

J.L. Fredrick is currently rediscovering the USA in an RV.